Flights of Angels

Also by Cindy Brandner

Exit Unicorns

Mermaid in a Bowl of Tears

Flights of Angels

Cindy Brandner

Starry Night Press

2 4 6 8 10 9 7 5 3 1

ISBN-13: 978-0-9783570-1-6

This book is printed on acid free paper

Cover design by Stevie Blaue

Printed and bound in the USA

Published in Canada by
Starry Night Press

First Edition

Rev. 02/29/2012

This one is for my own angels: Devon, Zoë and Larkin.

Acknowledgments

A book this chock-a-block with history and changes of geography requires the help and expertise of many people.

Thanks goes to the following:

All the people who allowed me the generous use of their names—Elaine Pontious for allowing me to use the birth name of her Czarina and for the small crate of books on Russian history, Lucy Murphy for allowing her own name to be used for Casey and Pat's grandmother, Richard Xu for the loan of his surname and Sallie Blumenauer for allowing me to name Jamie's childhood friend after her.

Paul Cowan in Belfast for answering all my questions, no matter how trivial. Also for the generous sharing of his own history.

Merci beaucoup to Isabelle Mulligan for vetting the Paris chapters and making certain my French is correct.

My team of good fairies that helped to whip this manuscript into a book: Tracy Goode, Denise Ferrari, Fran Bach and Lee Ramsey, thanks to each of you for your endless patience, discerning eyes and willingness to work through my tangled sentences and missing punctuation. Marcia Krol Petersen, Sandy Meidlinger and Lois Flanagan for being the first and last sets of eyes to read it before publication.

Stevie Blaue for the beautiful cover.

The ladies of Shamrocks and Stones, for being such a large part of my on-line life and my traveling life as well.

And last, but never least, to my husband Patrick, for all his hard work and faith which helps to bring these books into the world.

Table of Contents

Prologue

WE BEGIN OVER A GREAT SEA, THE WESTERN OCEAN ON THE RIM OF THE WORLD. *Only stars light our way, for it is still night, though our travels will take us toward dawn. This is an ocean of great storm-tossed waters and strange, still latitudes, where things disappear, never to be seen again. At its surface, it is a bowl of tears—of loss and new hope and of families left behind. Below the surface it is a place of mystery as unfathomed as the very universe. A place that is as much home to such as we as the waning of the moon or the whispering heart of the forest.*

For we are children born of sea foam and moon shadow, more dark than light and older than Time itself. We knew Leviathan before he had a name. We roamed the seas and the skies, the forests and the places of the earth as well as the places below it. We have been called by many names: angel, demon, faerie, spirit, ghost, to name a very few, but we are the unnamed and can only be summoned with wisdom and grace, and, once in a great while, by pure need.

But the sea, despite its allure, is not our destination. For we seek land, a land of myth and madness, of poets and politicians, rebels and raconteurs, of blood and brotherhood. A land unlike any other, half legend, half truth, wholly and terribly beautiful.

We fly through the night until a thin line forms on the distant horizon and we feel the relief of homecoming after such a very long voyage over the faceless, undulating ocean. And so we arrive at the edge of a country of limestone cliffs, soft-faced with moss and nesting gulls. In we fly across a patchwork quilt of a thousand shades of green and low stone walls with sheep dotting the dawn's landscape. But do not let this enchantment fool you, for this is a land that has known much pain, whose fields are watered well and deep with blood. This is an old land, and our people have lived here long, some saying we were the small dark ones that dwelt in the trees before the coming of the Celts—but we are older even than they. We knew this land before man, before God, before light.

Now we wheel North, which in this land is spelled with a capital 'N', defined by political lines rather than geographical. Here lie the cities of industry with musical names like Londonderry, Ballymena, Magherafelt, Newtownabbey and last—the city of our concern—Belfast, meaning 'sandy fort at the river's mouth'. A fitting name, for it is a city built on red clay, with politics girded in ropes of sand and lives that dissipate as quickly through the hourglass of time and chance.

On a hill apart, wooded and enchanted, a house sparkles against the first rays of sunlight. A house that looks as though mead-maddened cluricaunes were involved in its conception and building, for the back half bears no resemblance to the front, and surely that birdcage of glass and curling iron must owe something to the little folk. A house of wealth and taste, nevertheless, and no doubt, should we venture inside, we would find inhabitants of both imagination and discernment.

But even this is not our true concern, nor is it entirely where the story shall occur. For that we travel south to a soft dell of ferns and bracken and trees in which nestles a wee, recently whitewashed farmhouse from another century. Indeed this shaded hollow looks as though it might disappear into the mists, only to re-emerge every one hundred years or so. But the people that dwell within are real enough, to be sure.

We cross the wall, wooded and vined over with brambles and old roses, damp and misted on this mid-winter morning. Early as it is, we can see someone move inside the house, and the scent of peat smoke and hot tea curls out in invitation. We accept gladly for it's very cold this morning. It is a bit of a walk down into this hollow that, come spring, will be filled with flowers, for their seeds can be sensed sleeping beneath the chilled earth. We spy a tiny door set high near a much larger one. This one is painted red so that we might not miss it, and even has a small step for us to rest our weary wings, and a mat of moss to wipe our feet. And so, badger bristle boots well cleaned, we enter.

The kitchen is snug and cozy, a fire in the hearth and the homely sound of an Aga with a kettle boiling atop it. The floors bask in the fire's heat and the scent of the tea, darkly fragrant and redolent of hills far, far away. Deep windowsills laden with green things greet the morning light as it pulls itself up and over the horizon. We stop for a sniff of the green: lavender, lemon verbena, thyme and rosemary. Above one window hangs a St. Brigid's cross made of silvered reeds. Ah yes, this is a house that knows how to show the welcome of the door to the small folk.

And now, perhaps it is time to look at the inhabitants of this home. Some are two-legged and some are four. In the kitchen is a dog, a great grey woolly beast, watching a man pour out the tea and listening with a sympathetic ear to his morning chatter, while keeping a keen eye out for possible crumbs falling to the floor.

The man himself arrests our eye, as he would in any room in any country, for he is a young man, large and well-made, broad-shouldered and darkly bearded, with black curls and a certain twinkle in his eye that tells us he is not entirely immune to the lure of the fairy world himself. And so it is that we must be extra careful not to be seen nor sensed. But we linger a little still, because it is very

*pleasant here with the fire and tea and toasting bread and the dog and the first
sounds of morning.*

*But we feel the lure of the stairs just beyond the bookcase, for we are very
curious folk and must needs know what and who are in every nook and cranny
of a household. The stairway crooks back on itself like a twisted old elf, and this
only makes it the more imperative that we travel up, up, up, past a window with
eight sides—a most fortunate number that—and so all views from this window
will be happy ones. It is only five more steps now to the top floor, still dark under
its tightly thatched roof. 'Tis clear the inhabitants of this house understand the
importance of the old ways.*

*In the first room, there is a woman asleep, one arm under her head, the other
tucked around her belly in a gesture as old as the world itself. The first rays of
morning catch the edge of her jaw line and we see that she is lovely in the way that
humans sometimes are, a way that has nothing to do with what they call fads or
epochs. She is well matched to the man downstairs, for he is fire and earth and she
is water and air. We auld ones can tell such things at a glance, or merely by scent.*

*She stretches and opens her eyes, looking directly through the air at us. For
a second we fear she has seen us, for she has mermaid eyes and a water soul, and
both these qualities are notorious for catching glimpses of that which is not meant
to be seen by man. But then she sits up, rather awkwardly for a woman with such
grace in her lines, and we see there is nothing to fear. For at present her gaze is all
inward, which is as it should be, for she is with child and absorbed fully by the
tiny creature she harbors in the amniotic sea of her womb.*

*Ah babies, there is little about the human world we love more than those
smelly, howling little creatures. For they do still see us but have not the words
to reveal us. They communicate in the ancient way, through air and ether, with
laughter and tears. If one can catch a bubble of their laughter out of the air, it can
be made into a cloak that will warm one forever and never wear out.*

*We hear the quick tread of the man on the stairs, followed by the soft pad of the
dog's paws, if indeed something the size of a small pony can rightly be called 'dog'.*

*The man enters with two mugs of tea and the woman smiles at him, tilt-
ing her face up for a kiss. He hands her the tea and kisses her tenderly, bending
to greet the inhabitant of her stomach with morning salutations and soft words
of sweet foolishness, and so we know this is a child of love, much wanted. The
woman strokes the man's head and looks at him with her heart there in her eyes.
He straightens up and leans toward her for a goodbye kiss, but she gives him a
look from under her lashes and runs her hand up his thigh in a gesture that makes
us smile knowingly, for this too is as old as the ages and not limited to the ways
of man. He makes a mild protest, something about being late for work and then
succumbs, as he knew he would from the moment she touched him. This love is
both as fragile and strong as the tides of the sea and the movement of the planet.
It is a thing of sacrament, and so we turn away, for there are things even we are*

not meant to observe.

We return to the kitchen, where the heart of the home is found. Beyond the green things where we settle is a field wherein we scent the stirring roots of fairy soap, an entire wooded field of it—what humans call bluebells—such a plebeian name for an ethereal flower. On the edge of the field, we can hear the murmur of water and know this is indeed a right place, for water guards the boundaries between worlds, between dreams and dimensions, between man and that which is not man. Water opens the doors to the unseen. The woods too are important to us, for they guard and protect, but they also hide when hiding is needed. We sigh, for this is a good place to rest and rest we must, for even among our kind, we are ancient and feel the ache of bone and the pain of flesh, when the moon is dark and the tides run hard toward the horizon.

Altogether, it must be said, this seems as fine a place as an auld one might hope to find, to settle in for a while and observe and see what stories shall be woven before our eyes. Perhaps you will stay, for having come this far, you too must be tired and in need of rest. Here, come, there are wee chairs amongst the lavender. Let us sit and be still and see and listen...

Part One

...An Earlier Heaven
Ireland – January 1973

Chapter One

January 1973

Man of Peace

CASEY RIORDAN WAS STUCK IN A TERRIBLE TRAFFIC JAM and was going to be late for work. Which was to say that there was a flock of sheep lazing about the road as if they hadn't wool to grow nor a notion of moving in their wee addled heads, and he couldn't get around them no matter how much he honked the horn at them.

It was his own bloody fault he was late, and that did nothing to improve his mood. It was his wife's fault, come down to it. The woman needn't have pulled him back into the bed when all he was doing was delivering a cup of morning tea to her. He grinned despite the damned sheep still woolgathering in the roadway, for it was hardly a thing about which a man could rightly complain. Once Pamela had gotten over her initial nausea and exhaustion with this pregnancy, her hormones seemed to have gone wild and he swore he found himself horizontal more than vertical whilst home these days. Not that he was complaining at all, at all. In fact, he was half tempted to keep the woman pregnant for the next twenty years or so.

The sheep finally ambled off the road, blatting all the way, sounding purely indignant about having to move.

Casey drove as fast as the narrow lanes allowed, arriving at work some ten minutes behind schedule, his shirt half untucked and a rather wild look in his eyes. Pat was there ahead of him, already busy with a pile of blueprints.

"Yer late," his brother said and put a cup of tea on the desk in front of him.

"I know," Casey replied gruffly, hoping to hell Pat wouldn't ask what had him running behind every morning of late. To judge from the man's quirked eyebrow though, he had a fair idea. Well, it was likely, Casey thought, that he looked like a man fair depraved these days.

"Bring me up to snuff, will ye?" he said, unrolling a set of blueprints for a holiday cottage for a wealthy American. He had to give the plans one last look over and make a few minor corrections before shipping them off.

Pat sat on the other side of the desk and said, "We're near to finished the renovations on the Finherty place. The windows were delivered this mornin' an' we're waitin' on the rock for that retainin' wall. We've still to hear back about the bid we put in for the village center in Whitecross. But no matter that, we've got two more projects lined up before we can get to it anyway." Pat drank his tea down in three long swallows and stood, impatient to get on with the work at hand. Casey rarely managed to have more than a few words with him, and often their conversations consisted of just this, work talk.

"Pamela wants to know if ye'll come round for dinner sometime this week," Casey said, not looking at his brother, knowing all too well what the answer would be.

"Ye'll thank her for me, but I think—no—not just yet. Now, if ye'll excuse me, I've got to get on to Pete Simons about that load of schist he was meant to deliver yesterday."

Casey watched his brother go out the door, hard hat in hand. Pat had proved invaluable in the start-up of the company. No one worked harder or longer hours, not even himself. It worried him, though, for Pat seemed to have replaced any sort of life with working until he dropped with exhaustion. He understood why, but wished he could find a way to help his brother return to the land of the living. Pat seemed neither angry, nor sad, but rather as if he had turned to some form of stone, stone that moved with a great and restless energy, terrible in its burning. Yet, he was well aware there was little he could do, Pat had to find his own way through his grief, and certainly there were worse ways to mourn your wife than by burying yourself in work. He was grateful the boy hadn't hit the bottle. Frankly, he could not imagine what he himself would do should something happen to Pamela. He shrugged the thought away as though a cold hand had touched the nape of his neck. It was best not to think such thoughts, lest a man draw the reality into his life.

He stood, gathering his work gloves and tools. He was going to the Finherty place to finish the kitchen hearth. He looked forward to it, as there was a deep peace in working with stone and shaping it into the place within the home that would be its center.

Outside, as he headed toward the lorry, peace was in short supply. He had company. Not for the first time, nor unfortunately, for the last. Inwardly, he cursed and felt the tightening of his gut that always accompanied these visits. Outwardly, he put on his 'hard man' face, as Pamela called it, and steeled himself for the next few minutes.

Even the first visit had not been unexpected. A shadow economy was one of the side effects of war, illegal and unrecognized or otherwise. Neither side of the sectarian divide was averse to a bit of old-fashioned extortion, expropriation and a good dose of intimidation to encourage the locals to submit. Both sides already had a heavy grip on a variety of endeavors: drinking clubs, fruit machines, televisions and other electronic goods, moving vans, and electrical contracting, and where it touched him the hardest—cooperatives across sectarian lines that sold protection for construction sites.

His company was only months old, and he wasn't turning a profit beyond making his payment to the bank each month for both the business loan and his and Pamela's wee bit of land. He had put in what money they had managed to tuck aside during their time in Boston as well and he had no idea where exactly these bastards, who were strolling toward him thought he was going to find extra money to pay them not to rob him blind.

He didn't give them a greeting. He wasn't going to pretend this visit was in any way welcome.

He had christened them Pug and Mr. Spectacles in his mind from the first time he had seen them. The short one was stocky, with bad stubby teeth and small eyes. The tall one stood a good three inches above Casey himself, who was six foot three, and looked in dire need of a decent meal. He didn't find them particularly intimidating. It was more the notion of who was behind them, because these overtures they kept making had the feel of something personal about them. He wasn't on the slate for government funded projects, which was where the real money was and therefore worth a thief's time and effort. Small, private cottages and the occasional new home for a farmer was decidedly not worth the effort. This meant that he might be gone from the IRA, but he was, most unfortunately, not forgotten.

The tall one was the talker, the short one apparently, the muscle. The tall one put out his bony arm as though in cordial greeting.

"It's not worth the petrol it took ye to get here," Casey said, ignoring the man's outstretched hand. "Ye might as well get back in yer wee car, an' go home, I've nothin' for ye."

"Now that's hardly convivial, Mr. Riordan." The tall one fancied himself a bit of an intellectual and liked to use his manners and a variety of large words to prove it. Casey suspected that the gold-rimmed spectacles he wore were more affectation than necessity. Said spectacles were perched on the man's rather large nose and gave him the air of a befuddled stork. It did occur to him to wonder where the hell the lower echelons of the Provos were recruiting their enforcers.

"Ah well, pardon me, but I'm a wee bit busy this mornin' so ye'll have to forgive me for not rollin' out the red carpet an' servin' ye tea in the good china."

"Perhaps," said Mr. Spectacles, "Mr. Riordan, it would behoove us to come at this from another angle."

"Yer not goin' to convince me even if ye descend from the sky on a cloud with the Angel Gabriel as yer company. I've told ye three times now that I'm not cavin' in to extortion. I don't need yer protection, nor that of yer bossman."

The short man bared his teeth at Casey. Apparently he was the watchdog, brought in to nip anyone who didn't immediately buckle. Mr. Spectacles lost his own conviviality rather swiftly.

"Yer mighty certain of yerself for a man who is not protected anymore. Yer on the outside on yer own. Even those that counted themselves yer men a few years ago wouldn't have yer back now, so I wouldn't get too brave there, me boyo."

"I'm not yer fockin' boyo," Casey said through gritted teeth, "an' I can take care of my own damn back. Now get the hell off my property."

The man put his hands up and smiled the smile of a shark, all teeth and no humanity.

"Have it yer way, but we'll be back until ye change yer mind, an' if ye don't change it, bear in mind we know where ye live an' where yer wife is at any time of the day."

"Go anywhere near my wife or my home, an' make no mistake, I will find ye an' I will kill ye."

"Brave words, but ye can't be everywhere at once."

"Ye want to bet yer life on that?" Casey asked, a fury inside him such as he had not felt in a long time. He fought to keep his hands relaxed, though they wanted to curl up into fists and smack the smug look on the man's face right off.

"Oh, ye'll find I'm a gamblin' man, Mr. Riordan, an' make no mistake of it."

Casey merely crossed his arms over his chest and gave them a hard look.

"We'll be back, an' we'll only get more persuasive as time goes on."

"Well, until then, gentlemen," Casey said with no little sarcasm.

He watched them walk away, standing firm until they should be gone from his sight. They would indeed be back, but he knew if he crumbled to them now he would end up paying through the nose until he couldn't turn a profit on his own business. This grafting off your own people was, in his own humble opinion, beyond the pale. It hardly endeared the general population toward an already unpopular illegal army when they demanded protection money so that one might protect oneself from them.

Mr. Spectacles turned at the edge of the work yard and cocked an imaginary pistol at his own head, miming pulling the trigger, then pointing at Casey and smiling.

It was not easy, Casey thought, to be a man of peace, and he would be the first to admit that it did not seem to be a natural state of being for him.

Chapter Two

January 1973

The Doomsday Plan

NORTHERN IRELAND WAS CONSIDERED A PUNISHMENT POSTING for agents of Her Majesty's Secret Services, and so when one had royally (pardoning the pun) screwed up one's mission in said province, it was a bit of a puzzler where to send one after that. As MI6 currently had no need of his services in either darkest Borneo or a frozen mountaintop in Peru, they had settled for the next best punishment. Thus, David Kendall, rogue agent and master of disguise, found himself on a rainy Malone Road, staring up at a huge old Victorian house smack-dab in the heart of god-fearing Ulster. It would have been tragic if it hadn't been quite so funny. David had long been a victim of a sense of humor that, at times, made him feel distinctly unpatriotic as an Englishman.

He wasn't laughing at present, however, for it was time to come in out of the shadows and present himself in his new role—that of a young Protestant male, looking to dip his toes into the roiling waters of radical Loyalism. He took a deep breath of the damp winter night and strode up the path in the wake of two stiff-backed Church of Paisley types.

Even Patrick Riordan, who perhaps had known him better than anyone in Belfast, would have trouble recognizing him tonight. His hair, normally a soft butter color and cut short and neat, was long and dark, tied back with a leather thong and hanging down over the collar of an ancient leather flight jacket. The dark hair offset his pale English skin in a manner that made him look years younger. Young enough, he hoped, to pass for an underage boy. If the light were kind he ought to pass for he had always had the problem of fine-boned men in that he looked like a perpetual schoolboy.

At the door he slipped in behind the two stiff-backs, both middle-aged, both looking like good sash-wearing Orangemen, with the hard faces he had become accustomed to during his previous tenure in this city. Behind him were a couple of young toughs, so at least he wouldn't stick out like a sore thumb.

The man who greeted them in the foyer of the large and drafty house was either insane or the savior of hardline Loyalism, depending upon whom one spoke to. David tended to think the two psychoses were not necessarily independent.

Boyd McCarthy had the broad, red face that so many of his compatriots had, a result of too much drink and a hard city that carved the visage of its men in these lines through time. Crazy or not, David knew he was looking into the face of one of the most dangerous men in Protestant Ulster. He was also a compatriot that had worked hand in hand with Morris Jones, the man who had killed Lawrence. Jones might be dead, killed by the hand of a man only slightly less deranged than he himself had been, but his evil lived on within a ring of men. It was the main reason that David was here tonight, and had his bosses at MI6 known that, they would have indeed found him a posting in Peru and left him there amidst the snow and mountain goats for the next two decades. Their reason for putting him here under cover was to flush out the head of a new and extremely radical branch of Loyalism. The thinking went that Boyd McCarthy was close to the man who was striking fear in the heart of the Nationalist community. Three Catholics had been killed in the last month, merely for the great sin of being Catholic and in the wrong place at the wrong time. When the usual hardline Loyalist assassins were rounded up and questioned, they were unusually reticent. Blunt denials were expected. This strange hedging in men that little had frightened since they had graduated out of short pants was something else altogether. Something was afoot in the world of radical Loyalism and David had been assigned to find out what and who was behind it.

He only had time to take the briefest of impressions, of both man and house, before being hustled toward a room to the right of the dark foyer.

It was large and filled with dark furniture, as though it had been decorated during the high Victorian period and not updated in the slightest degree since. In one corner was a Chinese screen, dark blue in color and scattered with an opulent design of gaudy peacocks as well as years of grime. There were already six other men in the room, mostly of the sash-wearing, bowler-hatted variety.

McCarthy directed David to a fan-backed red chair with tufts of stuffing poking out, like an old man dressed in ancient red long johns. David sat on it and hoped that an errant spring wouldn't un-man him.

There was the usual small chat that preceded most meetings, but David, with his well attuned backbone, sensed a darker underlying mood, a frisson of expectation—but expectation tinged with dread.

McCarthy called the meeting to order, drab olive cardigan making him appear as harmless as a moth-eaten librarian.

"Gentlemen, I welcome ye here tonight with great hope and the expectation of a changed future. You do not need me to inform you of the gravity of the situation the Protestant community of Ulster faces. The responsibility for this situation lies squarely on the lack of political leadership and the splinters and fractures within the heart of our Loyalist brotherhood. The immediate need is for political unity to bring all the broken pieces of our community together under one umbrella. Thus, we can harness the true strength of our populace and face the future united against the evil that exists upon our very doorstep. I have taken the step, therefore, of asking a man to speak to us tonight, a man who embodies the very best of Protestant Ulster, a man who is not afraid to fight and bleed on the front lines in this ancient battle.

"Due to the traitors within our country and the laxity of our police force in protecting their own, allowing evil to flourish unchecked, it is not yet safe for this man to reveal himself. But we are very fortunate that he has agreed to speak to us tonight, for once you have heard his words, I believe you will understand that nothing less than the redemption of our people lies within his hands."

Boyd stepped back and looked toward the Chinese screen in the corner and David realized that behind it sat the man to whom this odd feeling of unease and darkness could be attributed.

He felt an odd slide in his stomach, a feeling he had encountered before, a premonition that the future was suddenly hovering right in front of him and something very bad was waiting there within its nebulous folds. Then the unseen man spoke and David's attention was riveted within the present, the voice sliding through his cells like a vaporous serpent.

"Ulster, my friends, stands at the crossroads of history and now is the crucial time for us. We have been betrayed by the state, abandoned by the British, the covenant of 1912 lies in tatters. The enemies of Faith and Freedom are determined to destroy the glorious state of Ulster, thereby enslaving the people of God. We are God's chosen as we have been since we sacrificed our blood in the service of Britain, on her battlefields.

"The aim of the enemy is the destruction of our Protestant Faith. It is no less than the total annihilation of our people, our traditions, the memory of our blood and sweat which have been poured upon this land and made it the strong nation it once was. Need we any proof further than that of the deal cut with those dogs in Dublin, the purpose of which is to give our power, our very institutions and parliament over to the Irish, the IRA, the Republican filth that insinuates itself everywhere now, from the bastions of Parliament to the secret meetings behind doors conducted by the British to throw us into the gutter of history."

The man was somewhat accurate, David mused, if over the top about it.

"It is our time now to take the path that leads to glory or to utter defeat. It is time for us to bring Doomsday to the traitorous forces that are thick upon the face of this land. It is time for the blood to run in these streets until the righteous are the only ones left standing, and from the righteous, we shall rebuild our nation.

"Toward this end there are things we must do now. We must embrace our Protestantism as we have not since the darkest and most bloody days of our Faith. We must show the people of this city, of this country, that to be a Protestant means living in a God-fearing, clean, ordered and industrious manner.

"Our children must be raised in the Church. If your ministers are not preaching the pure, true faith of our fathers, then we must have them removed and replaced with true and zealous men of God."

"Roman Catholic educational institutions must be outlawed. Religious education must only be taught at the hands of evangelical Protestants.

"The Roman Catholic Church must be declared an illegal body. History has shown us that the Great Whore of Rome conspires with the darkest forces against the liberty and fortunes of mankind. For generations this evil has blighted our land. It must be destroyed so that our fellow countrymen will have an opportunity to enter the True Faith. Only then will Ulster be undivided!"

David felt sick. Could this madman actually be proposing to take down the Catholic Church and apparently espousing any method of achieving that end?

"For God and Ulster!" The voices echoed in bloody counterpoint and David joined them, though adding an amen to what this man had just said curdled his insides.

The voice had been quiet, smooth as ice and twice as cold, despite the fire and brimstone content of the speech. Every man in the room was riveted, and David wondered if it was only he who was disturbed by the talk of blood running through the streets in rivers, and how the voice caressed those words as though the very thought of such savagery gave the speaker sensual pleasure.

He had an uneasy sense that he ought to know that voice, that it was buried somewhere deep in the memories of his last stay in Belfast. He felt a tingle along his bones and the quickening of his own blood told him here was the man he sought. This was the power behind the dark whispers, behind the movements taking place on the periphery of outright violence. This was the man that would, indeed, make the streets run crimson with blood.

After, there was tea but no pretense at civility. A dark force had arisen in the room with the hidden man's words and it tainted the very air, laying its staining oil on each of their skins. David was certain he was the only one feeling dirty though. The man stayed behind the screen for a short time, then left silently, but one could feel an ice-cold miasma in his wake. David felt he could breathe again, despite being surrounded by some of the most violent men in the kingdom. He listened to the talk and occasionally added some small comment himself, to make it look like he was a budding radical, though not terribly politically savvy. He wanted them to think he had potential as a foot soldier but little more. They were less likely to suspect him in such a role.

He excused himself a few moments later, asking for the use of the toilet. McCarthy directed him to the back of the house and the room two doors before the kitchen. He entered, counted to twenty and then slipped back out, hoping his luck would hold for a few minutes. He darted up the long stairs, years of subterfuge making the shadows his natural element.

He found himself in a long, dark hall with several doors branching off it. Christ, it would take a month of Sundays to search all these rooms, and there was no guarantee the proof of what this house harbored was even here. Yet, by the pricking along his backbone—a thing he had learned to trust during his years as an agent—he felt certain something was here.

About a third of the rooms appeared to be occupied. He could hear the murmur of voices behind some doors, the deep breath of sleep in others, and the muffled sound of crying behind one. He paused for a moment, knowing what it was to be a young boy, lost and alone in the world. One could have parents and a safe, warm house and still know such things all too well. For now there was nothing he could do to help these boys without compromising his cover. So he moved on, quiet, carefully avoiding the creaks such old houses always had in abundance.

A flash of pale color caught his eye halfway down the hall and he halted, freezing in place until he could assess the danger, or lack thereof.

Standing in a room to his left, the door slightly ajar, was the man from behind the screen. His back was to the door, but David didn't need to know what he looked like to recognize him. The presence was undeniable. Some people left an impression upon the air around them. Not many had such force, but he knew a few that did. James Kirkpatrick and Casey Riordan being the two that came immediately to mind. This man's presence was more of an absence, like that of a candle suffocated in the dark. A second ago it might have scorched you, but now it was only a tracery of smoke upon the air. Yes, an absence was what it was; an emptiness that sent skitters along David's skin like the touch of an icy wind. As hair-trigger aware of this man as he was, he knew without a doubt that the man also knew he stood there, watching him. He did not turn, because he did not need to acknowledge him. It was enough that they both knew.

He caught a glimmer of pale hair in the light from the window but no more. Not blond as his own hair was naturally, nor the distinctive light-catching gold of James Kirkpatrick, but a shade as pale as water. The silhouette was unnaturally still, yet the tension that came off the figure was almost febrile in its intensity. David could not angle his body any farther to see at what the man gazed, fixated. But knowing the topography of Belfast as he did, he would be able to narrow the possibilities once he was out in the streets.

He left quietly enough, not wanting to overplay his hand all in one night. Still, he didn't leave unnoticed. He could feel someone open the door at his back and come down the stairs as he headed for the shadows of the street.

The man followed him into the roadway, stride heavy, not bothering to disguise or muffle it. He didn't care if David knew he was behind him.

He made a small show of glancing over his shoulder. It was McCarthy himself. Either the man suspected him or he had fallen into the trap David had set.

"Hold up, lad," the man said, puffing slightly in an effort to catch up. David slowed and turned, a quizzical yet wary look on his face. McCarthy drew even with him and David had to stop himself from instinctively stepping back. The man put the fine hairs on his neck up. David had long experience of such men and he knew how dangerous they were.

"Yer the young lad from Liverpool, am I right?"

"Aye," David said, hoping he sounded truculent enough to pass for a boy in his teens.

"Ye'll forgive me for sayin' so, but yer lookin' a bit weary round the edges. Are ye in need of a meal or a bed? Only Donald didn't say where ye were staying. We've accommodation for young men such as yourself, alone in the world an' in need of some warmth an' the charity of our Savior."

David had to refrain from pinching himself, wondering if it could be this simple. Yet if his years in the spy world had taught him anything, it was that humans were very willing to trust blindly when it concerned something that they wanted. He was grateful, however, for the dark and the overhanging bough of the elm tree he stood under, for the man would not see the look of loathing that he knew was in his own eyes. Loathing and victory, for a part of tonight's goal had been just this, for David to find a more permanent way into this house.

"I'd be obliged to ye, Mister, for I've been sleepin' rough on the streets for the last three weeks."

"Come with me then, son. We'll have you set right in no time."

I just bet you will, you bastard, David thought and suppressed a little whoop of victory as he followed the man back toward the house.

He was in. Now he only hoped he would survive long enough to do what needed to be done. There would be blood indeed, just whose wasn't entirely clear yet.

Chapter Three

February 1973

The Map of Love

THE BED SAT IN A POOL OF FIRELIGHT, a safe oasis at the end of a long day. Pamela had warmed towels and a blanket in the oven until they were almost unbearably hot. She spread the blanket across the bed and Casey, naked, lay down flat on his stomach, heaving a sigh of relief.

"Are you sore?" she asked, straddling his back and reaching for the lotion she had made up expressly for this purpose.

"Mmhm," he murmured. "Spent half the day offloading stone for the retaining wall an' ye know my back doesn't take as kindly to that sort of work as another man's might."

She did know, for as strong as Casey was his back had been damaged too badly, too often, for it to have the sort of strength it once had.

In the half-light from the fire, the skin was a fine web of silver scars, the design that of a crazed spider, with long runnels of healed tissue branching off from the trunk of his spine. It was oddly beautiful, set against the broad and well-muscled canvas of his back. At the very edges, the scarring was fine as twigs outlined in hoarfrost.

She ran her fingers into the channels of damaged skin, her flesh and bone like ivory keys against the silver and shadow of his. She often thought she was more familiar with the nuances of his body than she was with her own. It had become a map of love for her, each scar a road, each bone and dip and hollow another feature in the geography that drew her as irresistibly as the moon pulled on the tide. This thought made her bite her lip to halt the laughter. With Casey's rather jaundiced view on large bodies of water, it wasn't likely he would care to be compared to the tide. Blissfully unaware of her thoughts, he groaned and took a deep breath of contentment.

"Lord woman, ye've a strong hand on ye. Ye've untied all my knots. Will ye tell me a story then, Jewel?" he asked as she relaxed into his back, the weight of her body keeping his muscles stretched and smooth beneath the skin. It had become a ritual between them. After she rubbed his aches and pains away, he would ask her for a bit of her history, a few bones of her past, dug carefully free from the mines of childhood. He had done this so gently, so slowly that it took months to realize she had finally shared her entire past with him.

"Will you want the time I went sailing with President Kennedy then, or the time I was kicked out of ballet class for bringing my horse with me?"

"Ye went sailin' with the President?" Casey half turned, giving her an incredulous glance.

"Well, technically he wasn't President at the time, just the junior Senator from Massachusetts."

"Oh well, hardly worth the tellin' or the hearin' then, is it?" Casey said with no small sarcasm.

"Then I'll keep my tongue still," she said.

Casey rolled an eye in her direction, no mean feat for a man on his stomach.

"If ye do it'll be the first time for it. Alright, then I give. How the hell did ye end up out on the sea with JFK?"

"My father and he moved in many of the same circles. They took me along sailing one afternoon. I remember it like it was yesterday. My father told me to pay attention because I was going sailing with the future President of the United States and it would be a memory to cherish someday."

"And was it?"

"Oh yes, he was magic, even to a small girl."

"Did he seem even larger than life in person?"

"Yes, he did. He was tanned and healthy and wearing an old unraveling sweater and jeans, if you can imagine. He was simply glorious; you know one of those men who are carved out from the air about them somehow and you know they won't live as ordinary mortals do, that fate and history have destined them for something much larger."

"Ye could," Casey said acerbically, "be describin' James Kirkpatrick here, ye know."

"I think Jamie seemed a tad glamorous even to the Kennedys."

"I should have known," Casey snorted, "the bugger is friends with the Kennedys, isn't he?"

"Well, he was with Bobby—Robert that is," she hastily amended, not wanting Casey to see just how tightly knit that summer community had been.

"Mostly just, is it? 'Tis alright woman. It wouldn't surprise me did the man have a direct line to the Pope."

Pamela thought it was perhaps best to let the subject of Jamie lie. Neither he nor Casey had ever spoken of what had happened between them but she knew there had been a confrontation of some sort and that neither man had emerged from it feeling particularly warm and fuzzy toward the other.

Casey must have sensed her mood for he switched topics himself.

"Do ye remember where ye were when ye heard the President had been killed?"

"Oh yes," she said, recalling with a terrible clarity the stark shock of that day. "I was in a store, buying a chocolate bar on my way home from school. It was on the radio and I remember a shock wave went all down my body, rippled from the top of my head to my feet. I dropped the chocolate on the floor and just stood there. The man behind the counter looked as if he'd turned to stone. It felt as though the world stopped just for a second. You could feel the earth skip a heartbeat and no one was breathing. It felt like we would never breathe properly again. I couldn't comprehend how he could be gone, how there could be a blank space in the universe where that strong, amazing spirit had existed. He and his brothers seemed immortal somehow. All of a piece with the American dream: sailors, dreamers, doers. I think the American dream was bruised for all of us after he died. It still existed, but it wasn't golden anymore."

"It must have been quite the time an' place while it lasted, though."

"It was," she said, aware that her tone brooked on the wistful.

"Ye miss it, don't ye?"

"What makes you say that?"

"Because, darlin', I saw ye in that element, didn't I? Ye fit with that world. With the sailboats an' big summer houses an' the politics an' all the glamor that goes with it. I don't doubt yer Da' wanted ye to marry a man of that ilk, someone like a Kennedy or a Fitzgerald. Didn't he?"

"Yes, it was what was expected of me, that I would marry well and within the Irish American aristocracy. The Kennedys were the stratosphere though. I'm sure my father would have settled for a lesser satellite."

"Yer Da' will have been fond of Jamie then, I suppose?"

"Yes," she said knowing there was little use in coloring the truth. "He was fond of Jamie. Apparently they kept in touch long after that summer on the Vineyard."

"I wonder what he'd have thought of me. Had he lived, Jewel, he'd likely have chased me off with a shotgun."

She had wondered herself at times what her father would have thought of Casey, an ex-IRA rebel who worked with his hands and had spent five years in prison. Likely he wouldn't have been terribly impressed until he knew the man behind the history.

"You're a finer man than any I've ever known," she said, stroking the side of his face with one hand, his stubble rasping pleasantly against her oiled palm.

"It's only that it intimidates a man a bit to know that ye came from such wealth an' privilege, that ye were meant for country clubs an' big homes on the ocean. I wonder that all this," he indicated the room with a wave of his hand, though she knew he meant the world beyond this room as well, "doesn't seem a wee bit shabby to ye? I took ye from that world, like pluckin' a jewel from its proper settin', an' perhaps I'd not the right to do so."

"That world was a lonely place for me, Casey. Maybe I would have found my place in it when I was an adult, but maybe I wouldn't have. No, I belong here with you, with the dog, the cat and the sheep, in a house that creaks in welcome each time I step over the threshold, in a wee hollow filled with flowers. A house built by a man who hammered every board into place with love. You're my home, man. I would never be happy elsewhere."

He took the hand that still rested lightly on his jaw and kissed it.

"I may not be able to give ye the sailboats and summer homes, but I can promise ye this one thing, Jewel. As long as I am alive in this world, you will always be loved."

"Thank you for that," she said quietly, depositing a kiss on the back of his neck. She moved awkwardly off his back and lay down beside him. She put her face into the hollow at the base of his skull, the crush of his curls soft beneath her cheek. His hair had grown long over the winter, though he kept threatening to shave it off the minute he found the time for it. She rather hoped he wouldn't though, for he had beautiful hair: thick, dark and loosely curled. Tonight it smelled of pine pitch and rock dust, elements with which he had worked that day. She loved the luxuriant silkiness of it and privately thought he looked like a wonderfully sexy pirate. It was not a thought she voiced aloud, knowing he would shave it off that second, lack of time be damned.

"Will we ever speak of it, d'ye suppose?" he asked so softly that it hardly registered.

"About what?" she asked on the rise of a yawn. The heat of his body near her own and the vapors of roses and lavender, chamomile and honey all combined to make her sleepy, not that she needed much of a nudge in that direction these days. Casey's next words, however, brought her fully alert.

"About you an' Love Hagerty," he said, voice still quiet, but now with an under-note of pain with which she was all too familiar.

She was silent for a long moment, heart thudding hard in her chest. She was certain that Casey must be able to feel it, as closely as their two skins lay together.

"I—I don't know. What would we say?"

"I don't know, Pamela, only that I think as much as it hurts the both of us, still we'll have to speak of it one day."

She didn't respond, though she knew his words were not framed in the form of a question, but rather a statement of fact that neither of them wanted to face.

Though they did not speak of it, she knew that didn't preclude either of them thinking about it, and she was sensitive enough to her husband in all his various moods that she knew when it was occupying him. A darkness would come down over him, visible even in the shade his eyes took on, and he would leave the house for a few hours. She never asked where he went during those absences, for fear that he might actually tell her.

The silence in the room was so complete that she could hear the tap of empty rose cane against the window, fretting in the night wind.

"Aye, not tonight then," he said, voice weary with all the words neither of them seemed able to utter.

"I'm sorry," she whispered in his ear.

"Aye, darlin'," he said and took her hand in his own, face still turned from her. "So am I."

SHE LAY FOR SOME TIME AFTER CASEY FELL ASLEEP, listening to the hiss and pop of the peat fire in the grate and the soft sighing of the wind outside their bedroom. Finally, she gave up on sleep and slid from the bed as quietly as her body allowed. She put Casey's discarded shirt on and went to sit by the window. The windowsills were a good eighteen inches thick and provided a solid seat for watching the moon cross the sky on restless nights. Tonight, however, was moonless, the yard below thick with shadows. She gazed out sightlessly, already chilled to the bone and knowing it had nothing to do with the temperature in the room.

For months now, this thing had stood between them, and she knew well that the longer it stood there, the more damage it was going to inflict on their marriage. Yet what could she say to him? What could she tell him to take away the things she had done? To wipe from his mind the images and feelings that she knew he could not help but imagine, in painful detail. She did not see how words could help, but was uncertain how they were going to get through this whole without her having to say them. Perhaps it would be better than what he was imagining, but what if it wasn't? What then? Everything between them was so terribly tenuous right now, their whole relationship as delicate as a spider's web touched by the elements and torn by the wind. If they spoke of it and he couldn't handle it—and she knew it was likely he wasn't going to like it one bit—then what? She could not lose him again, nor have him stay because he felt he had to for their child.

The night he had come for her at Jamie's those few months ago, she had hoped that they had mended things well enough so that this would not be necessary; the conversation that Casey felt must be had. It had been a foolish hope born of the sheer relief that Casey had come home to her, as much as he was able at that time. Being that she had waited months not knowing if she would ever see him again, it had been more than enough—then. But now it was all too apparent that something was missing. There was a constraint between them, if not in the small rituals of domestic life then in the bed where they had once given of themselves completely.

There had been the dreadful night when he had found out. It was still there, whole in her memory like a wound that hurt to touch but was impossible to avoid. She shivered and drew her arms tight around her chest. His scent was heavy on the shirt and she breathed deeply of it, allowing it to give her comfort. That night, she had tried to explain her infidelity, how the FBI had given her very little choice, and Love Hagerty had given her even less, that she had simply seen no other way out of their predicament and had thought her body a small price to pay for her husband's life. He had told her he would, all things considered, rather be dead. He had meant it and she had meant it too, and would do it again if it meant keeping him alive. But he was male and therefore could not understand her reasoning, not that she could blame him.

She had made a terrible mistake that night, but even in hindsight she did not see how she might have fixed it. When Casey had asked if she felt anything for Love Hagerty while she lay in his bed, she had been unable to answer. She had meant only that her body had, despite the revulsion of her heart, sometimes responded to the man's touch. She was afraid to ask Casey if he understood, afraid to open the wound that was her affair with Love Hagerty, for fear of what might be said. Conversations had a life of their own and that was particularly true of one that could not help but be volatile and emotional.

The night he had brought her home there had been too many emotions in the air to say anything, and after that, it had seemed best to let it all lie. But that night had given them back to one another, and so she would not touch the shape of it for fear of changing the pattern of their lives. He had taken her first to a small tumbledown cottage deep in the countryside and given her the choice of continuing their marriage, their life together and she had felt the gift of that fully. And then he had brought her home here, where they might begin to heal and he, she hoped, could forgive her enough to allow her back into his heart completely.

The house was warm, a fire glowing in the hearth. The light reflected in small shifting patches in the teacups that adorned the sideboard, and the floorboards gleamed softly. She sighed in relief. It was good to be home, like sinking into a warm bath on a chilly winter evening. She turned to Casey.

"How—"

He smiled. "I did hope ye'd come home with me tonight, Jewel. I didn't want to bring ye back to a cold house. That hardly seemed a proper welcome."

"*Thank you,*" *she said, feeling oddly nervous. Here they were home, just as she had wanted and hoped and prayed for these last few months, and now she didn't know what to do or say.*

Casey took her coat from her and she sat down in a chair by the fire, her legs suddenly wobbly as a new colt's. He came and knelt on the rug before the fire, adding a couple of bricks of peat to it. The heat steadied her nerves a little. She needed to tell him about the baby.

Casey rubbed his hands together and took a deep breath. Before she could utter a word, he turned to her with an odd look on his face and said, "Well, let's get on with it then."

"*Get on with what?*" *she asked, confused.*

"*Sex,*" *he said bluntly. "We need to get it out of the way."*

"*Oh,*" *she said, feeling a little dizzy suddenly as the full import of what lay between them hit her. There was no way for Casey to take her to bed without it conjuring up the pain that needed only the slightest breath to stir it to full wakefulness. How could she lie down with him, give him everything without any barriers between them, when she knew the images that would haunt him every time he touched her?*

"*I'm sorry, Jewel. That came out a bit more blunt than I'd intended. It's just that,*" *he breathed out heavily, "I want to make love to ye, but I'm afraid to as well. I'm afraid of what I'll feel. I'm afraid of hurting ye. But I know waiting will only make it worse."*

She swallowed and began to unbutton her blouse. Casey opened his mouth to say something and then snapped it shut as his eyes took in the changes in her body since last he'd touched her. She shrugged the blouse off, the firelight flickering on the ivory of her breasts, each one tinged blue with the dilated veins of pregnancy.

"*Oh,*" *Casey said, and it was a small shocked sound, as though someone had let his air out.*

"*Give me your hands, man,*" *she said softly and after a moment, he turned toward her and extended two hands that shook ever so slightly. She took them and placed them on the round of her belly.*

"*Did ye... did ye know ye were pregnant the night I left ye?*" *he asked.*

"*Yes, though just.*"

"*Oh, Pamela. Why didn't ye tell me?*" *His large hands spanned the small mound, eyes dark and riveted to the obvious pregnancy.*

"*I didn't think it was fair. I wanted you to stay for love, not for duty.*"

Casey bowed his head and took a deep breath. "Woman, there's never been a minute since I first saw ye that I haven't loved ye. I was angry. I was hurtin' somethin' fierce, but never doubt that I loved ye the whole time."

"*And I you,*" *she said softly, tears running freely down her face. "You scared the hell out of me, man."*

"*How... how...*" *words seemed to fail him, for he swallowed, the long line of his throat trembling.*

"Three months—so far, so good," she said, knowing the fears that haunted him as well as she knew her own.

He nodded, as though afraid to even give voice to hope. They had been hopeful so many times before, and been sorely pained at each loss. This time she felt it was different, that this pregnancy would result in a living child, a child that would help them heal.

He took her down gently, there on the rug in front of the fire.

She shivered when he touched her, though the fire was hot against her skin.

He brushed the hair away from her face and kissed her forehead tenderly before putting his lips to her own. She needn't have worried, for her response was immediate. Having been denied the touch of him for so long she found herself almost desperate, wanting him inside her, hard and needing, meeting her own need like fire striking tinder, setting off an uncontrollable blaze.

After, he stayed with her, skin to skin, his blood beating hard against her own. They were silent for a long time, both afraid to speak, yet content to be near one another for the first time in so many weeks. The night outside was silent with frost and cold, but inside it was snug and peaceful.

"Do you know how I love you?" she said suddenly, worried that after all that had passed between them, he still would not know this one crucial thing.

He propped himself up on an elbow and looked down at her, face tender.

"Aye, there are times, Pamela, when I get a glimpse of it an' count myself blessed among men for the ferocity of such a thing. Were it only half of what I feel for ye, I would still count myself the most lucky of souls. But I know it to be the equal of my own. We are, both of us, fortunate."

The kiss was long and spoke of many things neither of them could find the words for. Their mutual sorrow at the loss of the trust they had once taken as a given, the fear around this newly begun life they had created, the relief that their bodies still knew one another and responded with gratitude for the touch of the other. The knowledge that eventually they would heal this and the many other things that needed time and chance.

She got out of the chair, thoroughly cold now, and climbed back into the bed beside Casey. He was hot to the touch and roused a little at the icy contact of her hands. She snuggled tightly along his length and he murmured in his sleep, a sound of contentment and intimacy, then pulled her closer with his left arm, drifting back into the deep sleep she had disrupted.

Chapter Four

February 1973

The Boy from Liverpool

THE POWERS THAT BE HAD CHOSEN LIVERPOOL as David's cover. Liverpool with its centuries of Irish immigration and history or, as his boss had put it, "Liverpool has always been an Irish cesspit. No one could ever trace you there, and it's not likely anyone would ever try."

Not likely, but he had his facts in order just in case. His family and siblings, where they had lived—Merseyside of course—had been there since the first great influx of Irish after the 1798 Rebellion. The numbers were so high of those who had fled Ireland in those days, and the record keeping so poor that no one could trace a family in the tangled web of Liverpool's Irish history. He was meant to be the product of an English father and an Irish mother, thus explaining his sympathy to the Loyalist cause. He had spent a few weeks in Liverpool, familiarizing himself with the Merseyside and nursing a headache from his practice of the Scouse accent and dialect.

As covers went, it was less flimsy than most and he could occasionally take refuge in acting the foreign naïf. That didn't wash with Billy though, who was as tough a little cur as David had ever had the misfortune to meet. He was a touch leery of the child, for he had fixed himself to David like a barnacle to a weathered boat from the first day he had taken up residence in the big, drafty old house. He was a suspicious lad, with big white teeth in a narrow, pale face that made him look like a cagey squirrel. He was fifteen, a slip of a child who would likely one day be wiry and tough. Right now he seemed like a wee boy trying to stand in a full grown gangster's boots.

David doubted that much got past this child's screen. It had likely been a matter of survival for Billy much of his life. David had noticed the boy watching him several times.

It was as they were walking on the Protestant side of the Shankill divide near a particularly grimy drinking club on Centurion Street that Billy finally confronted him. David had been half expecting it, and half praying he was wrong about the boy's suspicions. He was not.

"So what bit of England was it ye said ye came from?"

The boy was direct if without finesse, David thought.

"Liverpool." He didn't offer any more explanation than that. It was always a mistake to offer more information than had actually been requested.

"Ye might have Boyd fooled, 'cuz he's so busy lookin' at yer arse that's he's not payin' attention. But ye don't seem right to me." Billy leaned up against the filthy wall of a betting shop and took a speculative drag on his hand-rolled. David was in no way prepared for the next question.

"Did ye know Lawrence?"

He schooled his face quickly to a bored nonchalance, fairly certain there was a method to the boy's queries and that he was going to have to play this situation carefully, but he saw little reason to prevaricate. If he was made, he was made. He had learned long ago to make the best of a bad or even lethal situation and he was highly trained in the art of playing both ends against the middle. Besides, if the child was going to rat him out, it was likely he would have done so already. If he hadn't, then he had an angle, and David was a big fan of angles because they could always be worked in both directions.

"Lawrence who?"

But Billy's attention had been sidetracked.

"Yer bein' stared at, well, glared at, really," Billy said and nodded toward a man who stood in the doorway of a corner shop, newspaper in one hand and a bottle of milk in the other. David looked and then looked again, thinking it was quite possible to jump out of one's skin in startlement. For standing on the corner, and most definitely not being fooled in the least by David's disguise, was Patrick Riordan, as tall and dark and even slightly more fearsome than the version David had held, somewhat gilded, in his heart and mind.

Pat tilted his head, hesitated for a moment and then stepped across the pavement, making toward David, who realized he had to move, and move now before disaster struck right here in the middle of this narrow road.

He walked toward Pat, fishing out a cigarette so that he could ask for a light and ostensibly have a reason to be chatting to this man should any interested eyes be observing him.

Christ, he breathed deeply through his nose as Pat came within feet of him, a look of furious incredulity on his face. He had forgotten how big the man was. Long and lean with it, so it wasn't as apparent, but a big bloody bastard nevertheless. They stopped at the same time, like two wary dogs about to square off.

"What the hell are ye doin' in this neighborhood?" David said, trying to avoid the dark eyes and look nonchalantly off into the distance.

"What the hell am *I* doin' in this neighborhood?" Pat asked indignantly.

"Point taken," David said, eyes low and scanning the area for potential witnesses to this unlikely and dangerous meeting. "Look, just pretend you're giving me a light for a cigarette or something, and then we'll move on and I'll get word to you on a safe place to meet. Just act like you don't know me."

"All things considered," Patrick said, with a pointed look at Billy still standing on the sidewalk, eyeing them with great interest, "I think maybe I don't."

"It's not what you think," David said, thinking that what it was was going to be even harder to explain—not that he owed him explanations—and yet he supposed that in some way he did. For this man was his friend, the best one he had ever had, and friendship was owed a debt, if nothing else.

"Oh, I'm afraid it probably is," Pat said with no small sarcasm, and kept on walking, "but I'll reserve judgement for now."

"Kind of you," David muttered under his breath, slouching his way back to where Billy stood.

"Know him?" Billy asked, his face suspiciously innocent.

"Aye, somewhat," David said, striving to sound as nonchalant as his pounding heart would allow.

"Really? Seemed as if ye knew him pretty well."

David shrugged as if to say it didn't matter to him one way or the other if Pat Riordan dropped off the face of the earth. He did not want the man targeted because of the last five minutes.

Billy tossed his cigarette to the ground, stepping on the spark of ash that was left. He was a small boy, even for his age but he more than made up for it in sheer bravura. David knew to be wary around him. If the child even breathed his suspicions to Boyd or any of his ilk, David would be found in several pieces out back of some grotty drinking club. He waited, drawing out the smoking of his own cigarette to give the boy time. He wasn't going to speak first. A mistake like that would only confirm the child's suspicions.

"Well then, here 'tis. Maybe I don't give a fock if yer a copper as long as ye take care of Boyd."

"How do you mean—take care?" David asked quietly, careful to keep his accent in place, even if it wasn't fooling this child.

Billy looked at him, a long assessing look, his blue eyes as dark and clouded as the sea that lay beyond this troubled city.

"I think ye know fine what I mean, Davey."

Unfortunately, David thought, that was all too true.

"I'll tell ye what though—there's one other thing I want in trade for my silence."

"Aye," said David dryly, "an' what would that be?"

"I want to talk to Casey Riordan."

Chapter Five
February 1973
Billy

D AVID HAD WEIGHED HIS OPTIONS before giving Billy an answer. However, in the end he had gone to see Casey, not trusting the telephone for discreet communication. He had bearded the lion in his den, so to speak, sneaking in the back door of the Youth Center on the one night of the week that Casey still worked there.

It had been a less than auspicious start to the proceedings, as Casey had greeted him with a gun and a brusque,

"Who are ye and what the hell do ye want?"

At least, thought David, swallowing hard to digest the heart in his throat, his disguise had fooled one of the Riordans. Then again, it was dark in the back entry and this was not a good neighborhood in which to be lurking unexpectedly around back doors.

After David had stated his name and purpose, Casey had eased back on the gun but still sounded as though he would be happy to shoot David should he move too suddenly or say something Casey didn't like.

"Well now that I know who ye are, I'll ask again. What the hell is it that ye want?"

David explained about Billy's request and the reasons behind it, then went on to explain how the request had come to him.

"Me?" Casey Riordan demanded, raising a black brow and giving his visitor a narrowed dark eye that produced a familiar clench in David's gut. Why he found Patrick's brother so fearsome, he wasn't certain. It wasn't as if the man had ever harmed him—threatened it by his mere presence and aura, certainly, but never actually *done* it. Perhaps it was just that he really looked as though he would like to occasionally.

"Yes, you," David said trying to sound assertive. "He won't talk unless it's you. I've done my best to persuade him without your help, trust me, but he says it's you and no one else. He was a friend of Lawrence's, you see."

Casey nodded and sat, rubbing his large hands over his face and sighing heavily.

"Aye, I see. Alright, tell the lad I'll listen to what he has to say, but whether or no' I can help is another matter altogether."

"You don't need to. I'll get him somewhere safe and set up. I'll do it myself if the company won't back me."

This received another raised eyebrow and a look of profound cynicism which David was all too well aware the British special forces had more than earned here in Northern Ireland. Often people who were lured into working for either the army or any of the more shadowy organizations that proliferated here like wheat on a threshing floor, were promptly and callously discarded once they had outworn their usefulness. At that point, the inevitable usually took place. If they were lucky–and they rarely ever were—it was a quick, if brutal, death. The unlucky ones found themselves bound and gagged and tortured in an isolated cottage for days until the merciful bullet to the back of the head was administered. Casey's cynicism might be profound, but it was also the opinion and experience of a realist.

"You loved Lawrence and he thought the world of you, so yes, I'd little doubt on that score alone that you would talk to Billy. We need to finish this for him, Casey."

Casey didn't reply, and the dark eyes were as unfathomable as a lake in winter, but he nodded curtly. "Bring him then."

He had given David directions to a location in the countryside where he felt they could meet unobserved.

The upshot of this consisted of David escorting a nervous Billy, who chewed his nails non-stop during the hour-long drive and was so tense that David's shoulders felt as though they were up around his own ears by the time they arrived. If arriving was the correct state to describe the location Casey had chosen for their meeting.

Ireland was scattered with small abandoned cottages, left as they stood generations before. The Irish did not believe in tearing down such buildings, for what if their inhabitants were to return and find their home gone? What if ghosts lingered near and sought shelter within walls that had once rung with laughter and song, once been both shelter and sanctuary?

David thought even a ghost would be hard put to find adequate harbor from the elements in this particular cottage, for there were only three walls remaining and a tumbledown chimney wound about with vines and mortared with moss and lichens. A fingernail paring of moon sat, gold and watchful, just above the scrim of stone.

The inside was empty, the only noise that of the wind moving through the trees and whistling softly against the ancient grey stone. A raven came flapping down and perched ominously on the top of what had once been a doorway. David felt an urge to quote Poe at it, but squelched it quickly for

Casey had come round the edge of one ragged wall, silent as a wolf in the night.

Billy quailed a bit when brought face to face with the man about whom he had heard much but never encountered in the flesh. David had a great deal of empathy for him, but pushed the boy forward with a gentle hand.

"Sit an' relax. I won't bite ye," Casey said to the boy, attempting to break the tension that lay over them all like glass.

"Yer a wee bit more imposin' than I imagined," Billy said and sat as though he dared not disobey the big, dark man in front of him.

"Aye, well, that may be so but Lawrence never feared me, not even when he first met me and nor need you. I'll not hurt ye lad, nor abuse ye in any way. Just be straight with me an' I'll give ye the same in return. Fair enough?"

Billy nodded and swallowed. Casey looked him in the eye and asked, "Will ye want yer man there to stay? I'm comfortable either way but I realize ye may not be, so what would ye prefer?"

Billy looked at David, who nodded in assurance that whatever he wanted was fine by him.

"He can stay. It's better if ye both hear what I have to say, I think maybe."

Casey nodded. "Yer right. Good thinkin', man." He nodded to David to sit and David wondered how he had so completely taken control of the situation. The man was a natural, if at times reluctant, leader and all in his aura seemed to respond immediately to this fact.

"So, let's start with this—why me?" Casey asked, his expression guarded.

"Because Lawrence was my friend. 'Course we only ever called him Flip. He was a wee bit older than me but he looked out for us younger lads, even if it meant he had to steal or... other things, to keep us fed. There were five of us who lived on the streets together when the season was right for it. Had a wee tent that we set up behind some bushes in a vacant lot. We stole fruit from the markets an' lemonade an' bread an' candy. 'Twas grand when it weren't rainin'. We was a ragged bunch but it was like havin' a family for a bit, one ye'd scrabbled together from odds n' sods, but a family anyway."

"So how did ye end up in the home?"

"Got pulled in by the police for stealin' a feckin' tub of margarine, if ye can believe it. An' once they realized I'd no family nor guardian, they put me in there. Boyd specializes in *troubled* boys, ye understand."

Casey nodded. "Aye, I imagine that makes it simpler for him to manipulate yez."

"He waits until yer likely to stay as not, because he treats ye like a wounded rabbit for a bit, aye. Ye get lulled into thinkin' it's not such a bad deal, three squares, a roof to keep the rain off and somewhere warm to sleep at night." Billy shifted on the pine stump, ramming his hands deeper into his jacket.

"Then ye hear steps on the stair an' outside yer bedroom at night, an' he pauses there as if he's checkin' to make sure everyone's safe an' sleepin', but it don't feel that way—ye know, like a parent checkin' on a child. An' then he starts with the rubbin' against ye in the cloakroom or the kitchen when no one else is about, but like it's accidental. An' then one night he's in yer bedroom an' he's rubbin' himself on ye, or makin' ye wank him with yer hand, or," Billy shrugged, "he wanks ye, dependin' on his mood, or he makes ye suck him off or take it in yer backside. It's the price ye pay to have somewhere to live an' most of the boys don't have anywhere else to go. They just see it as part of the deal. Some of them don't even have enough smarts to know it's wrong."

"An' what about yerself?" Casey asked, tone casual. "Did ye feel it was wrong when it started happenin' to you?"

Billy shrugged again, the blue eyes candid. "Aye, I did, but I was bein' fed, an' I figured I could stand it for a full belly. He didn't hit me, nor did any of his friends—though some were a wee bit rough."

"How old were ye—when it started?"

"Thirteen." Billy's voice was flat and his eyes no longer met Casey's but looked out beyond to the horizon, though David was certain he was blind to the beauty of the evening.

"Listen, it's more than that. There's a man comes round, but only after dark. I don't think he's there for any of the boys, but it's like ye can feel that he's there the minute he comes through the door. I've never seen his face, but I know his voice. It's more educated soundin', like he went to a good school or had money growin' up. There's somethin' not right about him."

David took a deep breath through his nose, seeing clearly in his mind the strange man from his first night in the house, the one who had never revealed his face but whose presence had hung behind him like a chill draft from a cave.

"I heard them talkin' one night. I'd gone down for a drink of water. I'm light on my feet an' the stairs don't squeak when I take them like they do for some of the other lads. They were talkin' about things to do with their wee club, rules an' regulations an' who owed money into the tea tin sort of thing an' then suddenly the toff one was sayin' somethin' about eliminatin' people. About makin' targeted hits an' havin' a kill squad for it."

"An' who were they plannin' to kill?" Casey asked in a steel-edged tone.

This news came as no shock to either David or Casey. There had been rumors of just such an organization for a long time, but to be told it was more than rumor still sat hard in a man's stomach. James Kirkpatrick had told him it was true, but that finding the men behind it was like tracing smoke on a foggy day.

"Republicans, Catholics—the toff said any Taig was as good as another." Billy shrugged apologetically. "It's not that I haven't heard that sort of talk before, when men drink an' get together for the drummin' on the 12th but... it wasn't so much the words he was sayin' as *how* he was sayin' them. He was so cold. I'll tell ye..." Billy looked Casey in the face again, his blue eyes dark with fear, "not much scares me, but that man does."

Casey flicked a look at David, who tilted his head just enough to acknowledge it. They would have to talk more about this later, privately. It was more than either of them had anticipated hearing from Billy. The boy was taking an enormous risk in order to show good faith. What they did with it was up to them. It was the sort of knowledge David knew that they both would come to regret having.

"Why would ye tell us this?" Casey asked, voice soft, but still with an edge that said he was wary of this boy.

Billy shrugged and looked up at the crescent of moon. "Because people might not care so much about boys gettin' raped, but this kind of information has real value. I don't know a lot in this world, but *that* I know. An' if this information should destroy the men involved, then they won't be free to do anything else either. It would kill all the birds in the bush with one stone. And," he gave David a slightly apologetic glance, "as a form of insurance, if ye know an' something happens to me then I can't just disappear with no one the wiser. Because I think that man knew I was listenin' and I don't know how he would know 'twas me for I was well hid in the wee notch at the top of the stairs, but all the same, there's a feeling in the pit of my gut that tells me he knows."

"Then ye'd best be careful, boy. An' you too." He nodded at David, then stood, signaling the meeting was at an end.

He didn't make any promises, and David understood the wisdom of that. Casey knew that boys like Billy didn't trust promises or tender words. They would only believe in a man who had walked the same streets and had to be as tough as they did, even if for different reasons.

Walking back through the twilit field with Billy in tow, David wondered if the can of worms they had just peered into was going to prove more than any of them had reckoned with.

CASEY SAT FOR A TIME AFTER DAVID LEFT WITH THE BOY, watching the whisper-thin crescent moon float over the hilltops. It was that lovely smoky gold that appeared this time of year. It was peaceful here, which was in part why he had chosen the spot. No one was likely to pass by. Sometimes it seemed as though no one had done so for several years, for it had that feel of a spot where there had been no human interference for a very long time.

The place in his chest where Lawrence sat was raw and tender. He had been hit hard by Billy's story. He wasn't certain he believed the boy entirely. There was something a bit sly about him, for all the appearance of truth. But what boy, having lived at the mercy of Boyd McCarthy, wouldn't be cagey and a wee bit sly? There were things that rang true, things that matched what Lawrence had told him. And David, who was living in the house, seemed to believe him and he trusted David's instincts. There was a great deal that could be said about the British forces in Ireland, but generally speaking, they didn't put complete fools in charge of the sort of operations David always seemed to be involved in.

He sat until he was chilled and the moon had gone to hide amongst the high branches of a yew. He realized that he was no longer thinking about Lawrence or what the boy Billy had told him. He was thinking about his wife and avoiding what lay under that, the way one avoided a live wire or a pot of scalding lye.

He had promised himself before their reconciliation he would not punish her for what she had done. He understood in a logical fashion that she had committed adultery in order to keep him safe, that she had believed—with a fair amount of cause—that she could keep him alive by going to Love Hagerty's bed. Logic had little to do with emotion, however, and emotionally he had been furious and hurt beyond anything he had ever imagined. He felt like the proverbial lion some days. Only the thorn wasn't in his paw, it was in his heart.

Thus far, he had kept his promise. Outwardly, he thought he had done well, but now and again he would see how Pamela watched him with a haunted look in her eyes. Or how there was just a millisecond of hesitation at his touch, as though she felt the reticence in his heart that he tried so hard to hide. In those moments, he knew, he was not fooling his wife in the least.

What they had between them was rare. He knew it, and he treasured it as something beautiful and whole that he had never expected to be blessed with. He thought of it sometimes as a pearl hidden away in the heart of an oyster, lucent and delicate, shimmering with an infinite variety of colors and lights. Now the pearl had been exposed, and there were flaws in it that he knew he would have to examine, but could not find the courage yet.

He moved out into the night, leaving the crumbling stone walls behind. The raven had long flown and the land was flowing into the dark, melding with the sky.

It was long past time to be going home.

Chapter Six
All or Nothing

SINCE LAWRENCE'S DEATH, PAMELA HAD DREADED COMING HOME to an empty house but tonight she was simply relieved to be in out of the rain. The sharp pain in her chest where Lawrence's memory sat was slowly dulling, and this in itself made her sad because life moved on even when it seemed hardly possible for it to do so. She and Casey had begun to talk of him, though it was still difficult and not something they did often. But she knew when Casey was thinking about him, from the look on his face and the fact that he usually went outside and did any sort of hard labor he could find for an hour or two, before returning, looking marginally less haunted.

She shut the door behind her, glad to be away from the city, away from today's job. It had been a long, unpleasant day of taking pictures for the insurers of a pub that had been hit with a pipe bomb. A group calling themselves the 'Redhand Defenders' was taking responsibility. No one had been killed in the blast but there had been some very bad injuries and blood and charred flesh on the twisted stools and splintered woodwork.

It was late and Casey wasn't home yet. She sighed, eyeing the clock and easing her body into a kitchen chair. The Aga kept the house warm even when they were both gone for most of the day. On a filthy night like tonight, it was ecstasy to come home to a cozy, warm kitchen. Not that she was away much these days. Since she had realized she was pregnant she had quit her old job of photographing dead bodies, mutilated and otherwise, that littered the ditches and streets of Belfast and the surrounding countryside, compliments of their unofficial and never-ending war. She didn't want to risk this pregnancy and she knew that her work was a bone of contention between herself and Casey. And their marriage was, she knew all too well, too fragile to bear much stress just now. Today's job was a one off, a favor to an associate who had a family emergency. The few jobs she had taken in the last months had been mainly weddings, christenings and communions. Even those were getting awkward and exhausting as her belly continued to expand. It was time to quit until after the birth, and maybe stay unemployed for a good long while. The idea of being home with the baby each day held enormous appeal. Casey was making enough money for them to get by, even if only just. Remembering her own motherless and rather lonely childhood, she was firmly set on being there for her child. Casey had definite views on this issue too, and they did not include his wife—*'haring about the countryside after corpses an' madmen,'* as he had succinctly put it.

She took her shoes off and rubbed her feet. It was an awkward task at present, and soon to become impossible. She eyed the round of her belly with both affection and chagrin. The word 'blooming' had been used by a woman in the butcher's shop yesterday, which she supposed was a kind way of saying 'large'. Casey being the size he was, she expected a good-sized baby, but the magnitude of her belly now, at not quite seven months, was a bit alarming. The idea that she had somehow, despite all the birthing books' assurances, to push this child out after another two and a half months of growing seemed utterly preposterous and entirely terrifying. As reassuring as Casey tried to be, she knew it was a journey that she had ultimately to make alone.

She took a deep breath and leaned back into the chair, letting the quiet of the house gather around her and take the worst of the day away. This house was a sanctuary in the truest sense of the word, a place of shelter, of refuge, but mostly of love. Suddenly she wanted Casey badly, wanted the strength of his arms around her and the comfort of his voice speaking any sort of words—the plain ones that told of his day, or the lovely, half-silly ones he spoke to the mound of her belly each night before bed. He had been late several nights this week, but he often stopped off for a quick pint with Owen before coming home. She thought the snug of Owen and Gert's kitchen would be rather pleasant on this rainy evening, and maybe Gert would make her some of that spicy ginger tea that always settled her stomach nicely. She went upstairs and changed into more comfortable clothes, part of her eyeing the bed with a great longing to just get into it and have a long nap. But the need to see Casey took the upper hand over weariness so she dressed, brushed her hair out, applied a little lipstick and blush to revive her pale face, and went on her way to Owen and Gert's.

When she reached their stone house the lights in the front windows of the wee pub were out. She went around to the back, bent over in the wind and rain that had howled itself up into a real temper. The kitchen light was still glowing so she knew Gert was up. She rapped on the door, anticipating the warmth and the smell of bread dough that Gert always put up before retiring for the night.

Owen answered the door, ushering her in out of the wet with his customary quiet hospitality. Over the last months, Gert and Owen had come to feel like family to her, and they were as excited about this new baby as she and Casey were. It gave her a feeling of warmth and stability to have Owen and Gert in their lives and she had come to depend on their friendship and open door. Childless themselves, Pamela knew they had come to view her as a surrogate daughter.

The kitchen was warm and the remnants of dinner were on the table, the heady after-scents of Gert's homemade German sausage still lingering on the air. Her stomach growled at the proximity of a decent meal, and Gert was already up fixing her a plate. She sat, though it was apparent Casey was not here. He had been here recently, though. His presence was as large and powerful as the man himself, and he left a certain energy behind in places where he spent any amount of time.

She tucked in to the meal gratefully. Her appetite had only recently returned and she was famished much of the day. The sausages were perfectly spiced and accompanied by a generous portion of floury potatoes and gravy, and a side dish of dilled carrots. Gert did not believe in making talk when someone was eating. First, she always said, a full stomach, then time for talk. Pamela was happy to obey and made short work of the meal. Her entire body seemed to sigh in gratitude when she finished and leaned back in repletion, hoping she had the wherewithal to drive back home. At that point she took in the strange mood of her hosts. They were both looking at her as if she either had a terminal disease she wasn't yet aware of, or there was horrendous news hovering and they couldn't decide who had the grim duty of telling her.

"I thought Casey might be here. He was, wasn't he?" she asked, wishing they would just come out with whatever it was that so obviously had them tensed as a bow with a nocked arrow.

Gert drew a hard breath through her nose and let fly. "He *vas* here, alright. With that *hure*, but I told him that he could go elsewhere. Imagine bringing that *rothaarige hure* into my home when he knows how much we care for you—I—"

Owen sent a warning look in Gert's direction and she snapped her lips shut, biting the sentence in half, but it was too late. Pamela's recently eaten dinner turned over in her stomach. Her German was limited, but 'redheaded whore' was fairly straightforward. She had long feared that the pain and anger of her betrayal might cause him to do something rash, like rejoin his old compatriots in the IRA. But this... this was not something she had thought he would do. There was no doubting it though, for Gert's face was drawn into a perfect portrait of Teutonic disapproval that spoke volumes.

"What is it? What's going on?"

Owen sighed, one hand ruffling the thin hair on his scalp. "He was in here earlier tonight then, but he's moved along now."

"Moved along?" Pamela said, feeling like a stupid and increasingly nause-ated parrot.

Gert shook her head. "Owen, ve haf to tell her."

"Tell me what?" she looked directly at Owen, knowing panic was plain on her face and not caring in the slightest.

"Gert asked him to leave if he was goin' to be drinkin' with that woman again."

"What woman," she said slowly, "and what do you mean *again?*"

"That woman with the red hair," Gert said. "You go see for yourself. He is vis her now."

Pamela looked to Owen, hoping he could give her some innocent explanation for why her husband was seeing this redhead behind her back. Owen merely sighed, gave her a look of sympathy, and shook his head. "It's true, Pamela, he's been seen about with this woman a bit. She's been down more than the once from Belfast. I think there's nothin' to it, but he did leave here with her tonight. I don't know what the laddie was thinkin' bringin' her here, mind."

"Excuse me," she said and ran for the bathroom, where she was violently sick. After, she took a moment to rinse her mouth and face, both numb and furious at the same time. How dare he? How could he? And then the inevitable answer. *You know how, you know why, and you cannot blame him in the least.*

She took a deep breath and looked into the mirror. She was horribly pale and there were great dark circles under her eyes. She wanted to simply go home, get into bed, pull the quilts up over her head and bury herself in ignorance, but something stiffened her spine. The same thing that had allowed her to break the faith of her marriage bed in order to keep her husband whole was not going to allow her to take the path of least resistance now.

She went back into the kitchen, the smell of sausage now curdling her stomach. She swallowed hard and waved away Gert's attempts to pat her down with a wet cloth.

"Thank you," she said, "for telling me. I needed to know, and obviously Casey wants me to know if he brought her here."

"Pamela, sit down, would ye?" Owen said, his kindly face drawn with worry. "I'll go fetch the lad an' be certain I'll not let him bring that woman with him. I'll bring him here to you. You look dreadful ill, lass, I'll not like the idea of sendin' ye out in this weather with such news in yer mind."

"Thank you, Owen—I—" she took a deep breath, and bit down on a fresh wave of nausea. "I have to face him myself. I can't explain, but this—please don't let this make you think less of him. This is my fault."

She left then, blind and deaf to their protests and not feeling quite as culpable as her words had made out. She was hurt beyond anything she had ever known and very, very angry.

Being that there were only three pubs to choose from in Coomnablath, it didn't take long to find him. When he didn't drink at Owen's he'd been known to tip his elbow occasionally at The Emerald, a slightly more up-scale establishment with seating for more than six at a go. However, had he wanted to be discreet, Casey hardly would have taken the woman anywhere in Coomnablath at all. To take her to Owen's meant he wanted her to know, to rub her face in it.

She saw the woman first, for she was in profile directly across from the door as Pamela stepped in. She was beautiful, even in the dim light of the pub, hair a deep, burnished red that glowed in the dim, like fire spread over dark water. Her eyes were a sparkling aquamarine, her skin fresh and dewy in the manner of true redheads.

And then she looked at her husband, bold features in stark contrast to the redhead's delicacy, his dark hair curling damply over his collar, the restless power of his body apparent even as he sat relaxed with a half-drunk pint of Guinness in one hand, his other hand gesturing broadly as he spoke.

It would happen now and again, to be taken afresh by Casey's physical presence, to remember the attraction he held was not solely for her, that other women had and did notice his particular charms and some even had the temerity to act upon it. He had never responded before, had always gently but firmly informed them that he was a married man and took his vows seriously. Except that right now he didn't seem to be thinking about his marital state in the least.

The redhead reached across and pushed an errant curl away from his eyelashes, a simple gesture that held a wealth of unspoken things, an act of intimacy that told Pamela the woman was very comfortable with Casey. So Gert was right. This woman had been around her husband on a regular basis while she sat at home like a fool waiting for him, blindly trusting that he would not take his revenge on her. Bile surged hotly at the back of her throat and she thought she might be sick right there.

And then he looked directly at her, standing frozen in the doorway, hair in dripping rat tails, skin bled white with shock. She couldn't breathe and understood suddenly that he had known she was there the entire time and thus the act had been one of deliberate cruelty. She didn't feel her legs move, nor her feet walk across the floor, but suddenly she was there within a foot of them, but it was only Casey whose eyes she looked into.

"You bastard," she said and slapped him across the face. "If you're having an affair, at least let me know ahead of time, so I don't have to wait up any more."

Casey's head rocked back slightly, a look of shock imprinted across his features along with the outline of her hand. His mouth opened but no words came forth, nor was she inclined to wait for him to make his excuses.

She turned on her heel and strode out the door, banging it so hard that she could feel the jolt of the heavy oak in her very bones. Fury was filling her with a hot-white light, making her feel disconnected from the wet pavement beneath her feet.

She heard his step behind her before she'd even crossed the narrow roadway, but was too angry to turn back.

"Pamela, for Christ's sake. Stop!"

"Go to hell," she said furiously.

"I think I'm there already," he said, and there wasn't anger in the tone, only resignation. The words stopped her cold. She turned, a brick wall at her back, rain sluicing down pipes like a minor waterfall.

"I'm sorry," he said, the rain already running in rivulets down his face, tracing the tight-held lines around his mouth.

"For what, whoring around the village while I stay home?"

"No—Jaysus, woman, I'm not havin' an affair with anyone—particularly not with that one in there. I'm sorry for lettin' her touch me like that."

"Are you?"

"Ye want honesty then? No, at this present moment I am not particularly sorry, but I imagine I will be soon enough."

"Why are you seeing her then, if you're not having an affair?"

"She's an old friend of Robin's an' she heard I was livin' back here again, an' so she looked me up. She has a wee girl who she says Robin is the father of an' she's been wantin' to talk about him. I don't know why she touched me like she did. It's not been like that at all, woman."

She shook her head, knowing suddenly that it wasn't about the woman sitting back there in the dim light of the pub but rather about the ghost whose taint spread between them like something dark and oily, clinging to their every interaction and all the unspoken words. The fury that warmed her went out like a light switched off, and she felt a great chill settle in its place.

"Ye can trust me, woman. I'm a wee bit insulted that ye jump to conclusions so swiftly."

"But you can't trust me anymore, can you?" she said so softly it could barely be heard above the pounding of the rain. She knew the words had reached his ears though, for he swallowed, his mouth twisting as if he would say the words she needed for comfort and yet could not bring himself to do so.

He leaned forward as if to touch her, then merely put his forehead to the brick wall behind her shoulder. Against her, she could feel his warmth, in the chill of the night, yet there was no intimacy in the touch, just a pulsing of pain that divided them no matter how physically close they were. The baby was kicking and turning as if it sensed the cracks that were opening wide between its parents.

"Did you want to hurt me?" she asked, words barely above a whisper over the pain in her throat. "Is that what this is all about—revenge? Well congratulations, you did it. I felt like someone had jabbed me in the windpipe, like I could hardly breathe when I saw her touch you."

"Hurts doesn't it?" he said, the pain in his voice apparent even through the pounding of the rain against the pipes. "Imagine what it does to a man to know that another has touched his wife far more intimately than that, over an' over again, an' with her permission to do so."

"I don't want to talk about it. I don't even want to think about it," she said, feeling the terrible drop in her stomach that the mere mention of Love Hagerty still caused.

"Well, I can't *stop* thinkin' about it," he said, breath chill in her ear. Then he pushed away and walked off into the rain without so much as a backward glance, leaving her against the bricks alone.

LATER, SHE NEVER COULD REMEMBER HOW SHE MANAGED the drive home, though the torrential rain had forced her to go slowly, wiper blades whipping like fury. Her own rage was entirely doused by the guilt that dogged her every step since the first time she had considered betraying her husband in order to save his life.

Inside the house, she went directly upstairs. She was wet and chilled to the bone so she stripped off in the bathroom, grabbing the white cotton nightgown that hung behind the door. She wrapped a towel around her hair and lit the bedroom fire, stacking pine in a neat tripod to give the fire the air it needed to burn hot. The baby was quiet now, a hard, solid weight firmly fixed within its watery world.

She sat down in the chair beside the fire and waited for her husband, eyes fixed on the flames but every nerve trained for the sound of the door, and for the weight of Casey's step over the threshold.

It was another hour before it came and she had almost given up hope that he would come home that night. She could hear him banking the fire in the Aga and checking the downstairs as he did each night, making certain the doors and windows were secured against the night and the world beyond.

He came up the stairs quickly, light step belying his emotional state. He hesitated at the bedroom door and she thought her heart might stop right then with the agony of not knowing exactly what had brought him home.

Several very long moments passed before the door opened and he came into the room. She sat forward in the chair, clasping her cold hands tightly in her lap. He didn't look at her right away for his face was hidden in the muffling folds of a towel. He was soaked to the skin.

"Are you alright?" she asked. Casey's head emerged from the towel, hair whorled in a clockwise spin of dark curls. He put the towel down and pushed the hair back from his face.

"I feel a wee bit foolish, truth be told," he said, and indeed he did look slightly shamefaced. "I don't know what came over me in there. I just wanted for a minute that ye should feel the pain as I do."

She took a breath, but it wouldn't force its way past the constriction in her chest. Casey wasn't one to waste time on small talk nor to pretend that the scene outside the pub had not occurred.

"We can't go on this way, Casey," she said softly.

"Aye," he swallowed, the line of his throat tight with emotion. "I don't suppose we can."

He sat on the edge of the bed, keeping a distance between them. She looked at him, noting the weariness in his face—as though he bore a terrible burden that he could not put down. And so if he could not, it was up to her to take it from him, no matter the cost.

A chunk of wood shifted in the fire, sending up a spray of sparks. The movement broke the tight silence that lay between them.

"You once asked me to let you in—to give you all of myself or nothing. You said," she fought for control of her voice, throat tight with longing and fear, "that half a loaf wasn't enough to fill a man. And now I'm asking you the same thing, to let me in that I may go with you."

There was wary surprise on his face. "What?"

"Casey, you've been holding back something every time we've made love since—since you found out about Love."

He took a deep, shaky breath and stood, crossing the room to where she sat, the fire's heat penetrating through the thin weave of her nightgown. Moonlight lay in a broad strip across the floorboards, lighting the bones of his face in stark relief.

He knelt on the floor and put his head in her lap so she could not see his face. His arms lay lightly along her thighs and she could feel how they trembled. His whiskers were like needles against the fine skin of her inner thigh but she wouldn't have moved for the world right now. She didn't even dare to speak, though she laid her hand gently on his head, feeling the soft springiness of his curls and the tension that lay along his skin.

"I wish I knew how to reclaim ye," he said quietly, though his tone was fierce. "I wish I knew how to wipe the vision in my mind of him takin' ye, of him makin' love to my wife. It makes me feel as though I've a rope chokin' me round my neck every time I think of it. I wish I'd killed him with my own two hands an' maybe that would have washed the poison out." The hands in question were clenched into fists, bunched tight in the cloth of her nightgown.

"Oh God, Pamela, I'm sorry, but I cannot seem to shut it out. Every time ye lie with me—I see his hands on ye—touching ye. I put my hand to yer breast an' I swear I can see the marks of his fingers there still."

It was what she had feared, that despite the fact that Love Hagerty was no longer alive, the ghost of what she had done with him would linger about their bed, that the mere knowledge of it would rip Casey apart and never cease tormenting him. He was a strong man, and secure in the fact of her love. But he was also a man who needed to possess his woman, just as she herself needed to know her hold on him was stronger than any other force in the world.

She had racked her brain for months now, trying to think of a way to bring him back to her as they had been before he knew about Love. She could only think of one way.

She unbuttoned her nightgown and shrugged her shoulders, the fragile white cotton puddling around her hips, leaving her bare in the firelight. Casey lifted his head, feeling the faint breeze of the falling cloth.

"What are ye doin', woman?"

She put a hand to the tight line of his jaw, forcing him to meet her eyes.

"You could do anything to me," she said, pulse hammering in her neck. "Do you know that? I would let you do anything to me if I thought it would heal this between us. I never was this way for him. I need you to know that. I always kept as many clothes on as I could manage. I closed my mind and my heart to him. I could never give him the vulnerability of my naked body. I've only ever given those things to you. I would let you beat me if I thought it would take this away from us. I would even step aside and let you go to the bed of another woman. The beating," she said, and the words came out half-choked, "would have to wait until well after the baby is born, obviously."

Casey swallowed, his fingers biting into her thighs, eyes so dark with pain that she could barely discern pupil from iris.

"Jaysus, Pamela—*beat ye*? Pregnant or not, I could never raise a hand to ye in violence, an' I think ye know that well enough. An' be honest, could ye really countenance me bein' with another woman?" His gaze was as merciless as the fingers that gripped her flesh.

"I could if it meant you'd come back to me whole afterward."

"Could ye? Could ye live with the thought of it, of me touching another woman the way I do you? Of me lyin' naked an' aroused in her arms?"

It was her turn to swallow. She could not dislodge the acid taste that flooded her mouth at the thought of him with another woman. And suddenly she *could* see it all too clearly—the long line of him, the dark hair of his chest and groin against the pale body of another woman, his mouth on her fine skin. She knew what it was to have that strength brought to her service, while at the same time being completely at its mercy. She gave a small cry of pain at the image, but Casey wasn't about to let her turn away from the mirrored vision of his own agony.

"What about the thought of me findin' release, of maybe findin' her touch an' taste to my liking? No, Jewel, look at me. Of me inside another woman, making love to her. Maybe *feeling* love for her."

"Is that what you think? That I enjoyed it? That I felt something for him? I hated every minute of being in his bed. Hated it, do you understand? His touch made me sick to my stomach. I threw up the first time, right after. I took showers so hot my skin was raw and I couldn't even look at myself in a mirror."

"An' how did ye feel about me when ye were there with him?"

"In the bed, I couldn't think about you. I would have killed him then and there if I had. Or I'd have gone mad. But after—later—" she looked into his eyes, her own dry and burning, "I hated and loved you in equal measure," she said. "Every time you were home, I wanted to keep you in bed the entire time. I wanted you to exorcise his touch somehow—burn it off me. I wanted you to be rough so I would feel you in me after you were gone. I wanted him to see your marks on my body when I had to go back to him."

"Aye, I remember," he said, "I did think somethin' wasn't quite right. But I wasn't likely to look too closely at it, was I?" He smiled but the expression didn't quite come off.

"I'd had sex with different women before ye came along, Jewel. Ye know that well enough, and I always enjoyed it, and liked to believe the woman in question was left satisfied as well. From the first with you, though, it was different. It was makin' love, an' it was sacred, an act of consecration in the dark or light. No one knows me like ye do, Pamela. There were doors I opened for ye that I never thought I could. The trust that lay between us—for me—was absolute. And to know that ye couldn't trust me when that man came between us..." his grip on her thighs was bruising but she welcomed the pain. "That ye didn't come to me and tell me what was going on—I—" his voice failed, the tears that stood in his eyes bright in the half-light. "Well, then I realized ye'd never trusted me in the way I thought ye had, and it like to killed me to know it."

She swallowed convulsively, wanting to break the lock his eyes held her in but knew she owed him this small thing, to feel the pain for a moment even as he did.

"What we have when we lie together, it's something rare. And I don't just mean the passion, though that's rare enough in itself. But that somehow I am both stronger and weaker in yer arms, that you gave me such trust even after ye'd been raped."

He closed his eyes for a second, breathing in deeply through his nose, in an effort to quell the emotion that had overtaken him. When he opened his eyes again, she saw that rather than mastering his feelings he had laid himself bare to her and for the first time in months, she felt as though she were looking directly through to the core of the man.

"I know what men see when they look at ye, Jewel. I understand that they lust after ye. But it never mattered because I never felt they knew the half of ye. They didn't really know what it was to love ye. Only I had the keys to that kingdom. Then Love Hagerty," he ground the name out between gritted teeth, "he more than lusted for ye, he loved ye. And I felt somehow that he desecrated what we had, as though he'd brought violence into the church we'd built together. And I am afraid," he bowed his head down to her knees again, "so afraid that if I let myself go entirely with ye again, I'll find out he desecrated it permanently."

She took a deep breath, knowing there was only one last thing she could offer him, and knowing it would kill her to do it. Still she could not continue to receive a love that was compromised. Compromised through her own actions, and she knew neither of them could go on much longer in this manner, not when they knew better.

"I would want to die if you left me," she said quietly. "I wouldn't know who I was if you didn't love me anymore, Casey. I wouldn't want to wake up another day. But I would let you go if it meant you could find happiness elsewhere—if you—you," her voice shook, but she knew it had to be said, "cannot find fulfillment with me anymore."

Casey's head snapped up, his face white with shock. "Oh Lord, woman, ye kill me, do ye know that?" He raised a hand from her thigh, the print of his fingers a shadow against the milky skin. He cradled her jaw, his thumb stroking the line of her cheek. "The way ye look there with the moonlight on ye, offerin' me everything that ye are." He shook his head sadly. "I could never love another woman, Pamela. I thought ye understood at least that much about me."

He stood and took off his shirt. It fell to the floor to join her nightgown. Then he unzipped his pants and stepped out of them.

He stood naked before her and she caught her breath at the sheer beauty of him. He seemed carved from the night, both silver and shadow, both man and animal, against the tamped glow of the fire.

He held out a hand to her. "Come to bed, my wife, my woman. Come with me. And I will go with you."

Chapter Seven
The Night Walker

I T WAS ONE OF THOSE NIGHTS WHEN EVERYTHING WAS SO STILL, it felt as though something momentous was about to happen and Nature was holding her breath in anticipation.

It had become routine, this wandering byways and streets at night, walking and walking until he was so exhausted he couldn't put one foot in front of the other. He knew the area here well enough to walk through the woods and leave the roads to their quiet slumber. The woods held their own charm at night, the trees keeping counsel with something ancient that hung in the air between their boughs, sighing and murmuring softly under the stars. This night he had come down to stay with Casey and Pamela, a thing he did from time to time when he could not stand to stare at his own four walls anymore, nor tolerate the silence that lingered there in the wake of her voice.

He was relieved to see the intimacy had returned to Pamela and Casey's marriage. They seemed happy together once more, and had taken up the rhythm of their life again, in tune with each other, speaking volumes across the room without saying a word. It gave bittersweet pause to him, the small intimate touches as one passed the other, the smiles, the little jokes that belonged solely to a couple. The way Casey watched her with pride in his face and a lessening of fear as each month of the pregnancy passed in good health and a growing belly.

He paused in the lee of an oak, putting a hand to a rough-barked branch, and took a deep breath. Sometimes he walked so long and so fast that he forgot to breathe and only stopped when his chest got so tight that he felt he was in danger of choking. In the wake of Sylvie's death, he had become unaware of his body. It became an enemy in some senses, one that he abused, overworked and forgot to feed until he collapsed from pure exhaustion. It seemed a limited thing, a boundary that he could not cross, a thing keeping him from what he truly wanted. There were solutions, he knew, to such difficulties, but something in him had shied away from such a definite answer.

And yet here he was, star stuff contemplating star stuff, able to look at the heavens once again, even if barely. It took courage to look up into the night sky. For so long he had kept his head down, his thoughts on a narrow track, not allowing the pain to swamp him, knowing if he did he was lost. For so many years, the stars had been his consolation and in another life, in another country, he might have become an astronomer. After Sylvie's death, he had not looked up for months. He had watched the ground burn beneath his feet as he walked endless miles at night, never once looking up. It had seemed grotesque that the stars were still there, forming constellations, that they didn't simply fall from the sky for the grief of losing her. He did not want to know if he could still feel beauty, if anything had the power to touch him.

Then one morning, he had started out early for work, the sky just beginning to lighten along the horizon and the trees sleepy smudges. And there it was—Vega, his father's star, so blue and bright, pulsing against the fleeing of night. He had stood transfixed, watching the sky band itself into a softer and brighter blue, and still that star had stood out like something alive against an unconscious world. He couldn't breathe, and though he might well melt into a panic, he could not look away from that star.

Finally, when Vega had all but disappeared, he had found himself moving again, placing one foot after the other, and he had known then, whether he liked it or not, he was going to survive Sylvie's death.

He looked up now, the night a perfect one for stars—frosted, clear and empty of other human beings. Intact if not whole, he stood there on a small island of *terra firma* with an illimitable ocean stretching out toward all horizons. Within that ocean, he knew, there were vast, dark spaces, bodies that moved in all directions at speeds that inspired terror. There was also beauty that stole a man's breath, and moments of awe and wonder that were like an oasis where a weary pilgrim might rest long enough to regain the strength to take that next burning step, and the one after that.

And maybe, just maybe, even for the walking wounded, for the terrified and the sick at heart, for star stuff with the ability to contemplate star stuff, there was still some form of life out there.

Chapter Eight
Should Old Acquaintance...

IT HAD BEEN A VERY LONG WEEK AT THE FAIR HOUSING OFFICE and when it ended, Pat had been more than grateful to head out into the countryside to look after his brother's stead for the weekend. He had meant to arrive before dinner but a last minute call from an utterly desperate family who had been evicted from their cold water flat had delayed him. His car had spent the week choking and coughing and finally died with a sigh two days before. He'd caught a bus out as far as Newry and then tramped the rest of the way. When he turned down the drive, the yard was dark as a nun's habit, the moon well hid behind cloud as dense as a bramble hedge. The trees only shapeless patches of greater darkness within the swallowing whole. The dark here did not disturb him. His brother had chosen well when he bought this house for there was a peace to the wee hollow that embraced one as soon as one left the roadway and took the ambling drive down toward the house.

He came around the corner of the house, still deep in his thoughts, to find someone standing there, face turned up to the night sky above. He startled, not expecting anyone here at this time of night. The person reached toward his waistband, a gesture so swift and automatic that Pat knew whoever he was, he carried a gun at all times.

He reacted swiftly, throwing himself to the corner of the house and rolling into the safety of the wall. He cursed himself roundly in his head, backing along the wall and trying to hear steps approaching. He had let his guard down in a way he never did in the city and now he was going to pay for that bit of foolishness.

He raised his head, eyes scanning the area. There was no sound of footsteps, but that could mean the bastard was circling the house in the opposite direction and coming up behind him. He doubled back, sliding along the wall, cursing Pamela's penchant for large thorny rambler roses up against the house. This time of year they had yet to sprout new leaves and the thorns were only the more brutal for the lack of protection.

He slid behind the largest one, which ran up the west wall to the windows of Casey and Pamela's bedroom. From here he would have a view both ways as the person circled the house.

He stood there for an agony of an age, slowing his breath and hoping his heart wasn't audible on the still night. There was no sound and he wondered fleetingly if the intruder had fled? No, his senses told him someone still lurked in the shadows, that even if he could neither hear nor see him he was still nearby, and no innocuous presence either.

The fine hairs on the back of his neck prickled suddenly, telling him someone was within feet of him. He turned his head slowly, not wanting to give his own position away.

The dark figure slid around the corner of the house, pistol at arm's length, silent as a snake in the grass. Something seemed familiar about the man, even through the adrenaline rush currently clouding Pat's mind. The hedge of cloud opened a little and a rogue beam of moonlight struck the intruder for a second. It was enough to see the shape of him.

"David?" he said blankly, his mind not quite able to fathom what a British spy might be doing in his brother's back yard.

"Patrick?" He stepped out into the light, tucking his gun back into his waistband as he moved.

"Aye, it's me," Pat said, extricating himself from the enormous thorns of the rambler. "It's the helluva shock to come upon yerself though, here in the middle of the night."

"I imagine it is," David said. "I think it might be best to take this conversation inside though."

It hardly seemed likely to Pat that anyone was lurking around the sheep pen in the hope of catching their conversation but he was chilled and damp from his dive into the leaves and grass and in need of a cup of tea to steady him. He had not expected to see David in this setting. Part of him was glad to see him, the part that had found in this quiet British soldier/spy one of the best friends he had ever known. Another part was angry. Angry because of the man's admittance that his feelings were more than those of simple friendship. Angry because as much as Sylvie's death had not directly been David's fault, it had been Pat's relationship with him that led to that tragic Sunday.

Once inside, Pat lit the fire while David put the kettle on.

David was the same and yet entirely changed. His hair had grown long over his collar and was dyed almost as dark as Pat's own, the planes of his face seeming harder and more forbidding than they had before. Well, Pat supposed, they were both changed and too much had happened, too much grief had been ladled out in over-generous portions, for them not to bear the marks of it. Some days he barely recognized the man in the mirror himself. And it was part of David's job description to be a chameleon, not to be recognized from one day to the next, to always blend, never to be in context. Part of the scenery, yet part of nothing. A life of loneliness lived by a man whose feelings ran deep.

"You've changed as well," David said, smiling and pushing the teapot across the table toward Pat.

"I know," Pat smiled, realizing his thoughts had played across his face as visibly as print in a book. "Life will do that to a man."

"How are you then?" David asked, as Pat poured out tea into the heavy mug David had placed near his right hand.

Pat shrugged. "As well as I can manage, I suppose." There wasn't any way to tell the man the truth because he didn't know the truth himself. How does anyone survive life-altering grief? How does anyone wake up every day feeling like he has shattered glass in place of the heart that used to beat in his chest?

David nodded, a wise enough man to know when to leave a subject lie.

"I wanted a wee break from the city, thought I'd come out an' stay. I've keys an' Casey is always tellin' me to come an' stay when I like so I thought I'd finally take him up on the offer. But yerself, well, that's a bit more puzzlin'. After all, Casey is my brother, an' the last time I checked him an' you didn't exactly have a warm relationship."

"No, we didn't and likely never will, but it was him that came to ask me to go see you after Sylvie died."

"Oh," Pat said, shocked that his brother would do such a thing. But if he were honest with himself, he knew Casey would do far more and far worse to ensure his well-being.

"I was hoping to talk to him tonight but when I arrived the place was dark and you were skulking about in the shrubbery. It's not the first time I've been here."

"What do ye mean, this isn't the first time ye've been here?" Pat asked, not bothering to hide the shock in his voice.

David took a heavy breath and gave Pat a hard look, one that reminded him that this man often had to interrogate people in his line of work. He saw clearly why David had been the one assigned to work with Jamie, one bastard spying on another.

"I've been in contact with your brother for a bit. There was some work that I felt he was suited to. We needed someone inside, so to speak, or at least someone who could access certain groups without raising too much suspicion."

"Ye expect me to believe that my brother *willingly* works for a British spy?"

David grimaced slightly. "Willingly might be an overstatement, but yes, that's the fact of it. If I tell you that he's helping me to get testimony about the ring of men who are running young boys as prostitutes, perhaps it will make more sense to you."

Lawrence. Of course. It made sense to him now, even as it made him furious at Casey. If anyone knew better than to hitch any sort of wagon to the British, it was his brother. If anyone was to find out it would be an automatic death sentence—no questions, no time for reasoning, just a bullet to the back of the head after lengthy torture. But if there was one thing that would cause Casey to behave in such a dangerous manner, it was Lawrence's death, and the notion that he owed the boy some form of posthumous justice. Still, it was pure goddamn nonsense. Justice was an airy notion when, no matter the verdict, it could not bring back the dead.

"Christ," Pat said, the tea tasting bitter as aloes on his tongue. "I should have known. Fockin' Brits can never resist sinkin' yer claws in when ye see an opportunity."

David raised an eyebrow. "I see you're still angry with me."

"Still angry? No, I'm freshly angry, ye bastard. Yer goin' to get my brother killed askin' him to work for the enemy, knowin' if ye dangled the idea of avenging Lawrence in his face he'd be unable to resist. The man has a family he's responsible for now. Or is nothin' sacred to your sort?"

"My sort?" David said, still maddeningly calm. In fact the man seemed almost amused by Pat's outburst. "Do you mean the spy sort, or the pervert sort?"

"The spy sort. I've never called ye a pervert so don't insult me by implyin' that I have."

David flushed slightly. "I'm sorry. That was uncalled for. I had forgotten how easily you get under my skin. My defenses are not quite what they would be, had I been prepared to see you."

"Nor mine," Pat admitted.

"Well, you wouldn't know it," David said, and smiled. "You're the same formidable bastard to me that you've always seemed."

It was Pat's turn to crook a brow in disbelief. "I hardly think, considerin' what ye do, that I put any fear in ye."

"Not as much as your brother, admittedly, but you're an intimidating man when you so choose, Patrick Riordan. Certainly you've a temper on you."

Well, Pat thought, that much was true. His fuse was long and slow to light, but as his brother had often said, when the explosion came it was best to stay clear of him for a good length of time. There weren't many people who had seen him angry, but David certainly was one of them.

"This—what you've told me about my brother. Ye shouldn't have."

"No, I shouldn't have. But I'll tell you, Patrick Riordan, in a world of people I either don't trust, or am not allowed to—you, I trust. Allow me that. It's been a rare gift in my life."

It was true, Pat knew, for despite the times and the country in which they had met, despite the tragedy and the loss, David and he had formed a friendship, and they had trusted one another regardless of being natural enemies due to politics and birth.

"So will ye be workin' with Jamie again?" Pat asked, and was gratified to see the flash of surprise in David's face.

"How on earth do you know about my connection with Jamie?"

"I didn't, just half guessed, bein' that I've an idea of some of Jamie's more secret lines of work. I know the man is well connected an' I doubt ye could do much on his turf that wouldn't have to somehow lead back to him, information-wise if nothin' else."

"Jamie," David shrugged and looked toward the ceiling, as though appealing to heaven for a way to explain the situation.

"I know him quite well," Pat said, smiling. "Ye don't have to explain. I was determined to hate him when I met him. He was everything I thought I stood against and now... well, now I can honestly say he's a very dear friend. The only people I trust more than him are my brother and Pamela."

"He thinks a great deal of you as well," David said. "He made it clear that if I hurt you in any way, shape or form he'd have me tarred and feathered and heading for the gibbet in short order."

"He tries to look after those he loves, though I fear it's been a bit like tryin' to herd mice at a crossroads for him, between Pamela an' myself."

David laughed, a light and charming sound. "I can well imagine. Your sister-in-law has a strong will and decided opinions. I doubt even Lord Kirkpatrick is immune to her other charms either."

"No, he's not," Pat said quietly. "It's why he left."

David raised a fine, dyed eyebrow. "Why he left?"

"He loves her."

"Ah," David nodded, as though a piece of puzzle had slipped into place that he hadn't realized he was holding. "And she him?" he asked, words light and hesitant as if he knew it wasn't quite appropriate to ask Pat, considering that the woman in question was his brother's wife.

"Aye," Pat replied, "she does, but she loves my brother as much an' it's him she's married to. It's not simple, but somehow they've all managed to get through it intact."

"More than intact, I'd say, I've seen your brother and Pamela together. There's enough passion there to singe an innocent passerby, much less those actually living inside it."

"It's been that way since the first time they set eyes on one another. They couldn't keep apart. It was like watching two magnets dance about in a limited space. But if ye'd ever seen her and Jamie with one another, ye'd understand there's another dance goin' on that's just as potent, but made up of entirely different steps."

"And your brother is alright with this? He doesn't seem one to be passive when it comes to his woman."

"Not alright," Pat said. "No, I wouldn't say that. It's caused some friction for them all, but Pamela has known Jamie for a very long time. He was a fact of her life and firmly in place by the time Casey met her. He's also one of her dearest friends and my brother is not fool enough to try to take that away from her. She might allow it, but it would never sit well with her. Eventually it would cause resentment and Casey wouldn't want that. He can be possessive of her certainly, but he's not stupid."

"Speaking of Jamie," David said, "does anyone hear from him these days?"

"Why do ye ask?"

"I ask because he seemingly disappeared some time ago, and I've not been able to get so much as a whiff of him since. And if he's not on our radar, then he's gone very deep underground."

"You keep tabs on Jamie?" Pat asked.

"To a certain extent, yes. The man is considered either an asset or a danger, depending on whom you ask on what day."

"An' what about you—do you consider him a danger or an asset?"

David laughed. "I don't think I've ever met a more dangerous man nor one better placed to help this country to a more peaceable solution."

"Ye sound like ye got to know him rather well," Pat said, shocked that David had revealed so much in a simple statement.

"It's alright, Pat. I don't have to shoot you for merely telling you that. You know Jamie well enough to know that he has a finger in several pies, politically speaking. It was inevitable that I would be dealing with him at some point. Odds are I wouldn't be the man for that task anymore though, were His Lordship still in residence."

"Which begs the question of just what they've sent ye back for an' why yer runnin' about lookin' like a hooligan in the streets of Belfast?"

"They couldn't think of anywhere worse to send me, so here I am, back in Belfast."

"As punishment goes, it's severe, that's for certain," Pat said dryly.

Pat felt suddenly exhausted and realized that all his adrenaline had ebbed. The heat from the Aga was like a sleeping draught that had filled his limbs with sand. His anger had gone along with the adrenaline.

"Ye'll take care for my brother, won't ye? He loved Lawrence like he was a son, an' he's been torn up inside since the lad's death. I don't want him rushin' in blindly an' gettin' hurt or worse."

"I will. I'm terrified of him but I find I rather like him as well, now that I'm getting to know him a little."

"Have ye..." Pat cleared his throat, uncomfortable and yet knowing a friend asked such things, "found someone?"

David gave him a long look before answering.

"I'm not good at celibacy, so yes, I have partners. My life, however, is not conducive to a permanent arrangement of any sort. If you're asking if I love anyone, well... some things in a person's life do not change." He placed his cup carefully on the table and took a measured breath. "I'm afraid, for me, this is one of them. Seeing you on the street that day told me all I needed to know about the state of my feelings. But I—I'd like to be friends again. I know you don't feel the same way and I understand that entirely. If you could find a small corner in your life for a friendship that's a bit like a rare plant, you never know where or when it might show up, nor how long it will last in each instance. Well then, I would be grateful for that. Do you think we can still be friends, Pat?"

Pat looked at the man across the table and knew, despite everything, he did indeed value him as a friend and had missed him in this last year. He nodded.

"We never stopped."

Chapter Nine

March 1973

Blooding

PAMELA WAS ON HER WAY HOME FROM TAKING PICTURES of a new baby for a couple down past Drumintree and she stopped in at the wee village market to buy milk and bread before continuing on the last stretch home. She had been to this shop a few times before and the shopkeeper, Mr. Linehan, nodded and smiled as she came in. He was a middle-aged man, father of five and ran a bustling little store that always had fresh produce and milk—something of a minor miracle in this area, where trucks were often at the mercy of the local Provisional IRA, the British Army, and the roadblocks and traffic snarls that occurred as a result.

"Not too much longer then?" he said, nodding at her belly.

"Another six weeks or so," she said, instinctively rubbing a hand over the occupant, who rewarded her with a firm kick. She headed for the back of the store where the tall old coolers held milk and butter. She was late in the day for the milk and only one bottle was left, near the back of the cooler at the bottom. She sighed and, taking hold of the handle, got down on one knee. How to bend over far enough to retrieve the bottle was the next question.

She felt someone behind her and turned slightly. It was a woman, young to judge by the fray-cuffed denims she wore. The woman kneeled down behind her, apparently searching the lower shelves for some item.

Pamela had just grasped the cool smooth glass of the milk bottle when she felt it, an inrush of people and a strange silence accompanying them. Her backbone understood before she did and she drew back, glancing up quickly at the mirror in the corner. It was old and had a soft green haze to it but she didn't need to see any clearer to understand what three men in balaclavas with guns held at waist height meant. She drew back sharply, knocking the milk bottle over in her haste. The noise was covered by the sudden explosion of glass and the spray of an automatic weapon.

She glanced up into the mirror, saw blood, and looked no longer. Mr. Linehan was most assuredly dead and so would she be if she didn't do something quickly. The storage area was directly to the right hand of the coolers. She grabbed the woman roughly by the arm and pulled her through the door, hoping to God the men were too focused on the till and the man they had just killed to realize the shop hadn't been entirely empty.

The storeroom was cool and dark and filled with boxes and crates. She pulled the woman in behind the tall stack of crates with *Kerry Gold* stamped in plain letters on the side. They found themselves in a corner with only one side of their hidey-hole open. Pamela motioned to the woman to stay put, and though she did not acknowledge the flick of fingers, she did move deeper into the shadows.

There were a few spare crates and Pamela thought if she could bring them over and stack them silently, it would made their hiding place far more secure. She held her breath, praying that the crates were empty because there was no way she would be able to move them if they weren't. They were and she stacked them swiftly, not taking the ones at the bottom for fear it would leave traces if the floor hadn't been swept in a bit. She slipped back into the space and re-stacked the crates to close off the entryway.

"What—" the woman began, her whisper soft but seeming to carry with the boom of a death knell.

Pamela hissed at her as low as she could. "Sshh."

She could still hear the men at the front, their boots crunching over the broken glass, but one set of footsteps was coming toward the back of the shop. She had no doubt that if they were found the men would shoot them, for the sin of being a witness and for being Catholic and thus, in South Armagh, considered an IRA sympathizer by default.

She thought about the open cooler door and felt her stomach drop a little more. The baby was kicking frantically, set adrift on a sea of adrenaline and all too aware of her own panic. She rubbed her belly as firmly as the tight space would allow. The woman laid a hand to her belly and kept it there. It was oddly calming to be touched so in the midst of such a fraught moment. Apparently the baby thought so too, for it ceased to kick with such vehemence and settled for a series of pokes instead.

The door opened and a waft of warmer air and light accompanied the man who walked into the storeroom. The sense of menace was tangible, with a taste to it like something bitter and hot on the tongue. He turned over crates, unworried apparently by the noise he was making. Then he turned the light on. Pamela fought the urge to close her eyes so that if he found them and killed them she wouldn't know the exact instant it was about to happen. Her mind was racing in a jumbled panic. The words, *'please let the baby survive somehow, some way, please let Casey find happiness again'* the only ones that bobbed out of the stew of sheer terror she found herself in.

They were deep in the shadows but it would be a natural place to look.

The open cooler door was going to make him search longer and more thoroughly than he might have otherwise. The only saving grace was that the crates were solid ones, no cracks between the slats. If he realized they weren't stacked right back to the wall though, they were as good as dead.

He poked at the crates and they swayed a bit, threatening to topple into their hole and give them away. The woman clutched her hand convulsively and Pamela clutched back. They were both holding their breath now, hearts pounding erratically. She could feel the woman's pulse hard and panicked against her palm.

She had learned the hard way how to be still, how to not move or breathe so that one did not attract unwanted attention. She had learned that some men did not see a person with a life and loved ones, they simply saw something to use or to kill when they looked at a woman. She had learned that one night on a train. It was a lesson that did not go away... ever.

He was lingering around the crates as if he sensed them, the way a fox will hear the rapid tattoo of a rabbit's heart as it lies paralyzed in its sights. She could feel him listening, hear him breathing, and smell the sweat of violence on his skin. Then, as suddenly as he had entered the small space he was gone, shouting in a rough voice that he had searched the back and there wasn't anyone on the premises. She let her air out slowly, feeling like a punctured balloon, not certain how her legs were going to bear her up out of this space. She turned to look at the woman and found herself confronted by eyes the color of fringed gentian. As clear as the remarkable color, was the fact that the woman was blind. As terrifying as Pamela was finding this, she knew that to experience it without sight had to be doubly horrifying.

"I have to check on Mr. Linehan," she said, though she knew it was futile. The man was dead, but on the one chance in a million that he had a thready pulse left, she could not leave him this way. "But then I'll come back and we'll go out the back door. It's just behind you. I'm going to put your hand on the knob so that you can get out if I'm not back in two minutes. Alright?"

The woman nodded, her face pinched and white with fear.

The shop was littered with glass and a spreading crimson pool, congealing already at its edges. The door to the street was open, the street outside as quiet as if it were three in the morning rather than the afternoon. One glance at Mr. Linehan told Pamela all she needed to know, he was beyond any sort of mortal help. She took a breath, careful not to step in the blood, though the men who had shot Mr. Linehan hadn't taken any such precautions. If she had to lay odds on them being caught, she wouldn't bet much more than the sheep shed. She walked swiftly back to the storeroom where the woman waited, hand still on the doorknob.

Outside, the air seemed to hum with a high vibration. Violence, she had found through experience, left a definite energy in its wake as if the moment kept playing itself over and over long after the actual event. The warm March day had disappeared in the time she had been in the shop and a cold wind ripped down from the slopes of Slieve Gullion, slapping their faces and stinging their eyes. She scanned the area quickly. The narrow lane, the overhanging trees. The closest houses were within sight and surely within the sound of an automatic weapon blast, but there was no sign that anyone had heard anything.

The car was parked beside the village's old church, only a minute's walk away.

"Take my arm," she said, guiding the woman's hand to her elbow.

"Is he... is he dead?" she asked, the gentian eyes near black.

"Yes, he is," Pamela said shortly, half her mind occupied with how to leave this village without being spotted, the other half trying to push away the image of Mr. Linehan's shattered skull, with one eye still intact, staring in that thousand-yard way that said whatever he saw wasn't of this world any longer.

"How did you get here?" Pamela asked. "Do you live in the village?"

"No," the woman replied. "Someone brings me in. I live down near the border. I'm not supposed to be here today though. I—if my brother finds out I was away from home, I'll be in terrible trouble. Please," she said, "ye don't understand, I have to be gone from here before the police arrive. I can't be found by the police. I simply cannot." The urgency fairly poured off the woman's skin, her eyes a deeper blue, pupils dilated in panic. Pamela herself wasn't entirely a stranger to not trusting the police, especially here in South Armagh.

She wondered what sort of character this brother was. Not someone you'd want to run into in a dark hedgerow, that much was apparent. She helped the woman into the car and cast a glance about the empty streets. Curtains were firmly drawn and she knew it was best not to linger.

She drove for twenty minutes straight, until they were firmly in the wilds of South Armagh, without fear of police or Army showing up. She pulled the car over on a narrow lay-by that was more hedge, ditch, and weed than it was a parking space. The events of the last hour had caught up to her so suddenly, that she felt swamped by it and unable to drive any farther.

"I'm sorry. I just need a minute to get my breath."

The interior of the car was washed with the flickering shadows of leaves fretting in the stiff breeze. Raindrops flew from the hedge onto the windshield. It was strangely peaceful. The woman didn't say anything but laid a soft hand on Pamela's shoulder. Pamela bent her head into the steering wheel and took several deep breaths. She could feel her body slowly calm though her mind swam with the images from the shop. She could still smell the hot copper stink of blood as though it clung to her own hands and skin. She knew she wouldn't calm entirely until Casey held her, his arms and the scent and touch of him, the final ingredient she always needed to restore a sense of order and security to the universe.

"How far along are ye?" the woman asked, her voice gentle.

"Seven and a half months," Pamela said. As though understanding that it was being spoken of, the baby poked a fist out near her ribs and Pamela touched it gratefully with her free hand. She knew stress wasn't likely to hurt the baby at this point, but she had lost too many babies ever to be completely confident until this one was safely delivered and lying in her arms.

"The baby will be fine," the woman said. "Ye need have no fears this time."

Pamela looked up to find the gentian eyes looking back at her in a way that was peculiarly comforting, despite the woman's lack of vision. "How can you—how did you know this isn't my first pregnancy?"

The woman shrugged. "I just know things sometimes. There's no explainin' it really, for it comes an' goes an' generally isn't there when I'd like it to be. But trust me when I say this babby is meant to thrive an' grow."

"Thank you."

"Yer welcome." The woman smiled, her face still pale and strained, but the smile was genuine and lit the gentian eyes to a soft glow that made it hard to believe such beautiful eyes could not see.

The checkpoint at Bessbrook Mill was swarming with soldiers. She had expected it but it still gave her a jolt as they waved her over to the side. She slowed to a stop and rolled her window down. This was all routine, massacre or not. This was life in Northern Ireland, day in, day out. The soldier cocked his head in the window, rifle in the crook of his elbow.

"I will need you both to get out." She nodded and opened her door, getting out slowly. The soldier was young. Most of them were, but this one looked especially newly minted. He eyed her stomach with a look of alarm. She sighed.

"I'm going to go help my friend get out," she said, speaking calmly but firmly as she had learned to do at every checkpoint. Casey had told her long ago, 'Make sure ye don't look nor sound as if ye've anything to hide, even if ye do. Nerves have a smell to them an' the soldiers are attuned to that—not to mention they're mighty nervy themselves an' as like to shoot ye by accident.'

She made certain to keep her hands out and visible at all times, to never make a sudden move and to look the soldiers in the eyes whenever they asked a question. She never volunteered more information than what was strictly required either. How anyone ever dared to go through these checkpoints with weapons in their boot or a fugitive in their back seat, was beyond her.

The woman got out and stood by the car, one hand resting lightly on it for a second, and then withdrawn. She looked directly at the soldier and smiled lightly. Pamela watched with growing worry. It was obvious that she did not want the soldiers to know she was blind for some reason. Was it a matter of pride or, and here Pamela had a frisson of fear shoot through her belly, was it a matter of identification? And if so, just who the hell was this woman?

They were through the checkpoint in short order, the soldiers already dismissing them as two harmless women, looking beyond them down the road, scanning the horizon, always alert for trouble, both the scent and sight of it.

"Now where can I take you?" she asked as soon as they were on the narrow roadway again, the hedgerows thick and dark above their heads, filling the car with shadow and a strange feeling of security.

The woman sighed heavily. "There's no avoidin' it further, I suppose. D'ye happen to know where the Murray farm is?"

"Noah Murray's farm?" Pamela asked, not even bothering to disguise her dismay.

"Aye," the woman's tone was dry. "I thought ye might be familiar with it. Ye see, Noah is my brother. I believe ye've made his acquaintance."

"You could say that," Pamela replied, mouth dry as dust. "He threatened to kill me."

"CHRIST," CASEY RIORDAN SAID FOR THE FIFTH TIME IN AS MANY MINUTES.

"I'm sorry," Pamela said softly. They were lying on their bed and Pamela had just finished telling him about the events of the afternoon. There was a fire in the grate, hissing softly, the house itself quiet and comforting as the night closed in around it.

"Ye've nothin' to apologize for woman, though I will say ye've a talent for findin' serious trouble." His words were terse, but the hand that stroked the mound of her belly was not and Pamela knew he needed to work his way through the fear of what might have happened to her and the baby that afternoon.

"Why Mr. Linehan though? He doesn't have any political importance. He's just a man with a shop and a family."

"It's likely there was no reason, or someone said something an' it rolled downhill gatherin' accusations an' more lies as it went until someone saw him as a viable target. They wanted to make a point. Bloody insane though, right there in the heart of Noah Murray's fiefdom."

Still, this hadn't been an operation by Noah Murray and his men. This attack was directed at him, a clear message that there was a group of Loyalists somewhere that had the effrontery and insanity to kill in the midst of his territory.

"Will the police go after them, do you think?"

"It's South Armagh, darlin'. The police have reason to exercise a great deal of caution down that way. They don't run the show down there, the South Armagh Brigade does, an' ye step too hard on Noah Murray's toes and he'll shoot yer feet off. Trust me, if the man finds out who's behind today's killin', the breaths remainin' to them will be in the single digits."

Pamela knew Casey was not exaggerating for Noah Murray had threatened her own life merely because she had voiced suspicion of some of the goings-on down in South Armagh some time back.

"I don't want ye to stop there anymore. I don't even want ye drivin' through there. D'ye hear? Christ, when I think what might have happened to you an' the babe today..."

He trailed off, his hand resting firmly over the bit of the baby that was sticking out. A wee foot, she thought.

He was right. Police were often targeted and just as often murdered in South Armagh. There was a reason the Armagh Brigade posted signs declaring their autonomy from one end of the county to the other; it was simply because it was true.

She touched him in the dark, seeking the reassurance of the big body, the shelter it gave her so easily. Also giving reassurance in turn, her presence and breath and warmth telling him all was well, she was here and she was safe. She breathed deep of his scent, allowing it to slide through her blood, cell deep, calming her.

After Kate—for that was her name—had dropped the bomb about her brother's identity, they had been silent for the rest of the drive.

The Murray farm straddled the border and was reached by narrow, twisting lanes, almost claustrophobic with thick blackthorn hedges that rose far above the roof of the car.

"Just drop me at the edge of the stone wall," Kate had said. "There's a space there where ye can turn about. The wall runs up to the corner of the house so I can make my way easily from there. That way if Noah is home and sees me I'll just say I was out walking and lost track of time."

Kate had sat for a few moments, as though hesitating over something.

"Do you need me to walk you closer to the house?" Pamela asked, thinking there were few things in the world she would less like doing but feeling she had to offer, considering the circumstances.

"No, I can manage fine once I touch the stones," Kate said. "It's just that—I—I should like to see yer face. Might I touch ye, to know how it is ye look?"

She said, "Of course," for the afternoon had forged an intimacy that more casual circumstances would not have allowed.

She recalled now the touch of the woman's hands on her face, light as rain, gliding over her bones, tracing the shape of her mouth, seeing with fingers that were as sensitive as a moth's wings, pausing on Pamela's scar, a question in her touch. So she had told her about the man with the board with the nail sticking out of it, about the raw hatred that had rendered him more blind than Kate could ever be.

Then the fingers had traced the round of her eyelids, stroking feather light along her lashes, cupping the shells of her ears, dipping down over her neck. It had been oddly intimate and yet, after what they had been through, not awkward in the least. Kate had bunched Pamela's hair up in coils and then pressed it to her own face, letting it fall slowly through her fingers.

Her skin had shimmered as though the woman's fingers had left heat and light in sensory pathways all over her. As swollen as her body was with late pregnancy, her skin felt fine as drawn silk and her nerve endings were as waterweed, swayed by the gentlest of currents.

The few moments had been surreal, a time scooped out of the horrors of the afternoon, and so it had seemed natural for the woman to seek out the round of her belly and cup the hard base of it in her hands, as though she could communicate without words to the child inside. The baby had responded with a slow, deep roll that shifted Pamela's entire body. Kate had merely laid her cheek, light as dandelion down, against the belly and stayed there for a moment. It had seemed more than natural to rest her own hand on the woman's head and feel their respective pulses echo with blood that was still warm and moving, that still gave life and breath.

She had felt an odd sense of loss when Kate got out of the car, as though this woman might have been, had their lives been different, a good friend. Now, here in the dark, she felt that pang of loss again like a small splinter in her heart.

"I liked her," she said, voice quiet with regret.

Casey squeezed her hand and gathered her closer to his comfort. "I know, darlin'."

Chapter Ten

April 1973

Conor

THE BIG ASH TREE HAD SUCCUMBED TO THE STORM AND LAY NOW in a welter of branches across the top of the drive. Casey swore, though the words were torn from his lips by the ferocious wind that still blew hard enough to bend a man double. The yard was a mess of broken branches and half-furled leaves, the pale mint green of new growth. The shed roof was partway torn off and flapping in the wind, making a sharp singing noise between hard cracks. He sighed, another thing that would need fixing. He'd battened Paudeen down securely in his small sheep shed. Built solid from two-by-fours and half-inch plywood, it would withstand the wind well enough, if the bloody sheep's bleating didn't cause it to fall down first. He turned and hunched his shoulders against the stinging rain. There wasn't much he could do until the weather died back a bit.

He ought to have known something fierce was brewing the evening before, for Pamela had been restless as a cat in a houseful of mice, saying she'd an odd taste in her mouth that she couldn't wash out with any amount of toothpaste and water. She hadn't slept much during the night either, saying the wind had gotten into her bones and she had to walk about. He knew it wasn't the wind but that her body was preparing her for the imminent arrival of the baby. Two more weeks before the child was due to present itself to the world at large. Thank goodness they still had a bit of time. What with the storm and all, it looked as though they'd be digging their way out for a couple of days.

Casey entered the house on a gust of leaves and horizontal rain.

"It's perishin' out there, darlin'," he said, shaking the rain from his hair. "Bloody ash tree came down across the drive so I hope the cupboards are stocked 'cause we'll be stuck for a day or two until I can get the thing cut up an'..." he trailed off for Pamela was clutching the sideboard with one hand, her belly with the other and staring at the floor in dismay, where a puddle of water was slowly spreading across the polished pine boards.

"What's wrong, Jewel?" he asked feeling a jolt of alarm shoot through his spine and settle in his stomach queasily.

"I think the baby is coming now," she said. "My water's just broken."

"Now?" Casey echoed, feeling the bottom of his stomach drop out. "What the hell do ye mean, NOW?"

Pamela glared at him, breathing out heavily through her nose. "I mean the baby is coming now, and it's too late to move me, or to go get a doctor or to saw the fucking tree up so you *can* actually get out of here. You're going to have to help me deliver the baby here, man, so if you want to boil water or get a knife to cut the pain, you better bloody fucking hurry."

The swearing convinced Casey as little else would have. In some respects, Pamela was a good Catholic girl and she only swore like this under extreme duress.

"Fock," he said, for lack of anything else that would sum up his current state of emotions.

"That's been done," she said, with what sounded like a laugh. "And now we're dealing with the consequences thereof."

"I can't believe yer makin' bawdy jokes at a time like this," he said as an irrational wave of annoyance swept through him. Bloody woman making jokes on the one hand and telling him he had to deliver a baby on the other. Jaysus Murphy and the little green men, was she mad thinking he could deliver a baby?

She gave him a pointed look and clutched at a chair as another contraction seized her.

"Come on, Jewel, we have to get ye up to the bedroom," he said, trying to infuse calm into his voice and failing miserably.

"What the hell are you doing?" she asked, as he put an arm behind her knees and one round her back.

"Carryin' ye up the stairs, woman, I'll not have ye droppin' the baby on the way up."

"Don't be a fool," she said crossly, "I can walk."

Casey merely shook his head and started up the stairs. "Lord, woman, ye've put on a bit of weight, no?"

A green glare told him that humor wasn't appreciated just at present.

He deposited her on the bed but she stood up again as quickly as her belly would allow.

"I'll not lie down just yet. I need you to go get some old blankets. There's a clean stack in the linen closet by the baby's room. Go get them, please." Her eyes were closed and a fine beading of sweat stood out against her forehead.

"Old blankets," he repeated blankly.

"Yes," she said in a tone that he'd heard her use on particularly slow and irksome people before. "I'm pretty sure this is going to be messy and I don't want to ruin the bedding."

By the time he returned with the blankets, she had the bed stripped down to the mattress and was kneeling on the floor gasping.

"Jewel, what's wrong?" he said dropping the blankets and going round to where she knelt.

"What's wrong?" she snorted, easing herself slowly upright. "The man asks me what's wrong! 'Tis nothing at all, just that I feel like my body is about to turn inside out and there's no doctor and the bed sheets look healthy compared to the color you've turned. Otherwise this is all just peachy."

Her sarcasm reassured him as little else would have. He spread the blankets out on the bed and then eased her back onto them, putting as many pillows as he could find at the top end to prop her up.

He settled her as best he could, astonished and terrified at the hard ball her belly became with each contraction.

"Now what would ye have me do, Jewel?" he asked, with the utter helplessness of a man corralled against his will into the mysterious world of women's business.

"Go boil the water," she said with a strange inward look that panicked him more than anything else had done. This was happening and there wasn't a damn thing he could do to halt it. "You'll need it to sterilize the knife."

"What the hell am I after needin' a knife for?" he asked, feeling much as Moses must have felt with the Red Sea and ten thousand Egyptians at his back.

"To cut the cord," she replied, her eyes once again closed, hands clutching the blankets hard. "Now hurry."

Casey had no memory of flying down the stairs but suddenly found himself in the middle of the kitchen with no idea why he was there.

"Boil water," he muttered to himself, "and get a fockin' grip man, while yer at it."

Just then someone knocked on the window, causing him nearly to jump out of his skin.

He looked up to find his brother peering back through the rain-lashed pane. He had never been so grateful to see someone in his entire life.

Pat came in a moment later, the rain still coming down hard enough to drive in the door behind him.

"I got caught short on the way back up from Armagh, thought I'd best stop over here until the worst of the storm passed an' make certain ye were tucked in yerself... good Christ man, yer white as a ghost! What's wrong?" Pat looked about the kitchen and then asked, "Where's Pamela?"

"Upstairs havin' the baby," Casey said tersely, putting the kettle on and straining his ears for any noise issuing from the upper floor.

"Seriously?"

"Do I look like a man who's in the mood for takin' the piss?"

"No," Pat said with the bald honesty Casey sometimes found rather annoying. "Ye look like a man who needs a stiff drink though. Telephone's out?"

Casey merely glared in answer, casting a swift and longing glance at the bottle of Connemara Mist on the sideboard but deciding he'd best keep a clear head for the present time. Besides, if Pamela smelled whiskey on his breath just now she wasn't likely to look upon him kindly. Still, it might go some ways towards calming his nerves. He took a step toward the bottle, only to be brought up short by a cry from upstairs.

Pat was already halfway out the door and Casey thought he looked a little too relieved to be heading back out into the wind and rain.

"I'll go for the doctor, but I have to warn ye man, the roads are littered with trees all over and so it may take me some time to get back. Can ye manage?"

"I pretty much fockin' have to, don't I then?" Casey said, feeling severely harassed.

"Aye," Pat said, "I suppose ye do. I'll be back as soon as I can find help."

Casey sprinted back up the stairs, still wishing he'd a few ounces of whiskey in him for fortitude. Pamela was lying on her side, an old shirt of his rucked up around her waist, her fists clenched tightly in the blankets.

"Pat came by an' he's gone off for the doctor now. He says he'll run in and tell Gert too."

She nodded, face pale, eyes wide and brilliant with pain.

"Casey, come hold me. I'm afraid and I need your hands on me."

"Sure an' who wouldn't be, darlin'?" he said in his most reassuring tone, sliding in behind her on the bed so she could relax into his body between contractions. They seemed to have gotten far closer together since he'd gone downstairs. He had a feeling this baby—nervous father be damned—wasn't going to wait for an engraved invitation or a waylaid doctor before making its appearance.

Pamela leaned into him, her entire body shaking with the force of the pain and pulling her out into deep water as surely as the tide. Water into which he could not follow, but he would bear her up as long as he might.

Skin to skin they lay, the world outside so far away as to seem impossible. Every few minutes she would pull into herself as though she were trying to curl up small enough to escape the agony, somewhere far, far inside the shell of her mind.

He sat behind her, rubbing her back in small, tight circles, kneading the muscles through each contraction with one hand while she held the other so tightly that he could picture the bones turning indigo inside his skin. Between contractions she fell back into his chest, her face turned into his neck, breath ragged but deep.

"Sing to me, Casey," she said after a particularly long contraction during which Casey had prayed to the Virgin Mary, thinking if anyone was likely to help in such a situation it was another mother.

"What would ye have me sing, love?"

"Something comforting," she said.

Something old, something soft and something he would naturally sing to her anyway. Something American for the country she had left behind to bring him home. He found one amongst the softer, simpler strains of the songbook he held in his mind.

> *It's not the pale moon that excites me*
> *That thrills and delights me, oh no*
> *It's just the nearness of you*

Casey kept his voice low and soft, trying to create with the thread of music a whole cloth of comfort for her. He kept the tempo of the music even while still counting the time between contractions. They were getting closer together and from the look on Pamela's face, he judged she was getting very near the crucial point. Even if Pat had managed to drive the entire way and then had the good fortune to find the doctor in, still it would take more time than he suspected was left for them to make it back here.

> *It isn't your sweet conversation*
> *That brings this sensation, oh no*
> *It's just the nearness of you*

> *When you're in my arms and I feel you so close to me*
> *All my wildest dreams come true*

He was little more than whispering in her ear now, stroking the line of her neck and shoulder and the hard, taut round of her belly between contractions, wishing to God and all his angels there was something he could do for her. He had never known such a feeling of helplessness in his life, nor such a deep and profound connection to another person. A feeling that went far down beyond the flesh, the blood, the bone and even the spirit. A thing he had known from the minute he first saw her, a thing that had been sorely tried so recently and yet for all that, still here, as present and undeniable between the two of them as it had ever been.

> *I need no soft lights to enchant me*
> *If you'll only grant me the right*
> *To hold you ever so tight*
> *And to feel in the night the nearness of you*

He finished on a low note, blowing gently onto her face to cool the heat that now seemed to consume her.

She closed her eyes and smiled. He stroked the hair back from her face and kissed her softly on the forehead.

"Casey."

"Aye, Jewel?"

"I just want you to know that I love you."

"I do know that," he said, worried at the intensity with which she'd spoken the words, as though she were afraid she might never have another chance to say them.

"In case I die, I want you to know that I have loved you from the first minute I saw you and that I don't regret anything I've done for that love. My only regret is the hurt I've caused you." She had hold of his hands and was pressing down hard on them, her eyes dark with pain. Despite himself, he stiffened slightly at the words, then forced himself to relax, not wanting his emotions to communicate to her.

"I've not a regret either, Jewel. I love ye more than the breath in my own body an' that's how I know yer not goin' to die. We're to grow old together here, an' yer not leavin' me with this wee person on my own. I'd fock it up surely."

"No, you wouldn't," she said, voice hardly more than a whisper. "You're going to be a terrific father. You could do it without me if you had to."

"Yer not goin' to die," he repeated in his firmest tone, as much to reassure himself as Pamela. If anything should go wrong, if she bled more than she ought, if the baby came out backwards or with the cord caught round its throat... he should have insisted they leave before the storm started. Christ on a piece of toast, where the hell was Pat with the bloody doctor!

"Casey!" she arched back into his chest hard, her entire body tight as a kettledrum. He eased out from under her carefully, knowing the moment had arrived and that he'd never been less prepared for anything in his life.

He knelt on the end of the bed, wondering how one assessed a situation in which one had no clue what was normal and what was not.

"Just make sure you catch the baby," Pamela said. Obviously, his wife was having no problem assessing him, Casey thought, chagrined.

"Here," he said, a strange calm descending over him, "brace yer feet against my chest, an' then push. We're almost there, Jewel."

She was propped up on her elbows, knees bent back and legs shaking with the effort of the last hour. He took her ankles and lifted her legs, leaning his chest into the soles of her feet so she would have something solid against which to push. He'd discarded his shirt earlier and her toes curled automatically into his chest hair. He hardly noticed though, for the entire universe had stilled to this point. He no longer heard the wind howling round the eaves nor the fire snapping in the grate, just the in and out of breath and Pamela's cries of pain and determination. He could see the top of the baby's head now, wrinkled and red, but nevertheless a head.

It was the most fiercely primal thing he'd ever experienced in his life, and exhilaration began to run through his veins despite his fear for Pamela. With each contraction he could see more of the head coming down.

"Okay, just a few more, darlin', an' the wee one will be here," he said, excitement infusing his words.

"Oh God, Casey, I can't," she cried, collapsing back against the pillows. He felt a jolt of fear run through him. She looked terribly pale and fragile, and he wondered if she had enough strength left to see this through.

"Pamela, look at me. Ye can do this darlin'. I'm here with ye all the way."

She shook her head, eyes closed, her entire body trembling with exertion. Her exhaustion was palpable, but he knew now was the crucial moment and he had to be strong for her.

"Jewel," his voice was gentle but commanding, "give me yer hand. I'm going to pull ye up, an' then yer to look in my eyes an' nowhere else, d'ye understand?"

She nodded and gave him her hand. He pulled her up gently, sparing a quick glance downward. The head was crowning now, a full round skull in evidence, covered with a fine haze of black hair.

She looked into his eyes then, her own a hectic and brilliant green, and he smiled in reassurance and nodded. She hesitated a moment and then nodded back. Fastening her gaze on his face, she suddenly groaned, her entire body gripped in another contraction.

"I'm goin' to have to put my hands down to catch the baby, alright?"

She nodded, the veins in her neck standing out, strands of hair plastered to her face and shoulders. She had never looked more beautiful to him than she did now.

"The head's out," he said a moment later, half in awe, half in astonishment that there really was a child, his child, their child in the world now. A good head of black hair and a wee, scrumpled face that looked terribly annoyed by this sudden arrival in a strange place. He could feel his wife's body beginning to tense again. "Alright then, darlin', one more, an' ye'll be done."

She pushed again, one last surge of exertion and the baby slid all the way out on a tide of blood and fecund water, and Casey's son slid surely into the large hands that awaited him.

"'Tis a boy, Jewel," he said, feeling slightly dizzy and unreal, yet more grounded than he had ever felt before in his life.

She leaned forward and touched the tiny skull and the baby opened his eyes, eyes the color of seaweed in storm-tossed waters. The baby turned his head as though he knew precisely where his mother was and opened his mouth in a loud cry.

"He's perfect," she said, her eyes filling with tears.

Casey met her eyes above the head of their son, the cord that tied him to his mother still pulsing with blood, and put one trembling hand to her face.

"Thank you for my son," he said softly and bent to kiss her. Under them, the bed was awash in blood and birth matter, outside the wind was still playing havoc with the world, and inside Casey felt a deep and utter happiness that he was certain he didn't deserve but was quite willing to accept nevertheless.

He laid the baby in Pamela's arms, uncertain of what to do now. Just then, a noise downstairs alerted him to the fact that help had arrived. He felt both relief and regret, sweet and sharp, for now this time alone, where the three of them had beat only to the heart of existence, was over and life, like the tide, had returned to its accustomed shore.

Gert poked her head around the door a moment later and with her came an awareness of the state they were all in. He was still bare from the waist up and Pamela was completely naked, both of them smeared with blood and sweat, the baby working himself up to a good squall now in his mother's arms.

Beautifully unflappable and solid as the Hoover Dam, however, Gert did not even blink an eye at the scene before her. She came over and touched one fat, red finger to the baby's nose. "*Ja*, is sweetheart, is he not?" she asked, beaming as though she herself had just produced him fresh from the oven.

She laid one rough hand on Casey's shoulder. "Go down and see Owen. This part is women's work." The bedroom became a whirl of activity after that, with Gert sweeping him toward the door and Owen waiting at the foot of the stairs to place a full glass of whiskey in his hand. He finished it off in three neat swallows, for the events of the last few hours had just hit him and he was strangely anxious, though his wife and son were only up the stairs being tended by Gert's extremely capable hands.

Pat came in with the doctor a few minutes later. Dr. Dooley was a brown chestnut of a man with a reputation for fearsome honesty, respected throughout the county.

"Upstairs?"

Casey nodded, not bothering to explain further. It would be obvious the minute the doctor stepped into the room.

"Well then?" Pat asked, shaking the rain from his hair as the doctor headed up the stairs, battered leather bag in hand.

"A wee, perfect little man," Casey said.

Pat grinned and gave his brother a hearty hug. "Can I see him when the doctor's through then?"

"Aye, sit an' have a tea first. 'Tis a bit mad up there right now. "

A half hour later, the brothers were well fortified with both tea and whiskey. The doctor came down and surveyed them with a smile of satisfaction.

"All's fine up there," he nodded toward the top of the stairs. "The mother has done beautifully an' the laddie's hale as a horse. Ye did just fine yerself too there, man. Yer wife says ye were a rock through the whole thing. Congratulations." Casey shook the proffered hand, feeling a relief so vast it threatened to take him to his knees that he'd done nothing to damage either Pamela or the baby.

"Please help yerself to a glass of whiskey before ye leave. Gert's not likely to let ye out the door without a bite either."

He turned to his brother. "Well then, Uncle Pat, are ye ready to meet yer nephew?"

The bedroom had undergone a transformation in Casey's brief absence. The bed was made with fresh linens, his wife sitting up against the pillows in a clean nightgown, hair pulled up and away from her face with a ribbon, and their son, wrapped snug in a blue blanket, in her arms. A pot of tea, a delicate china cup, and a plate of toast lay on the low table to the side of the bed. The fire was built up in the grate and all traces of the last few mad hours had disappeared.

"Can Patrick come in?" he asked.

"Of course he can," she said, her head bent in adoration over the tiny being in her arms.

Pat ducked into the room, bringing with him the scents of the rain and wind.

Pamela smiled up at him, her face flushed and glowing. "Hi, Uncle Pat."

Pat bent over the bed and stroked one long finger down the baby's cheek. "Who's a handsome boyo, then?"

"Would you like to hold him?" she asked.

"Are ye certain?"

"Of course I am."

Pat leaned down and took the baby gingerly from Pamela.

One tiny, splayed starfish hand came up out of the blanket and Pat caught it with a finger. The baby wrapped his own fingers tight around that of his uncle.

"He's beautiful," Pat said, a catch in his throat, and Casey knew that Pat was seeing in the baby's face all the children he would never have with Sylvie. "He takes after his Mam there." He grinned at his brother. Casey grinned back.

Pat walked over to the window with the baby. "Aye, yer a braw laddie. Yer Grandda' would have loved to have been here to see ye." He glanced up at Casey. "Daddy would be so pleased an' proud. I can hardly believe that yer a daddy yerself now."

"Aye," Casey said softly, his eyes on the tiny hands waving above the blanket's edge. I suppose I am at that."

"Don't fock it up," Pat said lightly, but Casey heard the harsher words beneath the light tone. *You have been blessed. Don't screw it up or I'll kill you.*

"Aye, point taken man," Casey said, tone just as light, but knew all the same that his brother too could translate. *If I fock this up, ye'll be welcome to kill me.*

He looked back toward the bed to find his wife eyeing them both with thinly veiled amusement. Apparently, she was no slouch at translation either.

THEY LAY FACING ONE ANOTHER, THE BABY CAREFULLY COUCHED between them. From downstairs came the sounds and smells of sausage and potato cooking. Gert had the entire household well in hand. The sounds of chat and laughter drifted up the stairs, for Gert had insisted on feeding the doctor as well as Pat.

Pamela was tired and knew she ought to sleep, but couldn't bring herself to rest yet.

"How are you feeling?" she asked quietly, not wanting to disturb the baby's peaceful contentment.

"Like a man who knows there's a God in heaven," he replied, index finger wrapped snug in his son's wee fist.

"And all's right with the world," she finished softly.

"All will be right with *his* world," Casey said firmly. "I'll see to that."

His eyes glanced up from where they'd been fastened to his son's face for the last half-hour. "Ye ought to rest, darlin'. I don't like how pale yer lookin'."

She laughed, and a small fist shot up, catching her directly under the chin. "Casey, I've just given birth. Pale is the least of how I'm feeling. Besides, I don't think I can sleep until we've named him."

"Aye, the laddie deserves a name after the day he's had." Casey ran a thumb over the small fuzzy head and the baby gave a stretch that seemed to involve every cell of his being and emitted a great yawn that gave his parents a good view of healthy pink gums and tonsils. "Would ye like to name him after yer Daddy?"

She blinked in surprise. "I thought we'd name him Brian for *your* Daddy."

Casey gave a slight shake of his head. "No, I thought of it too, but it doesn't feel right. I'd like the wee man to have a fresh start, an' that requires a new name, don't ye think?"

She nodded as the baby began to turn his head, small tongue working furiously in search of his mother's breast.

She sat up, Casey tucking pillows behind her back, and loosened her clean nightgown, baring one breast to the bundle now in her arms. He rooted impatiently, making small snuffling noises like a truffle pig.

"Ye can't fault the laddie for knowin' what he wants," Casey said, laughing even as tears filmed his vision and the baby's snuffles turned to outraged squawks.

"Ouch," Pamela said as the baby managed to locate a nipple and clamped onto it fiercely, his entire being visibly relaxing as his tiny jaw worked vigorously.

There was a slight draft from the doorway and Finbar stuck his big, tousled head in.

"Come in, *gadhar*," Casey said, voice gentle, knowing the dog was confused by the day's events. "See, she's alright. No one has hurt her." He moved back a bit so Finbar could rest his worried countenance on his mistress' face. The dog padded around the bed, big nose in the air, sniffing a whole array of new and elaborate scents. He sat by the bed, sagging against it when Pamela stroked his head.

"Look at ye, will ye? Yer like a queen surrounded by adorin' subjects," Casey said, taking in the air of utter contentment that surrounded his wife. She had never looked more beautiful, albeit pale and exhausted, yet with a glow that made her positively luminous—a Madonna wreathed in lilies. He leaned forward, tears stinging his eyes, feeling a profound and overwhelming gratitude toward whatever forces in his life had brought this moment into being.

"Have I said thank you for my son," he said, voice low and rough with emotion.

"Not in the last five minutes," she said and leaned toward him, bestowing a soft kiss on his forehead. "You had a bit to do with him as well, you know."

"Perhaps we're meant to name him Conor. Look—" Casey nodded toward the dog.

She looked to where the baby's hand lay curled tight into Finbar's fur, small ivory-pink digits pearlescent against the rough wool of the dog's coat.

"Conor means 'wolf-lover'," Casey said with a smile.

"Conor," Pamela murmured to the rounded head at her breast, "Conor."

"Does it agree with yer tongue then, Jewel?"

She took Casey's hand and laid it on their child's head as though in benediction.

"Conor Brian Thomas Riordan," she said, pronouncing each name distinctly as if to test the fitness of them.

"A new name for a new life an' two to remember those who live in his blood."

She nodded. "It's right. Conor it is then."

The newly named Conor was asleep, head falling back in the pure exhaustion of the newly born. One kelp-colored eye rolled back in his head, an eyelid, pellucid as the interior of an oyster shell, tipped over the exposed white, depositing inky lashes onto the flushed cheek.

Pamela turned to Casey, eyes half-shut with exhaustion. "Do you know what your own name means?"

"Casey?"

She nodded.

"Well, it comes from the surname O Cathasaigh, an' Cathasaigh means vigilant."

"Vigilant." She stroked a hand down the side of his face. "It suits you."

"Aye? Then go to sleep, Jewel, an' rest easy, for I'll keep watch over you an' the babe."

CASEY FOUND SLEEP DIDN'T COME EASY THAT NIGHT. He was too excited by the baby's safe arrival and with Pamela coming through it equally unscathed, being that he had been her only medical help through the labor itself. He felt a need to keep watch over everyone as they slept.

He lay down on the bed just to be near his wife and son, to listen to them breathe in the still of the house and know them safe and whole.

He could feel Conor start to move and stretch in his wee bed. Pamela had nursed him an hour before and the baby wasn't fussing. When Casey got up and bent over the cradle, Conor merely looked up at him with that inscrutable ancient look that newborns wear, as if they are a tiny bit confused by the world in which they've landed but are also the harborers of universal truths and unfathomable secrets.

"We'll let yer Mam sleep a bit more, aye?" He picked Conor up and tucked him tight to his chest, adjusting the blanket so that no cool air would hit his skin.

Pamela was resting soundly, Finbar on the floor by the bed, still worried about his mistress though he raised his dark eyes to Casey questioningly at this unprecedented disruption in the nightly routine. Casey clicked his tongue at him. Finbar rose on his gangly legs and trotted downstairs with them.

In the kitchen, he opened a window, letting the spring night flow in and around himself and the baby. The moon was a sharp quarter slice of pearl against the indigo of the April dark. The scent of green growing things was thick on the air and he could taste the tartness of sticky buds upon his tongue, the mint of new grass, the effulgence of fresh-turned earth. Conor stretched and wrinkled his tiny nose, blinking solemnly at his father.

"Ye've picked a fine time to make yer entrance, laddie," Casey said, tucking the blanket more firmly around the baby, realizing suddenly what he had come downstairs to do.

Outside the dew was heavy on the grass. He was barefoot and the wet didn't bother him. A soft wind ruffled his hair and stirred the flannel blanket that shrouded the baby. He took a deep breath to still the tremor he felt throughout his body, relishing the sharp and heady smell of rising pine sap in his very cells.

"Yer Granda' loved such nights, said he could feel his own sap risin' in the spring an' 'tis true that the man couldn't keep himself still, nor sleep much in the springtime. He was a fine man. Ye've the look of him about yer wee mouth. Pure Riordan stubbornness in the set of it."

Conor stretched up, tilting his chin to Casey as if to emphasize the point his father had just made.

A rift valley opened in the luminous clouds, exposing Vega low on the horizon. His Daddy's star, deep blue and twinkling in the restless night air.

"Look there, laddie," he turned so that Conor faced the horizon. "'Tis yer grandda' sayin' hello to ye."

To love someone with this immediacy was a little bit like being hit hard, when you weren't expecting it in the least. To be this afraid suddenly, so that the world seemed unbearably dangerous to someone so small and fragile and new.

He couldn't hold his son and not see, in some measure, the face of the daughter they had lost. Their time with her had been so brief, but he remembered every detail of her, how her tiny face looked like a translucent petal not ready to open fully. How perfect each finger and toe was, how like shafts of sea-drowned pearls her small bones were. And how, in the short hours they had been allowed to spend with her, he felt as though he had lived and died a thousand times and had seen the reflection of those feelings in his wife's face.

He always knew her age, and could see her as she would be now, an eager little girl proud and proprietary of her new brother. He thought of all the stories he would never tell her, the advice and wisdom he wasn't able to pass down, and hoped that she was with his Da' where she could have all those things that he so cherished from his own childhood.

"Take care of her, Da', an' watch over us too while yer at it, if ye wouldn't mind," he said softly.

He stood in the night, under the stars, until his son fell asleep, secure in the strength and love of his father's arms.

Chapter Eleven
Dirty War

DAVID SAT AT HIS DESK AND LOOKED OUT OVER THE NIGHT LIGHTS of Belfast. He had been sitting thus for over an hour in an attempt to marshal his thoughts and decide how to write out the events of the last several weeks in an official report. What to tell, what to leave out? It was always a fine line, a judgement call on an operative's part. Some things had to be told in order to reassure one's superiors that one was actually doing one's job in a satisfactory manner. Some things had to be hidden so they didn't suspect one was doing one's job a little too well.

He sighed, tapping his pen against his forehead. There was so much he could not even begin to describe, how he felt an utter stranger to the life he had left behind in England, how some days he thought with the facet of his mind which had become 'Davey'. In order to be effective, one had to become the 'other' until that other felt more natural than your own self did. Many days this life was the real one, the one you had put away seemingly the outer shell, the shed chrysalis left behind and, David thought, hollow at a distance.

Originally, David had been run undercover with the Military Reconnaissance Force, his youthful appearance and air of innocence a useful tool. But the MRF had become too corrupt, with agents gone native and no controls effectively exerted. The entire thing had blown up when it came out that a group of them had headquartered in a massage parlor and were dabbling in business that had little to do with espionage or intelligence gathering. David had disgraced himself in an entirely different manner and almost gotten himself killed one night down in South Armagh.

There were several intelligence agencies operating in Northern Ireland and little communication or cooperation between any of them. There was Special Branch, the elite of the Royal Ulster Constabulary. There was MI5, and even MI6—supposedly restricted by its charter to intelligence gathering outside of the United Kingdom—had a dirty finger in the Northern Irish pie. Once the MRF was disbanded in disgrace it had left a hole in the intelligence chain and thus, 14th Intel had been born. They were a handpicked crew, the upper echelons staffed with SAS officers. Nominally, he was attached to 14th Intel but his position within it had been left deliberately murky. Essentially he was on his own, and so if he got himself into a bad situation there would be no calling in the cavalry to rescue him. It hadn't been stated outright, but was understood nevertheless. Truth was, he preferred it this way, as terrifying as it could be at times. It did blur the lines, but at least it kept him free from the turf wars that the various intelligence companies engaged in as often, if not more, than the ones they conducted with the sectarian forces. Even there things were very murky, because it was clear to David that some high-end people were in bed with the more radical factions of Loyalism and screwing around freely.

It wasn't even a case of the right hand being unaware of what the left was up to. That was far too simple for Northern Ireland. There were hands without number here, and no knowing to whom they were attached, nor for how long, nor why. David had never seen a war zone so confusing. And it *was* a war zone, despite what the government and military mouthpieces said to the contrary.

Though that stance begged the question—if this wasn't a war, but merely a police action, why the hell had they brought in the army, the SAS and MI5? The government wanted to be seen to be actively doing something, but wanted no blood on their hands. Soldiers were trained to obey orders. The risk in not obeying was either court martial or death if disobedience occurred in a combat situation. Yet when the soldiers obeyed orders, and the resulting fallout was a black eye, they were left to take personal responsibility for their actions, as the government and army brass distanced themselves from the poor squaddies they played as pawns on their political chessboard. For boys that were often away from home for the first time, and wet behind the proverbial ears, this was more than confusing. It was a betrayal that would erode their view of life and country for the rest of their lives. David knew this only too well, for it had done just that to his own view of his country and her dealings in Northern Ireland.

The Catholic/Nationalist community had long accused the British forces of being in collusion with the Loyalists but the official voices had ballyhooed this as rampant paranoia or media huckstering. David feared it was neither. No one trusted anyone—and with good reason.

They were an odd people, the Northern Irish, unfathomable, hard as nails at times—hard faces, hard voices, hard lives. He had never seen a people more family oriented or who would take a bullet for a friend without hesitation. Their loyalty to tribe was half the problem. It was next to impossible to break that code, to get in under the wire. And even if you did, something would always be wrong—your accent too generic, your views not quite on target, your way of communicating and understanding revealing you as 'other' to a people who lived on trip-wire instincts.

Northern Ireland was, of course, too close to Britain. A part of Britain officially, though unofficially David knew they never really had been. The planting and partition of Ireland might be one of the most grievous historical errors any country ever made. But Britain could not admit she had a war within her own borders, and this effectively tied the hands of the army and intelligence services.

Everyone here was playing their own game, fighting a turf war that had nothing to do with bringing peace to this war-torn province. Everyone wanted a piece of the action. At times, to David, it seemed like a enormous game, without any hard and fast rules. Everyone looking to either snatch or broker power, to play the propaganda war, to justify criminal butchery by claiming it was provoked.

A half hour later he only had three things written down. First, his contact with Jimmy Sandilands and the information that had come from that association. Then the surveillance results from Boyd's office and home. There was next to nothing there; Boyd seemed to be a suspicious bastard by nature. David was certain Boyd didn't scent anything wrong with David, because he was blind where he chose to be. Lust would do that to a man. He shook off the distaste that he felt when he saw the look in Boyd's eyes or felt his breath on his neck.

The last item on his list was one over which he hesitated. He felt a marked antagonism toward involving the Riordans in anything official, of committing their names to paper, or admitting he had any contact with them. He never had put Patrick's name to any document, and he would not. It seemed a sacrilege to do so, as though he were laying something fragile and beautiful in front of strange eyes that would not see anything but information to be used against either himself or Patrick.

He laid the pen down and stood up. The last of the light was gone and deep night lay over Belfast, softening the lines of the hard little city. It might, in the view of the world, be a bit of a provincial backwater, but he was more at home here than he had ever felt in London. Sometimes he forgot that he had another country, that people here saw him as foreign, as other, as the enemy. It was a dangerous sort of amnesia and he ought to know better than to indulge in it.

He had long understood that his country was not innocent here in Ulster, that in fact Britain had much to answer for in the formation and continuation of the Troubles. In light of recently gained knowledge, he had to admit it was far worse than he had ever imagined. In England, only the glory of the Empire was taught in the schools. History was never taught in its fullness, hidden were the truths of man's unending cruelty to man, his subjugation of other races and the blood that bought colonies and kept them. What he had learned through his time with the Redhand Loyalists told him it was entirely within the scope of possibility that British military forces actively fanned the sectarian flames in Ulster to detract from their own culpability.

It was, he thought, as Voltaire had so succinctly put it, *'History is no more than accepted fiction.'*

It hardly needed adding that the accepted fiction was inevitably written by the victors.

He returned to the desk, picked up the paper with Casey Riordan's name on it and ripped it into pieces. Some things were worth saving, war notwithstanding.

Chapter Twelve

June 1973

Father to Son

CASEY SIGHED WITH RELIEF AS HE STEPPED INTO THE WARM WATER. It had been a long day, filled with a variety of difficulties: a stone mason who didn't seem to realize the workday didn't start at noon, a shipment of stone that was only half of what he'd ordered, and a set of painters who had argued from the minute they'd arrived until he had threatened to knock their heads together.

He kept Conor snugged tight to his chest as he lowered himself into the water, their shared nightly bath had become a ritual for the two of them. The warm water helped make the lad sleepy and Casey savored the quiet time alone before handing him off to Pamela to be fed and put to bed for the night. He settled with a sigh of contentment into the warmth, the baby splaying small hands in startlement as the water closed over his dimpled bottom and lower back.

He kissed the rounded curve of his son's head, breathing deeply of his scent: milk and talc and the sweet, green smell that was all the laddie's own. Conor clutched his tiny fists into Casey's chest hair, causing him to draw a sharp breath.

Every inch of him was a wonder, and it boggled Casey's mind to think he himself had once been this tiny, this vulnerable. From the near transparent shell-like ears, to the ten perfect wee fingers and the incredible velvet of his skin.

There were times that he noted the contrasts between his own scarred, hairy body and the delicacy of what had been created between him and Pamela. It never failed to humble him and yet people had babies every day, did they not? But not this baby, one much hoped for and often despaired of. They had tried for such a long time, and been sore grieved by the death of their daughter, Deirdre. And then another girl had been lost during his internment and he had begun to wonder if they were fated never to have their own children. For a bit it had seemed there might not be a chance for another child, as the tenuous threads of their marriage had been strained to their limits, then the miracle of this child, and a fragile new beginning between his parents.

He dipped a flannel washcloth in the water and poured a bit of the soap Pamela had made for the baby onto it. A waft of lavender, the dusty, sunny scent of chamomile, and the sweet summer fragrance of geranium billowed up on a vaporous cloud. He washed the baby slowly, paying particular attention to the crease of the neck. He had been nervous at first of handling the baby, his hands being bigger than Conor's head, but it had become natural within days, as though Conor were an extension of his own flesh—which he was, both literally and figuratively.

This time each night had become a time for rambling talk, of stars and trees and small gossamer creatures. It was hard to talk sense to someone so soft and tiny, and so Casey allowed his whimsy to take flight and knew that should anyone else overhear he was likely to feel a fool, but with only Conor listening, it seemed right. He remembered his father telling him how it was with one's own children.

"Ye'll understand when ye've yer own babby," his father had said. "Ye can tell them all yer soul in safety an' so ye find that ye do. Ye wish ye could give them the wisdom of the world an' keep their innocence intact at the same time, but of course ye cannot an' that's one of the hardest things about bein' a parent."

"Did ye feel that way about me?" he had asked, for he'd just received a rousing lecture on the virtues of celibacy not twenty minutes previous—for getting caught by the nuns with his hand on Theresa O'Dell's budding breast in the custodian's closet.

His father had reached over and ruffled his hair. "Aye laddie, I still do—every day. When I look at ye, I see a young man, but I still see the wee lad I held in my arms an' rocked to sleep nights too."

It was true, he did find himself discussing everything with Conor, from God to the squirrel that had gotten into last year's flower seeds. Tonight, however, it was time for a less philosophical discussion. As charmed as he was by this tiny bundle, still a man had other needs in his life which tended to be ignored when there was an extra tenant in the marriage bed.

"See, son the thing is yer goin' to sleep in yer own bed tonight come hell or high water an' that's an end to it. A man has certain needs, an' to be blunt, yer interferin' with the fulfillment of mine."

One seaweed eye squinted balefully at him.

"Ah, don't even try it on me, laddie. I'm a veteran of this particular war. Yer Mammy's an expert at those looks."

Conor's only response was to release a trickle of hot liquid down his father's chest.

"Well, ye've made yer point," Casey laughed, "but yer still sleepin' in yer crib tonight an' make no mistake of it, boyo."

Conor merely gnawed on his wet fist and loftily ignored this threat.

"'Tis a grand thing to have a woman that ye both love an' desire, an' I could wish no more than that ye'll know such a thing yerself one day. An' I'd hope that yer own child will have the good grace to allow ye some leeway in achievin' those desires."

Other than a brief '*unh*', Conor tactfully refrained from comment on this notion of his father's. Casey decided a direct plea might be more effective.

"'Tis rumored that a man can actually go blind from a lack of such things. Ye don't want to be responsible for yer own father losin' his sight now do ye, boyo?"

Casey couldn't have sworn to it, but it did look as though the lad rolled an eye at him.

"Alright, I admit it's not likely but yer lookin' at a desperate man here, son."

Conor appeared to give this some thought, returning to a reflective chew of his fist.

Casey suddenly realized that he and the baby were no longer alone. Pamela was standing quietly in the doorway, a towel cradled across her forearms.

"Oh, Jewel, I didn't hear ye come in." He flushed slightly, wondering how much of the conversation, one-sided as it might be, she'd heard.

She had a very tender smile on her face as she bent over the tub, lifting Conor out of Casey's arms and wrapping him snugly in the towel. The minute he smelled his mother, Conor began the snuffling bleat that precursored the lusty howl he put forth when he was hungry. She bent and kissed Casey's wet curls.

"The two of you are beautiful together." She looked at him from over the head of the increasingly indignant Conor, and said, "I'm taking this one to feed him and put him in his crib. So if a desperate man should find himself in the bedroom in, say, half an hour, I'll meet him there."

IT WAS A FULL THREE HOURS BEFORE EITHER OF THEM ARRIVED at their appointed meeting, as Mr. Guderson had unexpectedly shown up and needed Casey's help with fixing a tractor engine, and after that task had been finished he stayed for the cup of tea Pamela offered while Casey fixed her with a frustrated glare. She returned the glare in full measure and asked Mr. Guderson if he'd like a slice of pound cake to go with his tea.

When at last he took his leave of them, Casey was looking things too unlawful to be uttered.

"I'll be up in a minute, Jewel," he said, shutting the door behind Lewis' back. She knew he would do his nightly check of doors and windows, a habit long ingrained in him by a life in Belfast's rough interior. But after the watcher in the woods episode, she wasn't inclined to argue with his concern.

The evenings had been chilly, but the bedroom glowed with a delicious warmth. Casey had slipped up the stairs partway through Mr. Guderson's visit, leaving her alone to endure the lecture on the proper care of sheep. Now she saw that he'd come to light the fire. A sense of heightened expectation had her shivering, but not with cold.

"Oh Lord," Casey said, coming in behind her. "I did think the man would never leave. For someone who rarely has more than two or three surly words for a person, he was in rare form tonight. Pound cake!" he snorted. "If I lose my sight altogether, be it on your head woman."

She unbuttoned her blouse and Casey slid it off her from behind.

"How much time do ye estimate we have?" he asked, in the tone of a man who feels doomed to celibacy for the foreseeable future.

"Not much, judging by how these feel," she said, wincing as Casey unhooked her bra and she felt the full weight of her breasts.

"Oh God, that's wonderful. Don't stop." Casey was rubbing the groove lines in her shoulders created by the ungainly contraption that had been made, in particular, for nursing mothers. His fingers, long and powerful, made short work of the knotted muscles.

Conor had been asleep since eight o'clock and her breasts were full and tight, tingling with the need to be suckled.

"Do they hurt?" Casey asked, staring in a fascinated manner at the breasts to which, despite his daily contact with them, he still hadn't fully adjusted.

"Not too much anymore. They're just rather full right now." She looked down at them ruefully.

Casey traced a forefinger along the swell of one breast, following the line of blue vein visible in the low light of the fire.

"D'ye want me to get the laddie for ye, Jewel?"

She looked into his eyes, dark with the heat of desire.

"No," she said and caught her breath as he cupped the full weight of her breast in his hand, thumb stroking across the nipple, now taut with both milk and desire. She could feel the wet on his palm as the milk started to flow, needing only the barest stimulation to let down.

He laid her back on the bed, replacing his hand with lips that were warm and firm. She groaned with both relief and want. The very feel of his skin against her's was like coming in from the cold on a bitter night. Her entire body felt lit from within by a warm white light, each nerve ending pulsing separately as Casey's hands moved over her.

"Don't tease, man," she said arching toward him.

"Tell me what it is ye want, Jewel," he said, voice soft and husky. His lips moved across her shoulder, teeth sinking gently into the muscle, causing her breath to catch hard in her throat. "Tell me exactly what it is that ye want." His hand, hard and calloused, slid across her belly, readying her for a more brute intrusion.

"You," she whimpered low in her throat, desperate suddenly to feel him inside her, to make of their two respective beings, one. One flesh, one heart beating in accord, one purpose—seeking absolution of the body through passion, finite and fleeting as it might be.

Casey obliged most happily, drawing in a sharp breath as he slid inside her.

"Are ye alright?" he asked. "I'm afraid of hurtin' ye, Jewel."

"I'm fine," she gasped. "For God's sake, just don't stop."

He chuckled low in his throat. "Don't think I could even if I wanted to, woman."

He moved again gently and she felt that shift begin, where the world around dissolved and there was nothing but this—Casey against her, hot and solid, and time itself slowed, stopped, and this was all there was of existence, herself and the man she loved more dearly than life itself.

Her hands ran the length of his back from the firm round of buttock to the oddly smooth scars on his back, up across the arcing muscles of his neck and into the soft curls that cradled his skull.

"Lord, woman," he whispered, mouth against her ear. "I've missed this something terrible."

"Me too," she whispered back, crying soft and low in her throat as he moved again, an exchange of the flesh and spirit and a recommitment of their individual selves to this marriage.

She arched hard against him in the final moment, knowing the frustration of never being able to get quite close enough, even as her own body felt the shattering relief of release. Casey, with a shaking breath, joined her a moment later, then lay with his forehead bowed to her own, the thrum of their pulse in unison like a blood cadence.

"Wow," was all she had the presence of mind to say as Casey moved to lie full length beside her, managing to look smug and stunned in equal measure.

"Lord, that was something else altogether," he said. "I feel a bit like an owl that's been knocked from its perch."

"Mm," she sighed, "it's called deprivation." She cracked one eye open, surveying the blankets on the floor, the wet towel and the fine spray of milk across her husband's forehead. "Sorry about that." She reached up and dabbed the droplets off his face.

"For what?"

"The mess," she said. "I feel like a cow these days. If I'm not nursing, I'm leaking. I only hope you don't find it disgusting."

Casey gave her a bemused look. "Tis my son yer feedin' with it, so I'd be a bit of a jackass, darlin', did I find it disturbin'."

Just then a loud wail issued forth from down the hall. Casey laughed and sat up on the bed. "His timin' is a thing of beauty. I'll say that much for the boy."

"I'm glad you still find me desirable," she said softly, watching him as he stood and stretched, fingertips touching the ceiling, before he grabbed his pants off the chair. He turned and gave her a raised eyebrow.

"Jewel, I can't imagine a set of circumstances under which I wouldn't desire ye, but it's only the more so now that we've the lad. It's another tie between us. It strengthens the web of all I feel for ye, an' that, I can assure ye," he said softly, "is a very great deal."

She smiled and stretched, body feeling akin to softly melted silver ready to be poured and set. "Go bring me your son, man."

He leaned down and kissed her. "Aye, ye bossy wee woman. I'm goin'."

Chapter Thirteen
Muck

MUCK O'HAGAN WAS CONSIDERED IN SOME CIRCLES to be the best and most fearless journalist currently working in Northern Ireland. In other circles, he was considered a muck-raking bastard trying to fan the flames of Nationalist/Republican/IRA rebellion. Not that any of said organizations needed help in that area, for the bright hope of the Civil Rights movement had become a conflagration gone out of control.

Patrick Riordan had known Muck since the days of that bright hope, and had always liked him. He also admired his work. Muck might have a bit of a suicidal bent with the stories he covered, but he could sympathize with that. The stories needed telling and he was a great believer in the responsibility to truth that the press owed the public. It wasn't beyond Muck to write a good old-fashioned muck-raking scandal story filled with lurid detail and nicknames to cover the real identity of those he wrote about. But this fooled no one, for Muck would often write another story in the same issue of the paper where names were named and punches were not pulled, and the hooks and links to the veiled story were obvious.

Muck had been on the receiving end of more than one death threat, most of which came to the newspaper. He had a cork board over his desk filled with them.

Muck, whose real name was Clifford, had a gentle, dreamy exterior with roughly the same dimensions horizontally as he possessed vertically and glasses that would give a Coke bottle a run for thickness. People who had known him for more than five minutes were not fooled by that exterior unless he wanted them to be. He had the tenacity of an angry pit bull when he got his teeth into a story and would out the truth no matter the cost.

Patrick, not one to fear pit bulls in either their canine or human incarnations, had liked Muck from the beginning. The man, two years younger than Patrick himself, had grilled him mercilessly about his family's Republican background during what was meant to be a peaceful march protesting the imprisonment of six Irish laborers in a British jail. In exasperation after a full hour of such questioning, Pat had threatened to upend him into the next barrel or hedgerow they happened across. Muck had laughed and apologized and they had been firm friends ever since. Therefore, when his brother had come to him asking who in the press they might approach about this story, Pat had thought of Muck first and only.

Pat arranged to meet Muck upstairs at Madden's, a dark, cozy bar firmly entrenched in the Republican community. Like most Republican bars, it had seen its share of violence, and when he entered the door all the heads turned round to look at him. Once they ascertained Pat wasn't a Loyalist assassin they turned back to their drinks. A few nodded at him, or said hello. If they didn't know Pat by name, they knew Casey, and knew he was a safe quantity. The bartender, John, nodded at him and tilted his head toward the narrow stairs. Muck had already arrived.

He was waiting upstairs in one of the wooden corner booths, round head shiny as a bowling ball in the sun. One of God's more beauteous creatures Muck was not, but inside that round head was a brain as sharp as a stiletto. At this time of day, there wasn't a man behind the bar upstairs but Muck had two Guinness on the table, his own already half down the glass.

"Pat, it's good to see ye, man. It's been a bit of a while."

"It has, indeed," he agreed and sat across from Muck, tucking his long legs around the table post. After Sylvie's death he had disappeared for awhile, unable to face the idea of talking to anyone, of receiving condolences or having to convey the words that would tell of her death. He still did not want to speak of her and Muck, a wise man, simply skipped all the polite chatter that might inform the beginning of most meets like this one and got straight to business.

"So ye have a story for me, then?"

As Pat was also a man who knew how to get straight to the core, he simply sketched in the information in broad strokes, adding detail to make certain points, and leaving it out where there wasn't anything factual. Muck wouldn't appreciate guesswork and could fill in the gaps himself, which he did with the intuitive mind and enormous knowledge he held about his city and its labyrinthine deceptions and distortions.

"An' yer friend, the one inside—what is he? A British agent?"

"He is." Pat saw no reason to prevaricate. If Muck was to take this story on and hunt down the ends of it, he was going to need to know he could trust them implicitly with any intelligence that was passed along to him. He was too seasoned to be fooled by anything less.

"What's in this for him—why does he want to pass along this information? He's compromisin' himself, and if there's one thing I've learned about the shadow ops here, it's that they will usually throw a man to the dogs before they'll compromise their own security in the smallest way."

"Ye'll have to take my word when I tell ye, he's got his reasons for doin' this, an' they're honorable. He believes in things like that—honor and duty."

"Aye," Mick said, raising a skeptical eyebrow. "Well, if he stays here long enough, Belfast will beat it out of him."

Pat merely nodded, privately thinking it would likely take more than even Belfast could hand out to take David's honor from him.

Muck tapped a ruminative finger against his pursed lips. "Listen, this is between the two of us, man, but there's a whiff of rumor that MI5 has an agent in the deepest and foulest trenches of Loyalism, somebody that they've turned—an' in return they're looking the other way as the more radical elements arm themselves for a Doomsday they think is sure to come."

"They think Doomsday is comin'? Odd, I thought it had been here for years," Pat said.

"Aye, well, it's said they're waitin' on a big shipment of arms from South Africa."

"South Africa?"

"Aye, ye know they feel some kinship, livin' in a society under siege by an underdog that would like the right to jobs an' homes, maybe an education."

Pat felt slightly sick. This all tied in too neatly with what little David had told him, for it not to be true.

"Are ye sayin' it's too dangerous to pursue the story?"

"Lord above, no. I'm just sayin' this may set off a chain of events neither yerself nor myself can control. It's a filthy wee war we're involved in here, man, an' I know few understand that better than yerself. But even you an' I are relative innocents compared to what the secret forces here are willing to do, and how far they are manipulating things to their own ends—though what those ends are is merely speculation on my part." He paused to take a long drink of his ale. "Yer man on the hill called me before he disappeared into the ether an' told me to look closely at McCarthy but to be damned careful in what direction I was diggin', an' to keep it close until I was sure about what I knew."

"And what do ye know, then?" Pat asked carefully, his heart thudding a little faster in his chest.

"Nothing concrete just yet, but there's more goin' on in that home than just perverts interferin' with underage boys. It's not the first time someone has gone to the authorities over it. There's been allegations in the past, an' it goes to the police an' then it seems to stop dead there, which tells me that someone is protectin' the man who runs the place. Now why do ye think someone would do that, an' how high up would this have to go in order for such charges to simply melt away into the night?"

"Are ye talkin' across the water?" Pat lifted his own drink and drained it, trying to take the edge off the hollow pit in his stomach.

Muck shrugged and stood up, walking behind the bar and filling both their glasses again from the brass taps. "I don't know yet, but I'm almost afraid of what I might find. I joke about this job bein' the death of me one day, but I've an uneasy feelin' with this one sometimes, as though it might be the story that does kill me."

"Which only makes ye that much more likely to follow it wherever it leads," Pat said.

"Aye, yer right. It's my job, though if I don't get to the bottom of it—or top as it were—then I might as well hang up my pen an' paper tomorrow. It's a big, sticky damned web an' it may take me a bit to untangle the threads well enough to get a clear shot of the pattern beneath."

Muck sat back down and swallowed off half his drink in one go.

"Don't look discouraged, man, for we've something we've never had before—yer friend inside. He has access I can only dream about. He could be the key to actually finding out who is behind all this. Otherwise, I could spend years chasin' smoke an' mirrors."

They finished their drinks and parted ways after that, Muck back to the newspaper and Pat to the Fair Housing office to finish some calling and paperwork. There he put in a couple hours work, made three frustrating phone calls and found housing for one family of the three hundred on his list. What was needed, he knew, was a national council for fair housing allocation, not a hole-in-the-wall office that fielded calls from the desperate and poor in the Catholic community. What was needed was broad scale reform to the laws and to the people who were ostensibly in charge of upholding them. Unfortunately, for now, this was what they had—one man trying to stave off a tidal wave of despair and anger and to help people find what ought to be an inalienable human right—a roof over their heads and shelter from the storms of life.

What he needed for himself was something else, something more. Lying on his desk was an envelope with the crest of Queen's University embossed upon its thick vellum. Inside was his acceptance into their law school. He didn't know how he was going to make it work, he only knew he must.

Chapter Fourteen
The Bog Woman

CASEY WHISTLED TO HIMSELF AS HE TROD ACROSS THE THICK CARPET of white flowers and gorse that carpeted the north end of the bog straddling the line between his own property and that of Lewis Guderson.

It was a fine Saturday in early June and the air had the untroubled clear blue tint to it that often meant the day would go down bathed in sun, as well as having emerged in it. His current building was going up on time and, more importantly, on budget and he hadn't had another visit from Mr. Spectacles and his partner—though he wasn't fool enough to think they wouldn't be back at some point.

For today he would leave the concerns of work behind. He had left Pamela happily rocking Conor, the two of them blissful in the quiet of the early morning. Before leaving he'd bent to kiss her, and could still taste the oatmeal and honey flavor of her mouth. He smiled softly to himself. Having a family suited him well, and it felt like a warmth that surrounded him from morning to night and through the dark hours of bed and sleep. At the same time, such happiness was frightening. The worry that something might happen to any of his loved ones haunted his three o'clock in the mornings on the rare occasion he could not sleep. Today he would leave even those worries behind. Working with earth always freed him, his boot against the lug of the spade, its haft anchored firmly inside his knee, his spirit one with the thick, sodden, life-giving earth. It was good and simple work, paid readily with glowing winter fires that took the chill from a man's bones.

He reached the area he planned to work, and placed his bag of biscuits and hot tea upon the ground to the side. The scent of comfrey rose as the bag crushed the green juices from it. He would have to remember to pick some and carry the roots home to Pamela. She made an ointment from them that worked a wonder on bruises and cuts.

He eyed the area with a turf cutter's squint, judging where to start the bank exactly to inflict the least damage and yet maximize the amount of peat that might be pulled from it. The one thing he knew for certain was that he would have to dig well away from the ancient hawthorn crowning a slight rise in the land. The tree stood alone, more than forty feet high, though he knew the species rarely soared above thirty. It was in full bloom now, with great snowy corymbs of flower reaching to the ground. Such lone trees were said to mark the entry to the fairy realm and were best avoided unless one wanted to find oneself lost in the world of the Good Folk. Besides, even if he didn't have reservations himself, surely the neighbors would be after his head were he to meddle with such a thing. When he was just a lad himself, a man a few streets over had hacked down a small, stunted specimen that he claimed was a blight on his plot. The neighbors had been horrified and had shook their heads sadly when first the man's dog died and then shortly after he broke his back falling from a ladder. The Good Folk were not to be made light of and it was a fool man who did so in the face of such knowledge.

He set to work with the morning sun upon his back, laboring well toward noon before stopping for a rest and a cup of tea. A soft breeze blew across his body, drying the sweat from his t-shirt and carrying with it the scents of hawthorn blooms. It was an odd scent, and not one he'd ever cared for, as the Irish had always considered the hawthorn to hold the scent of death. Branches of it were hung over doorways during the Famine to indicate that someone inside the home was dying or dead. And to be certain, it did have an oddly decayed scent.

He leaned his head back against the trunk of the tree, feeling a mite drowsy. But just as he was about to close his eyes, a flutter in his peripheral vision caught his eye. He sat up quickly, casting about for a weapon and then felt immediately foolish, for it was only a bit of cloth the wind had caught. It was tied to the hawthorn tree, caught fast in its branches above a cluster of blossom. Odd that, for there wasn't a spring nearby, nor a well to his knowledge. These rags had once been common at holy sites, bits of material dipped in the sacred water of the well and then tied to the tree as an offering to the Goddess or nature spirit that was thought to guard the well. The hairs on the nape of his neck crinkled a bit, as though a pair of eyes were set fast upon him.

The cloth looked very old, a faded blue cotton without pattern of any sort. He reached out to touch it and shivered when he realized it was damp. He pulled his hand back sharply, looking around as a chill went arrow-sharp up his spine. It hadn't rained in days, and the breeze had been fair and warm that whole time. There simply wasn't any reason for the cloth to be damp. He backed away and picked up his spade. He would get back to work. A good sweat ought to banish the strange, shivery feeling touching the cloth had given him.

He set to digging with a grim determination not to give in to the feeling that someone here watched his every move. He dug for a good half hour, but the sensation didn't budge. Then, just as the sun ducked behind a puffy set of clouds, his spade stopped short, almost causing him to topple over into the wet earth.

He frowned to himself. The earth was soft enough but the feel was wrong. There was something obstructing the shovel and it wasn't bog. A strange chill feathered out from his spine and he considered moving away, digging elsewhere, ignoring whatever it was against which the tip of the spade now pushed. Curiosity, however, got the best of him, and he levered the spade up a bit, removing more of the wet soil. He knelt down, hand scraping away the thin layer that was left. Water oozed up through the peat, obscuring his view, but he thought he felt fur, smooth as an otter pelt, beneath his fingers. A dead animal? He had heard of whole cows being found, preserved as though they had dropped into the bog only the day before, though they had died hundreds of years earlier.

He scooped out two more soaking handfuls and then froze. It was definitely fur, but not upon the back of an animal anymore, for with the last handful of soil the outline and raised knuckles of a very human hand revealed itself. A woman's hand, the bones were too fine for a man. The fingers were wrapped around an object. He sat back on his heels, uncertain how to proceed. But curiosity once again took precedence. He couldn't simply leave it lest she had been the victim of foul play.

Another half hour of careful work revealed that the fur she was wrapped in was dark with age, though when the sun peeked over his shoulder he caught a hint of chestnut in its depths. Otter or elk perhaps? He wasn't certain, only that the skins must have been very fine and well cured, for the cloak was still intact. It was large too, and must originally have belonged to a man, for the woman's slight frame was dwarfed by it.

Skin, pale as ivory but taut as leather, revealed itself once the fur was moved aside. Strange that it should remain so white. After all this time in the bog it ought to have sustained discoloration. Her face, through the fine scrim of soil, was high-boned with no marks upon it, her hair a sodden stream of copper twined within the dark fingers of the earth. She had been a beautiful woman; even time could not hide that fact.

He turned his attention to the object in her hand. He was afraid to touch the fingers, to unfurl the bones that awaited only a breath to disintegrate. The object was small and stone, shaped by a rough chisel. It looked primitive in design, and yet—it seemed to give off a powerful emanation, as though the air around it pulsed with a potency that knew neither the constraints of time nor space. Crudely made, yet he recognized it for what it was—Sheela-na-gig, the Trickster Hag, the Crone, the archway into and out of life itself.

He had always held the beliefs of his childhood sacred, of a loving Christian God, and yet he would be lying if he said he had not always sensed something more behind that, something far older and darker in aspect. He knew what his wife would say—that it was the face of the Goddess that he glimpsed. The land itself had always seemed to him to respond to a more feminine rhythm rather than a masculine one. The Sheela—small, stone and vulgar—was one face of that ancient Goddess and a symbol of both the fertility and the power of the female. She was a figure of the in-between realms, of neither here nor there, but her power felt real nonetheless. He moved his eyes away from the squat stone figure, not wanting to acknowledge how much it disturbed him.

Against the woman's throat lay a necklace, a barbaric-looking piece with great chunks of amber, dark with wintery suns. He touched one of the pieces of amber carefully, for the workmanship was very old and delicate. It felt oddly warm for having lain so recently in chilled, streaming earth. He leaned forward, squinting to make out the details better. Between the nodules of amber were tiny flowers wrought in silver, perfect blossoms, some with out-turned petals, others curled in upon themselves with a small cluster of berries under the shade of each flower. Beside each triplicate set of berries was a thorn of silver, darkened with age. They were hawthorn, blossom and fruit and thorn together. In all the old tales, this was a way of knowing that one had crossed into the world of the Others, that both flower and fruit should reside together on one branch. Who had she been? One marked as 'other', that much was clear. No one else, with superstition as rife as it would have been in the countryside even a hundred years ago, would have dared to wear such a piece of jewelry. He laid the amber back in the shadowy hollow of her throat and set to clearing the rest of the soil away from her.

It was a long and arduous job for he did not want to damage the fragile corpse. He knew that brought to the surface and exposed to oxygen, bodies could begin to disintegrate very quickly, as though it were light and air that held the keys of decay. Strangely, the only thing he could smell emanating from her was the sharp green of herbs, as though she'd been preserved in them or had used them to such an extent that they had become a part of her very essence.

There seemed no marks upon her skin, leastwise, as much as he could tell. She looked as though she had simply lain down in the bog and fallen asleep, never again to waken in this world.

Now why had he thought that? That somehow she had managed to awaken elsewhere, but not in this world, or at least the world that human eyes could see.

"Who were ye?" he whispered quietly, even that small a sound sending a ripple through the air around him. He shuddered. The day had turned to twilight while he had been clearing the wet soil away from the bones and he should have been long gone home to his tea. The wind caught a lock of the woman's hair, a tendril already dried from the bog waters. It gave the illusion of movement to her face, and in the fading light it seemed she looked directly at him.

It was time to go home. He wrapped her carefully again in her fur cloak and returned the sods so they braced the frail cage of her bones and covered her skin. He didn't want animals getting at her. In fact, he felt guilty about leaving her alone as it was, but then, something about her didn't seem to welcome company.

He shook his head. His fancies and the fading light were getting the better of him. He gathered his tools and his lunch bag and after making the sign of the cross, strode from the bog, the feeling of eyes on his person never once leaving him.

Chapter Fifteen

August 1973

Internal Relations

IN THE LATE SUMMER OF THAT YEAR, CASEY'S GRANDMOTHER on his mother's side, Lucy Murphy, passed away peacefully in her sleep after a full day of working in her garden. Pamela had only met the lady twice, once shortly after their wedding when she had come to Belfast, ostensibly on a shopping trip but really to check out the bride, then again after Conor's birth when Casey's Aunt Fiona had brought her down to see this great grandchild. Technically, 'The Aunts', as Casey and Pat referred to them, were not actually aunts, but their mother's cousins. However, the tangle of Murphy relations didn't observe the difference between siblings and cousins, as Casey had explained to her, for Deirdre and Devlin had spent as much time in their cousins' house growing up as they had in their own and vice versa.

Casey's grandmother had seemed a little frail on that last visit. Much of her time had been spent in the rocking chair, which Casey had brought down from the nursery and placed by the Aga so that she would be both warm and in the center of the kitchen's activity. She had only been able to stay a few days before being whisked home by a brisk Fiona, and then the call had come two months later that she had passed away.

And so they found themselves, in the wee hours of an August morning, loading baby paraphernalia and themselves, plus Patrick, into the car on their way to her funeral.

Casey and Patrick both looked resplendent in their dark suits, Patrick in navy blue and Casey in a deep charcoal grey lightweight wool. Casey was always twitchy in formal wear, preferring the comfort of his workaday clothes, but today he seemed more agitated than was usual.

"Whatever is the matter, man?" Pamela asked as they cleared the limits of Belfast and were on the windy road to Ballymena where the majority of the Murphy clan dwelt and his Grandmother Murphy had spent the last sixty years of her life.

"I'm just a wee bit nervous about the day," he said, shifting in his seat and cricking his neck as if he was in a deal of discomfort.

"Why?"

"Because this side of the family is insane, that's why," Casey said grimly, sticking his finger inside the starchy white collar and pulling it like it was choking him. She reached across, loosened the knot of his tie, and undid the top button of his shirt. He sighed with relief.

"As opposed to the Riordan side? These Murphys must be real corkers."

"Ye've met Devlin, an' he's mild-like compared to the rest."

"Surely not?" she said, egging him on.

He cast a very black look in her direction. "Aye, we'll see if yer laughin' after my Aunt Sophy bends yer ear for an hour or two."

She cast an eye toward the back seat where Pat sat with his nephew. "Is he exaggerating, Pat?"

"No," Pat said matter-of-factly. "They're a mad bunch to be sure. D'ye mind the time, Casey, that Denny lived in the treehouse for a year?"

"Aye," Casey snorted. "I'd live in a tree too were Aunt Sophy my mother."

Pamela laughed. "I'm rather looking forward to this funeral."

"O-ho," Casey said, "don't be after thinkin' they won't grill ye mercilessly, Jewel. They're goin' to swarm at ye like bees to the honey tree. 'Twon't be pleasant at all, I assure ye."

"You're starting to scare me," she said, only half in jest.

"Dinna fret woman, ye'll survive it. Pat an' I have managed years of it, after all."

"Besides, everyone enjoys a good funeral," Pat said, and Casey nodded in agreement.

"It sounds like you were close to them," Pamela said, fascinated by the small threads of information about the brothers' shared history. It was a glimpse into the world they'd inhabited before their father's death, their mother's abandonment, and Casey's time in prison. Because her own childhood had been so lonely, she loved the tales that Casey and Pat could occasionally be induced to tell about their own relatives.

"We lived with them for a bit while Da' was in the Curragh. Split our time between them an' Granny Riordan."

"Your Granny Riordan was still alive then?"

"Aye, she died shortly before our Da' did. Otherwise she'd have taken Pat an' me in after Daddy died, whether we bloody liked it or not. Woman had a fierce will on her."

"That's stating it mildly," Pat said. "She once put a rifle to a man's forehead for askin' the time of day."

"Seriously?" Pamela said, twisting round to look at Pat. He looked up from a game of peek-a-boo that had Conor gurgling with delight.

"He was an old friend of Da's but he was in the Brotherhood an' she said that they'd taken her husband and her last son an' they were not havin' her grandsons an' that she'd put a hole in their heads did they come near either of us again. The man backed all the way out of the garden with his hands up above his head. Was comical, really. Our Nan kept the fear of God in yer man as well." Pat grinned and Casey snorted, while negotiating a hairpin corner that had a lorry pelting around it in completely un-Irish haste.

Casey slapped the horn a couple of times in a manner that had nothing hostile about it but seemed to Pamela more an exchange of greetings rather than an act of anger. Irish driving was a life and death sport and it was each man for himself on the narrow, twisting roads.

"Casey Riordan, were you ever *not* in trouble?" she asked.

"Well, I'd not like ye to think I was a complete reprobate, but aye, in the general course of things, I did manage to get myself out of one scrape only to find myself in another an hour or so later. Though it's not like ye were a milk-white choirboy yerself, Paddy."

"Aye, well, I did have ye right there ahead of me, leadin' by example, so what could ye expect?"

"O-ho, well I'll not be blamed for the time yerself an' Denny were caught in the convent then, will I?"

"In a convent? Patrick, I'm shocked," she laughed. "Casey, do tell."

Pat shot a glare at the back of his brother's head but Casey, being proof against both looks he could see and particularly against those he could not, ignored his brother.

"Well, see Jewel, I don't think I have the real story here, only Pat's version, which I suspect has been cleaned up like an Easter lily in comparison to what actually happened."

"Oh, aye," Pat rejoined with no little sarcasm, "because in Casey's version there's likely a dozen nuns defiled, a priest set drunk on communion wine an' no sheep safe in the hills."

"Oh, I don't think wakin' up in the Mother Superior's bed requires much embroidery, lad," Casey said, making a pointed gesture at a small car that was meandering on their side of the line. The driver returned the favor and all proceeded happily.

"A Mother Superior's bed? Patrick, I'm speechless."

"Aye? It's too bad we can't say the same for my brother. Besides the story is nowhere near as titillatin' as he's makin' it sound. Denny did have the job of deliverin' the fresh vegetables to the convent weekly, an' so we found ourselves there one evenin' with a bottle of whiskey he'd stolen from Uncle Ned an' they'd a convenient wee shed on the grounds. We sat out back of it, watchin' the moon come up an' drinkin'. I did remember Casey an' Da' sayin' a body should drink as much water as whiskey an' then ye'd not get sick. Didn't work."

"Well we didn't mean for ye to drink it from a pig's trough."

"'Twasn't a pig's trough," Pat said with injured dignity. "'Twas a sheep's bucket."

"Aye, so much better, that," Casey said sarcastically.

"A sheep's bucket and a Mother Superior's bed? This casts an entirely new light on your character, I must say." Pamela smiled over her shoulder at Pat, who winked in reply.

"Aye, but all I did was actually sleep in a nun's bed. I didn't turn one away from her calling."

"What?"

"Jaysus, Patrick, discretion isn't yer middle name today, is it?" Casey said, scowling out the windscreen to little effect.

"So this is true?" Pamela asked, delighted with all the confessions going on about her.

"Oh aye," Pat replied, giving his finger to Conor, who promptly champed down on it. "Sister Theresa Mary Francis—also known in her former life as Theresa O'Dell—or the girl who was willing to give up God for Casey Riordan."

"Patrick, I swear to God an' his wee angels when I stop this car I'm takin' ye out in the field an' makin' ye still that tongue of yers."

"No, you won't," Pamela said practically. "You'll dirty your suit. Now do tell me about Miss O'Dell, Patrick. Casey, mind the road."

"Mind the road, is it?" Casey snorted, but was then distracted by a large lorry loaded down with spilling hay.

"Theresa O'Dell was his first girlfriend," Pat said. "He was—what were ye Casey—maybe thirteen at the time?"

Casey merely raised an eyebrow. "Suit or no, boyo, mind what I said about the field."

Pamela waved an airy hand in her husband's direction. "Ignore him, and please continue."

"Well, at first she'd not give him the time of day. She was a bit in the way of bein' a grand one, her daddy was a solicitor an' all. But then the rumor got round after a dance, told about by Netty Blume, that Casey..."

"Patrick Brian Riordan—if ye tell this story I swear to ye—"

"He has to tell it now," Pamela protested. "I need to hear it."

"Oh trust me, Jewel, ye do not need to hear this. Besides, my son is in the car. It's not an appropriate topic to be discussin' in front of him."

"Nice try, man," she said, "but we could be having a riveting discussion about the benefits of prunes for all your son knows or cares."

"At this point," Casey sighed in a resigned fashion, "I wish we were."

"Pat?" Pamela prompted.

"Well ye see, he'd the reputation of bein' a wee bit of a Don Juan with the ladies already, an' Theresa had heard from Netty that—"

"I'll finish tellin' the story here if ye don't mind," Casey said, a tidal surge of red flooding up from his collar. "Now in my defense I have to say that she was a pretty wee thing, an' I was hormone-addled. My Da' always said young boys weren't fit for society between the ages of about twelve an' twenty an' I think he may have been onto something there."

He smiled, a fleeting nostalgia crossing his face. "Oh 'twas a desperate time altogether, I tell ye. If I wasn't playin' rugby, I was with Theresa, half undressed an' wholly frustrated. Behind the school, up in my room when Da' was at work, down by the rugby field. We were doin' everything but the act itself, an' to be honest I think I was a wee bit scared on the one hand an' certain I'd die a virgin on the other."

"I doubt that was ever a danger," Pamela said dryly.

"His innate charm was still a thing under cultivation back then," Pat said with a wink.

"So, did she put you out of your misery eventually?" Pamela asked.

"Oh aye," Casey nodded. "Though it left me a little confused to be sure. She cried afterwards, then when I asked her whatever was the matter she slapped my face an' then not even five minutes later, asked me if we might do it again."

"Oh God," Pamela laughed, "nothing is ever simple with you, is it, man?"

"I don't see how any of that was my fault," Casey said, grinning.

"So did you oblige her?"

"I did—though in hindsight, that may have been a wee bit insensitive of me."

"Well, you were only—what was it—thirteen?"

"Fourteen by the time we did the deed," Casey said.

"As old as that?" Pamela asked, voice rich with sarcasm.

Casey gave her a raised brow. "Listen, woman, 'twasn't my idea to talk about this."

She felt a slight twinge, despite the bantering tone of the conversation. He might have been only fourteen and was now a full grown man as well as legally wedded to her, but still... if she were honest, it made her jealous to think of him with another woman, even if it was years before they had known one another. Which made her, she was aware, a terrible hypocrite.

"She was a lucky girl to have you for her first," she said, trying hard for a charitable tone, though judging from the look Casey gave her, she hadn't succeeded in the least.

"Are ye goin' to tell her about Mahri then too?" Pat asked, a look of beatific innocence adorning his features.

"No, I think we've had enough of my confessions today, thank ye all the same. Perhaps though, while we're at it, we ought to discuss with whom ye lost yer own virginity, man," Casey said testily, the flush still dying back toward his collar.

"Janie Bell," Pat said promptly and entirely without shame.

"Janie Bell! She's—she must be about twenty years older than ye, man," Casey sputtered.

"She was fifteen years older, but I was always a good learner, as ye know."

"Yer shameless."

"Now that's more than a bit of the pot callin' the kettle names there, is it not?"

An annoyed *hmmph* was all the response Pat received to his question.

"Besides, we were talkin' about yerself an' Theresa. If ye don't want to tell the story, I'll be forced to."

Casey threw a dark look over his shoulder and then capitulated with a sigh, though a small smile tugged at the corners of his mouth. "'Tis true, Jewel, the girl did come to me before takin' her vows. But by then I'd met you an' that was that."

"This happened *after* we met?"

"Aye." He gave her a dark, slanted look. "Don't be after scoldin' me for that, woman. 'Twas durin' the first summer I knew ye."

"Oh." She could feel the dreaded flush creeping up from her neckline. That summer she had spent in Scotland with Jamie and though in the end she had returned to Casey, it wasn't a memory the man enjoyed.

Casey reached over, patted her knee, and flashed her a smile. "Dinna fret woman. 'Tis only that life went on even in yer absence that summer."

"How far on are we talking about here?" she asked lightly, though she knew her words didn't come across in as playful a manner as she'd intended.

"I was waitin' for ye when ye came home, was I not?" Casey's tone was no longer so light either. "But aye, I was a little sore an' angry at ye those weeks as well."

"Which means what exactly?" she asked, reminding herself that Pat was in the backseat and had become very quiet in the last few minutes.

"Which means we'll talk about this later, woman."

"Well then, man, what did she say to you?" Pamela asked, seeing the wisdom of not pursuing the present line of conversation.

"She said," Casey cleared his throat, the red flushing from his collar once again, "she said that those times we'd... well she said that was the closest she'd ever felt to God, more so than all the prayin' she'd been doin' in preparin' to take her vows."

"Oh," Pamela replied, feeling quite suddenly sorry for the girl.

"Aye, well," Casey said softly, "I think her experience of men after me wasna all that kind perhaps. So it stands to reason that she'd think of me fondly in that respect. She said if I'd marry her, she'd walk away from the church but that if I didn't care to, she'd stay. She said she knew that there would never be another man for her outside of myself. I felt awful tellin' her no, but the truth is, I didn't love her an' I did love *you*."

"Thank heavens for that," she said, and leaned over to kiss his already slightly stubbled cheek.

"So, Patrick," she turned and smiled at her brother-in-law, "just how did you end up in a Mother Superior's bed?"

He smiled ruefully. "Well, 'twas my misfortune that the Mother Superior herself did come across me prayin' to God to take me then and there, for I was so sick from the whiskey an' sheep's water that dyin' seemed a good alternative to how I felt. She took pity on me an' Denny an' put us up for the night. Aunt Sophy did be havin' fifty fits an' makin' us say ten rounds of the rosary the next day though she never could quite pinpoint which prayer would deliver our wee drunk souls from purgatory."

The rest of the drive passed in pleasant chat, with only two stops along the way to change Conor and once to feed him, and for Casey to wander off and have a smoke. Pat merely wandered, to give Pamela time and privacy in which to feed the baby.

The last twenty minutes before their arrival in Ballymena was slightly less jovial, and the two men grew increasingly quiet as each mile melted away beneath the tires. Pamela knew both of them were aware of the possibility their mother might show up at the funeral, though on the phone last evening Aunt Fee had assured Casey that they'd not heard from her and did not expect to see her.

Despite that reassurance, the tension was high enough to fly a kite by the time the car pulled down the narrow road to the church.

"We're here, then," Casey said rather abruptly, and immediately began fidgeting with his collar again.

Pamela reached across and gave his hand a reassuring squeeze, feeling a tad nervous herself. Pat was already out of the car, Conor in his arms, and Pamela could hear voices begin to call out his name. She got out of the car and walked around to Casey's side, determined to hide behind him if at all possible. But all was fine as the aunts converged on them in a rustle of black taffeta and veiled hats, smelling of everything from bread (Aunt Millie) to a wickedly spicy perfume (Aunt Sophy) to a strong draft of whiskey under mints (Aunt Fee).

There was much fussing and clucking over Conor, hugging of Patrick and Casey to matronly bosoms, and exclamations over how long it had been since the boys had been up for a visit.

Pamela hung back, waiting for the fluster and furor to die down a bit. Aunt Sophy, a short redhead with sparkling blue eyes, approached her first.

Pamela caught a waft of Shalimar on the breeze that preceded the woman, and then she was wrapped tight in a hug that had her face buried in clouds of fragrant red hair. Sophy held her at arm's length and scrutinized her with a narrowed eye.

"Well, yer entirely gorgeous, aren't ye, girl? Fee did say ye were a beauty but her description didn't quite do ye justice. Dinna bother denyin' it—no wonder the boyo married ye straight off as he did—without a single relative present, I might add." This last was said for Casey's benefit, for he'd come to take his wife's hand to go into the church. He merely gave his aunt the arm his wife wasn't on and led the women toward the church door. Pat, in tow with two more of the aunties and a happily squealing Conor, followed behind.

Sophy laughed a spangled sound that said the woman was possessed of humor on a regular basis. "Ah, yer just like yer Daddy. Ye know when to keep yer tongue quiet."

The church was overflowing with people, children of all sizes and ages and women, women everywhere. The Murphy family was overflowing with females, with only the odd male here and there to help keep the numbers steady.

Had Pamela not already known it, it would have been obvious that Casey and Pat took after the Riordan side of the family. The Murphys were a colorful clan, not only in nature as Casey had warned her—his tidy summation of the whole lot was 'fockin' nuts as a squirrel hole'—but also in physical features. Red hair, yellow hair, sparkling blue eyes, round, ruddy faces, with a few darker skinned ones who looked as though they might be direct descendants of the wee dark ones who had first inhabited Ireland in the mists of pre-history.

She followed Casey and Pat to a pew that was three back from the front, sitting in the midst of several female cousins who all had a hushed word or two for the men and stared at Pamela with frank and friendly interest.

There was a quiet apprehension underlying Pat and Casey's settling into the pew, during which time both men looked about in a far too casual manner. Apparently neither saw their mother, for they settled and Pamela could feel the worry flood out of them in waves of relief.

She smiled and laced her fingers through Casey's. He gave her own a squeeze and turned his attention to the priest.

The funeral itself was lovely, a proper goodbye to a woman who had obviously been well and truly loved by not just her own family but by her community as well. The family, along with friends, retreated to Lucy Murphy's home, a ramshackle affair in which she had successfully raised her children and occasionally small truant grandsons. Pamela met so many cousins and aunties, uncles and assorted family friends who were honorary members of the clan that her head was soon spinning. She retreated to a safe corner, having lost Casey to a gaggle of women with whom he was engaged in animated conversation. She sighed with relief, easing her feet out of her heels and taking a grateful swallow of the tea she had been handed by one of the aunts.

"He'll be a good man in the bedroom, no?" Sophy had slipped up beside her and was looking at her nephew with a fond smile.

"Pardon me?" Pamela said, barely missing choking on her tea.

"He'll be a good lover? Are ye deaf there lass? I've asked ye a question."

"He will be, indeed," Pamela said, nonplussed into simply answering the question honestly.

"Ah," Aunt Sophy said with some satisfaction, "I did think so. He'd the way of it about him even when a lad. The girls always buzzin' about him knew it to be certain even if he'd no clue himself at the time. I did be after instructin' him a bit myself."

"I—what?" Pamela sat her teacup down on the nearest table, certain she would drop it at the next shocking statement out of this woman's mouth.

"Ach, 'twas nothin' lass, though it's likely ye should thank me for I did teach the laddie the way round a woman's body."

"Indeed," Pamela said in stupefaction.

"I'd a wretched lover in my first husband, didn't know his arse from his elbow in the bedroom, nor mine come to that, an' I thought it'd be no bad thing were the young ones to be instructed a bit in what works an' what doesn't on a woman's body."

"And how—how exactly did you teach him those things?" she asked, not sure she actually wanted to know, yet unable to refrain from asking.

"Oh, with an anatomy textbook an' a few drawins'. Yer man was a quick study even when he was a lad."

"I don't doubt that he was," Pamela said dryly, looking over to where her husband stood in the midst of a nosegay of red and yellow-headed cousins, telling some story that had them all laughing fit to kill and touching him on the shoulders, arms and chest. She shook her head. The man didn't have the first notion of his effect on women.

"Be glad that he doesn't know his own power," Aunt Sophy said, apparently a mind reader as well as a sexual guru. "He'd be a danger to himself otherwise. Yer a lucky woman though, there's no doubt of that. The lot of us were mad for his Daddy when we were young but Brian never had eyes for any but Deirdre." Sophy paused to take a drink from her whiskey, a fleeting sadness crossing her face. "I did think she might be here today, bein' that it's her mother that's been buried, but then Aunt Lucy an' Deirdre haven't spoken these many years. Aunt Lucy never forgave her for leavin' Brian an' the boys. Nor, I suppose, did the rest of us. They were family, an' ye don't walk out an' leave family without a backward look nor explanation."

"Did any of you ever know why?"

Sophy shook her head. "No, not really. She could be a wee bit cold at times, wasn't one to confide her troubles to a person, but I never doubted for a moment that she loved Brian and the boys." She swirled the last of the whiskey in her glass and stared into the golden depths as though she sought an answer there to the riddle her cousin had left them with so many years before.

"Deirdre was different from the rest of us—didn't even look like a Murphy—sort of like yerself really, all fine pale skin an' dark hair, lovely delicate bones that looked like they wouldn't stand a stiff wind, though 'twas all show, for she'd a will on her like an iron poker. I imagine yer the same, aren't ye?"

"I suppose you could say that," Pamela acquiesced. Though she had never believed herself particularly strong, she had been sorely tried during their time of living in Boston and had emerged from the fires whole, if not entirely unscathed. Their time there had given her a far better understanding of what she could withstand if she had to and how ruthless she was capable of being.

Sophy gave her a knowing smile as if to say she knew a formidable woman when she met one.

"Brian wouldn't take the help after she left, though we had the boys for a bit while he was in the Curragh. Pat was about five when they came to live with us an' Casey ten. They were easy to love, those two. When Brian came an' took them home, I missed them somethin' fierce for a long time. We wanted Pat to come to us when his Daddy died an' Casey went to prison, but he'd not hear of it. Stubborn as mules the both of them." She smiled fondly at the two men in question, Casey now attempting to extricate himself from the vines and tendrils of cousinhood and Pat nodding politely to an elderly gentleman shouting in his ear.

"Well, lass, I've bent yer ear long enough. I'd best go make certain the food is about ready. If I don't feed this lot soon they'll rise up against me."

"Can I help with anything?"

"No, yer man is headin' this way an' yer wee one is well occupied. Why don't the two of yez sit down an' relax an' I'll bring ye a bite soon as it's ready." With that, Sophy made off at speed toward the kitchen, clapping a hand to the ear of a juvenile male Murphy and giving the evil eye to a cousin who had imbibed a bit more than was wise along her way.

Casey returned to his wife looking entirely harassed and sporting at least seven different shades of lipstick on his face. "Jaysus Murphy, I've been mauled completely now an' I've lost track of Conor. I only hope they're gentler on him than they were on me."

She dabbed at his face with a handkerchief.

"I swear to ye, Jewel, if ye spit on it I'll put ye over my shoulder an' take ye out of here. I've had my cheek pinched an' my hair stroked, an' that bloody Sophy patted my behind like I was eight years old again."

"She says I've her to thank for the fact that you're such a good lover,"

Pamela said straight-faced, rubbing at a spot of crimson near the corner of his lip.

"WHAT?!" Casey exclaimed in outraged indignation, his face flushing under the coating of whiskers he always had by midafternoon.

"Mm," she stretched up and kissed the corner of his mouth. "Not to worry. I minded my manners and thanked her profusely."

"Come with me, woman," he said, taking her by the elbow and weaving her through the crowd expertly.

"Are you going to give me a practical demonstration of your aunt's teachings?" she asked, laughing.

Casey snorted. "No, I'm in need of a cigarette an' a wee bit of peace, though it'd be no more than this lot deserves to see my bare arse wigglin' about in the bushes."

"I rather think they would enjoy it," Pamela said, red with suppressed laughter.

"Well, I'm glad *yer* enjoyin' yerself at least."

"Pat did say everyone enjoys a good funeral."

"Aye, an' this one is more entertainin' than most," Casey said.

He sought out a quiet corner of the garden, where the bees were humming in soporific content and the buzzing of the Murphy clan was barely discernible.

"Let's sit up here." He picked her up by the waist and deposited her on the stone wall that surrounded the garden, then jumped lightly up himself. He pulled out a cigarette, lit it, took a drag and exhaled on a long sigh of contentment. "Ah, that's good, that is. I've been wantin' one since we went into the church but I figured I'd better wait a bit or my Granny Murphy'd rise up in her coffin and have at me. She was always lecturin' me about the smokin'."

"So the Murphy women are a feisty lot, are they?"

"Feisty, is that what we're callin' it? D'ye notice the number of children runnin' about here, Jewel, an' how ragged-arsed all the men look? They're worn out but good, but they look happy, no?"

"And how about yourself, man, are you happy?" She was half-flirting, half-serious, for though she knew her power over him, like any woman, she needed reassurance now and again.

Casey grinned in a most lascivious manner. "Yer more than a wee bit feisty yerself, Jewel. But then Nuala did say as the O'Flahertys are bent that way."

"Are you up to the challenge of a feisty wife?" she asked, thinking how broad his shoulders looked, and how the vee of his throat—just there, where his chest hair curled up out of the crisp white of his shirt—was beating with a hard pulse. She swallowed and knew that Casey was as suddenly attuned to her as she was to him.

"Oh," he quirked a dark brow at her. "I am up for it an' then some, woman."

He leaned in and kissed her, softly at first, nibbling lightly on her bottom lip, causing her to open her mouth to him. His tongue was warm and restless and the taste of smoky whiskey spread through her own mouth.

"Would ye say I learned my lessons well enough then, Mrs. Riordan?" he murmured softly, his stubble rasping her skin in a way that made her tingle all over.

"I'd say you'd graduate right at the top of the class, Mr. Riordan," she murmured back, blood throbbing hard in every part of her body. She wondered if anyone would miss them if they disappeared for a small while.

As if reading her thoughts, Casey put his hand to her back and pulled her deeper into the kiss. Her hand slid around his neck into the thick silk of his hair and he gave a soft growl deep in his throat that vibrated right to her core.

"Ahem."

Pamela jumped and Casey had to grab her arm to keep her from falling off the wall. They looked up to find Pat surveying them with no small amusement.

"Thought ye might like to know that there's about twelve of the aunties an' cousins watchin' the two of yez out the kitchen window."

"Ker-rist," Casey said with heartfelt frustration. He hopped down off the wall, making a mock bow in the direction of the windows, put his hands to Pamela's waist and lifted her down.

"Come on, Jewel, if we can't have sex in the grass, then we'd best go in so I can eat. I'm determined to satisfy at least one of my appetites." He patted her backside in a most familiar manner and followed her into the house.

Pamela, flushed as a ripe apple, managed to avoid most of the aunts on the way in, but inadvertently caught Sophy's eye, who grinned at her.

The three of them loaded up their plates with sausage, potatoes and buttered cabbage. Casey snagged three Guinness out of a tub of ice to add to their repast and after they ascertained that their son was happily asleep in his basket, presided over by three of the redheaded cousins, they found a corner and sat to eat.

Pamela was famished, realizing she'd had little more than a cup of tea since breakfast. She barely spoke, used as she was to eating her meals on the run, as Conor was likely to fuss just as she'd sat down.

Casey and Pat made short work of their own food and re-filled their plates. They slowed down during their second helping and set to talking about the foibles and fascinations of the Murphy clan. And it *was* fascinating, for the Murphys were no mild-mannered bunch.

There was talk of an Uncle Peter who had run off with the merchant marines and returned many years later as 'Aunt Paula', and then there was a rather involved tale about Cousin Edna and her Protestant married lover by whom she'd had four daughters and with whom she had a house in the countryside. He had never divorced and Edna had defied the entire family by refusing to give him up.

Their talk naturally swung toward their father and reminiscences of their summers out west spent fishing, reading, and talking into the wee hours about history, literature, and life in general. It sounded like a bit of heaven.

One of the aunts went by and stopped to give Pat an emotional embrace, during which Pamela feared for his ability to breathe, as the woman hugged his head to her considerable bosom. She kissed him soundly on his forehead before moving off misty-eyed.

"Ye've lipstick on yer forehead," Casey said, waving a napkin at his brother and grinning.

Pat made a gesture toward Casey, similar in emotional content to several his brother had made during the morning drive. "I swear to yez, if one more person calls me 'wee Paddy' as if I'm no more than Conor's size, I'm not goin' to be responsible for my actions. Here, give over that sausage if yer not goin' to eat it."

"Over my dead body," Casey said, biting off half the sausage and chewing vigorously. Sated, Pamela leaned back into the crook of Casey's arm and sipped her stout, watching the crowd through a benevolent fug of food and alcohol.

The two brothers continued to chat happily about family memories, and the occasional cousin would drift over, join in the conversation and then drift out, or an aunt would pass, re-fill their glasses, tip another sausage onto Casey and Pat's plates, and run a fond hand across their curls in parting. Often they would reach across and stroke Pamela's cheek or lay a hand on her shoulder that let her know that she too was now considered family. There was a feeling of such mellow goodwill in the room amidst the chatter and laughter and the occasional tear that Pamela thought she could happily live in the midst of the Murphy clan for the rest of her days.

"...Ach no, he wasn't actually in the seminary yet, so ye can't fully blame Cousin Alice for that."

"No, 'twasn't Cousin Alice who did that, 'twas Cousin—" Pamela never did get to find out which cousin it was who had defrocked a potential priest, for Casey broke off mid-sentence and Pamela turned to see what had taken his attention. She felt a jolt of alarm at the terrible white set of his face. His eyes were riveted somewhere across the room and then she heard Pat swear softly. He was looking in the same direction.

They were looking at a woman, dark-haired, with delicate features that had been kept immaculately, for she was in her late forties, Pamela thought. She was still beautiful, upright and delicate as a reed, and she looked terribly familiar. Suddenly Pamela understood at whom she was looking.

"Casey? Is—is that your mother?"

"Aye," came the answer, "she is. Now, ye'll excuse me," he said shortly. He removed his arm from around his wife, placed his glass carefully on a table and stood, walking directly out of the house. The dark-haired woman watched him go with a tight set to her face.

Pamela felt certain that to go after him now would be a mistake. He needed a minute alone, especially now that his mother was walking toward them. She felt Pat stiffen beside her and she took his hand as a small gesture of support. His fingers were as cold as ice.

Up close, the woman's age showed a bit, though perhaps it was only the strain of her present circumstances that was putting the tight lines around her mouth.

"Patrick?" she said.

"Aye," he said coolly, and Pamela squeezed his hand.

"I think I'd have known you anywhere. You look a great deal like your father did at the same age."

"So people tell me," he replied, the tone of his voice giving no quarter.

"And this is?" she prompted, giving Pamela a look that made her feel like a bug under a microscope.

"This is Pamela. She's Casey's wife and the mother of yer grandson."

That set her back a minute, for the high cheekbones colored slightly and she studied Pamela's face with interest before she turned her attention directly back to Pat.

"I see your brother is as happy to see me as I expected he would be."

"He's just stepped out for a minute," Pamela said quietly.

The woman smiled, though the expression held no humor. "Stepped out, is it? He turned and walked out the minute he saw me, didn't he?"

"Yes, he did, though I think you can hardly blame him for that. He wasn't expecting to see you today."

"Or ever again for the rest of his life," the woman replied, a certain edge to her voice that made Pamela bristle in defense of her husband.

"And whose fault is that, do you think?" she asked.

"Mine." The woman said with a blunt honesty that was only too reminiscent of both Casey and Pat. "Patrick, do ye think we might have a moment?"

Pat looked at Pamela.

"Go ahead," she said, giving his hand a final squeeze. "I need to find Conor and feed him anyway."

Over the last few years she knew Pat and Deirdre had exchanged letters, and so this meeting between mother and son was not quite as fraught as it would have been otherwise. She stood for a minute, watching Pat wend his way through the crowd with his mother. There were similarities, despite Pat's overwhelming resemblance to his father, Brian.

Conor, when located, was being paid court to by a circle of women. He absorbed all this attention with the air of a tiny pasha, though upon sighting his mother he started to fuss. She retrieved him and looked about for a quiet spot to change and feed him.

She saw Sophy beckon to her from the hallway off the crowded parlor.

"Here, come into my Auntie's bedroom, love. Ye'll want a bit of quiet for you an' the babe, no?"

Pamela followed Sophy away from the din of the Murphy clan into the quiet of an old fashioned bedroom, thick with late afternoon sunshine and the smell of dusty rose petals.

"Well, that went about as well as could be expected, I suppose," Sophy said wryly, laying out a clean blanket on the bed for Pamela to lay Conor down.

"They knew she might be here but I think it's still a shock to see her after all these years."

Sophy nodded, looking very tired suddenly. "They're strong men. They'll manage it, but damn that woman. She never did have much sense of timing."

She leaned down, gave Conor a kiss and left the room, shutting the door firmly behind her back. To Pamela's strained nerves, the quiet was immediate and relieving.

She laid Conor on the bed and removed his tiny green outfit. He was always happiest in just his t-shirt. Like Casey, he had a small furnace inside that kept him warm at all times.

"Hello, love. Did you miss Mommy?" she asked, removing his diaper and exposing his dimpled bottom to the air. He cooed in delight, kicking his legs happily and not at all interested in having another diaper, clean and dry notwithstanding, placed on his bottom.

She gave him a few minutes, spending it stroking his tummy and kissing his face until she could feel the tension that presaged his realization of just how empty said tummy had become.

She sat with him in a rocking chair in the corner of what had been Lucy Murphy's bedroom. The windows faced west and the sun flooded the room with rose-gold, lending a gilt edge to the worn bedding and carpet. The room smelled faintly of the dried rose petals that filled a crystal bowl on a tall bureau. On the table beside the bed was a pair of reading spectacles and a picture of a young couple on their wedding day, beaming into the camera. In an era when the fashion had been solemnity in photos, their happiness seemed a living thing. The man was tall and thin with a full head of dark hair, and the woman tiny and fair. Casey and Patrick's Murphy grandparents, for she could see both these people in the aunts and cousins.

Conor set to nursing with a hearty appetite, the soft round of his skull edged in the same gilding, setting his dark curls afire. Here, in yet another generation, she saw the echoes of family for Conor, though still tiny, held traces of Casey in his face and what her husband might have looked like as a child. She wondered what a shock seeing the fully-grown man must have been for his mother, yet the woman had come here knowing it was likely her sons would also attend.

Pamela stroked Conor's cheek and when his mouth popped open, switched him quickly to the other side. Just then, the door to the bedroom opened and in walked Casey's mother.

She started slightly when she saw Pamela sitting in the rocking chair and then smiled tentatively.

"Oh—I'm sorry. I didn't realize anyone was in here. I just thought I'd come spend a minute in my mother's room."

"Please stay," Pamela said, making a quick decision and hoping Casey didn't kill her for it later. "I don't mind." She did wonder where Patrick had gone, and so soon after encountering his mother.

Deirdre turned back, shutting the door softly behind her.

Pamela sat Conor facing forward in the manner Casey always used to burp him, his soft chin in the vee of her fingers and her hand braced against his chest.

Conor perked up, holding his head straight in an effort to examine this new person. The strain left Deirdre's face and she smiled at him. Conor responded with a gurgle of joy and flailed his plump arms and legs.

"May I?" Deirdre asked, and though the words were spoken without intonation, Pamela noted that the woman's hands were trembling slightly. "I've found that babies will settle better for a stranger at times than they will for their Mam."

"Certainly," Pamela said, lifting Conor carefully off her lap and handing him into the arms of his grandmother.

Conor, who possessed his father's *sangfroid* when encountering new people, merely gave the woman holding him the eye and set to gumming on the lapel of her suit.

"He's a fine-looking wee man," Deirdre said, gazing down at the dark head, "like his Daddy was."

"What was Casey like as a baby?" Pamela asked, unable to resist asking the one person alive who would hold those memories of her husband as a child.

"Oh, he was a bonny, fine, strapping little lad. The women loved him even when he was a babby, always wanted to hold him an' fuss over him. He was restless though. Lord, the times I thought that boy would be the death of me through sheer frustration at trying to keep him safe. He wasn't happy until he was up on his feet and running about, knocking his head into something every other minute. He was only eight months old when he started walking. Stubborn as an ox and had a skull like one too. His father claimed he came by it naturally, the Riordans being hardheaded as the rocks of the field." She smiled at Pamela over Conor's fuzzy skull. "I imagine he's just as hardheaded now, but a good husband to ye still?"

"I couldn't ask for a better," Pamela replied softly.

"Aye, I thought as much. His Daddy was that way, tender with the women an' loyal as the day is long."

Pamela nodded and busied herself with setting her clothing to rights. She was surprised that Deirdre brought Brian up so casually when it was bound to be an incredibly difficult subject for her.

"Casey an' yerself," Deirdre gave her a quick glance, "ye love one another a great deal? I was watchin' the two of ye for a minute before the boys saw me, and it seemed to me you had something rare between the two of ye."

"We do. We're very fortunate."

"It's what I hoped for them, that they'd find good women, ones they loved. Patrick wrote me some time after his fiancée was killed. I was terribly sorry to hear of it."

"She was his wife," Pamela said quietly, for to speak of Sylvie was still an exercise in pain, "though only just. She was lovely and she adored him. It was a terrible loss."

"And what of you and Casey? It'll not be simple living in Belfast with his past being what it is."

"No—but then what marriage is simple? I love him beyond reason," she said in complete honesty. "I'd follow him through the gates of hell if that's where he chose to go. Belfast is his home as he is mine, so there we stay. Though we live a ways away from it now."

"But there are times maybe that it's a bit much, no? To love a man so?"

"No," Pamela said quietly. "Though it scares me now and again, I can't imagine a day without him."

"Aye, has he left his old occupation then?"

"He has," Pamela said stiffly. The familiar fear was never far from the surface and, like a barely healed cut, it needed little more than a butterfly touch to make it bleed.

"Mmmphmm," was Deirdre's only comment on this statement. "I don't blame him for being angry but I had hoped he might allow me a word."

"They felt forgotten, as though you'd walked away and never looked back. Casey maybe a little more so as he was old enough to remember you."

"You're a mother. Do you believe that it's possible to forget your children—to not think of them every day?"

"No," Pamela admitted. "But still, you can see why they'd feel as they do. It's not just that you left them, either. They loved their Daddy fiercely and they know the hurt you left behind with him as well. I can't imagine a woman getting over a man such as the one they tell me about."

"Would you?" The woman asked, looking very fragile in the sunset reds that were spilling all through the room now. "If you walked away from Casey tomorrow and never set eyes on him again, would you get over him?"

"No."

"Well, there's your answer then. Brian wasn't a man a woman would forget."

"The difference is I wouldn't leave," Pamela said.

Deirdre gave her a searching look and then said quietly, "No, I can see that you wouldn't. I wasn't that strong, though." Pamela was startled to see tears glimmer on the edge of the woman's dark lashes. "I've never lived a day without regret, not a single day. They can hate me or not, but I'd like them to know that, not a single day has passed that I didn't regret what I'd done. I loved their Daddy too. I think they need to know that and I missed him every day of my life. I still do. I thought I'd die too when word of his death reached me."

"Still you didn't come back." Pamela said, unable to keep a touch of anger from her words. "The boys needed you then, possibly more than they ever had before or would ever again, yet you stayed away."

"I sent the both of them the money to come to England. Pat refused, and Casey was already in prison by the time I learned of Brian's death. Pat never cashed the cheque either though I suspect he needed the money. I wrote Casey every week during his time in Parkhurst. All my letters were returned unread. I know he didn't owe me anything but still it was hard. I went to the prison and tried to visit but he refused even that, when I'm sure he was in sore need of the company."

"I think he couldn't afford any vulnerability at that point in his life," Pamela said, thinking of the few things Casey had actually shared with her about his life in prison. "Seeing a mother he'd not seen in years would have been far too hard for him under the circumstances."

Deirdre nodded. "Yes, I imagine you're right."

Pamela stood and smoothed down the front of her dress. "If you don't mind, I think I'll go see if I can find him now that he's had a bit of time to cool off."

Deirdre took her hand, startling Pamela. The woman's touch was cool but oddly comfortable. "I'm glad he has you," she said, before turning her attention back to Conor, who had his chubby hands entangled in her necklace now.

"Would it be alright if the baby stayed here for a bit with me?" Deirdre asked, dark eyes still slightly damp. "I swear I'll not kidnap him—you can tell Sophy. She'll keep an eye on the two of us."

"Alright," Pamela said, though she felt some worry at what Casey might feel about this. Still, the woman was Conor's grandmother, and this might be their only chance to spend a bit of time together. She gave the baby a kiss on his forehead. He seemed content enough to stay with Deirdre so she took her leave quickly, wanting a bit of time to find Casey.

She closed the door behind her and walked down the hall into the bright bustle of the kitchen.

Sophy, stirring something aromatic in a big black pot, beckoned her over. She tilted her head to the side, indicating an unopened bottle of Jameson's and two clean glasses.

"Take that with ye. The lad may well need somethin' to take the edge off." She nodded toward the west-facing window. "He'll be sittin' up atop the wee hill there. It's where he always went when he was a boy an' felt troubled. Ye just follow the path up an' ye'll have no trouble findin' him."

"I left Conor with Deirdre," Pamela said.

Sophy raised a red brow. "Aye, well, I think he's safe enough. She's not likely to run off with him, an' I'll keep an eye out as well."

Pamela bit down on a smile, for Sophy's words echoed Deirdre's so exactly that there was no doubt that, despite the years of estrangement between them, they were family.

All the family drama notwithstanding, it was a lovely night with a breeze blowing out of the west, soft and smelling of grass and the crushed thyme that bordered Lucy Murphy's garden.

The path was narrow, but there was still enough light to make the going easy. Sure enough, when she crested the rise of the hill, there sat her husband, with his knees drawn up and his back against the solid trunk of an oak.

Casey looked up at her approach. "A beautiful woman bearing a bottle of whiskey. Have I died an' gone to heaven then?"

"I thought you could use a drink about now."

He smiled wearily. "Aye, I could at that, darlin'. Where's Conor?"

"Fed and burped and in good hands. Your Aunt Sophy's keeping an eye on him," she said, thinking that it was best to omit the fact that it was Deirdre who actually had possession of their son at present.

Casey raised a dark brow at this.

"I quite like her," Pamela said. "Granted, she's a bit... unique, but certainly fit to watch over a sleeping babe."

"That," Casey said darkly, "remains to be seen."

"Well, there are about forty other baby-mad women down there, so I've no doubt he'll be well attended to."

She took the lid off the bottle of Jameson's and poured them each a stiff two fingers, took another look at Casey's face and added a third finger to his glass before handing it to him.

"So, how are you doing?"

Casey scrubbed his hands hard through his hair and sighed before answering.

"I feel a little like someone hit me over the head with a hot poker but

I'll be fine."

"Are you going back to talk to her?"

He shook his head. "No, an' I think ye can understand it well enough with yer own situation. Would ye look kindly on yer mother were she to show up out of the blue an' act as though she hadn't disappeared into the ether twenty-odd years ago?"

"No, I wouldn't. But mine isn't going to magically appear. I think maybe, whether you ever see her again or not, you should take this chance to talk to her."

"Why, Jewel? What can she possibly say to make me feel less bitter toward her?"

"Possibly nothing, but still she's here. It might be nice for Conor to have one grandparent."

Casey gave her a slanted look. "Now that's not playin' fair at all woman, an' well ye know it."

"Maybe not, but what's fair about being a parent?"

"If I tell ye I cannot talk with her right now, will ye think less of me?"

"Casey," she said, shocked that he would even think such a thing, "if you never spoke to her for the rest of her life, I would think no less of you. If you're not ready, you simply aren't. It was enough of a shock to see her."

"Aye, it was at that."

"I'm sorry," she said, putting out a hand tentatively and touching his arm.

He looked at her and raised a dark brow. "Whatever on earth are you sorry for, Jewel?"

She shrugged. "Just that this is so painful for you."

He sighed and put one of his hands over hers. "I feel that I ought to be able to be civil. I'm a grown man with a family and an entire history that's naught to do with her in there, an' yet I swear to ye Pamela that I felt about six years old the minute I saw her lookin' at us across the room."

"Oh, Casey." She held him closely and felt his body relax against her.

"Jewel, I don't know what I'd do without ye," he said softly. "Yer my conscience, always savin' me from the worst of myself."

"As you do for me, man," she said, laying her cheek to the soft coil of his hair. They sat so for several long moments until Casey finally sighed and stood, brushing leaves and needles from his pants.

"Come on, woman," he held a hand out, and pulled her up. "Let's go down an' face the lions."

Night sat soft about the house as they descended the hill, the lights glowing in hazy parhelia and the sound of talk ribboning out on the breeze.

There were fewer cars than when Pamela had ascended the hill, for some of the guests were taking their leave.

There was a chill thread in the wind, blown back by an autumn that lay only a few weeks ahead. Casey wrapped his suit jacket around his wife's shoulders and added his own arm for good measure. Pamela snuggled gratefully into his side. Despite sitting on the hillside for a good two hours, the man was still warm as toast.

"It'll be alright. We can go now, if you'd like. No one would blame you."

Casey smiled down at her in the waning light.

"'Tis alright, darlin'. I need to say goodbye to everyone. I think I can manage that well enough."

Inside the house, it was much quieter. Even the Murphy tongues seemingly had a limit. There was a fire in the hearth though the windows were still open to the night. Pamela collected Conor from Sophy, and sat down with him in a squashy wingback chair near the fire. Beside her on a mattress lay a crumpled posey of tiny Murphys, three buttercup heads with one small clove pink resting royally in the midst. The aunts and cousins were strewn about the room and Pamela instinctively looked about to place Deirdre, but if she was still present in the house, she was not visible.

Devlin was strumming his guitar softly, random riffs of plaintive chords that reminded them all of why they were gathered here under this roof.

He eyed Casey as he crossed the room. "Sing with me, boy," he said. "Yer Nan did always love the sound of yer voice."

Casey nodded and wove his way over to where his uncle sat. "What would she have us sing then, Uncle?"

"She was fond of *My Lagan Love*. She told me even I couldn't sing it the way you could, boy."

Casey sat on a stool, his shirt open and cuffs rolled up. He'd abandoned both tie and cufflinks some time ago, and looked relaxed as he sat silent. He was always quiet for a moment before beginning a song. She knew he was bringing his focus down to a fine point, preparing to do honor to his grandmother's memory.

His voice started soft, needing no accompaniment. She had heard him sing any number of times. He often sang while he worked about the house, unaware that he was even doing so, for it was that natural a part of his life. Still, his voice could surprise her for the sheer raw pure power of it. She could see the effect of it on the faces around him already.

Where Lagan stream sings lullaby
There blows a lily fair

The twilight gleam is in her eye
The night is on her hair

At the end of the first verse, Casey paused for a second and said. "Join me, Uncle." Devlin nodded and followed Casey into the second verse. The two men sang well together, Devlin's voice weaving a gossamer net under the falling stars of Casey's pure Irish tones.

And like a love-sick lennan-shee
She has my heart in thrall
Nor life I owe nor liberty
For love is lord of all.

From the corner of her eye she saw Deirdre come to stand in the doorway, still in the shadows, and knew that Casey would sense her there as well.

Her father sails a running-barge
'Twixt Leamh-beag and The Druim;
And on the lonely river-marge
She clears his hearth for him.
When she was only fairy-high
Her gentle mother died;
But dew-Love keeps her memory
Green on the Lagan side.

For a moment, the barest fragment of time, his eyes met those of his mother and Pamela lost her breath, for she saw there no hostility, no guard, but only the boy who had missed this woman every day of his life. Deirdre stepped back from the look, for it must have felt like a knife in her chest just to witness it, and the guard came back down over Casey's eyes. He turned his face away and continued the song, voice growing in strength like a flock of birds winging in ever closer across a winter sky.

And often when the beetle's horn
Hath lulled the eve to sleep
I steal unto her shieling lorn
And thru the dooring peep.
There on the cricket's singing stone,
She stirs the bogwood fire,
And hums in sad sweet undertone
The songs of heart's desire

The next verse he sang to his wife, dark eyes making certain contact with her own. His voice was soft and aching, pulling her by dint of his words alone, leaving her aching with the longing to take him to her bed, to soothe all the hurts of his past and shield him from the world.

Her welcome, like her love for me,
Is from her heart within:
Her warm kiss is felicity
That knows no taint of sin.
And when I stir my foot to go,
'Tis leaving Love and light
To feel the wind of longing blow
From out the dark of night.

His throat trembled through the sweat-sheened skin of his neck, the chords standing out in sharp relief. Pamela spared a glance toward Deirdre, who stood as though she'd been shot, frozen in place, eyes riveted to her eldest son's face and tears falling unchecked down her cheeks. She looked exactly as one might expect a woman to look whose heart had broken with a sudden and irrevocable snap. There was a space around her where none of the family came near, as though they did not want to feel her pain.

Where Lagan stream sings lullaby
There blows a lily fair
The twilight gleam is in her eye
The night is on her hair
And like a love-sick lennan-shee
She has my heart in thrall
Nor life I owe nor liberty
For love is lord of all.

He had closed his eyes during the last verse and they remained so for a moment, as he breathed in deeply, bringing himself back to the present world. And then he spoke, so softly, Pamela could barely make out the words. "*Slan leat*, Grandmother." Goodbye.

He opened his eyes and stood, looking directly at Pamela. He gave her a weary smile, and she saw written clearly there what the day had cost him. He moved across the room slowly, his aunts and cousins reaching out with lingering hands to touch him in passing.

Deirdre stood, still crying, a terrible thing of silence and loss, her face ravaged by the last few minutes.

Casey paused just for a second and laid his hand on his mother's shoulder, and then with neither word nor glance backward, he moved on through the strung silence toward his wife and son.

Pamela didn't dare look round, for a hush filled the place that spoke of emotion stirred to the point of physical pain, and tears still streamed down her own face.

Casey leaned down, kissed her wet cheek and gently lifted their sleeping son from her arms, tucking the soft, boneless warmth of Conor tight into the curve of his own shoulder. Then he reached out a hand and took hers.

"Come, Jewel, let's away home then."

Chapter Sixteen

Autumn 1973

The Dreaming Time

BENEATH HER FEET, THE PINE NEEDLES WHISPERED SOFTLY OF WINTER things. Of the coming cold and snow, of the dark half of the year when the quiet came down and enfolded the world in a mantle of calm. It was a time of year she had always loved, for the sense of the veil between worlds thinning was strong with her at such moments. This year that was a comfort, to think that perhaps of a chill night, Lawrence might come and warm himself beside the fire. Might sit beside Casey in spirit, if never again in the flesh, and they could once again be whole. That sometimes in the restless nights, perhaps when exhaustion bore him down, Pat might find solace in his dreams that Sylvie would be there for a moment, all light and lilacs.

In such times, she knew, when the air is chill and the night longer than the day, one cannot avoid certain truths. For her this truth had sat like a seed deep inside, a small kernel of worry that was now leafing out into real fear. For Jamie had not come home with the spring or summer and she did not think to see him now that the frost was heavy on the ground and the spiderwebs deserted in the hedgerows.

For this was the thin time when the earth laid bare her bones and showed her gems in the random berry left on the vine, the sheath of ice forming in perfect geometry across a pond and the black gleam of a naked birch branch. This was the threshold of winter, when the soil slept, harvests were put up, and life could hang by a thread. In this time, dreams came unbidden, rippling up from the dark wellsprings of the unconscious, murmuring things one would rather not know. These were the dreams that haunted during the daylight hours, spun fine as webbing round the senses, bringing hard questions into the light.

She dreamed of a man cold and lost in a forest so deep it was surely sprung from a fairytale, one of the ancient nebulous ones with old truths at their core. She did not see the man clearly, but she did not need to—she would know him anywhere, for she dreamed of Jamie.

The question that haunted her in the light of day was this—just where the hell *was* Lord James Kirkpatrick?

Part Two

Jamie
Hong Kong – February 1973

Chapter Seventeen

February 1973

The Flower-Smoke Room

HONG KONG, IT WAS SAID, WAS THE ONLY PURELY CAPITALIST CITY on earth. The city where one could get anything the heart desired—and many things the heart didn't know it desired—at any hour. Hong Kong was a city of endless rushing night, burning out hard in neon.

The messenger stood beneath one such flaming arc of the modern age, a crumpled map in his hand and a package beneath his arm. The sign, proclaiming the glories of carbonated sugar water, flashed alternatively in red and blue. The colors refracted against his spectacles, making him feel as if he were in church with light pouring through stained glass windows, spilling thick and terrible out of the glass heart of the bleeding Christ. He had to squelch the urge to genuflect.

Frankly, he'd expected something grander, but the number on the battered blue door matched the one in his hand.

The last flower-smoke room in the world was tucked behind a discreet address on one of the less traveled streets of Hong Kong, no more than a dark back lane overhung with crisscrossing arches of laundry. Directly above his head flapped a large variety of silken garments that his mother—good Presbyterian that she was—would have called *unmentionables*.

Robert took a breath, straightened his tie and knocked on the door. It opened a crack, one dark almond eye looking through it at him.

"What you want?" the eye barked at him.

He cleared his throat. "I believe there's a gentleman here expecting me."

The almond eye narrowed. "A gentleman? Wrong house. You go down street. We not got boys here." The door slammed emphatically shut.

Robert knocked again. The door opened again, a mere slit this time.

"You again? I tell you no boys here," the voice then continued on in a haranguing tone that Robert thought was likely the Chinese version of ranking him somewhere below the baser life forms that grew on top of pond water. He patiently waited the voice out, then smiling his no-nonsense smile said the magic words.

"Mr. Kirkpatrick expects me. This is the address I was given. Is he here?" The door opened slightly wider, a wedge of moonlike face joining the almond eye.

"Maybe he here, maybe he not. What business you got?"

"Will you please just tell him that Robert MacDougall is here?"

The voice mumbled something that sounded like 'Robber Donkey' and, giving him a gimlet glance, said, "You follow. Come. Come." These last two words given emphasis by the tiny creature in front of him clapping its hands together sharply. He followed the creature, for so tiny and wizened it was, he could not place a gender upon the wrinkles and silk-capped head. The legs, like dried sticks emerging from embroidered pants, gave nothing away either.

He was led up a set of stairs so narrow that his shoulders brushed the peacock-flocked walls on either side. At the top the landing broadened only slightly, dank, forbidding hallways leading off in either direction. The tiny creature clapped its hands again and Robert accordingly turned left. The entire floor was a warren of small rooms, miniscule dens for every decadence the East had to offer. Through partially opened doors Robert saw a variety of women in various states of undress, delicate amber sylphs, the Flowers of the Orient, for sale, for rent, for your delight. On his right a young girl stepped out, ageless in the way Oriental women are, her robe open down the front, breasts barely more than budding plums. She slipped her robe down to her elbows and waggled her shoulders at him.

"You like?' she asked in tongue-crowded English.

Before he could answer, the creature in front of him took a step toward the girl, yipped something sharply in her face and continued on its way. The girl shrugged her robe up as if to say, 'Your loss," and turned back into her room.

The door he sought was at the end of the corridor. Lacquer-red and brass-knobbed, it stood out in the murky atmosphere like a ruby in a pile of ordinary rock. The crone rapped on the door in a quick succession of birdlike taps and it was opened narrowly. A low, rapid, singing conversation followed, punctuated by the crone's bony finger being jabbed in the vicinity of the doorkeeper's nose. After several minutes of this, his erstwhile guide stepped aside and with a curt bow indicated he should proceed through the red portal.

From one world into the next, he passed with a single step.

The room seemed to be an antechamber of sorts, for a set of black-enameled double doors graced its north end, emblazoned with golden dragons, their eyes a flare of emerald. The doors, he suspected, guarded the man he had come here seeking.

The doorkeeper, a sylph in jade green satin, indicated with a tilt of her head that he should sit in one of the highly ornate chairs positioned about the little room. He sat with great trepidation, for the furniture in the room looked as if it were only meant to bear the weight of butterflies and birds. Robert was neither.

The sylph approached the double doors and pressing the eye of the dragon on the left hand side, entered the room beyond. The door closed behind her, the only sound that of her silk robe whispering against her skin.

What, he wondered, would his stout, blue-rinsed, orthopedic-stockinged mother make of such a place? Robert shuddered to think. In one corner stood a spinet, his appraiser's eye judged it to be of the Louis XV era, its value enough to make the most hardened dealer salivate. On the walls were a variety of paintings, some small prints in delicate, ornamental frames, others large canvasses. One was an impressionistic night view of Hong Kong's harbor with its junks and light-oiled waters, done in a thousand shades of blue. Another was one of the infamous flower paintings by an American artist, a poppy opening its dark-flame heart in flowing crimson and scarlet. This artist had vanished twenty years ago into the cigar smoke and gambling lairs of Cuba with this particular painting in tow, or so legend had it. Robert stepped toward it, looking for the telltale over-perfection of the reproduction and found instead the fragile flaws of an original. He shivered slightly, a bead of sweat running down the groove of his backbone. What sort of place had Giacomo sent him to? And what business could the Father General of the Society of Jesus have with the sort of man who frequented such a place?

Just then his doorkeeper re-emerged, inclining her head and one hand toward him. He started across the silk carpet, only to be stopped by a gentle smile.

"If you would remove your shoes, please," she said, her English a flawless ribbon of vowels and consonants.

He removed his shoes, grimacing slightly at the black and grey Argyll socks that he wore for luck and followed the shimmering sylph through the dragon-guarded doors.

He was escorted into a room of such opulence that his staid Scots heart thought he'd bypassed the road to Hell and gone directly to Its inner harbor. And if this was the Inferno, then the man upon whom his eyes had just lit would certainly qualify as Satan.

His mother had always told him that if a situation proved too much to swallow all at once, he ought to take it in manageable bites. He doubted very much that the creature laid out before him on embroidered brocade was in any way manageable but Robert, stout of heart and Scots to his core, resolved to give it a game try.

He decided to begin at the bottom and work his way up. Steam curled in elegant curlicues from the cusp of the toes. Steam, he told himself sternly, not the smoke of eternal fires. Long legs, well made, perfectly proportioned, a knee drawn up fine around opalescent bone. A scatter of golden fleece along the flanks and then a towel, likely for his own sense of propriety and not His Lordship's. Robert had a feeling that modesty was not one of the man's larger virtues.

Narrow through the waist, broadening to chest and shoulder, all of it well muscled and gleaming like distilled sunflowers.

A face, flawless in its execution and design, redeemed from perfection by a nose that had once been broken and, as a result, was slightly sharpened at the bridge. The hair, worn over-long, was gold and gilt as the proverbial prince.

He looked squarely at the man and felt the breath dam up in his lungs. Eyes the color of a shattered iceberg, a green beyond emeralds, olives or aqua, a green so pure that one felt snared in it, unable to get enough oxygen in order to think clearly. And Robert was a great proponent of thinking clearly.

"Robert, I presume," said the voice, which held within it components of many things: whiskey, butterscotch, dry ice, old schools, and money—great, crisp piles of it.

Robert, girding up his remaining courage, attempted to smile, opened his mouth to speak and finding no words yet willing to make their way forth, settled for a nod of his head.

"Well," the voice continued, smooth as buttered silk, "I've heard the Scots are miserly with words but this is purely ridiculous. Old Rabbie seemed to manage though," the lips, carnal by design, turned up at one corner,

> "Stay, my charmer, can you leave me!
> Cruel, cruel, to deceive me!
> Well you know how much you grieve me!'

The accent was indefinable, Robert thought in the one small portion of his brain that wasn't whirling. And what the hell was that burning on the brazier? It smelled like singed oranges and was making his thoughts drift dangerously.

"Perhaps a drink would loosen your tongue," the left hand, long-fingered, gestured gracefully to a narrow-necked crystal decanter. Robert, throat suddenly parched, nodded and then thought perhaps it was a mistake to imbibe during a job interview, even if one's potential employer wore no more than a large emerald and a small towel. However, he hardly saw any way to back out gracefully so he accepted the tumbler of grain-colored liquid and took a tentative sip.

> "Gie him strong drink, until he wink,
> That's sinking in despair;
> And liquor guid to fire his bluid,
> That's prest wi' grief and care;

There let him house and deep carouse,
Wi' bumpers flowing o'er,
Till he forgets his loves or debts,
And minds his griefs no more.'

The Rs, rolled with mocking precision, rollicked out in perfect imitation of his own High West Scotland tones. The man had all the mercy of a satiated cat playing with a wit-addled mouse. Even in watchful relaxation he'd the grace of a cat about him, something sleek and golden, a mountain lion perhaps. And the watchful stillness of a cat as well; Robert could almost feel him scenting the air, waiting to pounce. Robert took a larger, less tentative sip.

Strong drink indeed, he thought, the peat and smoke of the Spey swimming warm through his veins. Combined with the steamy heat, the scotch brought a thin skim of sweat to rest upon his forehead. He was only grateful no fellow countryman was there to see it.

One golden eyebrow, curved with the perfect symmetry of a gull's wing, arched delicately in his direction.

"Tongue found, sir," Robert said with a watery smile.

"So it is. I was worried there for a moment that we'd have to go in after it with chisel and pike. I believe you have something for me?" The golden head inclined and Robert, eyes squinting through the steam that was fogging his spectacles, started slightly and handed over the sodden bundle that had ridden between rib and elbow since his precipitate leave-taking of Glasgow some three days earlier.

An amber sylph, seemingly conjured from thin air, received the parcel from his hands and crossed the room to deliver it to His Lordship, who laid it to the side, the unnerving green gaze never once leaving Robert's face. He said something in a rapid, staccato singsong tone that Robert thought might be Cantonese, and the sylph dissipated back into the air as quickly as she'd apparated.

"Ah, look at him will you? Fresh down from the Isle of Skye with the moss still green between his toes and the final notes of 'Will Ye No Come Back Again?' fading from his lips. What shall we do with such an innocent?"

Robert cleared his throat and attempted to wipe a bit of the fog off his glasses. "To whom would you be speaking, sir?"

"To the leprechauns, of course. If they're not addressed three times a day they have terrible fits, turn the cream sour, salt the whiskey when your back is turned and let the grasshoppers out of their paddocks."

"Jamie," a voice soft as black lotus emerged more fragrant than the burning brazier. "Do quit toying with the poor man. He's only trying to do his job."

Turning, Robert wondered how he'd missed her. She was not a woman one overlooked, ever. Her beauty was Byzantine in its opulence, the face of the most favored odalisque in the sultan's harem. Skin neither black nor brown nor white but a combination that made all other shades seem coarse and inferior. Black hair, uncompromisingly straight, hung in a smooth sheet down her back. She wore gold silk, all but transparent in the heat, and even from a distance exuded the scent of spiced roses. Small-breasted and smooth-bellied, one leg lay in the part of her robe, gleaming with the rub of pampered flesh.

Robert momentarily underwent the misery of the plain of face in the presence of preternatural beauty, felt slightly nauseated, and took another sip of his drink for pity's sake.

"Of course," The Lord of Ballywick and Tragheda said, "I am being a boar. Robert, this is Quiyue Rourke, solicitor for the Far East holdings of the Kirkpatricks."

"I am more commonly known as Sallie," the woman said in a voice that bore barely a trace of inflection, but caressed his ear like a long ripple of amber silk.

Robert blinked. This woman, who ought to have well-muscled eunuchs waiting upon her every whim, was a lawyer? He stifled a sigh, thinking not all advancements in feminine equality were to his taste. He rose and extended his hand, feeling as overdressed as an Eskimo in the tropics. The woman with the prosaic name laid her own hand across his and Robert considered that there were situations that good, no-nonsense Scots Presbyterian mothers could not quite imagine. He kissed the hand and came away with the taste of cinnamon hot on his tongue and an overwhelming impression of liquid black eyes under high, painted, immaculate brows.

"If you can tear yourself away from Sallie, perhaps you'll be so good as to tell us the reason for this visit, Robert?" The Irish Lord was smiling, but there was little of humor in the expression. When the earls had fled Ireland in 1603, the Kirkpatricks had opted to stay. At that point only five percent of the land in Northern Ireland was left in the hands of Irish Catholics. The Kirkpatricks held on with both hands and never lost so much as an acre. Robert could see, rather clearly at present, the sheer bloody-mindedness such an act would require, well delineated on the face of their descendant. Of course, if one credited such things, there was the legend that Queen Elizabeth I, despite her double-barrelled abhorrence of Catholicism and the Irish, had been rather fond of one Silken James, an illustrious ancestor of the man who sat here before him.

"Well, sir, as you know, I've done work for Monseigneur Brandisi from time to time, and as he knew I was looking for a more permanent position—"

"He conveniently thought of me," Jamie said, eyes narrowing slightly. "Tell me, Robert, have you been sent to spy for him?"

"No, sir, it was only in the way of a favor."

"And how, may I ask, does a man of modest means from a tiny village on the edge of nowhere come to be in the position of having the Father General of the Society of Jesus owe him favors?"

"He is my father's first cousin."

"How is it," Jamie enquired with what might be mistaken for a gentle politeness, "that I always forget Giacomo's pack of Scots relations?"

Robert thought it a question that did not require an answer.

"And how, Robert, do *you* think you can be of service to me?"

"Perhaps, sir," Robert said trying to ignore the large beads of perspiration gliding down his back, "it would be more fitting for me to ask what you require?"

"I wasn't aware of having needs of any sort but as you've asked I'll answer. I have," His Lordship said sweetly, "three requirements of a secretary—he must be a man who knows how to hold his pen, his liquor and his tongue."

"A fair enough bargain," Robert replied, glass beginning to slide from his slick palms. "I think my previous employer can vouch for me. I am as discreet as the mythical monkey, neither seeing, nor hearing, nor speaking any evil... unless of course, sir," he chanced a smile, "you wish me to."

"Ah," the voice was as golden and drawling as a sun-drenched lion. "The Scotsman has a sense of humor. How unnatural. Now perhaps, Robert, you can convey the message you were sent to convey and I," Jamie put a hand over the one Sallie had laid lightly on his bare knee, "can get back to enjoying my afternoon."

" Well, sir," Robert began awkwardly, feeling his suit beginning to shrivel like a raisin in the unnatural heat, "there are some who feel, rather strongly, that now is the time to go home."

"By some," Jamie said, "I presume you mean that bossy little Italian, Brandisi."

Robert choked slightly on his drink. He had never met anyone with the temerity to call the Father General of the Society of Jesus 'that bossy little Italian', though no doubt many had thought it.

"It would seem that a certain man with rather definite religious beliefs has poked up his nose again in Belfast."

His Lordship's eyes narrowed slightly, "The fair Lucien looking for light, is he?"

"As you know, sir, the Republican party is split—"

"Yes I do know—the main philosophy of one being to shoot first and ask questions later and the other to talk you to death so there's no need of bullets. I'm well aware of the political platforms, such as they are, of our rebel friends. What I'm wondering, Robert, is if you've come all this way to enlighten me on the state of Northern Irish politics or if Giacomo actually had a message to transmit?"

"It seems the ground is fertile right now for a radical man on the Unionist scene too, a response to what's happening on the Nationalist side. The word is, the Reverend may be that man."

"He's hardly a man of the people," Jamie said in a relaxed tone, though a slight vertical line had appeared between his eyebrows. "And the vote in Northern Ireland has little to do with politics or the common good. The vote splits itself down tribal lines. Lucien belongs to no one's tribe."

"Unless of course, sir, if you don't mind me venturing an opinion, you consider how desperate these people are. We're talking about the hard core working-class Loyalists here, people who no longer trust the gentry or the new rich to make their decisions for them."

"A thug voted in by thugs. Rather appropriate, don't you think?"

"Sir," Robert shifted uncomfortably, all too aware of Sallie Rourke's amused gaze, "perhaps I am failing to purvey the gravity of the situation properly. It's thought by many that the stage is setting itself for confrontation."

"Enter," Jamie said dryly, "stage extreme left, the Provos, who've been waiting in the wings for war."

"Exactly, sir," Robert said with a tinge of relief.

"And how does this concern me, Robert? If you're Giacomo's agent, then who is he representing in this little masquerade of fools? Tell him the Tory minister will be satisfied with bouts of peace and quiet, interrupted occasionally by an acceptable level of violence and the odd bit of savagery. The British don't expect, nor do they want, any better from the Irish."

"The Father isn't complicit in the politics of the British."

"Robert, you're making my head ache," His Lordship said without a smile.

Sallie Rourke, silent to this juncture, rose from her couch, hair falling in a silent wing to hide her face as she retrieved a heavy glass bottle from a low, enameled table with carvings displaying amazing skill folded into its legs. She unstopped the bottle and poured into her hand a heavy stream of white powder that glittered in the fragrant light like milk-washed opals. From another flask, she poured a dark, viscous liquid into a small squat glass and added the white powder. This exotic brew she handed to His Lordship, who took it with murmured thanks and a look that conveyed many things, none of them well-bred.

"Ground pearls, doused in the blood of Scottish virgins," Jamie said in answer to Robert's raised eyebrows. "The ladies believe it lends vitality, stamina, and—shall we say—a certain luster to a man's abilities."

Robert watched as his potential employer took a deep swallow of the brew, the large square-cut emerald on his left hand catching the light in a dazzling display. If the rumors about His Lordship were true, the pearls were rather like bringing coals to Newcastle.

Both rumor and reputation had it that His Lordship lacked neither vitality nor stamina, and with amber sylphs fairly tumbling forth from the woodwork, Robert was inclined to put some credence in the stories he'd been told.

"Sir, I think you hardly need to be reminded that the Father General only has your welfare at heart. He is very fond of you."

"I've told him not to worry, but," Jamie sighed, "with Brandisi things go in one ear and out the other, like the wind whistling through dried honeycomb."

"While it is true," Robert replied with the patience of a born diplomat, "that the good Father tends to only heed what he wishes to, he does hear *everything*."

The cat eyes narrowed, considering him. Robert felt a sudden brotherhood to mice everywhere. Like a cat, the man's moods apparently could change at whim as well, for suddenly he assumed a different mask and a different tone. "Well, Robert, what is it you know of whiskey and linen?"

Robert could have told him a great deal and induced tears with a riveting monologue that began with the sincerity of the unseeded flax and ended with the frivolity of the distiller's ether, also known as the angel's portion. But he chose humility instead.

"Very little, sir, but I learn quickly."

"A wise answer, Robert. I see we begin to understand one another."

"Though the good Father thought perhaps I might be more useful in a political capacity," Robert said hesitantly.

"Ah, just when I thought we had found some common ground. I've taken a leave from politics. Things will go neither to heaven nor hell in my absence."

His Lordship had taken leave abruptly and without explanation in the fall, fueling rumors of scandal within the government where he'd sat as the Member of Parliament for West Belfast for the last two years. Even Giacomo didn't know the truth of the matter which, for a man who was reported to have the ear of a bat and the eye of a fortune teller, was endlessly vexing.

'In all things,' Robert could hear Father Brandisi's voice in his ear, 'he will use intelligence and reason. He is a man of great passions, but rarely will he allow passion to lead him.' Perhaps though, thought Robert, this instance would be the exception rather than the rule.

He'd saved his trump card for the last, thinking perhaps that it was unfair to use it unless the situation qualified as an emergency.

"The Reverend has been seen at particular meeting places in Belfast recently."

His Lordship eyed Robert coolly. "Does Giacomo actually believe I don't know that?"

Robert wondered wildly if Giacomo was punishing him for some unknown offense.

"Father Brandisi thought perhaps these appearances are an opening gambit, meant to provocate."

One golden eyebrow arched slightly. "Of course they are. At this point I choose not to take the bait."

"But you will in the future?" Robert cursed the words as soon as they left his lips. Giacomo had warned him to be careful on this particular issue.

"Predictability is a disease of the middle class and fanatics, and in neither group do I have membership," which Robert translated as, 'None of your damn business, meddling Scot.'

Robert nodded, glasses sliding down the increasingly slippery slope of his nose.

"Perhaps, sir, I have made a mistake in coming here." He quaked inwardly at the thought of having to relate his failure to Giacomo who, though a man of God, had a most worldly temper.

"Perhaps you have, Robert, but as you and I are both aware that Giacomo's will is rather like a horse cart from hell that runs down all in its path, I think we might as well find a mutually agreeable way to go under the hooves."

Robert blinked at this unexpected turn of luck, hoping his face didn't reveal too much of his surprise.

For the next half hour they discussed terms and conditions, His Lordship asking questions designed to test Robert's knowledge of the international finance market as well as his expertise in matters political. Robert, as instructed, remained deferential, displaying his knowledge while retaining his modesty. There would be little point in pretending to know more than he did. The man would catch him out, and the trust he was meant to cultivate would be destroyed before the ground for the foundation was even broken.

James Kirkpatrick was known as something of a magi in the financial markets, though no one understood how he took a dollar and made it not two, but two hundred. His instincts were infallible and investment bankers from Wall Street to Hong Kong clamored for his business. He'd been born to a sizable inheritance but had, in a few years of intense scrutiny and mind-numbing work, turned it into an emperor's fortune. Where the sizable inheritance originated was rather less clear. Rumor, tale-spinner that it was, had it that the original ancestor had come over from the Hebrides as a mercenary, responding to the call of the Irish chieftains who often hired Scots to fight their internecine tribal battles. Kirkpatrick was, after all, a Scottish toponymic, meaning very simply, 'church of Patrick'.

The main bulk of what Jamie had inherited came from whiskey, a heady brew called Connemara Mist that the Kirkpatricks had distilled by the side of a small river in Ulster for four hundred years. Only the Guinness family rivaled the Kirkpatrick name and money in the world of alcohol exports.

Another portion came from the linen mills that had also been in production for hundreds of years. Kirkpatrick linens, embossed with a graceful, arcing 'K' were famous the world over for the high thread count that made them the last word in luxury.

The present head of the house of Kirkpatrick had expanded the business far beyond the borders of Ireland and simple exports. He had investments from mines in the far north of Canada to offshore oil exploration in the North Atlantic, to several small loan companies set up in underdeveloped nations, allowing those without the means to start small cottage industries of their own. And these were only the thin end of the wedge.

Robert had not been averse to the notion of working for this man, if indeed the man could be persuaded to take him on. Until a moment ago, it had seemed extremely unlikely. Robert knew if His Lordship was willing to take him into his employ, however, it wasn't because he needed an able assistant but because he'd his own reasons for allowing a spy into his world. Robert felt distinctly pawn-like and yet intrigued by the man who sat before him in all his arrogant beauty, as though conducting job interviews in the nude were merely a matter of course. The man was now looking at him as one would look at a rather dim-witted schoolboy.

"I'm sorry, sir, I missed the last bit of what you were saying," Robert said, fighting the urge to stutter that pulled hard on his tongue.

James Kirkpatrick the Fourth, the Lord of Ballywick and Tragheda, did not apparently repeat himself for those hard of hearing or short on attention. He merely took another drink from the small glass in his hand and continued in his chilled whiskey voice.

"I have commitments I need to keep over the next several months. I do not plan to be back in Ireland until next autumn," His Lordship said. "If you still wish, after hearing the conditions I've set out, to be in my employ, you'll be there as well. Until then, you will receive instructions from time to time. The work will involve a great deal of travel."

"Indeed sir, I look forward to it," Robert answered courteously, wanting only to escape the hellish heat of the room and be on his way, mentally adding a codicil to take the beautiful and intriguing Sallie Rourke with him as he went.

The golden head inclined itself against the brocade pillows, fire-lit lashes tipping down over deep-bitten green. Robert saw that the man had not merely been acerbic, he had a headache and, judging from the tight line from jaw to temple, a very bad one. He cleared his throat quietly, disconcerted to find himself awaiting permission to leave, as though this man were a medieval king and he a peasant straight off the fief.

"Heavens," the eyes remained closed, but Robert knew the man did not need to see in order to read his mind, "is the wee Scot still here? You have my permission to leave, though perhaps," there was a flicker of amusement beneath the serene tone, "you'd like to kiss the ring before you go?" The emerald, seemingly on cue, blazed obscenely in the light.

Robert knew he'd overstayed his welcome and was in danger of compromising everything if he remained a minute longer. He stood, noting that Sallie rose as well, her movements as polished as those of a woman born a king's concubine. This, his practical Scots side admitted, was likely what she was.

She indicated with a slight movement of one graceful hand that he should accompany her to the door. She opened it for him, a waft of lighter air from the antechamber stirring the delicately jeweled Egyptian crosses that hung from her ears.

"What's in the brazier?" he asked, wanting to prolong his brief moment in her presence.

"Mugwort," said the sun strung voice behind him that did not belong to Sallie Rourke, "mixed with sandalwood, said to be useful in scrying rituals. Apparently," the voice continued lightly, "it prevents elves or evil spirits from entering at your door as well as being useful in the cleaning of crystal balls, or so," the words were punctuated with a yawn, "a gypsy told me."

Robert, being possessed of a certain amount of Scots cunning to balance his practicality, knew when he'd been issued a warning.

Sallie opened the door wider. "It's lavender," she said, casting a stern look at the recumbent figure, "to help him sleep."

"And the ground pearls?" Robert asked, wishing he dared to kiss her hand again.

"Headache powder in port," Sallie said tartly. "Don't let him fool you. He's a lamb under the wolf skin. He's good at throwing up smoke screens, though having been raised by Jesuits one would hardly expect less, would one?" She smiled coolly as she delivered the last sting and closed the door in his face.

Robert understood that her message was two-fold. 'All is not as it seems and those who create monsters ought to be wary of their creation turning back to bite the hand of origin.' He would, as he was certain he was meant to, communicate the warning to Father Brandisi.

Retracing his passage through the dark, perfumed corridors, Robert sighed with relief and thought, despite the rather exorbitant amount of money the man had just offered him, it was likely that every penny of it was going to be hard earned.

Chapter Eighteen
Irish Sal

THE KIRKPATRICK HISTORY IN THE FAR EAST WENT BACK to the time of the original tea trade with China, just as the stranglehold of the East India Company was beginning to ease and it was possible to trade in China without risking the noose with every cargo. This particular arm of the company had grown swiftly, by using the fastest clipper ships and the most ruthless seamen who could be found sailing the Seven Seas.

The Kirkpatrick Company put one of the first merchant steamers in the seas between Calcutta and Chinese ports as well, always keeping slightly ahead of the competition. When Japan opened for trade they were ready to establish themselves there with regular service between Yokohama, Kobe and the Chinese ports of call, and sub-offices in both Japanese cities.

They had to abandon their holdings in Hong Kong during WWII, leaving them to the invading Japanese, but Jamie's grandfather had rebuilt the company after the war and the retreat of the Japanese. He had wisely established offices elsewhere in China, thus never losing their commercial relationship with the Chinese.

The first time Jamie had gone to Hong Kong with his grandfather, the Kirkpatrick family had been in possession of wharf space in both Hong Kong and Shanghai, with the *godowns* in Hong Kong at a capacity of 750,000 tonnes of cargo. Since Jamie's tenure as head of the company had begun, he had increased their wharf space and built six-storey, concrete-reinforced *godowns* equipped with their own cranes and cargo lifts.

These warehouses had long been a favorite place for him. They were invariably hives of activity and hubs for various exotic goods that came here to be dispersed in all their richness around the rest of the globe. It was a more modern version of the Silk Road, both overland and maritime. One could sense the ghosts of those intrepid traders here, and the goods they bought and sold; the lingering scent of the frankincense and musk; the medicines and spices; the jewels and glassware; and the rivers of silk that poured out of China herself. They still dealt in wools and oils, spices, silks, teas, and remedies. And of course spirits of the finest sort, which was how Jamie's grandfather had originally met Daragh Rourke, the owner of Irish Sal's Bar.

Irish Sal's bar was legendary. Irish Sal, aka Sallie, had inherited the bar from her father, an Irishman of romantic temperament and a taste for Chinese women. He had come to Hong Kong seeking his fortune and met it in the form of Lily Xu. He had, as the legend went, fallen instantly in love with Lily when he encountered her selling chickens in the marketplace. Many men had done so before him, for Lily had a face on her as delicate and perfect as a lotus blossom. Before Daragh, all men had been rebuffed and sent on their way with a flea in their ear, for Lily's mother was possessed of a sharp eye and an even sharper tongue. Lily, however, was possessed of a rebellious streak and fell in love with the blue-eyed Irishman about five minutes after he succumbed to her.

The 'Bar' was a bit of a misnomer, for though it served spirits of all sorts, it wasn't traditional in any other way. Irish Sal's floated in Victoria Harbor and consisted of a rescued and refurbished opium clipper that had seen thirty years of service under the aegis of the East India Company. Some people swore they could still smell the sticky sweet scent of opium in its teak boards, brass and copper fittings and gleaming mahogany counters. The *Pearl Witch* had made the run between London and Hong Kong for those thirty years, her needle-nosed, sharp-raking masts and heavily-sparred topside cutting the waves like a hot knife through butter. When Daragh found her, she was a rotting hulk listing off Kowloon Point, more barnacle than sea-going substance. But he had seen the beauty of her lines beneath the damage and bought her on the spot, spending the next five years restoring every inch. And then, to recoup his investment, he turned her into a saloon. There were only two things, people said, that Daragh loved as much as he loved his clipper ship, and they were his wife and daughter.

Sallie was born to Daragh and Lily after seven childless years and was therefore that much more treasured for her late arrival. As if to make up for her tardiness, she was possessed of a beauty that was apparent by her second birthday and a fiery temperament inherited from both sides that brooked no nonsense and was fastidious in its choosing of both friends and foes.

Sallie, whose Chinese name was Qiuyue, meaning Autumn Moon, was only delicate in looks. In personality, she was as fierce as the monsoons that regularly tore across her island city.

James Kirkpatrick had first visited Irish Sal's in his youth, on a business trip with his grandfather to oversee their tea warehouses. When in Hong Kong, his grandfather always stopped in for a pint and to say hello to Daragh and Lily. By the time they visited the famous clipper ship, Jamie had already fallen under the cosmopolitan spell of Hong Kong itself and was in a mood to be impressed and enamored by all he encountered, including the Chinese girl with the name that sounded like an owl hoot to his Western ears. He made the mistake of sharing this thought with Qiuyue, who was neither in a mood to be impressed nor enamored of a rude Irish boy no matter how pretty he might be. Her pique only served to intrigue him more, and so he set out to charm her, always a tricky proposition with a girl of Chinese-Irish origins.

However, once he rescued a crow with a broken wing near her grandfather's apothecary shop and splinted its wing, then sang her a song in pitch-perfect Cantonese about the beauty of her mind and the delicacy of her ankles, she began to relent a little. As his charm, humor and ability to both lead and follow her on airy flights of fantasy weakened her defenses, she began to wonder how she had not been his friend her entire life. It became a defining state for her, being Jamie's friend and having him for hers. Once she had obtained her law degree, working for the Kirkpatrick family seemed natural. Neither she nor Jamie ever found it awkward that she was his employee, perhaps because he never treated her as one.

There were times that she questioned his approach to things, but she never doubted the results. She placed her faith in him, just as he placed complete faith in her ability to understand and negotiate her way through complex international trading laws and sanctions, as well as wily businessmen and all the various mores and quirks of the cultures they dealt with on a daily basis. They made, she knew, a very good team.

"WHAT A BEAST YOU WERE TO THAT POOR MAN," Sallie said to the man reclined in front of her. His eyes were closed and he was so still as to seem unconscious, but the voice when it answered was fully awake and deeply acerbic.

"He's faced far worse than me. He's a Scot. He wouldn't be comfortable with soft words and sweetness, and frankly I've a short supply of both those virtues at present."

Once the 'small Scot' had left, she led Jamie by the hand to the inner chamber of the warren of rooms, knowing that his vision was severely compromised at present and wanting to spare him the indignity of banging into a wall or ebony footstool.

The bed on which he now lay was old, but retained its imperial splendor. It was built of mahogany, six feet in length, five in width, its legs and posts carved in high relief. Panels shielded three sides of it from the rest of the room, giving privacy to whomever lay upon its silken mattress. Mother of pearl and jade crusted the base along with the archetypes of Chinese myth: dragons, butterflies, warrior monks, and fierce-faced demons. It was a bed fit for a merchant prince, which was a title, Sallie reflected, that defined Jamie rather well.

The room was dim, the only light that of a lamp with a cut crystal chimney, shaded by a jade dragonfly attached to the lip of said chimney. In that coddling dark, Jamie's hair blazed like a flag of gold against deep velvet.

The diamond-hard surface that he had presented to the small Scot only moments before was gone and he had succumbed to the pain that he had held tightly in check during the interview. Very few people were allowed to see him vulnerable in such a way, possibly only three that she could think of—herself, Jonathan Wexler and Yevgena.

Over the years, she had watched this man build a shield of reason and intellect to serve himself in the world. And certainly, though both intellect and reason were fierce within him, he was in truth a Romantic whose nature insisted on the pathways of intuition, imagination, and feeling through the senses, the world beyond, both visible and otherwise.

There were ways to break these shields, to release the body and allow the spirit the escape it needed from the fetters of body and mind. This she could provide, for there were times men did not understand the ways of their own being, but a woman knew these things by instinct and could give the necessary balm. He was at the fine dwelling edge of his own nerves and must be brought back from the brink in the manner that served best. Deprivation was as harmful as over-indulgence, and this man had lived long enough beyond his senses that he must now be steeped in them for his own good. For though she was beautifully versed in the laws of business and finance, she understood even better the laws of the human heart, which superseded all others.

One would not have known yesterday how severe the pain was. He had met in the afternoon with four of the Mountain Men, the leaders of individual sects of the Hong Kong triads. He had been chill as ice water, without a single outward sign that his head was fired with pain. These men were the most powerful and violent men in Hong Kong. Jamie, impeccably dressed in Hong Kong tailoring, had met with them and observed all the formalities and rituals so dear to the Chinese heart. He understood how to give face while keeping it perfectly intact for himself. It had been an especially arduous meeting, during which she had kept demurely in the background, though she did not miss one twitch or finger tap or any other sign that these men used to communicate beyond spoken language.

Even she had been slow to realize that Jamie was near blind from pain. The green eyes had been as sharp and penetrating as they always were and he had not missed a nuance nor conceded a point with men who were world class at Hong Kong's infamous 'squeeze'—the bribe money paid out monthly by businessmen for the 'protection' of the local chapter of the triad.

The meeting had lasted three hours, and Jamie had not agreed to higher pay for protection. But Sallie knew he had his own methods of dealing with the triads. Demanding higher pay was often a means of upping the ante and increasing their own face, something that Jamie understood. He granted what concessions he could, but refused to kowtow to those who cut too deeply into his profit margin or compromised the Kirkpatrick holdings in Hong Kong in any way. Once the men had left, Jamie had gone to look out the window of the large airy space they had rented for the meeting. It was only when she had gone to stand beside him to deconstruct the last hours, as they always did after a meeting, that she realized he was trembling like a leaf and his shirt was damp with sweat. And so she had brought him here and begun a series of treatments to alleviate his pain.

She put a cloth in a hot bath of water infused with lavender and orange oils and then wrung it out, releasing aromatic steam. She unrolled the cloth carefully and placed it over Jamie's face. He didn't protest, which told her he must be almost insensible with the pain, as neither meekness nor submission were traits he normally displayed. And so she knew he was to the point of being receptive to her cure. She knelt and pulled out an ornately carved ebony box. Inside lay the tools of the opium den. The pipe was simple, the bamboo that the Chinese preferred for its size and ability to hold and store the resins of opium which resulted in a more luxuriant smoke. The Chinese pipes distilled the drug rather than burning it. She had prepared pipes for her grandfather and he had taught her exactingly how to make a pure pipe, how to set the ambience and ritual that were an important part of the experience. But the pipe she prepared for Jamie wasn't going to be of that sort. He needed the concentrated morphine of the dross, and she had a small sticky ball of it ready.

She had only tried opium once in her life and it had been with Jamie in their younger years. What she remembered of the experience was a great deal of laughter and their total absorption in a caterpillar for what seemed several hours, that happened across their landscape at the time. She also remembered how her body had felt, vaporous and eased, without the heaviness of flesh. It had been quite wonderful.

Still, she had not smoked it since. She, however, did not get headaches that rendered her insensible for several days. She knew Jamie had certain tendencies in his personality that made narcotic substances unwise but she thought there were exceptions to every rule and this was one. She had brought every other remedy to his service, but none of them had worked: not the acupressure, nor the acupuncture, nor the massage, nor the burning of mugwort on his pulse points, nor the dark, bitter drink her grandfather had taught her how to make when she was a child. Because of their failure, she knew that the origin of his pain lay not in the physical realm, but rather the spiritual. Of this, however, he would not speak.

At the very least, it would quell his nausea and possibly give him a few hours sleep, something he sorely needed. Sallie was a pragmatist above all and unnecessary suffering, whether spiritual or physical, seemed like the worst form of self-martyrdom to her, especially when there were remedies at hand.

From a small ceramic pot, she took the sticky dark ball. She had acquired the *chandoo* from an old and trusted associate of her grandfather's. She had been explicit in what it was needed for and the old man had nodded and taken her behind his shop counter to where a long line of enameled jars stood, each holding a different grade of *chandoo*. What she wanted was usually reserved for addicts who were desperate for the direct hit of morphine, in which the dirtier grades of opium were rich. It was called the dross and was scraped from the leavings in the bowl of a pure smoke.

Sallie took the ball and skewered it. It was large enough to provide three separate smokes. Cooking opium required a dexterous hand and great focus. It was a delicate process and like a soufflé in that even if it was slightly burned, it was ruined. She held it over the flame of the lamp, at just the right angle and proximity so that it wouldn't overheat on one side and stay cold on the other. She picked up another ivory-handled skewer and began a gentle weaving, skewer over skewer, as though she were attempting to tie and untie knots with the needles. It had to be done just right, so the thebaine in it wouldn't evaporate and leave the smoker with a much harsher and unforgiving pipe. Patiently, patiently, needle over needle, slowly the color began to transform from black to syrupy brown, to tan and finally to the brown gold that signified it was done. Her hands described a dance of precise steps upon the air, winding up with one skewer holding the majority of the opium and the other just enough for the first fill of the pipe. This she spun briefly in the heat of the flame and then rolled it rapidly in a small bowl until it formed a small tight cylinder which she then inserted into the heated bowl of the pipe. One more spin of the skewer and the opium was in place against the sides of the bowl and ready to smoke.

Jamie had turned on his side, the emerald eyes dark and dense with pain. She positioned the lamp near him, placed the pipe in his hands with the bowl at just the right angle to the flame, and replaced the cloth over his eyes with a fresh one, knowing even the low, steady light of the flame, was an agony to him at present.

"Draw gently," she said softly, "but deep. It will take you where the elephants dream." She watched him draw, and draw again and again, until the weight of the drug stole over him. The smoke would caress each cell and float down the rivers of vein and artery, smoothing them and preparing the way for the darker notes of morphine which held the key to release. It would also provide the relaxation necessary for the second part of her cure.

This pipe was her grandfather's and inscribed upon the bowl were the words, *Spring Flowers and Autumn Moon*. She had not handled it since her grandfather's death and would not have brooked its use by anyone other than the man who lay before her now. She hoped that some of her grandfather's spirit still lingered with the pipe and would help to lift the fog of pain that Jamie was wrapped within.

She waited until the first pellet was entirely burned up and she had inserted the second before saying, "I have invited someone to share your bed tonight." Her tone was the same as she would have used in offering him a cup of tea but there were many butterflies below the belt of her robe. She was crossing a line she had never thought to cross with Jamie before. Under different circumstances, with a different man, she might have offered herself. But long ago she and Jamie had agreed that their friendship would outweigh any other concern and that they would not succumb to the temptation to bed one another. They had both, over the years, thought perhaps they had been smug in thinking that would be an easy pact to keep, but keep it they had, appearances in front of stout-spined Scots secretaries notwithstanding.

"You've done *what?*" Jamie said, though his voice, fogged with the drug, lacked the necessary impact.

"She is extremely well versed in the art of reflexes and muscles, she is an expert in relieving tension," Sallie said, imbuing her voice with just the right amount of rebuke.

"Is that what we're calling it?" he asked, sarcasm scattered heavily through the few words.

"Are you too weak for such activity?" she asked, tone light but unmistakably scornful.

One corner of the steaming cloth was lifted and a green eye looked out at her with a certain cynicism, tempered though it was by the opium veil. "I have a headache. I'm not dead."

"Good," she said crisply. "Then I trust you will know how to behave."

The green eye shot her a look of profound disdain before disappearing behind the cloth once more.

She was a woman forever divided between East and West. In some areas she was purely Western and in others the East, with all its opulence and art, held sway. In the bedchamber, she thought with the Qiuyue half of her mind and spirit. She had chosen Jamie's companion for the night herself, for in her business of international trade and finance, of complex negotiation between Eastern modes of thinking and Western, she had become expert in an array of things. Men came to Hong Kong for business, but when the sun sank into Victoria Harbor, they expected pleasure. From the depth of their gratitude on the day that followed such arrangements, she knew which woman was best at the business. And that was Li.

Sallie crossed the room and opened the small door hidden behind a silk screen. Behind it stood one of the most beautiful women she had ever seen. Though Li's name merely meant 'pretty', no such pale word could describe her. There were legends of a Mongol warlord in her ancestry, and if the cut-glass cheekbones and deep amber eyes were anything to go by, it was more than mere legend. Her business sense and shrewd management of both men and money led one to believe it as well.

She did not need to tell Li her business. She knew it well and could assess instinctively what a man needed to force the loss of his control. Even James Kirkpatrick had a breaking point, and right now he was very near it. Li understood this, just as she knew the effects of carefully controlled opium on a man's sexual nature. She would know when to prolong certain acts, and when to drive them to the finish.

Li nodded to her, a faint smile on her lips indicating, Sallie knew, that she was welcome to leave. She inclined her head to the side in a gesture of grace and gratitude, even if inside her feelings did not match these virtues in the slightest. This was the Chinese way. Face must be maintained despite whatever emotions roiled inside the body. She crossed the room on lightly padded feet, silent as moonlight on leaves.

At the door she hesitated for a moment, her hand on the ornate knob, and looked back into the room, hoping she was doing the right thing for Jamie.

Li had disrobed. In the dark her body was a ribbon of silk, pale as water and every bit as fluid, strong where she needed to be and melting where she did not. Yes, Sallie acknowledged with grim satisfaction, she had chosen rightly in this matter.

Li stepped into the opening of the bed enclosure and murmured a few words in Cantonese. Then Jamie spoke, his voice low and slightly jagged from the drug and pain, but flawless in the singsong cadence of Hong Kong's primary language. Sallie could not hear what he said, but the gist of it was clear for Li, sinuous as a wave, joined him on the bed.

There was a soft laugh and a gasp, and then the movement of two bodies. The laugh shocked her, for it was the laugh of a woman who well knew the night that lay ahead of her, which told her this was not Li's first experience of Lord James Kirkpatrick. Now many things made sense—Li's smile when she had requested this favor of her and her refusal of any form of payment.

"I do this favor for you," Li had said, "and later you do one for me."

Li's business here tonight was purely that of pleasure. Still, she was the right woman for the task. The only partner who might have served the purpose better in this regard would have been herself, but she had made a promise, and with this one man she knew she must never make the mistake of breaking it.

Li was a professional and therefore would not mind that there was another woman in the bed with them, invisible, but there nevertheless, for

Sallie could feel the shadow of her upon Jamie. It was this, she was certain, that had brought him to his current state.

She closed the door behind her and went down the stairs, the sound of the rain in tempo with her steps.

Chapter Nineteen

November 1973

Robert

IT WAS EARLY NOVEMBER WHEN A VISITOR SHOWED UP unannounced at their door. She was upstairs with Conor, having just fed him, and he had generously returned the favor by spitting up all down her clean clothes as well as his own. She had only managed to change him when Casey poked his head in at the nursery door.

"There's someone here to see ye, Jewel. Says he's Jamie's secretary."

She turned and gave him a quizzical glance. "Jamie doesn't have a secretary anymore," she said, wondering if Casey might have heard wrong.

"I'm only tellin' ye what the man told me, darlin'. He seems a decent enough sort. Come down an' see for yerself."

She sighed and handed Conor over to him. "Keep the man busy for a minute, will you? I need to change my clothes."

Moments later she descended the stairs, clad in a clean sweater and jeans, hair brushed and bound into some semblance of order but certain she could still detect a faint whiff of sour milk about her person.

A small man stood perusing the books on the shelf built into the wall that divided the kitchen from the stairwell. He was short and dark-haired, well groomed in an impeccable suit and wore a pair of glasses that lent his small face the aspect of an addled owl.

He turned at her entrance and smiled, holding out a hand as he crossed the floor in his argyle socks.

"Mrs. Riordan?" His Scots burr was as thick as porridge and just as comforting as that particular dish. She liked him immediately.

"Yes." She took his hand, hoping the smell of spit-up wasn't wafting off her.

"I'm Robert MacDougall, Lord Kirkpatrick's secretary. I've a few things I wish to discuss with you, if you can spare about a half hour?"

"Of course," she said politely, but her skepticism must have shown in her face for he said,

"He hired me several months ago but I've only arrived in Belfast yesterday."

"Please sit, Mr. MacDougall. If you'll give me a minute, I'll put the kettle on for tea."

In short order, the kettle was humming on the Aga, a plate was filled with tidy slices of lemon loaf and she was feeling slightly more ready to hear whatever it was the small Scotsman had come to say.

She joined them at the table, where Casey and their visitor were discussing the odds of Glasgow Celtic winning the League Cup this year. The small Scotsman had Conor deftly ensconced upon his knee. This caused her to raise an eyebrow in her husband's direction, who merely smiled and shrugged almost imperceptibly in response.

Robert caught the look. "I've twelve nieces and nine nephews. Babies are a constant in my life."

She sat and offered cake around before fixing the Scotsman with a pointed look. He laughed in response.

"Forgive me, but you remind me of him—Lord Kirkpatrick that is. You both can freeze with a glance."

Casey gave a slight snort of agreement and stood to fetch the tea. He brought back the pot and two cups, setting them on the table between Pamela and their visitor. "I've things that need attending to outside. Ye'll call if ye need me?"

"Actually, Mr. Riordan, what I've come to discuss concerns you as well."

"Oh," Casey said and sat back down, an expression of surprise on his face.

"Lord Kirkpatrick hired me some months ago, as I said, during a meeting in Hong Kong—"

"Hong Kong?" Pamela interjected, not from any real surprise. Jamie could turn up on a mountain top in darkest Peru, clad in silks, a chilled martini in hand and it wouldn't surprise her in the least.

"Yes, I'd been asked to deliver a package to him." He cleared his throat quietly, but in such a manner that told Pamela that whatever circumstances he had met Jamie under, they had not been dull in the least. "By the end of the interview, he had hired me as his secretary. Since then I've been kept busy with his various interests and only now managed to visit his home. I had expected to meet him here."

Conor, well behaved until now, reached up and took the glasses off Robert's face, promptly stuffing one lens into his mouth. Casey stood and took him from Robert, patting the baby's back to put paid to the howl of outrage before Conor could get it out.

"Come on, laddie. Let's find you something more digestible," he said, and walked toward the kitchen with Conor's small face peering over his shoulder.

"He ought to have been home this fall. Leastwise, that was his plan when I spoke to him." Robert said, polishing Conor's drool off of his glasses matter-of-factly before setting them back precisely on his nose.

"When did you meet with him, exactly?" Pamela asked, feeling a serpent of dread flick its tail in her stomach.

"It was early last February. Since then I have received instructions at regular intervals. I assumed they were coming from Lord Kirkpatrick but it turns out the instructions had been left with his lawyers who sent them off to me at preordained times."

"Are you telling me that no one has heard from him since last February?" The serpent unleashed a coil or two, making her feel distinctly sick.

"I can't ascertain that one way or the other," Robert said. "I didn't get the impression he was a man who could be easily trailed and he seems to have left a few smokescreens in his wake, whether by design or merely circumstance, I do not know. Only of late, I profess, have I become worried that he has been away far longer than he intended. To that end, I felt I should come here and see if I could trace his whereabouts through his household staff or his friends. Yourself being the obvious start to those enquiries."

"I—I," she glanced at Casey's back and made a silent apology in his direction. "The fact of the matter is, I don't know where he is and I haven't heard from him since he left—his departure was rather abrupt and he didn't say goodbye to anyone—well, beyond a letter of sorts," she finished, feeling as though she were the color of a pomegranate.

She could feel Casey stiffen slightly, for she had not spoken of the letter to him. Jamie being the loaded topic he was between the two of them, she had thought it best not to mention it.

"Might you tell me if the letter contained anything that might help us now as to his whereabouts?"

"No, it didn't. I have no idea where he might be."

"It's my understanding that if anyone other than yourself knows where Lord Kirkpatrick might be, it's his friend Jonathan Wexler. However, even if he knows, he's not likely to tell a total stranger."

"By which you mean you would like me to speak with Mr. Wexler," Pamela said, raising one dark eyebrow.

"Yes. I'm afraid, Mrs. Riordan, it's only the first of several things that I'm here to talk to you about." He shifted in his seat and adjusted his vest.

Pamela put her teacup down, aware that it rattled against the plate before settling. She didn't want to hear what this man had to say, didn't want to acknowledge that Jamie had been gone far too long for easy explanations and simple homecomings.

"There are several business matters that need to be attended to, things that only Lord Kirkpatrick has the power to sign off on—or in his extended absence, of course—yourself."

"Myself?" she squeaked, not daring to glance at Casey, though she heard his gasp clearly.

Robert furrowed his brow, clearly puzzled. "Mrs. Riordan, you hold the Power of Attorney for all Lord Kirkpatrick's businesses. Surely he made you aware of what that might entail when you signed the documents?"

"Yes, but I suppose I didn't think I'd ever need to exercise that power," Pamela said, a terrible chill spreading out from her core. "I—what does this mean for the immediate future? Because I'm certain Jamie will come home sometime soon."

The wee Scot had an inscrutable look on his face as he neither agreed nor disagreed with her statement. She clutched at the one straw in her possession.

"I do know that he keeps an appointment in February each year, but I don't know where that is."

"Yes, the Father General mentioned that as well."

"Father General?" she queried.

"Father Brandisi, he's the Father General for the Society of Jesus."

"The Black Pope," Pamela said, her own eyebrows arched now. "Jamie has mentioned him a time or two. Are you here at his behest?" The Father General of the Society of Jesus had long been nicknamed 'The Black Pope' both for the black garb of the Jesuit and for the immense amount of power the intellectual order wielded.

"No, I am in Lord Kirkpatrick's employ now, though I do know the Father General rather well. I am related to him through my father. It was he who had me take the package to His Lordship in Hong Kong." The small man cleared his throat again, causing her to wonder just what state Jamie had been in when Robert met him—in utter *deshabille*, with a courtesan on each arm? It wasn't beyond the man, certainly.

"Perhaps, Mrs. Riordan, you will know that Father Brandisi took a personal interest in Lord Kirkpatrick's education when he was a boy."

"I knew Jamie was educated by Jesuits, but I wasn't aware it was such a superior one," she said, and saw that Robert didn't miss the tart note in her voice. It seemed the man didn't miss much.

"I see he has told you somewhat of Giacomo's methods, at least."

"Yes, somewhat," she said, thinking it very likely that Robert had determined from the look on her face that Jamie's portrait of Giacomo Brandisi was less than flattering.

"I—what am I supposed to do now?" she asked, feeling as if her world were a glass globe that had just been given a severe shake.

"That will be for you to decide, Mrs. Riordan," he said matter-of-factly. "Perhaps we could meet at Lord Kirkpatrick's house, say, tomorrow morning. Much of what I need to go over with you would be better served there."

"I—ah," she swallowed and looked at Casey. His face was unreadable, eyes dark as onyx.

Casey gave her a long look and then turned to the small Scot. "She'll be there."

Robert nodded, swung his briefcase down to his side and walked to the door. Pamela joined him there, still feeling slightly numb from the information and below that, aware that her worry about Jamie had turned to real fear that something irrevocable had occurred.

The small Scot left after setting a time for their meeting, getting into a car that was fastidious in its cleanliness and neat lines. Conor had gone down for a nap, leaving her and Casey alone.

"Ye never said the man left ye a letter," Casey said quietly, face turned from her as he added peat to the fire. But his tone was slightly gruff as it was when he tried to mask strong emotion. Not for the first time, she wondered what the hell had taken place between the two men before Casey returned to her and Jamie abruptly left the country.

"It wasn't so much a letter as a book of poems with a small note in it." It had been more than that really, but it served no purpose to tell Casey. It would only hurt where hurt was unnecessary. Jamie had left her a small leather bound edition of Rilke's poetry and there had been a slip of paper in it so that the page fell open to a particular poem. Still, she did not know if it had significance or was merely where the paper had been placed.

The piece of paper had held only a few words... *'I wish you only joy, always—Jamie.'* No more words were necessary and Casey did not need to hear nor carry the knowledge of that with him in any way.

Thankfully, Casey did not say anything more on the subject.

She moved to sit down on the sofa near to the fire. Casey had built up a good blaze, but she was terribly cold and could not still the shaking that seized her the minute the Scotsman had explained why he'd come.

Casey sat down beside her and put one large hand over her own. "Are ye alright, darlin'?" he asked softly.

"Yes—or rather I will be. I'm in shock right now."

"All I can offer on that front is the fire an' a whiskey," he said and pulled her in toward him, warming her immediately with the touch of his skin.

"I don't know what to do," she said, still feeling knocked off center.

"Jewel, if Jamie needs ye to look after things then that's what ye'll have to do. The man is trusting ye with what amounts to an empire. That's a great deal of trust an' it was put in place for exactly the situation we find ourselves in now."

"Are you angry?" she asked, melting gratefully into the security of his body.

"No, darlin'. Ye didn't even know the man had left things as he had. It makes sense that he'd leave it with the one person that he most loves an' trusts."

She looked up at him, startled by his words. He crooked a dark brow at her in response.

"Aye, of course I know it. I may not like it, but it's been a fact of our lives together, hasn't it? Ye needn't look that way. 'Tisn't yer fault an' I can't say I blame the man for wantin' to leave things in your hands. He knows ye'll do right by him."

"So you're okay with all this?"

Casey sighed. "'Okay' might not be quite the word to describe how I'm feelin', but I don't see as ye really have a choice, Jewel."

"No, I don't suppose I have," she said, taking a turn at sighing, trying to budge the cold knot that sat frozen at the base of her spine. Jamie would be fine. Jamie had to be fine, that's all there was to it. And until he saw fit to come home, she would take care of business for him.

Chapter Twenty

November 1973

The Comfort of Romans

THUS IT WAS THAT PAMELA FOUND HERSELF SPENDING FOUR DAYS a week seated at the massive oak desk behind which several generations of Kirkpatrick men had sat running their various holdings. The first morning she had been nauseous and utterly terrified of doing something that would bring a four hundred year old company down within a matter of weeks. Some things could be dealt with summarily, other things were not so simple, requiring her to make decisions immediately or within a day or two, always a nerve-wracking endeavor that made her palms sweaty and her head ache.

By late November, though, she felt she was getting a handle on Jamie's business dealings. At least her head had stopped aching. Tuesday through Friday, she sat at his desk and sorted through the tangled threads of industry, philanthropy, correspondence, crackpots, international exporting rules and the fact that Nelson McGlory needed a new pair of glasses, yet again. This last was ascertained at the weekly chess game she now played with Nelson, though she was all too aware what a disappointing partner she must be in comparison to Jamie, who used to play this weekly game with the young boy.

How Jamie had managed to juggle so many figurative balls with such proficiency she truly did not understand. It also gave her a feeling of great accomplishment every time something that had seemed entirely incomprehensible only a week before suddenly became, if not simple, at least clear.

She saw that Jamie had laid the foundation for this for some time. That many of their conversations and much of what he had taught her, shown her and guided her through, had been in readiness for this possibility. Often as she looked through contracts, approval papers, bank transfers and assorted other pieces of Jamie's daily routine, she would hear the echo of his voice in her ear, feel his finger guiding her eyes to the line she was missing, and honing her instinct for this world out of its dormancy. She had always known Jamie ruled an empire, but just how far its tendrils spread across the globe, she'd been less knowledgeable about.

Robert was always on hand to explain the legal intricacies and to stop her from making snap judgments. On the days that she sat in Jamie's study, they took tea together while Conor was down for his nap in the afternoons. She was growing quite fond of the prim Scotsman with the mind of an arrow in flight. It was clear why Jamie had hired him to look after his affairs in his absence. It was this absence that hung most heavily in the air between them. As the weeks went by and the worry could no longer be put aside, she saw clearly that what Jamie had ultimately prepared her for was life without him.

It was on a dark, windy afternoon late in the month that Robert came to her looking as though he had a lime stored in one cheek and a chunk of bitter gall in the other. She knew whatever he was about to say would not be pleasant.

Pleasant it was not, even before he spoke. For on the desk he laid a thick white vellum envelope with her name in Jamie's elegant handwriting across the front. On the back was his seal with the bold imprint of the Kirkpatrick insignia.

He sat on the other side of the desk, then rose, taking the decanter of Connemara Mist and placing it on the desk between them. Teetotaler that he was, Robert couldn't possibly have taken any action that would have panicked her more. Being Scots, mind you, he had the profound good sense to know that whiskey should be administered before shock.

"In my instructions," he said, pouring them each a generous three fingers, "Lord Kirkpatrick asked that this letter be given to you should he not arrive home by a certain date. As that date," he passed her the glass and she clutched it gratefully, the fumes alone providing a homely comfort, "passed one week ago, I felt the letter needed to be given to you. Of course, you will want to read it later when you're alone."

She took a good swallow of the drink, knowing she needed the fortitude, though she wasn't a whiskey drinker by nature. Both Casey and Jamie had taught her the medicinal value of the drink in times of stress.

"Now," Robert took a deep breath and adjusted his glasses on his nose, "that dispensed with, I think it's time I spoke to you about your situation."

"Just how much whiskey do I need in me for this chat?" she asked, wishing she had started in on the bottle straight after lunch.

Robert merely cleared his throat in answer, which told her nothing. He could be the most inscrutable man when he so chose, which likely was a good part of why Jamie had hired him.

"There are several things we're going to need to go over, first of which are certain household items that need to be dealt with," Robert said. "Things that you will have to decide. Small things to be certain, but nevertheless decisions that can no longer be held off. The time has passed now that Lord Kirkpatrick set out as the terms under which all decision-making would be handed over to you."

Pamela found herself wanting to shake the stoic little Scotsman until he made some form of sense.

"What do you mean, *all* decision-making? It's one thing for me to sign papers as long as you explain them to me clearly first, but to take on decisions about the house seems rather more personal. Besides, Maggie has a much better handle on these things than I possibly could."

"I think you misunderstand," the Scotsman said quietly. "Because all of it, Mrs. Riordan, was left to you from the time you first came here. I believe you were nineteen at the time? Or was it eighteen? Should Lord Kirkpatrick fail to come home, this house belongs to you."

"What?!" She pushed her glass across to Robert and he obligingly refilled it.

"Yes, when I said everything I meant *everything*—the titles to the land, the house, the stables, the other homes he owns, the distilleries, the linen mills—and every other interest he has overseas. There's far too much to absorb in one sitting. That's only the bare bones of his assets."

"What?" she croaked again, feeling like a very stupid parrot.

Robert smiled at her, his wise-owl face sympathetic. "I can see all this will be a shock to you, so I'll give you time to absorb it but then we will, I'm afraid, have to sit down and take a look at what all this means. Of course, there are certain stipulations as well, to do with his grandmother and her cottage at the bottom of the property."

"Of course," she said, because there was nothing else to say.

"I'm going to see about tea. I'll be back in a few minutes," he said kindly, and absented himself from the study. She knew he wasn't going to see about tea. Maggie had never needed reminding and Robert knew that to so much as enquire was to risk his well-being and ability one day to reproduce. He had gone to give her a moment alone.

"Oh God, *Jamie*—what the hell were you thinking?!" she asked the air aloud.

Suddenly she bowed her head to the desk, throat tight with tears. She did not want this, didn't want any of it, didn't want the responsibilities, nor the rights and privileges that came with all this wealth and power. She didn't want anything to do with something that meant Jamie was gone, never to return. And she found she was not only profoundly terrified that he was indeed gone, but also very, very angry with him for leaving all this to her. For leaving her.

She stood, unable to sit at his desk in this current state of mind, and walked to the shelves that held his books, all the volumes that had informed that beautiful light-ridden mind of his. How could he be gone, how could all the poetry and prose, the bawdy wit, the wine and the song, be no more?

How could the man who had fed her knowledge as if it were no more than cake be gone? How could the howling darkness have finally overcome him? And where had he succumbed? How could the man who had taught her Latin, and how to sail a boat alone, the man who had given so generously of his time and heart, how could the man who loved her, be gone?

The letter lay like a ticking time bomb, guaranteed to blow this tidy world to smithereens if she should dare to open it. Well, she wouldn't open it. She wouldn't allow Jamie to do this. He would just have to return home, sound of body and mind, and tell her whatever he needed to tell her.

Her hands icy with fear, she pulled a book off the shelf, hoping as one does in such times that it would contain a prophecy as well as comfort.

> *A journey across many seas and through many nations*
> *Has brought me here, brother, for these poor obsequies,*
> *To let me address, all in vain, your silent ashes*
> *And render you the last service for the dead...*

No, not Catullus. He had never been a comforting poet—bawdy, witty, downright nasty and always entertaining, but not comforting. She moved along the shelf that contained the thoughts, great and otherwise, of the Romans. Her hand paused at Seneca. For comfort he was about right and his words were one of the bridges that had helped to form their friendship that long ago summer when she and Jamie first met.

It was an old, old volume and fell open naturally to its final page, where the great philosopher's words lay gold upon the onionskin paper:

> *'Death is not an evil. What is it then? The one law mankind has that is free of discrimination.'*

Seneca was not so comforting either. What she wanted was Jamie himself, to tell her somehow that he was safe, to reach across time and space and give her an indication that he was still somewhere here on this earth, with terra firma beneath his feet and the same stars overhead that she gazed at each night. To tell her that on this chancy planet, in the darkness of night, she still had her dearest friend. Now she must be his friend and take the steps to find out where he was and what had happened to keep him so long silent. Whatever steps they might be, they must be faced with courage for his sake.

She took a deep breath, replaced Seneca on the shelf and turned toward the living for help. The phone number was one she knew and kept in reserve for just such a time.

She sat back down at Jamie's desk and dialed.

In London a phone rang and was picked up. A voice said, 'Hello', managing to convey in those two small syllables a wealth of experience.

"Mr. Wexler," she said, "my name is Pamela Riordan. I need to talk to you about Jamie."

Chapter Twenty-one
Of Men and Angels

JONATHAN WEXLER ARRIVED TWO NIGHTS LATER. After initial formalities, Pamela preceded him to the study, where a fire was lit and tea soon to arrive. He stood on the Turkish rug and surveyed his surroundings with pleasure.

Casey was going to be late home from work and Conor was happily playing in the kitchen with Maggie's pots and spoons. Maggie's niece was visiting from Cork and had brought her two small daughters with her. They were fascinated by Conor and Conor in turn was happy to fascinate. So she was free for the moment to talk with John and see him settled here in Jamie's home.

"I forget," he said, "from one visit to the next, how beautiful Jamie's home is—I do love it here."

"It's very peaceful. One can almost pretend the city below doesn't exist."

Kirkpatrick's Folly had always been a place apart, a fairyland set upon a hill above a hard city. The front half was a Georgian beauty, with formally laid out grounds and lines that were as graceful as any perfect angle. The back half was pure Victorian whimsy, with fluted chimneys, leaded cupolas and octagonal windows. The grounds behind the house were filled with roses and vines and cottage flowers of every description. Further back was an ancient forest filled with storied trees: oaks, ash, elm, rowan and hazel. A bridle path ran through the woods down to the base of the mountain where the Kirkpatrick land ended. The house and grounds had a sense of timelessness, as though the world could be stopped and forgotten, and one would remain safe and content here amongst starlit rooms and roses.

Jamie's study was to the right side of the back entry and stood alone in a small wilderness of ivy and oak trees which shaded it deeply on summer days, but as it was made of glass and wrought iron, it was always open to the heavens no matter the season. Hidden within the wilderness was a tiny courtyard, laden in summer with the scents of bee balm and lavender, though in December such scents were a mere memory amongst the barren stalks.

"We have met before, though you may not remember. It was the night of Jamie's father's funeral," she began, but John held up one thin hand to stave off her explanation. He smiled wryly.

"I do remember you, dear girl—your entrance that night wasn't something a man, no matter his inclinations, was likely to forget."

John sat down in one of the buttery leather-covered wingbacks and stretched his feet toward the fire. He looked weary and far older than the picture of him her memory had held. "Would you happen to have a drink on hand, dear girl?"

"Connemara Mist straight?"

John inclined his head, hand adjusting his collar. "Your memory is faultless."

She handed him the drink and poured herself one as well.

Maggie came in with a tray loaded down with teapot and cups and a heap of roast beef sandwiches. Pamela suddenly realized how hungry she was. She put a plate together for John and one for herself, and then poured them each a cup of the aromatic Earl Grey.

"As I said to you on the phone, the one meeting he keeps every year is in Russia with his friend, Andrei."

"He has mentioned him a time or two," Pamela said, "but I didn't realize he went to see him. How is that even possible in the Soviet Union?"

"Andrei is an astrophysicist in the same league as Penrose and Sakharov. He's not allowed too many privileges for the total use of his brain by the Soviet machine, but visiting Jamie once a year is one thing they do allow. He is extremely important to the Soviet space program so they allow him a few things ordinary citizens can only dream of."

"He must be very dear to Jamie. It seems a rather risky thing to go inside the Russian border every year, permission notwithstanding."

"You'll hardly get a fair picture from me. I wasn't overly fond of Andrei."

"Why not?"

John took a deep drink of his whiskey without flinching and then sighed. "Because I was jealous. I was in love with Jamie, you see."

"I didn't know," she replied softly.

"No reason you should. I don't imagine it's something Jamie talks about over tea. He's been my dearest friend for many years and has allowed me to be one of his, but he's never been comfortable with the other feelings I have for him. I blurted it out one night when I'd had too much to drink and was, admittedly, angry with Jamie. I felt Andrei had stolen him away from me and that I had become little more than a figure of fun for the two of them. Oh, you needn't give me that look. I know well enough that Jamie isn't the sort to do that, but jealousy is hardly a rational state, is it?"

"No, it isn't," she said, wondering just how much this man knew about her own history with Jamie.

He laid his head against the high chair back, stretching his feet toward the fire. "Oh, to see the two of them. I was near eaten with jealousy. So well matched—fiery angels, the two of them—burning everything and everyone in their vicinity," John said bitterly, lines like bite marks around his mouth. "But Andrei's flame burned far colder than did Jamie's. I always told him to go wary there.

"Of course, it was at Oxford, as his professor, that I met Jamie. The cream of young minds are a dime a dozen there, from every land and every background imaginable. But even there, Jamie was special. It was as though Dionysus with all his spring rites had come that autumn to our grey and staid world. Everyone who entered his aura seemed to lose their ability to think rationally, including myself. You know what he is, though. You know what it is to be under his spell."

"Yes," Pamela replied softly, for Jamie was one of those rare human beings who seemed destined for something more than an ordinary mortality. He had the effect on others of making them feel special, of opening up the universe to endless possibility.

"Imagine him then at eighteen, before his marriage, before the lash of pain had laid him open so many times. Imagine all that fire, if you will, burning wild."

"Oh, I can imagine it," she said wryly, taking another swallow of the whiskey and relishing the heat that spread through her chest in its wake.

"Yes," John smiled, "perhaps you've drunk at that fire more than any."

"What makes you say that?" she asked, feeling the dreaded flush flooding up her neckline to stain her face.

"Because, other than his wife, you are the only woman I've known him to truly and deeply love."

"Oh," she said, because there seemed little else to say. John merely quirked a grizzled grey brow at her and took another swallow of his drink.

"Every March, just before his birthday, he would host a Mad Hatter's Tea Party. It was the event of the year, and one was just as likely to find a homeless fiddler there as the cream of Oxford society. Jamie never did discern between classes and he forced anyone else in his society to give up such notions too.

"The one I remember in particular was not only a mad tea party, but also the occasion at which Jamie stood and delivered a very blue variation on *The Hunting of the Snark*."

"All eight fits?" she asked, smiling.

"What do you think?" Jonathan returned the smile with interest. "And, of course, everyone there was *in* fits by the end of the first fit, and it flew downhill from there."

She could well imagine, having been the recipient of some rather blue, if elegant, verse from His Lordship's pen herself.

"In the middle of the party, he got up on the table, feet neatly placed between the butter and the tea, a large top hat on his head and the most dreadful purple velvet bow tie askew around his neck, and said the whole thing in a stream, with toasts to various people he'd included in the body of the poem. I leave it to you to imagine, if you will, what such a spectacle set up in each person."

She could see it only too clearly, and knew the effect Jamie had on others, how just to see him was to set up a craving that swiftly became a yearning that threatened to engulf one's life. That this effect was entirely unintentional on his part only increased its potency.

"He would lead everyone on a merry chase—it was such a time of enchantment—picnics in the country with champagne and strawberries, floating down the river in punts as though we all belonged to another time, one gilded in mellow golden light. A time that couldn't possibly exist in the real world, ever. One's own time is never a gilded age, after all. Sometimes he'd be on a reckless adventure for days, and then he'd disappear down the rabbit-hole as he so eloquently put it, often for days, and no one would be able to find him. Then he'd turn up at my door with that hollowed-out look and I'd put him to bed and knock him out with some sort of medicine until it seemed safe for him to re-emerge."

"He had to trust you deeply to allow you to see him when he was so fragile."

"He did, and I never betrayed that trust—not even once. I would rather die, frankly."

Jamie's friendship did that to people, made them pledge all in the name of it because it was a charm that could not be resisted and once warmed there, one could never find the equal elsewhere.

"Everyone found him irresistible, but when he was fully manic, he was a fire that drew every moth in the vicinity. It seemed even he couldn't control it. Others are inevitably singed by such fires. And as hypnotizing as such a conflagration is, it was very bad for him and he would regret his actions afterward, but it was too late. The damage had already been done, you see."

She stood, nodding to John so that he would not interrupt the flow of his narrative, re-filling his glass and adding a splash to her own. Any more and she knew her head would start to feel as if it was detaching from her shoulders.

"When he would listen, I would do what I could and say what I might to encourage him to keep himself as stable as possible. I'm sure you know the sort of thing I'm talking about: regular hours, proper diet, avoiding extremely emotional situations, avoiding the drink. I never could get him to take his medication, but I understood why he hated it so."

"He told me once he feels half-dead when he takes it, as if he's seeing the world through a thick film."

"Yes, but it's a very deadly fire he holds in his hands when he doesn't take it. He's wedged between Scylla and Charbydis constantly. Andrei only stoked that dangerous fire, threw fuel upon it, and it would leave Jamie wrecked in its passage. I hated Andrei for that, but Jamie had drawn a very solid line between the two of us and refused even to discuss Andrei with me."

He paused and gazed into the fire, and for a moment there was a silence in which the soft hiss of the burning peat was audible.

"His father was rather hard on him, considering that Jamie gave up his dreams for the man. Jamie was living in the most dreadful little attic outside of London, writing the most glorious poetry and prose, and his father came and told him he must come home. It was Jamie's last stab at rebellion, I think. But his father was in the midst of a nervous breakdown and had to be hospitalized shortly after Jamie came back here so I suppose it was inevitable no matter how one looks at it."

"He doesn't sound much like Jamie," Pamela said, feeling a sudden anger at the man Jamie had called 'Dad'.

"As I understand it, Jamie is much more like his grandfather, a light that draws all comers. His father was far moodier. I think the manic depression was more about the depression for him and he didn't experience too many of the manic highs. Jamie has always experienced both extremes. When he's in his manic phase, he's incredibly productive and he can write for several days straight without sleeping or eating. Of course, the crash afterward is particularly brutal, but the manic phase is a bit like an addictive drug—worth the pain to have the joy."

"Once he came home—was that when he married Colleen? I know they were young when they married."

"Yes, I think they married before the year was out. During his time in England, he never told me about Colleen. I think he wanted to keep her separate from the rest of his life, and I think he needed that time to burn before taking up his real life."

"I don't think that is Jamie's real life—the business and the day to day. I think he would say the life we live in our heart and mind, regardless of outward activity, is the true life of a man."

"Yes, I imagine he would in his more impractical moods, but reality does have a way of intruding on one's finer emotions, have you not found?"

She laughed, knowing no answer was needed. She got up, put more peat on the fire and re-filled both their teacups. The study basked in the low light, a place of comfort and peace. It hurt to think of Jamie being able to find neither at present, or perhaps beyond the... no, she cut the thought off firmly. He was alive. There were no other alternatives. He was a man of infinite and surprising capabilities who could survive things that would reduce other men to dust in a matter of weeks.

"At first, marriage agreed with Jamie. Colleen steadied him the way a rudder would a storm-tossed ship. Then the babies started to come and she was never the same, nor was Jamie. She shut him out, and his strength has always lain in his ability to help those he loves. She might as well have opened his veins and left him to hemorrhage, because what she did had the same effect."

"You didn't like her?" Pamela asked.

"Actually I rather did. I just didn't like what she did to Jamie. I know you will say I can hardly blame her. With such tragedy visited upon a woman, one should hardly have expectations of her as a wife. Yet I never thought she was the right woman for Jamie. She was a bit provincial and out of his league and she knew it on some level, despite how much she loved him. She knew it and took the first opportunity to bolt—oh, you needn't raise your eyebrows at me. I'm an old man and I'll tell it as I see it and spare you any false politenesses. Now you, you wouldn't have left. You would have allowed him the balm of taking care of you, of allowing his love to help you heal."

"I haven't always allowed my own husband that so I can't say I would have been any stronger than she was. What did she look like?" she asked, thinking it would be wise to steer the conversation off these imminent shoals.

John smiled, acknowledging her segue.

"She was lovely—very pale, made me think of something steeped in moonlight, so very fair and still yet somehow lacking the necessary fire. Something I believe you," he tipped his whiskey glass in her direction, "aren't lacking in at all."

"My husband would say," she admitted ruefully, "that I've more than an ample amount."

"Something I've no doubt he truly appreciates."

"Oh, most of the time he does, but not always. How was Colleen toward you?"

"By that you mean—I've called her provincial and you think it was personal reasons that made me say so. Well, she was very wary of me. I visited them a few times over the years and was always made welcome, but I could tell she was never comfortable around me. I came from a world that she was certain would take Jamie away from her. I think she still worried that it would claim him."

"You can hardly blame her for that," Pamela said, feeling sorry for the woman who had been Jamie's wife.

"Then, as you will know, the next several years seemed to contain little but heartbreak for Jamie and Colleen. I don't think anyone was surprised when she left, only that they had managed to survive with one another that long. She left for the convent and Jamie threw himself into work and drink with a vengeance. And after that... after all that... his father took his own life and Jamie didn't come up for air until after the funeral and your arrival on the scene."

"His relationship with his father sounds so different from what he's said—though he's said little."

"There were, I think, many good moments for the two of them. Jamie loved the man dearly, so there must have been. I always thought his father was jealous of Jamie, envied him the grace and beauty and the lightning-ordered mind that seemed to catch glimpses of God now and then while the rest of us only saw the world around us. Of course, the beauty Jamie experiences is always on the razor's edge, both perilous and savage, and yet I still long to see the universe, if only for a moment, through his eyes."

"But are any of us willing to pay the price for that glimpse of heaven?" Pamela asked softly, having seen how steep was the cost of Jamie's gifts.

"I have thought at times that no price would be too high," John replied. The answer of a born poet, Pamela thought, but not a man of sense. He stood up then and retrieved a box he had left by the study door. He placed it at her feet.

"I've brought this for Jamie. Perhaps you can put it aside for when he returns home."

Inside the box was a welter of paper and leather-bound notebooks bundled together, some tied with twine to keep them from bursting their seams and spilling with papered profligacy across the floor. There were also a few hardback books, cloth-bound, all in the same rather lurid lilac tone, with rough-cut edges and gold-lettered titles. She picked one up and glanced at the title, raising an eyebrow.

"Ah, yes," John said, "the works of the redoubtable Professor Swansea— purple prose and lascivious verse—but very well done if I do say so myself."

"Professor Swansea?" Pamela said, thinking about the small lilac book that she had in her own possession which had come to her via a Jewish translator in Dublin some years ago.

John merely raised one of his own bristly eyebrows and looked at her over the rim of his whiskey tumbler.

"I had no idea... Jamie wrote these?" she asked, pulling out another lilac tome with the title *The Adventures of a Bodleian Boy in the Orient*. Inside the flyleaf was a list of at least five other entries in this particular series.

"They're collector's items in the world of erotica," John said. "The bloody boy wrote them on a dare to begin with and then they were snapped up by a publishing house. They still sell very well to this day, but those are all first editions and will be worth a fair bit someday."

"Oh my," Pamela said, having opened one to the halfway point.

" 'Oh my' is an understatement, but I know what you mean."

"How much do you think—" she began and then halted, realizing the question was hardly appropriate.

John merely laughed. "Well, I don't know to be honest. Jamie has never been one to kiss and tell, but there was a dreadful amount of smoke during his time at Oxford for there to have been no fire at the base of it. He looked like a young god and was well practiced in Dionysian behavior as well. It does lead one to wonder," he mused, turning the cover of one of the thicker volumes, "how many of the Professor's scenes were the product of his fertile imagination and how many were purely autobiographical. There was a real scandal his second year. He had a not entirely discreet affair with a high-ranking parliamentarian's wife, that much I do know for truth. It was an utter disaster, because while he was sowing and dallying, she fell in love."

"Of course she did," Pamela said, still leafing through the lurid lavender tome and stopping here and there to grasp the nugget of a particularly evocative sentence. "Poor woman."

"Yes," John said with a sigh. "Poor woman, indeed."

"Why are you returning all this? I imagine he gave them to you, didn't he?"

John didn't answer at once, but stared into his whiskey as though deciding what to tell her. When he raised his eyes to meet her own, she saw a weariness in his face that aged him markedly, even in this low light.

"I'm not well and I wanted to be certain that I returned his things to him just in case something should happen. You know how people come picking like corbies over a carcass when someone dies. I'd rather that certain papers of Jamie's weren't left vulnerable. I know I can trust you to keep them safe here for him."

"I'm sorry," she said, seeing now what should have been obvious had her worry for Jamie not been so paramount.

"I'm not dying, dear girl, just not well, and with some of the things you'll find in that box, it's better to be safe rather than sorry."

The subtext being, Pamela thought, that the answer to Jamie's disappearance might well lie within those books and papers.

"I don't know where Jamie meets him. I don't know where they go or what they do. I don't know a damn thing and I'm sorely regretting how intransigent I've been all these years on the subject of Andrei."

"Does it still hurt when you see Jamie?"

He smiled and shook his head. "Only when I breathe, dear girl, only when I breathe."

A puzzle piece clicked into place suddenly. *"Gold is his aspect, gold his nature, his love given not...but that I think gold, too,"* she said quietly and saw the answer in John's face.

He replied, however, by quoting Donne. *"I am two fools, I know, for loving, and for saying so in whining poetry.'*

"It's a beautiful book. I keep it at my bedside for those nights when I can't sleep. It's always reminded me of Jamie and now I understand why."

"I didn't trust Andrei, and I made the mistake of telling Jamie that he shouldn't either. Still, I don't think I was wrong, but it drove a bit of a wedge between Jamie and me. There was a coldness in Andrei, a darkness to that fire of which I have spoken that Jamie did not see, or didn't fear as perhaps he should have."

"What do you think it was that drew the two of them together?"

"They were well matched," John said, "in intelligence, in beauty, in madness, two sides of the same coin. Only Andrei is the dark side and Jamie the gold. And Andrei resents the hell out of Jamie for that, only Jamie could never see it. Andrei is a dangerous man, and that's what frightens me most."

"You think he would deliberately cause Jamie harm?"

John took a long moment before answering. "Deliberately? I'm not sure of that—but if harm should come Jamie's way, I don't know how much Andrei would do to prevent it, or to fix the damage afterwards."

"What did your contacts have to say?" she asked, for they had discussed on the phone the means and ways by which they might discreetly trace Jamie's whereabouts.

"My enquiries haven't led me to anything concrete either. As best I can ascertain, the last person to actually lay eyes on Jamie would be the secretary, Robert. There has been verifiable correspondence since then, but as it turns out it was all pre-arranged. It was almost as if Jamie was readying himself to disappear, and didn't want anyone to realize it for a good long time."

"If that is the case—why?" she asked.

"That, my dear girl, is the million dollar question, isn't it? But don't despair, I have contacts, people who have reason to want him found, to whom I can appeal. I do agree with you, though, that it's time we started looking."

She heard a bellow from the kitchen that told her the evening, for her at least, was over. She smiled. "That's my son, I'd better go. It's time I was headed home. I just want to say that though Jamie isn't here, spending time with you has been like having him here for a bit, in spirit if not in body."

He nodded. "And with you as well." He took her hand in his own warm, dry one. "It was nice to speak aloud about him. Thank you, my dear."

She felt a pang leaving him on his own but he seemed a man used to solitude—by choice or otherwise, she did not know. Another bellow from Conor swept all concerns other than those maternal aside, and she left John where he sat, gazing out the study windows into the dark beyond.

John sat alone, watching the fire die to a small glow in the hearth, nursing his drink and allowing himself the luxury of sliding fully into memories of Jamie. It wasn't something he did often. The pain of it became too easily overwhelming, and he found himself living more in that world than in the one that surrounded him.

The memories were more real, more than life itself often was. Memory was the one gift love left behind when it took its burning leave of a man. Memory that one held as carefully as an ancient artifact, for to take it out too often and hold it up to the light would cause it to lose some of its wonder and rarity, and so he did not indulge in this sort of behavior very often.

Talking about it with Pamela had brought up memories both beautiful and awful. In particular the night he had allowed himself to drink until even his judgement had left in disgust. His original intent had been to find oblivion and stay there, wrapped away from the world. But, as had sometimes happened in his past, the whiskey had clarified that which he sought to obliterate and put sharp corners on feelings that he had wanted to dull and misshape. Waiting outside Jamie's door, he had found himself in a state of divine anger.

Jamie hadn't been entirely sober when he found John curled up there, looking and feeling about as dignified as a moldy dormouse on the mat.

"Oh Christ," had been the only salutation Jamie offered him, as though he sensed the tempest stirring in John's thin frame. He had slung him over his shoulder and John's head had been spinning too hard to protest this outrage to his sensibilities.

When Jamie dumped him unceremoniously onto the sofa, his head was already pounding and bitterness was flooding his mouth with a terrible bile. Had the drink given him what he wanted, he wouldn't have said the things that he did, or so he told himself later. And there had been a second, a small flash of an instant, where Jamie's eyes had looked into his and he'd felt his very soul seared within that look. That a mere look should have such power, a look not even of intimacy, without the tempering of tenderness in its scope, swept away the last vestige of caution he might have possessed.

"Why are you as you are? It's as though you were designed to torment me." Even he had known how foolhardy he was being, that the drink was making his jealousy flow upward and outward like a vile wine long past its drinking time. What had he hoped—that he might, in giving voice to these feelings, poison the friendship and leave himself only the emptiness such a draught will leave behind?

"John, leave it be." The patience in Jamie's voice was noticeably thin. Those words, with just a faint edge of anger to them, had been the straw that snapped what little sense he had left. John had begun to berate Andrei, always a chancy proposition. Even the expression on Jamie's face, the elongation of the eyes and the tightening of the mouth that always signaled anger, did not cause him to halt.

He ran down a list of what he felt were Andrei's most egregious faults, knowing how bitter and pathetic he sounded with every word that dripped from his lips. Jamie said nothing, merely allowing him to vent his spleen, though his eyes grew steadily darker throughout the recitation. This maddened John further, causing him to wind up with a snippy, "He exercises excess to the point of self-destruction."

"He's not the only one guilty of that," Jamie said tartly.

He knew Jamie did not mean himself by this, but had been unable to resist the opening, such as he saw it.

"I don't like to see you joining him in his debauchery. It's unseemly."

"Unseemly?" Jamie laughed at that and suddenly John felt every minute of the time he had spent on this earth, as though his age had deluged him, pinning him relentlessly with its dark weight.

"Yes, unseemly. Above we mere mortals as the two of you are, still some rules do apply."

"You forgive me the excess, why can't you forgive it in him?"

"Because, dear James, quite simply, I am not in love with Andrei."

"Oh," he said, and John felt the sharp sting of an answer that had been too quick to hide the dismay.

"Oh," John echoed back with no small bitterness. "Oh—I see. It's alright, dear boy. I know that your tastes do not run to old, failed, alcoholic professors. Had I been prepared… had I known…" he shook his head, a lock of grey hair falling in his eye. "But no, one cannot prepare for James Kirkpatrick because one cannot quite imagine that such a person, such a beautiful, brilliant bastard exists. So I'm not really to blame then am I, Jamie?"

Jamie had sat down opposite him, rubbing his face with his hands. More in an effort, John suspected, to give him a moment to compose himself than anything else.

"John, please—you're a very dear friend, and that is all I can ever offer you—friendship. That will have to be enough."

But the burden of admission had only stirred the poison in John's chest and once the spill had started, he found he had neither will nor want to stop it. So he turned, as he often had, to poetry to tell his anguish.

> *"TWICE or thrice had I loved thee,*
> *Before I knew thy face or name ;*
> *So in a voice, so in a shapeless flame*
> *Angels affect us oft, and worshipp'd be."*

"Oh Lord," Jamie said with some exasperation, "not Donne already. You usually wait a few hours into your agony to quote him. I am not an angel, John, merely a man."

"Oh no, dear boy, you are an angel and placed amongst us mere humans to torment us. You and Andrei both, fiery angels burning everything and everyone in your vicinity. But Andrei's flame burns far colder than yours, dear Jamie. Go wary there, my dear boy, go wary."

"I think I can exercise enough judgement to choose my friends. Which is, perhaps, more than we can say for you tonight."

"What is that supposed to mean?"

Jamie sighed in the manner of a man sorely tried. "John, what if some-one else had come upon you in this condition? This is utter madness. You could lose your position. I don't want to be the reason for this behavior, for these feelings."

"And yet, you are," John said, wishing his voice would fail him, that the words would stop up and stay buried where they could not do the damage he saw forming in Jamie's eyes.

"John, you can't make me responsible for your loneliness."

"Loneliness?" He laughed, but it was laughter that held no humor. "I've been more alone since I met you than I ever was before."

And then Jamie had done the thing that made John love him forever. Instead of reviling him as he had expected and had half desired, Jamie walked over, bent down, and kissed him gently on the forehead as one would a be-loved friend, and then had taken his leave. Only the scent of angels lingered behind—that particular scent of love and heartbreak, the one John could smell even in sleep, half waking from pained dreams of things that were never meant to be. The scent that made him curse God for making him love a man who could never return his love in the one way he wished.

They had gone on after that as though nothing had changed, but of course it had. In an odd way, it had strengthened their friendship, as though the admission had been a film between them before and now that it had been spoken, the glass had been wiped clean and there was no longer anything to avoid. The love had not gone away despite the confession, and over the years it had become a banked fire that warmed him and that he no longer resented. It had become his friend, for despite the pain this love had often caused him, despite the sleepless nights and the partners who were never quite what he wanted, despite all this... the thought of Jamie no longer being in this world left him breathless with an agony he knew he would take to his grave should it prove to be fact.

He was not a fool though, and he knew enough of Soviet Russia to understand the risk Jamie took by crossing that border each year. He also envied the love that took Jamie there, despite the danger.

He had been entirely honest with Pamela. He did not trust Andrei, not back then, not now. And so, that it should be Andrei who had drawn Jamie far across the world to a place where neither mercy nor love had a home, where there was no sanctuary in the heart of man... well, it made him breathless with fury. He had always worried that Jamie's friendship with Andrei would end up costing him his life. At present, he was worried it had done exactly that.

And yet—wouldn't he know if Jamie were dead? Wouldn't the clocks have stopped, the world have tilted on its axis and the dogs, in the words of that old bugger Auden, have ceased to bark? And if he were dead, how was it that the stars still twinkled mercilessly in the sky? Did they not know they were not wanted any longer? And if Jamie was gone, why did his heart still beat on, dumbly, like a beast that did not know to lay its yoke aside and crumble into the soil where at least it would find respite?

It was irresponsible to love an angel. They were bound to break one's soul in their passing. It was simply in the nature of angels to do so and they could not be held to blame for the results.

John had traversed around the study in his agitation and found himself halted in front of a picture of Jamie and Andrei, young, golden and immortal, daring the world to challenge them. Oh, the fragile and fleeting glory of youth. It was enough to break a man's heart many times over. Further along the wall there was a picture of himself from his first visit here to Jamie's home, a happy fortnight in a beautiful Irish autumn, the cares lifted from his face, if not the lines.

He took a swallow of his whiskey, the fire of it welcome as it burned all the way down his gullet. Above, the night was dark and heartless, and a great stillness had enveloped the house. Even the fire had gone cold, leaving only a phantom wisp of peat smoke in its wake.

He looked back at the picture of Jamie—that beautiful, bright flame could not be doused, for surely he would know, for surely he would die had such light been stolen. He touched the cool glass over that laughing face and found himself quoting Donne again. Bloody John Donne who had understood far, far too much about love's dark underbelly.

The day breaks not, it is my heart.

"Only my heart," John said and saluted Jamie's picture with the night's last swallow of whiskey.

Part Three

Down the Rabbithole
Russia – February 1973

Chapter Twenty-two
February 1973
The Package

ON THE RIM OF THE WORLD'S EDGE, A MESSENGER STOOD, weary and caked in snow like a shroud. He had been sent to fetch a man, and the description of his target made him less than enthusiastic about entering the premises where he was meant to find him.

"You won't be able to miss him. Hair like guinea gold, a bastard's grin on his face. He's likely to be the center of a circle of admirers he's leading merrily toward a night of debauchery such as they won't recover from soon, if ever. Oh," the man instructing him had paused and grinned, revealing a scar in the pocket of his right cheek and a gold tooth, "he's likely to have a girl on his knee as well. A beautiful one."

The messenger had voiced his doubts on the likelihood of a beautiful girl being found under the fur wraps and knee high boots of the natives in this godforsaken country. The other man, the Captain, gold tooth winking obscenely, said, "If there's one within a thousand square miles, she'll be on his knee, trust me."

"You know him yourself?" he had asked the man, a notorious sea dog with a reputation for ruthlessness and a peerless record for smuggling black market goods past the Iron Curtain.

"Yes," the Captain said with a bit of a wince. "He left me with these souvenirs last time we met," his tobacco-stained fingers split into a 'v', pointing to both scar and golden tooth.

The messenger quailed a little inside at the thought of the man who had the nerve, or idiocy, to knock the Captain's teeth out and leave him with a scar the length of a Cuban cigar, and wondered, not for the first time, what he had done to deserve this task? It was rumored that the man who had been assigned to fetch 'the package' last year woke up on a fur rug, naked, in the home of a toothless Laplander widow, with no memory of the previous three days. Such things did not go down well with the Soviet command to whom he was indentured. Even if he was already assigned to the ass-end of the Empire's postings, he was painfully aware of how much worse his own situation could get should he fail in his assignment.

Nevertheless, however monstrous 'the package' was, it was preferable to facing the wrath of Comrade Andrei Alexseyovich Valueve—a more icy, controlled and nasty bastard may he never meet.

He sighed, breathed in a small dancing vortex of snow and strode with as much courage and Russian stiff-spinedness as he could muster, buried as he was inside a wool greatcoat and stiff Army issue boots that came to his knees. He was aware of looking rather Yeti-like, though the fashion demands of a tavern located in one of the outer circles of a frozen hell weren't terribly high.

Vasily, which was the soldier's name, stamped his feet, shook snow from his fine dark hair and looked around the tavern. A more disreputable gang of thieves, pirates, and scoundrels it would have been hard to find, even given unlimited travel and time. A frozen hole at the end of the world, the wee village had one thing going in its favor, a narrow glut of water feeling with stoney fingers into the land. Due to the Atlantic current that washed across the headlands, this did not freeze in the winters. Hence, this collection of shacks, a church and a tavern was the way station for a group of international travelers of a very distinct class.

Vasily swallowed nervously. As accustomed as he was to vagabonds and crooks and all the other riff-raff that tried consistently to cross borders without papers, this crew looked more alarming than most.

The tavern reeked of wet herring-scaled wool and he saw in a blur the red-furred jaws of Norwegians, always among the world's toughest and most practical of seamen, the high flat-planed faces of the Laplander, the milk-skin of the Finn, and heard the dipping vowels and harsh-cut consonants of Slavic speakers. They eyed him with open hostility, but this did not concern him, for outside the borders of his own country he was aware the image of the Soviet soldier was not a flattering one.

He went to the bar and asked politely for vodka. He needed the warmth of it, and also the clarity it induced for anyone with Russian blood. When the taciturn barman, a squat specimen who looked at him as though he were measuring him for a rug, put a bottle of Kossu on the bar, Vasily took it and sat on a rickety chair as far away from the main body of drinkers as he could manage.

He looked over each man in the tavern in turn, no easy task, for the lighting was one bare bulb hanging fly-caked from the ceiling and supplemented only by a fire in the hearth and a couple of oil lamps flickering behind the bar. Still, there was no man answering to the description the Captain had given him. He sighed and took the cap off the Kossu.

His eye was drawn to a group off in the far corner, tucked away behind a filthy creosote post. It was a small group, but one man had a flamboyantly green and red parrot on one shoulder that kept repeating something over and over in what Vasily thought was Spanish. The shoulder the parrot sat upon was broad with muscle and covered in well worn oilskin, a fisherman from the set of him, and hair a pale gold above the ratty collar. Vasily perked up. Could this be the man?

With him sat three other men: a Laplander with his furs puddled around his hips and a look of furrowed confusion on his big face that said he had been drinking for some time; a short grizzled Finn with the callused hands of a long-liner; and a dark, greasy looking man with a wool cap squashed down over his head and a winter's worth of dirt worked into every line and crevice of him. Some sort of disagreement was brewing at the table, a dispute over the cards they each held. The man in the wool cap had tipped over the bottle of vodka that stood in the middle of the table in a brutish gesture of hostility toward the big blond man, and then slapped his cards out of his hand. The blond giant stood and slapped the table so hard the sound reported like a gunshot. It was a mark of the toughness of the tavern's clientele that they barely flicked an eye in the direction of imminent violence.

The woolen cap of the fisherman bobbed, his words delivered with force and apparent insult, for the big Swede backed up, fists balling in fury. Vasily was certain the big man was Swedish, for from the side he looked like a snow-cloaked Viking with that fastidious air so many of his countrymen seemed to be born with.

The fisherman was a Finn. Vasily recognized a few words even through the slurring. A drunken Finn—well, they never had been able to hold their drink like a Russian could—drunk and losing money like a cod sieve, if he understood the insults that were flying thick and furious. The lack of dignity was what appalled him. Even the louts in this place were watching the grubby creature with distaste. The Swede slapped the filthy Finn, knocking him off his chair.

Curled up on the floor like a wool-clogged shrimp, the fisherman spat at the Swede and said something in Swedish that to Vasily's ear sounded like a very discourteous statement about the man's mother. However, his Swedish was limited so it was just as likely that he had said something about a moose and a goat. Still, from the great roar that was now issuing from the Swede, Vasily thought perhaps he'd been right in his first assumption.

The big Swede grabbed the other man by the tatty collar of his navy peacoat and shook him to his feet before batting him away with a hand the size of a dinner plate. The fisherman's legs windmilled backwards, and in a vain effort to keep his balance, he upset the table and the parrot, knocked burning wood into the room, and lifted the fur hat off the Laplander before landing, with no small impact, in Vasily's lap.

The parrot was shrieking obscenities that were somehow translatable from any language, without necessarily needing to know the exact organs to which the person, or parrot, as it were, was referring. The fisherman patted Vasily's face, eyes bleared with drink and muzzy confusion.

Vasily curled his nose up in distaste. The man smelled as though he'd been soaked in a vat of Kossu for several days and then left to dry in a barrel of herring. He shoved at him, certain the smell would be impossible to remove from his greatcoat.

The man fell to the floor, a stinking heap, mumbling to himself in a polyglot of languages that Vasily could make neither head nor tail of. He was a pitiful creature, and Vasily, a soft-hearted boy at his core stood, and with a grunt of disgust helped the crabbed fisherman to his feet. Oddly, he was a good deal taller than Vasily had originally thought, and somewhat more straight-bodied. Seen up close he appeared younger, the dirt more of a smear than an actual settling into creases.

The fisherman smiled at him, revealing a set of teeth that were startlingly white and straight. Vasily began to get an uneasy feeling. Just then, a doe-eyed girl walked past him, skin aglow against her white furs like a night-bloomed peach. She glanced at him with a slow, fluid smile that made his knees want to drop in worshipful prayer, though like most good little Soviet boys the only god he was familiar with was Josef Stalin. He got a funny feeling at the nape of his neck, a small prickling that told him somewhere amongst this motley and filthy crew, was his quarry. But where? The girl was his only clue that the package was actually in the vicinity, because certainly she wasn't here with any of these brutes. Strange, but she was looking back over her shoulder now, as if beckoning him over.

Later he would blame the vodka, for after all the vodka wasn't likely to refute the accusation and he couldn't think of any other reason that he would agree to accompany the filthy fisherman into the sauna, housed in a small building out back of the tavern. That and the fisherman. When asked if he was aware whether a man with golden hair and a reputation for being a bit of a bastard was anywhere in the vicinity, he had assured Vasily that this man was one he knew but who wasn't likely to appear until the sun had disappeared into the sea.

"Why to seek him?" the fisherman had asked in extremely mangled Russian. "This is very bad man you are finding, young friend." He gave Vasily a look of pity that hadn't done a great deal to shore up Vasily's shaky spine.

"Come, we will sweat the poisons out while you wait for this…" the fisherman spat as though ridding his mouth of a vile poison, "…bastard." His new friend then all but dragged him by the lapels of his coat out back. Vasily felt a small trickle of unease but the alcohol had relieved him of actually paying attention to the feeling. Also, being Russian, he firmly believed in a sauna as a cure for almost all the bodily and mental ills the world could inflict upon a man.

The low-roofed hut looked as if a good wind would send it scuttling straight out into the frigid embrace of the Barents Sea. He eyed the sun still hovering on the horizon. He would have time to steam and go back into the tavern to await the package.

Inside, the hut was lathe and plaster, with a low roof and steam so thick that he couldn't find his own hand once the door was shut behind them. It clogged his lungs and lent a torpor to his head that increased the effect of the Kossu exponentially.

The fisherman could talk, that much was clear. Not that Vasily, neatly folding his uniform and placing it on a bench in the tiny vestibule, could follow much of what he said. He had a feeling it wasn't necessary and that the man would chatter glibly no matter whether his audience listened or not.

Vasily clambered up to the top of the two-tiered bench and settled himself against the wall. The fisherman handed him a bottle, his hand disembodied so that Vasily giggled, for it looked as though the bottle were floating to him out of the fog, a Russian dream come to life. He leaned back after several lusty swallows, allowing the vodka to lubricate his every cell. Later, he would think he must have drifted into a short sleep, for he had no recollection of the fisherman leaving. Yet leave he must have, for when Vasily next noticed, the fisherman was nowhere to be found though streams of dirt were running down to the floor, testifying to his recent occupation of the seat beside Vasily. With senses severely impaired by the litre of Kossu, Vasily felt little cat feet run up his spine and then he sensed a presence in the sauna that felt in no way benign.

He glared blearily through the steam and saw someone with hair slicked to his head in translucent streams of guinea gold and skin that had recently drunk sun in quantities not found in this hemisphere. He peered through the steam, the Kossu settling in sweet pools in all his joints, muscles and senses. A pair of eyes, cutting as viridescent steel, looked back at him. Somewhere far down inside his brain an alarm bell rang, but the tinny sound was quickly submerged in the river of vodka that kept emerging hospitably from the steam.

"You do know the old Finnish drinking game, don't you?"

One part of his mind noted with surprise that he was now addressed in flawless and stone-cracking Russian.

"*Nyet*," he said, the word acquiring the length of several slippery syllables in its traverse over his tongue.

"It goes like this—three Finns go into a sauna with a half litre of Kossu each, one leaves and the other two have to guess who left. Got it?"

"*Da*." He wiped a trickle of sweat from his cheek and was vaguely worried that he couldn't feel his fingers on his face until he realized he still had his mittens on. This in itself was worrying because he didn't remember putting them back on after removing his uniform.

"The advanced version goes like this—two men enter a sauna with a half litre of vodka each, they drink the vodka and one leaves, and the one left behind has to guess who left. So guess which one of us left," the voice said, floating disembodied through the steam.

Vasily scratched his face again, mittens sodden with Kossu and steam... and another scent... peaches or limes or something that he couldn't quite locate in his memory.

"I don't know your name," he said plaintively, feeling put upon by this game that he didn't understand. Silence greeted him through the steam.

"*Skazheete pozhluista*, (can you tell me please)" he said, with the inbred politeness that came of having far too many superiors in one's life. Still silence, and he moved over on the bench unsteadily, only to be jerked back unceremoniously by his mittens which appeared to be attached to a long set of threads that wove like an inebriated spider all over the small room. His inebriated state, however, made it imperative to follow each thread singly to its ultimate destination. This endeavor took some time, until finally the last thread led to the door of the sauna. But the door wouldn't move. It too seemed to be threaded shut in some ingeniously perverse fashion. He thought sinkingly of the messenger from last year and the year's worth of Siberian potatoes he had peeled.

Putting a shoulder to the plastered wall, he found it disturbingly solid. A small thrum of panic rose in his stomach though the Kossu was still numbing most of his bits into stoic acceptance. He rushed the door but his slippery flesh slid off with little effect. Still, he had the innate stubbornness of his forebears who had been farmers in the Ukraine for several generations.

He heard the roar of the UAZ and gave one last frantic rush on the door, which gave suddenly like a hot knife through butter and he shot out, naked as a cherub, into the blue banks of snow in time to see a man turn and wave at him—a man with guinea gold hair and a bastard's smile on his face. A man who wore the perfectly groomed uniform of a Soviet Red Army soldier, winter greatcoat and all. Vasily noted furiously that it looked better on the bastard than it did on him.

With a heart already lurking in the region of his appendix, he noted the doe-eyed stunner, furs framing her peachy face, blowing him a kiss from the passenger's seat before the jeep tore off in a spray of Finnish snow.

Beside him, the big Swede waved to the jeep, a broad grin on his face.

"You know him?" Vasily asked in the passable bit of Swedish he had learned during his Army training.

"*Ja*, is Jamie—I know him many years—he is—how to say—madman."

He noted then how cold his feet were and the interest with which several pairs of fishermen's eyes gazed upon his bare behind. Pulling together what dignity could be found nude and shorn of both his uniform and vehicle, he turned, pulled the threads of his unraveled mittens to him, and carefully bunching them over the area that was taking greatest offense at the cold, he walked back into the tavern, certain that anything was better than telling the Captain he'd failed. There wasn't, Vasily thought with sudden dark clarity, enough fucking Kossu in a glacier to make that palatable.

Chapter Twenty-three
The Dacha in the Woods

SEVERAL HOURS LATER, WHILE VASILY SLEPT CURLED UP in an Astrakhan rug in front of the tavern fire, the chancy bastard who had stolen his jeep and his clothing was pulling up to a long, low-eaved dacha heavy with snow and ice, his lips still tasting sweetly of peaches and vodka. Whether this cabin was on the Soviet or Finnish side of the border was debatable. He was in favor of it being on the Russian side because the stars here were closer to the ground and that seemed to him a Russian state of being. Cold beauty, seemingly within reach, but in truth not anywhere within the grasp of a man at all.

Russia—the very name was a dark, rich perfume upon his tongue. He had never been able to bring himself to call this country by its official name of the Union of Soviet Socialist Republics. No, she was Russia, indomitable and cruel, much like the nature of her own people. She was mysterious, dark, and unfathomable: from the far west where the city of St. Petersburg still hung like a sugar-spun fairytale of European architecture, European manners and European decay, a city of water, stone and sky, Russia's own Venice; to the east, Kiev, its outlines laid down in white marble and etched upon the skies in airy domes, so beautifully constructed they seemed like teacups awaiting the discerning tongues of angels on high to drink their exotic depths.

The Russians themselves were descended from the great horse warlords with their scythe-like cheekbones and ice-blue eyes. To the far north, with its vast, dark forests, tracts of which no man had ever walked within nor touched upon, was the land of fable, of Baba Yaga and the Firebird, the land of the sweeping amber-skinned hordes of Ghengis Khan... Siber, the very name conjuring icy steppes and dark-eyed women in wind-torn furs.

The armies of Ghengis Khan had numbered in the tens of thousands, men feared from one ocean to the other for their famed indestructibility. Neither hunger, nor cold, nor mighty Russian princes stood against them, the reach of their hooked swords extending from the frozen tundra to the warm-blooded waters of the Black Sea. They had shaped the modern body of Russia.

Ah, yes, the vast bloody, beautiful, terrible body of Mother Russia. No mother had ever been less nurturing to her children. She had succored her young on blood from the very beginnings of human memory. Never more so than now, with the heartless steel of the Soviet Empire and all its tin soldiers illustrating her might and fury. James Kirkpatrick stood in the cold embrace of her harlot's heart and knew himself ten kinds of fool for keeping this meeting as he did each year. Each year the risk of something going very badly awry increased, and he often felt his luck running down like a rope of sand, leaving little to which to cling.

But Russia gave him perspective. She was so huge, so brutal, so layered in history, beauty, terror and blood. So like Ireland, and yet nothing like it at all. For Russia owed nothing to the Western mindset. The Russian mind was inscrutable, owing to neither East nor West for its philosophy and way of viewing the universe. Russia was Russian, and could not be defined by the tenets of the rest of the world. She was a fact, a great dark Mother, whose mind and soul was slippery and often not understood even by her own.

"Yasha." A voice, strong, commanding, yet filled with a remembered laughter, came to him out of the snow and the dark.

There were only two people on the face of the planet who called him Yasha. One had been partly responsible for raising him, the other stood here now, outlined in the dark against the blowing pines. He had met Andrei Alekseyevich Valueve when they were both eighteen years old. They had three years of sublime friendship in which both were lucky to emerge with limbs and spirits intact. Since then this was all they were allowed, one night a year here near the Finnish border in a low log house whose eaves hung heavy with ice and pine boughs that scraped the roof.

"Andrushya," he replied, voice carrying quietly through the delicate spirals of snow that danced around the two of them.

They stood thus for a moment, Andrei Valueve's guards a dim blur behind him, the six feet of snow separating Jamie and his dearest friend filled with a wealth of memory and regret.

Then Andrei, always and in all essentials Russian, stepped forward to clasp Jamie in a bear hug which Jamie returned with equal ferocity. Emotion engulfed the men, from the sheer relief of seeing each other alive, and reassuring themselves that all nightmares could be woken from, even if both were very aware that such things were seldom true in the waking world.

"How is our soldier-boy? Have you left him in a brothel or afloat on an iceberg in the Arctic Ocean?"

"He was alive when I left him," Jamie said, his grin a flash of impudent white in the sea-darkened visage. "He's more scared of you than anything, so be a nice boy, Andrei, and take care of him."

"I will, just as I always do." He grinned back at Jamie, their shared history all around them suddenly thick with the memories of adventures that had often bordered on madness. "Now come inside before we freeze our *yaeechkas* off."

The dacha belonged to a friend of Andrei's but was never used except for this one night each year. Some mysterious person readied it for them so there was no creeping damp or ice-coated windows, rather a warm, snug interior filled with rugs and heavy furniture, food and drink for the night and the following morning and of course, a chessboard.

Inside, they shed their heavy coats, boots and hats, and turned to assess one another.

"Still the prettiest bastard on the face of the planet, excepting myself," Andrei said and flashed the white grin that had charmed any number of women out of their clothes and senses.

"I do my best," Jamie replied and grinned in return, the tension starting to leak out of him.

Jamie pulled two bottles of Connemara Mist from Vasily's great coat and handed one to Andrei. The other he gave to Andrei's guards, old soldiers who would welcome the whiskey's fire in their bellies and joints, especially on a frigid night such as this one. He always brought a few bottles because it bought them privacy for at least part of the night.

Andrei disappeared into the kitchen, giving Jamie a minute to look around and catch his breath.

Andrei returned with a tray that held caviar and thinly-sliced black bread, two glasses and a bottle of vodka.

"Let us sit and eat and drink—but most importantly, let us play." He put the tray down beside the chessboard and rubbed his hands in anticipation of the night ahead.

The chessboard was Andrei's, a beautiful confection of Baltic amber squares interspersed with onyx. The entire thing shone like a mirror and weighed close to forty pounds, heavy enough that no one thought to notice a few extra ounces.

Jamie sat and leaned back in the chair, stretching his legs while Andrei poured them each a generous measure of vodka. He took the glass from Andrei and sighed in anticipation. It did not disappoint. The vodka was smooth, near frozen, gelled to perfection, creamy with the silk of silver birch coal in its under notes. Andrei always brought him a bottle of this, the only alcohol he drank these days.

There was at first a mellow quality to the evening, the light from the fire flickering drowsily, and the old camaraderie between the two of them present enough to form a third entity in the room, a troika of memory and affection.

"Do you hear from Colleen these days?" Andrei asked lightly. Too lightly.

"No, but she is well and, I think, happy now."

"And what of you my friend, are you happy now too?"

"Near enough," Jamie said, "and you?"

"Near enough," Andrei replied, with only the slightest undertone of mockery. He took a swallow of his vodka after moving his bishop into a confrontation with Jamie's knight and eyed Jamie speculatively. "So, what is her name?"

Jamie looked up sharply. "Was I talking about a woman?"

Andrei nodded, blue eyes remarkably sober. "Yes, I think you were."

Jamie looked down at the board with his hand tight around the glass of vodka. "Her name," he replied after a strung silence, "is Pamela." He noted with annoyance that Andrei's face was alight with interest. It meant that he was about to ask uncomfortable questions. Questions Jamie had no desire to answer.

"I am going to just say this, and then I don't want to talk about her anymore. She's married to another man. She loves him and anything beyond friendship is impossible between us, and even friendship has become insupportable."

"Does she love you?"

"Obviously not," Jamie said. "She's married."

It was Andrei's turn to raise an eyebrow. "Where the heart is concerned there is nothing obvious at all, and so I'll ask again, does she love you?"

"Yes, I suppose she does, but it's irrelevant, isn't it?"

"Love is never irrelevant," Andrei said, and his tone alerted Jamie to the fact that they weren't really talking about his own love life, or rather, the lack of it.

"You sound like a romantic, Andrei, not a state you've been bothered by before, so now tell me—what is *her* name?"

Andrei laughed. "Her name is Violet."

"And what of your Ilena and the girls?"

"They are well looked after. Ilena does not know, and so it need not matter."

Jamie leaned forward, rolling his glass in his hands, casually surveying the room to make certain the guards could not overhear.

"Are you mad, telling me this here?" he asked, easing his grip on the tumbler for fear of shattering it.

"Yes, I'm mad, completely and entirely mad, like a March hare."

Every year he waited for the words, every year he waited for Andrei to tip his queen into the waste ground and tell him he was ready to escape. And every year he left with fear in his heart that next year at their appointed time, Andrei would not appear because Andrei would be dead.

It was a terrible game the two of them played, choreographed down to a dance whose moves were meaningful on several levels, for each move told a very specific story. Each move telegraphed information to the player across the board, who must never let his concentration falter lest he miss a subtlety. At all times, they kept up a seemingly relaxed patter, a strain in itself. But they had perfected a sharp and stinging banter long ago which always held in its under notes a far more serious conversation.

It had started as a lark, something that Andrei's acrobatic mathematical mind found amusing. Code was in his blood, both the formation of it and the unlocking. Jamie's mind, equally nimble, had taken each challenge thrown at him by Andrei. Challenges that often involved great physical risk and acts that were definitely outside the boundaries of law.

To this particular game they had added the quote as the key that unlocked the interior door to their shared history. Now here, a long way past those two schoolboys, Jamie waited and then his heart stopped for a moment for Andrei, still chatting as though he hadn't a worry in the world, had tipped over his queen. Jamie smiled and said something inconsequential through lips that were frozen with sudden panic.

Andrei's eyes met his, the blue flame in them glowing as though cupped in a dark hand. There was a smile on his face, but it wasn't one that reassured. As though there had been no halt in their conversation, Andrei said,

"I am, of course, *mad as the mist and snow*, but what else would you expect of a Russian?"

Many years ago, when they had worked out their code on paper and then burned it, each piece, according to its movements, had several meanings. The queen, tipped over in this fashion and coupled with the quote meant only one thing—'I am ready.' Ready to leave Russia, ready for the plan to go into effect. He wondered suddenly what had changed, what had finally tipped Andrei into defection from a country that he both loved and hated in equal measure. The woman? Could that be it? There was no doubt something had changed immeasurably since last year.

Sitting here still, drinking his vodka, was akin to free-falling down a mountainside and being expected not to react. Andrei was apparently studying the board with great concentration, yet the queen still lay upon her side as though he had merely knocked her over accidentally and forgotten to pick her up.

Jamie said something. He wasn't even sure what, for adrenaline was hammering in his ears like the roar of the ocean breaking against a rocky shore.

With Andrei's words, the last piece fell into place. The Yeats quotation was one they had agreed upon years ago on a mad night when they had nearly died.

How many years ago were you and I unlettered lads

Mad as the mist and snow?

Jamie sat barely breathing, for he had long ago despaired of ever hearing those words cross Andrei's lips. Coupled with the tipped queen it could only mean one thing—there would be no time for planning. They would have to go tomorrow.

They played through to the end of the game. They had to, there was no choice with eyes upon them. Jamie focused on the game as well as he was able, sipping his vodka and allowing Andrei to re-fill the glass twice. Andrei won the game, though narrowly. Afterward, they made a show of sleepiness and bid the guards a formal goodnight.

Andrei hugged him as he always did at any parting, no matter how brief. "*Spokoinoi nochi,*Yasha." Good night, Jamie. And so to bed with a million unanswered questions ricocheting around in his head.

"*Spokoinoi nochi,*" he replied, voice relaxed and tired. It was an effort to appear unconcerned, to move easily, to stretch and tell Andrei he would beat him tomorrow at yet another game. It would be a miracle if the guards didn't simply sense the tension that strummed the air, tight as the strings of a violin.

He readied himself for sleep but kept his day clothes on, his boots by the side of the bed so that he could slip them on at a second's notice. The room was small, the bed a narrow one but comfortable and warm, the latter quality being the virtue that mattered most in this country.

He lay on the bed, blind to the low, dark-timbered ceiling, heart still thumping hard, adrenaline running like a steeplechase through his blood, and thought about the path that had led the two of them to this night.

On the other side of the wall, another man remembered, his boots by his bed, his heart in his throat.

Like two stars burning in opposition, it was inevitable that Andrei Alekseyevich Valueve and James Stuart Kirkpatrick, existing within such a small galaxy as Oxford, were going to collide. It was just as inevitable that the resulting smash would be seen for miles around.

Andrei Alekseyevich was a genius, one of the new mathematicians known as ambidextrous for his facility in both pure and applied mathematics. Genius at Oxford wasn't entirely rare, but Andrei had that extra facet—the divine spark of intuition that illuminated his mind with a light like that of a dying star—incandescent and burning, and as surely as the heavens were distant, it set him apart. As did the fact that he was Russian and would be emerging from behind the Iron Curtain, a rarity granted only by his father's stature in the Communist Party.

Andrei, entirely comfortable with the status his genius, his looks and his

White Russian ancestry had bestowed upon him from birth, was less comfortable about sharing his bit of the stratosphere with a man similarly endowed. Granted, James Kirkpatrick was the darling of the English department and wasn't infringing upon the sacred ground of Andrei's discipline. Still, he was managing to make his presence known and felt.

Standing six feet in his stockings, with a shock of white-blond hair and the high imperious cheekbones of his Slavic forebears, Andrei had long been able to take for granted his pull on the opposite sex. Add to this his genius and natural charm and he had never had to brook competition of any sort. Enter James Kirkpatrick.

By the end of his first week at Oxford, he had heard the man's name mentioned six times and found his interest piqued. By the tenth mention he was feeling slightly annoyed: by the twelfth he decided he had to seek the man out for himself. He dropped a casual word and had himself invited to a country weekend in Surrey where he knew Jamie Kirkpatrick was also to be a guest.

Their initial meeting, it could be fairly said, did not go well. At first Andrei had been suitably impressed, for James Kirkpatrick was indeed and in a word—gorgeous. He also proved to be witty and quite funny, for he had the entire drawing room in stitches with his stories. That he was brilliant was in no doubt. Andrei felt grateful to the gods that it was in a useless discipline such as English, and not in a field that mattered, such as mathematics or physics.

Andrei had been holding court in the library of the country house, a group of mathematics scholars clustered around him as he showed them a proof on which he was working. At some point, Jamie Kirkpatrick had joined the ring of fascinated faces, sitting casually cross-legged on the Turkish carpet, a look of intense interest on his face that informed Andrei the Irishman actually understood the proof as he'd scratched it out on the paper. Andrei sniffed, for few people had the sort of facility with mathematics that he had. In all of history there had been a golden string of mathematicians, rarely more than one or two to a generation, to which line he belonged.

The golden head had inclined over the paper on which Andrei had roughed out his theory and while other faces were suitably impressed, this one was not. The green eyes elongated in thought, the mouth drawn in an inscrutable line. Andrei was irritated. He did not trust people who were not suitably impressed.

"I think," said the voice, which was also completely lacking in awe, "you'll find that if you take this step out, you can come to the same conclusion much more quickly."

*The bastard, for this is how Andrei was now thinking of him, scrawled the same formula below, took out the step he had pointed out and added in two other components. The proof was indeed solved, though the arrogant **svoloch** could not be bothered to write in the answer, he simply left it blank for Andrei to fill in himself.*

Andrei suddenly wished dueling wasn't out of fashion. Had Jamie been a mathematician himself, Andrei would have received it in the spirit intended, as one mathematical mind easing the path of another. Mathematics was often a collaborative effort, with a free flow of ideas leading to an inevitable conclusion.

But to have an English major show one the flaw in a problem, to have the insufferable gall to make him look a fool in front of all those people... well, that wasn't to be countenanced. And yet, after the man left, Andrei had seen what he meant and that he'd merely made one of those intuitive leaps that set great minds apart from good. Suddenly he regretted his absence, but the man, like quicksilver, had disappeared from the premises. Andrei though, was quite certain they would meet again. He felt it inevitable, and Russians were great believers in the inevitable.

WHEN THEY DID COLLIDE, IT WAS TO BE ON THE FIELD with horses and great whacking mallets, and if it was not heard for miles, it was certainly seen by several hundred people.

'Let other people play at other things—the King of Games is still the Game of Kings.'

Polo had been the game of choice for Persian princes, Chinese emperors and dark-eyed Mughals. Therefore it was a sport that Andrei played, for he was as royal as Russian blood allowed in such times as he found himself.

His team, clad in scarlet jerseys, trotted out onto the field. It was a warm day and the sun glittered off the expensive cars parked behind the stands, stands which were filled with glorious English girls. Andrei inclined his head at a particularly sumptuous redhead, who flushed a lovely pink in response. He would have to remember her for later.

The opposing team wore emerald green shirts, and when James Kirkpatrick rode out, it was in the position of the number three man on the team. Andrei's own position. It required one to be the most skilled player, for the third man was the team's playmaker, setting up the shots for other players, hitting in the long balls, and taking the penalty shots and knock-ins.

Andrei knew a natural horseman when he saw one and had to admit that he was looking at one now. He had seen him earlier sitting upon his horse like a King, relaxed, chatting with the inevitable girls who seemed to gather and turn their pretty faces up at him as would delicate cupped flowers toward the sun. There had been a cluster of girls around his own horse, though not, he thought irritably, quite so large a cluster. The man was seriously starting to annoy him.

Jamie Kirkpatrick rode a chestnut mare sixteen hands high with a gleaming coat and form that said she was both well exercised and well fed. Andrei's own mount was a sturdy steppe pony, fourteen and a half hands at the withers and a descendant of those tough little horses upon which the Mongol hordes had conquered the Eastern world.

James Kirkpatrick rode as though he'd been born on horseback, for the horse checked and swerved like water parting around reefs and shoals, with no more than a slight movement of the man's hands or a whisper low to the pretty mare's head. Andrei rode just as well, for he had trained on the wide open steppes of the Ukraine without a saddle or bridle, and had learned the hard way how to control a horse with muscle and will, how to coax the best from the animal, and how to become a part of the flow and stretch so that one no longer knew which was oneself and which was horse.

The first chukka consisted of the two teams getting a feel for the other. Andrei even managed to eke out a goal. It was hard won, for the Irish bastard played a hard opposition and gave absolutely no quarter. He was damn good, but that was fine by Andrei because he was quite certain he was better. By the end of the first chukka, he was no longer feeling quite so superior. He had been ruthlessly checked, and he was of the mind that the ball was somehow magnetized to that bastard's stick. Still, his goal remained the only one.

First chukka down, five to go.

Andrei started the second chukka in high humor. His horse was warmed up now and prancing under him with barely restrained energy. They were up one point and his blood was thrumming in a most pleasant manner through his veins.

His humor did not last long. The play in the second chukka was brutal, but this Andrei did not mind. It was that bastard James Kirkpatrick that had him riled.

He turned in the saddle, only to the find the bastard on his left flank, going like fury. The next thing he knew was a sharp knock and scrape that felt like his head was being re-positioned in an ungentle manner and his helmet was gone. He raised his stick ready to smack the bastard, only to find he was gone in a sleek ripple of emerald silks. Andrei kicked his pony's sides and tore after him, though the demon was partway across the field with Andrei's helmet no longer in hand.

For Andrei's helmet was currently soaring in a glorious parabola, high up into the sun and then came down, mud and all, into the silken lap of a brunette with good teeth. The crowd roared with laughter and Andrei felt a surge of pure Russian fury ice his veins. Then the crowd was roaring in approval for the man had flown upfield and knocked the ball in from half a length of the course away while the rest of the players were distracted by the sailing helmet.

The man smiled and removed his own helmet, his golden hair wet and gleaming as sunflowers. He tossed it into the stands where the curvy redhead who had drawn Andrei's eye earlier caught it with a smile that bespoke a wealth of promises, none of them polite.

It was mad to play without helmets. A ball in the temple was certain death. The play ought to have been stopped but it was a game played for fun, not to be taken seriously and Andrei knew no one was about to try and stop either him or Jamie at this point. They were enjoying the spectacle too much.

Three chukkas down, three to go. And the emerald bastards were ahead by one.

Half-time was spent changing horses and switching ends so no one could complain of a wind disadvantage, and assessing oneself for injuries.

In the second half, Andrei felt as though he were playing against the Devil himself, for the Irish bastard rode like the wind upon the back of a mythical winged horse.

They tangled over and over, a mesh of horseflesh and men and mallets and elusive ball. Setting up play after play, knocking the ball in for the other players, some of whom were giving them a wide berth each time they slammed together. Neither of them particularly noticed, for the universe had narrowed to the two of them.

During one tussle, when the ball was between them, caked with mud, horse's withers also thick with it, Andrei had voiced his displeasure.

"Svoloch," he hissed at the man, then curvetted his pony in an arc and brought the mallet down to hit the ball with a backswing. Instead, it hit with a furious crack on the chestnut mare's foreleg. It had been an accident, though Andrei knew it looked like anything but, and made no effort to correct the impression. A penalty was called.

"Bljad," Jamie said, green eyes narrowing like a furious jungle cat. The sight was pleasing to Andrei, who trotted away, back held straight as a Cossack. A string of seriously rude Russian followed him down the field, turning his milky white ears red at the tips. A Russian sailor would have been impressed; Andrei was not.

The buzzer went before play could be halted.

Four chukkas down, two to go.

The field was little more than churned mud, for though the inconstant English sun was now out on glorious display, it had rained all the morning and night before. Andrei's thighs were numb and he knew they were bruised black. One shoulder felt as though it had been pulled out of its socket and popped back in by a giant's hand. In other words, he felt roaringly alive and ready to show that Irish bastard to whom this game belonged. He used the four minutes to check his pony, to calm his anger and to refocus his mind on the game. He took a breath, feeling the hard pound of his blood and the quiver of his muscles, and then he turned the horse and started back up the field.

The Irishman was already pounding down the field toward him at a furious gallop, the new mare beneath him glittering like dark Baltic amber. Andrei set his own horse to a hard canter, seizing it expertly with his knees like a Cossack and demanding the run of its life.

Later, the women would speak of it with a flush in their faces and even the men would have a spark in their eyes, for it had been great sport. The two men engaged, the only two men anyone had eyes for had been golden princes—sun sparking from their bridles, gleaming off boots and saddles, and glittering off the blinding gold and shimmering white of their respective heads.

It occurred to Andrei halfway down the field that if he didn't improvise, the Irishman would, if not outright kill him, at least maim him permanently. He should have apologized for the bloody horse—that had been a miscalculation, but it was too late to stop. Whatever was meant to happen was already rushing headlong at him and he was Russian. And any Russian worth his salt knew that Fate would have Her way.

The Irishman reached the ball first, but only a bare second before he did.

His hair soaked to his head, golden ends curling up, green eyes narrowed to slits, the man said something so exceedingly indelicate about Andrei's mother in flawless Russian that Andrei was impressed despite his immediate wrath. He returned the favor in the coarsest words a Russian could summon up, which was to say extremely coarse, and then set about taking the ball away from the bastard. But the ball was gone. It had, through some devilish sleight of hand, been shot halfway across the field to the number one seated emerald player. And the Irish bastard was smiling.

The crowd was now focused on the number one seated players, locked in furious combat over the ball just as, Andrei saw with a lurch, the Irishman had intended they should be. He swerved, intending to jump the pony over to the right and avoid the man's mallet. But in a movement too quick to even be seen, the mallet was tossed into the man's left hand, which served a numbing crack to Andrei's shin before being tossed back to the right. The Irishman's mare did not miss a step and they flowed on like a golden stream down the field, where Jamie caught the ball as it shot out from Andrei's number one's mallet. He deftly shot it with his right hand straight between the posts.

Andrei shook his head in outraged admiration. The bastard was left-handed, but had been playing like some ambidextrous demon the entire time. His shin was starting to throb horribly.

They were even at four goals each.

Five chukkas down, one to go.

All hell broke loose in the sixth chukka. The field was slushy, the horses tired and the players all in the grip of a royal fury. Scarlet and emerald jerseys were near to indistinguishable under a thick veneer of mud and bruises in shades of vermilion and puce, ochre and verdigris were flowering on every bit of visible skin.

Andrei knew it was time to dispense with tactics and go for broke. There was only a minute and a half left when he managed to get his mallet behind the ball.

Number four in emerald green was a bruiser, broad shouldered and looking about as friendly as a pissed-off bull who'd had scarlet jerseys waving in his face for the past hour and a half.

Andrei gritted his teeth and bore down as hard as he dared on the horse. He fixed his iciest Russian glare on the man. The bruiser in emerald green appeared entirely unimpressed and began to canter out from the goal posts.

The big bay swung round and Andrei snapped his own pony's bridle hard, forcing it to jump sideways.

His pony was lithe and limber, almost acrobatic, and could dance around larger horses. He could, with a little fancy footwork and his own sleight of hand, keep the ball and then all he needed to do was get clear of the big bay and take the ball home. He had made such plays a hundred times before and was as certain of his mount as he was of himself. But then the big man, one minute seated like a warrior, fell from his horse and his shoulder—the size and consistency of a warship's hull—hit Andrei's helmetless head with the full force of the fall.

For a moment the world went dark but Andrei shook his head and, with no small effort, kept his seat, and swung the mallet back, knowing the bruiser had neither intended nor had the opportunity to remove the ball.

The ball was gone and his mallet swung across empty air. Andrei turned, confused, wondering if it had gone through the goal without his realizing it. But no, there it was swooping upfield like a gull in flight with that green-eyed svoloch on the wing beside it. The ball lofted through the posts in a straight and perfect line. The crowd went wild and the buzzer sounded.

Six chukkas down, game bloody lost.

Andrei threw his mallet down in disgust but managed to sit high and lordly in his saddle when they shook hands with the other team. Jamie Kirkpatrick took his hand in such a good-natured manner that Andrei wished he still had his mallet within reach.

*Later, they'd ridden off the field, Jamie and Andrei with both flowers and small bits of paper containing numbers and personal information raining down on them. Jamie had, in a gesture of both sportsmanship and a certain sarcasm, tipped his helmet to Andrei (returned to him by the blushing redhead, who had skin the consistency of milked apricots, damn the man anyway). At least the damned horse was going to be all right, Andrei thought, even if he himself never walked again. Then Jamie Kirkpatrick flashed him a grin that was both mocking and infectious as though to say, 'Now wasn't **that** bloody good fun?'*

The great Arctic flow of Andrei's Slavic blood found itself in melt and he was laughing at a joke that needed no words to find the humor. He fully expected the man to cross the field there and then, for had he not summoned him by his laughter? By the silent moment shared across the arc of sunlight, reeking with blood and sweat—both that of horse and human?

But the man did not cross and was even now sliding from his horse with champagne still dripping from his brow, checking his horse over, the redhead glowing with expectancy off to the side. After that Andrei lost sight of him, for he was busy seeing to his own horse and having his bruises tended by the brunette with the good teeth, who had returned his helmet along with a suggestion that seemed terribly hospitable of her.

A few hours later, bruises well salved, Andrei decided that if Mohammed would not come to the mountain, then the mountain, Russian haughtiness not-

withstanding, was going to have to bloody go to Mohammed.

He knew where to look, for the man favored a dark, down-at-the-heels pub where workingmen and locals drank rather than the cream of England's youth that clotted the pubs near the university.

James Kirkpatrick was in a snug at the back, eating a green apple that nearly matched the shade of his eyes. On the table in front of him was a bottle of whiskey partnered by two glasses. He'd cleaned up and changed into a perfectly pressed pale blue shirt and grey wool pants. His hair was still damp from his ablutions and other than an indigo bruise on his collarbone, there was little proof that this was the murderous opponent from the polo green.

"I did wonder when you'd turn up."

Andrei sat, not without a visible wince, but with remarkable grace—or so he felt.

Eyes of Russian winter looked into those of an Irish spring in torrent and knew they had found their match, in mischief, in daring, in recklessness, in genius and in sheer bloody-mindedness. It was a heady feeling.

"And so at last—James Kirkpatrick—or the next Pushkin—I'm told?"

"Pushkin? I thought I was the second coming of Byron."

"Well, if you prefer to be compared to an English hack rather than the world's greatest poet, so be it. Give me anything he ever put pen to that stands against Eugene Onegin."

James Kirkpatrick smiled, appeared to give it a second's thought and then green eyes gleaming, recited in a mockingly Irish drawl—

Now, I'll put out my taper
(I've finished my paper
For these stanzas you see on the brink stand)

There's a whore on my right
For I rhyme best at Night
When a C—t is tied close to my Inkstand.

"Touché," Andrei laughed. The man took another bite of the apple in his hand and smiled in that familiar mocking manner. Andrei narrowed his own eyes. He wasn't used to people discomfiting him in such a manner.

"Your hair is too long," he said imperiously.

"Your lips are too red," James Kirkpatrick replied in a maddeningly calm manner. "And you owe me forty pounds for the vet bill."

Andrei, who had always been rather vain about his lips, considered kicking Jamie with his good leg and then limping off into the sunset. But Andrei had an itch that was driving him mad, and from what he had heard this was the only man at Oxford who might be capable of providing the desperately needed and highly skilled scratch.

"I hear you play chess."

"I do." Jamie raised an eyebrow. "Are you asking me to play?"

Andrei drew a deep breath to rein in his famous temper. Was the man completely ignorant of who he was dealing with?

"If you want me to play, ask me—it's called civility."

"Do you know who I am?" Andrei asked, looking down the length of his aquiline nose in his haughtiest manner.

"Aye," Jamie said and reached down beside him. Andrei frowned, and then smiled as he saw what the man had brought with him. An old chessboard, with a worn velvet bag that held the comforting clack of King against King, of Bishop about to bow to Queen, and of Queen taken by Knight. Andrei swallowed down a surge of electric excitement.

Three hours later, brow furrowed in astonishment, he lost.

Jamie re-filled his glass with amber nectar and said, "Again?"

Andrei's leg hurt like a polar bear had bitten it. He'd drunk half a bottle of that poison the man kept offering him and he'd never felt so happy in his life.

"Yes, again."

"This time, man, give me your best game. Otherwise you're wasting your time, and what I find most offensive, mine as well."

And so Andrei gave him his best game and won, but only narrowly and after a nerve-wracking, mind-numbing two hours. He was dumbfounded, but only had one question for Jamie.

"How?"

"I see the board exactly as you do, three dimensional and with the lines running through it of every possible permutation. Mine are blue, what color are yours?"

"Red," Andrei replied, flabbergasted into revealing a secret he'd never told anyone. There were visible lines, like whisper thin threads, that ran between the pieces on a chessboard and allowed him to see in a lightning glance how many moves he could make and what the consequences of each move would be one, two, seven moves down the game.

"What are you looking at?" For that disconcerting green gaze was upon him again, the golden head cocked to the side.

"I'm trying to decide which of us is prettier. I'm quite certain it's me, but I can see that in certain lights and if you were to wear pink, it would definitely be you."

"You are just as much of an outrageous bastard as they say," Andrei laughed.

"Isn't that why you sought me out? Because you're bored?"

Andrei responded with an eloquent Russian shrug. "I think the very least you owe me is the redhead."

Jamie grinned, a flash of impudent white. "Ah, she's sworn off other men now. Says I've ruined her for all men in general but for Russian prima donnas in particular."

"Svoloch," Andrei said.

"*Takes one to know one,*" *Jamie replied and set the chessboard up once more.*

SLEEP CAME HEAVILY THAT NIGHT UNDER THE LOW EAVES OF THE DACHA, for he was exhausted from his travels and had fallen into a heavy doze in the midst of his remembering...

He hears the drumbeat of hooves, one horse, one man coming across the white wastelands, a black cape floating around him, hanging in the falling snow. There is a sense of menace so deep that it is like falling into a well with no bottom. He has to keep away from the man, hide as deep in the forest as he can. The snow is so heavy, up to his knees and it is hard to make headway. His breath comes in heaving gasps and he is afraid that the exhalations of air will hang shroud-like, making a cloud-path by which to track him. He does not know why the man pursues him, but as prey will always know its predator, he knows the man does not mean him well.

He has been running for a very long time. He must find somewhere to hide soon and somehow cover his tracks.

Just ahead, the trees are dense, long swooping boughs heavy with the shadowed snow. He can hear the horse's chuffing breath, can feel the icy trails of it sliding along his spine. His feet are shod in rough leather shoes and they make little sound on the snow, which is lighter here under the trees, allowing him to move faster.

His mind is a blur. He is in the natural state of prey, running solely upon instinct, upon the knowledge that lives in the blood, not the mind. Ahead is a windfall where a few fir trees have fallen in a ferocious wind. If he can make that before the rider catches up with him, he might have a chance.

He makes it to the windfall, dropping to his knees and crawling in as the branches scrape his back and head and the needles fall in a stinging shower into his eyes. Whether this will be shelter or trap he does not know and does not care, for he has to stop before there is no breath left in his lungs.

It is pitch black under the shelter but dry and thick with the scent of resin bled out from the dying trees. He catches at his breath the way he would at a falling branch, trying to pull it in, keep it from the hound's nose. His lungs hurt, scraped raw with running and breathing in the ice-crystalled air. It is, at the very least, a moment of respite.

He lies in the carpet of needles, grateful, drinking the scent as though it is the essence of salvation though he knows this is not so. But humans live in hope, and he is, after all, a mere man.

He dozes, or at least thinks he must have, for suddenly there is a woman in the trees, naked, skin tinted palest green under the moon. Her hair is wet, frost limning the pale stripling color of it, like the underside of birch bark when it is torn away in spring. He can smell the water and the wood of her, and knows she is of these things, just as he is of blood, bone, and the warm density of flesh. She walks atop the snow and does not seem to feel the cold. She does not look his way but he can feel that she is aware of him, just as she is aware of everything that moves and breathes and scents in these great cold Northern forests.

He longs to follow her, the way day longs to follow night, the way water yearns after fire, even if it should mean death, and he is certain it would. But he knows her, in some wordless way, a knowing that is in the cells, in the blood and not of the mind at all.

He moves, ready to leave his shelter to follow her and then she is gone as if she had never been, a willowy flicker in the snow-light. Suddenly he is aware that the man and horse have come upon the windfall, the horse's hooves silenced in the needle carpet beneath the snow. It is the horse's eye upon him that alerts him.

The great clouds of the horse's breath fill the space between himself and the stars, and its eye, lit with the blue light of the moon, gazes at him with neither violence nor tenderness. He can feel the man's instincts roving out, probing the night for him, for the prickling flesh of the prey. He tilts his head slightly, afraid to set off another shower of needles, so that he might see his enemy more clearly.

The man is faceless, his black hood obliterating so much as even an outline of his features. Upon his chest is a strange insignia, that of a severed dog's head and a broom. He is an oprichnik, a man apart, an instrument of terror set loose upon the country to scour out betrayers. He rides the night winds and with him, as his constant companion, rides Death.

There is a knotted cord around the man's neck, made of saints know what, and strung on it is what he would swear is a child's jawbone. He closes his eyes and hopes that Death will be swift about his duties.

But Death is always a chancy fellow. Suddenly the horse whinnies, a high-pitched noise almost like a woman's scream, and lunges off through the snow away from the windfall. He is safe, for the moment.

He lies under the trees for a long time, or it might be no time at all. One can never tell in these in-between landscapes, populated as they are with demons from bygone times and snow-walking mermaids. But even this suspended time cannot last, for he is cold and knows he must move if he is not to freeze and be found there someday, perfectly preserved in the frost.

He leaves his shelter reluctantly, for the cold out in the open is much worse. It bites into his skin like a thousand needles but he walks forward, for he knows numbness is worse. It is the sleeping dwarf that heralds death.

He keeps on through the forest, under the heavy boughs, ears alert for any movement, for the stealth of a spray of snow, a branch that shouldn't be moving, a noise that does not belong to night in the forest. He comes out into the open so suddenly that it is a little like falling and he has to stop to get his bearings.

In the open field, the snow blushes silver and a silence like the moment before the world began hangs there, holding him fast. Across the field, skimming its edges, there is a ripple, sinuous as water, in and out of the shadows, cream against the snow, a creature that belongs to moonlight, to cold blue taiga, to trees that bleed gold upon the ground. A tiger, one that could kill a man with a single swipe, and it is as if he can already smell his own blood upon the snow, spilling hot, scenting the field with chilling copper. The blood, which in its heat and movement under fragile skin, sings to the tiger the oldest siren song of all.

And then he sees them as they move out from under the dark branches that ring the field, upon their black horses, swathed in their black cloaks with their severed dog heads and icy brooms. He is surrounded, and there is no way out. The tiger has melted into the shadows as though it never existed.

The black horses step forward in unison. He can hear the cloaks snap upon the rising wind and knows himself trapped more surely than a winter hare in a hunter's cruel-jawed trap.

Later, when there was time for thought, he would wonder if he had sensed them coming in his dream. Those men in the long coats moving even then through the darkness toward the low-eaved dacha in the woods.

From the Journals of James Kirkpatrick

May____, 1955

The past rises up in layers, slowly surrounding me until I feel that if I were to slip down that side street, enter that house, I would come face to face with the men we have followed down through these hundred years and more. When we first arrived, they were mere shadows, ink-stained angels or demons, depending upon the day's view, but now they have acquired form and shape. They slip in and out of the sides of my vision. Ah, there, that auburn-haired fellow, slim as a wraith wading into the sea—certainly that must be Shelley. Shelley who foresaw his death, who felt the sea rise and overwhelm his house, his family, and his very soul.

But it is Byron I came to seek more than any other and find the man as elusive here as he is in his own writings. Just when one thinks one has caught a handful of his coat tails and will be able to ride the starry trails of his imaginings with him, one realizes he is away laughing, off in the distance, eluding understanding. He hid so much of himself from public view in life, even leaving his own country so that he might live less in subterfuge.

I imagine him passing in his coach, that resplendent vehicle that cost such a fortune in its day, with its dinner service, its traveling library and plate chest, and its lounging sofa for the days after the nights of excess. I hear the jangle of harness, the snort of horses still warm from the stable, stamping their hooves in the pre-dawn light of Pisa.

But here it is not possible to think of Byron without conjuring Shelley, pale, tired, worn from his ever-whirling household and all the people who wanted things from him. I see him walking along the shore, his mind on fire with all the words there would not be time to write down, all the feverish-winged thoughts that went out in the Gulf of Spezia forever. It was upon a shore not far from here that Shelley's body was put to fire, though his heart, held in Byron's grieving hands, would not, they say, take the flame. Perhaps Shelley was tired of burning, for he had been in the crucible all his life.

Why are we haunted by all the things poets do not live long enough to say?

May____, 1955

We have found a place to stay for the next several weeks, a crumbling, decrepit casa with its feet in the sea. Behind us rise hills, rolling and heady with cypress and olive trees and the smell of ripe lemons wafting in through the windows—which is just as well as it helps to overpower the mildew.

The house was owned by nobility until early this century but the war put an end to that. When I asked the old caretaker who rented it to us what happened to the family, he shrugged, one of those Italian shrugs that are more eloquent than thousands of words from a different race and said—'They are all gone, disappeared after the war.' This could mean any number of things—they were all killed, or they had to leave for their own safety, and for one reason or another never returned.

Like all good casas worth their salt, it also comes, Giuseppe assures us, with its own ghost. He told us this as the night rolled in, blanketing the house like thick muffling velvet. He said it's the ghost of a woman who lived here in the 16th century, who was imprisoned in the stone tower that looks out over the sea for the crime of not producing a male heir for her lord. She eventually died there, still imprisoned in the tower. It is said she roams the house in the night, looking for a doorway out but never finding it. Andrei looked suitably alarmed at this news, for he is used to Russian ghosts who tend to come back only for vengeful purposes. I am used to Irish ghosts however, who are an altogether milder species.

My room looks out over the sea. I opened the tall windows and left them that way for the night, the shushing of the waves lulling me to sleep.

May____, 1955

We spent a sleepless night here, due to the peregrinations of the ghost—or so we thought at first. It occurs to me that an Irishman and a Russian ought not to share such old, decrepit lodgings. It seems inevitable we would summon a ghost eventually.

I was fully asleep, having imbibed too much grappa during the evening, when the most unearthly moaning woke me up. I sat up in bed, rather startling the woman who had accompanied me home. It didn't take her long to understand what had wakened me, and she set to jibbering in Italian in a manner not designed to pluck up a man's courage.

I left the bed swiftly, for the moaning continued, seeming to come from both the rafters and the window and then quite suddenly from the tree outside my window. I shook my head to clear the cobwebs and immediately regretted it—perhaps I was only having a grappa-induced hallucination. I felt it was time to put on some pants, as no man can meet a phantom with dignity when he's naked as a new-minted babe.

Pants on, I opened the door to my bedroom, feeling a bit like Shelley going off to face the terrifying apparitions that heralded his own death. Colliding with an angry Russian in the hall somewhat dampened this Romantic illusion. Andrei was, like myself, only half-clad, but ornamented with a signorina wrapped in a sheet. She too was letting loose a stream of Italian invective which I felt certain would either banish said ghost or bring it down upon our heads in fiery vengeance.

A thing—a wafty, white sort of thing—was floating up in the tower near the cap in spiraling loops. In the gloom of the night, with the sea moaning and crashing in a lugubrious manner outside our walls, it looked utterly terrifying. There was no making head nor tail of it, for it was most oddly shaped and drifted in no comprehensible manner. Truly, it seemed that we were being paid a visit from the other side. As we stood there craning our necks, trying to rationalize it, the women very sensibly began praying loudly to Mary and went to retrieve their clothing, after which they made haste to leave our lodgings. I can't say I blame them, for had I anywhere to run, I might well have done so. A ghost is hardly like a bug. You can't merely eject it from your lodgings with a pat of its wings and a blessing to guide its path away from your door.

This left Andrei and me looking at one another in blank dismay, neither of us being versed in the finer points of how to exorcise a ghost. Admittedly, a damp, crumbling casa by the sea in Pisa does not lend itself to a feeling of jolly calm. In fact, I was beginning to feel rather like a vapor-given character in a Gothic novel when the ghost—how to say this delicately—emitted a rather worldly substance that landed squarely on my shoulder. That, I am assured by our housekeeper Gina, is a sign of great fortune. We shall see.

Our phantom was an owl that had somehow not only managed to fly in through the gaps in the tower, but arrived with a pair of commodious ladies' underwear attached to its head. The resulting confusion had understandably upset it, hence the mournful moaning.

How to get it down became the issue. And get it down we must for it was bumping about up there like a demented ghoul intent on dashing its brains out.

Before I really thought about it, I started to climb the sides of the tower. It was an exhilarating climb, though in retrospect, suicidal. I could feel the stones crumble in places as my feet left their purchase. I felt as though I had quicksilver along all my limbs and that I merely flowed along the wall as if I were as much part of it as the stone and lichen, wind and rain.

I managed to shove the shutters open so that the owl could fly out. Feeling the air, it did, though not before flapping furiously around my head for what seemed a very long time. Just as the owl gained its freedom, letting out a screech into the night that would have chilled a Viking to his core, I felt the stone under my hand give. There wasn't time for thought, only blindly flailing and hoping for some solidity in a suddenly precarious universe.

It is difficult to give truth to this scene, so ridiculous was it. For there I was, hanging from a chandelier that was clearly about to tear itself out of its crumbling moorings and take me with it straight to the pits of hell—or at the very least, to the cold stone floor of the casa.

Andrei, seized with inspiration, grabbed the sheets from his bed and returned, frantically knotting them. I was still hanging on despite the chandelier groaning in a manner that indicated it was about done with my nonsense. He knotted the end with what seemed to me sadistic thoroughness and tossed it to me. I had a moment of free fall as the chandelier gave way and crashed to the floor below. I caught the knot of the sheet and fell like a stone. The sheet snapped tight. Andrei had the other end braced over the balustrade, the tendons in his neck and arms standing out like an anatomical drawing. I shimmied up the sheet with adrenaline booming through every cell, crawled over the shaky stone of the balustrade and collapsed at Andrei's feet. I started to laugh, for the sheer ludicrousness of the situation and for the immense relief of being alive.

Andrei looked down the haughty length of his exceptionally aristocratic nose and said, "You are fucking mad, Yasha. Oh and by the way, you are welcome."

"Thank you," I said, suitably chastened as the adrenaline ebbed and the various contusions and cuts began to assert themselves.

Then being a good Russian, he poured us each a shot of vodka from the store he carries everywhere with him. We drank it back, said goodnight with what dignity remained to each of us, which is to say, none, and departed to our respective beds.

June____, 1955

We visited the ancient Bay of Baiae today, taking a boat over its drowned columns and cracked mosaics, the heaved blind arches thick with swaying mosses and the pearled remnants of ancient marbled cisterns. Here is the home of Poseidon, here where Caligula built his bridge of boats, giving lie to Thrasyllus' prediction that he had no more chance of becoming Emperor than riding a horse across the Gulf of Baiae. Rome suffered famine for Caligula's conceits, and here many drowned in the rose thick water as boats overturned after nights where wine spilled upon lip and over gem-studded prow with a profligacy only the most crazed of emperors could have summoned forth, even from a land as fertile as this one. It was here that Hadrian died, wasted away and bleeding from nose and mouth. Here that Caesar and Nero summered. Here that Cleopatra studied while waiting for her lover to return... but it was not Caesar that came to her, only the ghost of his violent death.

I could see, if I half-closed my eyes, the scented women and men, the warriors on furlough, the philosophers and hedonists all come to this aqueous garden that Seneca called a 'harbor of vice'. How different they were and yet how much the same, drinking deep of the sun's nectar, seeking pleasure, wanting love, planning battles and dreaming new philosophies amongst the terraced gardens. How many affairs were begun and ended amid the summer's pleasures? How many hearts were broken briefly or, perhaps, permanently?

June___, 1955

Andrei and I have gathered round us a social group of mathematicians, poets and philosophers, students and vagabonds who are resting here before continuing the journey onward after the call of the Siren East. The evenings are pleasant, spent with the local wine and grappa, and the food that Gina makes for us. The weather has been perfect, as though we exist in some idyll in a story rather than a climate that can be brutally hot in summer. And if the days are perfect, the nights are beyond sublime, the stars so thick and heavy that they bring to mind Joyce's words about the 'heaven-tree of stars hung with night-blue fruit.' And, of course, there are the Italian women. Andrei seems to be trying to sample as many of the locals as possible before the summer is over. I prefer to linger over the meal and find its secret delights. There is a beautiful divorcée living in the hills above us here who intrigues with smoky silence and a fierce hunger of infinite variety that leaves me hollow-eyed and making my way home in the pre-dawn silence with only the thick cypress and lemon and olive groves for my companions. John lectured me roundly on gluttony, debauchery, and the regrets that are their constant companions before I left Oxford for the summer. I know he referred not to food but to women and I have tried to keep his advice in mind, because I do not like to take a woman to my bed without feeling, even if it is only fondness and desire.

I wonder though, if it is ever possible to leave a woman's bed feeling entirely whole, not as if something, however small and unidentifiable, is missing. If such a place exists, I have yet to find it.

There is nothing missing, however, in all the talk and speculation that gathers itself around our table each night. We have a small gnome of a man who comes once or twice a week, named Pietro, who is an amateur local astronomer and has shown me the heavens in a way I have never seen them before. He has a dreamer's soul, and therefore we speak the language of one like spirit to another. Often we can stretch out on the grass behind the casa and stare at the heavens for hours altogether and never need to say more than a sentence here or there.

July___, 1955

I noticed that terrible brilliance at the edges of my vision today. At first, I thought it was merely aftershocks from the sun on the sea, or rather I hoped it was. I do not want to have one of my episodes here. I do not want to have them anywhere, for that matter, but somehow I know this will, should it arrive, be a bad one. I dare not run, for it runs with me, fleet and dark, taking off the chains that bind it even now. Like Shelley, I would find a wild wood and stretch my frame in the gloomiest of shades to try to quench the unceasing fire that gnaws at me like a beast with an insatiable appetite.

But I cannot find the wood. The pit looms and I will fall.

July____, 1955

    It is never easy to describe time spent with the Crooked Man, not even to myself. I shudder to bring such thoughts into focus, as I only want to travel away from those times, as far and as fast as I can. It is like being in and out of focus in your own emotions, your surroundings—in short, reality—whatever constitutes that fragile state. Sometimes it is like a broken mirror afterward. You can only summon the most distorted of images and make out fragments of a picture you don't particularly want to see. This time, I carried something clear out with me, as though I held something precious and knew it, so took care to protect it through whatever dark and filthy landscape must be crossed to get to the other side.

    It was a woman. It sounds mad now but I could swear I felt someone take my hand and pull me toward a sanctuary where the noise stopped and the whisperings of the Crooked Man were silenced. A place where it was cool and I could just rest. I don't know if I saw her face, felt her skin or... what? I didn't carry the memory of those things out with me, but I feel the trace of her along myself, as though she wrote directly upon my soul. But I don't know the words that were carved thereon.

    I knew her. She was as real as this paper beneath my hand, as real as the broken colonnade that runs down to the sea. But she was more than these things. I knew her in a way that seemed to have little to do with time. She was my 'soul without my soul', as Shelley once put it. But even Shelley, with his passions and loves, did not truly believe in the 'Epipsychidion'—mourning the loss of this ideal. For poets know better than others that such things do not happen in this realm. But oh, how we all long for it. Whether we can express it in words or not, still we yearn.

    She lay down beside me and took my hand in hers. A strange peace descended over me at her touch and I could feel her weight on the mattress, smell her scent, fresh and somehow soft. She touched her hand to my face and told me to sleep. And I did.

    I awoke and, of course, she was not there. She had only been a fevered dream, a beautiful dream that seemed more real than the waking world, but a dream nonetheless. I felt a terrible loss, as though I had lived a life with her in some other time, some other place, but now we could only meet in dreams, in that fragmented landscape of my brain and heart at its lowest and darkest.

    Tonight I sat by the window in my room, the scent of the sea strong, and found lines of Rilke running through my head.

You who never arrived
In my arms, Beloved...

I don't know her. She never existed and yet tonight I feel the cut of loss as deeply as if someone had torn my heart out.

"I miss you." I said it low, looking toward the sea, but I said it to her—she who never arrived.

July____, 1955

Andrei has been stalking around in an icy silence for two days, since I managed to get up out of my bed and rejoin the world. I finally confronted him today and asked him what the hell was wrong with him.

He flashed me one of his haughtiest looks and said, "If you're planning to commit suicide, I'd rather you didn't do it on my watch."

I refrained from pointing out that this was somewhat rich, considering his tricks on the Eiffel Tower.

"I have no idea what you're talking about," I said, though my heart was thumping in my chest. I have no memory of the last few days other than the dream of the woman.

He gave me one of his iciest looks, the one that makes you feel like an undesirable bug caught in someone's soup. Then his expression changed.

"You really don't remember, do you?"

"Remember what?" I asked, fear making me peevish with him.

"Yasha, you were walking into the sea when I found you. If I hadn't wakened in the night, you would have drowned. You don't remember, do you?"

I shook my head, feeling sick. I have done some very stupid things during previous episodes, but not to this extent, not something that might actually have killed me, and without even a vague memory of it.

"I was yelling at you as I ran down the shore. You never even turned your head. You seemed completely unaware that I was there, as though you were in another place altogether, even after I grabbed you and dragged you out. I shook you hard, I was so angry, and you just looked at me like you weren't sure who I was or why I was shaking you."

There is no way to tell him the vision I was caught up in, how I did not even feel the waves wrapping round me, ready to pull me in and down, that I was on another far plane where the Crooked Man rules and it is always night. There are no words to explain and so I did not. Andrei seemed to sense this for though he is normally given to large and very verbal fits on anything that upsets him, he merely shrugged and said, 'Yasha, you are well now. That is all that matters. Eat, for the love of God, before you disappear.'

One cannot explain a journey with the Crooked Man to one who does not travel those ways. It is to touch the drought, to know such aridity of soul that one thinks one will never know water again, either spiritually or mentally.

July____, 1955

A letter from my father arrived today. It was, as usual, filled with paternal admonitions to come home for at least part of the summer. Guilt had begun to dribble in at my toes the minute I took it from our postman. I even contemplated putting it aside and not reading it. But filial guilt did its work and I read it.

I just want this summer free of the yoke that comes with being a Kirkpatrick. I just want to be me for a few months. How weak that sentence sounds yet it sums up all that I feel, what I want right now. I see my life stretching out before me. I know my duty, and for now I want to run in the opposite direction, for I know my feet will take me back to what I must do eventually.

Such is duty and Catholic guilt, a powerful cocktail.

August____, 1955

We went sailing yesterday on the Gulf of Spezia, just as Shelley and his friends had done so long ago. As it turned out, our trip mirrored a little too closely the one Byron and Shelley embarked upon in Switzerland.

The day was perfection, the sun on the water, a slight breeze in the air and the sails unfurled against a sky so deep blue that it seemed a sea entire that we might dive into and lose ourselves swimming amongst celestial bodies.

Such are the ruminations of mad poets not sensible sailors. The sailor would have noted that the sky was perhaps a shade too deep, that the breeze was ruffling the water in more than fanciful play. Still, it seemed that the storm broke very suddenly, for when next we looked up the sky was a dreadful mottled green and the wind turned from sprite to banshee in the space of a few heartbeats.

I knew we could not outrun the wind. We'd have to run bare poles into the waves and hope to ride it out until the weather cleared.

Andrei is not a natural sailor and had turned roughly the color of seaweed. It occurred to me, between trying to reef the sails and bail the boat simultaneously, that it wasn't the least bit Romantic to be doing exactly as Byron and Shelley had done—albeit neither of us has a pregnant cousin back at the house. But in all other aspects this was a moment of poetical déjà vu. Byron and Shelley had survived it, mind you, though the terror Shelley felt at the time, being that he could not swim, must have been horrific. Andrei and I are both strong swimmers and I felt sure we could manage if we had to. I just prayed, fervently and aloud, that we would not have to. Andrei meanwhile, clung to the edges of the boat for dear life, soaked by the waves that were lapping over the sides.

I suggested, in what I felt was a mild manner considering the circumstances, that he help bail some of the rapidly accumulating water out of the boat, only to have him glare at me out of a face that was a rictus of terror. I realized any rescue we affected was going to have to be purely by my own efforts.

It was a full hour before we made shore and there were times that I thought *we were going to end up down with the weeds and crumbled roads at the bottom of the Gulf. But as often happens with such things, the fear of what the outcome might have been didn't hit me until later when I was entirely safe.*

My main emotion upon stumbling, drunken with relief, onto solid ground was that sense of ridiculous joy in one's own existence. Andrei, bilious and furious, did not share this feeling in the least.

He faced me on the shore, obviously in the grip of his operatic Russian temper. This image might have been more fearsome if he hadn't had seaweed hanging off one ear like a pirate's earring. I made the mistake of laughing and thought for a second that he might hit me. Instead, he drew himself up in his very haughtiest White Russian stance and said,

"If I die young and tragic, I do not—James—intend to do it in water!!"

And with that, he strode up the shore toward the house. I stood there bemused, for the man surely could not be blaming me for the weather. But he only calls me by the Anglicized version of my name when he is truly upset.

Russians are impossible.

August____, 1955

My lovely, cool divorcée has proven to be less than cool about separation, as the autumn puts its head upon the horizon. She hasn't been happy recently, because since my visit with the Crooked Man I haven't been as frequent a visitor to her expensive linens. She wants me to go to Rome with her, says the universities there are as fine as anything England can offer, tells me that her house is big and lonely and that she needs her Apollo there to warm its halls. She did not receive the word 'no' well, despite how gently I tried to phrase it.

After last winter, after the mess and the potential scandal, I have been careful to disentangle myself once I thought a woman's emotions were becoming too deeply involved. I think I lingered too long with Francesca, for which I am sorrier than she will ever know, but I do not love her and will not pay her the disrespect of pretending that I do. Besides, I am no one's Apollo or Dionysus. I am merely a human being with all the failings of our species.

Women want me to say things that I can't find it within myself to say. They want promises that are empty, and they would know they were empty as soon as the words fell from my tongue.

August____, 1955

I have spent the last three days with Clothilde and feel ruthlessly sorted. I forget how perfect in its alignments and elements her world is. I feel ironed out and far more sensible than when I left Italy. I have used good china, slept on flawless linens, had my mind scoured out with pithy and remorseless Gallic good sense and been restored to myself fully.

August____, 1955

You cannot avoid what must be done, not forever. Only perhaps for a short time and maybe that's why older people sigh over youth and think it was some halcyon time. But it isn't, is it? We are aware of how brief this span is, and are already feeling the weight of expectation that hangs over all our heads—of what others want for us and from us. From the beginnings of youth, one can already see the end on the horizon.

August____, 1955

Andrei accuses me of having grown a Catholic conscience and leaving him to fend on his own with the entire female population of these redolent hillsides. It's not my Catholicism that has reared its head, rather the girl that came to me in my dream—or was it a dream? Since my episode, I haven't been able to shake the feeling that I am, in some way, being unfaithful to her when I am with another woman. It's ludicrous, not something that can be explained, and so I don't. Andrei is welcome to believe that I am struck with religiosity rather than insanity.

Myself, I do not feel insane, but I am intensely aware of the absurdity of remaining faithful to a woman who does not exist. Why then can I not shake the feeling that she does indeed exist, some where, some time?

August____, 1955

I have been shot at by an irate father, not through any peccadillo of my own but through Andrei's dallying. The bullet missed me by about an inch while I was sitting reading Shelley, half asleep and dreaming about the poet's last demon-haunted days. The bullet was a sharp alarm that lodged in the bookcase just behind my head. At first I thought I was having some dreadful hallucination, being that I saw a white, furious face at the window with my own reflected back right beside it. However, I soon recognized Signor Martelli and managed to duck before the next shot. I suppose Andrei and I look enough alike that I could see how easily the mistake was made.

I managed to duck the next two bullets while yelling in Italian that he should cease and desist, and pointing out that I wasn't the promiscuous Russian rogue he was after. Said promiscuous Russian rogue was thankfully absent, giving me time to bring Signor Martelli in and calm him down with a boatload of grappa and pecuniary promises. He was in an altogether more receptive state of mind by the time Andrei returned, though I had hidden the pistol in the meantime in case the mere sight of his daughter's seducer inflamed him back to the heights of Latin revenge.

The upshot of all this is that we are leaving Italy slightly ahead of schedule, in a flurry of recriminations and tears. A settlement for the child's future well-being has gone some way to ameliorating everyone's temper other than Andrei's, who has shown a sudden streak of sentimentality about this future offspring of his. Considering that he has no intention of marrying Gina, nor of taking up olive farming on a Pisan hillside, I have pointed out that the sentimentality is somewhat misplaced, not to mention late. But a Russian sodden with vodka grief is not open to pragmatic opinions.

I put him to bed and now I sit, having packed and made arrangements to leave, knowing our absence and the settlement, will go farther to lessen Papa Martelli's fury than will our presence and false promises.

The night is deep and fire-lit and even here in this sun-laden land I can feel autumn's approach, a chill thread amongst the bright-flowered tapestry of summer. It is so quiet tonight that the sound of pen against paper is a loud scratch. Even the sea is quiet, as if it broods, as I do, upon something which has no answer.

I have a sense that something has ended here in Italy, and that all things will be changed in the autumn. I can't put my finger on why, only that I feel restless and at the same time there is a strange void in the normal framework of my world.

Though my soul has sojourned here this summer with Shelley and Byron, it is with Rilke's words that my thoughts now lie. For indeed, the summer was immense, the fruits were full heavy, and the sweetness of the grape beyond compare. But it is time now to go home. But oh, how I long for just two more ripe southern days...

'For he who is alone, will remain alone... as the leaves begin to blow.'

Part Four

Bandit Country
Ireland – December–February 1974

Chapter Twenty-four

December 1973

The Contact

"YE DO PICK THE ODDEST PLACES FOR YER ASSIGNATIONS," Casey grumbled, seating himself on an upturned cask of whiskey and promptly lighting a cigarette.

David gave him a pointed look, and Casey sighed, taking a long drag before stubbing it out.

"This is the only bloody time I can have a smoke in peace. Pamela keeps confiscatin' the damn things on me. Besides, I don't think my wee cigarette is goin' to blow us up, man, unless there's some strange bog gas leakin' out of the walls down here."

"There isn't, but I don't think it wise to take risks either," David said, sounding rather prissy.

They were seated in the cask room below Kirkpatrick's Folly, where Jamie's own private reserve of Connemara Mist was held. The space was dry and cool, and, most importantly, extremely private as well as accessible from a location to which only Jamie and David were privy.

"So, why are we here?" Casey asked, his eyes roving around the casks that lined the walls. "Does the boy have more names for me?" He was referring to the list of names that David, via Billy's sharp ears and nimble fingers, had been passing along to him over the last months.

"Yes," David said, "only two this time, but it's two more that will be saved. But that's not the only reason I asked you here."

That got Casey's attention. The dark eyes swivelled back in David's direction. "No? Then what exactly are we doin' here?"

"I have a proposal for you and I'd like you to hear me out before you say no."

Casey raised a dark brow at him. "That's not the most promisin' beginnin' I've ever heard."

David ignored the cynicism and began to speak before he lost what was left of his nerve.

"Look, here it is—Jamie's extended absence has left a bit of a hole in our communications. No one has his connections within the Nationalist community and the British establishment. I don't think I'm telling you anything you don't know when I say he was the man bridging the very precarious divide between the two communities. So as not to slide completely backwards, we need to fill at least one side of that equation. In short, we need a contact man who has strong ties within the Republican world. Your name is the one that came up over and over again."

"That wouldn't be because ye brought it up yerself, now would it, David?" Casey said caustically.

"I wasn't the first to mention your name as it turns out. Believe it or not, Casey, I do not take every opportunity to place you in harm's way."

The man actually looked shamefaced for a moment. "I know ye don't. Only ye'll forgive me, but trusting any deal the British put on the table is a bit like kissin' a viper an' hopin' it doesn't bite ye. Why me? Last I checked they were wantin' to either put a bullet in me or stick me in prison for the rest of my natural life."

"Because the Provos trust you—for the most part anyway. You understand that world, you know which expectations are realistic and which aren't. The truth is, the government is at sea about this. They don't understand the issues that matter to the Republican community but they want to put feelers out a little further because they would like to start the process of disengagement."

David felt a frisson of smugness when Casey's jaw dropped.

"What?" Casey mimed digging at his ear, as an indication of his disbelief. "Did ye actually say 'disengagement' in regards to the British Army?"

"I did," David said, his voice quiet. "It's not generally known, and they haven't even advanced the idea to the Provisionals, because that's what they would like you to do, and then set up a series of face-to-face meetings so that both sides can hammer out a timeframe and plan for making this a reality."

Casey took a moment to absorb the impact of the words. "Yer certain it's not some kind of trick? Something to make the Provos declare a ceasefire an' then draw them out on what their plans are? It wouldn't be the first instance of double-dealin' or sleight of hand for yer men in London."

"I believe they're in earnest, and I am not especially gullible, particularly when it comes to my own government. It's very hush-hush at this point. Even the Northern Ireland Secretary doesn't know this offer is on the table."

"An' yet yer tellin' me?" Casey gave him a shrewd eye. "I'm not entirely comfortable with that sort of knowledge."

"They simply want you to get the lie of the land, see what the Provos are willing to compromise on, and what they absolutely won't."

"That'll depend a great deal on which ones I talk to," Casey said. "There are some that have a long view an' some that most assuredly do not."

"Talk to the ones that you believe understand what implementing a peace process will mean. The others will get swept aside in the torrent should this take hold."

"If this gets out—an' it will have to eventually—those others could become the torrent. Ye know that, right?"

"They are aware of the risks and that this may all blow up in our faces without any forward movement or resolution, but I think we have to try. Don't you?"

Casey nodded, shifting on the cask. "What about the Loyalists? The army is never goin' to be able to withdraw slowly enough for them an' it's not goin' to be able to move quickly enough to please the Provos. It's a bit of a rock an' a hard place, is it not?"

David laughed. "This whole island is a bit of a rock and a hard place, not to mention its people. All I can really tell you is that the government wants to deal with the Republicans. They aren't putting this offer out to the Loyalists—probably because they know what the answer would be. They know the real change has to come from the Nationalist/Republican side of the divide."

Casey sighed and stood, large frame restless within the confines of the room. David knew it was likely the man wasn't entirely comfortable being in Jamie's house. He knew enough of their history now to realize that while they held each other in a certain esteem, neither man had gone out of his way to seek the other's company. For, he knew, quite obvious reasons.

"Look," Casey said. "I'll do it, but it will have to be on my own terms an' in my own time. Because I'll be honest with ye, Pamela would have my bollocks for breakfast if she ever got wind of this. I made a promise to her to stay out of trouble, an' to be entirely honest with her. An' I'm pretty damn certain this isn't information I can whisper to her across the pillows at night."

"Fair enough," David said crisply, "but they would like the first approach to be made within the next two weeks."

Casey raised an eyebrow at him. "I'm thinkin' ye don't quite understand what 'my own terms' an' 'my own time' means here. David, I don't have as tight of links with the IRA as ye seem to think, an' there's more than one within the organization that would be happy to see my head on a pike in front of City Hall, so tell yer superiors to have a bit of patience. We've put up with yer presence for eight hundred years. I think ye can give me a month, no?"

"A month then," David agreed. "We'll meet here again. It's the safest place."

"Why is that?"

"Because Jamie had it swept every week and I have kept up the tradition in his absence."

"Well, no one could accuse ye of an absence of paranoia, leastwise," Casey said dryly. "Here it is then. But heaven help us both if Pamela catches us colludin' in the cellar. She is, to all intents an' purposes, the mistress of this house right now."

"Maybe for good," David said.

"D'ye know somethin' the rest of us don't?" Casey asked.

"No, and that's what troubles me—we can't track him down, and there are people trying. People who can find anything or anyone, given the time."

"Perhaps they only need a bit more of that particular commodity. Would ye not say the man is the sort to escape all notice, no matter how professional, if he should wish to stay off the radar?"

"Not even Lord Kirkpatrick is quite that good, modern-day Percy Blakeney that he might be."

"I wouldn't be so certain of that," Casey said. "He usually manages to surprise people when they least expect it."

David left then, trusting that Casey could find his own way out of this malted underworld.

Instead of heading straight back outside, Casey wandered a little further down the dark corridor, the top of his head brushing the ancient beams. If his bearings were correct, the first tunnel that branched off when he came down the ladder led straight under Jamie's study and looked to be a newer addition than the rest of the corridors. He had a good idea of just what its uses were.

There was a warren of rooms underneath the house, most with obvious uses, some merely empty and gathering motes of dust and silence. He poked his head in a few and found more casks—these empty—shelves of decorative bottles and undecorated ones as well. Cobwebs abounded, unlike the cask room where everything was clean, dry and orderly.

Suddenly he could hear his wife's voice as though she were standing next to him. He looked up, eyes roving the ceiling. It was likely the room was vented to keep it properly dry. It must have a grille in the kitchen for he heard the clink of pottery and the slow rumble of a kettle put on to boil. Conor was winding himself up. The laddie liked his meals on time and made his wants known in no uncertain terms. Casey might have been standing in the kitchen with them, the sounds were so clear. Old houses were like this sometimes, the acoustics performing strange and wondrous permutations so that you could hear a conversation one floor down and three rooms over as though it was right next to you.

Pamela was singing to Conor now, distracting him until his food was ready. Her voice was soft, bubbling with laughter at the edges. He stood and listened, his heart suddenly aching and full with love for his wee family. His wife, his son, all that was most precious to him, right there, singing and laughing in the kitchen above his head.

It came to him then that when you are lucky, when you are redeemed by love, when you have in your life a full measure of goodness, of happiness, that you have to try, at least, to set other things right. You have to extend a bit of faith and hope for, if not believe in, miracles.

He left the room a moment later to walk back up the tunnel and out into the smoke and fog of the winter woods.

THE CONVERSATION WITH CASEY RECALLED TO DAVID one with James Kirkpatrick. They had been sitting in his study late one night, curtains drawn and fire lit, whiskey at hand, chessboard laid out and a game in mid-play. David had made a comment—light enough in itself—about the labyrinthine nature of any sort of dealings in Ulster, both political and business. Jamie had laughed.

"David, if you think you can accomplish anything here in the North without severely compromising everything you believe in, thought you believed in, or were about to believe in, think again."

"Is that what you've done?" David asked. Jamie had looked up from the board, one gull-winged eyebrow arched, but seeing that it was an honest question he answered in kind.

"More than I care to admit, even to myself, David. Unfortunately, I've found that it's utterly impossible to get anything done without enormous amounts of compromise. There isn't a lot of black and white in this country. It's about a million shades of grey instead. I imagine your next question is—do the ends justify the means? That I do not know, but I hope for it. Otherwise I wouldn't be up to my eyeballs in this mess, would I? And nor, I suppose, would you."

Jamie's tone had been light but David had understood the implied threat. That if he had an agenda with Jamie beyond the sharing of information and the actions that sometimes resulted from that information then Jamie would not hesitate to take him out. And David had absolutely no doubt that he could and would do it, and not lose too much sleep over it either. This had only increased his fascination with the man, for he had never met anyone quite as skilled as Jamie Kirkpatrick at presenting a glittering façade of civility while underneath being as ruthless as a shark in pursuing what he felt was right for his country. David had been warned what to expect by his handlers when they had set up the first meeting with Jamie. Still, he had not been prepared for the man himself—and all credit to his handlers—no one could really have prepared him adequately. The first meeting had left him feeling as if His Lordship had whisked his brain with a gently-applied eggbeater.

The hour was late and David knew he must leave soon. He loved this house, loved the mellow ambience of it, the feeling of all those generations having lived here imbued in the very air. And he enjoyed Jamie's company immensely. The man cut little slack and suffered no fools, and David enjoyed the effort required to keep up to Jamie's mind, or at least to bask in the illusion that one was keeping up.

David sipped contemplatively at his whiskey, reveling in the smoke-gold taste of it, allowing it to purl at the back of his tongue before swallowing it. When David put his glass down, Jamie refilled it from a decanter he kept near the chessboard. Jamie's own glass, though filled with the requisite two fingers, remained untouched. As it always did.

"I'm frustrated with how things work, or don't work, in this business of ours." David said, thinking of the naïve soldier he had once been and of the cynicism—hard-earned—that had become a central facet of all his waking hours. "People are naïve about what it actually takes to get anything accomplished, especially in a society where the dealings, by necessity, are dirty from the word go. I can never make my handlers understand that compromises are necessary for even the smallest deal here. Which I suppose is why they keep the Secretary in the dark as to what's on the table."

Jamie smiled, but it was a tired smile.

"David, you know as well as I do that foreign policy often consists of polite diplomacy in public and a deal of compromise and dirty dealings behind the scenes, well away from the sensitive gaze of the public. It's the only way to get things done."

David had always found Jamie's honesty refreshing. It was indeed how things were done, only not many people would admit to it so baldly.

"Just how many languages do you speak?" David asked, for Jamie was well used to his curiosity and never had trouble following his *non sequiturs.*

"Adequately—maybe twenty. Fluently? Less than that. I only know the vulgar words for some."

It was the way many of their conversations went, David noticed with no small frustration and yet an admiration for the man at the same time. He answered any question asked, only the answers often left one feeling more confused than before. David often found himself so enthralled with the answers that were given, he didn't realize until hours later that Jamie had not addressed the heart of the actual query.

"Why do you stay?" he asked. "You have money and the talent to live anywhere, do anything. Why do you stay here?"

The green eyes looked long over the gleaming chess pieces before Jamie answered. But when he finally did, the answer took David by surprise in its simplicity and honesty.

"Because this is my home, and there are people here whom I love. I have three sons in the family burial ground and an ex-wife out west in a convent. Such life as I've lived, and by that I mean the things that have true meaning, has been lived, in great part, here."

In hindsight now, he realized that one of those people who Jamie loved was Pamela Riordan and that he likely stayed in some part to watch over her. Which, knowing what he did of the woman, must have been no small feat on Jamie's part. It also spoke of a love that was selfless. He was a little surprised by it as well, for Jamie had, at times, the brutal practicality of a freshly-sharpened scalpel. He wondered too, as he watched Jamie remove his bishop from the board with a move he had not seen coming, what it would be like to know that this extraordinary man loved you?

"I had a brother," David said, surprising himself by the admission.

"Had?" Jamie said, voice casual, as he moved a knight up diagonally.

"Yes, he's dead." David cursed under his breath, realizing the man across from him was anticipating him at least three moves in advance.

"I'm sorry," Jamie said with such sincerity that David suddenly missed his brother, Edward, as he had not allowed himself to in a very long time.

The evening ended with Jamie beating David with a combination of moves that was Machiavellian in its simplicity. Somehow it never bothered David to lose to him, for Jamie created, from various twisting strands, a whole cloth of congeniality and mellow goodwill, and David had long known it was the game that mattered, not the winning.

Standing now on the edge of the Kirkpatrick land, breathing in the smoke from a not-too-distant peat fire, he remembered what Jamie's final words had been that night.

"We will none of us come out of this unscathed, and that's only if we're lucky enough to come out of it at all."

Chapter Twenty-five

December 1973

The Soldier

BELFAST, SOME DAYS, SEEMED LITTLE MORE than a crematorium. A crematorium for cars and lampposts, tires, baby buggies, piles of rubble, blasted brick and tossed doorways thrown about by the latest bombing episode. A crematorium that held the ashes of a thousand dreams and hopes and false starts and talks and prayers.

Walking through the dank evening air, a chill wind blowing straight through him, Casey smelled the sharp tang of cordite and heard in the distance the popping of sporadic gunfire. Ballymurphy maybe? It was always a hotbed of trouble, though no more than his own old neighborhood, the Ardoyne.

It had been a long day and he longed for the warmth of his home in a visceral manner: fire, food, bed, and warmth with a full belly and the sweet respite of unconsciousness. The car was parked away from their latest building site, if one could call it such, for they were merely repairing the structural damage from a pipe bomb thrown through the open doorway of a pub. Still, it was a chancy site and he had no desire to leave his car to the mercy of the feral hooligans who infested the area.

He thought about leaving sometimes, moving to the Republic, making a fresh start in a community near Dublin or Cork. But something in him always retracted a bit at the mere idea. There was no place in the Republic that was home to him in the way this burning wee city was, no place that called to his bones and blood the way his own bit of land did. The house and the property surrounding it had felt right from the moment he clapped eyes upon it. Something in his soul had settled in right then, and wasn't happy about the idea of being rooted up once again. And the North was his country; the Republic was not.

But for the sake of his wife and son, perhaps he ought to give up this notion of country and tribe and belonging. Because in some ways it wasn't his truth anymore. Leastwise, he didn't belong, not in the circles that he once had. And he was more aware each day of how dangerous such a position was.

He was still on the British Army's hit list and he wasn't entirely in favor with the local lads either, though not so out of favor that he hadn't managed to convey David's message. The gentlemen with whom he had spoken throughout a tense hour had not been quite as skeptical as he himself had been regarding British withdrawal. Which made him think it wasn't the first time they had caught wind of such a thing.

He was jolted from his musings by the sound of steps behind him and knew through long experience that it was the measured, heavy gait of a soldier—of a nervous soldier. And well he should be nervous. He was a little off the beaten path for a soldier. The man must have taken a wrong turn somewhere.

"Hoy—you there, stop!"

He kept walking, hoping to disappear into the shadows that sat heavy between the narrow, dirty buildings. Bloody boy must have a death wish patrolling in this area, because this was Republican territory and a British army uniform was as good as a pulsating bullseye in these streets.

"I said stop—you there!"

There was a point at which a man had to stop or risk having his spine shattered. Casey was all too familiar with exactly where that point lay.

"Get on your knees!"

Casey stopped and put his hands in the air, pushing the fury down under his immediate concern for breathing. He lowered himself down to one knee, making sure to keep all his movements slow and steady. The slightest unexpected move and he would have a bullet through the brain, and there would be none to enquire whether his killing had been justified or not. It was the way of things for a Catholic in Northern Ireland. The cobblestones glistened under his knees, the damp immediately soaking through his trousers.

These boys lived on their nerves, and many of them were just that—nervy boys, ready to shoot at their shadows. Northern Ireland wasn't exactly a prime posting and they only sent in the big guns when the natives got truly restless.

He could hear the rhythmic steps closing in behind him, and kept his head tucked down, eyes fixed to the pavement, but every other sense was alert and scanning for overt hostility and itchy trigger fingers. If the soldier was older—say his own age—the trouble could be much worse. The young ones were never as hard, nor as willing to kill a man in cold blood. The veterans didn't have as much compunction about it. They tended to suspect even Prods of nefarious acts of terrorism. And if they had been posted here long enough, they might recognize him. He knew, by virtue of past acts and his family name, that he was on every watch list.

The muzzle, cold and intrusive, was on the back of his neck now, the soldier breathing heavy—scared or angry? Probably scared. He sensed a boy behind him, not the full menace of a man. A boy he might be able to talk his way round.

"What are you doing out here?"

"Walking," Casey said, unable to keep a weary dryness from his tone, though he knew it was foolhardy to behave so.

"Walking where?"

"Home. My car is parked just another block from here."

"Why isn't it parked closer to wherever you were?"

Casey understood the subtext of this question all too well. If a suspicious looking Irish bastard like himself was walking the streets of his own city, it could only be that he had planted a bomb and was now casually strolling back to IRA headquarters. Tempted as he was to say this aloud, he had learned the hard way to bite down on his tongue and keep his thoughts to himself.

"Because I'm workin' on a building site where there's a few gangs of boys about who slash tires an' such for after-school entertainment, so I don't park there."

With every encounter he endured of this sort, he felt more and more that his luck was running out. What were the odds of coming through an unofficial war, that was seemingly never-ending, unscathed? With family and life intact? These boys came and went but he lived here. This was home, and home was an unceasing battleground.

The muzzle was still there on his neck, intimate in a cold and stomach-dropping way. A split second was all it would take. He felt the fragility of his body all too clearly at present. Unbidden, a vision of Pamela sitting up in the bed that morning—sleepy, hair a wild corona around her head, nursing Conor—flashed through his mind.

No, no—he couldn't think about his family or the panic truly would set in and he might do something that would cause this boy to pull the trigger.

"Go then," the boy said roughly. Casey rose up an inch at a time, not wanting to give the soldier any excuse for leaving his body in the roadway as so many others had been left. His knees were stiff and there was that itch in his backbone that one got when it was a target. It was an itch that had been present much of his life, only of late he seemed to be aware of it all the time.

He walked a small distance away before turning back, the drizzle making the boy's face little more than a flushed blur in the night.

"Ye were hopin' I wouldn't stop, weren't ye?" he asked, though it wasn't really a question and the boy knew it as well as he did.

"Maybe I was," the boy said, caught off-guard into answering honestly.

Casey nodded. There wasn't anything to say to that, and the entire idea of it lay at the bottom of this ungodly war in which they were all engaged.

He could feel the soldier's eyes on him until he reached the end of the road and turned the corner. But Casey, having lived in this city too long, did not look back.

Chapter Twenty-six
Bandit Country

SOUTH ARMAGH HAD LONG EXISTED AS A PLACE APART, even from the rest of Northern Ireland. It was a Republican stronghold with roots in rebellion that went back to the hanging, so the locals claimed, of Big Charley Caraher. Big Charley had, so the story went, stolen a cow and paid for it by having his privy parts cut off before he was hanged. After his death, his body had been quartered and sent to the four corners of the country, and his head displayed on a pike set high so that none might miss it. If this was meant to scare the natives into behaving, it didn't have its intended effect.

Just as some land was sacred, some seemed to foment trouble in its very soil, and South Armagh was such a place. Its entire history was one of betrayal and murder, of disappearances and deceptions that led to some of the bloodiest crimes committed on the entire island. The very geography seemed to encourage such acts. Slieve Gullion rose out of the mists of legend. The mountain was home, it was said, to the Irish hero Cuchulain. Finn McCool was reputed to have been lured into the mountain's lake by the trickster hag, Cailleach Beara, and to have re-emerged from the lake, no longer a young warrior but an old, bent man. The mountain itself was ringed by the depressions of a ring dyke, ancient sentries guarding it since time immemorial.

It was some of the most beautiful country on the entire island, but like a woman whose countenance is exquisite but whose heart is cold, a man took up with South Armagh at his peril. From the beginning of its history, it had been a frontier zone, the no-man's land between the English Pale and the gateway to the world of the Gael.

Certainly there was no piece of ground in the six counties more steeped in blood and violence. It was by far the most dreaded posting for a British soldier. The odds of dying in South Armagh were far higher than in other parts of the Six Counties—even rubble-strewn Belfast was relatively safe in comparison. A soldier's closest companion in South Armagh was pure terror.

Republicans in South Armagh did not see the Troubles as a recent event but rather a continuation of the struggles of the past, one long war of attrition against an enemy who could no more understand their mentality than could an alien from another planet. At the heart of this culture of rebellion was a powerful folk memory, with tales passed from one generation to the next like a precious chalice. In an enclosed community, such tales became part of the blood and code, and the past was as real as the present if not, at times, more so.

It was a land of hard men and the king of the hard men was Noah Murray. The Murray farm straddled the border between the Republic of Ireland and Northern Ireland, a location that gave it certain advantages that Noah Murray had exploited to the full. He had built an empire on smuggling and it was said that much of his money found its way into IRA coffers. Any bit of country close to a border lent itself naturally to smuggling, but Noah Murray had taken it to a new level and become like a pirate king of old. To say he was respected in his area was to belittle the man's stature, for he was feared to the extent that when his name was merely mentioned, even in private company, people went dead silent and averted their gaze. It was as though those who knew him suspected him of psychic powers and were certain he would know if they so much as breathed against him, much less said a word in criticism or anger.

Noah Murray lived with his sister on the farm and he was called 'The Monk' behind his back. No one had ever known him to have a woman in his life, and it was said he made his sister keep his house as clean and spartan as a monk's cell. The Murrays had a long history in the Republican movement. Noah's grandfather had fought in the 4th Northern Division in the War of Independence. Noah's father had been involved in several border skirmishes and was a member of the IRA himself. But even the IRA was a different creature entirely in South Armagh.

In fact, David had noticed in going over the files that many of the names that were on the security forces files from the 1920s were still on them now, with the legacy of the fight passed from father to son *ad infinitum*.

The Murray farm was isolated, its position on the border notwithstanding. High hedges surrounded the property and bounded the narrow track that served as a road into the house. It made surveillance both easier and distinctly more uncomfortable.

The morning was shrouded in mist. Crouched in a ditch just northeast of Noah Murray's farm, David Kendall, secret agent, thought the espionage business was nowhere near as glamorous as Hollywood and spy novels made it out to be. In fact, it was fucking miserable most times, especially when you had slept the night in a ditch and been wakened by an inquisitive sheep, *blaaa*-ting in your ear just as the dawn broke. Then you had to piss in a bottle because you couldn't afford to venture out of said ditch. All in all, not terribly glamorous.

Noah Murray had been under surveillance for some time, but despite the fact that the man was known to run more than one racket from his farm and a variety of bolt-holes around the countryside, they had never been able to get anything concrete on him. David had another motive altogether for taking a turn in this ditch, for the Redhands were planning to take their crazed campaign into the heart of Republican Armagh. Being that he was along for the ride, regardless of how insanely risky it was, he wanted the lie of the land in advance.

Frankly, the entire county made him twitchy. Just last month an innocuous-looking tractor had trundled up to one of the watchtowers that dotted the area and sprayed great arcs of petrol all over it. Then the man inside the tractor had thrown a match, sending the tower up in a whoosh of flame that lit the countryside all round. The guardsmen didn't dare try to get out, knowing the PIRA would be waiting on the ground to pick them off. They had called for help and only managed to survive by taking turns wetting themselves down in the shower.

Watching the activities on the farm had not been dull. It was apparent that Noah's smuggling operation extended beyond pigs, grain and cattle. His assets were hard to assess, and it was rumored that he had hundreds of thousands stashed in foreign banks and in the country under relatives' names. He was also—if even half the stories could be believed—one of the coldest, most ruthless bastards David had ever had the misfortune to run across. People said he only loved one thing in the world and that was his blind sister, Kate.

It was hard to say how much Kate knew about her brother's professional life. Word was he tried to shelter her from it as much as possible and that she turned a literal blind eye to the rest. As if thinking of the woman had conjured her out into the open, he saw her walking across the field. He was impressed by how well she navigated in her world, for she took care of many of the animals, including a few pet lambs. Mostly she walked the property alone, but today she had company. David peered through the binoculars and swore out loud.

Both women were headed directly toward him and he was unhappily aware that he was very familiar with one of them. There was no way out of the ditch without one of them seeing him, being that her eyes and mental acuity were both extremely sharp. He sighed. He liked Pamela Riordan a great deal but would just as soon not run into her at Noah Murray's farm whilst on reconnaissance duty. What the hell was she doing meandering about Noah Murray's land, baby in arms?

There was no way to avoid Pamela spotting him. He took his balaclava off, thinking she wasn't likely to react well if he crawled out of the ditch thus disguised. Being that she was married to Casey Riordan, she might well have a pistol tucked in her sweater pocket.

She started a little when he came out of the ditch, for apparently she hadn't spotted him. When he waved weakly she covered it with a laugh, as though some small rodent had popped out into her path unexpectedly. He could, he swore, feel her glare across the fifty yards of frosted pasture that lay between them. Now Kate was asking questions and looking around as though she sensed his disturbance on the air.

Pamela pointed to something on the horizon and started to talk in an enthusiastic tone whilst making a not entirely polite hand gesture at David behind her back. David took the hint and darted across the bit of pasture between the ditch and the surrounding trees. It could be, even though the girl was blind, that she would be well able to sense him if they came closer. Noah Murray wasn't home, for he had seen him leave just after dawn with a lorryload of pigs destined to make a dizzying loop of a journey, with several different drivers.

David was familiar with the woods hereabouts for a variety of reasons— some professional, some personal. He ducked in and kept his feet to the drifts of dead leaves, slick with frost, so that his footprints would melt away quickly. He knew the twists of the road and followed them roughly, walking cross country and finding himself not surprised in the least when a car stopped on the roadway beside him. He glanced briefly through the tangle of brambles and stone, and then hopped the wall that ran for miles along the country lane.

Pamela was waiting, wrapped in a heather-purple sweater and scarf, passenger door open. She indicated with a nod that he should get in. He slid into the seat, glancing over his shoulder to the baby snugged into the back in his basket, blissfully asleep. The child looked as much like his father as it was possible for someone so small and possessing minimal teeth to look.

She drove off at once, bouncing down the narrow laneway and keeping a sharp eye out the windshield for stray sheep, meandering cows and snipers. Such was the countryside of South Armagh. The baby, seemingly immune to rough roadways, continued to slumber happily.

"David, if you don't mind me saying so," Pamela began without preamble of the small and polite sort, "you're insane. The British Army is insane, the Special Forces are insane, 14th Intel is insane if they think they can make inroads into South Armagh or even touch Noah Murray. I've met a lot of scary people in this country, but nobody quite like this man."

"How the hell do you know about 14th Intel?"

Pamela sighed and raised an eyebrow at him as she slowed to go over a cattle guard. "David, please."

David decided it might be better if he didn't know. This woman often seemed frighteningly well informed.

"What is it about Noah Murray that gives you special pause? After all this is the land of the hard man. What's one more?"

"He doesn't have a conscience. Only when it comes to Kate does he have a soft spot, and even then I think it's limited. I saw some of the things he did when I was still working for the RUC—there aren't words to describe the brutality that went into some of those deaths. He owns this countryside. Surely you know that, and he has a grip on the people here that's almost unimaginable. He rules through absolute fear. I'm sure you know a great deal more than me about how well armed the PIRA are down here."

He did indeed know more, and all of it made him very uncomfortable about what the Redhands wanted to do. It was, as Pamela had so succinctly put it, insane.

"Then surely you ought to be keeping your distance as well."

"I don't go into the house," she said soberly. "Kate is used to it. She isn't anyone's fool and knows what her brother is. She can use a friend, and so can I."

She pulled the car over into one of the overgrown lay-bys that served as stopping points or a passing lane in the countryside. David looked out the window, surprised at the vulnerability in Pamela's tone. Away from them the pastures tumbled, shimmering with frost, the green beneath richer for the contrast. Horses were miniature figures on the horizon, shaped delicately in pewter and roan, bay and chestnut. Closer were the omnipresent sheep, soft rolling bundles of fleece and plaintive calls. An amber haze of sunlight fell, thick and sweet, over it all. It was a bloody gorgeous country, David thought, feeling a sharp ache in his chest for all that had gone wrong here and would continue to go wrong.

They sat quietly surveying it, the sun's warmth an unexpected balm through the windows. The baby shifted and cooed softly in his sleep. David wondered what someone so new would dream of, what soft thoughts occupied someone so tender and fragile, someone so loved and protected?

"I miss Lawrence," Pamela said suddenly and David turned to her. He had forgotten how direct this woman was, even about deeply emotional topics. It was a trait, however, that he found refreshing in this country of subterfuge, where he was rarely allowed the luxury of truth. He waited, for he had a sense that it had not been a statement made merely for its own sake.

"I miss him," she continued, "and I know Casey does too. I know Casey is having a hard time because he didn't know what was happening to Lawrence, and couldn't save him from things he did not know about. But I know," she fixed David with that lucent green gaze that reminded him of James Kirkpatrick in no small degree, "that there is nothing I can do that will bring him back. I also know how much harm might be done by trying."

"Pamela, I—"

She held up a slender hand to forestall him, her silver wedding band turned to gold in the sunlight.

"David, I don't want false promises. They never serve in this country. Just understand that my husband is a man in the finest sense of that word. He believes in protecting and providing for the people in his care, even if those people are gone from him. I understand that, I do—but I am more concerned with protecting the here and now." She glanced back at her son and David did likewise. He still slumbered, cheeks flushed rosily, long thick lashes like fans against his skin.

"I understand," he said, uncertain of how much Casey would have told her.

Point made, she pulled back onto the narrow road. They drove the rest of the way in silence, comfortable enough with one another for this to be acceptable. He watched the wee towns go by, the high, dark hedges dotted with frosted berries, the lanes that twisted and wound and ultimately petered out on the doorstep of an abandoned cottage or a tumbledown of stones that had once been a church. A beautiful country indeed, though 'a terrible beauty' as Yeats had once said.

She stopped short of her own property, near the head of a crooked lane with which David was very familiar. He raised his eyebrows at her but she merely smiled in return. While it was true that she couldn't risk taking him any further and this spot was appropriately isolated so that neither of them would be compromised, he was starting to think the woman might be a witch, what with her knowledge of a variety of things he had thought closely-guarded secrets.

"David," she said softly, and he turned back, facing her in the last of the day's sun. Her face was lit with shades of red and violet. She looked up at him, eyes wide and deep with emotion. "Please take care for him in this thing you've got him involved in. He cares too much, and that blinds him to danger at times."

"I will, Pamela, I promise."

She gave him a slightly weary smile, as if to say she had learned the hard way not to put too much stock in promises in this land and then she was off, car bumping along toward her home.

David walked up the road a small distance and then turned down the lane that led to an old grey farmhouse. The lane rolled down to where the light was deeper, and to the west, a church spire stood dark against the flooding sunset. The scent of peat smoke was on the chill air and there was, up ahead, a light that was kept burning just for him.

Chapter Twenty-seven

January 1973

The Partnership

FRESH SNOW LAY OVER THE GROUNDS OF THE KIRKPATRICK LAND when Robert arrived in the early winter. It was late afternoon, the sun laying a soft burnish over the snow, kindling blushes along the dark oak branches that lined the long, winding road to the house.

When he glanced back, the city below had become something remote—lights blooming in small houses, the snow taking the edge from the darkened brick and narrow streets and coating the rubble of the most recent bombings.

He crested the long ridge and came around the final corner to where the house stood. Bathed in the late afternoon light, it glowed a rosy umber, the long front windows gleaming opaque mirrors that reflected back the trees and sloping lawns that fell like velvet blankets down to the tree line. Vast old oaks clustered like ancient guardians near one corner of the house, a funny structure within them that resembled nothing so much as a Victorian birdcage. He was, from that first encounter, enchanted.

After seeing the inside of the house, and walking the grounds in the damp twilight, this sense had only been heightened. It was a home, not merely a house. Even with its master absent, Robert could feel that much.

The enchantment had continued. Now, walking out beyond the stables, hearing the comforting whicker of horses within, he thought about the letter he had received from His Lordship, penned in a graceful hand. It had a certain amount of economy that reaffirmed Robert's initial impression that Lord James Kirkpatrick was not a man to suffer fools gladly.

It had been clear to Robert from the beginning that he had been chosen specifically to help Pamela Riordan do whatever was necessary to take the reins of the company, that he had been hired to guide and sometimes protect when the waters of commerce and cutthroat business found her out of her depth.

He need not have worried that day in Hong Kong that His Lordship would reject him, for he knew now that the man was farsighted and usually ten moves ahead of everyone else. Robert had been hired for this job, Robert was certain, before Robert had ever heard of it.

The letter had laid out exactly what would be required of both him and Pamela, what it meant to head such a variety of companies, what sort of mind was needed, what sort of makeup would be assumed for meetings with men who would think a young woman could not possibly understand the complexities of corporate collusion and double dealing, men who would happily rob and cheat Jamie's companies blind if they believed they could get away with it. Grimly, and with his Scots Presbyterian backbone appropriately stiffened, Robert was determined not to allow this.

He had been duly warned about Mrs. Riordan's appearance and thought, having witnessed and worshipped the charms of Sallie Rourke, that he was proof against such things and would be able to comport himself with dignity and an absence of awe. It was not to be, however. When he met her in her home, in the presence of her rather large and daunting husband, she had been clad in jeans and a sweater, without cosmetics of any sort and with her hair in a hastily pulled back ponytail. He had barely refrained from letting his mouth hang open. Her husband had smiled as though enjoying a private joke. No doubt the man was used to it but Robert did not envy him. Then again, considering the looks that passed between the two, and the presence of Mr. Riordan himself, the man had little to worry about.

When she arrived at the Kirkpatrick House on the following day, clad in a pale linen dress, hair in a chignon that didn't quite manage to contain all her curls, and with her face lightly made up, he understood absolutely what James Kirkpatrick had meant by his warning. She was—in a word—exquisite, with a wild edge to her beauty that would make many a man think utterly ridiculous thoughts and wish that there was a dragon handy so that he might slay it on her behalf. This, he realized, once his initial astonishment had passed, could be used to their advantage in meetings and in brokering deals.

Working together over the next few weeks, he came to see there were more reasons that Jamie had chosen him as a complement to this woman, for they worked together well. Their minds were fitted to an understanding of not just the nature of the empire they were dealing with, but also the man who had built it from a more modest fortune, with investments spread in so many areas and countries that Robert had thought he might never finish absorbing the Kirkpatrick portfolio.

He only had to sit through one meeting with Pamela to realize that she was politically savvy far beyond anything he had expected in so young a woman. She briefly sketched in her background for him and he felt another piece of the puzzle slide into place. The piece that did not fit, however, was why James Kirkpatrick had left his entire fortune and properties to her, a woman not related to him in any way and married happily to another man, for he had witnessed Pamela and her husband together enough to know that it was indeed a marriage of both joy and passion.

Still, it was not his place to surmise what had prompted Lord Kirkpatrick's decision, only to make the consequences of it as painless as possible. It was a piece of work which was about to become much more difficult than he could ever have anticipated.

HER OWN HUSBAND NOTWITHSTANDING, PAMELA RIORDAN thought that it was possible she had never been so grateful for the presence of a man as she was for that of the small Scot, Robert MacDougall. And that it was also possible she had never been as furious at a man as she was with Lord James Kirkpatrick. Without Robert's steady and sensible hand, she was certain she might simply have set fire to all these sets of papers, documents, ledgers, figures, facts, webs, entanglements, and walked away cursing Jamie roundly.

She had a headache for the first week, trying to understand the labyrinth that constituted Jamie's empire. She had more than a passing acquaintance with it already, having worked as his secretary for a brief time, but this was more a baptism by Greek fire—all-consuming and without mercy. She was still trying to absorb the fact that, in some fit of madness, Jamie had decided to hand all this over to her.

In its entirety, it overwhelmed her—the flaxes and barley crops, the presses and parts, the boilers and reducers, the forests and mills, the forges and farms, the refineries and warehouses, the ships and silks, the cogs and wheels, both literal and figurative that in one way or another bore the imprimatur of the Kirkpatrick name. Jamie had taken all of it seriously and understood the nuts and bolts of every investment he had made. And as much as he made, he was also generous with it. The charities, thank heavens, were administered by a lawyer and weren't something she had to deal with directly, except for those things that Jamie had done himself face-to-face, such as Nelson McGlory and his eyeglasses, chess games, dinners and outings. There were many Nelsons in Jamie's life, and she felt guilty that she had not understood just what Jamie's life truly entailed in all its details. But then, she supposed, there was no reason she ought to know. She was only a small corner of his life, and therefore her view was bound to be limited.

She was shown clearly though, that Jamie's life was lived on a level that affected entire nations and the ties between them, tenuous as they might be. It made the political world in Boston, of which she had been part for a time, seem very small potatoes in comparison. She was quick-witted enough to know there were still some very dark corners into which she could shine no light. She also knew that those dark corners were best left as they were.

Robert was one of the lights, and had quite obviously been chosen very specifically to help her. His very presence was calming and he understood instinctively how much she could absorb on any given day. He had an extremely good mind for both finance and organization—was brilliant at it, really—which left her to wonder why he had chosen to take a position with Jamie in this manner. He was also as solid a personality as she had ever met, and completely unflappable under pressure. Which was why, when he came into the kitchen one afternoon with a very particular look on his face, she felt an immediate flutter of anxiety.

She was having a late lunch, feeding Conor apples mashed with strawberries and chatting with Maggie.

"What is it?" she asked.

"We have company," Robert said and there was no mistaking the warning in his voice.

"Who?" she asked, trying to detach Conor's small sticky hands from her hair.

"Jamie's great-uncle—he says he's Jamie's grandfather's brother. As far as that goes it seems to be, most unfortunately, true."

His tone became clear. She stood upright and looked him in the eyes. "Most unfortunately. Obviously this is not a welcome visit, nor a restoration of a family member that was missed. Would you care to fill me in?"

"No, the tiny Scot couldn't possibly do the story justice," said a voice that skittered along her spine like a many-legged insect. She turned and thought Robert's tone had not done justice to the situation, nor the man about to create it.

It was like seeing Jamie through a long, dark glass, a glass that distorted through time and vice, through uncontrolled appetite and corruption. He was tall, but soft around his edges, with heavy hands that held several rings. The clothes were expensive, well cut, but could not hide that they shrouded a man well past his prime. Even money could not sweeten this particular visage.

He walked toward her and her body stiffened. She had known men like him before, men without kindness, men without moral fiber or honor in even its palest shade. She was determined never to be a victim of one again.

As he came closer, the initial illusion of him bearing any resemblance to his nephew dissipated. His eyes were a cold shade of blue, his hair was darker than Jamie's and, she suspected, its color came from a dye bottle rather than any endowment of nature.

He took her hand and she repressed the shudder that came naturally as he lowered his lips to touch them to her skin.

"Well," he said, "I certainly understand what my nephew's thinking was when he signed over this entire estate to you."

"Really and what would that be?" she asked, affecting a cool tone, though he was still holding onto her hand. His touch felt like that of a reptile—

clammy, chill and ravenous.

"I don't know his precise thoughts, but I certainly know which part of his anatomy was doing the thinking."

She took her hand from his with no small effort. She laid her other hand on Robert's arm, feeling the angry words before they traversed his tongue. Neither of them was going to give this man anything he wanted if she could help it.

"Perhaps you would be so good as to join Robert and myself, in the sitting room? Maggie, could you bring tea?"

Maggie nodded, her look stabilizing Pamela's backbone and resolve. From the sharp glance directed toward him, Pamela thought, Uncle Philip would be lucky if there wasn't arsenic in his tea. She left Conor with Maggie, happily playing with a pot and spoon.

She chose the sitting room for its formality, and because she did not want this man in Jamie's study, even if the bulwark of the desk would have been very welcome to hide her shaking knees.

A fire was already crackling in the grate. Maggie lit the fires in the downstairs rooms to prevent damp this time of year, despite the presence of the central heating that had been installed many years ago. It was warm and the furniture, though formal, was also comfortable. Pamela chose a chair with a stiff back, to keep her upright and placed no lower than this man. The Chinese, she knew, called it 'face' and she was determined to keep hers firmly in place. Robert sat to her left, slightly back, so that it would be clear to Uncle Philip that he was there guarding her side, but that it was she who was ultimately in charge.

Maggie brought the tea, placing it on the low table that sat between them all. Pamela poured it out, the delicate scent of Earl Grey filling the air. She handed a cup to each man and then took her own, grateful for the small warmth it provided against the chill this man had brought with him into the room.

Philip chose to go on the offensive immediately.

"You have much to learn, my dear. In my day we didn't allow the help into the sitting room and certainly did not let them attend on private conversations."

"Robert is my right hand," she said coolly. "Any concerns you may want to place before me will also be heard by him. Now, perhaps you will be so kind as to tell me what it is you want?"

"I think that ought to be clear," he said, and picked up his teacup, taking a swallow of the hot brew, icy-cool eyes never once leaving her face. There was an avidity to his gaze that touched and defiled everything he looked at, as if he, like a greedy child, would eat all of it, swallowing before he could even taste.

"Oh, it is," Pamela said tartly. "But I should like it spelled out all the same."

"If my nephew is dead, and it seems that he must be, then this will," he invested great scorn into the single syllable, "cannot be allowed to stand. While you are lovely, you are not blood and in this case, blood will out. This estate should have been mine when my brother passed and now, with all other heirs dead, it will be."

"This estate," she said quietly, "passes to the eldest child, of which you are not one. As Jamie has no living heirs to pass it to, it was to his discretion whom he wanted as its guardian until such time as he returns home. There was no mention of you in any of the papers and we have a team of solicitors who went over all of it in fine detail with us."

"I too have solicitors," he said, placing the teacup on the table. "They do not share your belief that Jamie had the legal right to leave the guardianship of this estate in the hands of whomever he pleased. They believe I have a very good case and I intend to prosecute it to the fullest extent."

"I believe that will be a waste of your time and money," Pamela said, keeping her tone pleasant. "But if you wish to squander both commodities that will, of course, be your own business."

"Indeed it will," his tone was pleasant too, but not without challenge. "Long ago, I approached my nephew, Jamie's father, and asked him for what was rightfully mine. And then when he died, I asked his son. Now I find I am no longer inclined to ask but rather to tell. This house and all that is in it belongs to the Kirkpatrick family and I am, despite being Fortune's outcast, most assuredly a Kirkpatrick. Family should administer the estate. It is unfortunate that young James has met with some terrible fate, but while it is tragic it does not alter the fact that this estate is mine, should have been mine long ago and, of course, it goes without saying that I will be claiming all the assets that go with it."

"I believe it shows a somewhat less than familial feeling to keep insisting that Jamie is dead, which I assure you he is not." She smiled, for Jamie would not want her to give in to her anger at this man. She had her own fears as to the state of Jamie's well-being, but refused to believe he was gone. This man, despite his words, had likely long wished Jamie dead. She could almost hear Jamie's voice in her head, cautioning her to never underestimate even the most obvious adversary.

She stood to refill the cups, adding the sugar and lemon in exact measurements. She would not allow the standards of hospitality to slip, even when the guest was overtly hostile. His eyes seemed to pluck at her neckline and pry through the very seams of her clothing. It was nearly time to nurse Conor and her breasts were taut against her blouse. She felt as though the man sensed this, or could see the change since they had left the kitchen. She felt in need of a shower, merely from the touch of his gaze. It was, she knew, very deliberate on his part.

She sat back down, fighting the desire to wrap her sweater around herself in defense.

"Satisfy my curiosity, will you?" he said, stroking one puffy finger along his lips. "Tell me what that much money and property buys a man?"

"Not what you seem to think it does," Pamela said dryly, averting the hot words she could feel bubbling up in Robert beside her. She knew, though just how she could not have said, that it was imperative that they keep their cool in the face of this threat. And that this man was a threat, she was in no doubt.

He canted one leg over the other and leaned back. The gesture echoed his nephew, though this man's elegance seemed a practiced, conscious part of his arsenal, whereas with Jamie it was merely a natural part of him.

"You might be surprised what I'm thinking." He paused for effect, "I have a very fertile imagination."

It was as though Robert were not even present, for the man was very clear about whom he was inviting onto the sparring field. Jamie had this skill as well, to make it seem as if there was no one else present, even when the room was crowded. But this was the inverse of Jamie's skill, a dark feeling, as though he could touch without moving, could sense the fears that moved inside her about what sort of damage he could do, and that he fed on it.

It had been one innuendo too much for Robert, for the small Scot stood, tone brisk.

"I think sir, that you've taken up enough of Mrs. Riordan's time and hospitality this afternoon. I believe it will surprise no one if I say that next time we meet, it should be with legal representation in attendance and in a less private venue than Lord Kirkpatrick's home."

Pamela rose to stand beside Robert, aware as she did so of Philip's eyes skimming the length of her body. She ignored it, for there was nothing else to do.

It appeared Uncle Philip had gotten whatever it was he wanted from the meeting, for he rose as well, again with that inverted echo of practiced elegance.

She walked him to the door alone, after giving Robert a look which conveyed that he should stay behind. She needed to show Philip that she was not afraid to be alone with him, that she had indeed been left with Jamie's trust for reasons other than what he believed.

He bent once again over her hand, and she allowed it, for she would not give him the pleasure of having her shake him off. He could not know how much he had discomfited her in a single meeting. His lips were cold against the back of her hand and his tongue flicked lightly along the edge between two of her fingers. The inference was inescapable, and she repressed a shudder of revulsion before gently disengaging her hand.

"You will be seeing much more of me," he said as he stood, "and I, of you. It would be better if you were pleasant with me, Pamela. It will go far easier for you in the end."

She merely showed him out the door, unwilling to give him the engagement he was looking for until she was on more certain ground.

She let out the breath she had been holding, after barring the door behind him. Then she went to the kitchen, picked up her son, and took him to the study to nurse. The normality of it and the soft weight of Conor's body in her arms siphoned away some of her agitation.

Robert, who had the timing of a master statesman, rapped on the study door just as she finished nursing. He came in looking slightly grim.

He poured them each a small tot of whiskey and set hers on the table beside her. She left it for the moment, putting Conor to her shoulder and letting his sweet weight and warmth finish the job it had begun. She felt more relaxed, though not much more capable.

"How much of a threat is he?" she asked. She was sitting in the wingback leather chair Jamie favored. She needed some vestige of his presence to shore her up in the face of this menace.

Robert sat across from her and took a deep breath. "I'll not know yet, but if he's right and Lord Kirkpatrick is dead, then your hold on things—despite the will—may be more tenuous then we would like. As the man pointed out, he is blood and, as you are well aware, Jamie made a very unexpected move by entrusting everything to your hands. I know he had very good reasons for doing so, many more than I perhaps realize, but blood is blood and will often win out in a court of law. If nothing else, he can tie our hands badly and cost us hugely in time. He could be distracting us for some other purpose, as well. Certainly it's clear he is neither a good nor scrupulous man so we will have to be very much on our guard. Pamela—we can't afford a single mistake or so much as a ha'penny to be unaccounted for in the company ledgers."

Conor sighed in repletion, his breath warm against her neck. She wanted to close her eyes as he did and go to sleep, anything to avoid thinking about this newest problem. However, it wasn't merely about her and what suddenly seemed her frightful inadequacy. There were many other people depending on her to be strong.

"Then that's what we will do. Jamie trusted us to protect what he built. I refuse to let him down. If he had wanted his uncle to have anything, he would have stipulated as much in the will. Jamie is a very generous man, so if he didn't put his uncle into the will, there's a damn good reason why."

"What if...?" Robert began, but did not continue, for the words were already there between them, had been there during the entire conversation.

"No," she said fiercely, "no! Jamie is not dead. He will come home."

Robert's face looked more owlish than usual, the soft light playing off his glasses.

"I think perhaps," he said gently, "we have to consider that he may not be able to come home, that perhaps we are indeed on our own here, Pamela."

"No. He will come home, Robert. He will because he has to."

From the Journals of James Kirkpatrick

June____, 1962

I am hiding. I know that well, but as hideaways go it would please even a hermit. The path down to the house runs between thick stands of pine and the pathway itself is so deep with needles you can't even hear your own footsteps. A wee weathered gate hangs crooked as sin between two pines and is thick with a rambling rose of unknown provenance. The house itself—well, hut if we're being strictly technical—is held together by the most frighteningly large and vengeful-looking wisteria, though from a distance the overall impression is one of great charm. Up close, you realize that without the vine the whole place would likely crumble into dust.

Inside, it's just rough pine planking for both floor and walls, well weathered to a deep amber and thick with the scent of summers past. A small iron bedstead holds a lumpy mattress and worn bedding that is nevertheless clean and smells of the salt and sand that impregnates every atom of air here. I can rest here. I can hide here, and maybe if I am very lucky, I can find a way to solidify this amorphous jelly of a universe I inhabit.

June____, 1962

In the night, this is a different country, when the fields do lie under some dark enchantment. In the night, when humanity sleeps, you can feel the ancient bones of this land twist and groan and rise ever closer to the surface. In the night, the shy creatures are abroad, the fox who gazes at the moon transfixed, the owl flying on silent wings through the mountains and streams of the air. In the night there is no law. The borders of daytime float away and the wild rules at will.

When it's dark, I feel the planet as she must once have been, a free and dreadful thing growing rampantly, suckling dread young who were born with the taste of blood upon their grasping tongues.

I walk amongst all this darkness and hear the whispers of wild things, and the language of earth and thrusting weed, of the sea and its own dark creatures—things that will never see the light of day. Yet I sense their bodies, floating, diaphanous, dreadful, simmering near the surface, drawn there by the moon's silver lure. They prick their claws along my spine and make me glance behind to find my shadow a grotesque thing, reminding me who the true monsters of this world are.

You can feel the planet spinning at night in a way that the busyness of day precludes. I cannot seem to rid my head of the words of Walter de la Mare in these dark hours—

The waves tossing surf in the moonbeam,
The albatross lone on the spray,
Alone know the tears wept in vain for the children
Magic hath stolen away.

Would that it had been magic that had taken my sons away, that I might believe them gone to a far land, where flowers storm like snow and boats dip and stream along the Milky Way.

Colleen said to me that we cannot produce anything but children born with broken hearts—I suppose it stands to reason at this point, as both of ours are broken.

A broken heart does not mix well with sleep. It keeps one awake for the fear it has of death before morning. Yet I do not fear my own death. Instead I think of it with something akin to longing because it would be a release from these awful, shivering thoughts that I cannot obliterate from my mind. Perhaps it is why the night seems a natural home for me now. I understand the dark things, the yawning abysses of the world, the things that exist beyond the realm of today's laboratories. The dark is for magic, good and bad, woven from realities and the deep dreams that lie fallow in the base of man's brain.

I often look up to the night sky during my rambles and wonder as man has wondered since he crawled up out of the blood warm seas—Are we alone here? Am I looking for God or little green men?

I cast my mind out far, over the great depths and fiery dance of the countless suns, moons and stars to the edge where the tide of infinity laps against those original starry shoals and ask—what, who, how? Is there another mind out there that could recognize the firing neurons of my own? Is there a yearning as vast as that of humanity, the hope that if we reach out with radio waves, spaceships, telescopes—that our grasping fingers will touch more than... nothing? And what would we hear inside that great silence, which seems as though it would be the most terrifying sound of all?

June____, 1962

I miss my wife. There, I've admitted it. I miss the woman I married. I want to be able to comfort her and I cannot and it makes me feel entirely impotent as a man. I feel like a shell here, as I wander the woods and the shore. Even sailing does not bring the needed reprieve. Nothing does, and the light is changing, making that imperceptible shift that warns me I'm nearing the edge of the abyss. The trouble with falling into that abyss is that even if one can manage to climb out, one cannot shake off the ghosts that cling and crawl out with one, for the abyss is haunted. I know, because those ghosts keep me company tonight. They cluster close and whisper the things I wish I could deafen myself to, but I hear them. I hear them well and their voices rise higher each moment, until I cannot hear anything else for their clamor.

June_____, 1962

I was out for a solitary ramble this evening, when I came across a most enchanting sight. At first I thought I was seeing things—always in the realm of possibility with my quixotic and unreliable grey matter—and even rubbed my eyes to be certain I wasn't hallucinating. But no, the vision remained. There was a creature dancing on the small shingle just down from my hut, dancing light and joyous under the full moon that was rising on a twilit sky. She can't be of this realm, I thought, for she seemed impossibly 'other', as though she had never tasted of man's disillusion or bitterness, and knew no such word as pain. I told myself a pretty fancy, as I stood there watching her. She was born of the sea foam, and rose right there from the mysterious waters for a dance on the solidity of the earth, and that when she was done she would slip back into the waters with barely a sigh in her wake, and return to that deep blue kingdom from whence she had come. And there was I, mortal clay, having caught a young oceaniade cavorting on the sand.

I could be forgiven my fancy, I believe, because she looked like no earthly child, carved out against the background of dark dreaming pine and old mossy stones, with the surf foaming around her ankles. Her hair was wet and streaked like seaweed down her back, the color of indigo in the moonlight. Of course I would find her dancing there on the edge of the earth, feet in the water—that place where two elements meet and are neither here nor there has long been considered a place of magic, and making of the impossible, possible.

How long I stood there, I do not know, but suddenly she turned as though she sensed human interference in her fairy revels, and her eyes cut across the gloaming so that I was certain she had spotted me. I couldn't have moved though, not for all the tea in China, for I recognized her and the recognition rooted me there. There is no way to say this without sounding foolish—or mildly insane—but it was one of those moments that do not come in all lives, where I just knew someone—all of them. I knew that if she could see me, she would know me too—without words, or explanations—as though we both belonged to another race, another time, and were the only two survivors left here stranded on a strange planet, where neither of us truly understands the rules.

A fool's fancy, and sitting here now with the fire crackling away, and a very prosaic cup of tea at my left hand (unable as I was to find mead in these sensible cupboards), I feel a fool even writing the words. Perhaps she was merely a vision born of a wildly romantic night of moonlight and amber-scented pines and the great wild body of the sea, not to mention the lack of medication in my bloodstream.

Perhaps.

June____, 1962

I spoke briefly with Colleen today. Briefly, because it seems neither of us can find words to bridge this terrible span between us. I cannot comfort her and she cannot forgive me.

It was a dull day, with the sort of oppressive humidity that sits on this coast occasionally during the summer. I could feel the weight of it reflected in my mood. So I forced myself to take care of the business that has lagged in my absence, the thousand small decisions that never fail to be good for one, especially when I consider the people who make up the companies and how even the finest details affect their lives. It is good to know there will be plenty to keep me busy once I return home.

July____, 1962

My moonlight oceaniade is real.

I was fishing below the tiny bridge that spans the stream near my hut, when I heard the unmistakable thump of horse hooves approaching. I was in no mood for company so I only poked my head around the struts of the bridge, where I would have a view of the trespasser. She stopped just short of the bridge, apparently having some difficulty with the horse's bridle. Now, I ask you, would a creature of sea foam need a bridle?

I was equal parts relieved and disappointed to know that she was an actual flesh-and-blood child. Mind you, even in the suffering light of day, she did not look fully human—except that she was exceptionally grubby and clad in a shirt printed with cabbage roses—surely an oceaniade would not be caught in such a thing. And she was cursing volubly at the horse she rode. Then again, who is to say even enchanted sea creatures aren't given to fits of temper and astoundingly coarse epithets. Sailors would have blushed to hear the tongue on her. I myself was quite impressed, and stood with my mouth open as she passed, without noticing I was there.

She sorted out her troubles with the bridle, though it took several minutes, during which time she had plenty to say to both the horse and the universe in general. Surely it is only my imagination but she seemed to have a lilt in her voice, as though the green hills of my own country were somewhere in her background.

She wore no shoes—well, an oceaniade wouldn't be aware of something so prosaic as footwear, now would she? The shirt she must have stolen from a drying line on a moonlit flit inland. Otherwise, surely she would be clad in Neptune's robes.

As she ambled away, good relations restored with both bridle and world, I felt slighted—for no sensible reason—that she didn't sense me there, even if I was standing in waist-high bracken in the shade of the bridge.

I really ought to take my nasty little pills before I find myself dancing on the seashore too.

July ___ , 1962

Well, my oceaniade most certainly is human if broken bones and vomit are anything by which to judge. The former is her ankle and the latter caused me to throw my shoes out. I saw her out early this morning on a big, black brute of a stallion that she had no business whatsoever riding. I would have trouble controlling him, never mind a slip of a girl, which to him probably felt like a minor irritation on his back, to be quickly disposed of.

As befits a sea creature, however, she was pounding down the beach, barely clinging to his mane. Whatever on earth possessed her to ride bareback on such a beast, I do not know—or rather I do—but that's neither here nor there at this juncture. I could see disaster coming as clear as the crash of the Hindenburg. Like most disasters one sees rolling out before one's eyes, I could not reach her in time to prevent it.

There was, literally, a snake in the grass, and the horse reacted as horses will in such situations. He reared up and flung his rider off as if she weighed no more than a bit of oat grass. She might have been fine, only jarred and bruised, but his hoof glanced off her ankle on the way down. I think I will hear her screams echoing down the next several weeks. I ran to her, but she was mercifully passed out by the time I reached her. I carried her to the nearest house and had them call the local doctor.

*She woke briefly before the doctor shot her full of morphine and seemed to think I was an angel hovering over her. I would have found it funny, considering how I mistook **her** for a mythical creature at first, but her eyes were so filled with pain and terror and confusion that I only sought to reassure her. She passed out again, and when she came to after the ankle had been set, tried to sit up. The result is splattered all over my discarded shoes.*

When I asked about her origins, I was told she is Thomas O'Flaherty's daughter, who is rather famed as a financial wizard here. With the sort of old, quiet money that resides on this Island, that is saying something. A flesh and blood child who spends her winters in New York, I am told, and becomes a wild solitary creature each summer on the Island, with the unlikely name of Pamela. I was right about the lilt of her tongue though. Her father is a born Irishman who emigrated some years back, but she has spent many of her summers on an estate in County Clare.

Her father is, at present, on business in China, and she is under the dubious care of a woman named Rose. When I went to inform her of the girl's injuries, she reeked of drink. Being that it was just noon when I knocked on the door, the woman must be a rampant alcoholic.

I fear that bringing her home to that cottage and leaving her under the aegis of such a woman is tantamount to some sort of sacrilege. Can one leave such a creature in the hands of a rough-mouthed Irish scrubwoman? This isn't elitism speaking, for this Rose has the soul of a scrubwoman as well as the demeanor. At least the mystery of Pamela's merchant marine lexicon is solved.

Pamela—the name sits oddly on my tongue—for oceaniades surely are not meant to have names.

July____, 1962

After a few setbacks, Pamela is on the mend. The poor child has suffered horribly during these hot days, an allergy to morphine and the bones in her ankle having to be re-set being the worst of it. She is out of hospital now and able to hobble about, and so today we took ourselves out among the tall pointed firs and into the salt-sticky day, thick with sunshine and the scent of wild roses.

She hasn't made friends with the local girls nor the summer visitors. I suspect this is because she is too singular and because the girls can see already that she will one day have a beauty that will, even on its simplest days, eclipse their brightest entirely. Girls see and know these things and act according to the dictates of their tribal pecking orders. Such a girl never fits within those confines and therefore never lives the charmed life that so many others envy her.

For now, it would appear, I am her only friend, and she mine.

July____, 1962

It's interesting how summer seems to be the season in which one can retreat back to one's childhood pleasures and savor them again as much as one did at ten. Today we went sailing, and it turns out that Pamela is a bit of an oceaniade in more than just appearance, for she sails like she was born to it, as though water is a more natural home to her than the earth. Well, it stands to reason, doesn't it?

Afterwards we had dinner at a ramshackle hut near the shore that serves the most ambrosial lobster stew imaginable. She has regained her appetite and so, oddly, have I. I feel as though I have been sleeping for a long time and now, in the presence of this pure spirit, I am waking up and finding life still holds a sweet, sharp joy.

She truly is a most arresting child. I barely understand my own emotions around her, only that in her I have found a friend such as I never hoped to find again in my life. Her mind is far beyond her years and she's conversant in poetry, prose, cabbages and kings. Last night she quoted Patrick Kavanaugh to me as we came through the gate into the field—

> And then I came to the haggard gate
> And I knew as I entered that I had come
> Through fields that were no part of earthly estate.

"Doesn't that give you the most delicious shiver?" she asked me. "I feel it sometimes in this field, as if I've stepped out of time and place and I expect to see strange creatures in the brush that are nothing to do with this world."

She was right. There is something about that particular field, a sort of magic that isn't entirely wholesome and is therefore a tad more exciting. She often seems to anticipate my thoughts, and will finish sentences with an eagerness that tells me hers is a mind that has been starved of the sort of company it needs to flourish. And so I do what small things I can, bring her books of poetry and the ancient classics. She has picked up enough Latin and Greek already to make her way slowly through short passages of Ovid and Virgil. I am learning to love them again through her thoughts and interpretations. She halted no more than five lines into the first eclogue yesterday and, fixing me with that terribly honest and rather stern green gaze of hers, asked if I, like the narrator, was exiled from home. I found myself saying 'yes' before I could think to halt my tongue.

In truth, I am exiled at present—not through choice—but rather through circumstance. I could go home if I chose, but what waits for me there except further proof of my own shortcomings and failures? I know come autumn there will be no more avoiding 'home' and I will return, for good or ill, to resume my real life. For now though, I linger with this strange and lovely child, telling myself I do it for her good, yet knowing it is she that is so very necessary to me.

When our lesson was done, she seemed preoccupied and then looked at me very seriously, those green eyes like a rake on one's soul and said—"A gem cannot be polished without friction, nor a man perfected without trials."

Just that and no more, that light, slightly grubby hand resting on my own as if it had been formed there and was as natural as the sun setting in the evening. It is worrying that I need not express my thoughts or the streaks of melancholy that come across me from time to time. She understands, and has no compunction about calling me out on them.

And that, I suppose, is what I get for teaching the child about Roman philosophers.

July____, 1962

In the way that I always do, I've attracted a few strays. I swear there's a siren call that goes out when I settle in anywhere for more than a day or two that only animals can hear. The most disreputable looking marmalade cat has taken up residence on the front porch and even the suffocating wisteria cannot muffle his howls. He is the veteran of a thousand battles, to judge from his scarred hide, like some old Roman soldier who hasn't been home for decades and knows nothing but the fight. He is missing an ear, and his nose looks like it was split by a fairy axe.

His appearance is not one of beauty, but Pamela is smitten with him and talks to him as though he were Prince Valiant. Lord knows that beauty is no requirement for love, and a bloody good thing too.

For her sake, I am feeding and watering him, though come the autumn he will once again be cast upon the mercy of nature.

I did say a few strays, didn't I? We also have in residence an ancient and rather moldy-looking raccoon who looks in the window of nights, giving me the fright of my life. I think he passed his sell-by date about a decade ago but isn't aware he was supposed to lie down quietly and die beneath a leafy green tree, or at least have the good grace to eat a poisoned bit of meat.

I suggested perhaps the cat might be happier residing at her cottage.

"Louis won't go," she said. "He likes living with you."

"Louis?" I echoed, feeling as I often do with her, slapped with tangents.

She gave me one of those lucid green looks that manages to say, 'Keep up, you thick sod,' without her ever moving her mouth. All the while hand-feeding the cat—oh, pardon me, Louis—tunafish.

"Besides, Rose is allergic to cats." She sighed and leaned down to kiss the filthy cat on the top of his ratty head, managing to convey the idea that Rose is also allergic to herself. Certainly the damnable woman acts as though she is, for she has given this girl up into my care as though she has been waiting for someone to come along and lay claim to her. I know how society views such a relationship, but she is hardly Lolita and I am not in the market for a prison sentence.

But what if—just what if—you found the dearest friend of your life in the body of a twelve-year-old girl? Written out, it looks perverse, but it doesn't feel so when she is sitting here discussing Plato or the Ulster Cycle with me, or making me laugh as I no longer thought it possible to laugh.

When I queried the universe as to whether there was an invisible sign out there that had denoted me as a flophouse for the world's strays, she asked me if I considered her such. She has not learned the art of coyness, therefore I knew it was an honest question and so I answered it in kind.

"No, you are not a stray, Pamela. You are my friend."

"Thank you," she said back to me, with the grave look that penetrates right through to my soul.

What I did not add was that it is myself who is the stray, and that someday she will be old enough to know that. For now I am grateful for her ignorance.

August____, 1962

I have a manuscript due with my publishers in London at the end of this month. The last tome from the purple pen of the Professor, I hope.

With this deadline hovering, I was in the back garden—such as it is—scribbling, cat upon my knee, when she came on me.

"What are you writing?" she asked, plunking herself down in the canvas chair opposite, Louis abandoning me with yowling meows the minute he saw her.

I started and flushed as guiltily as if she had come across me naked, doing something reprehensible to a sheep.

*"Oh, it's **that** sort of thing," she said, then raised a brow at me and smiled. For a single moment, it was as though the woman that she will one day be looked straight out her eyes at me and I was struck to the spot. I envy the man who will one day have her for his own. He is fortunate.*

*"I have read Catullus, after all," she said, and gave me a look that can only be described as bold. Sometimes I wonder if it is I who is not old enough for **her**.*

August_____, 1962

I can no longer reach Colleen. The nuns say she has asked to be left in silence for awhile. I do not know what to make of this. I only know it felt as though someone had stabbed me hard in the chest when the good sister said, 'I regret to tell you, Mr. Kirkpatrick...'

Yes, I regret too, dear Sister Anne. I regret so many things. I regret that I do not know how to pull my wife back from the wasteland into which she has wandered. A realm that she has traveled so far into that I fear I may never be able to retrieve her and bring her back into the warmth of what we knew for such a brief time. For I am no white knight, nor do I possess a steed that can carry me through the thicket of thorns and pain that separates us now.

In fairytales, the princess always ends up with her prince, but this is not a fairytale and I cannot cross wastelands without water or forge pathways through fire. What the fairytales don't always tell you is that in real life the prince sometimes has to let the princess go, even if she is taking his heart with her and he doesn't expect ever to have it returned.

What if all she needs is for me to let her go? Do I have the strength for that? For I truly believed, in that mute core where we all hold our most unshakeable beliefs, that we would love each other through this lifetime into old age and infirmity. And now—now I do not know what I believe anymore.

August_____, 1962

There are ghosts in my head tonight, dreadful, rattling things with the wind singing laments through their bones. That poem by Sorley McLean is brought sharply to mind—

Who is this, who is this in the night of the heart?
It is the thing that is not reached,

the ghost seen by the soul...

That is so exact, the ghost seen by the soul—elusive, yet I am never able to rid myself of it. When the days are especially sharp and bright and the very air tastes like wine, I know I will soon see that ghost. I can hear the faint echo of its chains rattle most clearly when my mind is fire bright and I can write without sleep or sustenance for days.

Tonight, however, is not a firelit one, and I can see the outlines of that ghost clearly, and how very dark and nasty is his shape, his visage that of hell itself. The shade of him is on the wall, flickering in my peripheral vision but not to be seen face on. He is too clever for that, this dark slitherer that infests my brain at will.

Tomorrow morning I may well wake up in another world, another universe even. I will be able to see the old one from my vantage point, but I will not be able to touch it nor find my way back to it. For there are holes between this world and that, fractured panes of glass through which one can view events and people though the broken glass always distorts them, shapes all interactions oddly, changes the light and the sound so that voices come from a great distance yet are overly loud and grating—as though every word slaps my skin and flicks at my nerves. But there are no maps for this dark planet.

Sometimes I really do believe the dead can walk. Because there are nights I'm certain I'm one of them.

August_____, 1962

*I have lost three days, just like that, as though the planet whirred round triple fast on its orbit and flung three days out into space. I might even think this **had** happened except that it appears the rest of the world did indeed experience those three days. I haven't had a blackout like this since I was nineteen and it has shaken me to my roots. I don't know where I went or what I did and can only hope that I holed up somewhere and did no damage to anyone or anything.*

I woke up two nights ago in a mist-chill field with no idea of how I came to be there, nor what field it was or even if I'd managed to stay on the Island. I set out walking in an easterly direction for I could hear the sea faint on the night air and knew if I could make my way there, I could navigate back to this shambling salt tossed cottage and lock myself in until I could turn the world back from its upside-down orientation.

I have that dreadful arid feeling in my head, as though my mind and memory are nothing more than sand blown about by any chance ill wind. I write here in the vain (I fear) hope that something will swim up out of the pitch dark of my subconscious and shine a small light on what took place these last days. Even in my bipolar state, I know this sort of incident is not normal—as much as anyone can apply the term 'normal' to a mental illness.

Apparently I have been cared for during this episode. Once I was lucid enough to realize how much time had passed, I stumbled out to the stable to check on Pelargonium, worried that he was half-starved and dehydrated with neglect. But there was fresh hay in his stall, unsullied water in the trough and a look of smug contentment on his face that said he'd had adequate exercise. It's as though a fairy has stolen in and out and arranged things so that my disappearance would leave no trace upon either myself or my surroundings. There is fresh milk in the fridge, tea (loose—so I know the Irish preference is understood) and the place has been dusted and aired. The sheets are fresh and there is a vase stuffed willy-nilly with the wild roses that fill the roadsides here.

It is, of course, Pamela who has been, done, and cared. Sometimes she seems a child and others, like now, she is far older in soul than anyone else I've ever met. I tried to thank her, to ask her what had happened, what she'd witnessed but she only looked at me long and soberly, and said, "It's alright, Jamie. We don't need to talk about it."

And that, it seems, is to be the last word, for she refuses to speak to me on the subject. Which begs the question of what the hell I may have done or said to her during that time. I shudder to think, because I have no memory and feel like I am only now inhabiting my body once again. I try to judge by the way she holds herself and the look in her eyes—normally so telling—but currently she is a closed book where I am concerned.

August_____, 1962

My oceaniade refuses to leave me to the mercies of myself and has been here each night since I came up out of the abyss. I suspect somehow, in some way, she is responsible for my reappearance in the land of the living.

That first evening after I returned to myself, she sat propped in the ancient chair at the end of my bed, a worn copy of Seneca's 'Letters From a Stoic' spread open on her knees. I told her she needed to get herself home before dark, to which she replied, 'I've brought my things, and am staying the night.' To which I replied, 'No, you are not.' She merely looked at me with those terribly candid eyes and said, 'I hardly think you're ready to be alone. You might wake up in a field again. Besides, I've told Rose I'm staying at Katy Lipton's house so going home now would only get me into a heap of trouble."

"And what if Rose finds out?" I asked.

"She won't,' she said. "She never checks anything." As this is only too true, I had no following argument. I hardly knew how to broach the subject of how inappropriate it was for a girl of her age to be staying with a man of mine. I knew such arguments would hold no sway with her. But as usual, she read my mind and laid it out for me in black and white.

"I can tell by the crease in your forehead that you're worried about what people will think and say, but as you live at the end of nowhere here, I hardly *think we need to worry about it."*

She manages to silence me in this way at least three times a day. I imagine it's good for my character but it does get a tad annoying to be anticipated in this manner.

So she stayed, safely tucked up in the other room, yet with a good view of the door, should I try to make a night flit again. Oddly, I was comforted by her presence and slept as I have not in many months.

And so it is with words and the fresh heart of a young girl that I am drawn forth through each circle of hell, until I find myself standing once again on terra firma and recognizing the face that looks at me with those green eyes as pure and beneficent as spring after a bitter winter. A child has been my salvation and my rock, and suddenly I am afraid to be without her.

She closed the journal there and laid it down on the desk in front of her. Outside the afternoon light had faded into a chill spring evening and a wind had come up, causing the rose canes to scratch against the study windows as though seeking entrance. Her tea break was long over and she had been caught up in reading Jamie's thoughts for the better part of an hour.

The journal made clear something she had always suspected—that there were things he did not remember—had not even been aware of when they happened. He didn't know the reason she would not leave him for that first week after his collapse was because she was terrified that he would kill himself, either accidentally or with full intent. He could never have known, of course, the things he had shouted during the worst of it. Nor the way his eyes had burned hollow with a pain that was so tangible it became an entity unto itself, a third being there in the room with them.

Even now the remembrance of it made her stomach cramp.

During the very worst of it, she had barred the door and slept curled on the mat in front of it like a dog guarding its master from the wolves that howled incessantly outside. Only the wolves were within, and there was no earthly guard against that. And then there had been that night when he had lain there with those lightless eyes wide open, yet she knew he was not present—as though the bright spirit that lived within was submerged in a primeval swamp from which it could not surface. That night, she had crawled into the bed with him and held his hands in her own. And she had offered up as sacrifice every bit of beauty her young life had known, every song, every story, every ripple of light on water—all of it was said and sung, words to build a webbed bridge by which he might safely cross the chasm of the night.

Though she had been only inches from him, she knew he did not see her, did not recognize her presence, for certainly he never would have allowed the proximity had he been even vaguely aware. So it was she was able to wipe his face with cool cloths and smooth the golden hair out of his eyes. To this day she could feel the fear of that night, how it had wrapped them both as in a thick and cloying shroud—he lost to his own demons, swarming up endlessly from the abyss—and she in terror for him. It had been that night she had told him, because he could not hear nor protest, that she loved him. The words had seemed natural, despite the fact that she had never uttered them to anyone outside of her father in all her life.

Because she was neither a child nor yet a woman, she gave him her heart in a way that a child could not have, and a woman would have had the wisdom not to. Only he did not know and she did not have the words to tell him of the gift he had been given.

Through him, in those three days, she glimpsed the edge of the abyss and found herself so afraid that she was physically ill with it. That the human mind could turn on its owner in this fashion, rabid as a hellhound, she had not known. That a mind could subject someone to such torment, could seize and grasp and bind to the point of madness, was not knowledge most would encounter in a lifetime. To witness it firsthand bound her to this man as little else could have done. It did not occur to her to call for help, to find someone in the medical profession to come with needles and pills, because she knew Jamie would not want it, that somehow the abyss was as necessary as it was dreaded.

So it was that they crossed it together, Jamie in its depths and she walking the tightrope above, never losing sight of him, and dragging him inexorably to that far shore where sanity, arid and overly bright, awaited him. She suspected he would not thank her for it, but she would do it nonetheless, for there was nothing in her young life that had taught her that there might be choice in such a time.

In any event, he was too sick when he regained consciousness to either thank or castigate her. The sickness he could deal with himself, dragging himself back to the bed, hair translucent with perspiration, eyes dark but no longer hollow. He was too weak to order her away from him, and for that she was grateful.

She lived a strange life that next week, slipping in and out of the cottage that she shared with Rose, pretending to go to sleep in her own bed, only to slip into the moonlit shadows and onto the long sandy road to that other cottage after dark, for she would not leave Jamie for more than a few hours at a time. Rose, thankfully, fell into an alcoholic stupor early in the evening and as long as Pamela made a show of going off to bed, barefoot and clad in her nightgown, she never checked further.

Jamie, without much choice in the matter, left the door unlatched for her. Stripped down to his essentials both mentally and emotionally, he gave no time to remonstrating with her, for he sensed, she thought, how little good it would do him.

The nights were the most difficult for him. That was clear. As though the darkness itself came and sat upon his shoulders, a great and weighty bird of prey, waiting to clutch and claw at his brain. And so from dusk to dawn she read to him, curled in the tatty chair that she had pulled to the foot of his bed. She read the books from which he had read to her and many others besides, songs both of innocence and experience, books of dry wit, and books of fulsome beauty. She read poems from other ages more golden than this one, but just as fraught with all the foibles of man and womankind.

In this manner, over the course of that week, she put her hand in his and drew him step by step away from the lip of the abyss. And so it was that a friendship whose bonds had been forged in the darkest of hours was woven into an unbreakable pattern.

Part Five

Back in the USSR
Russia – March-August 1973

Chapter Twenty-eight

March 1973

The Frozen Forest

HIS LORDSHIP JAMES STUART KIRKPATRICK was about as far from the glamorous world of high finance and corporate piracy as one could get and still be on the same planet within which he had once moved. He was, to put it succinctly, at the arse end of the world, in a prison camp where he was being held against his will for sins he wasn't aware of committing. This was where he had awakened after the furious scuffle and world-eclipsing blow to the head. He had not seen Andrei since that morning. He had no idea if he was alive or dead, injured or himself imprisoned.

The Soviet euphemism for this state was Repressed in the Second Category. Repressed in the First Category meant you were no longer breathing. He wondered what they would call his first week of incarceration, when they had not allowed him to sleep, questioned him under bright lights all night and then left him to sit on a stool during the day, kicking him if his eyes closed. He was given a minimum of water and an occasional heel of bread to eat—just enough, he supposed to keep him from fainting. Torture was hampered, after all, by an unconscious victim.

He was all too well aware how much worse it might have been. He had heard tales of the tortures the secret police were capable of dishing out. They had tried a few on him, from soft-voiced persuasion of the 'if you just tell us what we want to know, we'll feed you, you can rest and then you can go home', to screaming in his ears at the top of their voices about making his death long and painful, using the sudden reversals of tone to unbalance him. But they hadn't gone further and, beyond the bruises and cuts he had sustained, they hadn't used pain as a means to pry a confession from him. He knew how it might have been, and felt fortunate not to have had that sort of wreckage inflicted upon him—removal of fingernails, immersion in acid, strait-jacketing and something called 'bridling' where they put a rough length of toweling in a man's mouth, pulled the ends over his shoulders and tied them to his ankles so that he was arched in agony for days, often until his spine snapped. These were only things he knew about, for there was no limit, apparently, to the lengths a well-fed, rested man could go to in the name of getting information out of another.

They had seemed to believe he was a spy who had infiltrated the Soviet Union to make contact with Andrei, one of their most eminent scientists, in an effort to convince him to defect so that the West might plumb his brain and steal the secrets of Soviet advancement. His spying, they said, went back to his and Andrei's shared years at Oxford. He was, they seemed to believe, an agent of the British government, in league with the Americans.

He had the sense, even as his interrogators alternatively yelled and coaxed, kicked and stroked his psyche, that there was far more going on here than he was aware of. He wondered what the hell Andrei had done, what plans had been made, what contingencies put in place, before he tipped that goddamn chess piece over on the board.

They had put literally hundreds of pictures on the table in front of him, grabbing his hair and forcing his head down to them until the images blurred beyond recognition. It was years of him and Andrei, the annual meetings on the border, the travels they had taken to various places around the globe. More than a few made him recoil, for they had been taken at very private moments with various women. He had been nauseated after that, wondering if any moment of their friendship had been free of the stain of surveillance. There were, he had to admit, some photos that compromised his protests of innocence—with the British Foreign Minister, with various high-ranking politicians both British and American. Useless to try to explain that himself was a politician and these people were in his natural milieu as a man of wealth and head of a company with far-flung interests.

Then the bald man with the badly scarred face who had been his main interrogator slid a picture of Pamela in front of him and said, 'She is spy too.' It hadn't been a question, but Jamie had denied it nevertheless. She was safe in Ireland. They could not touch her there. At least he prayed they could not. The picture had been taken outside his own home, when the two of them had been working in the garden together, in those autumn days while she had waited for Casey. Still, the idea of them watching her made his blood thick with rage.

When they had not received the answers they wanted, they had become more inventive. Time had stretched itself out to unbearable lengths, the nights as long as a month. But he did not have the answers within him and could not give them what he did not have.

He had been dumped in the camp, secured behind machine guns and high, barbed wire tipped fences after a full two weeks of 'persuasion'. By that point, he could hardly tell up from down and thought he might well die if he wasn't allowed to sleep.

It took time to get his bearings. He had needed sleep first, and food, and then to get through the shock of what had happened. He wasn't a big enough fool not to have a realization at the back of his mind that this was always a threat, that both he and Andrei had known they were playing with fire. Still, the reality was far different from the most vivid of imaginings.

There had been no way to tell where the camp was, for he had been unconscious for the duration the journey. As best as he was able to make out, they were some distance south of the Karelian Isthmus—and not so far from the border then, leastwise not as the crow flew. The Karelian Isthmus was originally Finnish Territory, but Finland had lost part of it to the Soviets during the four month Winter War that began in November of 1930. The closest city was Leningrad, formerly St. Petersburg, the Venice of the East, raised from bog and forest by Peter the Great. But 'close' in Russian terms was measured in hundreds of miles across unforgiving terrain and weather that could turn on a dime from blisteringly hot to a cold that could shatter bones.

The camp had been built around the remnants of an ancient monastery. The chapel had been all but destroyed under the godless regime of the Soviets, but the huge bell tower that rose from one corner still loomed over the camp like a dark specter. The monastery was hollow, some walls entirely gone, leaving behind cobwebbed cells through which the wind howled on chill nights.

He and Andrei had played their game one time too often. Knowing the risks, he had played the fool to a very high cost. Because one day you could be anchored securely in the world with home and friends and family, anchored by love and tradition and familiar roads and pathways both literal and figurative, and then the next day, without warning to either yourself or those who loved you, you could vanish like smoke upon the air, leaving no trace in your wake. It wasn't as though this was a thing peculiar to Russia, for every country, every town, every lonely forest road had that same ability to swallow people whole, telling no tale on its unmarked ground, in its silent buildings. But Russia had swallowed millions entire, held the bones and mute cries of untold numbers who would never be found, who would sink into the soil, whose bones would become porous sieves and leave no trace for those who might one day seek answers.

It was how he felt himself, porous, made of some amorphous material, as though he were slowly ceasing to exist in the real world. Locked away here, surrounded by a dark fairytale wood, as though he and all who lived here were under the enchantment of a dark sorcerer. Except this was Russia, and therefore the fairytale would not have a happy ending.

His one stroke of luck was the sort of camp to which he had been assigned. It was a logging camp, immured in the dense boreal forests that covered northern Russia. Many years before, Jamie had spent a summer working in the coastal forests of British Columbia. It had been hard, dangerous work, and he had loved every minute of it. He was no stranger to hard work, had found in the past it served the dual purpose of keeping his spirits on an even keel and allowing him to escape the mind for the brute pleasures of the body. He had always been an avid sportsman as well, so that his muscles and flesh were not averse to hard, long hours. Here in the prison camp he spent twelve hours of his day in the forest, felling trees by hand, partnered with an old man who wielded a crosscut saw like it was a tinker toy. He kept up that first day through sheer stubbornness, his muscles screaming in protest and his flesh exhausted beyond comprehension. At least he knew the work. Still, it had taken two weeks of cutting above quota to gain even a nod from the old man.

The old man was also his bunkmate, along with a Georgian dwarf named Shura and a man named Volodya, who reminded Jamie forcibly of the dormouse in Alice, if the dormouse had been a clerkish entity of the Soviet Empire. They had all eyed him with great suspicion, as well they might, and had been doubly disturbed when they discovered that his ability to speak Russian was the equal of theirs.

The huts in which the prisoners were housed were long, low buildings built of native logs, roughly hewn, chinked with moss and settling into the soil. He had been put into one of the smaller buildings, meant to contain eight inmates. There were only four of them on bunks that were nailed to the walls and fitted with thin mattresses that must have been there since the '30s. A cast-iron potbellied stove sat at the center of the hut, it too a relic of days gone by.

It was here he had awakened after being thrown into the back of a truck—to find that two days had melted away. This information was received from the dwarf, who upon his awakening was standing over him with a cup of hot tea. Jamie drank it gratefully and would have even had he suspected it contained arsenic. It wasn't any sort of tea he was familiar with, but it had been hot and fragrant and warmed the ice that had settled in his core. It had also eased the pain in his legs and arms, which made him think it was medicinal in purpose.

Shura was the first to speak to him, and Jamie realized quickly that it was more because Shura could not keep his tongue still than from any trust of the stranger in their midst. Shura's coloring was classic Georgian: black hair, black eyes, swarthy skin. His nature was pure Georgian too, filled with music and merriment. His was a soul that not even the camps could break. Through Shura he learned who ran the camp and who the real power was, he learned what to expect, what would earn extra rations of food and what would bring punishment down on his head like a hammer. According to Shura, the power did not lie with the camp administration, but in another direction altogether.

"Is not the camp commanders that run this place. It is Gregor. He is *vor y zakone*—are you knowing this term?"

"Thieves in law," Jamie had said, nodding his head to keep Shura on the conversational track.

"Yes, he is real power here. Gregor says jump, we all take off our shoes and ask how high and for how long—except Nikolai—Nikolai is exception to every rule here in camp. He has been here so long he has no memory of life before, and he is hard like Siberian ground. Gregor fears no one, but he respects Nikolai and keeps his distance. The camp governor and guards fear Gregor too and so they do as they are told."

Jamie knew who Gregor was from the first day. He was hard to miss. Gregor was a large man, built like a predatory animal, all muscle and sinew but with flesh enough to know he was getting more than his assigned share of food. He stood firmly atop the pyramid that comprised the thieves' society here. He was called *nayk* behind his back—'the spider'—because he sat at the center of the camp's web, feeling every shiver and tug on the strands and reaching out to strike and bite when least expected. Jamie could feel the man's eyes on him several times a day, sending fine, primitive threads of danger down his spine. He was a man to be avoided until one could not avoid him any longer. Jamie was no fool, and so he knew that the time would come when he would have to reckon with Gregor in one fashion or another.

He had absorbed the environment quickly, observing the various groupings and camp hierarchies, knowing that if he was to survive with his skin intact he needed to get the lie of the land as quickly as possible. The camp OC was a small, slightly oily personage with sly, lurking eyes that always looked for some infraction or misdemeanor for which he could punish one of the unfortunate inmates. Those who were not under Gregor's keeping, that was. Those were victims of an altogether different sort of punishment, one which Jamie strove not to think about too deeply.

The work, as hard and mind-numbing as it was, seemed to be the one thing that kept them all going, because it induced such exhaustion that one didn't have the wherewithal by nightfall to dwell too long on the accumulated misfortunes of the day.

Jamie asked about the old man when Shura was shaving his head. It was a necessary evil, Shura told him, to avoid the plague of lice. On the subject of Nikolai, he had shrugged in his eloquent Georgian manner and said, "Nikolai will only speak when it is absolutely necessary. Otherwise he gets by with grunts. Even the guards let it pass. Nikolai is like big oak tree that has been here so long, and is so immune to pain and fear that everyone just walks around him."

"And what about Vanya?" Jamie asked, curious about the beautiful youth who came each day to the forest with them to look after the horses that were used to haul the logs away and helped to serve the two-legged beasts their lunch ration. Vanya, who was disturbingly androgynous and had eyes the color of smoked violets, was also shunned by most of the inmates. He did not speak when he handed Jamie his bread, but there was something in his eyes that looked like a question, or an appeal, depending on the day.

A funny look passed over Shura's face and he shrugged. "Vanya is *peed-eraz*. You understand?"

Jamie feared that he did indeed understand.

"*Peederaz* is like camp whore. He is chosen by the long timers. He is at their mercy, to use as they please, to rape, to humiliate. The *peederaz* sleeps on the floor, he's not allowed at the table to eat, nor in the showers when others are there. He cleans the hut and he's forced to have sex with anyone who wants it, any time. If he refuses or complains, then he's beaten or stabbed and then those long timers," Shura spit to the side in disgust, "will simply move on to another victim."

Jamie felt sick to his core for the boy, though the situation did not surprise him. A young man who looked like Vanya was always going to attract the very worst sort of attention. To a certain extent he understood, for all his life his own face and form had brought him attention which, at times, he had been ill equipped to manage. There had been a period during his late teens and early twenties when he had been propositioned by older men on a weekly basis, merely because his beauty had made them lose their normal sanity to the point where they no longer cared what they risked. But his inclinations had not led him that way and he had broken at least one heart very badly over it.

"Any other advice?" he asked, trying to ignore how naked his scalp felt now that Shura was done shaving it.

Shura ruminated for a minute, mobile mouth drawn down. "Just this—*ne veri, ne boisia, ne prosi.*" With that he collected his tools and tucked them away under his mattress.

It was sound advice, Jamie thought, if a tad bleak.

"Don't trust, don't be scared, don't ask."

Chapter Twenty-nine

March 1973

Prince of Thieves

JAMIE'S FIRST ENCOUNTER WITH THE *vor v zakonye* was less than pleasant, though he had never expected tea and civility.

He had been here six weeks and had acquired the rhythm of camp life soon enough. It was as unimaginative as the food. But under the daily routine, under all the head counts and quotas and the unvarying diet, under the exercises and obedience to regime there was a tension that simmered like the cauldron over a witch's fire, waiting to boil over and wreak havoc.

He had been noticed. He had expected it. One could not be a new quantity in a prison setting and not be an oddity, but when one was foreign and fair, as Shura had so succinctly put it to him, one was in for more than a normal share of attention. It was not possible to skim beneath the radar in such a place. Their lives were lived within breathing distance of each other and sometimes not even that. Privacy was a commodity that came at a very high price. One he did not have the coin for at present.

He was walking back to his hut one evening after choking down the thin soup and hard, crusty bread that constituted supper. Though it was still bone-chillingly cold, he thought he noticed a slight warming in the temperature. The compound was long and narrow, with the *vor* hut sitting in the center so that one had to pass it to get from the dining hall and administration to all the other huts in the compound. There was no avoiding it, nor the harassment of Gregor and his minions if they felt so inclined.

Rounding the corner of the long hut, it was immediately apparent that some sort of commotion was taking place. He cast a quick, surreptitious glance at the guard posts but none of them seemed to have noticed—or they were being selectively blind and deaf, because it was something to do with Gregor. Shura had been completely accurate in his assessment of the camp hierarchy. Gregor ran things and anyone who didn't like it wisely kept his opinion to himself.

He took in the scene in front of him. A crowd of men had the boy

Vanya cornered, a dove surrounded by wolves and, like a true dove, there was nothing he could do to prevent what was going to happen. The camp whore he might be, but Jamie could see clearly that the boy was terrified.

Vanya looked at him, desperation tightening the fine skin over his high-planed bones, and he held Jamie's eyes for a second before he was shoved through the door of the hut. Jamie took a deep breath, trying to ignore the adrenaline that flooded through his body.

He knew he ought to let it alone. Vanya had a role to play in the camp and earned extra bread by it. Shura had told Jamie that it was little different from how the boy had earned his bread before the gulag. It might make no difference to him how many or who. And yet... the look on that delicate face and the dense appeal in the violet eyes said otherwise. Jamie sighed and swore softly under his breath. There was no choice in the matter and little use standing out here in the snow telling himself there was.

He strode forward and hit the door hard, braced for what he knew he would see. Jamie was no stranger to the world's darker pleasures, nor to the odd turns lust often took, but he knew this act had little to do with desire and much to do with a violent domination that Gregor sought to impose on each person in the camp.

Vanya was bent over one of the rough-framed beds, his shirt in tatters on the floor, his face shoved into the reeking mattress to the point of suffocation. His pants were down around his knees, and the fragile line of his backbone stood out in sharp relief against his pale skin. Blooms of red washed the surface of his skin where he had been manhandled.

No one turned around at his entry for they were too intent on the spectacle in front of them. Jamie moved further into the hut, steeling his senses against the reek of male lust.

"Let him be. Surely even you can find someone more willing," Jamie said loudly, though his knees were fully aware of the fool his tongue was making of him.

Gregor turned, his large frame gleaming with menace, a blaze of white-hot lust smearing his features and Jamie understood at once the magnitude of the mistake he had just made. Behind him, he felt the men close ranks, blocking off any escape he might have imagined making.

Gregor took his hands off Vanya, who immediately scrambled into a corner, huddling into himself in a pitiful effort to cover his naked form. Gregor stood and stepped closer. The heavy scent of the man's brute carnality hit Jamie full in the face.

Instinctively, he stepped back but was shoved forcefully forward by the men at his back. Gregor grabbed him and spun him round, shoving him up hard against the rough wall of the hut. His left arm was hiked up excruciatingly high against the ridge of his spine. It would take no more than another inch to break it. He gritted his teeth and pushed his forehead hard into the wall. There was no room to move, no space to draw a breath between him and the man that held him with such terrible force.

"Are you willing to take his place? Are you willing to be my *sdelat kozyol?* Are you, Jamie? Because that's a trade I'd be very happy to make. Oh very, very happy, indeed." Gregor laughed, a low, oily sound that made Jamie's stomach roil like a terrorized snake. He knew the term. A *sdelat kozyol* was a homosexual slave, a person apart in the camp, used for his body but not considered human. Like Vanya.

He couldn't breathe, couldn't move. The man's hold was like iron locked against his back. Panic built under his breastbone, spreading up his windpipe in a cold, greasy slick. He had to stop. He needed to breathe. If he passed out he knew exactly what would happen to him and he wasn't sure he would survive it, either physically or emotionally.

A rough finger curled around the shell of his ear and stroked down his neck to his collarbone. The man's mouth whispered in his ear, wet and hot.

"You are very warm-blooded, Yasha, no?"

The long body pressed even harder against his and he felt the man's erection pushed into the small of his back. Panic was close to taking over now. Never mind what harm he might incur. It no longer mattered. There was only the animal drive to survive.

The utterance of his name was an obscenity in the man's mouth. Jamie knew what the use of the diminutive of his name from this man meant. It was a sign of disrespect, of placing him on a lower level, of saying they could do with him as they liked and that they would.

Gregor grabbed him by one shoulder and spun him around again, huge callused hands pinning him swiftly, though even had he been able to slip in a punch, it would have done him little good. The men were packed around him like hungry wolves that could smell blood on the air. Each one had the congested look in his face of lust for blood, lust for another's pain, salivating for something Jamie prayed he would not be forced to give.

Gregor's eyes were nearly black, dense as tar with hunger. Jamie did not blink. He knew he must not be the first to look away. Men like Gregor fed on fear, glutted themselves with it and were never satiated. Their appetites would always call for more. Jamie knew if the man smelled or sensed it on him, he would never be rid of him short of killing him, which wasn't a measure he was prepared to take... yet.

Still, his throat was dry with fear, his entire body panicked at the thought of what was about to happen to it. There was little choice in the matter. He could not talk his way out of this, nor could he overpower the opposition. It made him think of Pamela and that terrible night so long ago when she had been raped by four men on a train. Then he had felt a murderous fury, and now he felt the fine edge of a terror that she had experienced for hours.

Then from the doorway, a deep voice, heavy with the rumble of disuse, spoke. "You leave him alone or I will shoot you where you stand. Don't doubt my word. I have nothing to lose."

"Go away, old man," Gregor said, though he eased his hold on Jamie's arm a little.

Nikolai's response was to shoot the air directly above Gregor's head. Gregor swore but backed away from Jamie—not far, but enough to allow Jamie to take a shaky breath.

Gregor turned, his entire frame one of killing menace. Yet standing so near, Jamie sensed a hesitation. Jamie remembered Shura's words about Nikolai and how he was the one exception to all the rules.

Nikolai never wavered. The gun was as steady in his hand as though he merely held a flower. Gregor must have read the intent in the old man's eyes for, much to Jamie's relief, he took his hands off him and backed away a little.

Nikolai nodded at the men in a way that must have been command enough, for they began to file out of the low-slung hut, one by one, some muttering curses under their breath but most silent and avoiding eye contact with the old man who held the rifle in his clawed hands as if it were an extension of his own arms.

But Gregor, it seemed, was not quite done with him yet. Before he followed his coterie out the door, he turned to Jamie and smiled, a thick cloying thing that spoke of horrors Jamie had never imagined.

"Not tonight then, my sweet," Gregor said, pupils still dilated with lust, "but soon. I promise you, very soon." And then he was gone, vanished into the night without a sound, as if he had truly become the demon he seemed.

Jamie fell to his knees in relief, furiously rubbing his ear where it was still wet from the man's tongue and breath. He wanted nothing so much as a hot shower to wash the man's insidious touch from his skin.

"You shouldn't have done that, but thank you all the same." Vanya said. Nikolai had seemingly vanished into the evening air without a word.

"You're welcome," Jamie said. "Don't worry. He won't touch me."

"How can you be so certain?" Vanya asked, pulling himself up into a sitting position.

"Because I'll kill him if he tries it again," Jamie said, and knew he meant every word.

Vanya stood and pulled on his pants without shyness.

"How—?" Jamie began, but halted his tongue, for it was none of his business.

But Vanya seemed to understand the unspoken words for he shrugged, the amethyst eyes opaque with some emotion Jamie could not put a name to, and thought perhaps it was best that he did not try.

The boy turned back and looked at him. There was no shame in him, only a sort of singularity that Jamie had encountered once or twice before in his life.

"It is only a body. It is not who I am."

ANY RECKONING WITH GREGOR WOULD HAVE TO COME SOON. Jamie knew he could not afford to wait too long, and waiting only stretched the agonizing tension out to its limits, leaving him with the feeling that it could snap back on him without warning.

The compound itself was secure enough, and the guards would often retreat to their hut to play cards and numb their boredom with the anesthesia of cheap vodka. They made a patrol of the area once an hour, more time than Jamie needed.

The ground was hard as steel, the dirty snow caking thickly in his cuffs. Jamie crouched beneath the window of the long hut, waiting for the last of the grumbling conversations to die down to the small night noises of sleep. Then he used footholds he had mapped out during the last week to climb up, silent as a snowflake drifting upward through the air, onto the roof.

All his senses were heightened, the scent of the smoke from the guard's hut thick and gelid in his mouth, the wind sliding with chill fingers around his body like a frost harlot. His thoughts were slippery and he knew this wasn't the best time, yet could not think of a better to do this deed.

The windows were shut, but it was only the work of a moment to open the one he wanted. A fetid fug hung in the hut, where multiple men slept. He slid over the lip of the roof, grasped the upper edge of the window, and slipped through noiselessly. He landed on the floor lightly on the balls of his feet, ready to spring, scenting the area like a cat. He knew that Gregor's bunk stood alone to the far left of the hut. He had chosen a window some way from the bunk so that his eyes would have time to adjust to the dark before he made his way there.

The end of a crossbeam hung over Gregor's bed, smoke-blackened and soaked with the animal miseries it had witnessed. It was his silent ally. He swung up lightly, the wood rough under his palms. His blood was fizzing and he knew he needed to keep a cool head or risk making a mistake. With Gregor being the size and temperament he was, it was not a risk Jamie could afford to take. He could not let Gregor dominate him in any way, shape or form.

He hung above him, and the man stirred in his sleep, softly mumbled words slipping from his mouth. Jamie froze, hanging like a spider on a very dangerous web. It took a few moments—moments that seemed like hours—before the man settled again. He began to snore, just as Jamie felt his hands slipping on the beam. He let out a little of his breath and then let himself down onto the bed carefully, so that his weight was distributed evenly, no more than a vague disturbance on the air.

For a criminal, Gregor slept deeply. Jamie slipped the knife from his teeth into his left hand. His knees were to either side of the man, who slept on his stomach. He grabbed the man's chin hard and pulled his head up, clamping the jaw shut so that he could not yell and alert everyone in the hut. He put the knife to the prominent adam's apple.

"Don't fucking move," he hissed, his Russian guttural with threat. The pressure of the knife was enough to kill the man with the slightest move, but not enough to draw blood. Not a fool, Gregor didn't move, but lay taut beneath Jamie. Jamie's knees held his arms to his sides as effectively as a vice. He didn't have the Russian's size, so he had to take him at a disadvantage like this and hope that his size wasn't equalled by agility.

Jamie pulled the massive head back a little further, the neck arched at its apex. Any further and it would break. His own muscles were strained to the point of snapping but the hand on the knife remained steady, increasing the pressure inexorably. He would not cut him, for that would be to shame the man and he could not afford to do that. He leaned in to Gregor's ear and spoke in a whisper as intimate as a lover's but as cold as the ice that surrounded their prison.

"Touch me again without my permission, and I will kill you. Make no mistake about it. I know how to make it slow and hard for you. Do you understand?"

He eased the pressure just enough so Gregor could nod ever so slightly, not enough that he could so much as grunt for help. He wasn't quite so jazzed on his own adrenaline as to think he would make it out of this stinking hut alive if even one man awakened and became aware of his presence.

It was time to go. His point was made and now he needed to move like the proverbial greased lightning. With a last judiciously placed squeeze of the man's neck, he was up and off him, hitting the floor as lightly as a cat and with as little noise.

He slid out of the window, tumbling into the trampled snow, coming to his feet like an acrobat and running low and fast before he was fully upright. Behind him, where he had expected a roar of outrage and a flurry of movement, there was only stillness and the sound of his own breath. The guards were still in the hut, their raucous laughter spilling out onto the night. He kept his body low in the shadows, half expecting a knife to land with a thunk between his shoulder blades. He had squeezed the carotids just long enough to daze Gregor and give himself the needed seconds to slip out the window and away.

Moments later he was in his bed, lying on his back, blood lurching through his veins like a rabbit that had narrowly escaped the wolf's jaws, and was hiding in the hedgerow trying not to die from the resulting heart attack.

There was something strange in the hut, something unfamiliar. It was the silence, he realized. Nikolai wasn't snoring or muttering in his sleep.

Jamie found he wasn't breathing, but anticipating, afraid that if he made the slightest noise the man would not speak, for he was certain he was about to. The very energy in the room testified to it. Nikolai's voice, when it came, was as deep and dense as the oak tree everyone claimed him to be.

"You have done what needed doing. Don't look back, don't regret, no matter the price."

"I won't, Nikolai Ivanovich," Jamie said quietly, as ridiculously grateful for the old man's few words as he would have been for the blessing of a saint. For with that one sentence, the man had made him feel that he was no longer alone, no matter what terrors the days and months ahead held.

Chapter Thirty

April, 1973

Seanachais

JAMIE THOUGHT THE OLD SAYING THAT A MAN could get used to anything, given enough time—including being hanged—had never perhaps been proven truer than in his current situation. A man could get used to having every liberty and right he had ever taken for granted stripped from him. He could get used to constant hunger with no hope of alleviating that terrible gnawing in his belly. He could become accustomed to standing to attention in the frozen dawn while Soviet platitudes and diatribes were broadcast over a squawking PA system. He could get used to the inhuman quotas that had been designed long ago to work a man to death while providing him the minimum requirement of nutrition in order to draw his death out to vulgar limits. He could even get used to being cold all the time, so cold that sleep did not come easily despite an utter and complete exhaustion that sat deep in every cell of his body.

Despite his repeated demands that he be allowed to contact someone at the British embassy in Moscow, that he be allowed to make a phone call, that they in fact acknowledge in any way, shape or form that he existed and had even a snowball's chance in hell of ever getting out of here, or that they contact someone on the outside to let them know why and how he had disappeared off the face of the earth—he had not been allowed any of these rights, for rights were a rather foreign concept in the Soviet Empire. He might as well have landed on another planet in a far off solar system for all that a gulag resembled the life he had left behind.

Life was brought down to its bones here. What was necessary and what was not became clear very quickly.

Everything had its uses: tin cans became cooking pots, bits of string were used to tie foot wrappings in place, scraps of paper could be used to line boots and mittens. Every item had use as barter as well. Even things not material had their place in the complex trading system of the camp. The item of greatest value Jamie had, it soon became clear, was his ability to tell a story.

Storytellers resided near the top of the prisoner hierarchy, as any sort of distraction from reality was very highly valued. And so he became the camp storyteller through the simple expedient that the previous storyteller had dropped dead in his boots only two weeks before Jamie's unfortunate incarceration. This new occupation bought him extra rations of bread, small bits of chocolate, and favors when he needed them.

He had long believed that novels had a life of their own, far beyond that of an individual reader. For a good novel lived on in the minds of hundreds, perhaps even thousands or millions of readers and thus became another entity outside and beyond the rough-cut pages and black-type words. This became truer as he told stories each night near the pot-bellied stove. His memory had always been an unreliable sort of fellow when it came to certain events in his life, mercifully perhaps, for there were things it shielded him from that he suspected he did not need nor want to know. Books he remembered, though, with a near photographic clarity that served him well in his role of storyteller.

He pulled from the well of memory other stories, ones he himself had invented during an adolescence that had been both unbearably dark and incandescent to the point of scorching his spirit. These stories he changed, for he was not that boy anymore and did not see things in the same light. But it gave him a feeling of grounding himself here in Russia, as though by saying words he had written down long ago, he had rooted the lodestone of his soul.

Memory, however photographic, was like water, in constant flux so that one perceived things differently depending upon the angle one approached it from or, as the case might be, the age. Some things flitted beneath the surface, flickering, a flash of scale and fin, and others tore the surface of that still pool, glittering and arcing, spraying a thousand other droplets of time and remembrance. So it was for him with tales, finding something different with each telling, another layer through which to peer or sink wholly, depending upon the angle from which he viewed the story, or the mood, easily sensed, of his listeners that particular night.

And so he became the camp Seanachai. He thanked God for his fluency in the Russian tongue, for between Yevgena and Andrei, he could speak it as though he were a native. He knew many Russian stories and could recite Eugene Onegin from memory. He was also familiar with many of the other great Russian poets—Blok, Pasternak, Akhmatova and others. He gave them the poets of his own world too—Yeats and Byron, Shelley and Wordsworth, Keats and Rilke, and the stories that sat closest to his soul—*Les Miserables*, *The Idiot*, *The Inferno*, *Ulysses* (that was a challenge and a half in Russian—his brain felt like a pretzel twist during the telling), *Dr. Zhivago* and the whole lovely world of Trollope's Barchester Tower series. He told Dickens in installments, just as the great man had written his stories, instinctively knowing where to leave off to create the maximum anticipation for the next session.

He knew if they were caught he was likely to be punished severely. Western literature had long been banned in the Soviet Union, and despite Kruschev's thaw and the phenomena of *samizdat*, it was still a punishable offense. But he knew that to take a people's stories was to kill something in their soul, to strand them on a far shore where nothing seemed familiar, for people were their stories and the re-telling of them in all their facets had the power to keep a man sane. Stories knew no national borders, nor politics, but rather a truth universal to the human condition, no matter the regime under which the minds had been captured.

His own mind had been molded in the traditions and teachings of the West, whether from the ancient Greeks or the less ancient Jesuits. The teachings of the Jesuits had been many, but if they had left him one gift of lasting power, it was this: he was able, when it was most necessary, to build himself a fortress of the spirit to keep safe that which was most imperative in a man. It was a place within which to seek the eternal and unchangeable, to fix one's sight far beyond pain and humiliation and to roam unhindered in a place of beauty and peace. It was a sanctuary that he carried everywhere with him, and had for as long as he could remember. For this he was grateful to those men who had the teaching of him in his youth.

He noticed Gregor and his lackeys sometimes hung about the edges of this storytelling circle, close enough to hear, occasionally close enough to menace. If he was unfortunate enough to lock eyes with Gregor, the man would give him a long, slow smile and then run his tongue suggestively across his lower lip. Jamie merely held the look long enough to be sure the man knew he was not afraid, even if his insides felt slippery with the thought of what the man wanted to do to him.

Gregor, however, was happy enough for now merely to play with him. Three days after Jamie's nighttime visit with the knife, he had come back to his hut to find Vanya sitting on his bed, his meager sack of belongings on the floor by his feet. When he raised an eyebrow in question, the reply was simple.

"I am sent to stay with you. I am told I am now *your* bitch."

"Pardon me?" In his shock, he had spoken in English, to which Vanya could only respond with a brow wrinkled in confusion.

"I—no, this is not possible. I do not want anyone to be my bitch," Jamie said in exasperation, thinking to himself that in the revenge department Gregor was far wilier than he had expected.

Vanya raised a perfect eyebrow at him in return. "It is no hardship to be such to you."

"That is not the point," Jamie said, not sure if he had a point that was going to make an impression on the beautiful young man.

Vanya lay back on the bed, amethyst eyes alight with mischief. "Well, if you do not want me to be bitch for you, what *am* I to do?"

Jamie contemplated him for a moment. "As it happens, I find myself rather short on friends just at present."

Vanya's face lost its mischief. "To be friends in Russia is a serious thing. We do not take such offers lightly. It is an engagement for life, more serious than marriage."

"I'm in here because of my friendship with a Russian," Jamie said.

"And he is still your friend?" Vanya asked, perfectly serious in his query.

"Yes," Jamie said, and knew it for truth.

"Then you are understanding what it means to be friends in Russia."

Jamie considered the head that lay upon his improvised pillow and sighed. "I'm beginning to."

Chapter Thirty-one
April 1973
Spy Games

SPRING CREPT UP FROM THE SOUTH, ACROSS SALTED SEAS and the rich soaked soil of the steppes. With it came a gradual thaw, though the air was still raw with winter's leaving. The evenings were still laden with frost and the occasional fall of snow, but spring was undeniably in the air, though it came with its own problems—mud and voracious mosquitoes as well as a host of other pests that were impossible to control in a camp where so many people lived in close, not terribly clean, quarters.

Coming through the gates that night, exhausted, and aware of the perpetual guns at his back, Jamie was not in a good frame of mind to receive a summons to the OC's office. There was not a decent bone in the man's body and a summons would not mean anything good. Every face that turned to him before departing for the dining hall wore expressions made up equally of pity for him and relief that they had escaped the net this time.

The administration building shimmered with warmth after the chill of the forest. Jamie thought the sheer pleasure of the heat might well drop him to his knees if it wasn't for the trickle of fear in his stomach as he wondered what the hell Comrade Isay wanted of him now.

He had learned quickly here that to be invisible was to survive. But without a physical disguise, James Kirkpatrick was not one of life's natural chameleons. His beauty had always singled him out for attention both welcome and not, much as the man seated in the office awaiting him had never been invisible either. He felt relief at first, quickly swept away by anger.

Andrei looked well—rather too well—Jamie thought, with nary a bruise or cut or broken bone in sight to explain his long absence.

"I see you aren't dead," Jamie said dryly.

Andrei came away from the window and seized Jamie by the shoulders, searching his face as though he would read there how Jamie fared.

"Yasha, it is the first time they have allowed me to see you. For two weeks I didn't know if you were alive or dead."

"It's likely they weren't certain either whether I would be alive or dead at the end of those two weeks," Jamie said. "I was in Lubyanka—where exactly the hell were you?"

"Under house arrest. I don't move, I don't breathe, I don't speak a word without them knowing about it. I work, I go home, I work some more. Not that that is new, but they aren't even trying to hide their presence anymore."

"And how exactly do I play into this?" Jamie asked. "You realize I have not been allowed to contact an embassy or anyone outside of this hellhole? It's as though I've ceased to exist in the last month."

Andrei's hands dropped from his shoulders, his blue eyes dark with emotion. "Yasha, you must believe I knew nothing of this. I would have somehow warned you. You cannot think that I..."

"I don't know what I think. A couple of weeks in Lubyanka will do that to a man."

"Did they hurt you? I had begged for them to show you mercy."

"My interrogators were Russian. How much fucking mercy do you think they showed me?"

"I am sorry, Yasha. I cannot begin to tell you how sorry I am."

Jamie merely raised an eyebrow.

"I begged them to allow you to contact someone at the British embassy, or even to allow you to contact someone in Ireland. They refused. I was only allowed here because I refused to do any work on the project unless they let me see you and know that you are alive."

"Well, as you can see, I am alive, so you can go back to your comfortable little nook with your adequate food and shelter and rest easy."

"You are not supposed to be in the forest. I specifically—"

Jamie held up a hand. "It was offered. I chose to stay on the cutting crew." He did not say that much of his reason for that foolhardy decision was the stubborn old ox who was his partner. As long as he could take some of the weight from Nikolai's shoulders, he would do so.

"Why are you so stubborn, Yasha?"

"Half the inmates already think I'm a spy. I start pulling cozy indoor duty and they're going to be certain I am."

"The forest could kill you," Andrei said.

"And if it does?" Jamie said.

The words hung there between them, the accusation implicit.

"You think I want you dead? Why on earth would you think such a thing?"

"To be honest, Andrei, I'm not sure I know what you would or wouldn't do. Nothing makes a hell of lot of sense after you're tortured for two weeks and then wake up in the middle of goddamn nowhere in a gulag."

"They believe," Andrei said tightly, "that you are a spy."

"A spy?" Jamie said and laughed.

"So they believe, Yasha, and you know in Russia that is not a matter for laughter."

"It's not a matter for laughter anywhere that I'm aware of," Jamie retorted, "but as it's an accusation completely without foundation, it is a matter for some humor, if of the particularly grim sort."

"Don't you understand?" Andrei hissed. "It doesn't matter if it's true or not, suspicion alone can land you in Lubyanka, from which there are very few return journeys."

"I've already had my Lubyankan holiday, and even if they take me into prison and torment me with hoses and bamboo slivers—which are about the only two things they didn't do to me last time—I can't tell them anything different."

Andrei stood, putting his hands on the desk between them, his blue eyes dense with some meaning Jamie wasn't eager to translate.

"We are too long friends to prevaricate."

"What do you mean by that?" Jamie asked sharply.

"Only, Yasha, that I remember that spring at Oxford too. You were not the only one approached."

Jamie felt a deathly stillness descend over him, as though he stood suddenly on the broad plains of this country, with snow falling in every direction and no human aid anywhere in sight. Why Andrei would speak of this here was beyond him. It could mean a long and messy death for both of them.

"All I remember of that, Andrei, is that I turned them down. Did you?"

"It wasn't as simple as a mere refusal. You, of all people know that, Yasha. We both came from countries that had caused Britain no small problems."

"That's an understatement in the extreme," Jamie replied. "But it still doesn't change what I said. I turned them down. Did you?"

"Sit down, Yasha. I did not come here to interrogate you."

Jamie sat, for he saw little choice in the matter, and the warmth of the room was too seductive to resist. Andrei had set out a chessboard with the pieces neatly aligned. And there was food, more than he had seen in a very long time.

"This they will allow, and for the time it takes, you are warm and fed, my friend. It is the little I can do for you."

Part of him wanted to take the chessboard and throw it and all the exquisite pieces out the window, and the other part merely wanted the comfort of the game, the warmth, the company and the food.

There was bread, soft black rye, and thinly sliced beef and boiled eggs and vodka.

"And what of Violet?" Jamie asked, so quietly that he could not be heard even over the soft crackle of the fire from the cast iron stove. "Does she get these dinners, the warmth of a fire and your attention for an hour or two?"

Andrei's face tightened visibly. "She has refused to see me these last two months. I do not know why. From her end there is only silence. If you—"

"We know of each other. Beyond that we have said little more than hello," Jamie said. He had been made aware by Shura that the small, copper-haired woman who worked in the infirmary, was named Violet. After that, it had been simple to make the connections. After that, it had been hard not to suspect that there was far more to his capture and incarceration than had originally met the eye.

The food was more plentiful than what his stomach had come to expect over the last several weeks, and slightly more flavorful. He was warm too, so warm that he took his coat and hat off. He could see the changes in himself reflected in the quick flash of Andrei's eyes as he took him in, weighing and assessing against the last evening in the dacha. He knew the comparison wasn't good.

Chess provided them with common ground, though, and Jamie felt a visceral relief in the absorption of the game. The warmth had heightened his senses, his hearing so sharp that the *whoosh* of felt against wood was audible.

A drink was placed into his hand at some point and he sipped at it slowly, the warmth alone inebriation enough.

The familiarity of the game allowed their talk to be light, ribboned about with their own special code, coloring the weft of their communication. And so there was what was said and what was meant.

"You will have to forgive my appearance. I am still getting used to life in the gulag."

Why the hell am I here?

"I am sorry for that, Yasha. You must believe me."

Me, you are here because of me and my mistakes.

"Work going well?"

What are you involved in?

"Yes, it is interesting as always."

I can't tell you, but it's something more terrible than your worst imaginings.

"Good to hear. I miss my own work, my home, spring in my own country. The Russian spring is not a soft one."

I want to go home before they kill me.

"It will warm up soon. The summer will be wonderfully hot."

I will not let them kill you.

"I'm Irish. I burn if the sun is too hot."

You will not be able to stop them.

A silence and then softly, moving his bishop, Andrei spoke aloud.

"I am doing what I can, Yasha, but it is not easy. Right now they hold all the chips and I am, as you might say, between a rock and a very hard place."

Jamie merely gave him a hard, green look, for he was painfully aware that there was much more going on here than met his limited view. Things that Andrei could not tell him. He himself was the rock, Violet the hard place. They had Andrei neatly cornered.

"You remember that night on the tower? What we promised?"

"Yes," Jamie said stiffly.

"I still mean what I said that night. The question is—do you?"

To mention that night here, now, was cutting too close to the bone and Andrei knew it. But that had never stopped him before. He had always known how to make his cuts deep and lasting so that the scar only partially healed. So that with the right touch it might bleed again at his command.

PARIS, CITY OF LIGHT, CITY OF LOVE. Paris—le Grand Siecle of Louis XIVth— a city of astrologers and artists, of writers and philosophers, of great minds and grand hearts. A city, too, of riff-raff, pickpockets and prostitutes, peddlers and organ grinders, inspiring in their ability to graft and mold themselves to life and the survival of a poverty that ought to have ground the spirit from their very bodies, yet did not.

The ghosts of all these people wound about amidst the narrow streets and topple-roofed houses, the France that had risen like a red-gold sun over the rest of the western world, whose rule had been absolute, formed as it was under the hand of a wildly ambitious cardinal.

France had been the finishing school for the entire continent, where one must come to acquire the graces and discipline to fit one for the life of the diplomat, merchant prince, grand philosopher, prophet or priest. Until you had boiled yourself in the cauldron of her learning, you were not fit for the higher life.

Jamie had acquired some of his own finish in France—though it had been of a less academic sort. He looked toward the Arc de Triomphe, to the western limits of the city. There in the privileged Chaillot Quarter lived the woman who had provided learning of another sort in his life, and his body still bore the traces of her teaching. It was strange indeed to be in Paris and not under the tutelage of Clothilde in one manner or another, for she had been a friend of his mind before they were lovers. For no man, she had stated in her straightforward manner, should have his mind entirely formed by Jesuit priests.

Together they had read books, ones with fragrances that still lingered with him, scenting his vision of the world. The Jesuits—Father Lawrence and Monseigneur Brandisi—had given his mind the soil, but Clothilde had planted the flowers in it that grew up in a profusion of brilliant color. Had he been in Paris alone, he would not have hesitated to visit her but he knew instinctively that she would not approve of Andrei and that Andrei wasn't likely to warm to her, beyond the obvious qualities of grace and beauty.

Jamie and Andrei visited Paris at least twice a year. It was one of their great shared loves. Since that fateful polo match, their friendship had grown by leaps and bounds as it will when two minds are well matched. Jamie understood that they were cut of the same cloth, that they possessed in equal measure that fire in the brain that could both ignite and incinerate. Such a thing made their friendship dangerous in and of itself, for they had established early on their shared penchant for reckless endeavors. In Andrei Alekseyevich Valueve, Jamie Kirkpatrick had found a man who was both friend and competitor, whose blood stirred to the music of the spheres as wildly as his own. And someone who was willing to partner him in outrageous and dangerous games. Jamie could smell a kindred spirit and had known Andrei for one from the first time he'd seen him skimming a church spire to hang a professor's robes from it.

"How does it come to you?" Andrei had asked as they walked in the misty air of a Paris evening. They'd had coffee and so many Sobranies earlier at a grotty little hole in the wall in the Latin Quarter that Jamie had insisted they walk off the resulting caffeine and nicotine haze.

"How does what come to me?" Jamie asked, waving away Andrei's offer of yet another cigarette.

"You know, the fire in your head."

Jamie shrugged, noting the droplets of mist coalescing on the sleeves of his coat like impossibly fine silver mail. "Like a tidal wave at times, so much that I can't process it. It overwhelms me. At others, it's like I'm fogged in and separate from the rest of the world. It's a bit like being underwater. You can hear things and see shadows passing overhead, but it's distorted and you feel as though that world is another realm that you can't enter. What about you?"

Andrei laughed, a black sound as only Russian laughter could be. "I just get somewhat suicidal, think about ending it all. When I think about it during those times, it seems like it would be a relief. To be set free of my mind."

"I wonder why—when at times the mind is a thing of such beauty and wonder. Then at others, it sinks into such cesspits of despair."

Andrei shrugged. "Some say it's chemistry, biology or fate. I think if you are going to be granted the gift of wonders in your mind, you're going to pay for it equally with the darkness."

"How very Russian of you," Jamie rejoined. He understood what it was Andrei meant, though. There was always a price to be paid for gifts. He was about to add his thoughts on the line between genius and madness when he noticed Andrei looking up, an expression of excitement on his face that didn't bode well for the health of either of them.

Jamie's eyes traveled the same path as Andrei's—up the shimmering length of pure structural iron that was the Eiffel Tower. He had an uneasy feeling he knew what Andrei had in mind.

"Let's climb it," Andrei said, the electric glow he gave off when in the grip of one of his less intelligent ideas, lighting the pewter-toned air around him.

Jamie did not ask why, even though it was insanity to consider it. It had rained that day and cleared only toward evening. The puddle iron structure was gleaming with a thin sheath of ice now in the clear, cold evening air. Even if he did ask, Andrei would only answer, "because it's there."

And that was reason enough when Jamie was in a mood to match Andrei's.

The iron was brutally cold and Jamie knew if they didn't move fast it would rip the skin right off their hands. It also hardened the flesh, making it slide against the ice in a manner that didn't assure their safety. But both he and Andrei had the grace and bearing of natural athletes and had someone viewed them from a distance they would have seemed merely to skim the surface of the imposing structure.

Jamie hugged tight to the inner arch of the base, leaning into the thick strut and feeling his shoulder start to cramp immediately from the searing cold. Hand over hand, one slippery foot after another, they managed with straining muscles and numbed flesh to make it to the second balcony, where they tumbled laughing and out of breath onto the cold, dirty floor. It was deserted, for even the tourists had abandoned the tower for the warmth of restaurants and hearths. They leaned out, arms wide to the city, the illusion of flight sending both spirits soaring.

Over a blue void they hung, the city stretching itself endlessly in every direction. Below was a carpet of stars in which one could fall into infinity and be young forever. The wind was stinging like ice in their faces, but they merely laughed with the joy of it, the sheer beautiful pain of having little control over their lives, yet here for a moment believing that one could alter destiny, conquer fate, and the expectation of one's family, friends and country.

"Do you ever want to just let go?" Andrei asked suddenly, blue eyes electric with a fevered glow and his expression deadly serious.

"Sometimes," Jamie said slowly, "sometimes. Yes."

Andrei nodded. "I thought so. I recognized it in you. I have seconds where I truly think I will fly and the temptation to let go is almost more than I can bear. Like I'm an angel and would soar upward into the stars instead of smashing onto the pavement.

> Come, night; come, Romeo; come, thou day in night;
> For thou wilt lie upon the wings of night
> Whiter than new snow on a raven's back."

Andrei quoted, his Russian vowels rich and black with a strange yearning. "I long to be that snow upon the raven's back, Yasha. Sometimes I think it's the only thing that matters."

Jamie did not need to ask what that one thing was, for there was only one subject on which Andrei waxed poetic, and that was freedom. Freedom of a sort that men with countries, with blood ties, with love hardly ever knew. Perhaps *only in the heat of battle, at the edge of a death that seemed certain, there one could drink from the well, never more than a taste, but enough to addict one for life.*

"What about you, Yasha? Would you fly with me?" *Andrei's eyes gleamed in the cutting light, and Jamie felt an electric surge in his blood that such moments had occasioned in him times before. The same surge flowed in Andrei. It was like a call and response between the two of them. It was the thing that made his tongue hesitate.*

"Not tonight," *Jamie said, tasting a strange regret, sharp as the taste of metal, sweet as the taste of love.*

Andrei smiled, a gesture that held a wealth of ghosts in the mere turn of his lips. "Perhaps tomorrow then."

"Tomorrow we have to see that friend of John's," *Jamie said, in an attempt to return some practicality to the conversation.*

"Must we?" *Andrei blew out a cloud of blue smoke that twined with the crystals of breath Jamie had exhaled.* "You know what sort of afternoon it's bound to be, Yasha. Some dried out old **pedik** who will serve us tea that tastes like horsepiss and then try to get us drunk in the hopes that we'll let him screw one or both of us."

Jamie blew on his hands in an effort to warm them. "I promised John," *he said, bound even at nineteen by his word.*

"He's in love with you," *Andrei said, blue eyes piercing as an ice-tipped arrow.*

"I know," *Jamie replied as quietly as the wind would allow.* "I feel sorry about it, but I don't want to give up his friendship either. Is that selfish?"

Andrei shrugged, a gesture of Russian absolutism. "Of course it is." *He rapped Jamie's aching knuckles hard.* "Come on, you selfish Irish bastard. Let's climb up the rest of the way."

Jamie looked up to where the spire trembled in the wind. "Race you!" *he shouted and began the mad, suicidal scramble across and up the iron bars.*

The wind slapped sharply against him and for a fleeting second he was weightless and he felt it—the brutal glory of youth, of being strong and seemingly invincible. He looked over at Andrei, who was just moving from one strut to the next. Their eyes met and they both grinned, eyes streaming in the bitter wind—and that was when Andrei, normally nimble as a goat, lost his footing.

To catch him meant risking death for them both. It meant risking the plunge into that starry field with no knowledge of what came after. Or if indeed there was an after at all.

Jamie sucked in a breath of air and flung himself across the divide, grabbing Andrei's hand just before he hit the iron hard enough to knock his wind out. His own fingers were sliding, slipping and numb, though he could feel the slick of blood and knew they were cut. If Andrei gave into the temptation he would kill both of them, and Jamie's risk would be for nothing.

He slammed Andrei's hand into the iron and bent his fingers to the strut, Andrei's hand slippery with blood beneath his. He held their two hands there together until he felt Andrei's grip assert itself.

Andrei's face was frost-limned against the cold air, his eyes hot as the heart of a blue star, and the man behind them just as inclined to self-immolation. Jamie's eyes held Andrei's for a space of eternity and around them there was only this—the still beating core of the universe, no world at their feet, neither light nor time, merely space, dark and limitless below.

"Not tonight, my friend," Jamie said through clenched teeth. "Not tonight."

Andrei must have seen something in the green eyes that made him understand. If he went over the edge, tipped toward that starlit abyss, he would make the journey alone. He nodded and then found his footing, easing his cut hands and cracked wrist off the iron for a moment, his face paler than normal.

"Can you climb?" Jamie asked, giving his own hands ease before the trip down to the second balcony.

"I think so," Andrei replied, uncharacteristically subdued. The journey down was long, and Jamie cursed Andrei soundly every bated-breath, crawling inch of it. Rather than cursing him back, Andrei bore the abuse in silence. This told Jamie that the man had scared not only him, but himself as well. Good. The bastard could stew in it, could drown in it for all he cared.

They came off the last strut simultaneously and Jamie, taking one look at Andrei's calm appearance, promptly hit him on the chin, knocking him flat on his cashmere-clad bottom.

"You bastard," Jamie yelled. "You did that on purpose!"

"I needed to know if you'd save me," Andrei said calmly, as if he weren't lying flat on his back, fingers bleeding and his face already flowering with bruises as multi-hued as an Impressionist's garden. And yet there was an exhilaration pulsing off of him, that Jamie knew the taste of all too well.

"Why?"

"Because someday, Yasha," Andrei replied, "someday I will fly and I will need you to catch me. I cannot make that leap in faith, unless I know I can trust you absolutely."

"I'll be there," Jamie said, and meant it.

Andrei had been forcefully returned to Mother Russia shortly after that. Jamie had not seen him for five years and then suddenly had come a message, through Yevgena, that Andrei was living in Zvyozdny Gorodok, which literally translated meant 'little town of stars'. It was Russia's ultra secret cosmonaut training center. Jamie understood at once that the very thing that gave Andrei the freedom to dream had also taken away his freedom entirely.

Neither would forget though, for on each man's shoulder they bore witness to that night's promise in the form of an angel rising from a spray of stars—a spray of deepest night blue flowing upward over shoulder blade with a lone star tipping onto the shoulder itself. A moment of madness that had become a pact.

With age, he understood that when Andrei had offered to step off into the dark with him it had been, for both of them, their last chance at freedom—the sort which addicts forever, but rarely offers more than one taste.

A strange taste of regret, sharp as metal, sweet as love.

Chapter Thirty-two

May 1973

The Crooked Man

VIOLET STEPHANOVA MATTVEEVA WAS EXTREMELY ANNOYED with herself. For weeks now, she had been conducting an internal argument between her own good sense and native Russian suspicion against her inevitable downfall in any situation—a large dose of good old-fashioned curiosity. The object of this curiosity was the man her lover had called the only true friend he had ever known.

Physically she had avoided entering into the charmed circle this man seemed to create everywhere he went. She felt that many in the camp had lost their minds and reserve far too quickly. For all they knew, this James had been planted inside to ferret out their secrets and before they knew it they would be headed to Lubyanka to have their secrets pulled out in a much less charming manner.

She found herself objecting to everything about him and surreptitiously studying those qualities at the same time. To begin with, he was not Russian. He could not even know what it was to be Russian, to always have to separate the personal from the public. To have two lives that did not mesh, that barely touched at the edges despite being lived in one body.

But he did not have the open book quality that most Westerners had. He knew how to wear a mask so smoothly it appeared entirely at one with the man he presented to the world. She wondered what had made such a thing so. For Andrei had told her that Jamie had all the world could offer: wealth, women, intellect and beauty. The latter two were already apparent to her. She had never heard a non-Russian speak like a native, but this man did. The beauty too, despite his shaved head and lack of proper nutrition, could not be hidden. In fact, it was of a sort that seemed ridiculous—that the universe should lavish such care on one individual whilst others ran about with harelips and bulbous noses, hunched backs and wandering eyes. She had felt something of the same when she met Andrei, as if his physical beauty were an affront to humanity, for he too had been carved by a generous hand.

But there was something more to this man, a strange sort of light that drew everyone. She saw the results of it even in Nikolai, who was as hardened by tragedy as anyone she had ever known. It was, she knew, what saved Jamie from much harsher treatment at Gregor's hands, and what had pulled Shura and Vanya to his side almost immediately. He inspired an intense loyalty, and though she found it annoying, she could feel the siren call of it herself. Thus far, she had resisted the lure. She was determined to do so for as long as she was able.

It was his storytelling ability that proved her undoing. At first, she avoided the fire at which he sat telling his tales to a few, but gradually the circle grew, and the spinning of his narratives grew in accordance. She understood that he was gifted this way, as though the fairies of whom he sometimes spoke, the dark ones of his own land, had both blessed and cursed him in his cradle. Some nights she drew close enough to hear a sentence or two, of things both dark and light, of eastern winds and sweet spices, and magical birds risen from ashes, of mares whose milk poured across the heavens and gave rise to a foaming river of stars.

He seemed to draw his words from the wind and the earth, the water and the fires. He moved his hands in accordance with the rhythm of those words, and creatures came forth and lived in the ears and eyes of his audience for that enchanted hour or two: deer with silver-white coats, wolves made from star-spittle, great slumbering mammoths who, when awakened, could shiver the earth with their roars, and silken-eared hares that contained the wisdom of the ages. There were astrologers and princes and stubborn girls with hair like crow feathers and nimble minds, there were dwarves of good intent and shape-shifting wild things that could not be counted upon in times of trouble. There were fields of blue poppies that gave clouded, lovely dreams and sleep that lasted a hundred years. There were ponds of black lotus that pooled like ink, in which shadows lived and frogs lurked that held golden keys within their oily bodies.

Her own father had told stories well, had made them for her out of what fabric she knew not, for Soviet Russia did not lend itself to enchantment.

But this man made stories for the lonely, to draw each shade into the warmth of the fire, then give them something they lacked, even if the lack was not recognized before.

He knew the old Russian tales and understood quite well the Russian need for blood and bones and caves and cold dark forests, for bears that governed great iced lands and deformed old women with spiteful wisdom gnawing at their gaunt frames. He understood the peasant that lurked under the most sophisticated of Russian veneers and so gave these tales earth and grain and hovels dug into hillsides. He told of a great Mother who slept in such silence that even a spider's weaving might be heard within it, and when that Mother awoke it was with torrents, twisting roots and smoking soil.

Some nights his stories felt like mist curling around her senses, intoxicating but invisible. Other nights it was as if threads both dark as secret mosses and bright as spun gold wove themselves into her brain and her heart, pulling her inexorably to the fire where he sat. The stories wound one within another, the teller speaking through the mouth of one far older, and that one speaking through gold-furred foxes, arctic-eyed wolves and old women who knit the threads that held the world together. It was as confusing and as wonderful as the results of drinking too much vodka, mixed with cloudberry wine.

She drew even closer to the fire when he told tales in which his own land figured, tales of bright, shining people who lived beneath the hills and mermaids with glass green eyes and night-furled hair that lured men into vast cold waters where soul cages slept at the bottom of the sea. Tales of a land where the green was like no other, and small cottages were wreathed in earthy smoke and fresh misting rain. There were enchanted pots with strange brews in these tales, and lineages of common folk who had mixed and mated with the Auld Ones and bore odd, gifted children as a result. Stories of swans frozen into winter lakes and stolen feathers that kept them from flight. And always, always in these tales of his own land, there was the sea, as present as a missing mother, tracked silver-blue by the passages of whales and mermaids, dazzling with seals' diamonds in the daylight. She had never seen the ocean but she dreamed of it often, so to hear it woven so casually through his stories was to understand that it was part of him, just as were his blood, breath and golden hair.

The night he lured her fully and finally, as a master would pull his falcon to his arm with a note or two, was the night he began to tell his own tale. How she knew this story was particularly his, she could not have said, but it had a dark ring to it, a truth that could not be denied, for it came from a deep wellspring within this man and he did not look happy nor comfortable in the telling. There had been something in his voice, some strange incantatory quality that had made his listeners shiver and hug themselves tight and look over their own shoulders into the dark night.

I am the Crooked Man and I come by crooked ways, along the phantom roads of a country that is no more. I walk by night, under the moon, both dark and full. I have seen all the foibles and furies of man, his tempests and his tragedies. I have known what it is to lose all and gain it back, only to lose it again. I remember a time when my country was still in the mists, before history, when the white stag roamed in the forests and the wolves called from hilltop to hilltop.

I am the Crooked Man and I carry within my bones the shells of the seas and the dust of the heavens. In my blood are the waters that covered the land long ago, the ice that gouged the canyons and hills, the valleys and streams, the lakes and rivers.

I am the flicker in the corner of your eye, there and then gone, seen only in passing and then dismissed by your eyes and your head, though your backbone knows better. I stand at the dark crossroads. You know, you have seen me there, deny it though your daylight self will. I am the chill that quivers your flesh and makes you look behind on dark nights.

There is a world beneath the one you know. You have felt it, occasionally thought you glimpsed it. The real world, such as it is called, lies over this other one lightly. The other can be sensed, known, entered even, but most are blind to it, for it is safer that way. But the world is a labyrinth and one turn down the wrong path, one fork too many and people lose their way, disappear and are never heard from again. Or are they? For in the labyrinth there are those who watch, those who wait. The human world will have its remedies for such, the coat turned inside out, the cross upon the chest, the chanting of familiar prayers, but those things are as dust in the world that lies beneath.

At night the worlds merge, the old pathways open and other ones walk abroad, sometimes making mischief, sometimes doing things far worse. Maybe you have heard them, maybe you have heard me—your name said quiet on a slipstream of shadow, so low you thought you were mistaken and shook your head, chiding yourself for daft notions but walking faster nonetheless. Be assured, it was my voice that touched your ears. I am the wheel that creaks in the night when no coach can be seen to pass.

There are always some who can see, who have had the ashes washed from their eyes and know the night creatures even when they walk the day. They can see the edge of things, how one world overlaps the other, how there are cracks in between through which many things come and go. This is more curse than gift, for if you can see me, let me assure you, I will come to you.

Write my name with ink upon paper and you will scent the smoke of my arrival as I writhe my way up out of the page. For I am the Crooked Man and I come by crooked ways.

Jamie paused in his telling and took a drink of water. The pause stretched out until Vanya said, arms hugged tightly to his middle, "You will not stop there please. There is more, yes?"

Jamie nodded and with a strange smile upon his face, continued.

Once there was and once there was not a boy named Jack who lived in an emerald kingdom by the sea.

Like most boys, Jack kept the things that mattered to him in his pockets. One pocket held the stones he collected: some amber, some of interesting shape, some with odd sparkly bits to them and some just because he liked the heft of them in his palm. In with the stones were other oddments: a ball of fuzzy string, a piece of heavy glass, the wing of a dragonfly and the skull of a dormouse that he had found one day in the field by the stream that ran past his house. In his other pocket he kept his dreams. Some of them were solid things, others were delicate wispy things that were only starting to take shape. Some would start to form and then blow out like smoke dispersing from a fire. He never knew from one day to the next what he might find when he pulled his dreams out of his lefthand pocket and examined them. Some days there would be lovely cloud horses that trotted off his hand and out into the air before turning and coming back, and once a sailboat that just kept going and disappeared over the horizon. Sometimes too, they were dark things, a little nasty—like the smoke-toad that had melted into a grubby puddle right there and dripped through his fingers. Once there had even been a little girl made of lavender fog who had turned on his hand and stuck her tongue out at him before hopping off and skipping into the bramble hedge.

The thing with a pocketful of dreams was this—you had to be careful with them, had to pay attention to which ones disappeared and which ones stayed and grew more solid day by day. Because sometimes when you weren't looking, a nightmare would slip itself in and take charge of the rest. That was how the Crooked Man had gotten into his pocket and stayed. He wasn't always visible but Jack knew that he was there, or if he did go off for a bit—and he never wanted to know where the Crooked Man's journeys took him—he always came back, and Jack was aware that he would return. The Crooked Man was hard to explain for he had only started out as a wee smudge in Jack's dream pocket, nothing to claim much attention. But then Jack noticed that if he had a bad day or was particularly angry or lonely, the smudge would gain size and start to shape into something.

He wasn't ever sure, after, when the Crooked Man actually became a man, or if he always had been only Jack didn't know it at first. He thought perhaps it had been the day he discovered the hole in his pocket and found to his dismay that a few of his dreams had fallen out. He had looked everywhere for them but hadn't been able to find a single one. They weren't in the hedges, nor in the puddles, nor in the flower garden, nor in the big glass birdcage where his father kept his books and important papers. He had been distraught but then, in the way of young boys, he had gone out skipping rocks and forgotten about the lost dreams.

It was only a few days later that he was playing in the forest at the edge of the Kingdom, even though his nanny had told him many times not to go there alone. He had been happily absorbed in building a fire using only acorns, when the most horribly shivery feeling slid along his back, as if an icy snake had wound its way up his spine. He was scared to look round, for he knew suddenly that he wasn't alone and that whatever or whoever was there with him was most definitely not a good thing or person.

His grandmother had told him that it was wrong to think only humans know desire, for the moon was born of the earth's desire, the ocean stirred to the call of the galaxy each and every day, and the forest had its own dark and silent

desires. Any boy or girl could feel it once they stepped into the forest's embrace,
when home was too far behind and the path faded out from beneath their feet.
Then before they knew it, the entire world was made of great looming trees that
knew far more than men, knowledge passed through roots and rain, through dark
ground slitherers and eyes that only opened at night.

He turned round slowly, putting on his most scowlingest face, thinking it
best to look fierce for whatever he was about to confront. At first he couldn't see
anything. There was only the familiar forest—the rowans with their bright spark
berries, the hazels with the milk-capped mushrooms on their branches, and the
heavy oaks that always seemed like old stern men with great grey beards to Jack.
Nothing seemed out of place, yet...

No, he couldn't see anything in particular, but he could feel it. The woods
looked much as they always did, being trees and having little choice about it. But
then—there—he saw a disturbance amongst the leaves that lay thick upon the forest
floor. They were moving as though something writhed beneath them.

The leaves crept and slithered into the air, just a few inches at first, swirling
slowly in a dreadful vortex, taking shape, becoming worn boots and then legs
and a trunk and chest and neck. Before him stood a tall, headless man, spectral as
a scarecrow in a shorn field on All Hallow's Eve. Jack knew he should turn and
run, but he was frozen to the spot, acorns smoldering at his feet. Terror slowly
filled him, from the toes up, the sort that made you feel sick and light at the same
time, as though you were unable to run because your whole body would just float
up and stay hovering in the dreaded spot.

The leaves kept rustling ever higher, forming a face, high cheekbones, a long
mouth with terrible lips, hollowed out holes that burned like the eyes of a jack-o'-
lantern and long hair that hung lank to the man's shoulders. The leaves clustered
and built upon the head becoming a hat, with a deep, tattered brim that put a
shadow over the man's face, leaving only the sharp chin and hideous smile in view.

The figure slid forward, and Jack felt hypnotized by its strange sibilant hiss-
ing that was more like the sound of dead leaves scuttling down an empty laneway
than any sort of speech. Still, Jack knew the man was calling him, beckoning him
with those long leafy fingers, wanting to take him down, down, down into a very
dark place.

He could smell the man, and the scent of him was burning leaves and water
that lay still and dank in deep pools. It was blood and hot marrow and the crack-
ing of bones under a predator moon. It was secrets that you didn't ever want to
hear, and knowledge that would shame the devil.

The fingers reached out, unfurled slowly and touched Jack's cheek with their
cold frond ends. It was the touch that broke the spell and Jack ran, ran like quick-
silver flowed in him instead of boy's blood, ran like the wind was his mother and
the white stag his father. He ran for so long and so far that when he finally stopped,
he had no idea where he was. He had a vague memory of crossing a stream, run-

ning over hills and the day becoming night, then once again becoming day... but no, that was impossible. No boy could run for that long.

When Jack stopped to regain his breath and rest his legs, he found himself in a strange world where nothing looked familiar. Surely he couldn't have run right out of the kingdom, for its lands ran to the horizon and beyond.

Perhaps in his exhaustion he had taken a wrong turn somewhere—but where? He was certain that it was only moments ago that he had seen the blasted rowan tree, the one that had been struck by lightning three harvests ago and scented the air around it with cinders ever since. And if that was so, he had to be on the right pathway. Yet nothing looked familiar. But then the forest never did look familiar once twilight settled over it. The trees kept their own counsel at night and were no friend to man, his mother had often warned. Indeed, the forest did feel very different at night, though not this different.

It was cold too, and there were no lights anywhere, not a hint of warmth through the dark and twisted branches of the trees. He turned in circles, panic spreading through his limbs, desperately searching for something, anything that would tell him which direction would set his feet on the path home. For Jack realized that home was what he wanted more than anything right this minute—a fire burning in his old nursery room, the scent of hot buttered toast and the stiff rustle of Nanny's petticoats, the lovely heat of a cup of tea in one's hands, and a bed with a feather mattress and quilts heaped high. A small sob escaped his lips as he realized what he had left behind. It was then that Jack realized, with a terrible shiver across his soul, that he was well and truly lost.

Chapter Thirty-three

May 1973
Underneath the Stars

THE CHAPEL ATTACHED TO THE ANCIENT MONASTERY had long ago been stripped of its sacred vestments and was used now as storage for supplies by the camp administration. The main body of the chapel was open, with a rough workbench left under a section of the roof that had fallen in long ago. It was a stark place, yet the sense of sacred communion remained and Jamie could well imagine what it had once been. For above the onion towers, all five of them, representing Christ and the four evangelists, still soared toward heaven, their shape designed for the easy slippage of prayers upward. The bell tower stood empty. Once the bells would have tolled out many times a day, a ringing reminder to the faithful. But that had been long ago, much longer in the hearts of men than in the actual passage of time.

If he closed his eyes and let his mind slip to another time and place, he could conjure it up—the thousands of candles lit in continual prayers, the heavy torpor of the incense. Here they might well have used the resin of the great fir trees that surrounded them, sweetened with the oil of flowers, the smoke of which took worship with it as it left, seeking God.

The floor would have been a mass of movement, for in the Orthodox tradition they stood to worship. The interior of the church would be a blaze of color, for the Russians had believed that God was not only the God of Truth, but also of Beauty. The iconostasis, that frontier between earthly life and heaven, would have been filled with icons painted in the distinctive Russian style, an open book reminding one always of God, the saints with their thin-bladed noses and great deep eyes signifying the peace of the life to come. Icons were a song of faith to remind man of the redemption possible through the creation of art and beauty. The Soviets had destroyed as many as they could find.

Stripped of its ornaments it might be, but it was also empty, and Jamie sought the solitude and peace of it as much as he was allowed.

Tonight he was extremely tired, and knew he should seek his bed rather than hold a conversation with an absentee landlord. Nevertheless, here he sat on the rough bench beneath the hole in the roof so that he might have a view of the stars overhead.

He was too tired to form words or even coherent thoughts, but some things were simply part of his memory's lexicon, to pray for those he had left behind, to hope that they fared well and were safe and happy. To hold for a minute the pictures of home and to turn it over in his mind and then banish it before it could twist in his heart and take hold with thorn and root. Here too, he could allow the injustices and angers of the day to accumulate, to fall away, to become dust and to make room for the injustices and angers that would follow on the morrow.

He closed his eyes for a moment, feeling as though he could sleep here, sit until he crumbled from time and inertia and be swept away with all the other human detritus of the Soviet machine.

He missed things. Without warning, longings would hit him like a splinter in the chest, digging hard under the skin: the taste of tea in the morning, the view out of the kitchen over the city, the homely smell of toast, the sound of Maggie's heavy footsteps and how her tongue had never spared him except when he was small, but he had always known she loved him. He missed his stables, late in the evenings when it was just him and the horses, the scent of them and hay and well-oiled tack. He even missed the piles of paperwork on his desk each day, the invitations to events he had no wish to attend, the long columns of numbers that his brain had always loved for their ability to straighten out the universe. He missed things that he used to feel as burdens, for he saw them now for what they were—an involvement with and a love of the world, the world within which he had moved with such ease.

He missed his dog and his favorite chair in the study, the one his grandfather always sat in, and he missed the way the moon rose over the oaks outside his study, spilling light across the floor in the evenings. He missed his small Protestant friend, Nelson. He thought of how the firelight turned Nelson's brown hair into a burnished chestnut, how the child did not have a poker face at all but was a burgeoning chess player. He hoped that someone was making sure Nelson had pants that were long enough and lenses in his glasses to keep up with his weakening eyesight. But he knew, of course, Nelson would have those things because Pamela would see to it.

Pamela. He tried not to remember, but sometimes a stray moment snuck in when he was too tired to ward it off. There was a night, just before Casey came to take her home, when the despair of waiting for her husband had been more than she could bear alone. She had crossed the space between herself and him in the study, knelt down on the floor and put her head in his lap the way a child would who desperately needed comfort. There had been nothing strained or awkward about the moment, and he had stroked her head, watching the play of his emerald ring against the night-blue silk of her hair.

Around them, the old house was silent, peaceful, the only sound the fire in the grate hissing softly and the only feeling that of Pamela's breath warm against his knee. In that deep silence, her hand had come up and lain softly over his, and so they had sat for a very long time as the night flowed over them and the stars pinwheeled across the heavens and slipped off to set in another sky, far away.

"May I sit with you?" The voice seemed to come out of the ether and startled Jamie in his fugue of exhaustion. "I'm sorry, I did not mean to frighten you."

At the edge of the bench, copper hair a dull glow in the dim, stood Violet. He was momentarily stunned into open-mouthed silence, for she had done no more than nod curtly in his direction in all these weeks in the camp.

He regained his faculties enough to nod and clear the dust from the bench.

She sat down, tucking her hands between her knees, her shoulders rising up to meet the shorn edges of her hair.

"You were praying?" she asked, a quiet curiosity in her words.

"No—or yes, but only in a broken-down way. My relationship with God has always been difficult."

"On your side or on God's?" she asked, smiling.

"Both. Likely it's more problematical for him," he said returning the smile, despite his exhaustion. "Mostly I just come here for the peace."

"You can feel it though, can't you? There's something here, a presence. It's more than mere emptiness."

"Yes," he said, grateful suddenly for her company. It was true there was something here, whether the echoes of a faith that had been practiced once, or the presence of a spirit beyond the trappings of earthly woe. Still, it was here, indefinable as things of the soul always were, but undeniable.

Her nose was tipped pink from the cool evening, charming against the camellia white of her skin. She was tiny, yet had a persona much larger than her physical size, and she exuded a kind of peace that quieted others merely by her proximity. He had been careful in his observations of her, once he had understood just who she was. He understood what it was that had drawn Andrei away from his elegant and icy wife to this woman. The fire that never left Andrei in peace would be tempered by this woman, and in her arms he had likely found brief moments of peace, that he had not been able to find elsewhere in his life.

She touched the hollow of her throat, and closed her eyes. It was a gesture with which he was long familiar. He looked more closely and saw the glint of gold hidden beneath her uniform. Almost as invisible as faith, but somewhat more tangible.

"You pray?" he asked. She looked at him sharply and he realized he had made a Western gaffe for in Russia, religion was more private than sex. God had never left Russia entirely, but had remained within hearts and minds, hidden in secret cupboards and the memories of the peasants and the grandmothers. For her, it would be natural to think he prayed, for it was part and parcel of the Irish soul, but in Russia that same flame of faith had to be hidden to the point of snuffing it out.

She spent a long moment studying his face, and he allowed it, not masking his thoughts.

"Yes, I pray. I was raised by a peasant woman named Masha, as my mother was too busy with her Party duties, and the Party did not allow a true believer to show great affection to her child. Nights she studied at the Institute of Foreign Trade. Often it was just Masha and me, for my father was exiled and I was not allowed to speak of him. Masha was a devout Old Believer and she prayed morning and night and included me in all the rituals of her religion. When I was small, it was like believing in a fairytale or a ghost, something delicious that made me shiver. But as I got older, it became something deeper, something that formed a strange lifeline with a presence, an idea beyond the cold empire into which I was born. I suppose you could call me an internal immigrant. Outside I am a Soviet: inside I have left for a far country."

"Why are you here?" he asked.

"For much the same reason as you are, Jamie—my relationship to Andrei."

He raised a questioning eyebrow and she smiled in response. "I see you are not the man for a simple explanation. I was the daughter of an exiled economist and that alone would have been enough. But I was also part of a group that started an underground newspaper called *The Record*. The idea was to make a record of all the unpublicized news events in the Soviet Union: human rights abuses, arrests, trials, demonstrations, *samizdat* publications—and hope that we could smuggle it out to the West to bring attention to what was happening inside Russia.

"You have to understand that when the thaw came after Stalin's death, we really thought everything would change. No one could have imagined that it would all stagnate under Brezhnev and that many of the old repressions and punishments would come back. It was exciting to believe that we could change, that our generation would be the one to break the chains of Communism." She shrugged, face clouded with old memories.

"The KGB waged war on us, which told us we were hitting a nerve, that word was getting out beyond our borders. They searched our homes, offices, anywhere we might have papers. Once they stormed in on me and I had to dump a bunch of papers into a pot of soup boiling on the stove. I knew it was only a matter of time before I got into really hot water. Then I was sent to work on a project at Zvyozdny Gorodok and I met Andrei."

She looked down at her small hands. Jamie waited in silence. She would continue her tale, or not.

"I would not have you think I went lightly into the affair with Andrei. You are not Russian, so perhaps you do not believe in Fate as we do—the knowledge that your life is meant to have these meetings, these interstices where things are supposed to happen—and you cannot avoid them no matter if they are going to break your heart or ruin you entirely. This is what I felt when I saw Andrei. Fate. I knew I was meant to love him, to sacrifice my entire being to him if that was what he wanted. Oh, I know it sounds very dramatic, but that is Russian love. I was fully prepared to love him in vain, to have no return of my affections. But then a miracle—he did."

She looked at him openly, grey eyes dark in the old chapel. "Sometimes it has felt like all my life has been a suppression of feeling, of avoiding emotion, of not longing for that which was not possible, of never allowing yearning to take root in my soul. When I met Andrei, I decided that I was not going to suppress anything, no matter the price. So I am here in this camp, for that sin—for feeling when I should not have. They used my ties to *The Record* as an excuse."

"Does your family know what happened to you?"

Another shrug. "For myself," she said slowly, "there is no one left to mind. My father died in a gulag much like this one. My mother disowned me, and Masha went to her God long ago."

She took a deep breath, and smiled, a gesture he felt more than saw.

"We have holey memories in Russia. So much is lies in this country and we are fed the Party line from our cribs. We are also taught to look the other way, to be quiet, to keep our mouths shut. It does strange things to your mind after awhile. You can't remember what was true and what was false about a given incident. It is better sometimes to just believe as you are told to believe. It makes life more livable."

"Does it?" he asked, for the night was one of those oddities that allowed such questions as daylight would not.

"No, but it is better not to admit that too often," she said and stood, leaving him alone in the church. There had been both admission and warning in her words.

Chapter Thirty-four

June 1973

Gregor's Story

JAMIE AND NIKOLAI HAD CUT ABOVE QUOTA FOR A MONTH STRAIGHT, earning them extra rations for a week. The bread was hard and the meat stringy, but it was edible. Still, he put away part of the bread and meat for Volodya, whose meals were even smaller than the norm. Volodya often cut under quota, as the skill of sawing seemed to be something he could not learn, and each day in the forest was a struggle for him.

He took the opportunity of his extra rations to sneak off to the showers during suppertime. To have a moment alone was as rare and precious as stumbling over a hillock of diamonds and he had no intention of wasting it. He intended to get decently clean for a change. Gregor held court at the supper table, he and his *vor*, taking up one long table entirely, eating their meals like the wolves they were but lingering afterwards unless they had business to attend.

He had decent soap from a trade with Vanya who had access to mysterious channels of black market goods. Jamie had given three cakes of it to Violet and kept one for himself. It was dense hand-milled soap and heaven only knew where the man had found it, but Jamie wasn't going to look this particular gift horse in the mouth.

The water, heated in the cistern by the day's sun, was hot enough to sluice the dirt from his skin in great waves, rolling down his body in blissful comfort. It made him long for the ocean, to be totally immersed in water, to have the force of it sweep him away, to take him home.

He scrubbed his hair, which had grown out to a downy half inch upon his scalp, until it squeaked, and then lathered his body with what seemed a sinful amount of soap.

The night before he had dreamed of the forest maiden. She had, as before, remained in the shadows but this time she had spoken to him in the ancient language of water and woods and she had touched him, her fingers smelling of green and movement, of the dark light that lived within water and the thickness of cold amber in the trees. Her touch had been both dreamlike and real on some shifting level, and his body had responded to her with an ache he had not known in some time. She had felt as fresh and raw to his flesh as the first flicker of green upon a spring willow bough, as sweet as a cold green apple, fetched from a well.

His dreams, other than the strange dream language of the *rusalka,* were beginning to speak to him in Russian.

The dream of the water woman had lingered with him all day, like webbing around his senses that he could not shake. With the extra rations restoring some of his strength, he had found some of his other hungers returning. Even now, the memory of the forest maiden's eyes meeting his and her mouth opening to speak sent a surge of warmth through him.

His body, starved as it was for touch of any sort, stirred at the dream memory and he was grateful to be alone for the moment. It wasn't uncommon in the camp to see men in various states of arousal. Men, after all, were men. Even half-starved and worked to the point of collapse, the desire for sex still somehow rose to the top and flouted itself, looking for any sort of release. He had experienced bouts of abstinence before, but never one quite this long.

"Now *that* is what I call a proper welcome," said a thick, lazy voice behind him.

Jamie turned slowly, wiping the water out of his eyes one-handed. Inwardly he cursed himself for letting his guard down.

Gregor stood at the edge of the showers, Jamie's towel swinging from the end of one hand. He would have to brazen it out. There was nothing to cover up with anyway, and he couldn't afford any show of weakness with this man.

"I'm afraid you have me at a disadvantage," Jamie said, certain he had never felt more naked in his entire life. He was also very aware that the last time he and this man had been in contact, he had been holding a knife to Gregor's throat.

"Ah well, Jamie, as long as I have you," Gregor purred, "I am not fussy about the terms."

"Could I have my towel?"

"Mm," Gregor pulled the towel suggestively across his mouth. "You look like you would taste good, all clean skin and golden hair. I have wondered, you know," he looked directly at Jamie's erection, "if you would disappoint, but I see now that things are even more pleasing than I had hoped. You are, as your good book says, 'most fearfully and wonderfully made'. So what do you want? You need Gregor to be the *peduh* for you? It has been many years since I was any man's bitch, but for you I will make exception. You want to be on top, is okay with me."

"Is there anything, aside from the obvious," Jamie said dryly, "that I can do for you?"

Gregor sighed. "It is a shame to waste such a thing, but this I did not come here for. He tossed the towel at Jamie. "Get dressed. We need to talk."

Ten minutes later, dry, clean, clothed and more than a little irritated, Jamie joined Gregor who was waiting for him, minus his minions, outside the bathhouse.

"Come," Gregor said, tossing aside the clover he'd been chewing on. "Take a little walk with me."

"Where?" Jamie asked, wondering if an ambush was waiting for him in a secluded spot.

"Not to worry, Yasha. Your virtue," Gregor smirked unpleasantly, "such as it is, will remain intact tonight."

"It's not my virtue I'm worried about as much as my ability to breathe," Jamie retorted.

"The only weapons tonight will be those of words. Now, will you come along?"

Gregor strode toward the camp boundary and Jamie followed, wondering what sort of reckoning awaited him, because even if it did not come tonight, he knew it would eventually.

The evening held remnants of the day's warmth, the sun filtering through the fir trees at a low angle. The nights were not as long; the change perceptible by several minutes each day.

Gregor and his *vor* had a meeting place to which everyone else gave a wide berth. It was only a scrubby ring of pines that had somehow survived the mowing down of everything else within the fences. Here they held meetings, drank themselves senseless, and occasionally were permitted bonfires. To Jamie's knowledge, no one else was ever allowed to enter this sacred ring. He wondered if he was about to be offered up as a virgin sacrifice or if something less ominous was brewing.

"Sit," Gregor said, as expansively as if he were offering Jamie the depths of a buttery leather armchair, rather than a fir stump bleeding sap.

Jamie sat, glad there was a solid tree trunk behind him to guard his back. Gregor sat across from him, clasping his large hands together and leaning forward so Jamie could feel the aura of brute menace.

"So you are brave, maybe crazy. I see this now—after you sticking that knife to my throat."

Gregor fished a flask out of his back pocket. "Here. It's vodka, though it should be fucking poison for what you did to me."

Jamie took a swallow, knowing it would be one step too far to refuse the drink. A Russian might tolerate a knife to his throat, but a refusal to drink with him was a far graver insult.

"So I tell you this. First I am wanting to kill you—for no one has had the nerve to put a knife to my throat, crawl into my bed and threaten to gut me like a pig before. I am furious, thinking who does this fucking Irishman think he is? But I am not a fool. I see how others are drawn to you. I see that if I do not make truce, that even if I kill you, someone then will kill me. Probably the old man, maybe the whore. The whore I can manage, the old man I am not so certain about. Because the old man has those eyes. They see right into and through you, and he does not care any longer if he lives or dies, which makes him very dangerous."

Jamie made no comment, for it was an exact and unsparing portrait of Nikolai.

"I owe you for sparing my life that night. You could have killed me, but you don't. This makes me a little worried. For what, Gregor, I ask myself, has this man spared you the knife? And I cannot find the answer, and this itself worries me more, so that I am losing sleep."

"Really? I slept like a baby after threatening to gut you like a pig."

Gregor threw his head back and laughed. "You are bastard, Jamie. I am liking this very much. Don't look scared, my friend, I am liking this in a man—not a *peduh*."

"You promised to be the *peduh*, if you remember correctly," Jamie said.

"You are making joke, no? This is good. You are relaxing and understanding Gregor better now."

"Are you going to tell me what you want? Why we're out here?"

"Not to rush, good man. Talk takes time. Have another drink first."

Jamie sighed, but took the drink. If the bastard wanted a pissing match, he would give him one. He'd practically been suckled on whiskey and Connemara Mist carried a punch more subtle than vodka but no less lethal. Some men needed to go toe to toe in this way, or they would never trust you. Though Jamie was not thrilled about having to prove his manhood by drinking himself into a paralytic state, he understood the psychology behind it and knew he couldn't afford to walk away from this challenge, for there was more than a hangover at stake.

Gregor, it seemed, was in a conversational mood.

"I am *bezprizorni*—this is a word you are knowing, Yasha Yakovich?"

"Yes," Jamie replied, for he knew his Russian history well.

The *Bezprizorniye* were originally the 'wild children' who had roamed the roads and forests, the cold cities and abandoned byways of Stalin's Russia after the purges began. Children who had been orphaned by Stalin's fist coming down on thousands of people: mothers, fathers, brothers, sisters... for Stalin's fear and rage knew no boundaries and no one was safe under the aegis of Papa Joseph.

The *Bezprizorniye* had morphed through need, and the feral anarchy that will come with abandonment of all social mores and parental affection, into a criminal underclass from which the *urkas* would often pluck promising candidates to come up through the hierarchy of the ruling *mafiya*. The *Bezprizorniye* formed their own mafia as well, and such criminal enterprises became the only family these children knew. The ties were forged, literally and figuratively, in blood. They were also unbreakable outside of the release of death.

"I am pickpocket when I am small. Children make the best ones for their fingers are soft and light. But I also have a wolf. She makes me stand out, so I have to leave her each morning chained up. She howls like I am killing her but I can't take her into the city with me. I work the streets of Kiev, but I live like animal on the outskirts. This suits me though—I am half wild thing, much as I am now. Then one day I pick the pocket of the wrong man. I do not know that he is a feared gangster, that he is the *vor y zakone*, the vor that rules over all other vors in Kiev. His name is Viktor and I think he will kill me when he catches me with my hand in his pocket. At the very least, I know he is going to break my fingers. Suddenly my wolf shows up out of nowhere, growling and walking slow toward him, threatening, making it clear she will rip out his throat. Viktor tells me to call her off, but I just shrug and say, 'No, because then you kill me, or hurt my hands and my hands are my bread.

"He swears he will not hurt me but I still am not trusting him so I make him let go of me and back up behind my wolf. Then she and I, we walk backwards, keeping an eye on him and finally when I think we are out of harm's way, we run. I am a fool to think this man will not find me, but I do not know he is *the* Vor, and that many shake in fear at the simple utterance of his name.

"He does find me a week later. This time I know I am dead. There is no way out from such a man. But he is impressed with my nerve and wants me to work for him. He offers me a place at his table, a bed under his roof. I say yes, though I am still, you understand, a fierce thing from growing up in the woods with only a wolf as my companion.

"Once Viktor Dmitriovich takes me under his roof I am treated as family, as a member of the vor, whose ties are stronger than blood. I have to wait until I am much older to be sponsored in, and to become a prince among thieves takes even longer.

"I am sent to school. I find it very hard to sit still in the desks and I cannot abide the discipline and authority of the teachers, so Viktor Dmitriovich has me tutored. I still pick pockets, and once I am older, I move to larger theft, bigger crimes. Always, I defer to Viktor Dmitriovich, for I owe him the loyalty of blood.

"This is how I grow, this is what makes me a man, and so I know no life but that of thief and enforcer. I spend much time in prison. This too makes man's shell grow harder. I am strong though. The bastards put me in chains for a year. I cannot walk far enough to piss without having to sit in it later and there is not enough chain to lie down for sleep. This does not break me. Because the vor are my family and I will not betray those ties and I do not recognize the authority of the Soviet. The vor and my own strength are all I have. Now only strength is left. So I make family wherever I am, with those that gather round a man such as myself, a man such as yourself."

They had come, Jamie saw, to the crux of what Gregor wanted to say to him. The subtext being, *'I see you as a threat and I take threats very personally.'*

"I am a vain man at times. This I know about myself—vain of my power, vain of my position, but I am no fool and so I see that you are a man who draws others without effort. I see the camp dividing along these lines already, slowly, but it is happening. I decide that I have two choices—to kill you, or to call a truce. I kill you and I am going to spend much longer in this hellhole than I am already condemned to. And I am man enough to admit where my weakness lies—and such as you are is a very big weakness for me."

"Such as I am?" Jamie said, and took another swallow of the vodka before passing it back to Gregor. He knew what the weakness was. He had seen it in the man's eyes clearly.

"Uncle Viktor is always saying to me to stamp out all weakness, to take that which lures you most and put fire to it. For others this is drugs, alcohol, gambling, women. For me, it is beauty—all beauty is my weakness—buildings, music, art, men, women. I crave it, want to take it into myself, have it for my own soul. I want it like a junkie wants heroin. I cannot stop the craving in my veins. I think if I can consume enough of it, with my eyes, with my mouth, with my body then I will be satiated, will know some peace, will perhaps have beauty always inside, will be beautiful myself. This is not how such a drug works, of course, it only makes me want more and more and I can never fill that place that yearns for beauty."

He stretched his arms out, flexing them as though the ghost of the chains he had once worn still lay there, heavy upon his wrists.

"Your beauty has heat, it has passion. You have done and seen many, many things and yet it has not jaded you, I am thinking."

The statement seemed to be in the form of an observation rather than a question, so Jamie didn't answer to it.

"And this beauty, this experience," Gregor sighed, "is only for women."

"Yes," Jamie agreed firmly, "it is only for women."

"That is a pity," Gregor said, dark eyes reflecting the feral wildness he had never left behind.

"The women don't seem to think so," Jamie said, but his tone did not match the lightness of his words.

"No, I am sure they don't." Gregor held him in a hard look for a moment and then changed direction.

"The tattoo on your back—the good Comrade has one to match."

"Yes, we got them at the same time," Jamie said.

"Why?"

"Because we were drunk, and because we'd done something incredibly stupid earlier that night and in the way of the young and stupid, felt the need to commemorate the moment."

"He is good friend to you?"

"Yes."

"Yet, you end up here because of him. This doesn't make you angry? Make you want to kill him, maybe take his woman?" Gregor quirked an eyebrow at this last suggestion. Jamie ignored it.

"How do you know that Comrade Valueve has the same tattoo as me?"

Gregor shrugged. "I see him one time with the woman. He is naked, and his back is to me. Nothing is secret in the camp, nothing."

"You watched them having sex?"

"Yes, was nothing else going on at the time, so I watch. Your friend is very beautiful too, not quite like you, but still worth watching. I don't like him so much though. His soul is missing."

"His soul is missing?" Jamie echoed, wondering exactly what Gregor meant.

"There is something very cold in him. I see it in his eyes. When he looks at you, it's like there is a snake curled up at the bottom of a lake, waiting to strike. Myself, if I am going to kill you, I tell you. I put knife in your belly while looking in your eyes. He would send flunkies to do this work and a man would never get to look his own death in the face, and die like a man should, with honesty."

"He is my friend," Jamie said in a tone that warned the man to let it lie.

Gregor held up one hand in mock surrender. "I am only making an observation and saying that your being in this camp may be more than meets the eye."

He stood then, making it clear their interview was over. "So do we have a truce then, Yasha Yakovich?"

"Do I have a choice?"

"No."

"Then yes, you have a truce."

Jamie stood and extended his hand. Gregor allowed several seconds to lapse before he took it, making it clear that he was in the position of ascendency and that Jamie would do well to remember it.

Gregor walked from the circle first, turning his back to Jamie so Jamie would know the man did not fear him. Just beyond the border of the trees he turned back, eyes cold as black ice.

"One more thing—end of story so to speak. My wolf—Viktor made me kill her when I was twelve years old to show my loyalty to his command.

I loved that wolf, you understand? That wolf was my only friend for years. She protected me, slept by my side, ate with me. My wolf and I are one blood—but I killed her when I had to."

Jamie nodded, holding the man's eyes with his own, showing him the message had been received and understood.

Chapter Thirty-five

July 1973

Camp Wife

IF THE CAMP COULD BE COMPARED TO A SPIDER'S WEB then Svetlana, the OC's wife, was the black widow at the center of it. Which made Jamie, at this juncture, the juicy fly on the edges of the web, struggling in layers of sticky silk, making his predicament more precarious with every flail of his limbs. He had felt it from the first, the way one felt the various tugs and disturbances in the weft of one's own universe.

Shura had warned him. Jamie had visited the infirmary one afternoon after cutting his thumb with a barking axe and ran into Svetlana just outside the doors. He stopped, as was expected. She stalked directly to him and bent her head over his thumb. The cut was not serious, neither ligaments nor vessels had been severed, but she clucked over it as though the digit were in danger of falling off before personally escorting him into the infirmary.

"You will look after him, Comrade Shura," she said. "We would hate for such a lovely man to bear scars."

Shura raised an eyebrow at him behind her back. Jamie swallowed, for her finger was drawing the smallest of circles in his palm, its message unmistakable.

"You have been observed," Shura said after Svetlana left.

"Yes?"

"She has her sights on you and that means only one thing. Right now, she has a young one but she will soon discard him. But you," Shura finished wrapping the gauze around Jamie's thumb and tied a precise knot to keep it in place, "I am thinking, are no stranger to women so perhaps the task will not be troublesome."

"I'm not in the habit," Jamie replied, "of being commanded to service women."

Shura looked at him, perfect seriousness in the crooked face. "It does not matter what you do or do not want. This is the Soviet Union. None of the rules of your old life apply here."

At first, it had not worried him over much, for it was to be expected.

Once Gregor had asserted his dominance and they had settled into a wary truce, he had thought he would manage. However, he felt Svetlana's observation more than the watchful gaze of others, an observation that was neither distant nor benign.

He had seen from the first that the camp commander was weak. It showed in the filth of the camp environment, in the lawlessness that prevailed even within barbed-wire fences. What order did prevail, prevailed because of Gregor.

Svetlana was not weak, but she did not pair her strength with kindness or an ability to organize. However, it did not take Jamie long to realize that outside of Gregor, this woman was the true power in the camp. He knew well enough to keep her in his sights and do as little as he could to draw her attention to himself.

It was only a couple of weeks after the infirmary incident that he was commanded to stay behind one morning, for which small favor he was not terribly grateful, as it would not endear him to his camp mates. He would be suspected of everything from currying favor to outright spying. Either could cause a convenient accident with a saw, or a tree that suddenly fell in the wrong direction.

Since that first morning, he had been called in for numerous small chores—to mend a chair, to repair leaking faucets, to chop wood and stack it deep against the sides of the snug cabin—all while an armed guard trained an automatic weapon on him. Sometimes he was held back from his work in the forest for this. Other times he was ordered to use his evenings. This he resented, though one resented in silence in Russia. Today he had been called to fix her radio.

He was not anyone's fool, and saw immediately that the radio had been tampered with, just as the washers on the faucets had been deliberately loosened. He knew there were prisoners who had earned the easier work of chopping wood or repairing such things as needed repair, whereas he had not. He had been chosen for these things for one reason only. He was fully aware that many would count themselves fortunate in his shoes. It was his misfortune that he did not.

She was attractive enough and kept herself as well as life in such a god-forsaken post of the Empire had allowed. But it wasn't her physical attributes that were the problem. It was her soul, and he meant that in the most Russian, emotional, dramatic sense of the word.

She walked toward him now, like the spider to which he had compared her, navigating the silk thread in her web. She was all red, in both character and physicality. Her hair was red and had been deepened to a scarlet flare with henna, her mouth full and crimson with some cheap rouge. Her body was full too. Not even the drab uniform she wore could hide that. She was carnal in that way he had encountered a time or two before, like fruit full and tempting, but once you bit beneath the skin, you discovered it had begun to decay. He met her eyes, for there was no other way. Deference did not serve with a woman like this one, at least not in his case.

"Today, you will stay and take tea with me in the afternoon."

An innocuous enough invitation, but he understood the implication. Her appetites were not hidden and God knew he himself was no untried virgin. It shouldn't be such a difficult thing. He was, most nights, too tired to ask himself why it seemed to be just that—difficult. For he had known this was inevitable, the way a man will who has known such a woman before.

Until today he had been able to deflect her but had known too that she was merely toying with him, drawing out her own pleasure. He sensed that pleading his Western ignorance would not help him, the language of the body being universal in its phrasings. Hers was speaking in full sentences.

He ignored her and replaced the back of the radio, putting the screws in with careful deliberation. She came around to where he sat, her hand running across the back of his shoulders. He went still, weary with the pantomime in which they were engaged.

"Did you hear me?" she asked, her tone that of a woman attempting to seduce, but only accustomed to one note, that of command. Her eyes held all the ice-blue hauteur of her ancestors. He wondered once again what egregious sin had landed her with such a weakling for a husband, in a remote outpost that had long been forgotten by central command.

"I heard you, but think I mistook your meaning. I am not, after all, a native speaker."

"Do not even try to play the fool with me. They tell me you are extremely proficient in our language." She had one red-tipped finger on his chin now, forcing him to meet her eyes.

"Alright then, I am saying no."

"What?"

Jamie knew she had heard him but that it did not matter. His opinions were of no account in this matter but he could not desist from voicing them.

"No," he repeated, just as quietly, but with more force than before. His temper was fraying rapidly. It was the first time in his life he had hated a woman. It was not a pleasant sensation.

She slapped him hard across the face, jerking his head to the side and filling his mouth with blood. The second slap promised to be even greater in force, but he stopped it by grabbing her wrist hard and holding it up in the air, suspended in mid-violence. He realized his mistake at once, for he saw the flare in her eyes and understood its meaning. She was breathing heavily through her nose, face flushed with excitement. He felt suddenly very weary, and wanted nothing more than to crawl back to the hut and pull the covers over his head. He did not want to deal with this woman.

"I can have any of them flogged or put into isolation. I believe the little one who works in the infirmary would suffer under such attention." She let the words linger on the air, strong with import. "I think you understand my meaning."

He did, and it hit him with force how narrow his world had become, how without choice or places to turn. She was still breathing in short, sharp bursts and he understood far too well what she wanted and how she wanted it.

Inside himself he shut a door, weary, for he knew when a man is forced into a corner and there is nowhere to run he must fight with whatever weapons are at hand or submit to what is demanded of him so as not to cost others. There was, as far as he could see, only one path currently open to him, and fury had its own intoxications.

He took a breath and bared his teeth in a bloody smile, hearing Vanya's words in his head as he moved toward the woman.

It is only a body. It is not who I am.

Chapter Thirty-six

August 1973

Mother Russia

HIS COUNTRY, THIS RUSSIA, WAS A LAND BEYOND CONCEPTION—eleven time zones, six thousand miles from east to west and three thousand from north to south. It laid claim to the world's longest coastlines and boasted every kind of geography known to man: arid desert, inland seas, frozen tundra, thick fairytale forests, semi-tropical beaches, long sweeping steppes that were so treeless that a man could be lost for days without sight of any sort of landmark, rivers that flowed on forever and surging rugged mountains. This land that made one feel the terrible frailty of existence as a man.

Did the brutality of such a landscape inspire brutality in man's heart as well? For Russia had treated her children harshly, and as children will, they loved their mother all the more for her chill indifference.

If you listened long enough in the great silences such a land held, it would speak to you—of its past, of its future and of all that had sundered it. Russia speaks to him of the great horsemen that once swept her plains, and the armies that even now marched by the hundreds of thousands across her frozen heart. She tells of falling stars that laid waste to the abundance of her bounty and the rifts in her body where enormous stores of water, the largest in the world, are held. She speaks of her peasants, her shamans, her priests, her emperors and queens, her poets and musicians. She whispers of the long iron girders that trace her spine for the distance of seven days. She speaks of the empty spaces in her soul, of the migration of dancing cranes and herds of reindeer. She speaks of her amber hair—seductively, her pearls, her minerals and the rich, loamy fertility of her plains. She tells him the story of all her peoples: the haughty, mysterious Slavs; the silent Sibers; the earthy Ukraines; the Balts and Turks and Tatars; and the Yakuts, whom she claims can walk through hordes of white men like smoke and never be seen nor felt. She tells of the thunder of foreign troops who have come again and again, and of the vast silence of her winters that have inevitably defeated her foes. Her voice is as dark as a terrible perfume, as she tells of the secret police and the fields sown with the blood of the forgotten innocents. She speaks in contradiction and secret languages that have not been spoken in hundreds of years. And under all her words, her seduction, her coldness, her heat and succor, he hears her heart—the great, thundering heart of Mother Russia. And he hears that it is a heart forever in the process of breaking.

He understood such a country, for Ireland showed little mercy to her children either. It was an odd thing to love a land so, for it never loved one back. It too was prey to the vagaries of weather, meteorites, man's misdeeds, fortune, or lack thereof, and that entirely fickle mistress—chance. And yet, each land had its own characteristics, due to the great shift of mountains and seas, and the inner boiling cauldron of the earth itself. Each land had its own nature, soft with heat or laid upon by winter's iron hand, some fertile with life and pungent with decay, some with skies so large they made a man want to drop to his knees and hide his head for the terror it could inspire. Or a land could lull you, the way Ireland often did, hiding its capacity for the taking of blood and the breaking of hearts in the soft swell of its verdant green hills, and the windswept beauty of its coastal zones.

The forests here had silenced him with their grim, dark grandeur. They spoke of trolls and goblins, of the soft, sibilant cackle of the Baba Yaga. At twilight they were positively spooky with the dark falling long before it did on the open plain. Being Irish, and therefore no stranger to the idea of trees having a life and world of their own, he imagined they spoke to one another through the aspect of air, with the stir of leaves and the scratch of branches and the high wail they emitted during a storm, or the horrible grinding moan that echoed throughout the forest when they fell.

The resin was thick and heady as golden honey, the scent released by the day's heat to linger in a still torpor in the late afternoon. He paused, allowing the group to walk some way ahead of him.

He longed for home in a visceral way, the deep-rooted longing for familiar surroundings, to be in a place where you understood instinctively what was required, where you could lie down in a patch of sunlight and not worry about being punished for it.

He still thought about escape each and every day, but where would that leave Violet, Nikolai, Shura—the motley crew of people that looked to him for sustenance to help them face another day? The thought of what vengeance might be wreaked on them always halted him when he felt the pull at the forest's edge, the ever-present beckoning west, so strong at times that he had to wrench himself away to ignore its call.

And so for now, it would appear, Russia was his home. Russia was his country and he would have to hope that, as her adopted son, she would see fit to allow him one day to leave, taking his life with him.

Part Six

Soul's Ransom
Ireland – January-March 1974
Russia – November 1973- April 1974

Chapter Thirty-seven

January 1974

Just Kate

IT WAS A DARK AND STORMY NIGHT, OR RATHER, PAT RIORDAN thought, gazing out his brother's kitchen window, a somewhat poorly lit and intemperate afternoon. The air was heavy with the expectation of snow, the light that odd grey-pink that heralded a big fall.

He didn't mind a good storm. It shut the world out and allowed a man to dwell with his own thoughts. Today, his own were to be confined to his law books. He sighed. The table was loaded with books and papers, and though he found the law in all its labyrinthine convolutions fascinating, this morning's reading combined with the impending weather had given him a mild headache. He had already cut kindling, done dishes, taken Finbar for a long tramp through the moisture-laden woods, and made a sandwich. Half of it had been eaten by Finbar, who always managed to convey the impression that he was on the verge of starvation.

He turned to his book on criminal law as it pertained to the Northern Ireland court system and began reading, thinking with no small cynicism that many of these laws only seemed to apply to half of the population, and them only some of the time.

He was thus absorbed, taking in a statute from 1778 concerning the theft of a cow, when he heard an engine chugging along the narrow lane at the head of the drive. He frowned, not feeling in the mood for company. It was likely Gert, who seemed to be of the opinion that he hadn't a notion on how to feed nor care for himself.

The car stopped at the head of the drive and then drove quickly on. Finbar cocked his head toward the door. Pat, dog in tow, went to see what the disturbance was. The wind shoved the door in when he opened it, bringing with it a whirl of snowflakes. The storm had begun.

A woman was making her way down the drive, the wind pushing her along and flaring her skirts around her, making her resemble a violet petal blown about in a seastorm. Blown about she must be feeling as well, for she was clutching the trunk of a young birch as though for dear life.

Pat crossed the yard, the wind whipping his hair into his eyes and the snow whirling around his head. He coughed loudly as he approached, for she had not noticed him yet and seemed disinclined to let go of the tree. She looked about wildly, settling eventually on the air just over his shoulder. He realized with a small shock that she was blind.

"Can I help ye?" he asked, coming within a few feet of her. He was scared to go any closer as she seemed so like a startled deer that she might bolt at the least provocation.

She was clutching a parcel tightly to her chest. "I'm looking for Pamela. Is she here?"

"I'm sorry, but they're away just now. They've taken the babby an' gone for the weekend. Was she expectin' ye?"

"No, she wasn't. I came on the spur of the moment like, because I have a gift for her. I'll just leave it here, if I may?" She was slightly stiff and formal in her manner, considering the snow was now coming down in earnest and she was quickly turning from windblown violet to frosted blossom.

"Of course," Pat said. "But won't ye come in? I'm Pamela's brother-in-law. Ye look as though ye need to get in out of the weather for a bit. I'll make ye some tea. I'm here lookin' after things until they get home."

She hesitated, and he stood patiently waiting for her to decide. Not that there was much choosing as far as he could see, for the car had dropped her off at the head of the lane and gone onwards. And it was far too cold to hang about in the dooryard.

He gave her his hand to guide her into the house. Finbar wagged his tail and ambled over to her. Not for the first time, Pat thought that the dog lacked somewhat in the way of vicious guard-dogging abilities.

"How about I seat ye near to the stove?" he asked, uncertain what to do with the woman now that she was in the house. He had offered her tea, so that was likely where he ought to start.

A few minutes later he had her seated in a chair, her wool coat hung to dry and the kettle on the boil.

"Do ye have a name, then?" she asked, fussily brushing melting snowflakes from the folds of her skirt.

"Aye, it's Patrick. An' yer own?" he inquired, feeling a tad testy and not knowing quite why.

"Kate Murray," she said briskly. "Just Kate, not Kathleen, or Katherine, or Katie—just Kate."

"Alright then, Just Kate, how is it ye like yer tea?"

"Just a bit of lemon," she said, crossing her heavily stockinged but very dainty ankles.

She picked up the damp parcel that had been clutched to her chest, removed the brown paper wrapping and shook out the contents.

"Would ye be so kind as to hang this up so that it might warm an' dry?"

Pat took it, the weight of it hanging nicely from his hands. "It'll be a gift for the wee man?"

"It will. I did want to give it to him for Christmas but I didn't finish it until a few days ago," she said primly, clasping her hands together in her damp lap.

It was a quilt, done in various shades of blue, the fabric in blocks of velvet and sateen and cotton prints. It was a beautiful piece of work.

"Did ye sew this yerself?" he asked.

"Yes. I tell my brother what I want for materials and he picks them out for me an' then we sit an' he describes each bit while I touch them. He cuts the blocks an' then I tell him what order to put them in, but I do the actual sewing myself," she said with a note of pride. Well justified too, for the stitches were near to invisible.

"Yer brother?" He had a sudden memory of Casey saying Pamela had encountered Noah Murray's sister some time back. He was rendered mute for a moment at the idea of the feared Noah Murray cutting quilting blocks.

"So what is it that ye do for a living, Patrick?"

"I run the Fair Housing Association," he said, still studying the intricate stitching of the quilt and wondering how she had managed it. "I work with my brother part-time with the construction, an' I go to law school."

The kettle was whistling and he stood to fetch it and fill the brown betty with fresh tea leaves and water.

"A solicitor is it? What will ye hope to do with that?"

"Well," he said slowly, for his own thoughts on this were only half-formed. "I should like to be part of justice in this land, rather than ignorin' the problems we have." Then he swallowed, realizing just how much a part of the crime equation this woman's brother was.

"That's a fine ambition," she said, "but maybe none so easy to do in this country."

"Aye, maybe not, but a man has to try or what's the point of livin'?"

He brought the tea to the table along with two clean blue mugs, wee crooked things that Pamela had made at a pottery class at the local church. They held the tea fine though, and were charming if not pretty. He poured out the tea and cut up the lemon, putting a slice by his own plate and picking up a wedge for hers.

"Are ye a handsome man, would ye say?" she asked suddenly, startling him into squeezing the lemon into his own eye.

"Damn it!"

Apparently unruffled by his profanity, she asked again.

"Well, would ye say ye are?"

"Are what?" Pat asked, dabbing his face with the tea towel, which he realized belatedly he had wiped up the dog's water with earlier.

"Handsome?"

"I—I—well..." he took a breath and frowned. He wasn't given overmuch to thinking about his looks and being that he didn't think about women very often these days, it seemed moot. Between that and his studies he rarely thought to get a haircut and beyond making sure his clothes were clean and neat, he didn't give his attire a great deal of attention either.

"Hmm—ye must not be, I find handsome men usually know as they are handsome, so if ye don't know, ye musn't be."

Pat was starting to feel persecuted by the woman's sharp assessments.

"Well, I don't shame the dog when I take him out walking," he said, tossing the tea towel aside and putting the abused lemon on the woman's saucer. She could bloody well squeeze it herself.

"Yer tall though? Six one?"

"Six two," he said through his teeth.

"Will ye tell me what the kitchen is like, the layout?"

He looked about the comfortable room, which was really half kitchen, half sitting room. It had a squashy couch at one end, covered in a tatty old blanket to save it from Finbar and Rusty, who often curled up on it together. A copy of one of the *Father Brown* books lay face down on one end. Bookshelves flanked the couch, for Pamela was of the opinion no room was whole without books. Across from the couch was the hearth, built of rough stone by his brother's sure craftsman hands.

It was indeed a cheery room, with the blue Aga taking up part of one wall, the pine floors a golden brown as they started to age with use, the deep windowsills filled with herbs and flowers. The countertops were thick and serviceable, and dotted with crockery in various shades of blue. A print of John Singer Sargent's *Carnation, Lilly, Lilly, Rose* graced the wall above the sofa, bringing the soft strains of twilight into that corner.

He described it to her in detail, both the dimensions and the colors, the decorative touches and the atmosphere, which was one of lovely, cozy homeliness. Pamela might not be the world's greatest cook, but she certainly knew how to make a home feel just right to whoever stepped over the threshold. He even described the views out the windows, the stone wall so thickly covered with brambles and rose cane that even now, in the depths of winter, it looked like a hedge, rather than an ancient stone retaining wall.

"It sounds wonderful, but I could feel that. It's a home with a great deal of love soaked into its walls, no?"

"Yes, it is," Pat said, thinking of all that Pamela and Casey had overcome, and how it had knit something incredibly fine and strong into the weft of their home and life together.

She stood suddenly, startling him.

"I've two hours until my ride comes back to fetch me so I'll cook ye somethin'. It's likely, bein' male, ye don't feed yerself properly. An' to be honest, I'm less nervous when I've spoons an' bowls to hand."

He opened his mouth and then closed it. His father had often said that if a woman offered to feed a man, he ought to mind his manners and let her do so unimpeded.

"I'll need potatoes, a bit of chicken if some is handy an' some herbs an' such. A few veg as well. Is there an apron about?"

Pat gathered the things required, and ducked into the cold room that Casey had built off the kitchen's boot room. The potatoes and vegetables were kept here, as well as the cool stone crocks for milk. It smelled pleasantly of the autumn harvest of onions and fat potatoes in burlap sacks, the dirt still clinging to their skins. Carrots too, still with a sweet snap to them, and the bittersweet earthiness of leeks. He gathered a bit of each and brought them back to the kitchen to find Kate with her face buried in a pot of herbs. She nodded to herself and switched two pots around.

"I know them by scent," she said, briskly tying the apron he had taken off the door hook for her around her waist. "Then I order them alphabetically, to make things quicker. Now dump the potatoes and veg in the sink for me an' I'll give them a scrub."

Her hands were long and narrow, with short nails and pale skin. She was efficient and made short work of the scrubbing, lining the vegetables up across the counter and chopping them up on the oak cutting block. Then she broke off a sprig of thyme, some savory, and a bit of basil and chopped them up fine as grass. Her dexterity with a knife was something to behold, Pat thought, as she ordered him about to fetch a pot and get a bit of flour and where was the salt an' pepper anyway? He wondered if she bossed her brother around in this manner, and felt his first pang of pity for Noah Murray. She was a wee harridan, to be sure.

An hour later he was seated to a chicken stew such as he had never tasted in his life. There were even wee dumplings floating in the golden liquid. The pot, used to his sister-in-law's cooking, wouldn't know what to make of it and nor did he. But well instilled with his father's teachings, he ate it and was grateful for it.

Kate ate only a little, and then fed part of her portion to a grovelling Finbar. Rusty, curled up in her lap, eyes half closed in bliss, was treated to tiny pieces of chicken as well. Pat leaned back in his chair, surprised by how relaxed he felt.

He took a leisurely look at his guest. She was quite pretty when she smiled, which she did now as she murmured to Finbar. Eyes deep blue, reminding him of the violets that hid amongst tree roots and under thick covers of bramble. Hair a color somewhere between dark brown and black like the winter woods. She was upright and slim, and the color she wore flattered both her eyes and skin. He wondered if her brother helped her decide what to wear as well. It was the first time, he realized, that he had really looked at a woman since Sylvie's death. It caused a wave of guilt to flush over him and he looked away.

"Have I done something to make ye uncomfortable?" she asked, and he was mildly annoyed at her perspicacity.

"No, I was just musin' on something," he said, feeling to lie was the lesser of a few evils. Just then, the chug of an engine reverberated through the still of the early evening. She stood abruptly, dislodging Rusty, who made his discontent clear with several loud meows.

He walked her out into the sparkling evening. There were several inches of snow, mounded softly over posts and icing tree branches. The sky was still light with snow-laden clouds, and what was on the ground sparkled bright as a field of diamonds.

She turned back at the gate, dark hair and slender figure framed against the snowy branches of an elm. One hand rested on the gate latch and she put the other to his jawline, startling him. The scent of herbs and onions rose from her skin, mingled with the quixotic scent of violets.

"Thank ye for a pleasant afternoon."

"Yer welcome. Thank ye for a delicious meal."

He watched her get into the car, partially hidden by the high hedge that bordered the lane. It was clear the driver did not wish to be seen. He wondered who it was she could trust so far.

He walked down the drive, the scent of snow fresh in his nose. He felt oddly twitchy, as though there were an itch beneath his skin that he could not scratch.

He whistled to Finbar, who bounded up with something thoroughly disreputable clenched between his teeth. He sighed, contemplating the law books awaiting him inside.

Finbar looked up at him eagerly, long body a shimmer of excitement over the possibility of another tramp through the woods.

"D'ye think me handsome?" he asked the dog, who cocked his head to one side as though giving the question serious thought. He even paid him the compliment of dropping whatever disgusting thing he had been clutching in his jaw.

"Don't take too long about answerin'. 'Tisn't flatterin' to a man if ye have to think on it for more than a few seconds."

Finbar wagged his tail vigorously. Pat was wise enough to accept a compliment when one was offered.

"Ye may not be the world's best guard dog, but ye've fine taste in humans," he said. "Now, let's go off on the tramp again, shall we?"

Chapter Thirty-eight

February 1974

Shades of Bruising

ROBERT HAD APPROACHED HER EARLY IN FEBRUARY with a pile of papers, and a worried look on his wise owl face. He had pointed out a few small discrepancies, mostly in Jamie's foreign holdings, and a small bleed of shares that had been purchased under names that led to small companies appearing to be mere fronts for something larger and anonymous.

"The entire thing reminds me of a Potemkin village," Robert said. "Complex fronts to fool the onlooker but nothing of substance behind the façade. Yet whoever it is, is doing damage."

They put their heads together and followed the trails that seemed to leave only the occasional breadcrumb to guide them. The result was that Robert went off to Belgium to check on a potential lead and she stayed behind to man the fort and see if she could make any more headway in discovering what was going on.

It was like trying to follow the strands of a spider web in a snowstorm. Just when she thought she had found the end of the trail, it branched off into another direction. Something this well plotted would have taken immense time and patience, the sort of cunning that—well—that a spider would have.

She kept most of the files under lock and key at home now for she put nothing past Philip. The man had made good on his promise and was obviously not going to go away without his pound of flesh or fortune. Solicitors for both sides had come to a stalemate and she and Robert had quickly realized that her position, despite Jamie's wishes, was very precarious.

This evening she had put Conor down for the night shortly after dinner. He was exhausted after two fretful days of teething. The tooth had broken through this afternoon, and he had eaten his dinner, had a bath and after a cuddle in the rocking chair, gone deeply to sleep. Casey was working late to finish up a job, so the house was quiet around her as she sat elbow-deep in neatly stacked ledgers, papers, account books and correspondence. It wasn't long before the papers were sliding toward the edges of the table, the ledger books were crisscrossed, and the correspondence had been consigned to her knitting basket to be dealt with later.

The learning curve had been exceptionally steep, and she had been barely keeping abreast of things when she and Robert were thrown the curveball that was Uncle Philip. And now there was the elusive evidence that things were in no way straightforward on the edges of Jamie's kingdom.

Casey came in some time later on a gust of frosty air, riffling the papers around her and startling her out of a doze.

"That excitin', is it?" He bent over and kissed her, and the smell of wood and water filled her senses. She breathed in deeply, his scent always a restorative.

"Your supper's in the warmer," she said, and got up to stretch. "I'll get it for you."

"No, sit back down an' tell me what's got ye so frustrated," he said, putting his coat on its peg, then filling the kettle and placing it on the Aga.

"How can you tell I'm frustrated?"

"Because yer hair is standin' out around yer head like a porcupine caught the wrong way in a windstorm. Ye always twist yer hair about when yer troublin' over something."

She gave him a very green look and indicated the papers strewn all over the table.

"These damn numbers, I can't make head nor tail of them. I don't know what the hell Jamie was thinking, putting me in charge of all this. Robert noticed there have been discrepancies and brought it to my attention. But now he's in Belgium for the next two weeks and can't help me figure them out. Ultimately, it's for me to get to the bottom of it and I can't seem to. It's like a maze of numbers and it's only a hint here and a glimpse there, nothing to make a whole picture from to see what's actually taking place."

"Would ye like me to take a look?"

"Would you? If you can figure out what's going on, I'll be your slave for eternity."

Casey grinned. "Don't be after makin' such rash statements, Jewel, because be certain I'll hold ye to it."

She gave him an affectionate cuff on the shoulder and went to finish making the tea. Casey had a natural affinity with numbers and she trusted that if anyone other than Robert could untangle the snarl of financial threads, it would be him.

It took two hours, three cups of tea and one of whiskey, and his own hair bearing a decided resemblance to a small prickly mammal, but figure it out he did.

"Here, come sit with me an' I'll show ye what it is, Jewel. It's not easily seen, so don't think that ye made a mistake in not seein' it sooner. Someone has been very sneaky."

She gave him a questioning look. The headache was creeping back in.

He showed her where the pattern to the fraudulent share purchases was, and why it wasn't apparent on the surface.

"It's all on the manufacturin' end of the process if ye notice—the bare bones, the part of the businesses that build things, and the inner structure of the companies themselves—it's the support beams of the companies, if ye'll forgive a buildin' metaphor. If ye control the supports of all these companies, ye can also destroy things right at the foundation. They've thrown in a few purchases designed to distract from the overall pattern, but it's there. It would take some time an' doin', but I imagine it would amount to a fair bit of the company after awhile. Someone is very patient is all I can say."

"Someone who obviously knows Jamie is away."

"Aye, I'd say so."

He sketched it out for her. "I'm no expert on this sort of thing, darlin', but someone inside the company has to be helpin' your mystery party. It looks as though the books are bein' cooked, only so subtly that it's not goin' to bring attention to itself until it's far too late."

He showed her what he meant and it was even more damaging than she and Robert had suspected. Concerned as they both were with a thousand details each day, it would have been easy for someone with an ally inside the house, so to speak, to wreak havoc upon the edges, slowly opening a way directly into the center.

She stuck her hands in her hair tugging at the roots, as though she could loosen the ache inside her skull and possibly stimulate some idea about how to deal with this latest problem.

"When ye want to defeat an enemy, ye use his own tactics against him," Casey said, as though he had read her mind.

"Are you saying we start buying our own stock and hiding it in shell companies?" she asked, not certain how that could work.

"Aye, that's exactly what I'm saying. It might be high finance, Jewel, but it's all just a shell game when ye get right down to it, no?"

"I suppose so," she said, knowing what he meant, but thinking it was a far more complicated shell game than she wanted to play.

"It is that simple, only ye would have to have nerves of steel to pull it off. Here's how I think ye might start, though."

Casey might have thought it was simple, but to Pamela it sounded less like a street-side game than a walk across a high wire in glass slippers. She could see the simple genius of using their own methods against the thieves, still he was talking about millions of pounds, about people's livelihoods and well-being, about a legacy that had been handed from generation to generation.

"I'm scared that I'll make a mess of this whole thing, Casey. That I'm going to lose Jamie's companies. What if someone is staging a coup? How the hell do I stop them?"

"By playin' their game better than they can, Jewel." He frowned and looked back down at the ledgers, now stacked neatly at his right hand. "Ye know what's oddest about all this?"

"Yes," she said, for it had occurred to her before anything else. "It's the dates you mean, isn't it? It started before Jamie left—he would have surely noticed."

"Aye," Casey said. "It's as though he were allowin' it to happen."

"I can only think of one reason he would do that, Casey."

His eyes met hers over the piles of papers and long columns of figures.

"He was tryin' to draw them out, whoever they are."

"That and..." she let the thought trail off but Casey, understanding, finished it for her.

"He never meant to be gone this long, but I think we knew that already, darlin', didn't we?"

"I suppose we did," she said, glaring at the piles of papers as if that would make them snap to order and pull in their tails of long, trailing, misbehaving numbers. "I bloody wish he would have left all this," she gestured at the mess of paper, "to someone more competent than myself, someone who knows how to fix this."

Casey eyed her soberly. "Well, in the first place, Pamela, if the man didn't think ye entirely capable, he wouldn't have left everything in yer hands. An' furthermore, I think ye need to quit lookin' at them as Jamie's companies an' take the reins like they're yours, because for all intents an' purposes, an' if—God forbid—something has actually happened to the man, they are yours."

"Sometimes I am so mad at him for leaving me all this."

"Aye, I imagine the man knew that ye would be, an' yet he left it to ye nonetheless. Ye might ask yerself why, rather than fightin' against it. An' then ye need to dig yer heels in and start fightin' for it. I know ye can, Pamela, an' I think sooner will be better than later. Ye owe him that."

She ruffled her hair hard, trying to clear the cobwebs from her mind. "I don't need reminding," she said testily. "But sometimes I just want to stay home, be Conor's mam, make dinners, knit sweaters and plant a garden."

"Would ye really?" Casey said, in a rather too dubious tone. "I don't see it myself, woman. In fact, I'm grateful the man did leave it all on ye, as it's kept ye too busy to go harin' about the countryside, chasin' down machine-gun totin' bandits an' hitmen. An'," he added picking up the mugs and the whiskey bottle, "the pay is a bit better too. Now," he said, regarding her with a very serious look, marred only a wee bit by his dimple, "about that promise ye made... Get upstairs, woman, because I'm about to call ye on it."

WHEN SHE LOOKED UP FROM JAMIE'S DESK, it was far later than she had realized. She had sat down to catch up on the endless pile of correspondence that landed in the mailbox each day, intending to give it an hour before heading home. But the rosy twilight had now faded into an inky dark outside the windows. It was chilly in the study, the fire had burned down to ash while she was absorbed in letters from everyone from a Dutch farmer from whom they bought flax to an Italian Countess whose memories of Jamie were exceedingly fond.

She stood and stretched, yawning and pushing her fists into the small of her back to ease the tight muscles. She needed to get home and start dinner. But she would have to take the time to pack up today's work and take it with her, for she didn't dare leave anything here at the mercy of Philip's prying eyes.

As though her thought of the man had drawn him like a demon out of smoke, he entered the study without knocking. She frowned, certain that she had locked the door behind her when she returned after lunch. He had taken to showing up unannounced this way, every other week or so.

"I was just leaving," she said, striving to keep her tone civil but not quite managing it.

"I should like to speak with you. What I have to say will only take a few minutes."

She was sorely tempted to say no and order him out of the study but knew she could not afford to antagonize him any further.

She sat in the wingback by the hearth, wishing she hadn't let the fire go out. She was chilled through now, as she always seemed to be in this man's presence.

"I have a friend—" he began.

"Do you?" She allowed a good dose of skepticism to salt her tone.

He ignored her and sat himself down in the chair opposite, somehow managing to convey that he was lord of the manor and she the rather unwelcome guest. She sighed, thoroughly tired of these meetings.

"This friend told me something about you that I found interesting."

"Yes, and what was that?" she said feigning unconcern but feeling an inky pool of anxiety begin to spread in her stomach.

Philip looked at her directly, settling his hands over his belly and sliding his tongue over his full bottom lip. "He told me about a night on a train, and about you and four men."

She made a concentrated effort not to move her hands, not to betray anything by movement or change in the color of her skin, even if the blood was dropping to her feet at present.

"If you have something to say, just say it."

"He told me these men—all four of them—made good use of you, in every way men can make use of a woman—physically that is."

She was grateful that she had little more than tea and fruit in her stomach.

"He also told me that all these men died as a result of that night."

"Did they? I can't say I'll mourn them, but I have no idea how they wound up dead." Her voice was the consistency of needles.

"Don't you?" Philip said and stood, walking over to where she sat frozen in place, unable to think or move or to deny, even had it not been futile, and she saw clearly that it was.

"Men do seem to wind up dead around you. Oh say—Love Hagerty for instance. This friend tells me the relationship there was far more than employer/employee and that when you tired of him, you set the mafia on him."

"Who is this friend?" Pamela asked, her tone no longer calm.

"Oh, that's for me to know. Let us just call him an interested party. I did find it fascinating that he seemed to believe that my nephew and your husband may have had a great deal to do with the demise of those four men."

"That is ludicrous," she said, tone sharp in spite of herself, for she could not allow this man to touch Casey or Jamie because of this.

"Oh, I don't think so. You might be partially blinded by my nephew's charms, but I think you well know how ruthless he is. How could you not know when you are exactly so yourself?"

"Is there something in particular that you want from this conversation? Because if not, I should like you to leave."

"Oh, as tempted as I am by that idea, I have no desire to find myself another pint upon your bloody hands. As much as I should like," his finger caressed the line of her neck, "to part those lovely white thighs and partake of what's between them, I think—in the interests of breathing—I will pass on your charms."

"I would rather die than allow you to touch me," she said quite calmly, all things considered.

"I would be careful about making such sweeping statements. One never knows when one might need to go back on them." His voice was as insidious as a scaled, oily creature creeping upon her skin.

"It's a puzzle to me, you know."

She gritted her teeth as she felt his breath upon her neck. She would not move until she understood just what he wanted.

"It's a puzzle how a whore like you can look so untouched, so beyond the reach of most men and yet apparently—as my friend tells me—not beyond so many at all."

She stood, unable to bear his looming presence any longer. She faced him, eyes blazing with anger, her entire body deadly cold.

"I think you had best get to the point."

"The point, my lovely, is the same as it has always been. I want what is rightfully mine: this house, the companies, all the assets that my nephew left to you."

"I don't know how many times you require to hear the word 'no', but I am saying it again. Jamie trusted this to me, and when he returns I plan to turn it back to him as he left it, if not better."

"Jamie is dead, dear girl. He isn't coming back to rescue you. I will get what is mine one way or the other. I can take it without an ugly and protracted fight or it can be as bloody as you like. It's up to you."

"You aren't getting any compromise from me, so sharpen your sword," she said.

"Have it your way, Pamela, but don't say you weren't warned. Coups can be extremely ugly."

She sat for several long moments after he left. The scent of his aftershave was stuck in her throat and she still felt as though she was going to be sick.

His words had conjured up the image of that night on the train when four men had indeed used her in every way they had time and imagination enough to do. She had long ago left the shame of it behind. Or so she thought, for somehow Philip had managed to pull it up in front of her again, to make her skin crawl and shudder with the memory. The shame was still there, sunk under the skin like delicate pools of paint in shades of bruising. Dip in the brush of another's words, red and harsh, and they spread once again through her body in ripples of blood and bone memory.

In the aftermath, each of those men had died, but she had never asked Casey nor Jamie about it. She had not wanted to know. She was certain, though, that between the two of them they knew how each man died. There were only two other people who knew the truth of that night. One was her brother-in-law, who still suffered his own scars, and the other was a man she had hoped never to encounter again.

It appeared that the Reverend Lucien Broughton had returned from the pits of hell to which she had wished him.

Now she wasn't just angry, she was deathly afraid.

Chapter Thirty-nine
The Spinning Orb

EACH WEB BEGAN WITH A SINGLE STRAND, a bridge by which all others would be built and sustained. His original strand had grown over time, fed carefully on his own sense of injustice, and out from there had come the structural threads, the foundation on which revenge could be built, one sticky strand at a time.

Each stage took patience, but he understood that waiting and planning and taking the time to utilize each step of that plan was the only guarantee to capturing the prey you truly wanted. Years had gone into the framing of his web, the finding and training of the right people through which he could begin undermining the House of Kirkpatrick. The radius threads then were laid, the small holdings at the outer reaches of His Lordship's empire into which he had placed people, the little flies that were his own, and through them he would feel every vibration, come to see every weakness, every crack through which an able spider might creep. And then there was the careful, slow spiral of the auxiliary thread, the hidden pathway that allowed him to build the silken trap in parallel while keeping himself safe but close enough to observe who came along the more dangerous path.

There were obvious prey, and then there had been some surprises. Jamie's own will had given him the most desirable prey, had placed her near the center of the web like a beautiful, fragile butterfly whose sheltering calyx had been shorn away, leaving her open to the winds of fate. He knew not to underestimate her though. Other men had and lived—or rather not lived—to regret such folly. He enjoyed this contest, for under the tutelage of his own arch-enemy she had become a far more interesting opponent than he had previously found her. Still, she was only the foretaste of that for which he truly hungered.

Philip had not been a surprise, though his venomous spite was certainly a bonus. He had groomed Philip for a long time, making the insinuating threads both inviting and tight, so that the man was entirely his with which to toy, to maneuver, and yet the fool had no notion of himself as anything other than the predator. There was time enough to disabuse him of that notion, and for now his ego blinded him most effectively to the true design which he wished no one to see except Lord James Kirkpatrick himself—and him only when the entire arrangement had played out and he would be able to understand what had been done to him and those he loved.

The real surprise on that sticky pathway, the treasure, had come along unexpectedly, and he had barely felt the vibrations of it at first. But when he had... oh, when he had... it had been like finding an exquisitely jeweled dragonfly trapped by its own iridescent beauty within those winding silks. A dragonfly that didn't understand its own power and therefore was malleable by one who did.

Some time back, James Kirkpatrick had destroyed all his careful planning, had in one stroke wiped out his work, forced him to destroy his own creation, to crawl backward eating his own web as spiders were forced to do occasionally in order to rebuild. But a smart spider knows that during daylight one hides at the edge of the web or retreats into a secret nest, one foot delicately poised on a signal line invisible to all other eyes, so that no movement, however slight, goes unnoticed. He had kept his original bridge, and that was all a good spider needed to rebuild the entire structure.

And so he did just that—rebuilt his web slowly, walking it by the secret pathways, checking and re-checking his lines, keeping in his peripheral vision any bright flashes that would warn of the enemy. There had been none such in a very long time, for the enemy was lost, prey to stranger forces than he himself had foreseen. Meanwhile, there were all sorts of interesting vibrations to keep a spinner entertained through the long days and weeks and months of waiting. Time to let the lines out so that they might wind back into places both old and new, fasten themselves and begin to do their damage. He was aware too, through those filaments, of which were the dangerous ones that landed in his web, for their vibrations were different—like those of a wasp, something a spider had to be far more wary of tangling with. The British agent who had seemingly fooled everyone but himself, the woman's husband, the more volatile factions within the Redhand Defenders and the fat Jesuit. Wasps of varying degrees of threat.

For now, he held the most interesting pawn hostage to himself—that beautiful bejeweled dragonfly that he had brought into the web through careful coaxing and golden promises. A dragonfly guided along the threads with such careful, delicate handling that the dragonfly never even guessed at his true purpose. For such a creature could end the game, bring it all down prematurely, the way an early hard frost could kill a spider. But that, of course, was not how this game was played. One waited for one's true opponent to return to the web. One allowed him time to struggle against the ties that would bind him inextricably in a weft from which he would never be able to free himself. That was going to be his greatest pleasure. For his patience was greater than that of the spider, that could after all succumb to seasons and time or simply fall to a predator greater than itself. Only he understood all the intricacies of this web. Only he knew every drag line, every net, and every sticky silken prison to which his prey could be consigned.

For only he understood the elements of this game fully. Only he knew the motivations, the injustices, the great wrongs that underlay it and why it must be played out to its very end. Fate had decreed it so long ago, and Lucien Broughton was a great believer in Fate.

Chapter Forty
Two's Company

FOR MUCH OF HIS LIFE PAT RIORDAN had been an incurable, if cautious optimist, but of late he was finding his optimism at a low ebb. How he was to keep the Fair Housing Association going and get through law school, not to mention working with his brother in order to pay his bills, he did not know. Seated behind his overflowing desk at the former institution, he looked up towards the dingy ceiling, appealing to whatever power might be up there. But if it were hovering outside in the pissing rain, it could hardly be considered a sane entity. Then again, the Irish weren't terribly picky about the mental health of their many saints and deities. Take Saint Columban for instance, a man prone to trouble if ever there was one, but deified by the Irish Catholic Church.

He was tired, and it was a bloody filthy afternoon outside, making the thought of the trip home terribly unappealing. He often kipped here though, for the wee home he had shared so briefly with Sylvie was merely an empty shell now, a place to store his clothes and occasionally eat a meal and rest his head. He slept more soundly here, despite the cramped quarters and the inadequate length of the chesterfield.

He looked around the small space where he often grabbed naps between bouts of studying and keeping this mad wee business going. Though he didn't suppose he could fairly call something that leaked money like a sieve a business. He suspected Jamie funded it partly as a tax deduction. Instinctively, he crossed himself as he always did when he thought about Jamie and his long, inexplicable absence, and offered a wordless prayer for the man's safe return.

Fifteen minutes later he was well stuck into his studies, even if there were times the law seemed like a mess of snakes wherein a man could not tell head from tail—much less which head belonged with which tail—when the door opened letting in a gust of rain and cold air. He looked up in surprise to find the woman who had piqued him so recently at Casey's house. Just Kate.

She stood in the doorway, umbrella in hand, clad in a smart raincoat and sensible shoes. She looked in his direction without the slightest trace of a smile. Rather, she looked thoroughly businesslike.

"Can I help ye?" he asked, thinking it wasn't likely she had come seeking his help for housing and at the same time wondering what it was she did want, and how she had managed to get herself to his own doorstep.

"Kate Murray," she said briskly. "Perhaps ye'll remember meeting me at Pamela's house a few weeks back?"

"I could hardly forget it," he said tartly, immediately regretting his tone, for a soft wash of pink ran up her neck into her face.

"I'm sorry. That's hardly a hospitable greeting." He rose from behind his desk and walked around to where she stood. "Ye'll come in, please. There's a chair here, an' then perhaps ye can tell me how I can help ye?"

He helped her with her raincoat and she sat, waiting for him to sit back down, for she faced herself toward his vacant chair as if she saw its exact placement. She was neat as two pins in a white twinset and charcoal grey skirt. He sat, folding his hands together and placing them on the desk. The woman made him nervous though he couldn't have said why, and he was also suddenly aware that his face was in need of a shave, and his sweater had seen better days.

"Now then," he cleared his throat to give himself time to form his next thought and the woman hopped in neatly as a bandbox sprite, cutting off his words before he could even think them.

"I've come to work for ye."

"Pardon me?" he said, for whatever he had been expecting, it had not been this.

"I've come to work for ye," she repeated, as though he were particularly slow, which admittedly he felt in her presence. "Can ye honestly say ye don't need the help?"

He opened his mouth to protest but realized he really did need the help, though he was mystified about how she thought to provide it.

"I don't mean to be indelicate," he began, and wasn't surprised to be cut off before he could finish his thought.

"I won't be able to take on the paperwork, but I can deal with people for ye. I'm good with people. I'll answer the phones, make the tea an' keep the place tidy."

Pat wondered how she knew the place was untidy—which it was to an egregious extent.

"Ye don't need to pay me, if that's what yer worried about. I don't need the money. I'd just like to do something useful other than keep house for my brother. I thought perhaps ye could use the help."

Her tone had become a tad snippy and Pat sighed. He looked toward the ceiling, thinking the universe had an odd sense of humor in how it arranged to answer one's appeals.

Within two weeks, he wasn't sure how he'd managed before she came along. When he arrived on the days the center was open, there was already tea prepared, the mail sorted and the filing done. When he queried how she managed it, she explained that she wasn't stone blind and could see things if brought up very close to her face... which made him wonder why she had allowed him to believe she couldn't see a blessed thing upon their first meeting. However, he knew when a universal appeal was answered in such an efficient manner, one did not question it too closely, especially when the answer was—it was soon clear—far better equipped than he to sort out the riffraff from the people who genuinely needed his help. She did not suffer fools gladly, but had endless patience for those who needed assistance filling out paperwork, and the fortitude to push through all the bureaucratic red tape they encountered on a daily basis. She freed him to do what he did best, and that was get out into the community to deal with people face to face and decide how best to meet their needs.

They took to having afternoon tea together on the days when they were both in the office, sorting out the paperwork, answering each other's questions and just generally decompressing from another day living in the wilds of Belfast.

It was on one of those afternoons, when the phone had managed not to ring in twenty minutes and they were both comfortably quiet over their afternoon biscuit and tea, that he asked her why she didn't have a man in her life. A question which, he ought to have known, would cause her to bristle.

"You needn't worry yourself on that score," she said, in her straightforward manner. "I'm not in the market for a man, and if I were I wouldn't set my sights on you."

"Whyever not?" he asked, half to egg her on, and half out of real curiosity. Kate, lovely as she was, didn't seem to have any sort of social life outside her secluded existence with her brother. There were obvious reasons for that, but he sensed there was more to it than what met the eye.

She gave him one of her crisp looks, as though she were assessing how big of an eejit he was just at the moment. At such times, it was hard to believe the woman could not see more than the vague outlines of things.

"Because I had a man I loved very much, but he's gone now and I am not fool enough to think I'll find his like again. As to why not yourself—well, it's clear to me, Patrick Riordan, that your own heart is well and truly broken. I'd be an eejit dyed in the wool to take on such a thing."

"Oh." He nodded, nonplussed—mostly because it was baldly true. "May

I ask what happened to yer man?"

"He was a Prod and a soldier, and he's dead now—shot on duty."

"My God. I'm sorry, Kate." He thought it was a miracle the man had been killed on duty, and not tortured to death by her brother.

"I don't need your pity, man, any more than you need mine."

"Right," he said briskly, feeling as though she had verbally smacked him in the head, not the first time he'd felt so and not, he was certain, the last either.

"Ye will have had yer own loss as well." She said in a more conciliatory tone.

"An' how do ye know she's dead? Maybe she just left me."

"Because her presence is everywhere that ye go but ye never speak her name. So I expect that she died, an' did not merely leave ye. Besides, I suspect yer not the sort of man a woman leaves voluntarily."

"Aye, she died," Pat said quietly, "died by a car bomb that was meant to kill me."

"I'm sorry."

He was tempted to bite back at her that he had no need of her sympathy either, but her tone was so sincere that he kept his tongue still.

In an odd way, they fit one another, he realized. They were both broken, both wanting to be left to get on with the tasks at hand, both keeping their heads down and moving forward as much as one could in this uncertain land.

In another odd way, he realized he didn't feel quite so alone anymore.

Chapter Forty-one

March 1974

Finola

THE COTTAGE SAT AT THE BOTTOM OF THE KIRKPATRICK ESTATE, buried in the surrounding woodland. It reminded Pamela somewhat of the quintessential crone's cottage in fairytales. When she had first stumbled upon it, she had questioned Jamie as to the occupant. His rather cryptic answer had been that he was the tenant of the woman who lived there. She had her suspicions about the mysterious woman, though the cottage had sat empty for quite some time now. Today it looked as though someone had been around, if not in residence. She rode Phouka up to the low wall where a weathered gate hung between two ivy-clad posts.

She was not here on a pleasure ride today, as she had been that Christmas morning long ago. She thought it was high time she and the occupant met.

She slid down off Phouka, looping the reins over a gatepost.

"Can I help ye?" said a sharp voice directly behind her.

She let out a small yelp and clutched at her heart. "I—I'm sorry, I didn't realize that—"

"That anyone was home."

"No," she replied, tone tart enough to match the woman who faced her. "I just didn't realize you were right behind me." She turned. "I wasn't snooping, I usually ride this way and this is the first time the cottage has been occupied."

"Aye," the woman said, narrowing her green eyes in assessment. "That's true enough. I've been away for a time, and am only now come home."

Pamela took the opportunity to study her features, looking for genetic traces of James Kirkpatrick, but saw few. She was small, but not with Jamie's whip-like grace and her skin darker than Jamie's simmered gold.

In the bones of her face, though, Pamela saw echoes of Jamie's feline grace, distilled by time and sex into something softer but no less formidable. Her hair was a pale chestnut with a haze of silver hoarfrost glinting out here and there. And her eyes... there genetics had played its arrow straight, for she had eyes of dark jade, elongated and as capable of cold fire as were her grandson's.

"You must be Jamie's...?"

"Grandmother. Not that it's any of yer business, one way or 'tother, but yes, the man is my grandson on his mother's side. Before ye ask—don't deny it. Ye've yer lips pursed up to ask just that."

Which rather, Pamela thought, put her in her place for she *had* been about to ask that very question.

"Well, as long as yer here," the woman said, "ye might as well come in for a cup of tea."

"I really shouldn't—I—" she stuttered, completely unnerved by the sight of Jamie's eyes looking out of an old woman's face.

"Ye'll come in for tea. It doesn't take that long to drink a cup, an' frankly 'tisn't anyone I ask in, so feel flattered that I have."

Pamela was certain 'flattered' wasn't how she felt. Terrified came close, but didn't quite describe the array of emotions currently set loose in her stomach.

She followed the woman inside, her head almost grazing the lintel for it was low in the fashion of cottages built a hundred years before.

"Sit where ye please," the woman said, putting down the leather bag she had been carrying.

Pamela sat on a low stool by the hearth and took a steadying breath.

"Have you been traveling?" she asked, sitting upright, hands folded in her lap as if she were back in Catholic school with a particularly strict nun for her teacher.

"Ye could call it that, I suppose."

She wasn't one to share more information than strictly necessary, Pamela saw.

"My name is Finola and you, I expect, will be Pamela."

"Yes, I am."

"Well, it's past time we met then." The tone of the woman's voice indicated that while the meeting might be overdue, it was not necessarily one considered a pleasure.

Finola was silent while she made the tea, her movements quick and light but firmly no-nonsense. There was something of Jamie about her there too, for he also was a being of precision and grace. She wondered how much he saw of her when he was home. It struck her as very odd that he had never mentioned his grandmother other than the cryptic comment about tenancy, and Pamela had never chanced upon her in all the times she had stayed under Jamie's roof.

"He comes for dinner most Saturday nights," Finola said and handed her a steaming mug that smelled beautifully of catmint and lemon balm. "That's what yer wonderin', isn't it? Why ye've not seen me before?"

The woman sat down across from her, tucking her neat little feet upon a low footstool.

"Are you a mind reader?" Pamela queried, starting to feel a tad nettled at having her thoughts so easily read. Jamie had the same annoying habit.

Finola laughed at that. "No, but every thought ye have shows in yer eyes, lass. Here, drink yer tea while it's hot an' save yer breath to cool yer porridge."

Pamela obediently sipped her tea, which tasted lovely and had an immediately soothing effect. She looked about the tiny cottage with interest. It was rather spartan in its furnishings, and all the pieces that were in it were well made but not ornate. The hearth dominated the main room, and had a brisk fire crackling in it. Overlying the warm smell of burning peat was the scent of herbs, both fresh and dried. She could identify the sharp spike of rosemary and the oiled pleasantries of lavender, as well as something peppery and warm. A narrow set of twisting stairs led up to the second floor, where she assumed the bedrooms were.

"He doesn't speak of his mother a great deal," she ventured, thinking that someone had to start the conversation. "But I've seen pictures of her. She was lovely."

"Yer not one for the small talk, I'll see. Aye, my daughter was lovely, but she was a wild spirit from the day she was conceived. Always restless, always burning. She loved her wee lad to distraction, don't get me wrong, but her mothering was of the hit and miss sort. Smother him with love one moment, flit off the next. It wasn't good for him, but he had others in his life who kept things on a more even keel. Kathleen and I never saw eye to eye. She was an artist. If ye've seen the painting with the strange wee faces an' such in Jamie's bedroom, then ye'll know she had a gift. Even that was unstable though. Sometimes she could paint an' draw, but often she couldn't settle herself enough to work at it."

Pamela knew the painting Finola meant. She had liked it so much that she had moved it from the master bedroom to the study. The scene was of a bewitched hollow at night, with all the nocturnal creatures abroad and a full silver moon setting the scene aglow. Every leaf seemed a thing of trembling movement, the neat-faced foxes on the brink of putting a paw forward. But despite the moon, it was a work with a dark, diaphanous quality, enchanting one moment, chilling the next, depending on the light and the mood in which one viewed it. She had spent many long minutes studying it, for it seemed that no matter how often she looked, there was always some element she had missed before. A new face would show up as part of a leaf, or eyes seemed to be watching her though she could not locate the source amongst the small faces, some wizened as walnuts, others round as a wheel of cheese yet as mysterious as the depths of a lake.

"She was very talented."

"Aye, talent she had but art is a demanding mistress, an' Kathleen could never devote herself to one thing for more than a day or two at a time. I could understand that when it came to her art, an' every other career she thought to pursue, but a husband and a wee child are a different kettle of fish altogether. That's where Kathleen and I disagreed, an' rather permanently, I might add. I lived away for a long time, an' wasn't here when she died."

"I'm sorry," Pamela said, meaning it.

"Aye well, 'twas my own fault. I was stupidly stubborn an' paid the price of it. I imagine though, yer here to speak of Jamie, not his mother."

"Yes, I am," Pamela said, aware she was a glass pane through which this woman could see very clearly.

The woman's gaze was assessing, the green eyes sharp as a needle. Her hands, small and brown, cupped her mug of tea and when she spoke it was in a manner Pamela had not expected.

"I suppose grandparents always think their grandchildren are special, something beyond the ordinary. Jamie, though, truly was different. Most children have the ability to see into that next world—the one beyond, just over the hill or off the edge of the horizon—but what if that ability never left you? What if you still could see those other realms, no matter how dark many of them were? Because that is the world Jamie inhabits, one without the normal boundaries of the one most of us live in. Some call it a mental illness or think he's crazy. Does he seem like a crazy person? No, he functions well within the boundaries that we all do. He even flourishes in a way most can only dream about."

She leaned over and poked at the fire, stirring its flames, the peat crumbling and sending up a shower of cherry sparks.

"Ye know him, likely in ways that I do not, an' so ye know that he's handicapped in more ways than one. I expect yer aware of his particular difficulties."

Pamela saw her thoughts must have been clear, for the woman said, "I don't just mean the black moods that come upon him. Havin' seen ye in the flesh now, I think perhaps ye know too well yerself that beyond a certain point beauty becomes more of a burden than a blessing. Jamie's beauty has always been beyond that point. Perhaps if he had been stupid or mean or small-souled, it would have evened things out but, of course, he is none of those things."

"No, he is not," Pamela said quietly, "and how dearly that has cost him. I say this knowing that I am more guilty than most of returning to that well each time I've needed safety and security."

"The man is no one's fool. He has spoken of ye often, an' I know well enough he was more than happy to provide those things for ye. I think perhaps ye both have understood for a long time what it is ye are to each other. There is no blame in such a friendship."

Finola got up to re-fill their teacups and Pamela's eye turned to the sideboard where sat a chess set. The black pieces were carved from a deep mahogany and the white of palest birch, though long usage had stained the birch a mellow gold. The pieces were from Tenniel's illustrations of *Alice in Wonderland,* the Knight carved in meticulous detail right down to the beehives, brushes, candlesticks and watchman's rattle that loaded down the Knight's saddle. The Red Queen pointed an imperious finger and one could almost hear her yelling '*Off with her head!*' Alice was the White Queen, the pawns carved in the form of the White Rabbit, while the bishops were served by the Mad Hatter, and Tweedledee and Tweedledum bookended the back row in the position of rooks. Finola noted her gaze and smiled.

"His paternal grandfather had it made for Jamie. It's one of the boy's most prized possessions. It ought to be up in the big house but he still likes to play with me of an evening now and again, so he leaves it here."

"It's wonderful," Pamela said, leaning over to look more closely at the detail on the White Rabbit's pocket watch.

"He taught me how to play," Finola continued, "though his paternal grandfather was the only one who could really challenge him. As he was away a great deal, Jamie taught others to play. None of us could come up to his ability. He was so young when he taught me that he had to stand up on his chair to get his favorite view of the chessboard. He told me later that each piece has a lingering light like a comet tail and that he could see how it might be moved, ought to be moved, all the lines of tension, possibility, beauty. He said it was what he loved best about the game, all that could happen and how he would have to choose, and lose all the other games it might have been. Ye could almost see him storin' the limits and permutations of each piece in his mind so that he could pull it out later, an' turn it about on its head."

Pamela could see Jamie, in this cottage, a small golden boy already kindled from within by that light that could flare into incandescence and enchant all around him—even if it burned the bearer—leaving scars in its wake that only Jamie knew the depth of, and sometimes, though rarely, those who loved him.

"He had his own world. Only children often will. When he was of an age, I gave him blank books so he could write some of his thoughts an' fancies down. It seemed to me that his head was too full an' I thought perhaps writin' it down might help to calm him."

Finola bent down and opened a cupboard beneath the settle. When she stood again, she held a leather-bound notebook in her hands, darkened with age and usage much as the chess pieces were, yet this had nothing of the feeling of mellowness about it. Finola was holding it out to her, still speaking, though her tone changed to something that had pain way at the back of it, like a sliver of glass caught in her throat.

"He started this when he was fifteen, and then around eighteen he simply stopped. I think it frightened him, how real an alternative reality could be, so I stole it, and hid it away because I knew he would destroy it at some point. He never knew I had it, but I wanted to preserve some part of that beauty from that time in his life. He was an amazing child. Even then people were drawn to him, animals too. He came here when he needed to be away from the big house, and all the drama it contained. We would have our days roaming in the woods and fields. I taught him all about plants and told him the old stories of Ireland. Then we would have a quiet meal by the fire in the evening, and I'd read to him until he slept, or when he was older, he would read to me."

Pamela took the leather-bound book in her hands and felt through its weight and the silky texture how treasured it had been.

"Why?" she asked, longing to sit down right there by the fire and start reading.

"Because there's not many of us who love him well enough to tell him when he's wrong. You are one and I am another. An' I think," the old woman's eyes met hers, "that he would have wanted ye to have it."

She opened the cover, uncertain of what she expected to find. Another journal, one from when he was very young, but it wasn't that at all. The title page bore the words *The Tale of Ragged Jack*. She shivered, half in anticipation, half in fear of what the pages would reveal. The book had lain undisturbed for some time, for it had the scent of paper long shut away from light and air. The edges were brownish gold and she felt as though she were touching part of Jamie himself, for his presence was here in the first few sentences. Jamie had always had the ability to travel that crooked pathway, to feel the wild eyes staring in from the snowy night, to hear the whoosh of bird wings that flew too close to the sun.

"So will we get down to the crux of what ye came here for?"

Pamela, still caressing the book's worn cover, took a second to adjust her thoughts.

"Yer here to ask me if I can help ye find the boy, are ye not?"

"I am." She saw little reason to prevaricate, for the woman would know a half-truth when she saw it. Just as her grandson always had.

Finola picked up the White Knight from the chess set and held it cupped in her palm. "In a way this is responsible for his being lost."

"So you believe he is in Russia too?"

"Yes. If he is lost, it is because of his friendship with Andrei."

She replaced the White Knight on the board and looked up at Pamela.

"The question is what are we goin' to do about it?"

The Tale of Ragged Jack, continued.

WHEN NIGHT FELL, JACK HAD NO IDEA HOW FAR HE WAS FROM HOME. *Even the stars did not look familiar. The Teapot constellation, with its familiar spout drawn in blue stars, was nowhere to be found, nor the Saucer Nebula, normally a comforting smudge not far below the Teapot's spout. He knew he had to rest, for exhaustion would only lead him further astray, if indeed one could go astray when one had no idea where one was.*

He sheltered in the hollow between the roots of a huge oak tree, bedding down amongst the dusty leaves shed at its feet, and drawing his coat tight as he could around him. He peered out over his collar to the night sky above, searching in vain for a star that he knew—one to hang his hat upon, as his grandmother would say. But there was still nothing by which to orient himself. Finally, he closed his eyes, unable to bear the sight of all those cold, shimmering stars that could not guide him home.

In the morning, he breakfasted on the bit of bread left in his pocket from yesterday's tea and drank from a clear stream that he could hear when he awoke, burbling away to itself just beyond the roots of the oak. He had slept fitfully and awakened in the dim hours before dawn with an owl glaring at him from its perch not far above his head.

He tossed a coin to choose a pathway to follow for the day, for one seemed as good as another when one was lost. The path he chose ambled through fields that were a heavy amber with grain needing to be harvested and the autumn scent of apples falling red from the trees to lie like rubies along the dusty roadside. Jack filled his pockets with them, eating one as he went along the winding road.

The sun was high above the horizon when he heard a commotion on the road ahead of him, and the terrified yelps of a puppy. He hurried his steps, not thinking about what sort of trouble he might be running toward. Jack had never been able to resist the hurt of any helpless creature.

When he crested the hill, he saw a farmer with a wagon heaped high with golden hay, standing at the roadside and kicking at a thin, miserable little creature

*that was cringing away from the heavy hobnailed boots into the long grasses of
the ditch.*

Jack ran toward the farmer, yelling, 'Stop that!'

*The farmer turned on him and Jack realized how he must look, a small
ragged boy already filthy as a vagabond with the dirt of his travels. The farmer
was formidable, a hulking brute with small piggy eyes that had little but anger
and meanness in them. Jack stood his ground. He knew you couldn't give bullies
an inch or they would chase you a mile.*

*"Leave him be," Jack said, far more stoutly then he felt. "What's he done to
you?"*

*The farmer spat a filthy stream of snuff onto the ground, before answering.
"He's useless. Let a fox in the chicken coop, an' now hides in the grass, hopin'
I won't find him."*

*"He's only a baby," Jack said angrily, having seen a toffee brown eye peering
through the grass at him. "You ought to be ashamed."*

*The farmer took a menacing step toward him as though he would happily
kick Jack into the ditch along with the dog. But then he stopped short, though Jack
did not know why. He only knew he wasn't afraid, just filled with a fierce anger
that left no room for fear.*

*"Bloody cur, just like the dog—useless too, I'll bet. Well, have him then,
I don't want him."*

*Jack stood in the roadway until the farmer's wagon was a moving spot about
to disappear behind a hill. The dog was still crouched in the ditch, completely silent.*

*Jack walked to where the dog stood, crouched down and held out his hand,
with the palm cupped open, so that the dog would know he meant it no harm. It
huddled in the grass for a moment longer, but then its natural curiosity got the
better of it and it emerged from the grass on long, trembling legs. The dog sidled
toward Jack slowly. One eye was the soft brown Jack had spied before, the other a
glacial blue, the sort of eye that saw things beyond the obvious.*

*Jack carefully unfurled his fingers one at a time, as gentle as waterweed in a
slow current. The dog tilted its head, as though measuring Jack's trustworthiness.
Jack kept so still that he was barely breathing, knowing that trust is a slow thing,
built up by time and care, but there has to be a seed to begin that process.*

*The dog sniffed his fingers one at a time, and then sat down, sighed and laid
its muzzle in Jack's open palm. He had always had this way with animals, though
he did not know what it was they sensed in him to make them so immediately
trustful. Perhaps it was only that he understood what it was to not always know
how the world worked, or what was right when presented with choices. Perhaps
they simply knew he would not hurt them.*

*He knew then that he would take the dog with him, for even the most unlikely-
looking creatures could contain within themselves a noble heart and great gifts.
They only needed someone with the eyes to see them. The pup was gangly to be*

sure, but its coat glowed like the moon on a frosty night and its eyes looked straight into Jack's soul. Yes, it would be a valuable companion, though Jack would have appreciated any sort of friend on his journey.

When they stopped for the night, Jack made a fire, for it was cold and the dark seemed filled with watching eyes. They ate potatoes that Jack had found in a deserted field. He baked them in the coals, and they had them with milk that he had stolen from a creamery window. For dessert, there were tiny wild berries that tasted like the color of a sunset, all crimson and gold, with seeds of violet.

Replete, they lay down side by side. Jack was amazed at how much warmth the dog provided and how much easier sleep came with another creature by his side.

Aengus proved to be a trusty companion, and Jack's heart was considerably lightened by the dog's comforting presence trotting behind his heels the next day. He named him Aengus in honor of the poet in his kingdom who was famed for his wanderings to exotic places.

Over the next couple of days, Jack chose their pathways by a toss of his lucky ha'penny. It was little more than guessing, yet after each toss they would get some way down the road the penny had chosen and he would pick up a thread on the wind, something that smelled of burning leaves and dim, still water, and he would know that they were on the trail of the Crooked Man. Lost, but heading in the right direction, with only foreign stars to guide their way.

They had walked for three risings of the moon and they were both weary and very hungry. Jack knew they needed to sleep and to eat. But he was a child of the woods and knew that to lie down now would mean death, for there was cold upon the face of the moon tonight, cold that would dig into a boy's marrow and freeze him forever.

It was with great relief that they came upon the cottage. Tucked away as it was in briars and vines, it was a wonder they saw it at all. But some stray gleam of moonlight had lit upon it and brought it to their attention. There was smoke puffing from the chimney and the smell of something savory stewing. Jack's stomach rumbled loudly.

Distracted as he was by his stomach and weary limbs, it took a moment before he realized that someone was standing by the corner of the cottage, in the lee of a hanging vine.

She was the smallest woman he had ever seen, with a face as sharp as the tip of a needle and hair like the wing of a crow. She had nut-brown skin, wrinkled as a walnut shell and was clothed in a green dress, with small bristled shoes on her feet. She stood upright, with her hand on the hoe that she had been using to turn earth, her eyes piercing him through, eyes that could see straight through a lie or deceit of any sort. Jack knew her kind. His grandmother was just like her. The best tactic was to answer truthfully whatever questions were asked.

"What will you be wanting?" she asked, her voice nearly as sharp as her eyes.

"Some food if you can spare it," Jack said, "and a warm place to sleep for *the night."*

She fixed him with a narrowed eye, and Jack swore he could feel her reading the pages of his soul as though they were boldly printed upon the air. Apparently she found something there that she liked, for gruffly, she said, "Come in then, boy, and bring your dog with you."

The inside of the cottage was snug, a huge fire roared in the hearth, and over it hung a large cauldron from which the savory scent issued.

"Sit," the woman said, and though her tone was gruff, it was not unkind.

There was stew in the cauldron and a round of fresh-cut bread on the table. The woman served him a steaming bowlful and set another to cool for the dog. She gave him two thick slices of bread, heavy with butter. Jack tried to eat slowly, but found his hunger would not allow him his normal manners. The old woman merely sat down by the fire and drew a spinning wheel between her knees.

She spun the finest thread Jack had ever seen. His own mother was good at spinning and her threads soft as silk, but this lady spun thread that was almost translucent, like a spiderweb. At the same time she was grinding corn with her foot on a peddle that turned two silvery whetstones. He rubbed his eyes. Surely that couldn't be right. But, indeed, she was managing both tasks at once.

"Why is a boy so young on the road alone?"

"I'm not alone," he said stoutly, his hand on Aengus' silvery head.

"No, of course not," the woman said kindly. "I only meant to ask why you are away from your mother and father?"

And so he told her about the Crooked Man and asked if she had ever heard of such a being. She had slowed in her spinning, her face in shadow so that he could not see her expression, though he sensed that mention of the Crooked Man had disturbed her.

"Aye, there are always tales of such a one in all times and places, but I think this one is more than a bit of myth pasted together with half-truths an' dreams, for there be times the stories take a turn an' become something more so that ye know he is travelin' the hills an' dales hereabout."

"Have you heard such stories of late?" Jack asked, half dreading the answer.

"I have, indeed. I did meet one such as you describe, long ago. Maybe that's why ye've found yer way to my fireside tonight, for little is chance in this world of ours, spin an' tilt as it will."

She pulled the thread she was spinning out long and fine. It was the color of a rainbow, which was to say no clear color at all but rather one misty shade blending into the next for something altogether beautiful.

"'Twas a very long time ago. I was only a wee girl then, knee high to a cricket an' bold as a brass penny. I'd a good mind an' well I knew it. Ye'll maybe be too young to know this, but 'tis a gift to know what ye are meant to be in this world. I knew long ago, for I could grow plants an' knew their uses from an early age. I could feel the healing in my hands, like a green thrum that needed release. My

grandmother was a healer before me an' saw what I was from early on."

A ginger cat, hardly larger than a thimble, climbed up the worn linen of her sleeve and sat down upon her shoulder and proceeded to lick his paws with great gravity. Every so often, as the woman spun her tale along with her thread, the cat looked up and fixed Jack with an uncanny golden eye.

"I had gone out one afternoon, in the green time when the plants are waiting to be picked, just this side of the full moon when their medicine is most potent. It was my first time out gatherin' alone an' I was half excited, half afraid, for the woods are never empty even when it seems they are. I got lost in the searching and picking, an' without my realizin' it, the sun had sunk low an' the shadows were grown thick and long. When I looked around me, I didn't know where I was. Everything looked the same an' yet not the same at all."

Jack leaned forward, almost toppling off the stool in his eagerness to hear her next words.

"I'd strayed across the boundary between worlds, lost the path entirely an' had no idea where I might be. 'Twas soon full dark an' there was mist comin' up out o' the roots of trees and from under the fallen leaves. Then the leaves started to move, though there was no wind, an' the boughs of the trees creaked as though they were in pain."

Jack sat bolt upright, the quiver of a cold arrow flying up his spine. It sounded like the same sort of mist and wind that he had experienced just before the Crooked Man appeared. The same dancing leaves.

"I was frightened near out of my wits, an' clutchin' the amulet my grandmother had made for me." She patted the small silver vial that hung about her neck, near black with age and use, and strung from a bit of leather.

"'Twas as if one minute there was little but leaves whirlin' in the wind, an' then before I knew it a man was standin' in front of me." She shuddered expressively. "An' such a man too, dark an' silent, but 'twas as though I could hear a terrible laughter from inside him. My ears couldn't hear it, still my spirit could. I wanted to run. My whole wee body was shaking, but I was rooted to the spot."

Jack nodded without realizing he was doing so, for it mirrored his own experience almost exactly.

"He touched my forehead, an' it was as though I could feel somethin' wild within myself tryin' to get out an' follow him, or maybe 'twas only the bit that he would take an' tuck in his filthy bag. Is that what he did to you? Took somethin' of value?"

"Aye, he stole some of my dreams—put them in his bag just as you said. Though I never saw him do that exactly..." Jack trailed off, suddenly confused.

The old woman looked at him sharply, and he could feel the prick of her eyes like a needle poking gently at his skin. "Oh, it's likely he did exactly that. He's a master of the sleight of hand is the Crooked Man. Steal the shirt off yer back an' have ye lookin' at the moon whilst he does it. I will tell ye this for free though, laddie, he cannot harm you, unless you allow it," she said, and bit the thread off the spindle neatly, winding the remains into a tidy ball and tucking it into the pocket of her apron.

"I don't understand," Jack said. How was he, just a boy himself, supposed to fight off such as the Crooked Man?

The woman smiled, sadly. "You aren't meant to understand. It's a sort of knowing that goes deeper than that. When the time comes—and it will, for you have seen him already—you will either know what to do or you won't."

"That seems stupid," Jack said angrily, turning his face away from the woman so she would not see the tears that stood in his eyes. He was tired, and the warmth of the fire, a full belly and the woman's kindness had him undone.

"It's long past time for you and your wee dog to be abed," she said crisply and rose from her low stool, setting the spinning wheel neatly into its corner.

She put a pallet by the fire, sweetly stuffed with rosemary and lavender, and once he and Aengus were tucked up cosily on it she covered them with a quilt that made his throat go tight with thoughts of his warm bed at home, his blankets that smelled like sunshine and hay and the scent of lilacs that sometimes drifted through his windows at night. Maybe that was why he dreamed of home that night, of his mother crying and his father roaming the hills and valleys of the kingdom, calling his name. He must have cried out in answer to his father, for he awoke in the ashy light of dawn with the old woman above him, her hand on his arm, steadying him out of the dream world into reality.

In the morning, she fed him on oats and honey and filled a satchel with bread and cheese and goat's milk for him to take away with him. During the night she had mended his breeches and the tear in his shirt, for which he was very grateful.

The sky was rosy with dawn when he was ready to leave. Aengus had been fed too, and stood eager to go, scenting adventure on the horizon once again. For a moment Jack felt a spear of ice drive through his stomach, for he was afraid of what lay ahead and wanted nothing more than to be here with the old woman, do chores for his keep and to stay well away from the borders of the forest. But he knew he could not, for though Jack was young and sometimes foolish, still he knew that some paths are chosen and guided by an invisible hand and cannot be avoided.

The woman halted him outside the door of her cottage before he set out upon his lonely road.

"I have three things for you to take on your journey. The first is a length of thread, the second a bag of bones and the third is a weight of salt."

The length of thread was from the wool she had spun the night before, neatly coiled and, in the morning light, an odd green in color—not like a rainbow in the least—yet he knew it was thread of the same spinning. Jack couldn't swear to it, but he thought it wriggled a bit when he tucked it into his bag. The bag of bones was light as air, and the bones rattled about inside as though chattering one to another. The sack of salt was a solid weight in his hand, yet when he put it into *his satchel it was light as a feather.*

"Now drink this," the lady said, and handed him an old silver flask, dark with age.

"What is it?" Jack asked, for a very dubious smell was floating out of the neck of the flask, forming a small black cloud.

"It's a potion, one that will allow you to see and hear and speak in a different way. These are skills you will need on the rest of your journey."

Jack drank it and could not decide if it was the sweetest thing he had ever tasted, or the foulest. It tasted of earth and berries, pine needles and willow bark, of moonlight on the forest floor and of the things that scuttled there, but it also tasted of sunshine and afternoons spent haying, of ripe apricots and pomegranates and honeyed dates.

"There can be no honey without bitter gall," the lady said, and put the cap back on the flask, though the tiny cloud of its scent still hung in the air. "No rose without thorns. You must always remember that. Now open your eyes."

Jack felt a faint buzzing sensation in his forehead, as though a nest of bees were stirring lazily. He opened his eyes and closed them again, shook his head to clear his vision and opened his eyes again, but it didn't help one whit. The forest was absolutely teeming with tiny people, animals, carts, chatter, laughter and the odd screech or two. These people were dressed much as the lady was dressed, in things that looked as if they were made of leaves and tiny skins, with willow wands for crowns and birch bark for hats.

The women—for they were women despite being no taller than his own longest finger—had baskets over their arms and babies on their hips. The baskets were filled with all sorts of things: lovely floury loaves of bread, stone bottles of whiskey and mead, tiny apples no bigger than a sparrow's beak. One woman had a basket filled with sparkling powders: deep gentian, brilliant scarlet, gooseberry green, and pigments he could hardly have imagined before—stardust and the gentle pink of a mole's paw. And there were pigments for things he had before only smelled or thought—like the scent of bread fresh from the oven, or the way rain felt on your skin on a hot day, or mud between your toes after you'd pulled off shoes and socks, and other darker colors that were like a good sharp bang on your head, or a deep bruise that hurt to touch, or the way that a cut felt when the air moved across it.

He turned to look at the lady and his jaw dropped open in shock. She was no longer the old, needle-faced woman with worn hands and stooped back. She was beautiful, like a queen in a tale told over and over, whose beauty is never diminished by the telling.

"Never judge someone by her exterior, Jack. It's important to remember that as you go on your journey."

"Aye," he said, "'tisn't likely I'll ever see anything in the same way."

"No," the woman said, and touched a hand to his face gently, as his mother used to do. There was both kindness and sorrow in her voice, and Jack knew that

he had crossed some boundary since his encounter with the Crooked Man that could not be uncrossed, and that he had left something precious behind in doing so.

Chapter Forty-two

November 1973

Red Raven

AND THEN AS IT WAS WONT TO DO IN RUSSIA, winter came once again. The cold was so severe that breathing hurt and talk was unthinkable. Words would surely freeze and fall to the ground before ever making the journey to another's ears. He had heard tell that the natives believed that each winter all laughter, tears, words and stories fell to the ground and froze, only to be awakened by spring's thaw, when suddenly the air would fill with chatter, laughter, gossip and tragedy, a cacophony of humanity borne on spring's gentler air. But what *this* ground would have to say was likely more than any human could bear to hear. For in what tone did blood and grief speak?

Fragments and tendrils of the people who had once walked here, lived here, died here were left behind. You could feel their ghosts walk in step with yours, like a shadow that you could not detach from yourself, until the time came when you wondered if you were seeing through your own eyes or viewing a vanished world through theirs. To be here was to live in a place apart, to feel as though you inhabited a planet out at the very limits of the solar system, where the sun's warmth could not be felt and there was no home other than this.

Russian land was once measured by the counting of the souls that tilled its earth. Thus an estate with one thousand able-bodied male adults was valued at one thousand souls. The value of this earth since Stalin's time was incalculable, beyond the measurements of feeble humans. Russians also referred to ghosts as 'souls', giving a whole other element to what a land was worth.

Russia had stripped him down psychologically until he felt there were no hidden crevices in his life or mind anymore. Some days, he felt as cold and as alien as the landscape. Life here was survival—bread rations and cutting above quota to increase that meager bit of food allowance. It was keeping an eye half open at all times because someone always wanted the little you had, and you had to be willing to kill to keep it. It was life at its most raw and fundamental.

It was late November and Jamie had now been in this camp for almost ten months. It had been a long and bitter day of cutting timber, and now they were returning to camp for the night. They walked in a shambling line, heads down, for the wind was too bitter to face. Even Gregor, normally one to spit in the wind, no matter how frigid, was silent today, merely putting one foot in front of the other on his way back to the camp, to a bowl of soup, a crust of bread and a chilly sleep in a drafty hut. Only to get up and go through this numbing routine again tomorrow, and the day after tomorrow, and the day after that, and the day after that one, *ad infinitum*, a dreadful dark fairytale without a hero to ride in and rescue them, without an ending of any sort.

In Russia, however, there was no line between the here and there, between nightmare and waking. There was no way to tell when one had gone through the glass, for there was no glass, no partition between the creatures of the night and the realities of the day.

A close packed line of ravens sat on the ruins of some long dead peasant's hut by the track they trod. The ravens were silent in the grey gloom of the day, huddled close for warmth, beady eyes intent upon the ragged line of humanity that filed toward and past them.

As they approached, the string of birds broke apart croaking into the twilight, an omen that shivered in a man's spine. It was as though a voice, old and inhuman, had spoken aloud on the cold air and imbued it with the portents of tragedy on its way, drawn fast and light across the snow and tundra, but coming with merciless intent.

An involuntary shudder rippled through his body.

"What is it?" Vanya asked, trudging beside him.

"Nothing," Jamie replied. "Goose just walked across my grave is all."

Vanya raised his eyebrows at him in puzzlement. "I do not understand this, Yasha."

They were nearing the camp gates and Jamie felt an odd relief. He would be glad to be in out of this day with its strange forebodings.

"It's just a way of saying the day feels eerie and haunted. The weather and the light are giving me chills up my backbone."

"Ah," Vanya smiled. "This I understand. But it is to be expected, for there are many ghosts here, so many that we breathe them in each day. You can feel them in the forest, but where they speak loudest, where they are thickest is up there." Vanya nodded his head toward the old bell tower that loomed over the camp, a huge, ugly Gothic structure that was the stuff of nightmares, even without its particular history. There, at the height of the purges, people had been led up the long hill in their underwear, for no camp uniform was to be wasted on a corpse, and shot at the top of the stairs to the tower's cellar. The corpses would pile one upon the next, removed when the pile got too deep. No one in the camp ventured near the tower unless expressly ordered to, and even then, they travelled the pathway there with dread and slow feet.

"Shura is here because of a ghost."

"What?" Jamie asked, startled out of his grim musings by Vanya's words. Shura had never been forthcoming about how he had wound up in the camp. Jamie had suspected there was a story there worth hearing, and that it contained something dark that Shura was still haunted by. However, he had not thought a literal ghost was at the core of it. His face must have shown a hint of skepticism, for Vanya eyed him seriously and said, "You maybe don't believe in ghosts? Once you hear Shura's story you will believe in them. You ask him to tell the story tonight. Maybe for you he will."

"Why would he tell it for me?"

Vanya laughed. "Sometimes I am thinking you are blind, Yasha. Many people would happily do whatever you might think to ask of them. It's only that you never seem to ask."

IT WAS A NIGHT FOR GHOSTLY TALES. The wind had risen to a wail through the trees and it shoved through the tower, making the ancient bell echo with a strange metallic whine. Beyond that lay the dark, looming presence of the forest, the trees soughing eerily. There would be a storm before morning. He could taste it. But inside the hut it was warm, the potbellied stove glowing with heat. Nikolai sat next to it and Violet knelt at his feet, massaging the old man's hands. Nikolai's hands were horribly crabbed, and it was apparent that all the fingers on both hands had been broken—and badly—at some point. The harsh winters without adequate protection had done their share as well. Violet gave his hands a thorough check each and every night unless she was dropping from exhaustion, and then Nikolai wouldn't allow it.

They made a beautiful picture. Violet's copper hair floated in a halo around her face, the fire's glow burnishing it a bronzed gold. Nikolai leaned back against his bunk, eyes drowsing with the pure pleasure of having the stiffness rubbed from his hands, and from the compassionate touch of another human being.

When Jamie made his request of Shura, the small Georgian had looked at him long and hard before answering. In the end, he had acquiesced in a manner that told Jamie it was not a story to be shared lightly.

Shura now took his seat nearest the fire, as was his privilege as the evening's storyteller. He took his feet from his boots and stretched them toward the heat. The stink of wet, scorched wool soon permeated the air. Normally voluble to the point that everyone in his vicinity wanted to suffocate him, tonight Shura seemed reluctant to begin. Jamie poured him a small glass of the peppered vodka he had been given in exchange for fixing an ancient transistor radio.

Shura took a long sip of the vodka and looked at the faces that surrounded him. He drew in a heavy breath and began.

"I was in the Merchant Marine and the ship I was on was called the *Krasny Bopoh*. I was junior to the ship's doctor, a glorified sort of nurse."

"*The Red Raven?*" Jamie said, thinking it was one of the odder names he had heard for a ship. It caused a ripple of unease, the ravens sweeping silent across the field coming into his mind's eye. In Scandinavian folklore, ravens were thought to be the souls of the murdered, and in Germany the souls of the damned.

"Yes, it was a bad name for a ship, but the ship itself was ordinary enough. We sailed the commercial lanes all around the globe. I loved the life on board. I was kept busy enough, but rarely had to deal with a true emergency, though that changed near the end of my time aboard it. We mostly shipped coal to Japan, but plenty went to other countries. We picked up other cargoes to bring home, sometimes grain, electronic goods, sometimes other things that a man did not look at too closely. On this particular trip, we were coming back from a supply run to Cuba and we got caught in a terrible storm just north of the Faroe Islands. It was autumn and the seas were getting rough and cold anyway, but this storm was like nothing I had ever experienced before—snow and hail, and a wind that felt like Thor himself was howling down our necks. We put up near the northernmost Island and tried to weather it out. But we were driven onto some rocks and sustained enough damage that we needed assistance.

"The Captain decided he had to go ashore to find help, or at least try to contact someone to let them know we were having trouble. He took one man with him, Vanko. The rest of us were to stay behind and wait.

"When we awoke the next morning a heavy fog had set in. I've never seen another like it. It was an entity unto itself, so heavy and with such a presence—not a good one, something malevolent, spine prickling. I swear you could feel something hiding in that fog, waiting. The afternoon came and went and it became clear the Captain was not returning. We could not raise him on the radio either. We knew we had to send a scouting party ashore. I volunteered to go because staying on the ship in that fog was making me crazy.

"The entire island was blanketed with the fog and it muffled everything. I cannot explain how spooky it was scrambling over those rocks onto the land, wondering where the village was and why we couldn't even get static on the radio from our Captain. It's amazing that none of us drowned that day, as the fog made the land indistinguishable from the sea. Nothing felt solid, not even the rocks. The island was very hilly, and the cliffs suicidal. We were fortunate not to lose anyone, though later we thought it might have been a blessing to simply fall off a hill to certain death.

"It was late, near nightfall, when we came across the hut. There was just one wee light, but the fog was starting to clear off and it seemed as bright as a bonfire on a hilltop, we were that relieved to see it. It was a fisherman's hut, but no one in our crew spoke the Faroese dialect so communication was limited.

"Vanko was there, sitting in a corner, staring off into space as though he saw something the rest of us could not. We gathered that the fisherman had found him lying amongst the rocks on the shore when he had been down to check if the storm was abating. As best we could determine, Vanko had been in this state since the fisherman found him, almost catatonic, but able to move if guided. Of the Captain, however, there was no sign."

Shura paused and took a breath, and Jamie felt a shiver of prescience pass down his spine.

"We found the Captain on our way back to the ship. He was lying on the rocks where we had tied up the rowboat that brought us to shore. Understand, there is no way we could have missed him even in the fog, so we knew he could not have been there when we arrived. His body...well, it is best to say little, only that sailors usually have strong stomachs and there were many puking their guts out on that shore. I do not know what manner of beast does such things, but I do not care to find out either.

"There was nothing to do but head back to the ship. If Vanko knew what had happened to the Captain, he wasn't saying, because he was no longer saying anything. We took him back to the ship, along with the Captain's body in a canvas bag. We had to sail, and hope that the ship would make it to Russia in one piece. We would limp into port, but at least our engineer had managed to effect repairs enough that we were seaworthy. No one wanted to stay on that island. We would rather risk sinking.

"Vanko had always been a very happy sort who could drink most of us under the table. He was Ukrainian and had the prosaic good nature of his race. But after that night on the island, he was changed. It was as though he had brought something back with him, something dark and terrible. He was a big man, used to his meals being regular, but after that night he barely ate, he never slept and he wouldn't speak about what was ailing him. We gave him medicine and he would fall asleep but wake up screaming and raving. It seemed to do him more harm than good, and after a bit he refused to take anything. He was terrified of falling asleep, said something was waiting for him in his dreams. Three days after we left the islands he was running a terrible fever and raving like a lunatic. I was the one who stayed with him in the infirmary. I could make no sense of anything he said, but I was frightened nevertheless. We had to put him in restraints because we were afraid he would harm himself.

"On the fourth day, somehow he got free. I was out on deck when it happened. He came running like a wildman, his wrists all bloody and raw. I don't know how he managed to get the restraints off, but it had to have been very painful and difficult. I am sure he must have broken bones doing it.

"I saw his face as he went by but I could not stop him. He was terrified, terrified enough to take his own life. The waters there were very cold. A man might survive five minutes, maybe ten. Even then he would require immediate medical attention. Vanko had no intention of being rescued. He knew sure death lay in those waters and he went in knowing it would mean his life. I will carry that look of his all the way to my grave.

"Things got worse after that. Sailors talk. A ship is a small world, and soon we were hearing stories that had many things in common. The night watch said they often sensed something watching them, something evil they claimed, but when they turned around there was never anyone or anything there. They only knew there was something in the shadows that raised the hair on their necks and terrified them. They were certain it was whatever had killed Vanko, for no one believed that he had taken his own life willingly. Too many of us had witnessed his death."

Sailors are a superstitious breed but do not frighten easily, which could only mean that something was very wrong aboard the *Krasny Bopoh*.

"We feared the sunset each night. For it was when the shadows swarmed and deepened, that they released whatever it was that laid low during the day." Shura shuddered in remembrance. "Oh, how we dreaded the night. Two days later, another man threw himself over the side. Same as Vanko, raving, terrified and before we had a chance to tranquilize him, he was gone. We searched the waters but never found his body. The next one though, was different.

"Pavel was a quiet boy, not a terribly good sailor, but he did his work as he was told and didn't question authority, which was what the Soviet state has always wanted from its sons. We never even knew anything was wrong. He had been on night duty and in the morning the man taking over his rounds found him laid out on the deck in a pool of blood. He had cut his own throat—the knife was still in his hand. He had never said a word about anything bothering him. But when they put his belongings together to send home to his mother, they found his journal. It was as if some force had come back with Vanko off that island and was driving us mad one by one, forcing us to kill ourselves.

"Things got worse on the ship after Pavel's death. Everyone was certain he would be next. We were only a day out from Arkhangelsk and everyone seemed to feel if we could make it into port, we could rid ourselves of this curse.

"Once we were on land for a few days, it seemed that we had half imagined it. How could there really be a ghost aboard ship that was driving men insane? The truth was we had little choice about getting back onto the ship.

It was go back to sea or starve. Still, there were a few men who didn't show up when it was time to sail. I went back because I had a young wife and son to support, so what could I do?"

This was news. Shura had never mentioned a family. The surprise in the room must have been apparent for Shura smiled a little, though it was not an expression of happiness.

"It was another life." He took a slug of the vodka, stretched his legs further toward the fire, and continued with his tale.

"We were five days out to sea when it happened. As if the thing," his mouth curled as though he would spit on the memory, "had waited until we could no longer turn around and run back to port. One of the junior officers killed the cook and then took his own life, and we knew then it wasn't over, that the thing would not be satisfied until we were all dead.

"We had to go back to port since a murder had taken place. It took five days to get back and we knew we were all going to be in trouble for bringing the ship in without completing our run. Mass panic took over, as though we were losing our collective minds. I tried to rationalize it, tried to tell myself that we'd all ingested something that was causing a terrible hallucination. Before the boat even turned back for Arkhangelsk, I felt it—on deck, in the hold, it didn't matter. I could feel eyes watching me, waiting for something, an opportunity to strike. I couldn't sleep, couldn't eat. When I did manage to fall asleep, I had terrible dreams, and woke sweating and screaming. I wasn't alone. Two-thirds of the ship was the same way. Later, those of us who survived asked ourselves if we had indeed experienced a mass hallucination, if there was a mold on the ship that could cause such a thing. As human beings we have to seek those answers to keep our sanity. When it was happening there was no explaining or rationalizing it. We were too terrified, too exhausted. And then one night, I saw it standing on the deck. It wasn't anything solid, but I saw it nonetheless. And I knew it was looking straight at me."

The fire had died back some, the stove no longer glowing red. The wind outside had risen to a terrible screech, and Jamie could feel gusts of cold air coming through the chinks in the hut. He put more wood in the fire, building it back up to a blaze. But the chill they all felt was more than just the weather. Violet was huddled up next to Nikolai, her small face pale, and Vanya, who had heard the tale before, looked as spooked as if he himself were witnessing the events firsthand.

"What did it look like?" Vanya asked, tone half eager, half horrified.

"Like a man, yet not a man—something awful that wasn't one thing or another, but some abomination in between. There is no way to say how it was—like a terrible dark mist yet more substantial than that. Capable, I was certain, of choking the life from me should it get its miserable hands about my throat. It was more how it felt, as if it were wrapping something dreadful around you, insinuating things into your ears, for which there are no words in any language."

Shura held up his broad hands. "It sounds unbelievable now, but that thing wanted me to kill myself, wanted me dead and it made it next to impossible to resist. I imagined it over and over, just throwing myself into those icy waters. I knew it would never leave me alone until it had taken the breath and blood from me. Death seemed the only release.

"One after another, it took us. It was a waiting game, and we started to envy the men who had already gone into those dark waters. Time had ceased to have meaning, and yet meant everything. Even an hour was an eternity, stretching itself out beyond the horizon. The day was a haven, the night a horrifying dream only dawn could relieve."

He paused to wet his throat. The only sound was the soft crackle and hiss of the fire and the occasional rasp of Nikolai's breathing. The rest of them were holding their collective breath, waiting for Shura to resume his chilling narrative.

"There is little more to tell, my friends, only that three more of us died before we made port. I was not one of them, why, I cannot say. But it was a fight, as though God and the Devil were warring over my soul that entire time. Mostly I felt like the Devil was winning. In the end, I walked off the ship which means God must have triumphed."

"You are a believer?" Violet asked. It had been asked in innocence, but it was a loaded question. A belief in the State was one thing, belief in God quite another in the Soviet Union.

"Yes, I am a believer in all sorts of things, not all of them good, or things I wish to have knowledge of—but once you have seen and felt such things, you have no choice but to understand there is much in this world that is not easily explained. I begged God to deliver me during those days and nights, and He did. I would be an ungrateful fool to not believe in Him after that."

"How did all this lead to you being sent here?" Jamie asked, moving the conversation quickly off dangerous shoals. He did not wish for Shura to compromise himself.

"I set fire to the ship," Shura said, a distant look on his face. "I had help. Those of us who walked off that boat in Arkhangelsk knew it had to be destroyed. There was no other way to rid ourselves of whatever was on it. And the company would have kept using it, kept finding crews who did not know the story and sending them out to sea to certain death.

" We tugged it out into the mouth of the river where it flows into the White Sea and soaked it with gasoline—every inch of it, for no one wanted to take the chance of the ship being salvaged. Then we sat on the tug and drank ourselves senseless. I waited to get drunk until I knew nothing came off the ship. I knew whatever it was Vanko had brought aboard, went up in the flames or down into the water."

"How can you be certain?" Vanya, always the devil's advocate, asked.

Shura fixed him with his dark eyes, and there was a look in the depths of them such as Jamie had not seen before.

"Because I heard it scream and then when the flames got higher it stopped. Nine men had died on that ship, and still they kept crews on her. I was one of the few who knew what had happened and it wasn't good knowledge to possess. They sentenced us all without trial for the burning and sinking of the ship. Here I am as a result, sentenced to twenty years for the destruction of state property, but I consider it a small price to pay to have rid myself and others of that thing on the ship. And now, Yasha Yakovich, you know my story."

Normally, when the evening's tale was done, people left chatting quietly amongst themselves, their breath gilded streams on the cold night air. But tonight everyone was silent, as if the spectral hand of Shura's ghost had touched them all in the telling.

Jamie walked Violet to her hut as he did every night, waiting until she went inside to turn back to his own quarters. He spared a look for the guard tower, seeing the small, bright coal of the guard's cigarette flare like a star in the wind and cold.

When he returned, the aura of something dark still permeated the hut, despite the sight of Shura in his red long johns, perched on a chair trying to chink the worst of the drafts with moss.

"Thank you for telling your story, Alexsandr Kobashivili," Jamie said, using Shura's formal name, to show him due respect for the sharing of his tale. "I will be lucky to sleep tonight."

Shura shrugged, the dark Georgian eyes still with memory. "It is only one story of many and not so special, Yasha, for we all have souls—or ghosts as you would say. We are all haunted, in one way or another, *da*?"

"*Da*," Jamie agreed, for he knew the truth of that particular statement all too well.

It was as he fell asleep that a memory came to him, of himself and Andrei telling stories one night as the level in first one vodka bottle and then another slowly fell. They had been telling folk tales from their respective homelands and Andrei had just related a particularly gruesome fairytale that involved a young maiden having her eyes taken out, and then later being cut into little pieces and buried in the forest. When he had commented upon the darkness of the tale, Andrei had merely shrugged.

"It's a Russian story. They don't end well. Russians don't believe in happy endings."

It was a Russian story he was caught in now, one of those dark fairytales where there was no hero to ride in on a white charger and rescue them all.

No, he told himself, on the edge of sleep, if one wanted a hero in a Russian story, then one had to become the bloody hero oneself. Russians might not believe in happy endings, but occasionally Irishmen did.

Chapter Forty-three

March 1974

'...For Blood and Wine Are Red'

J AMIE ENTERED THE HUT ON A SWIRL OF FROSTED SNOW, the heat of the room
hitting him in the face as though he had stepped too close to the fire. He
breathed it in, allowing his lungs to take the sweet, shocking pain of it. The
small kitchen and dining area was empty, but clean. She was here though, he
could sense her as one senses a spider ensconced in her web, where no thread
moved or breathed without her knowledge. He could smell too the oil she
liked to drop into her bath that was scented with black gardenias.

On the cracked countertop there was a bottle of wine—red and breathing out in dark, fragrant notes—pomegranates and deepest crimson grapes,
the ones whose juice poured forth like fresh spilled blood. She had already
poured a glass for him and left it waiting. He drank as he was meant to, for it
was part of the game. It was delicious, tasting of Georgian earth and Saperavi
grapes and the deep undernotes of the vessels it was aged in, the ancient clay
of the *kvevri*. It was as heady as liquid roses on his tongue. He wondered
where she had sourced it, what deeds had been committed to bring it here
to this godforsaken hole. He drank it like a Georgian, swiftly to the dregs
and then poured himself another glass, taking a slow contemplative swallow,
before walking through to the bedroom.

On the bedside table was a bowl of white peaches, a sharp silver knife
beside them, waiting to quarter and bleed them. Their delicate flesh was veined
with coral and garnet, their perfume heady as opium. He knew well enough
their purpose, nestled there in their lacquered bowl, for he had taught her
this particular pleasure. An open jar of honey glinted crimson-gold in the
firelight. Oh yes, he had schooled her well. Too well, perhaps. He still had
a bruise on his face from their last encounter.

She was already on the bed, naked. The sheets were clean, candles blazing
in profusion, lighting the entire place with a rubescent glow. She was a study
in red: red lips, parted in carnal expectation, lower lips suffused within the
claret hair, breasts tipped vermilion with a generous brush, full and aroused

in the cherry coal light which spilled from the stove and lent its carnelian flush to her skin. Her hair was loose, fanned across the clean pillows like flames burning the cheap cotton. She was desirable and his body, despite his mind's aversion, took this in and did with it what it would. He had become a whore, knowing that whether the ends justified the means or not, he was still whoring his body to keep his soul intact. At some point, as he knew from previous experience, his soul would present him with a bill for that fractured wholeness.

In the extremes of blind need, there comes a place where thought is obliterated and all is sense and feeling. But after—when the body loosens its hold and the mind reasserts itself along grey pathways—comes regret, fine as soft falling snow at first, but building until, like the avalanche, it breaks and suffocates. There was, however, no room for such a luxury as regret in the Soviet Union. The obliterating of history had eliminated the need for regret, for without a personal history, how could one have regret? How could one experience such a thing when one was no longer a self, but merely part of a machine, a nameless cog without a voice?

The bill, he knew, would only be sent from his depths when and if he found his way home, and so until then he would keep running up the cost, for he might never survive to pay the debtor.

He allowed nothing of his own world to come here, not even the life of the camp outside these walls. He made of his mind a compartment, and within it there was no one he loved, no places of familiarity, no memories of other bodies touched, nor eyes met, nor thoughts enjoined. He was merely a vessel.

He had been tutored in the arts of lovemaking long ago by women far more sophisticated than this one. He knew how to touch, how to play upon the skin and the nerves until his partner cried with need and want. He knew when to stop and when to begin again, and again, and again. He knew how to ruin her for all other men who would share her bed after him. It was his small revenge and he did it with precision and great skill. He also did it with hatred, the one thing he had allowed into the vessel, into the compartment emptied of self—hatred for her, and for himself. It added an element to the events that she responded to with vigor, and his body, barren in all but sensation, understood and replied.

He watched her now, his own clothing shed, appreciating with the male eye what her female form offered—the narrow waist and full breasts, the hips already tilting upward in expectation of what he had been ordered to bring.

He joined her on the bed and did what he had been contracted to do.

HE HAD COMMITTED THE CARDINAL SIN. He had fallen asleep in her bed, something that was not permissible and foolhardy in the extreme. He awoke to confusion and an awareness that the fire must have burned down hours before for it was cold in the hut, frost already forming on the inside of the logs. The light was no longer in hues of red, but those of dawn—blue and violet, ash and mist. His head felt unnaturally heavy and he remembered the wine dimly, tasting of flowers and smoke and dark Georgian earth. It had soured in his mouth through the night and now mixed with the peaches and honey in a rancid brew.

The silence was thick in the small room and he tried to remember how long Isay was meant to be away. He hoped there was enough darkness left to to hide his return to his hut. He tried to raise his head and found it seemed to be filled with molten lead, his arm stuck to the sheet by a substance he could not define, for his vision was swimming with dark spots.

He smelled the blood before he saw it. The rank copper stink was unmistakable, as was the cold, clammy feel of it under his body, on his body, everywhere. He sat up, waiting for the dark swimming in his head to stop.

She was still in the bed, and 'still' was the operative term. She was motionless with the sort of cold flaccidity that only came with death. Her throat was a scarlet slash, clotted around the edges to a crusted black, her skin blue and flaccid. Her hair too had been drenched in blood, was stiff and dull with it. He himself was covered in blood—all hers presumably, for he felt no mortal wounds in his own flesh. In fact, other than a headache, he felt as if all his parts were intact.

He stood, legs wobbly and stomach surging. He had to get out of here, wash the blood off, he had to... his thoughts trailed off here... had to do what? There was nowhere to run and certainly no place to hide. The knife was on the bed. He had been lying on it, for he could feel the imprint of the handle in his hip as his senses began to return. He had been drugged—Svetlana too, or she would have fought. There was no other way for him to have slept through this carnage and he had clearly been meant to sleep through it. But who and why? Everyone hated the woman, but she was merely the devil they knew, and no one fretted about that too much. Except for her husband. The bottom of his stomach dropped out. If Isay had done this, he meant for Jamie to hang for it.

He stumbled to the bureau, cracked the ice on the basin of water and splashed it on his face. He needed to clear his head, to think, though it wouldn't matter if he had a map to the labyrinth he was currently in, he could not see his way out. He was naked, covered in Svetlana's blood and the knife would have his fingerprints all over it. Not that it mattered because there wouldn't be any testing, or even a pretense at charges or a trial. He was already dead if that was Isay's desire.

He looked at her, mouth slack, death's blue mottling her skin and suffusing her face. He wanted to feel pity for her, for the fact that she had once been human, but inside he only felt terribly hollow.

There was a noise at the door, a sound of footsteps in the kitchen and Jamie froze, the drug still carrying him in its clutch but starting to ebb with the effects of cold and adrenaline.

Gregor's head came through the doorway of the bedroom a second later. "Volodya sent me to find you. I was certain this was where... fuck."

"Agreed," Jamie said, putting a hand to his head and wishing the spinning would stop. Of all the people who might have found him, he was somehow relieved that it had been Gregor. Dangerous he might be, but he would not be afraid.

"Yasha?"

Jamie answered the unspoken question in the dark eyes. "No, I did not kill her, though I am fully aware of how ridiculous that sounds given the circumstances."

"If you say you did not do it, I then believe you. Whoever did that..." Gregor nodded toward the blood-soaked bed and the terrible gaping throat, "hated her very much."

The name was there between them, the thought as clear as the knife that still lay upon the bed. Who, other than her husband, could hate this woman this much?

"Wash the blood off your body," Gregor said. "I am going to find you some clothes."

Jamie looked in consternation at his own clothes. They lay stiff and maroon with dried blood where he had dropped them by the bed. His head whirled, trying to find the thread that would unravel the horrific tapestry of the previous night. He remembered drinking the wine, getting into the bed with her, and he would swear neither of them had been drugged at that point. So the wine was not the culprit. Which left only the peaches and the honey. They had spilled at some point and mixed with the blood when it was still hot and pulsing with life. The blood was gelling now, fixed incarnadine tributaries that branched from the river of her throat.

They had both partaken of the peaches and honey, and considering just *how* they had partaken of them, the drug would have hit Svetlana first and doubly hard. Another roil of nausea twisted in his guts and he bit back hard on it.

Gregor returned posthaste with a set of clean prison garb.

Jamie attempted to put the pants on and would have toppled over had Gregor not caught him by the elbow. Gregor merely took the pants, steadied Jamie and dressed him as though he were a particularly hapless three-year-old—admittedly, a fair summation of his current state.

"Who told you to come to her last night?"

"She did... I think. Or... it was understood." His memory seemed to be a slippery thing, like a frog sliding over ice unable to find any traction to force a direction. "I—I don't remember things very well right now."

Gregor fixed him with a dark, hard look that bade him pay attention.

"You see," Gregor said slowly and Jamie, through the torpor of the drug, understood there were two levels of conversation going on, "it snowed last night, but there are no tracks in the snow. It is pure out there, though melting now. So, you see, Yasha, things do not look very good for you."

Jamie squinted at him, trying to clear his vision. And suddenly he understood. If he didn't kill Svetlana, and there were no tracks outside the hut, then whoever had killed her had been here when he arrived, and was still here in the cabin. What exactly they were to do about it was another matter altogether.

"I have muddied the snow outside so that they cannot tell how many came or went. But now, Yasha, I think you should go. Take this and drink it." Gregor thrust his daily flask of vodka-laced *chifr* at Jamie. "It will clear your head. You cut your quota and keep your silence. I will see you tonight."

"But..." Jamie protested. Gregor cut him off immediately, the hard *vor* showing clearly in his face and tone.

"Do as I say, Yasha. If you want to keep breathing, just do as I say for fuck sake."

When Jamie walked out into the cold still of the camp, nothing moved. The entire world appeared lifeless, suspended. The guards and the crew were leaving and he fell into their ranks as though it were a normal morning, under a normal grey Soviet sky. The cold not as severe today but enough to help cut into the fog of his drug-addled wits.

The day in the forest was exceptionally long. Later, Jamie could not remember it. He simply cut and cut, and obeyed Nikolai's every grunted command. His head slowly cleared as the drug, whatever it had been, wore off. The bleary memory and pounding head pointed to barbiturates of some sort. No one commented on Gregor's absence and Jamie was certain more than one surreptitious glance was directed his way that day, though it may have been his imagination, for he felt as though there was blood in every line of his skin, stinking, declaiming a guilt he could not remember.

When they returned to the camp in the thick twilight, snow was falling again, and the camp was deathly quiet. Jamie had tensed in expectation of lights and military police, barking dogs, and a swift answer to just what the consequences of Svetlana's death were going to be.

Gregor met him outside his own hut, where Jamie was surprised to find himself having made it so far unmolested.

"It is fixed," Gregor said, offering him a cigarette as though they were talking about a dog race, not the murder of a woman whose bed he had been sharing on a regular basis. Jamie took the cigarette, in need of any sort of calming device.

"How the hell can it be fixed?" he hissed at Gregor's dark, stoic expression.

Gregor took a long drag on his cigarette and blew the smoke out before answering. "Both you and I know, Yasha, who really killed her. He was hiding in the closet the whole time. He admitted that he drugged the honey and watched the two of you until you passed out."

Jamie felt a chill of another variety pass through him, as he remembered snapshots of the night before. He had hated the woman but physically they had not held back with one another. He felt sick.

This tiny corner of the universe was lawless. He knew that in most camps he would be dead already, without any sort of charge or trial or even a pretense of wondering at his guilt. And there was guilt, for if he had not gone to her bed repeatedly, this would not have happened. It didn't seem to matter that he had not had a choice in the original decision, for he had understood what the consequences would have to be. There had been something dark hanging there in the air between them before she had ever laid a hand on him.

"I have him within my power but only to a degree. There is only so much I can do, Yasha," Gregor said. "But I have brought him to a place where he agrees to settle this honorably."

Jamie looked up at the big man and wondered how he thought honor could be found in this situation.

"It is not as though I was the first man she took to her bed that was not her husband," Jamie said, feeling a deep longing for his own uncomfortable cold bed, for the privacy it afforded if nothing else.

"No, but you are the first, I think, that she loved. And so it matters to him."

He was suddenly unspeakably weary. "What does he want, then? Whatever it is, I will do it."

Chapter Forty-four
Ring of Fire

THE RING WAS SIMPLY A SPACE INSIDE A CIRCLE OF SNOW-HEAVY pines that had been raked. A fire had been lit to one side, for the warmth of the spectators, he assumed, and it lent a falsely celebratory glow to the night. The ground was damp, for the snow had been cleared away. At least his feet would have purchase. How much that might matter when the intent of the evening was to kill him was up for debate, but he was glad of it nevertheless. The only thing he had on his side was his background as a boxer and the fact that no one in this country knew it other than Andrei.

They were out beyond the borders of the camp, deep enough into the forest that no shouts for help would be heard, no pleas for mercy granted. Guards, picked for their un-seeing eyes, kept guns trained upon all present.

When his opponent stepped into the ring of fire. Jamie knew a moment of free-falling terror. He should have known Isay would not play fair, that he, cowardly to the bitter end, would send someone else to do the dirty work for him. This man he now faced was more bear than human, big and thick, arms like great slabs of beef and solid with muscle. Jamie took a deep breath and hoped for a quick death. It was about the most optimistic thing he could think of at first glance.

Gregor, ever the master of the succinct summary, uttered the Russian equivalent of "Fuck my mother, that bastard is huge."

"I noticed," Jamie said dryly.

He danced at the edge of the light, assessing the man, knowing that even the largest and strongest will have a weak spot—throat, kidney, a soft patch in the belly, or a weak knee. But there was no way to know this man, so he would have to find it out the hard way. His own advantages were what they always had been: quick thinking, lightning agility and always staying one step ahead. Unfortunately, he was going to have to get in close enough to take a couple of hits in order to get a better idea of the man's reach and speed. He took a deep breath. It was best to get it over with.

The first hit took him in the midsection and made the world go entirely black for a second. The second one glanced off the side of his head and he thought he heard angels singing. He managed to jab in a swift uppercut to the man's jaw and then danced back from him. The big man was slow, not agile, and he was going to wind quickly—though maybe not quickly enough—and he could hit like a piledriver. Jamie could play for time but not for long, for he couldn't risk exhausting himself, because once this man had him, he was toast.

He was careful to avoid the fire, skirting its edge, but skirting it fine, as it was a weapon he could use to his advantage. He had to take a hard-knuckled blow to his left eye to manage it, but he got his opponent to step into the hot coals, his great weight sinking him in to his ankle. He roared with pain and stumbled out, scattering bright coals in his wake, his boot smoking and sizzling on the slushy ground.

Jamie took a second to catch his wind and wiped a hand across his face, for despite the cold the sweat was dripping from his hairline. Somewhere in the night, Isay's dark eyes watched him. He could feel them.

Though he was left-handed, Jamie could lead with either, which had always given him a distinct advantage over other fighters—they never knew which direction the hit would be coming from. His trainer had once said he had never seen a fighter with a faster strike and it was what he used now, tapping the man hard around his head, in the soft part under the ribs. They danced for a long time, Jamie light but tired, for the drugs still lingered in his blood; the other man heavy and ponderous but coming on like a slow-moving train. Spinning, dodging, weaving, the faces beyond the fire a blur, though he could feel the strange lust that bloodsport brought surging up in the male animal. The night was thick with it.

The bear-man had a longer reach even if he was slow. The power behind the blow was stunning, though it glanced off the side of Jamie's head, for he had managed to half step out of range at the last second. But the man got in under his defenses as Jamie reeled back. He was grabbed in a hard hug, it was like being mauled by a bear, for the air left his lungs in a rush and his ribs creaked under the pressure. He was lifted off the ground, his opponent grunting, slippery with sweat and the raw stink of brutality. The world was dancing with tiny black sprites against the background of crimson flame and inky sky. He dug his thumb hard into the brute's eye, the only leverage available to him. He was dropped like a hot coal, smacked away like a bothersome fly. Jamie fell backward into the filthy snow, allowing the fall to take him all the way over and regaining his feet in one fluid move, even though it hurt like holy hell.

His left ear was ringing and his eye was starting to swell shut. If the bastard got a hold on him again like he had a moment ago, it was over. He had to think of something quickly or accept death here and now. It would not be without honor, nor freedom—it would be a better death than he had come to expect here in the Soviet Empire. He could choose it. It could be on his terms.

The fire leaped higher, the sparks touching his hair and skin, the small sting of pain clearing his mind. Gregor came into his field of view. He could only spare him a split second but saw him look pointedly toward the northern edge of the circle where the pines, thick with snow, hid a drop-off. He understood Gregor's message, but thought it was next door to suicidal to attempt it. Then again, there was little doubt this man had been ordered to beat him to death, so inflicting some damage on him in the process seemed fairly attractive.

Jamie angled himself around, putting his back to the drop-off. He knew it was there, but he had no idea how steep it was, nor how far the fall. He danced back to the edge, feeling it yawn behind him. He needed to bring the man to him, and bring him fast. He still had one hand clapped to his eye and blood was trickling out from beneath his palm, but the other eye was locked on Jamie with dull hatred, thick with the promise of death.

"Yeb vas," he said as they closed together and Jamie made an incredibly indelicate comment on the state of the man's mother's morals, in the most gutteresque Russian he could manage. He heard Gregor's shout of laughter, just as the ground began to give way. He was hit with the force of an ox, all muscle and brute blind fury. They hung there for a desperate instant, suspended over the void and then fell through the scrim of pines, tree branches whipping at them, ice cascading, snow falling with them, gathering branch by branch into a cataract that enveloped them within its cold, plunging embrace.

They hit the ground as one, a twisting, writhing mass of furious muscle and pumping blood, adrenaline rendering them impervious to the cold, stone, and ice that shrouded them. The fiend had his hands on Jamie's throat, and a red tide began to rise behind his eyes. He brought his knee up hard, using the one advantage he had against such a large brute—his agility. The man grunted and cursed, falling to the side with a thud. Jamie gasped for air, lungs burning, throat nearly closed. He knew he had to get up, get away, but oxygen was the first priority. The world was red from horizon to horizon, and he could hear himself wheezing, desperately trying to pull air into his starved cells.

Suddenly he sensed someone else near, there was a hot sliding burn in his hip and a spreading warmth that blazed across his skin. Blood spilling from a knife wound, pouring from his own body. He could feel the hot seep of it into the snow and the numbness that spread out across his nerve endings. He felt he should sit up, but could not find leverage in the snow. This was more frightening than anything else, for he could already feel the strange drift that blood loss caused in a man.

Then the snow and stone were alive with movement and he knew Gregor had jumped down to even the odds. He heard the thunk of stone hitting a skull and knew the mauling brute next to him posed no more threat.

He noted that the moon was especially bright and large and found this pleasing, as one ought to have something lovely to look at in one's final moments. Then the moon, with Gregor's face in the middle of it, drew down to a tiny spot in a great sea of blackness and disappeared. It was all, he thought, a little anti-climatic.

HE CAME TO FACE DOWN ON A GURNEY with a view of the ugly green linoleum that floored the infirmary. He did not remember the journey back to the camp, but had an uncomfortable feeling that Gregor might have carried him there. Sensation was still hazy. He was aware that he had been stripped of what little clothing remained to him and that his backside was now being viewed with varying degrees of concern by Shura, Vanya and Gregor. Despite blood loss and several blows to the head, he felt rather twitchy under such an examination.

"Another inch or two lower..." Gregor said.

Shura's long drawn out "aieeee" did not require translation. It was universally male in its consternation. He patted Jamie's shoulder companionably and said, "Is not too deep," and bustled off to the counter where the sterile instruments were laid out. Gregor proceeded to pour liquid fire into the wound while Jamie suddenly wished he had a propensity to swoon.

"Christ," he hissed between gritted teeth, "hold back on the vodka a little, would you?"

Gregor merely laughed and poured the last of the bottle into a glass. "Drink this. You're going to need it, Shura says we're out of anesthetic and he thinks you need at least twenty stitches. The wound is clean now."

"You don't need to sound quite so gleeful about it," Jamie said, sweat breaking out on his forehead at the thought of twenty stitches without any sort of numbing.

"I will hold your hand, if you need me to, Yasha," Gregor said and there was no mistaking the scorn in his voice.

Vanya took his hand, without saying a word and Jamie squeezed the boy's fingers in gratitude.

The ludicrousness of the situation could not fail to impress itself upon him. That he was currently naked with a dwarf on a stool looming over him with a large needle, a male prostitute holding his hand and that Gregor had his own big hand on Jamie's bare rear end—suffice it to say that it wasn't likely that the joke of it was being missed by Gregor either. Suddenly the humor of it was more than he could contain and a snort of laughter slipped from him, causing Shura to pause for a second, halfway through pulling a stitch. Jamie sucked in his breath at the sensation before another laugh slipped out, and then Gregor and Vanya started to laugh. Shura said something admonitory about ruining all his careful work, then he too chuckled. By then Jamie, Vanya and Gregor were laughing so hard that they wouldn't have noticed if Shura had done a tap dance on the gurney.

At this less-than-fortuitous moment, Violet entered the infirmary.

"Oh, God," Jamie clutched the edges of the gurney and attempted to pull himself together, but it was hopeless because he could see the tableau laid out in front of her in his mind's eye. Apparently so could Gregor, Vanya and Shura, for they too clutched at the shreds of their sobriety and failed miserably. Shura was still on the stool, the needle in hand but totally unable to attempt another stitch. Gregor had his head on his knees trying to catch a breath between bouts of laughter, Vanya had his on the edge of the gurney, and he himself, mother naked, head swimming with vodka and pain, was equally unable to exert any control.

"Men," Violet said, crossing the room like a small battle ship under full sail, and taking needle and thread from Shura's shaking hand.

The stitching was finished three-quarters of an hour later and Jamie was stone cold sober by the time it was done. Violet washed down the suturing with icy cold vodka, all the while delivering a low-voiced diatribe on the stupidity of men. The vodka he had taken internally had worn off. Both Shura and Gregor had been ordered about so that he was covered with a hot blanket and given another tot of vodka. He took it gratefully, for his body had finally formed an understanding of what had happened to it and was shaking with cold and shock.

Gregor brought the low doctor's stool to the head of the gurney and sat on it facing Jamie. His dark eyes were sober now, his voice no longer teasing nor prodding.

"You want that I should finish this?"

"No," Jamie said, "this is my fight."

"Yasha," Violet said sternly, "he will not stop until he kills you."

"I know," Jamie said, and succumbed to unconsciousness.

Chapter Forty-five

March 1974

Tyger, Tyger...

THEY CAME FOR HIM IN THE NIGHT—faceless men in the dim of the infirmary, manhandling him with no small viciousness. He understood where they were taking him and knew it was inevitable. What was less certain was what path inevitability was about to take him down.

Isay was seated in the kitchen of the modest hut, a hunting rifle propped between his knees. Jamie was lightheaded with fatigue and the drugs Shura had given him for pain and fever. There was a lantern on the table but to his hazed vision it seemed only a smeary slide of dancing light, Isay's thick features swimming in and out of focus. He could smell Svetlana's blood, could almost see it splashed all over the bed and up the walls. He wondered what the man had done with her body, if she would be buried with respect or tears.

"You sit there," Isay pointed a meaty finger toward one of the kitchen chairs. Jamie sat, hoping it would help him restore some sort of equilibrium. Isay had been drinking, and Jamie knew his capacity, like most alcoholics, was near to limitless.

"Where I come from in Siber we have a game we play sometimes. It is called 'Tiger'. You know this game?" Isay was shining the length of the rifle barrel and Jamie felt certain that he knew this particular game, only the name changed sometimes. But he replied the only way he could.

"No, I'm not familiar with this game."

"This is fine, for I am going to tell you how this game is played. I am going to tell you the rules."

Jamie fought to clear his head, knowing he was going to need every wit he possessed very shortly, despite the man's seemingly friendly tone.

"Not all men have seen the tiger, even those who live in the taiga all their lives. But I have seen him many times. I have taken him down. You know what they say about the tiger—for every time you have seen him, he has seen you one hundred times and remained invisible to your weak human eye. They also say that the tiger, he never forgets a slight, never forgets what each of his enemies smells like, he never forgets the taste of a man's blood once it crosses his tongue, no matter how briefly."

Isay stopped polishing the rifle but his hand remained on the stock, caressing it as though it were a woman.

"Where I grew up, you have to know how to kill from the time you are small in order to survive. There the tribesmen say that every man has an animal inside that he will recognize as his own soul. I had dream about you and in that dream you and I were both tigers. Two male tigers cannot be in the same territory. One must die. It is how nature deems it to be."

"What is it that you want, Isay?" Jamie asked, tired of the man's story, and wanting only to end it.

"Tigers hunt, that is their nature. So you and I will hunt. I will be fair." He tossed a pile of clothes at Jamie. "That will keep you warm enough to survive," he chuckled, "as long as you don't quit moving."

There were felt-soled boots lined with wool, woolen pants, mittens and a coat. A hat too, lined with fur.

"Put them on. There is no room for false modesty here, not between us, no? We have fucked the same woman after all."

Jamie put the clothes on, not daring to turn his back on the man. Adrenaline was coating his every nerve ending but it had the advantage of clearing his head. At least he was steady on his feet now.

"You are ready to play our little game?" Isay's grin was a leer, anticipating several hours of blood sport.

"Ready as I'll ever be," Jamie said tersely.

"Then go," Isay said. Jamie stepped toward the door, knowing his time was finite. Something in the air flicked at his primal brain and he stepped away from Isay, almost out of reach, but not quite.

"Oh, one more thing."

Jamie turned just as the knife took him in the hip, a sharp blade of pain like ice slicing through his blood, destroying Shura and Violet's handiwork and buckling his knees with the agony of it. It might have been worse had he not checked at that last second.

Isay smiled down at him, a feral, dark thing. "Now run, tiger, tiger," he said. "I will give you a half hour head start, but then be ready because I am coming for you. I left the gate behind the woodshed open, so choose your path carefully."

Because there was no choice, Jamie ran. Where the knife had cut him, he could feel the blood welling hot, the scent of it would draw every wild animal within the trees and the droplets of it in the snow were going to provide Isay with all the trail he needed to chase him. It wasn't a fair fight, but then he had never expected one from this man.

The night was bitter, clear like the finest vodka, hung with fire and stars.

It hurt to breathe in, both because of the cold and because every breath caught at the stab wound, dragging jagged over bone and open flesh. The gate was indeed open, the snow beyond virgin and silver. He went through the gate, drawing in the fiery air despite the pain for the clarity it brought.

Inside the perimeter of the trees he stopped, reaching under a fallen birch to retrieve a canvas bag, a bag filled by his own premonitions, a bag that Svetlana had helped him hide though neither of them could have foreseen just how this situation would play out.

He stopped a few minutes later in a spot he remembered where sphagnum moss grew in a boggy patch. He stuffed as much as he could into the pack, pulling up more to staunch the blood at his side. It would have to do, and he hoped the reek of his own blood would not prove to be the calling card that drew his death to him. He needed to keep to the forest tracks. There was less snow there and he would be less easily followed where the trees grew especially dense. He might not survive this, but he wasn't going to make it easy for that son-of-a-bitch either.

He set a pace he thought he could maintain without weakening too badly. Behind him he heard the spine-shivering noise of a hound baying. Isay was bringing his dog.

The birches rose like ghostly maidens from the snow, the firs dark way-posts by which to guide oneself—if one had any clue where one was. He pulled in his focus. If he was going to be treated like an animal, hunted like an animal, he was going to have to think and move like an animal. Observe, decipher, catalogue. It wasn't impossible, he had done it before, but never bleeding and weak as he was now. When you were prey you kept moving, or you went to ground, as well camouflaged as you could manage. When you were the predator, you kept moving too, for to stop in this land of the long winter was to die, whether you were tiger, bear, wolf or man.

So he moved, putting the pain to one side. The soft-soled boots allowed him to run lightly and as long as he moved swiftly he didn't sink into the snow, for a hard crust overlay the softer snow underneath. This current cold followed a few days of unseasonably spring-like weather. Isay would likely wear snowshoes. Isay would take every advantage he could. Isay did not know that Jamie had a few advantages of his own.

Long ago, he had been trained in the ways of tracking both animals and men, how to shift one's vision so that one saw the invisible. It was about abandoning your normal parameters and seeing through the eyes of primitive instinct, about realigning the borders of your normal human perspective to something far older and less civilized. You couldn't rely on visual prints in the forest. You had to understand other things, other signs that said either man or animal had come this way. He had also been trained well in the art of evasion, and how to turn the tables.

He understood from the start that Isay would drag this out to savor the game before the kill. He wouldn't want to finish it tonight, with only a couple of hours before the dawn. But that did not mean he wouldn't taunt him, harry him, and try to drain what strength he had, out in the cold and merciless forest.

It was a strange night, both beautiful and terrible in its lineaments. He had found this a few times before in his life. Stripped to the essentials of survival, one saw the naked heart of human existence, the dreadful fragility of bone and flesh against the elements, against every force that conspired against survival in the first place.

Thoughts ran fleet through his mind, of friends and loved ones left behind, by now realizing his absence was longer than it ought to have been. These thoughts tangled with other things, the great starry dome above, fretted with a darkness that was different from the darkness at home. Here it was both steeper and longer and filled with echoes of that which had come this way but would not pass again. He thought of his sons, each in their turn, and of the towering firs that surrounded him, deaf to human need and grief. And he thought of an afternoon in a meadow and of the woman who had been there with him, and stumbled a little—which saved him from death.

The bullet whined through the air beside him, close enough so that he felt the heat of the forged metal. He had let exhaustion and sentimentality get the better of him in a moment when he could least afford it. He sprinted off the trail, which he realized he had been mindlessly following for the ease of it. He was so tired, the loss of blood muddling his head and instincts. The near miss had the effect of waking him up, sending adrenaline in a slick pour through his blood.

He stopped some ways into the trees. In the distance he could hear water moving under ice and the soft croak of a crow wakened from its sleep. His senses were dulling and he knew he could not go on much longer.

It was time to head for shelter. Dawn was near, and Isay had to be getting tired himself, not to mention that his absence from the camp would be noted. He was far off the trail now and no longer sensed the man or dog behind him. He took the precaution of backtracking through some of his own footprints, before heading for a windfall of trees he had seen earlier in the night. A covering of snow at least two feet deep lay over it, which made it the perfect shelter when he could not risk lighting a fire. He came to it from the far side, out from a large grouping of fir so that his footprints were indiscernible.

The stiffness in his side became pronounced as he knelt to dig out a small opening between the trunks of two fallen trees. Crawling in under the windfall proved difficult and opened the wound in his hip again. He could feel the heat of the blood spill out and into his clothing. Removing the bloody moss, he opened a small bottle of distilled alcohol from his rucksack and poured some directly onto the wound. He passed out for a few seconds from the pain, then came up gasping like a landed fish. He repacked the wound and bound it with a clean strip of cotton. He refastened his clothes. There was nothing he could do about the smell of blood. There was nothing to be done about the scent of his humanity, come to that.

The small hole he had entered through he re-packed with snow, except for a very narrow tunnel for air. He positioned the rucksack a few inches from the opening, dug a hole in the bed of needles and grasping the hatchet from the bag, rolled himself up in a sheet of canvas left over from some Red Army prisoner. Wedged carefully with his back to the lip of stone against which the trees had come to rest, he fell asleep.

The fever came on while he slept. He awoke stiff and shuddering, and knew immediately that his temperature had increased, for the ache in his body was due to more than just having slept rough and cold. He was parched as well, but not hungry. The knife he had been stabbed with had likely been filthy and the wound too deep for the moss to be entirely effective.

Outside his shelter it was twilight and time for him to move again, to get his blood flowing and some warmth into his extremities. He ate a few handfuls of snow to alleviate the fire in his throat. It tasted strongly of the cold amber of fir needles.

The stars were out, Saturn dimmed in the glow of a three-quarter moon. He took a breath of frigid air, shouldered his rucksack carefully and set out, light as a cat across the moon-limned landscape of the northern forest. Casting his senses out, he could feel Isay near. The hunt was on again.

The crisscrossing tracks he had so painstakingly laid out had given him the result for which he had hoped, for the prey was now stalking the predator. The edges of the dog's prints were soft, crumbling to the touch, telling him that he was not far behind and must be careful not to stumble upon them.

The best trackers always had a sixth sense, that natural radar that swept the area surrounding them and told them when to stop and take notice of something that wasn't quite right. With Jamie, it had always come like a whisper threading his senses that told him where to look, how to see, when to hesitate. And so he knew when something had changed on the trail ahead and when they stopped.

He reversed his path, stepping carefully in his own prints, and angled off through the trees, the hatchet an outgrowth of his own hand now after holding it all night, ready to strike if need be. He found a thick patch of rhododendron and hid behind it, careful not to rustle the dry leaves that still clung to the branches. He had traced an arc through the trees so that now he was almost directly behind them.

He crouched in the shrubs, breathing into his cupped hand so that the vapors weren't out on the wind. He was downwind of the hound, though the dog's ears pricked and its nose drank in the air as though it was identifying each molecule and storing it for future reference. Something of greater interest was on the airy pathways tonight, and Jamie thanked God he had befriended the dog and that his scent was likely on Isay's own clothes, which would further confuse the issue.

Man and dog were lit with cold fire, standing upon the edge of a narrow river, thick with ice, each as clearly outlined as if they stood in bright sunlight. The fever had given his vision a surreal focus, making things painfully sharp. All his senses were preternaturally fluid and heightened, though he knew this was dangerous, that fever held its own delusions and they could kill a man. He was too far away to be certain of hitting Isay if he threw the hatchet. It would have to be in the head and it would have to land with enough force to split his skull.

He crept backwards out of the shrubs, easing his hold on the hatchet only slightly and headed in a northwest direction, checking the sky as he went. The moon had set and shadows cloaked the tops of the trees. Down here in the snow, the light was silver-blue and his eyes flowed along the landscape almost by feel—rock—stream—snag—his skin attuned to the wind and movement of branch and creatures that moved as he did, to the rhythms of the dark.

He knew the line between this hyper-sensitive state and exhaustion was extremely thin. He needed to find shelter again, somewhere he could light a fire before it was too late. Somewhere he could lie down and likely die, perhaps even before Isay and his hound found him. That was about as much favor as he could expect from the universe at this point. Dying from cold was supposed to be peaceful, though he begged leave to wonder just who had reported on that particular finding.

He smelled the animal before he saw it. Being outdoors for any length of time sharpened a man's senses, but the scent of blood was so familiar right now that he could not mistake it. It was hot and thick on the air. Something recently killed lay in his path. He slowed to a walk, the scent pulling him the way a woman would, to a place beyond thought that lay in the primordial brain, shivering along the spine in tiny branching pools.

The kill was fresh, a stag, felled, blood still steaming, the snow around stained a rich crimson. He was very hungry, the fever no longer hiding basic bodily requirements, and he needed the nourishment if he was to continue. But this stag had been killed by something very big and very lethal and if it was still nearby Jamie knew he risked being killed himself. Predators were known to share, but one never knew when the meat was an open invitation and when it had merely been left for a few minutes. In the latter case, it was viewed as robbery and punished accordingly should the thief be caught at the kill.

He would have to risk it. He knelt in the snow, and put his hand in the blood that still pulsed slowly out of the throat. The blood was hot on his tongue, and slid down his throat easily, his stomach gurgling in response to the first sign of nourishment in days. He cut away some of the meat with his hatchet, well away from the bite marks that had already taken much of the stag.

He felt the eyes on him suddenly, a ripple up his backbone, a warning as old as man. The warning of an apex predator, a creature that was a perfect killing machine, against which there were few defenses. A creature that did not belong this far west, and therefore a creature for whom there was no rational explanation, yet it was as undeniable as the carrion scent that hit him with the force of a fist. He turned his head slowly.

The tiger stood looking at him, twenty feet away, a distance that was not even a full jump for a such an animal, eyes a blaze of green-white fire in the night. The fur of its ruff stood out, a gleaming frost white, the black stripes moving across its body like shadow over snow. Jamie knelt frozen by the stag carcass, knowing not to move until the tiger moved. If a tiger stepped forward, then a man could take one step back, but until the tiger advanced any move on his part would be seen as aggression or an open invitation to attack him.

He could feel the tiger's breath, and heard his own respond in the rhythm of hot blood. They stood suspended between worlds, that of man and wild animal, where only the rules of one applied. For a moment their separate worlds overlapped, hanging there in the cold blue splendor of the night. With the taste of the same blood upon their tongues, they were one and understood each other with ease. To be the predator, one must not be seen, nor heard. One must become as a ghost, no more than a passing sigh upon the wind, which could turn into a tornado of killing claw and tooth in a mere second.

"Thank you, Amba," he said softly, using the Udegai name for the tiger, conceding his right as czar of the taiga. One must thank the tiger and acknowledge the debt. The tiger continued to watch him, the green eyes as hypnotic as those of a forest djinn. Finally, it became clear that the tiger was not going to attack. Jamie stood slowly and backed away, one step at a time, with no clear idea of where the tiger's territory began or ended.

It stepped forward, and for a heart-stopping second Jamie thought he had made a fatal mistake, though he knew already he would rather die under the tiger's aegis than under that of a cuckolded husband. But then the tiger turned, its tail as long and thick as a grown man's arm, glistening silver against the snowy forest trail. Jamie followed, compelled for a reason he could not put into words. Only that within the *umwelt* in which he and the tiger had met, he knew it meant for him to follow.

Time held no dominion that night. Fever brushed it aside as unnecessary to survival. He trotted behind the tiger, keeping pace, keeping a respectful distance as well. He felt, against all common sense and experience, that it had a purpose in taking him this way and that it was not, ultimately, to kill him. For the tiger was wounded too. It was there in the measured marks of his stride, small drops of garnet, glistening jewels on a bed of white velvet.

A strange strength entered his blood, his muscle and bone, allowing him to be fleet, to flow with the tiger, even as they both bled from their respective cuts. Together they had ventured across some boundary between reality and dream, though the substance of the cold and the taste of the stag's blood seemed beyond question.

The air had lightened infinitesimally when the tiger stopped, turned and looked at him, eyes fired emeralds in the waking dawn. It was clear this was where they would part ways, for even a tiger knew when to hole up and rest, to nurse both wound and rage until strength returned. Jamie stopped and stood watching the animal melt away into the snow, becoming mirage-like in the pale morning.

He had not heard the dog since before spotting the stag the night before, but he knew this did not mean that Isay had lost his trail. Isay would have to stop and so would the dog, and Jamie knew that he needed rest now too, for with the tiger's disappearance he had become aware of the burning pain in his side and how very cold he was.

He would never understand how he recognized the small hump in the snow for what it was, only that it reminded him of the fairy mounds back home. There was no trail, no pathway leading to a door and yet he had sensed the door there, waiting, covered in white. A sod hut, three-quarters underground. He had to clear the snow away from the door with his hands. Inside, when he stumbled down the short incline, it was little more than a root cellar. There was a potbellied tin stove, shelves with a few canned goods, some kindling and dry birch for the fire, two bottles of vodka and—most blessedly—a low-slung bedstead made from rough lumber and rope, with a straw mattress on top. He wanted nothing more than to collapse on it, but knew he had to light the fire first or he would die from the cold in short order. The smoke could and likely would lead Isay to him if he was close on his trail. Jamie would have to take that risk for he needed to change his dressing and to rest. And he needed to eat, if he could manage to cook the frozen lump of meat before succumbing to his exhaustion and blood loss.

The tin stove didn't take long to heat to a cherry-glow. The low-slung bedstead was close beside it and Jamie sat there to remove the moss dressing from his side. The slash was swollen and angry looking, a flush of heavy red spreading out from it, heralding the infection that lay under the skin. But the moss had done its job, even if removing it was almost as painful as the original cutting. Moss, processed properly, had antiseptic qualities, but he had not had time to dry or clean it properly.

He cracked open one of the bottles of vodka, lay on his good side and poured the alcohol liberally into the infected wound. It wasn't as painful as the last time, and he thought perhaps this wasn't a good sign. He repacked the wound with moss again, this time taking care to remove as much debris from it as he could.

He cooked the meat directly on the tin stove, the sizzling blood scent of it simultaneously nauseating and enticing him. When it was cooked, he ate all of it, for he could not afford the scent drawing the dog to him. And then he lay down, pulling his coat tight around him, leaving his boots on and hoping that he would wake again. He thought about the tiger as he fell toward the fever's dark abyss, and said a wordless prayer for both their souls.

SHE CAME AWAKE IN THE MOMENTS BEFORE DAWN, heart thumping unpleasantly in her chest, breath short and limbs aching with cold. The dream still clung dense and thick, and it took several moments to get her bearings, to smell the warm, musky scent of Casey still deeply asleep beside her, to hear the soft hiss of the peat he had banked the fire with before they had gone to bed.

The covers were still heaped over her and heat pulsed from Casey's recumbent form so she didn't know why she was so cold. She listened carefully for Conor, but heard no sound from the other side of the wall. She eased her way out of bed, the dream still there in echoes and pulses—the snow, the cold, the dark. She shivered, trying to make sense of the jumbled images.

Pamela wrapped her robe around her body. It had been lying over the chair near the fire and the heat was like a shield between her and the strange dream world that she still felt as if she had one foot in, metaphysically speaking.

She checked on Conor, to find him sleeping heavily, turned on his tummy, mouth open, cheeks warmly pink. She adjusted his blankets, for his internal furnace ran high like his father's and he tended to kick the covers off during the night. She breathed in his scent of milk and sweet dreams and then left the room.

She was too unsettled to go back to sleep, so headed down to the kitchen to make some tea. It was the wee hours, but she knew her slumber was done for the night.

Pouring a few teaspoons of dried lavender heads into the teapot, she filled it with water from the humming kettle. Around her, the house was quiet, whispering only of night things.

She sat by the fire, adding two bricks of peat and stirring the coals until they flared ruby-bright, throwing out a tremendous heat. Once the tea had steeped, she poured a cup and brought it back to the fireside.

She stared into the flames, sipping her tea, focusing on the pulsing glow of the coals and emptying her mind in order to bring the dream back. There were pieces of it there: a great snowy forest, a man on a dark horse, clad in a black cloak, coming remorselessly on through the snow, cloak hanging on the wind and the movement of the horse beneath him.

In daylight, she knew, she would chide herself for allowing this to worry her so, but here in the depths of night there was no such homely comfort. Rather, she had the distinct feeling that she had entered some strange realm, beyond dreams, and touched... what?

There was only one person she thought might be able to help her understand what was happening. She recalled the last words the woman had said to her before she left her cottage that day. She had taken Pamela's face in her rough, brown hand, the scent of rosemary like sun-warmed pepper on her skin.

"How far can ye suspend yer disbelief? Ye've the eyes of one whose proper dwelling place is between the worlds, but do ye? Can ye believe in something which may make no sense to yer logical mind? That may go against all that ye've been taught for much of yer life?"

The woman's green eyes had held her as though she was pinned to a board, her gaze searching in the dark corners of her soul. There was no point in lying to her, not if she wanted her help.

"Yes, I can," she replied firmly. "Now, tell me what it is you have in mind?"

AWAY FROM THE DARKLY ENCHANTED FEEL OF THE COTTAGE and without Finola's sharp presence to shore her up, explaining all this to one's rather pragmatic husband and asking him to take part in it was a task that required gathering all of one's courage into a tight ball and then just blurting it out—rather less eloquently than one had hoped.

"Have ye the drink taken?" Casey asked calmly when she had finished, the look on his face one of amused bemusement.

"No," she replied indignantly, "I haven't taken a drop of anything in months, as you well know."

His next question was phrased in a deceptively mild manner. "Well, if yer not drunk, then perhaps ye've lost yer mind entirely?"

"I have *not* lost my mind," she said firmly, trying and failing to judge whether this was going better than she had foreseen, or worse.

"Really? D'ye have the faintest notion of how fockin' mad what ye've just suggested sounds? An' when I say that, I don't mean yer average garden variety mad neither. No, this is lock-ye-up-an'-throw-away-the-friggin'-key madness."

"Well, yes," she said, with some asperity, "I do know how it sounds, but it's the only thing I can think of to find out if my dreams are really telling me something or not. And the thing is—well, the thing is, I need you to come with me."

Casey's eyebrows, already raised, shot up into his hairline. "Might I ask why *I* now need to be involved in this insanity?"

"Because I've need of your hands on my skin," she said, meeting his eyes despite the ice water gathering with force in her stomach. Casey's eyes were the color of heavy smoke, a sure sign of a good fury building in him. "To bring me back. Finola says it's the only way to be certain—to be certain that I don't die in the trance."

"Well, I've the need to put my hands on yer skin, but it won't be in a way you fancy, let me tell ye, woman," Casey said, and she swore she could see small puffs of steam emerge with each word.

"I'm goin' out for a wee walk. I need to think." She could hear him grumbling under his breath about 'fockin' mad women who would never leave a man in peace'.

He was gone long enough that she had time to bank the fires, feed Conor one last time and put him down, then have a warm bath and put herself to bed. Once there though, sleep proved entirely elusive. She tossed and turned, tried to read, but couldn't focus on the words and finally lay on her back staring at the ceiling, listening to the rain start on the roof. She tried counting sheep, but gave it up once the sheep started to turn and glare at her, with a suspiciously familiar dark-eyed gaze.

She was about to get up and go downstairs to add another few rows to the sweater she was knitting for Conor when she heard Casey come in. Feeling a surge of cowardice, she remained in the bed, pulling the quilt up to her nose.

Casey came directly upstairs and into the bedroom. She chanced peering at him over the top of the blankets. He was wet with rain and still looked hot enough under the collar to ignite small fires but the lines about his mouth told her he had come to a decision.

"Ye needn't hide under the blankets like a wee dormouse, woman, as much as I'd like to stick ye over my knee an' give ye a good tannin' at times, I've never done so, an' I don't intend to start now. Though I'll tell ye, it was a near thing tonight."

She pushed the quilts back and sat up. "Well?"

"Well, what?" His voice was muffled, as he pulled his sweater off over his head.

"Will you do it?"

He drew in a deep breath and sat down on the side of the bed. He gave her a hard look that made her squirm and wish that she had stayed under the quilts.

"Did it ever occur to you two meddlin' women that he might not *want* to be found?"

"But why..." she trailed off at the look on his face.

"Why—why because the man can't fockin' have ye, woman, that's why. An' frankly if that shoe was on my own foot—an' I've thought it was goin' to be a time or two—I'd leave too. I wouldn't want to see ye, if I couldn't have ye. The bloody man told me it was him or me before he left."

"What?" she said and Casey blinked as though it had only now occurred to him what he'd said.

"Aye," Casey replied, tone a trifle grim with the memory. "He staked his claim to ye in fairly clear terms. But the truth is, Pamela, I owe him."

"You owe him?" she asked, feeling that she sometimes did not understand either Jamie or Casey very well at all.

"Aye, I owe him, much as it galls me even to say it. He was more than fair—he walked away when ye were vulnerable an' he could have pressed that to his advantage. He didn't have to do that, an' I can only imagine how much it cost him. So," he breathed out heavily, "if ye honestly feel he's in danger, if ye think these dreams of yers are tryin' to tell ye that he needs help, then I suppose we have to do whatever we can to help the man. So yes, I'll come to the witch's wee cottage with ye, an' I'll lay my hands on ye if that's what ye need from me. But," he glared down at her, eyes lit with black flame, "I think it's fockin' mad what the two of ye are doin' an' I swear, woman, if anything happens to ye..." he shook his head as words failed him.

She drew him down to her, cradling his head to her breast. "Nothing will happen to me as long as you're there with me. Finola said you are my anchor and I know it for truth."

He moved his face up toward her own, his eyes no longer smoky with anger but dark with feeling.

"I need yer hands on me too, Jewel, now an' always—an' if..."

"Shh," she touched her mouth to his own, silencing his fear with the warmth of her touch, the security that her own body provided his, a connection to life itself and a reassurance that this would always exist between them. For it always had, this heat and light and fire, a sustenance that fed them and bound them together each time until the web was so tight she often felt she didn't breathe fully until Casey came home at night.

She settled herself under him opening to him and he buried his face in her neck, whiskers rasping like stiffened velvet, causing her to gasp and arch up against him. He sighed softly, and in the language of his skin and her own, she knew that though he had agreed, he was afraid of the deal he had struck.

Chapter Forty-six

March 1974

All the Colors of the Rainbow...

To say the drive to Finola's cottage was fraught with a white silence would be to vastly understate the tense and rather grim mood that surrounded both Pamela and Casey. They had discussed themselves blue about the probability of this 'focking plunge down the rabbit-hole', as Casey was calling it, amounting to anything that could be quantified on the scale of hard, cold reality.

His wife, during one of these conversations, had given him the delicate arch of one sooty eyebrow and said, "What is reality though? In the time of the Greeks, they only saw a few colors, rainbows were tri-colored. Did that mean that all the colors we can perceive now didn't exist? Or that we merely were not equipped to see them yet? And that there aren't dozens more colors that we can't see now, but will someday?"

Casey suspected that the foray into a discussion of the Greeks and their color blindness was merely a diversionary tactic and refused to be thus distracted. He had then been treated to an exegesis on inward evolution, and being tuned to the 'finer' vibrations of the universe. She wound this up with a tart, 'a man who had a ghost save his life ought to be less of an obstinate ox in his thinking.'

They had been touchy with each other for the next few days, though they had discussed the drugs that Finola would be using on Pamela—aconite and hemlock. Looking them up in one of Pamela's green-stained herbal primers had done little to soothe Casey's worries on that front.

"They induce a sort of delirium that will allow me to leave my body, so to speak," she had said calmly, whilst spooning pureed apples and oatmeal into their son's mouth.

"Did the good Lord in all His wisdom not hand ye a dose of fear an' common sense before ye landed in the world, woman?" Casey had asked in exasperation.

She shrugged, making plane noises to encourage Conor to open his wee mouth for the last spoonful. "It's been done many times before. Finola is well learned in the ways of medicines and herbs. She won't let anything happen to me. Witches did it for centuries to induce the sense of flying."

Casey had thrown his hands up at that particular bit of logic and gone out to feed Paudeen and to work on the barn. Then he'd gone for a long walk and smoked far too many cigarettes for a man who had quit months before.

What it came down to was Jamie, and Pamela's complete belief that his life was hanging in the balance of all this occult mumbo-jumbo, and that was where, Casey admitted ruefully, his wife had him over the turnstile. He owed the man, for Jamie had given him back his life in a few angry and ultimately clarifying moments.

All of this had brought them here, on this March night, to the far reaches of the Kirkpatrick land. They had to walk the last couple of miles, after leaving the car parked at the cypress gate. There was no road into the cottage, and indeed Casey wondered if they were going to be able to find it at all in the dank twilight.

"Perhaps ye have to be drugged ahead of time to actually find the place," Casey said, shivering and clutching Pamela's hand tighter in his own. She squeezed back and after contemplating the fork in the narrow pathway that extended ahead of them, chose the left-hand option.

They had to walk single file after that, the trees clustered tightly around them in their spare spring garb. Oak trees, dense with tightly closed buds, hissed in the night. The air was chill with mist, and the sounds of the city did not penetrate here. It might have been another world entirely, far removed from the small battered streets of the city below. Though he was well used to the country and as comfortable as any man amongst the fields, trees, and hedgerows, Casey found that Jamie's land unsettled him. It was almost as if it belonged to an entirely different sphere, an enchanted fairy hill where one could disappear and re-emerge several years later, confused and confounded by the changes of the world around.

The path they trod continued to narrow until Casey had the sense that the trees limbs were trying to ensnare them. Certainly he had enough twigs in his hair to testify to it.

They might have missed the cottage if it weren't for the flickering light that shone from its windows. It was low and built partly into a small hillside, so that it seemed an organic outgrowth of the bracken and the trees and stones that surrounded it.

A small puff of wind, chill and thick with the scent of decaying plant matter, blew into their faces.

"Is that a whiff of brimstone?" Casey asked, only half in jest.

"It's dill," Pamela said in the matter of fact tone that was starting to annoy the hell out of Casey.

"Are ye not a wee bit frightened by the thought of committin' what amounts to black magic?"

"It's not black unless you use it to harm others," she said, raising her hand to knock on the door. It swung open before her knuckles could make contact.

"Good, I see ye've managed to convince yer man to help," said the small figure in the doorway.

Pamela went in without hesitation and Casey wondered just how well acquainted she and Jamie's grandmother had become. He had a feeling that Jamie wouldn't be any more impressed than he himself was by this friendship.

The lintel was old and low, the cottage must date back to at least the sixteen hundreds, though it was obvious to him it had been modified in the last decade or so. Still, the original bones were in evidence enough that his builder's eye could date it to within a few decades. He ducked in behind Pamela, closing the door against the spooky atmosphere of the night.

He eyed the woman directly, a challenge in his stare that clearly stated he would brook no harm coming to his wife and that he was here to prevent such a thing from happening, the woman's grandson be damned.

She eyed him just as directly in return. Yes, she looked a woman fully capable of both the knowledge and implementation of dark arts. The cottage, lit only by the fire, was warm and seemed far too snug against the chill night to be the stage for this insane act to which they were all committed. The kitchen was the center of the home, with the ancient hearth against the south wall. Near the fire was a bed—undoubtedly the scene of the sacrifice, he thought.

"Come and sit," Finola said, and Casey realized he'd forgotten his manners in the face of coming events.

He put his hand out to shake the woman's own, but she took it and held it between both of hers rather than shaking it. Casey felt an odd vibration where her skin met his—a heat as though energy were crossing from her to him and then looping back again. She merely continued to hold on, her fine fingertips searching the web of lines that crisscrossed his palms.

She tilted her head to the side and nodded. "Interesting."

Casey cocked a brow. "What's interestin'?"

"The lines of yer hand. They're a wee bit odd. I've only ever run across one other set like yer own. But never mind, we're not here to discuss yer future." She let go of his hand suddenly and turned to Pamela.

"Ye'll need to drink the tea right off, and then we'll get the herbs on ye." She handed Pamela a steaming mug, which she drank down quickly, not even flinching at the heat.

"Will it hinder things," Casey asked, seating himself on a low stool by the fire, "if I don't particularly believe in all this..." he made a gesture with his hands to indicate that he didn't have words to describe the situation in which he found himself.

"Ye don't have to believe. Ye merely need to be here. Ye'll hear a great deal about this sort of thing in scientific studies, where they try to put it under a microscope in a lab, but it's been practiced for thousands of years. Some people are more open to it than others, an' some have a natural talent for it. Yer wife falls into both those categories."

"An' how can ye know that?" Casey asked, a suspicion growing in him.

"She's done well on the last two tries, and I trust it'll be even easier with you here this time."

"The last *two* tries?" Casey gave Pamela a look that said volumes in both content and context.

Pamela merely shrugged and pulled her sweater off over her head, and then proceeded, to Casey's immense consternation, to unbutton her blouse.

"What the hell are ye after doin', woman?" he asked, standing and blocking any view of her with his own body.

"She has to be naked for this," Jamie's grandmother said calmly. "The ointment needs to be rubbed on bare skin."

Casey, quelling a desire to pinch himself, asked, "An' what am I meant to be doing?"

"Nothing just yet, other than calmin' yer nerves. Yer purpose here is to keep her safe, an' to bring her back should ye sense something that ought not to be there in the psychic landscape."

"Aye, an' how am I to know what should be there an' what shouldn't?"

"Trust me," Finola said, "ye'll know if somethin' is wrong. It'll present as a dark presence an' there's no mistakin' the feel of such a thing."

Despite himself, Casey felt a chill snake down his backbone.

"Now, do ye know what I mean by a dark presence?" Finola asked, pouring the same steaming concoction she had given Pamela into a mug for him.

"No, I'm afraid I've left my 'Field Guide to Demons and Malevolent Fairies,' at home," Casey said sarcastically.

"Yer a wee bit skeptical for a man who's seen a ghost or two in his own time," she retorted dryly.

Casey cast a sharp glance at Pamela, but she shook her head. Which begged the question of how this woman knew he'd any familiarity with ghosts.

"Drink yer tea," Finola said, handing him a red pottery mug that had stars and moons etched into its round-bellied frame.

"What's in it?" Casey asked, sniffing suspiciously.

"Eye of newt, wing of bat. What else?" she said, and Casey smiled despite himself.

He sipped it cautiously, but tasted only the green of fresh herbs with a hint of exoticism lent by a bit of cinnamon.

"Why does it have to be Pamela? Why can't I do it?" he asked, though he feared he knew the answer well enough.

"Because he loves her, so her hold on him is greater than anyone else's. It's a slim chance this will work, but she's the only one with odds in her favor."

He merely nodded, uncomfortably aware that his face had noticeably tightened at the mention of Jamie's love for Pamela. The fact that it was the bald truth did little to alleviate the anger that roiled low in his belly over the idea of that love.

He took another sip of the tea, tasting something dark and earthy now below the herbs and the cinnamon. He wouldn't put it past the woman to drug the both of them witless. Ah well, in for a penny in for a focking pound, he thought, and took a large swallow.

Casey turned his attention to his wife, watching her in the low firelight, and was struck by how even now, when fear gripped his innards as hard as a clenched fist, she took the breath from him with her beauty. To see her stand there limned in fire, with the old woman rubbing the ointment in broad strokes across the orchid white skin, her hair held up by her own hands, a curving shadow under each full breast... he shifted uncomfortably on the stool, but found he could not look away. Even after five years of marriage and countless nights spent in heat, in abandonment, in love he still was entranced by her and could understand why the man they were here to summon had never been able to let this woman go, and so had left instead.

"Don't turn yer thoughts from it, it's why yer here, man—the hold your body has on hers. It's love, but it's the physical aspect too. Yer bound to her by a million threads, but this one is one of the strongest. 'Tis at the center of the web and binds the two of you fast when other things have failed. Ye know it well enough. Ye've used it on her more than the once and she, in her own turn, has used it on you."

Casey looked up, chagrin written as clearly as the shape of flames on his face. "That transparent, am I?"

He saw his wife and the old woman exchange a glance of female knowing as old as the hills. Women, they always bloody knew where they had you, and most times it was in a position of distinct disadvantage.

Pamela bent down and kissed his forehead, leaving the acrid scent of herbs in her wake as she got into the bed. She settled on her back, the delicate rose-hue of her skin in sharp contrast with the dark blanket that now covered her from her shoulders down.

Casey could feel the misgivings begin to build again. What the hell sort of dark forces might they be playing with here? He could be a starkly pragmatic man, but in matters such as this, where one was jumping into the murky world of spirits and astral travel... well, he, like any true Irishman, had his doubts about the wisdom of such a venture. Might they not stir up something they could not control, something angry and dark and—he wrenched his thoughts away from that particular direction, training his attention on his wife once again.

She writhed slightly, the fire glistening along the curve of shoulder and neck, and moaned softly. Casey knew that particular sound all too well, and felt a hot surge of blood rise in him. But for whom was her body rising like that?

"Don't take it personal. It's the drugs. Ye need to get in the bed with her." The old woman raised an eyebrow at him. "Ye'll need to take yer own clothing off as well."

It was Casey's turn to raise an eyebrow.

"Ye need to be skin to skin with her. It means a bit of the drugs will seep into yer own system, but I suspect yer not as susceptible to them as she is, so it's not a danger.

He cleared his throat and the old woman gave him a sardonic green eye, as if to say 'I've seen plenty of naked men in my life, laddie,' but she turned and he quickly shed his clothes, shivering despite the heat of the fire.

He slid into the bed, glancing over his shoulder to be certain the old woman was still turned away.

Pamela's body was like fire against his own, pungent with the herbs, slippery with the ointment. He couldn't be near her this way and not get hard, not have the blood in his body rush toward her, seeking entry.

She turned in his arms, restless, eyes open, pupils dilated until her eyes were almost black.

She touched his face delicately, and looked at him as a blind woman might—through him rather than at him—and said in a soft voice, "Jamie?" For one mad moment, he thought the man was behind him.

"Relax, close yer eyes an' empty yer mind as well as ye can," said the old woman, her voice much softer than its normal tone, almost hypnotic in its rhythm.

She began to hum, something very old that stirred at the base of Casey's spine, but which was oddly soothing at the same time. He closed his eyes as bid, and relaxed into the warmth of his wife's body.

The cottage around him seemed to slide away, though his mind sought to maintain the root of it, to ground some bit of himself in the here and now—the feel of the bed beneath him, the warmth of the fire against his back in contrast to the sudden and terrible cold of his wife's body. But all he could see was a heavy grey mist that threatened to swallow him whole, to take his wife from the security of his arms. She felt less substantial already, as though she were becoming part of that mist.

He peered through the fog, willing it to clear from his eyes, and suddenly there in the dark was a cold pair of green eyes, cutting as a shard of ice, staring back at him. Not his wife's eyes, but a gaze with which he was all too familiar. He had no sense anymore of what might be real and what not and so it seemed only natural to reach out toward the hand that lay upon the blanket, long fingered and shaded a delicate blue.

He took the hand, freezing and stiff, into his own and did not know if he held Pamela's hand or Jamie's. It looked like Jamie's and yet how could it be? Jamie was thousands of miles away and there was an aura of being neither there nor here, but rather suspended in some twilit space that had no connection to life or the world with which he was familiar.

The hand clutched his, and he knew with certainty it was not his wife he touched. He jerked back, though the feeling of the hand clasping his was fading already. But he knew, for a second, he had felt the other man, the cold of him, the longing that bound the three of them in this eternal triangle. He had felt it too, the love that his wife and Jamie shared between them, and found himself a part of it, enmeshed in threads too sticky to ever disentangle. And he knew that the old woman was right, only Pamela could find Jamie, only Pamela could reach him, when he was beyond the reach of all else.

THE WHITE TIGER HAD BEEN STALKING HIM FOR DAYS. Jamie knew if he did not find shelter soon, it was going to stop sliding in and out of the blue shadows of the forest and claim him for its own.

He was exhausted and had been walking for so long that he'd lost any sense of time other than what was given him by the position of the sun and the stars. He did not know what day of the week it was, nor even the month. It was only winter, endless, white and cruel winter. Even the sounds had their own season, all the noise about him in shades of white and silver: the crunch of his own footsteps, the howl of the wind as it slapped his face relentlessly, the soft slither of the tiger always just far enough behind to scent his blood, caged within the fragile skin of a human being. He was slowing badly. It was only a matter of time. The night before... or had it been morning... he had found himself paralyzed and fascinated by bolts of ruby light glistening in the snow until he realized it was blood that patterned the white with jewel-like pinwheels. He had no comprehension of how long he stood there, but only knew the light was much dimmer than when he had stopped. And now the tiger was getting close enough that Jamie could smell its hunger and feel the echo of its pulse in his own veins, its footfall with each step of his own, each exhalation of its lungs with the crystallized outpouring of his breath, the yearning in its very cells for the repletion of another's blood.

He could not remember the last time he had eaten, and though the hunger cramps had left him some days ago, he knew this to be a bad sign. He was sure it was lack of food that was making him see the odd streaks of color that flashed in front of his eyes now and again. The only thing he had drunk was handfuls of snow. Nor did he know the last time he had seen another human being. Was it weeks ago, a month? Had it been in the camp, and for that matter, he didn't have a recollection of leaving the camp. Had he been released? Had he escaped? These holes in his memory were very troubling but he turned away the thoughts as too tiresome.

He staggered on for some time more, but the landscape seemed to barely change and he wondered if he was simply moving in ever-increasing circles. As the sun started its rapid fall toward night, he simply could not put one foot in front of another anymore and fell to his knees in the snow, his blood seemingly replaced by lead. He longed with a violence that was drowning out his survival instinct, to lie down in the snow and go to sleep.

He fell down into the snow and barely found the strength to roll over on his back and prevent suffocation. Just a minute, or maybe two, and then he'd get up and keep moving. He lay there with eyes open and watched the skein of day unravel into the full of night. First came flowing grey-blue to tint the trees and then ribbons of lavender, shot through with reds and purples until finally the ink of night absorbed all colors and the stars came out blazing through the cold air, one by one. It seemed an entirely separate world from the pain and hardship of the one below. Against that indigo background he could see trails and roads built upon the air, bridges by which to ascend the night and walk off into universes both terrible and beautiful. There were delicate oceans of frost, breathed out, breathed in, on which flew translucent ships, with sails rimed by the fine-grained salt of stars. How he longed for the ease of such a universe, to set sail in a celestial sea. He could feel his eyes closing, and the sweet lethargy of sleep wrapping its arms about him.

It was the tiger's roar that woke him. Jamie started, heart pounding, scrabbling to his feet, snow falling down his collar and into his boots. Dear God he was so cold, aching in every joint and cell. Dazed with sleep, he cast around, not knowing in which direction to move. The tiger had sounded very close. He couldn't see anything now, adrenaline clouded his vision, blurred the periphery of sight, his ragged breathing fogging the air with crystals. Then directly to the west a shape on the horizon caught his eye, a house, perhaps fifty yards away. He shook his head, confused, certain it hadn't been there when he had fallen down. It was a structure certainly, but still looked like a thing of dreams or wishful thinking, built as though it had sprung from the pages of a Russian fairytale, onion domes capping low towers, with great hoods of snow adorning them, and steps leading up to a broad, railed porch that was almost buried in ice. But in the midst of all this, he saw a glint of gold and knew it was a latch. Please God let it be unlocked. He stumbled toward it, panic giving his legs strength to move.

Somehow he managed to run, and knew if the tiger was going to strike, now was the time it would happen. His back was braced for attack even as he made the stairs, scrabbling up them, half crawling through the masses of snow and ice. He was certain he felt the tiger's breath hot on his neck, could taste the blood-craving upon its tongue, but he knew to look around would be fatal. He grasped the door latch and heaved himself up. The door gave all at once and he fell into the entry, kicking the door shut behind him as he went down.

He lay there for a moment, half worried the big cat had somehow leaped in behind him. But there was only silence, not even a snuffling or scratching outside the door. He sat up slowly, the world spinning around him. He braced his back against the door and looked around, which was, other than a hint of drifts and an echo of shored ice, an exercise in futility. For it was night and the light, even here in this ice castle with its cupolas of snow and frescoes of sparkling frost, was of the blue variant, thick with shadow, and laced with deception.

He sat for a long time, fatigue so heavy that he knew he could not move, even if it meant to light a fire and save his own life. And so sleep, like the oldest of friends came to lay its cape of oblivion gently down.

Jamie awoke to view the world through the finest of silver-linked spiderwebbing. At first, he wondered what sort of fantastical eight-legged beastie could have woven such a virtuosic netting and then realized it was threads of ice that had formed from his breath and floated down to settle upon each curve and line of his face. He sat up slowly, snow and ice raining off him in great glittering drifts. He looked around and gasped out loud.

It was as though he had awakened inside a Faberge egg, where the enamel was translucent enough to allow the heart of the jewels to stream through. In the ice was every color: the sea-blue of azure, the blood of rubies, the sand of topaz, the blush-rose of quartz, the delicate lavender hue of amethyst and the warm butter of pearls. Stairways of emerald, with railings that glittered like sugar, but that would, he knew, crumble at a breath. At the top of the stairs spread a deep and mysterious lapis lazuli that hinted at another world altogether in the upper story, but he dared not attempt the climb. The one floor was enough, for light such as this was infinite, could not be pinioned nor harnessed. Its very essence was that of eternity. It fell in vortices and lattices, swirled in coruscations of brilliance, shot in rays of spangled thistles.

He got to his feet, every muscle protesting, and walked slowly across the room to where a large Russian heater stood, delft tiles gleaming bluely through a thick coating of frost. There was a stack of birch next to it, though no kindling, and a small box of wooden matches. Jamie struck a match against the icy flint and was more grateful for that small violet and gold flame than he could remember being for anything in a very long time.

Despite his gratitude for the matches, the fire would not catch, the wood was frozen solid with a layer of ice. He pounded it against the floor to no avail, other than setting a shower of ice particles free to swirl around him. He needed to go outside to gather dry sticks, but when he scraped a hole in the frost of one window, he saw the tiger tracks clear as a water print upon silk. He looked from every window then and saw that the tracks encircled the entire structure. He was trapped like a rabbit inside a snare, one move toward the outside world and it would snap him straight through the bone.

He returned to the fire, knowing there was little else he could do. After another half hour of profound effort, he managed a small flame on the cold wood. The flame hissed and spit like an agitated rattlesnake, but let out a tiny bit of warmth. He blew on it gently, afraid of eclipsing it but more worried that it would fizzle out on its own if it didn't build up some strength. Once it seemed like it would hold, he stood, stamping his feet to keep the blood flowing, sluggish as that process might be. The frost had begun to melt on the window nearest the stove, water running in rivulets through the remaining ice. It was through this small opening on the world that he spotted movement outside, a speck against the unending fields of white.

He peered until his eyes felt like they might freeze in place, widening the hole in the ice so he could see more clearly. The figure continued to advance, though the drifts of snow that blew across the landscape obscured his view of the person every few seconds.

He had gone so long without seeing another human being that he thought, were the person an Urdu-speaking flame-eater recently escaped from the Armenian circus, he would fall on him with tears of gratitude, merely for the sight of another human face.

But what if it was someone hostile? He dismissed the thought—how on earth would someone find him out here anyway? It had to be a hunter, of one of the nomadic tribes who wandered the frozen vastness of Russia no matter the season. The figure advanced close enough that he could see by both movement and form that it was a woman.

A woman? What in the name of all that was good and holy was a woman doing out here in the midst of nowhere? Now there was nothing for it but to risk that the tiger was still lurking about and go out and warn her.

He sighed, looked at the fire with regretful longing, and flung the door open. The wind slapped him in the face as if to tell him he was a complete fool to venture out again, which he thought, wrapping his ragged coat more securely around him, he bloody well was. He slid down the ice and snow that coated the stairs and bounded to his feet at the bottom, eyes watering from the cold, but still looking around for the tiger to come, sleek and boundless, from the side of the house.

The woman was cursing, a streak of words so blue that there was an indigo cloud all around her. More startling than the words though, was the language in which they were uttered, for they were English. Jamie narrowed his eyes against the stinging cold, trying to make out her features, but her head was down as she navigated drifts of snow, almost up to her hips. He knew that voice though, knew it as he knew all the geography of his soul. It was impossible that she should be here, utterly impossible... and then the woman looked up and he thought perhaps he was dead, or that he had crossed entirely into another dimension.

It simply wasn't possible and yet there was only one pair of starred green eyes like those, only one face that he held in his memory in such finely drawn detail. He moved across the snow toward her, feeling oddly weightless as though he were merely floating along the top without effort, but his feet felt a terrible distance away from his head, now that he thought about it.

And then she was there, wrapped in furs, the white of them lying against her skin like torn silk on orchids. She leaned forward and kissed his cheek, as though she'd only seen him a week before. The smell of strawberries flooded his senses and something new, a note he did not recognize in the melody of her scent.

"Are you going to invite me in, Jamie? It's bloody cold out here."

"I—I—"

"Dream or not, Jamie, certain rules still apply."

Jamie was about to retort that he hadn't known her to ever wait upon an invitation before charging in where angels feared to tread, but remembered the tiger and hustled her toward the house.

She pulled the hood back, her hair tumbling out in wild disarray. Her cheeks were a deep rose with the cold and her eyes spilled light that warmed far more than did the fire. She laid down a bundle of sticks and opened the door on the stove to shove several inside. The fire grasped them immediately, grateful for the sustenance.

"Really, Jamie, this fire wouldn't warm a newt," she said, shaking her head in disgust.

Jamie, nonplussed now that the immediate danger of tiger attack was over, merely stood and watched her add a few sticks of dry pine from her pack until the fire was roaring in a life-saving blaze.

Again from her pack, she unrolled a bundle of furs, thick and rich and black as night—sable if he knew his furs and he did. What he didn't know was why she was here or how she had managed to find him when even he had no idea where he was.

"I kept dreaming you were in danger," she said, "so I went to see your grandmother to find out what we could do about it."

"My grandmother? Well, it all makes sense now," Jamie said with no small annoyance.

"Does it?" she asked.

"Well, no," Jamie admitted. "It's just that anytime my grandmother gets involved, things tend to get confusing and complicated to a truly impressive degree. So the fact that she's connected with you showing up here without warning, when even I don't know where 'here' is, does make things a bit clearer. Though the fact that my grandmother is in the mix does beg the question of—"

Pamela cut him off from that avenue of inquiry, by handing him a tiny bottle, saying, "Drink this."

He took it, surprised at the weight of it. It was silver, though dark with tarnish, strange words inscribed on its sides. But because it was Pamela, he simply unstopped the bottle and drank down what it contained. It was thick and stung his mouth like nettles, but it tasted oddly ambrosial as well. Heat flooded his body along the path of the drink.

"Now get undressed and get into the furs."

Jamie was tempted to look around to see if there was a tiny door with the address 'W. RABBIT' engraved upon a brass plate, but squelched the thought under the stern look Pamela was giving him. And though he had no memory of shedding his clothes, he soon found himself under the furs, disturbingly bare.

"Where is Casey?" he asked, thinking it would have been wise to ask the question before getting naked.

"Oh, he's here too, just a bit behind me is all." She waved airily and producing another flask—this one copper—she drank its contents.

"Would you mind terribly," he asked, buried in a sable quilt that reached his chin, "pouring a bit of hot tea on my nose?"

"Jamie," she sighed, "please quit messing about. This isn't a tea party and you are most certainly not a dormouse, by any stretch of ludicrous imagining."

She was speaking in an odd mixture of Gaelic, Russian and her own native English. Jamie wondered if the drink had been absinthe or something akin to it for he seemed to be lost in dreams that made only a dream world sense. There was no flavor of either wormwood or gall on his tongue, however, only that strangely warm and stinging taste that lingered all the way down his throat.

Feeling giddy or drunk or high or poisoned, or possibly all of the above, he found himself declaiming in verse—

"In my youth, said the fool, though I was learned and fair
I was considered both a rogue and a wit,
My reputation was sullied and bruised as a pear
Though 'tis true that I liked to be bit."

Pamela sighed as though taxed by a small, badly-behaved boy. "Alright, have it your way, but I refuse to wear a hat or drink from a dirty teacup and I insist on fresh butter for my bread."

And then, clad still in her furs, she said,

"You are fair, said the maid, as I've mentioned before
But I find you uncommonly glib
And if you give tongue to rhyme anymore
I shall give you a dig in the rib."

The fur slid from her shoulders and dropped to the floor. Underneath she was completely naked. Jamie found himself wordless with surprise. Dear God, but he had forgotten how beautiful she was. She was the poem he had never written, as perfect as unspoken thoughts traced upon an orchid.

"Poets make the most conceited lovers," she said. "For instance right now you're comparing my skin to orchids, but are not sure how to tie that in with the ink of blood that runs in traceries of a thousand rivers beneath my skin. Aren't you?"

"Are you reading my mind?" he asked, thinking she looked rather like a stern and wildly seductive nun at present.

"Maybe, I'm not sure. You're a bit transparent right now. It could be that **you** *are reading* **my** *mind."*

"Now you're being contrary," he said, still trying to see around her, wondering what in hell 'a bit behind me,' meant concerning her husband's presence.

"He's not terribly happy about me being here, but he came with me, so it's alright," she said in a manner Jamie found incredibly blithe for a woman wearing no more than her socks. "Besides, this is a simple thermal exchange from one body to another, the best way to warm you up."

The heat from the stove was intoxicating. He was drunk with warmth and when she slid into the furs next to him, he gasped aloud at the fire of her skin. She shimmered with heat from head to toe and Jamie moved toward it as life will toward the sun that sustains it.

"Let me warm you," she said softly, turning under him with the ease of water.

"But—I—"

"Jamie, it's simple. I'm not really here."

"I know," he said softly, "because I've dreamed this too many times. Still, I can feel you and smell you. I don't understand—"

"Neither do I, Jamie, but I don't think it matters."

"But—"

"Shh," she put a finger to his lips to still his protest, and the white scent of water lilies rose up, a pale-tinted cloud to fill his senses. She was all velvet fire against him and his body could not help but respond.

She touched his face and said his name softly, so softly that he thought he might weep for the pain of hearing it so after all these months.

He felt himself shaking and could not stop. She merely held him tighter, her skin melding into his own, its heat thawing the frost at his core.

Now he could see the two of them from above, as though he were hovering over his body from somewhere near the ceiling. Was he dreaming, or was he dead?

And then he was lost in her heat, her scent and the feel of her beneath him, taking him down into a haze where he couldn't define direction or thought, where nothing mattered but the two of them, stars caught fast in the crimson fire of the night. Her skin against his own, her scent mingling with his, the night silk of her hair in his hands and raining along his body.

Her eyes were a spring river into which he fell, the water of her dividing at his entry and then surrounding him in heat and life. She was the only solid point in an amorphous universe... the finding of his own forgetting, the substance that filled his missing parts.

Thought and time were lost to another world, one that did not exist for them. The warmth of the fire was still there, but he felt as though she were drawing him far, far away from this palace of ice, over seas and into a far country of summer wine and warmth.

"Don't give up, Jamie, because you are needed and you are loved." She took

his face in her hands and kissed his forehead gently and he looked down, down into her eyes and felt as though he were a boat long lost at sea and now in sight of a harbor, where humanity might be rediscovered. The world was terribly still, and he wished...oh, how he wished to stop it here before she began to dissipate in his hands like smoke and stardust. No sooner did he think the thought then it became reality and he couldn't feel her anymore. And the warmth, so recently found, began to drain from him like sand from an hourglass. He was so tired, so very, very tired...

Without warning, a big hand grabbed his and a jolt of heat ripped through him like lightning. A pair of dark eyes met his own and a decidedly rough and masculine voice said, "Don't die. D'ye hear me, you bastard? Do NOT die!"

Jamie began to fall, the walls of the ice castle crumbling around him into grey, formless mist. He tried to grab for purchase, but there appeared to be no walls, no solidity in this place that Casey's shout had banished him to. Then without warning, he hit and hit hard, as though a wave had spewed him onto a rocky shore. Above him was a Russian voice—a female, agitated. Each eyelid felt weighted with lead and he couldn't find the strength to wiggle a finger.

An inch at a time, his spirit and his body rejoined and he became aware of his surroundings. The smell of antiseptic, the strange hissing silence that always seemed to reign at night in infirmaries and the scratchy wool of the blankets that covered him—no mistaking that for sable. The camp. Inside him something bowed its head in despair, for he had not escaped. It had been a dream after all.

He tried opening his eyes, but it was a Herculean task, and he was feeling anything but mythological at present.

"Don't try to move, Yasha, you're very weak—here." Around him the blanket was loosened slightly, the pillow under his head fluffed.

It was too quiet and he wondered where the soft shoe of the aide was, the occasional clatter of instruments or bottles.

"Where?" he croaked, and though he felt he was shouting, it emerged only as a reedy whisper.

"We're in the infirmary," said the woman, confirming his suspicions. "You've been in and out of consciousness ever since Gregor found you. You had a terrible fever from where you were stabbed. Don't you remember anything?"

He shook his head, a mistake as it turned out, because a pain like lightning ripped through him. A cool hand on his forehead steadied him.

"Violet?"

"Yes, it's me."

"I... but..."

Confusion was ribboning in and out of his synapses still, dark and sinuous, twisting the real from the perceived. With it came an odd sense of desolation as though he had lost something immeasurably precious, something that had never been intended for him but was no less yearned for despite the fact. Yet he could still feel traces of heat on his body, like lines of passion written into his skin, yet it had not been real. Or had it?

Violet was slowly swimming into his line of sight, copper hair smooth as a shell against the curve of her face, the grey eyes dark with worry. Her hand still rested on his forehead.

"We thought you were going to die. You scared the hell out of Shura."

He took her hand, and the scent of water lilies hit him as hard as a slap to the face.

"You should rest," she said quietly, and he knew it was a delicate avoidance of the look she had just seen on his face.

He did not protest, for he was indeed very tired. Before Morpheus drew him down to that deep place of healing, Jamie felt once again the bruised bones of his hands. And for a moment he brought those same hands to his face and smelled the scent of strawberries and love.

And then he slept, no more to dream.

Chapter Forty-seven

March 1974

Katya

H E CAME BACK TO AN AWARENESS OF HIS WORLD SLOWLY, the first truly conscious moment arriving in the wee hours when the dark was so profound he could not at first see anything. He sat up, head spinning, but needing some form of movement in the suffocating, visceral darkness, like a blanket laid over his face that he could not push away.

In the far corner a frail light glowed, a candle's worth, curling into a small portion of the night, and lighting it as valiantly as such a tiny light could. He could see a hand at the edge of that glowing pool, a hand crabbed and broken, bent around the handle of a smoking kettle. He was grateful that it was Nikolai who was present when he awoke.

The old man shuffled over to him, his slow gait belying the powerful presence that moved with him everywhere.

"You are awake, Yasha Yakovich," Nikolai said and put one gnarled hand to Jamie's brow. "You are much cooler. This is good. For a while we are worried that your brain is cooking."

Cooked was how his brain felt, Jamie thought. But all things considered, it was preferable to dead which, he was aware, had been the only other alternative. The area between what was real and what was not still seemed like a strange no-man's land. And he wasn't certain which side of it he was on yet.

"I am making you tea," Nikolai said, before sitting heavily on the stool next to Jamie's bed. He smelled comfortingly of pinesap and tobacco and the sweet cut of fresh snow.

"How long have I been asleep?" Jamie asked.

"For more than a week. Today was the tenth day of your great slumber." Nikolai chuckled and then coughed, his lungs crackling like frosted leaves underfoot. Jamie winced. Nikolai's lungs were getting worse by the day.

He could smell the tea as Nikolai poured boiling water over the leaves. Every sense seemed heightened, as if he could smell the Indian hills where the tea had been grown and taste the soil where its roots had taken hold. The heat of it was almost more than his mouth, still sensitive from the fever, could bear.

He was horribly weak and tired and drifted off shortly after drinking half the tea. When next he woke it was late afternoon and dark again, but not as dark as it had been the previous night. Shura was there when he woke, having just come in from the dining hall, a soft halo of melting snow on his thick black hair and shoulders.

"I'm being allowed a long recovery time," Jamie observed in an effort to avoid the steaming cup of green sludge Shura presented him with a few minutes later. Shura, however, was having none of it and forced it on him.

"All has changed on the outside while you have been dreaming, Yasha. We have a new camp commander. As far as such things go, he seems like a fair man, not insane like our previous boss."

"Why—when did this happen?" Jamie asked, sitting up in the narrow cot.

Shura smiled. "It seems, friend Yasha, you have angels on your side. When you are well, you will meet the new commander."

Twenty minutes later, Jamie had managed to choke down the vile concoction that Shura insisted would restore his strength much faster than if it was left to his weak non-Georgian constitution. Then he managed to convince Shura that if he didn't soon shave and wash, they would all wish he had expired. Shura set him up with a basin of hot water, soap and a razor in a screened off corner of the infirmary.

Jamie was horrified by the weakness in his limbs and how erratically his heart beat from the short walk across the infirmary floor. He managed an abbreviated shave and a barely adequate wash before succumbing to the bed once again. He fell back to sleep almost immediately.

He awoke in the wee hours to find Nikolai sitting vigil once more.

Nikolai had made him tea again, not as strong as the *chifr* that Gregor liked to drink, but not far removed from it either. The brew tasted as though it had been strained through a smoked fish before landing in his cup. It was, however, hot and bracing, so he drank it down.

Nikolai pulled the wooden stool that Shura used over to the side of the bed and sat his rangy frame down upon it. "I would speak to you, James."

"Of course," Jamie said, the use of his name in its Anglicized form seeming foreign to him now.

"We are thinking you will die, James, and I realize this makes me very sad. For very long time I have been detached. It was necessary not to care when people came and went, whether released from prison or put under the ground. I have lived a very long time, and so there have been many, many people I have known who are now gone. But I realize I care about you, and I find this strange. I ask myself why this one Irish boy? What is so special or different that you can't just shrug and cut same amount of wood tomorrow, whether he lives or dies? Why should he matter?" Nikolai sighed. "I still do not have answer to this question, James, but I think it does not matter so much why I care, just that I do."

Nikolai then came to the heart of what he wanted to say. "You are good with stories, and so I think to myself that maybe I need to tell this man my story so he can keep it inside him and carry it out of this place."

"Is there something in particular making you think that I'm more likely to leave this place than you are?" Jamie asked.

Nikolai arched a grizzled eyebrow at him. "You will outlive me if nothing else, Yasha Yavovich."

"That," said Jamie, "is rather debatable at present. However, I would be honored to hear your story, Nikolai Ivanovich."

Nikolai rummaged about in the pocket of his threadbare winter coat, emerging with a battered flask that contained, Jamie had no doubt, some of the rotgut vodka that was brewed inside the camp.

He unscrewed the cap, took a healthy slug, sighed and passed the flask to Jamie, who eyed it with trepidation. The vodka brewed in the camp wasn't subjected to any sort of alcohol limitation, so it wasn't impossible that it could blind a man. On the other hand, one did not refuse vodka from the hand of a Russian. It was considered bad manners of the worst sort.

He had to bite down on a gasp as the searing liquid tore straight down to his stomach and did away with its lining. He handed the flask back, knowing it was fruitless to hope it wouldn't be passed to him again. The only thing Russians liked better than their vodka was poisoning someone else with it.

There was a small silence as Nikolai stared down at the flask in his hands, as if seeking the correct place to begin his story. Stories, Jamie knew, were like that. They required the right words to begin, for if they were begun with the wrong words they would quickly go awry and wander down pathways they were not meant to.

"I have lived in camps such as this much of my life," Nikolai said. "But I was born in St. Petersburg. Those of us who lived there simply called it Piter, though you may know it as Leningrad. And once, once I was such a musician. I played the piano, or it played me—as a good instrument will."

Jamie could not help but flick a glance down at the man's twisted, broken hands.

Nikolai saw the look, brief as it had been. "They were not always so. Once they were rather beautiful, the hands of a musician, straight and long. Then they were broken during an interrogation."

Jamie looked at him enquiringly.

"I think that tale is not one that needs telling, and I am easily distracted these days, so allow me to return to my original story." He cleared his throat and took a breath, sending a crackle through his lungs. He hit his chest with a blunt fist as though that would clear it and continued.

"Leningrad is not what St. Petersburg once was. Stalin destroyed St. Petersburg's soul, the purges there were worse than almost anywhere else. Entire stratas of society were wiped out: fathers, mothers, children and sweethearts. It became a ghost town, with the memory of people I had once known seeming to walk at my side down the streets. We were so proud of our city. We were the new Paris, the Venice of the north, the re-birth of ancient Palmyra, an oasis of art and light and literature in a cold, harsh country. We were a reminder, I suppose, to Papa Joseph that he was no more than a peasant boy who had come to power through betraying and murdering his friends, and then through a reign of terror such as has never been known before.

"That last spring before the Siege the weather was awful. In fact it seemed that it would never turn. Then suddenly it did, right before the summer solstice, right before that whitest of white nights. We had a series of storms and then it was summer. The lime trees came out in green, the forsythia bloomed in violent golds and the roses began to spill from the balconies. The girls came out in their summer frocks, windows were opened to the streets and one could walk in the dusk and hear the strains of Scriabin or Mussogorsky drifting out into the summer night. With the night when no darkness would fall fast approaching, it seemed almost enchanted, as if there was hope. We had no idea what forces were at work in the world and how they would soon mobilize against us.

"I remember as if it were hours ago, rather than the many years it has been, strolling down the Nevsky Prospekt. It was the grandest avenue in the world, a piece of poetry with its stone and water, its granite and low skies, its light—oh, that cursed endless light. We Petersburgers were very vain about our city. We felt we were light years removed from Moscow and its backward ways. There was arrogance there, no doubt, but to us it was just the city we loved, the city that had birthed such brilliance into the world."

Nikolai paused, his crippled hands rolling the flask back and forth between them. The light of the fire caught it and sparked silver in the night.

"I would wish, though, to tell you of that first winter, for it was in many ways the most difficult of all the seasons of the Siege. You will understand," Nikolai said, passing the small flask back to Jamie, "that there is a certain madness that comes with hunger, that arrives like a specter on the doorstep of humanity, when death is always just around the corner, or breathing down one's collar. I was once a man of great civility, so such things were shocking to me, until finally there was no room left for shock in my body or mind."

Jamie nodded as Nikolai put the flask in his hands once again. He took another swallow of the oily vodka and barely noticed the fire that swept up his gullet in return. He didn't dare so much as flinch at this point, for he would do nothing that might halt the flow of words that fell from Nikolai's lips, like water thawed after decades of winter.

"That first winter was eternal. We were a city of silence and ice. We were a city of the dead and the dying. There were street cars frozen in the snow, everywhere, frozen in time, exactly where they'd been when the electricity failed. There was one tram on the Nevsky Prospekt that I would stop in each morning. I was so weak by that time that I had to break up my walks or risk collapse in the snow, and to collapse was to die. I was not alone on that tram. I had three friends: Masha, Boris and Natasha, or so I named them, for I had no idea who they really were. Corpses all three, frozen as they had sat, perhaps only to rest as I had, only they never got up again. I think Boris and Natasha were husband and wife. His mitten was still frozen around hers. They had clutched hands at the end. Masha had a book in his lap, Gogol's *Dead Souls*, which seemed ghoulishly appropriate. I took to reading him a page each day on my way through. It was a way to keep my own sanity. The entire winter passed in this fashion, and I came to look almost as corpse-like as they did.

"I knew they were dead but it didn't seem to matter. It was a form of companionship. And they did not complain, nor cry aloud with hunger pains and the terrible cawing of the ill. And then one day, Masha read aloud to me and he turned a page. I actually saw the skeletal bone of his fingers take the page by a corner and turn it over. I ran from the car in terror. When one is in a hallucinatory state, it is simply one's reality and so I truly believed that those corpses had come to life. I thought I could feel Masha's bony hands around my muffler, that he would pull me back to that tram car and I would be forever one of them, part of a gruesome quartet condemned to that iced purgatory."

Nikolai shook his head, the glow from the stove limning the mane of leonine hair in hammered silver. "I had gone a little mad at that point, but I missed them later, as though they had been more real to me than those who still shuffled the streets of the city. As though we were more ghosts than those skeletons on a train, but," Nikolai shrugged with dark Russian absolutism, "perhaps we were. For are the dead less dead merely for breathing and moving? I admit I envied them at times, for their pain was over, their bellies no longer clawing at them to find sustenance of any sort—even the most putrid kind."

"How did you survive it?" Jamie asked quietly, the heat of the stove, the thick plant smell from Shura's remedies and the order of the infirmary swept away in the vision of that icebound city.

"You get numb," Nikolai said bluntly. "You think that you've finally achieved the point where you can no longer feel anything, and it's a relief. After that first winter, I thought I had achieved that. Then someone killed my dog and ate him. He was all I had left of the world I had once lived in. He was the only being I loved anymore and it broke my heart, the heart I had thought frozen and beyond feeling, hurt as though someone had sliced it open and left me to bleed out." Nikolai shuddered. "Strelka had been the only warmth in my life, and then he ran off after a stringy cat and never returned, so I knew someone had eaten him. He had always returned to me before. I was his best friend too, you see. I stood there in the street calling and calling him for hours, my voice echoing off all those grand buildings, all those empty homes with the wind scouring my face and knew that I would never love anything or anyone again.

"I did not cry, for it is true what they say, that all Leningraders' tears were frozen that winter. I felt as though I were a river inside that had once flowed with humanity and joy and thought and anger, and now it was winter, the most terrible of Januarys in my heart and that river was never to know a spring melt again. My heart had been frozen from the time I lost my wife."

"Your wife?" Jamie could not keep the surprise from his tone, for Nikolai had seemed so ruthlessly alone, so self-contained within his worn exterior that he had not thought the man had once had a family.

"My Yekaterina."

Jamie saw at once that this was the true point of everything Nikolai wanted to tell him. He sensed that the man had not told anyone of his wife before. He understood such things only too well. He himself did not speak of Colleen or his sons, or rather, he had once, and then not again.

"How to tell you what she was... She was music, like hearing a wild gypsy fiddle in a dark wood, haunting and perfect and never truly the same twice. I met her at the university. I was rushing from one class to another and heard the most wondrously sad music coming from one of the rooms. Someone was playing the cello. I stopped and I swear the earth stopped with me, just to listen to her. I hesitated to enter. I did not want to interrupt such music and I was afraid, you see, that to have a soul to make such music, she was going to be ugly—uglier than Baba Yaga—why else such suffering, such music as could plead with the very stars to rain mercy?

"But she was a vision, so beautiful that she struck me dumb. Hair like moonlight on water, that blonde that is more silver than any sort of yellow and eyes so dark that I knew I would never find the bottom of them, even if I were to try for a lifetime. I did not know what to say, and she was blind and deaf to any world except the music. And so I sat at the piano, my heart swelling out of my chest, closed my eyes and started to play with her. I followed her through each glissando, each vibrato. She began to play faster and faster. I was determined not to let her elude my grasp. Somehow, I knew this was a challenge I must not fail and that it was far more than a mere sonata being played and fought for in that room. I was wet through my shirt by the time the music came down from the skies and we were suddenly just two people in a room together who did not know one another.

"She stood, this woman. So slight, it seemed impossible that she had such mastery over her bow, for was such a creature not made only for fairytales, where suitors would fight mythical bears and dreadful old witches merely to set eyes upon her face?

"To me, she said, 'Well, Nikolai Ivanovich, I wondered when you might get around to introducing yourself', as though she had been expecting me all along. Later, she told me she knew as soon as she saw me that I was meant to be significant in her life. And once she heard me play she knew she would marry me. I must have seemed a dolt at that moment, mouth hanging open like some country bumpkin."

The memory of his first meeting with his wife lit the old man's face with a glow that was painful to witness, yet Jamie felt profound gratitude that there had once been such joy in Nikolai's life.

"How to explain when someone knows you before words are even uttered, before more than a few glances are exchanged, when someone knows all that you are without explanation, and you feel it the minute you are in their presence?"

"Soul mates," Jamie said quietly, thinking of his own soul friend, who had never needed explanations, and had understood him from the time she was a young girl. Then he pushed the thought away, for she was not his to have, and thinking of her here when he might never see her again was the act of a masochist.

"Ah yes, soul mate, that longing for the other half of one's soul that humans spend their entire lives in search of but rarely find. I was fortunate there. Katya was the other half of my music, my thoughts, my soul. Before her my music had been good—many thought I had great talent. After Katya, it became something more, far richer and fuller. The notes seemed to take wing and the compositions flowed under my hands as I had only dared to dream they would.

"Some said it was too fast, a whirlwind courtship and that we would live to regret such haste. But I think we are wise at times in such things, and know when there is not time. We sense its limits may be fast approaching and that we must grab life with both hands while we still can. So we married that very month, quietly, only her family and what there was left of mine.

"That spring in Leningrad, the lilacs were so heady that their scent felt like honey in a man's mouth and the cherry blossoms rained down through the air. When the winds blew we were caught in a snowstorm of petals. It was perfect, despite the past, despite our tenuous grip on the future, it seemed the grandest, most beautiful place on earth. Love will do that. It makes you see only the good and not the flaws, even when they are glaringly obvious. Of course, the flaws were unavoidable and coming toward us at the speed of furies.

"There had been rumblings of war, that Hitler was determined to take Russia and crush Leningrad on his way to Moscow. But Stalin declared it wasn't so and no one seemed too alarmed at the prospect. And I—I was in blissful ignorance. I had a beautiful wife and soon we were expecting our first child. I didn't want to believe that heartache, pain and starvation and all the other horrible realities of war were already on their way. It was casting a terrible shadow over us all, but most of us could not see it. Some did of course, but as is always the case, we called them Doomsday prophets, crazy men, wishing ill fortune on us without proof.

"The prophets, of course, were right. The Nazi jackboot came down on us with the force of a hammer. In a moment, for it seemed little more, everything was gone—all the beauty and the passion... and the music, the music lasted longer than other things but I could no longer bear to hear it, and certainly not to play it." Nikolai shook his head.

"By late fall, all our lives had become about bread rations, about how many grams, what you were warranted according to your age and station in life. Bread became the measure of a man's worth. What is the use of cherry blossoms and the taste of lilac on your tongue when your entire life becomes about the size of your bread ration?"

"What happened to Yekaterina?" Jamie asked softly, for the night had closed in around them as Nikolai told his story, and the hush, along with the old man's words, had given their small space a sense of something sacred.

"She left just before the blockade. I wanted her gone from Leningrad and I promised to join her later. I sent her to her parents, thinking she would be safer with them. Of such small things are tragedies made. They came to take her father away while she was there, and so they took the entire household: father, mother, her younger brother Dmitri, and my Yekaterina and our unborn child. I was never able to find out what happened to them. For a long time I imagined they had escaped and that she made it out of this godforsaken land. Then one night I dreamed that she came to me and laid her hand on my chest. I could smell her scent, and feel the calluses on her fingers that her music had left behind. She bent down and kissed me, so soft, and I knew she was gone, that the dream was her goodbye to me. I only hope when..." he swallowed, the pain still thick and tangible after all these years, "when they took her, it was quick, that she didn't starve to death or die in childbirth."

"They?"

"Stalin's henchmen, Beria's thugs—take your pick. They were all the same. Corrupt and vile men who used every bit of their power to bleed the country and commit such atrocities as the world has rarely known. Katya's father had known Kirov and suspected that his killing was not the work of a random assassin, as Stalin wanted the world to believe. He kept quiet about his suspicions, knowing the eyes of the secret police could fall on him next, as apparently they did."

Jamie took the old man's hand in his own, feeling the swollen knuckles and ropy veins and beneath them the shimmering ghosts of long flexible fingers that were a pianist's signature. He wanted to speak words of comfort, to tell this man that even the Soviets, even the henchmen of Stalin must have mercy in their hearts for an expectant mother, but he knew this was not true. He knew some hearts were frozen from birth.

"It hurt to touch the piano after that, for how could there be music when Katya was gone? And so I closed my piano and never touched it again. I hated the damn thing and had someone take it away. An instrument never really goes away though, not one that you play for years as I did that one. It becomes an extension of your very self, a part of your being. I have often wondered if it went to a home where it was loved, where children learned their scales and played 'Chopsticks' hour after hour, if it ever forgave my abandonment. Do you believe instruments have souls, that with all the love and precision we put into them, with all the music we make upon them, if somehow that energy doesn't turn into something more?"

"A friend once told me that music is proof that God loves us," Jamie said, "so yes, I believe that an instrument has a soul. All the music that you made, with your wife and on your own, left its imprint behind somewhere."

Nikolai nodded. "I have hoped such things myself, but do I believe them?" He shrugged, a gesture that held a wealth of expression. Jamie suspected that despite the very necessary stone walls the man had built around himself over the years, the soul of a Romantic still lived and burned inside.

"Thank you for listening to my tale. I have never told anyone of my Katya before. It was too hard to say the words, and I had put her memory away deep down so that the camps could not touch her, nor tarnish what she was to me. I believed that to speak of her would take her away. I see now that it has given her life once again. You will remember her story, and that once she was so well loved that the very universe seemed to turn to her breath."

"I will remember her," Jamie said softly. Just then, a rush of wind came down the chimney and sparks sprayed out into the infirmary, smoldering on linen and linoleum. Nikolai took a towel to the sparks, beating them out swiftly. Small wisps of smoke traced their way into the air, and the scent of scorched cloth filled the space.

Nikolai turned back to Jamie, his face grey in the dim light.

"Good, I am glad knowing this. It makes the rest of my journey simpler, easier."

"The rest of your journey?" Jamie asked, alarm playing down his spine along with the draft from the chimney.

In reply, Nikolai merely reached over and squeezed his arm, then stood and went to bank the fire.

Chapter Forty-eight

April 1974

Spirit and Flesh

JAMIE'S RECOVERY CONTINUED with what seemed infuriating slowness. He had been placed entirely at the mercy and dictates of Shura, who was, when it came to the infirmary, a dictator of no small demeanor. His visitors were monitored and timed. Even Gregor in an entirely uncharacteristic show of obedience, was utterly and meekly lamb-like under Shura's medicinal boundaries.

The new commander had visited his sick bed, a move that was unprecedented and mildly unnerving. He was a strongly-built man with thinning blond hair combed over a well-formed skull, intelligent blue eyes framed with gold-rimmed glasses and an organized manner about him. He had given Jamie polite assurances that he would not be expected to return to the forest until he was fully recovered and could be found something less arduous in the meantime, but for now he must simply rest and rebuild his strength.

It was an afternoon a week later when he awoke to a familiar scent: sweet, acrid, bitter, and entirely seductive. For a moment he thought he was dreaming, but then he heard the familiar thud and grind of a mortar and pestle. Shura was making medicines. Where he had come across a cake of raw opium it was probably best not to ask. From the sounds and the astringent scent of alcohol, Jamie thought he was making laudanum. Shura paused, and Jamie sighed inwardly. There was little use in pretending sleep, Shura was as attuned to his varying states of consciousness as a mother elephant to her tender young.

He took quick refuge in a quotation sprung up vivid in his head. Translating it simultaneously into Russian woke him up nicely.

'...*taken together with violets, roses, lettuce, mandrake, henbane, nutmegs and willows, or you may smell at a ball of opium as the Turks do, or anoint your temples with a mixture of opium and rosewater at bedtime, or, less agreeably, apply horse-leeches behind the ears and then rub in opium.*'

Shura turned, face piqued with interest. "Horse leeches?"

"It's very messy. You wouldn't like it," Jamie said.

Shura grinned. "I believe you are most definitely on the mend."

"I still don't understand," Jamie said, the light sarcasm gone from his voice, "how you saved me. But I am very grateful."

"You are welcome, Yasha." Shura paused to roll the pulverized golden grains, sweet as honey upon the air, into the waiting alcohol. He then put it aside and covered it with a heavy cloth before he poured several balled-up leaves into a different stone mortar, and began grinding industriously.

"The others believed you were in a coma. This I did not agree with. I have seen comas before, and you were not like that. Gone somewhere far away, surely, but not like a coma and therefore, I believed, retrievable. Someone else believed that too."

"Your medical training," Jamie said dryly, "must have been highly unorthodox."

"My Babo taught me most of what I know of plants and people. She could find the right plants for healing this or that ailment merely by following her ears."

"Her ears?" Jamie asked, sitting up. His own grandmother could do much the same by scent, or so he had always assumed. Leastwise, it was how she had taught him. His grandmother had an exceptionally keen nose, amongst other attributes.

Shura nodded, taking several small glass vials from the hoard he kept in one of the less visited drawers.

"She told me that the plants sang to her, each in their own note, and that was how she knew which was to be used for what sickness. If you had known my Babo, you would not doubt it, for she could cure almost anything, even the terrible diseases of the blood. I asked her to fix my size once, for I believed she could do it. She told me that God had given me a larger heart than most men, so I had to be content with the small body. I did not see why I could not have had the big heart and the big body, but," he shrugged, "such are the questions of life."

"What drugs did you use on me?" Jamie asked.

"How do you know that I did?" Shura asked, curiosity rather than accusation in his tone.

"I am well acquainted with the traces they leave behind. This signature was rather unusual."

Shura shrugged. "Does it matter now? I will not apply them again. I imagine it was something similar in nature to what was used on the other end."

"The other end?" Jamie echoed.

"The woman who came to you in spirit, though not in flesh—the one you seemed to require for your survival. I believe she used similar medicines to make her journey as were used for you, to meet her there."

"That's impossible," Jamie said shortly.

"And yet it happened." Shura dusted off his hands and poured the powdered leaves into a tincture of alcohol, creating a swirling green mist within the glass.

"I still don't understand how I survived, or how I ended up back in the camp."

"You must ask Gregor about that. He's the one that brought you back. You were very sick. The infection from your wound had spread through your body and you had lost a great deal of blood. Gregor said he would kill me if I didn't manage to save you. He sat with you for many nights, he and then Nikolai, night after night."

"Are you telling me I owe my life to Gregor?"

Shura smiled grimly. "Yes, at least in part, unless you believe his story about the tiger."

"He's telling a story about a tiger?"

"Yes, he says he followed tiger tracks to find you. He said the only trace of Isay he found were his boots and some bloody clothing. The hound came back alone to the camp and has been cowering in corners ever since."

"You sound as though you don't believe him."

"I think the tiger that saved you," Shura said, "walks on two legs and has a spiderweb tattooed on his neck, but that is only my opinion."

Jamie considered the implications of this, and then decided he wasn't well enough to consider such things yet and turned his mind to another subject that had been vying for his attention.

"Violet has not come to visit," Jamie said, knowing Shura would understand the question within the simple statement.

Shura was to the point, a trait Jamie appreciated.

"It is a matter of embarrassment for her, I believe. There is no way to explain to you what it was like in this room that night. I have known strange things, some of which I have shared with you, things that have no explanation in the rational light of day, and I will say to you, that night was one of the strangest I have known. We will all deny it now, but there was someone else here in the room with us, invisible but undeniable. She came because you needed her, and your need of her was in all possible senses. You know what happened, I am certain. You can see why it might be of embarrassment for the woman whose body is used as substitute."

Yes, he could see quite well how it might be from her point of view. He was more than embarrassed from his own limited view. He had no need to speak of it further because there were, perhaps, things he was not ready to know.

Shura went on with his work of grinding, the warm scent of herbs hovering in the air against the crackle of the birch in the stove.

Jamie was still tired and prone to dropping off into a heavy sleep without warning, but this afternoon he felt alert enough to allow his thoughts to drift along the plane of sunlight that arced across the infirmary floor. What had happened apparently was not merely a dream, unless, of course, he was still stuck fast in the amber of fever, paddling in place, and only dreaming that he was awake.

How far could time and space bend, and could both become a function of the human will and heart? What did he himself believe? Viewed from either a religious or a scientific angle, it was possible. Even if one had to go out to the bleeding edges of current scientific wanderings to make it possible, still it was. He could hear Father Lawrence's quiet, careful tones inside his mind telling him it was so, and was glad today of the Jesuit's mold and grasp upon his own mind, for it was steadying in his current state.

"Shura? I must ask a question of you."

The dwarf went still, his head bent over his mortar and pestle. He answered before Jamie could find the words to ask his question.

"She did not suffer, Yasha. By the time her throat was cut she was entirely oblivious."

"Thank you."

Shura turned, dark eyes curious.

"It matters to you?"

"Yes, it matters. I did not love her, but it matters."

The Tale of Ragged Jack, continued.

I T WAS A FAIR AUTUMN, WITH LONG, LIGHT-SPILLING DAYS that stretched to the farthest edges of the horizon. The fields were heavy with bounty, the stalks of grain bowed down with weight, the apples dropping fragrant as perfume along the roadside. The chestnut trees handed down their fruit directly into Jack's hands, so weighty were their boughs.

Along the way there were others who had seen the Crooked Man, or thought they had, though their memories seemed oddly porous and so they were never truly certain they had seen him. Maybe it was only a story they had heard told on dark, chilly nights by the fire. It was always this way, Jack thought with frustration—whispers, hints and small traces on the wind of a scent that lingered and then was gone before you could name it, or register it in memory. Something dark with a moral at its center to frighten children in from the dark, or to make them avoid isolated pathways.

He wondered at times if he was mad to continue on this journey, to follow a man who only left a trace upon the air. What was the worth of a few dreams anyway? Surely he could live without them, slightly diminished, but alive.

The snow fell on the night of Hallow's Eve and it continued to fall for four days and nights after. It was achingly cold, the wind blowing the snow up into whorls, where they hung like frosted diamonds upon the air. The cold had stiffened Jack's hands and he could no longer feel his feet. Even Aengus was cold, his coat frozen into frosted tufts that stood up across his back making him look like a silver-dipped hedgehog. A fringe of ice hung in the dog's eyes and both of their breaths furled out upon the air, freezing into small sailing ships that skimmed off along the ice and disappeared.

He did not know how much further they could keep going, for he was very tired and could feel the same exhaustion echoed in Aengus. The thought of lying down and simply allowing the snow to cover them both in a final blanket was almost dizzying in its appeal.

By late afternoon of the fourth day, the snow was coming down so hard that

Jack knew they would have to stop for the night. They had lost the path some way back, the snow filling it in great drifts. Where to stop was the question, for nothing looked familiar or sheltering.

Then something caught his eye, a puff of steam—though surely it was only the snow stirred into a whirligig by the incessant wind. But there it was again, and it was unmistakably steam.

He blinked the snow from his eyelashes, unable to believe what he was seeing. There at the roadside, was a huge copper teapot and a column of steam emerging in great clouds from its spout. He thought he was hallucinating, even down to the sound of a rolling boil. But as he drew close and could smell actual tea and feel the heat of the enormous copper pot, he knew it was real.

There was a cup there, with a small note fixed to the side. Jack took it out and carefully unfolded it and then read the few lines it contained.

> Please drink if you will
> 'Til you've had your fill
> But leave a jot in the pot
> For the next vagabond
> That comes along.

The cup had a spider or two inside, but Jack shook these out gently near the heat of the teapot so that they might not freeze. He got a glare from each for his pains, before they scuttled off on hairy legs to the dark and warmth under the pot.

The next problem was how to pour the tea out. There was no way for him to move such a huge pot and he risked giving himself a scalding shower if he tried. But they simply had to have something warm if they were to survive the night and unless the note was designed as some special sort of torment, there had to be a way to get the tea out. The scent of it was overwhelming, making his mouth water and his stomach tremble.

Several minutes later, he was ready to kick something in frustration. It didn't matter how he approached it, there seemingly was no way to get at the tea. The sides of the pot billowed above his head, too slick and far too hot to climb. He sighed and sat down in a pile of melting snow, feeling utterly defeated.

"Try stickin' the cup under the spout, ye wee eejit."

Jack thought he was hearing things at first, for the voice seemed to issue straight out of the teapot itself. Though this was a strange thing in a strange land, still he didn't think teapots would talk, no matter where in the universe they found themselves.

"Over here. Are ye blind as well as thick?"

Jack looked toward the irritable words and found, to his great surprise, the head of a frog, or a very small unhandsome man, sticking up under the edge of the teapot. He crawled forward on his knees to peer more closely at the strange being.

There was a big gap under the pot—under the fire as it were—impossible as that seemed. In this gap stood the frog, or man, for even up close it was not clear which he was. In this world perhaps one did not need to be either, but could exist as something in between.

"It's the Hanging Fire of Wick. You don't know of it? This fire came from the original Wick Fire, deep in the heart of the Perilous Peaks. My own grandsire brought it back with him from the Wick Wars and it has burned from that day to this."

Jack placed the cup beneath the spout, and the hot tea poured out, filling the cup to the brim. It was scalding, but his hands relished the warmth, and his senses filled with the scent of black tea with cardamom to warm the blood. He took a sip. It tasted delicious and his stomach growled at him to send it down.

The frog spoke again, startling Jack into spilling a little of the tea onto the snow. A small fire started where the drops had landed.

"You and your dog will have to come in out of this weather, for it's a dark moon and the night will be terrible cold as a result. Neither beast nor boy will survive it without fire. Come, give me your hand. I'll pull you in."

Jack hesitated. Was the frog proposing to pull him through the flames?

"It will not burn you, not even singe the gold of your hair. It's special so 'tis, an' not made to burn the flesh of a child nor any other innocent creature."

Jack wasn't sure if this could be true but they would have to risk it, for if they stayed out another night in the cold they would surely perish. The wind beyond the teapot was howling, a ravening beast waiting to swallow small boys and dogs alike.

The frog-man had surprising strength and Jack tumbled into the hole, straight through the Hanging Fire. That it wouldn't singe him hadn't been quite true, for the frog had to beat out sparks lighting in his hair. Aengus tumbled in behind him and landed in a furry mass on his lap. He smelled slightly smoky but was none the worse for wear beyond that.

It was beautifully, intoxicatingly warm beneath the pot, though it occurred to Jack that he had left the cup of tea, mostly full, up above.

"Not to worry, I've a pot on the stove a-brewin'. Come with me."

The frog-man lit a reed off the Hanging Fire—a curious violet color when seen from below—and indicated that Jack and Aengus should follow him.

The walls seethed with chill vapors, oozing a strange liquid that glowed a sludgy green in the dark. The light from the Hanging Wick fire was strange, pulsating rather than flickering the way a normal fire would.

The frog-man was most odd looking. His nose looked exceedingly frog-like, as did the glistening folds of his head, yet he walked upright, even if his legs were springier than a man's would be.

"You needn't pretend not to stare. It's as you think, I'm neither this nor that, neither man nor frog."

The frog's home was merely a hollow dug out of the ground, part cave, part earth, shored up by thick, gnarled tree roots.

The frog gave him a hot drink as soon as they entered. It smelled odd, a hot, bitter smell like the drinks his father sometimes had after dinner. He had a strong feeling that to drink it, despite his thirst and hunger, would be a grave mistake. He poured it down the wall behind the bench upon which the frog had bid him sit, hoping the earthen floor would soak it up.

He wasn't comfortable in the frog's home, for it had a shifty feel about it, and he could swear that things moved about when he wasn't looking, He was certain an old copper pot with a strange insignia had been on the second shelf when he first sat down and now it was on the floor. Small bits of metal and strangely twisted pieces of wood cluttered every surface.

He caught the frog giving him odd looks as the night wore on—half sly, half wondering, and wholly worrisome.

The frog chattered away about all sorts of things, but Jack was so tired he could hardly make sense of the words, much less answer the questions the frog posed. Still, he had a strong sense that he musn't fall asleep here. He would have to wait until the frog himself slept and then sneak away into the frozen waste of the night.

The evening seemed terribly long. Supper consisted of a thin soup and bread. Jack watched to see if the frog would eat and when he did, determined these two things, at least, were safe. It seemed as though days passed by the time the fire had died to embers. The room was so dark that Jack could only make out the frog's outline, and the strange lambent glow of his eyes. The silence was so thick that Jack could hear the frog breathing, heavy hissing breaths and each exhalation releasing something vile and cold.

"My home is humble and is only this one room," the frog said, breaking the silence, "but you and your dog may sleep on the settle nearest to the fire, for let no one say I am not a good host."

The settle was uncomfortable and the thin blanket that he drew over him smelled strange, like soured smoke and dirty copper. Jack feigned sleep, though every cell in his body shrieked in protest at the idea of closing his eyes or turning his back on the frog.

The house was silent except for the hissing of the fire and the pulsing of some-thing else there in the night, something dark and slithering, something waiting for him, Jack, to fall asleep and leave himself vulnerable. It seemed as though an aeon passed before he heard a sibilant snore issue from the frog where he lay on the hearth.

Jack had clutched his bag to his chest when he lay down and over the last hour had slowly slid his hand inside. He took a pinch of the salt and put it on his tongue. He wasn't sure what the woman had meant by clearer sight, but he knew he had to do something and hoped the salt would help him decide what that might be.

His vision went entirely black, causing him a moment of horrible panic, but then it cleared just as suddenly. Everything looked different and quite awful. The shelves were still cluttered, the floor still shiny, but not in the way he had seen it *before. The various pots, medals and bits of copper were now skulls and bones, of small animals and of children. The floor was sticky with blood and other matter that Jack had no wish to identify.*

He slid his hand back into the bag of salt, heart pounding and his breath caught hard in his throat. He felt rather than heard the frog slide off the hearth, the sucking pop of his feet against the sticky floor, and knew the frog meant him great harm, that he would be the next skull on the shelf, his blood the freshest layer on the revolting floor.

He could feel Aengus straining at his side, ready to attack or to bolt. He dug his hand deeper into the bag, clutching it into a fist, feeling the crystals of salt cut into his palms. Then as the frog leaned down, his breath a fetid swamp upon Jack's shoulder, the long webbed fingers trailing the nape of his neck, Jack turned quick as a whirlwind and flung the handful of salt into the frog's wide, staring eyes.

The frog howled in pain and reeled back. Jack and Aengus bolted, running for the hole above which the teapot sat. The tunnel seemed infinitely longer than it had on the way into the frog's lair. Jack was terrified that he had taken the wrong way and would be hopelessly ensnarled in blind tunnels, running until he collapsed, and then the frog would be able to claim him as yet another victim.

He dug in his bag for the bones and held them out in front of him, knowing they were not a real defense against such evil as the frog possessed. Yet there was a strength in them that hummed through the skin of his hands and steadied him as he began to navigate his way through the dark. As he chose the left branch of a tunnel rather than the right, he began to realize that the bones were guiding him, pulling in one direction insistently, telling him where he must go. Still, it felt like hours passed and he was certain more than once that he felt the frog's hot breath on his neck, the strange penetration of those pupilless eyes. After what seemed miles of endless muck-oozing walls, the ground beneath his feet began to rise toward the upper world.

They came out into the sun, to fields that were green and flowering with wee paintbrush blooms in all the most delicate spring shades. Jack reeled back in shock. How was this possible? He had gone into the frog's hole only hours ago, in the teeth of a terrible early winter storm, and now it was spring.

He and Aengus paused only long enough to put the bones back into the bag and then they ran far and fast, to put as much distance as possible between themselves and the opening to the underworld.

They did not stop until the sun was sinking into the west, a mass of carnelian flame against a background of dark pointed firs. Jack was still dizzy from the passage of time whilst they were with the frog. He had felt entirely off balance all day, unable to understand how so much time had passed, and frightened of what it meant. Was he losing his grip on reality altogether?

The field where they finally sat to rest was sweet with the smells of timothy hay and the twitter of birds putting their young to bed. Aengus lay beside him, long snout on his paws, a worried look in the deep eyes. Now that he looked at him, it seemed to Jack that Aengus had grown remarkably. More than just a gangly pup now, his chest was deep as a ravine, his bones more solid within the pewter-silk fur.

Jack decided they would sleep there in the long grasses that smelled like lavender honey, for he had not the heart, nor the legs to go any further that night. He lay back, hungry, but at least not thirsty for they had come across a tiny stream earlier in the day, and he had filled his leather water sack. He and Aengus had drunk until the water made their bellies ache.

Aengus curled into Jack's side as he did each night, his solid ribs and big paws a great comfort. Soon the dog was asleep, though from the way he twitched, his dreams were troubled.

Sleep did not come for Jack right away. He sought comfort in the constellations, and then realized to his horror that he did not recognize any of the formations in the sky. They had changed once again. The stars, bright as they were, blurred into a mass of cold fire that smeared the sky from horizon to horizon. The tears in his eyes were hot and prickly, but there was no one to see nor mind so he let them fall unchecked for he was so tired and confused. The tears seemed to let a little of his sadness out, as if it could be absorbed into the ground and he could leave it behind in the morning.

He put his hand into his pocket, something he did for comfort, even though he knew his dreams were no longer there. But something was, something that he did not remember being there before. His fingers curled around smooth shapes, cool as spring water, and drew forth three perfect white pebbles that gleamed with the soft luster of pearls.

Where on earth had they come from? For if the frog had slipped them into Jack's pocket he knew he would have to get rid of them immediately lest they were some sort of scrying glass through which the frog could trace him. Yet they did not feel as if they were anything other than ordinary pebbles, unless one counted their polished glow. Holding them was oddly comforting, as though he had regained something that he had thought lost forever.

He fell asleep with the pebbles lodged in the lines of his palm, which his nanny had long ago told him was the tributary of his heart seen clearly there in the skin of his hand.

Part Seven

Another Country
Russia – April–September 1974

Chapter Forty-nine

April 1974

The Poet Commandant

UNDER THE NEW COMMANDER, the camp assumed a semblance of order. As such things went in Soviet Russia, he was a fair man and earnest in his desire to improve life for the prisoners as much as he was able. While there was no disguising the barbed wire and automatic weapons and the glowering guards, things did improve. In the spring, the garden had been enlarged, with Violet and Shura to be in charge of what was planted when the weather was auspicious enough. The food had improved as well, with larger portions, the bread was fresher and far more edible, and more meat and vegetables in the soup. The vegetables weren't always identifiable but they were edible, if one didn't linger too long over the texture or taste.

There had even been a shipment of new blankets, which were greatly appreciated and added to their worn predecessors, kept out the chill Russian nights far more effectively. The ground within the camp was cleaned up, the huts scrubbed down, the dining hall scoured from top to bottom and new uniforms issued. All in all, James Kirkpatrick reflected, it was about as good as a gulag was likely to get.

He was currently standing in the commander's office. The room looked out over the small exercise yard and beyond to the gates and heavy tree line. There loomed the omnipresent Russian *bor* that had spawned hundreds of dark fairytales, and the home of the great Mother Goddess of the Slavs, Baba Yaga. Home too of the Amba and his own recent brush with death. He shivered and turned away from the window, wondering with no small worry, why he had been summoned to this meeting with the new commander. The man was not yet present and Jamie had simply been told to wait.

He went automatically to the bookshelves, the smell of ink and paper drawing him like fine wine. His fingers itched with the desire to touch them, to run his hands along the leather-tooled bindings, and feel the impression of the letters against his fingertips. It had been so long since he had had lost himself to the delights of a fictional world. Telling stories was an altogether different process, and did not provide the same sort of escape. It was the difference between building a world and fleeing into one. His eyes ran along the titles greedily. The great Russian poets were present; Blok and Akhmatova, Pushkin and Pasternak, and many English ones too. The Greek philosophers were well represented: Aristotle, Xenophanes, Plato and Heraclitus. There was a crumbling volume of Seneca's *Letters from a Stoic* too. He had his own well-thumbed edition of that particular book at home, and often referred to it on the nights when he could not sleep and the questions of life seemed insuperable. Once, long ago, the words of the Roman philosopher had been a bridge by which he had returned to life.

"Please feel free to look at the books. You may borrow some if you would like."

Jamie started guiltily.

The new commander was much as Jamie remembered him from his hazy sick visit. He was a tall man, thick through the chest and shoulders. He wore spectacles that belonged to another era and had the slight squint of the perpetual reader.

"I meant what I said. You are welcome to choose a book or two to read, should you care to."

Jamie's hands clutched tight with the desire to take the man up on the offer right there and then, but he had lived long enough in the gulag to distrust even the simplest act of kindness. So he kept his hands tight and turned toward the desk where the man now sat, relaxed, a bemused expression on his face.

"It is not a trick nor a trap, only that Volodya tells me you are a man of some learning, and so I assume you must miss books and reading."

"I do," Jamie admitted.

"Please sit, and we will have tea."

Jamie sat, realizing how weak he still was. Extended activity of any sort still put him on his knees in short order.

The commander made the tea himself, proper hot Russian tea in a glass pot, the scent of the *zavarka* heady before the second pour of boiling water. He poured it out into two silver-based glasses when it was done steeping.

"Your tea will want cheering," the Commander said, pouring a generous dollop of vodka into Jamie's glass.

The liquid went straight to Jamie's blood, sending out tendrils of billowing warmth that relaxed him. His head naturally turned toward the bookshelves once again, the way the needle of a compass cannot help but point north.

The commander gestured toward the books, the steam from his tea fogging up his spectacles.

"I studied the Russian poets. By rights I should have been one of those intellectuals who are imprisoned in an asylum."

"So why weren't you?"

"My father was friends with Stalin," the man said.

Jamie did not respond for such a statement did not require commentary—nor did he know if it was safe to do so.

"It's alright," the commander smiled. "I'm not proud of it, but it's the only reason I'm not dead or locked away in a mental institution."

What followed was something for which Jamie no longer felt equipped—small talk, pleasantries, food, and an entire lack of hostility or Soviet subterfuge. It had the effect of putting him off balance, which was, perhaps, the man's intention.

There was more tea, two pots of it, and jam with which to drink it. Black bread spread with cold, salted butter and sour cherry preserves with blinis. Jamie ate sparingly, for his appetite had not fully returned since his illness.

If he had expected interrogation, he was to be disappointed. What the man wanted was rather different.

"I should like," the Commander said, awkward suddenly, "to hear of your country. It is rare to have a foreigner under one's care and I should like to take advantage, if you do not mind."

"My country?" Jamie said, feeling a strange emptiness below his ribs.

"Yes. Describe it to me, if you would."

He looked up, curious, and saw the hunger of a man who was meant to travel the world, to see its many strange corners and beautiful haunts. But it was hard to think about Ireland, for his own country had become something distant to him, partly through necessity and partly because he felt like a different man entirely from the one who had left there eighteen months ago.

It was as if he saw his country in miniature, a wet, green island that he had once read about in a fairytale, with far distant castles and crumbling towers barely glimpsed through a crystal scrying lense. He found that those he had left behind became figures in a painting, set upon idyllic backgrounds: verdant greens, thick and swirling; delicate blues; deep reds and soft earthen tones; contours drawn watery in outline and narrow winding roads that led off over hills he could not climb, nor see beyond the twists and runneling turns. He would picture Casey and Pamela in their home or moving about in the environs of Belfast, and found they had become figures caught in some strange romance—the tall dark stranger, the beautiful maiden, now a wife and likely a mother. But now and again, he found her head turning and gazing out of that landscape and himself looking back, like to like, and would be surprised at the power it still had to wound and bind even at this distance in time and space. He knew this was not so, that their lives moved on in parallel or as much parallel as this limbo existence of his afforded. Time was the only common denominator he had with his friends, and even that moved differently here, and certainly had a different meaning.

He realized that he could not think of it as more than a strange painting because it was home and he knew he might well never see it again. He could not think of it because it lived in that crack inside himself that he dared not visit for fear that it would open wider and wider, until it swallowed him whole. A country could do that to a man, countries always did when you loved them. So you did not think of a country in its truths or as your home, but as a picture, painted in colors that faded along with memory, and it was that you spoke, not truth, just a picture. It was a painting on cobweb, layered with artistry, composed with a brush made from the feathers of a phoenix. It was the exact placement of things, that magic of spatiality, that kept a man safe.

And so, because it was what he could give, Jamie yielded up that Ireland, the one he had sold so often to the world with his linens and whiskey: the drenched green island populated by poet priests and madmen, by fairies and blarney-blowsy politicians, a land where the rivers ran sweet and slow enough to bottle for the angels and even blood vengeance came wrapped in mist and music.

The painting in which he sometimes glimpsed Pamela moving and breathing was different, for it was personal. And there were other things in that painting, things that he wished now he had told her about, or had in some way prepared her for—the dark figures that lurked beyond the horizon's edge, or crept about the crumbling tower at night, the shadowy cloud that passed over the verdant landscape, the cold wind that was a harbinger of storms to come. There were things in that painting that he did not understand himself, things that glimmered out beyond the edge of the canvas, where one could only guess at them the way geographers had upon ancient maps by designating it to the dragons.

He could only guess at the form of the dragons that would come and what sort of fire they would bear in their bellies. He hoped that he had given her what she needed for this fight, that he had put the sword in her hands that she would have to wield against enemies he thought perhaps he did not know as well as he had once believed.

Chapter Fifty

April 1974

Vor, Like Me

THE NIGHT AFTER HIS MEETING WITH THE COMMANDER, Jamie made his way to Gregor's hut harboring no small misgivings in the pit of his stomach. But the hut was empty of both Gregor and his assorted flunkies, which meant they were either in the ring of trees or in the banya trying to sweat their demons out. With luck it would be the ring of trees. But luck was not on his side that evening, for the banya was puffing like an asthmatic chain smoker and there were a few men wearing swatches of cloth around their hips outside, all members of Gregor's tribe.

He walked into their circle, feeling the hostile wave spreading out from them at a hundred paces. He merely eyed them coolly in return, knowing that any show of fear was akin to the scent of blood in a shark pool with these men.

"I need to talk to Gregor," he said.

The man shrugged. "You want to talk to Gregor, you will have to talk to him in the banya—that's where he conducts his meetings."

Jamie gritted his teeth and nodded. "Tell him I'm coming in."

It was a sign of Gregor's power in the camp that he had been able to convince Isay to allow him to build a banya. The Russian obsession with steam bathing no doubt also played into the decision to allow it. Russians were of the strong opinion that between steam bathing and the internal and external application of vodka, they were the possessors of the most rude good health on the planet. Jamie thought they had a point.

The banya was built of fir logs tightly chinked with moss and had a low, peaked roof. Unlike the white steam baths in the cities, there was no changing room between the outside world and the steam bath itself, so Jamie removed his clothes behind a bushy shrub and wrapped his hips in his shirt before entering the miasmic atmosphere of the banya.

A low bench ran along one wall, and a small stone stove sat in one corner. A man was bent over the stove, pouring a pail of water onto the rocks releasing great billows of steam. Gregor sat with one of the omnipresent flunkies at his side, unselfconsciously naked and brilliantly colored, like some huge and unpredictable chameleon with very sharp teeth.

"I'd like to speak to you privately," Jamie said, not bothering with any sort of greeting.

Gregor took a long look at the expression on Jamie's face and nodded to the men surrounding him. "Go."

"You don't want us to check for weapons?" Sergei asked, favoring Jamie with a narrow look, that said he'd be more than happy to find a knife on his person. Though precisely where the man thought he might be hiding a weapon didn't bear thinking about.

"No, if Yasha has come to play, then Gregor will play with him accordingly," Gregor said and flicked a hand at them, indicating that they were trying his patience by displaying less than immediate obedience. Once the flunkies had departed, Gregor looked at Jamie.

"Please, you will sit," Gregor said, indicating the bench beside him. Jamie sat, his skin already slick with steam and his hair starting to drip.

"So, you reconsider my offer, Yasha Yakovich?" Gregor's heavy-lidded eyes were in their usual insolent position but Jamie did not miss the new respect accorded him by the term of address.

"No," Jamie said firmly, "but I do have a request to make."

"You come for favors without offering anything in return? This is bad manners in my country."

"And in mine also," Jamie said. "I have come with an offer, as they say, that I think you will find hard to refuse."

"Oh, Yasha, I don't doubt an offer of yourself would be very hard to refuse."

Jamie sighed, a Russian sigh that Gregor could not mistake.

Gregor stood to throw more water on the stones. He turned and took fresh birch branches off the wall opposite the bench, tossing one to Jamie, who, long familiar with Russian bathing habits, wasn't surprised when the man sat down sideways, making his back accessible to him.

"Are you sure you want me doing this?" he asked, as dryly as the atmosphere would allow.

Gregor grunted, flexing his broad shoulders. "*Da*, and do it hard. I don't like little girl taps."

"Alright, just remember you asked for it," Jamie said, and set to whipping the man's back with a crisscross motion of the birch branch. Green and freshly plucked, it was springy and must have stung like hell, but Gregor never flinched. It was a curious form of massage, but one the Slavs had been practicing since time immemorial. It was said to increase circulation and metabolism and to clean the blood. The oils from the leaves were reputed to have anti-aging properties as well as giving the skin a wondrous glow. Jamie had had it done by a lovely Swedish girl many years past, and could testify to its invigorating effects, which had not, as he remembered it, been strictly limited to his back.

He took the opportunity to look more closely at the tattoos that spread so thickly across the man's back. It was hard to tell where one ended and the next began. A pair of angels was the main feature, one looking west, the other east.

"The angels are past and future," Gregor said, and Jamie wondered how he knew what he'd been thinking. "This is Russian way, unable to let go of past and so we cannot move into future. I refuse this though—the past is important, and right now we are mired in it, but I think the future is more important, even if we have to drag ourselves there in the chains of the past. It is necessary, maybe it will even kill us, but it must be done."

Between the angels was a flock of sparrows. "What do the sparrows represent?" Jamie asked, continuing with the flagellation of Gregor's back.

"Freedom," Gregor said, "that someday I will fly away from this, that the Soviets cannot keep me under their thumb, and if nothing else, my soul is free. It is not the back that tells most important things though, it is the chest."

He turned, presenting Jamie with a massive width of chest and shoulder. Jamie understood the language of much of it. The dark stars that surmounted the thick muscle of each shoulder were thieves' stars and there was, of course, the inevitable barbed wire, with a barb for each year spent in Soviet prisons. Jamie counted fifteen barbs on the chest alone. A wolf with bared fangs was framed inside a star, but it was a smeary blue crucifix that took pride of place across the pectorals, surmounted by a crown that identified Gregor as a 'Prince of Thieves'. A dragon executed in rich tones of purple slithered across his stomach, its fiery breath falling into the belly button. The arms were sheathed in a variety of symbols, some of which Jamie could read and some he could not. On his knees were two crimson and black compass roses, signifying that this was a man who neither bowed to, nor acknowledged, any authority greater than his own. A snake curled in brilliant emerald green up Gregor's left calf, the tail tickling his ankle, its forked tongue flicking at his kneecap.

There was one last tattoo, a rose that held within its petals a single word 'Beauty.' It was the placement of the tattoo though, rather than its presentation that made Jamie raise an eyebrow.

"That must have hurt," he said.

"It did," Gregor laughed, a mellow sound that surprised Jamie with its fluidity. Here was a man who had laughed easily and often in his life. "To paraphrase your own words when you were stabbed, it hurt like fuck."

"How—" Jamie began, and then reconsidered the wisdom of the question he had been about to ask.

"They gave me a very pretty artist for it—to keep the canvas taut."

"Still." Jamie gave a visible wince.

Gregor grinned, his broad white teeth a flash in the swarthy face. "I am tough bastard, is no problem. I am not always minding pain in this fashion—you are understanding this, I think?"

Jamie laughed. The man was bloody incorrigible. "Yes, I am understanding this—somewhat, not in that exact fashion," he nodded toward the tattoo in question. "Nevertheless, I know what you mean."

"Ah, Yasha, see, I am telling you we are same under the skin. I knew this about you. On surface, you are not quite as pretty as me, but underneath we are same dark spirit. Now—to business. What is it you want, and what do you have to offer in return?"

It always amazed Jamie how quickly Gregor could snap out of his transsexual persona into the sharp, hard *vor* that he truly was at heart.

"I want a piano," Jamie said, and threw another ladle of water onto the stones. The resulting clouds of steam gave Gregor a decidedly Mephistophelian aura.

Gregor laughed, a long peal of hilarity that bounced off the low-ceilinged hut. "Oh, Yasha, you do amuse me. You are funny, funny man. A piano? Even if I could find one, how on earth would we have something that size transported here and smuggled past the guards?"

"I have already cleared it with the Commander. I just need you to find the piano for me. It has to be a good one too, not one whose wires are rusting from sitting in some abandoned school room collecting six feet of snow every winter. Understand?"

Gregor leaned back against the rough wall of the banya, a smile playing about his full lips while his eyes narrowed speculatively. Jamie kept his own features flat and expressionless, but allowed himself a small inward pulse of satisfaction. The bastard was intrigued and that was more than half the battle. He understood instinctively that Gregor, being the creature he was, loved nothing more than a challenge to his abilities. Jamie suspected they had been too dormant of late and were wanting some strain. He was more than happy to supply the exercise for this man's particular talents.

"So, I find you piano—and what do you give me?" Gregor asked, flexing one long arm and making the spiderweb on his shoulder ripple, a movement that had the effect of making the spider within the web appear to be crawling up his neck.

"Whatever you ask," Jamie said and met Gregor's dark eyes fully. "I owe you my life, as I understand it. You may have what you want."

Gregor eyed him shrewdly, black eyes narrowing to slits. "This is too easy—where is—how do you Westerners say—the catch?"

"No catch, only that I think you're not going to choose sex with me.

That's too simple for you. You're going to want something more, something permanent."

Gregor ran a finger over his mouth, and nodded. "You know me too well, Yasha. As much as I would like to avail myself of your considerable beauty, still I want to give part of myself to you in the bargain. I am thinking you would let me use you, but not allow it to touch you in here." He tapped his big blunt fingers over his heart.

Jamie knew that to do a deal with the devil, you had to be willing to give up at least a corner of your soul. This he understood. He might not like it, but he understood the necessity of it.

"Here is what I am proposing. I am going to tell you a story, Yasha, but it will, I warn you, take many nights for the telling. Also, the telling will be painful at times, but you will bear it well, I think. But first things first. To tell this tale, we will have to go to my hut and we will need more vodka, because a storyteller's throat must never be allowed to go dry. We will finish this bottle," Gregor flourished a bottle that had been sitting under the bench, "and then retire to my hut. Drink."

Jamie drank. The vodka was flavored with pepper, a sure cure for the common cold and guaranteed to sweat out a man's ills in the banya.

"This story," Jamie said, handing back the bottle and feeling rather relaxed between the steam and the drink, "does it feature anyone I know?"

"Ah yes, Yasha, someone you know very well indeed. And someone I think I am knowing far better than he would like. But before we leave the banya, I am returning the favor of the *veniki*."

Jamie thought it was fortunate that the vodka had settled in sweet glowing pools in his brain so that he couldn't examine too closely how he felt about having his back whipped by a naked Russian who was quite clearly aroused by the situation. He stuck his hand out and growled, "Give me back the damn vodka, I have a feeling I'm going to need every ounce of it before this night is through."

MORNING WAS TINTING THE HORIZON WITH ROSES the color of a ripe peach when Jamie stumbled out of Gregor's hut, reeking of vodka, with a head filled with lead and a chest that hurt as though glass had been scraped over it all night. This wasn't, Jamie thought blearily, too far from the truth. He shivered, pulling his shirt together where it had been ripped unceremoniously from his back before he could take it off. All he wanted right now was the blessed anonymity of sleep.

But before he could reach the sanctuary of his hut, Violet stepped from the shadows of the women's building, her delicate face lighting with relief upon him, while at the same time assessing him for visible bruises and contusions. Well, she would be disappointed. The bruising was well hidden and not likely to heal anytime soon. He wished she had stayed in her hut and would not look at him with such an expression on her face. He wished the entire world would just go away and leave him in peace.

"I was worried," she said, the dark circles under her eyes testifying to her words. "Nikolai came looking for you first thing this morning and I noticed all of Gregor's crew slept elsewhere last night." At this juncture, she flushed like a frosted rose, a deep pink coming up under the morning light on her face.

"Are you asking," he said acerbically, "if I lost another sort of virginity last night?"

Violet was nothing if not brave and so she stepped in where other angels might be wise not to tread.

"Yes, I suppose I am asking that, Yasha? Have you made some sort of bargain with the devil?"

"Gregor being the devil in this case, I assume?"

"Yes," she said, her small mouth pursing in annoyance. "Are you being contrary on purpose, Yasha? It's not amusing."

"Well," he replied, "I can assure you I wasn't laughing a great deal last night. But to answer your question, I believe I was nearly naked at one point, and things did get fairly intimate but I don't think he did anything to me that hasn't been done before."

She stepped toward him, reaching out a hand to touch his face but he recoiled, weary suddenly of people needing assurance, of people wanting to touch him, comfort him, wanting more than he was capable of giving.

The hurt flickered across her face briefly, and he felt a small whiplash of regret but was too tired to apologize.

"Why?" she asked. "For what would you do this when he had finally come to respect you, when you were safe from him?"

Jamie shook his head wearily. "I was never safe from him. That's an illusion, Violet, and you more than anyone ought to know it. Gregor is a wild animal, and any appearance of tameness is only that—an appearance. He wanted something from me and he wasn't going to rest until he got it. What it was is more complicated than I could have anticipated, that's all. And now if you don't mind, I need to go wash up before breakfast and the twelve hours facing me in the fucking forest."

Later when the forest had sweated the majority of his anger from him, he regretted his sharpness with her. She did not deserve it and it had been wrong to take it out on her. How to tell her what had happened though? How to explain what had passed between him and Gregor that long night? The disturbing thing was that in the end it had been more intimate than sex. Technically, the man had not raped him but what he had done was more insidious and longer lasting. He had shown his soft human underbelly during those long hours. He had branded Jamie with his time here in Russia, had made indelible the imprisonment of both mind and soul. He had done what he had set out to do, link the two of them eternally. Jamie hated him for it yet understood why the man had done it. For he had written Russia into Jamie's skin, permanently carved it into his body. With ink and needles. It had seemed a small enough price to pay for Nikolai's piano, but he had underestimated Gregor, as always.

Shura had told him that Gregor was an artist with a needle and he hadn't exaggerated, for Gregor had taken his time, as though Jamie's chest were the Sistine Chapel. It had been tedious and painful and talk had been inevitable. It was, as well, only the first night of the deal he had struck. There were several more awaiting him.

His first mistake had been to ask Gregor why he hadn't simply killed him after Jamie had threatened to do the same to him.

"Is because you fascinate me," Gregor said simply, stretching a hand out for the vodka. The bottle was half empty, their second of the night. "And also, I am finding you attractive sexually—this you find disturbing, so I use it."

"In the way a mouse fascinates a snake?" Jamie said, ignoring the provocation of the second half of Gregor's statement.

"A mouse—oh no, Yasha, not snake to mouse, snake to snake—that is why I find you irresistible. You are my soul's mirror and a man does not find such a one more than perhaps, once in life. If you were not such a one, I would have raped you that first night in the hut and been done with it, used you when I pleased for your beauty and that would have been the end of it as far as you and I were concerned.

"But instead, instead my sweet Yasha, I see something in you, something that can hypnotize others, something that I cannot resist myself. This annoys me, so I set to study you, to see what it is no one can resist, and I find myself. All my life I have, how to say—demons in my chest and this makes me angry. This makes me do things I do not always like. I see you have done these things too and so I look longer and one day I see you have demons in your own chest. I see this haunts you—at first I scorn this—I am Russian. I know blood is life and life is blood. There is no escaping this fact. I think maybe your country is soft in comparison, that you are a man with guilt, weak with regret. But I see this is not so either, only that your masks are held firmly in place, maybe because they have been there all your life, no?"

Gregor had hit too close to the truth, for Jamie had always been a master of dissimulation, of distracting from the truth of what was truly happening, of what he felt at his core. Gregor was right, there was blood on his hands, though he did not regret all of it, for sometimes, it was necessary and that was all there was to it. Gregor had seen this, had seen him for what he was, because they were two sides of the same tarnished coin.

"Yes," Jamie said, "they have been there all my life. Except once or twice."

"We are both harlequins, you see. We are too fond of our masks. We lose ourselves in them. This is the danger."

Jamie had merely nodded and taken another drink. Gregor contemplated him for a moment, the dark eyes like a quiet scourge.

"You have killed men?" He asked suddenly. It was phrased as a question but Jamie knew from the man's expression that Gregor already knew the answer.

"Yes," Jamie said, because there was no reason not to tell the truth. Frankly, if anyone was ever going to understand, it was this man.

"You don't kill coldly though. You kill for vengeance, I think."

"Yes."

"So you know then, the feel of this, how it is hot and angry, but good. It gives release."

"Yes," Jamie said, because it was the truth—the bloody, terrible truth—but no less honest for that.

The strange thing was that even though he was never going to fully trust him and would always be aware that there was a chance the man would kill him for the least provocation, there was an element of honesty in Gregor that had opened that same well in himself, where admittance of the dark things that rode a man's soul was accepted and could be spoken aloud. He thought it was possible that he had never been as open and honest with anyone in his life as he was with Gregor that night. It was insane that this man who had been alternately threatening to either rape or kill him since they had met, was now someone he could talk to as he had never talked to another, except perhaps for Andrei, and in some respects, Pamela. But even with her, this sort of brutal honesty was not possible. Certainly it was no longer possible with Andrei.

Gregor was silent for a long while after that, absorbed in the pattern he was ink-carving into Jamie's body. When he finally spoke, Jamie had to ask him to repeat himself as he had been half-asleep, the vodka numbing his senses enough to allow some level of unconsciousness.

"They tell me you dream of a woman," Gregor said, stopping to change needles and inks.

"Do you want me to empty out all the grit in the corners of my soul?" Jamie said, the vodka settling in a hum behind his eyes and drifting through his blood like a flock of ice-winged stars.

Gregor eyed a bottle of green ink as though he were an Antwerp diamond merchant who had just found a flaw in a large stone. Then he shrugged his shoulders and set to inking the needle.

"The night is long and the story is but half told, Yasha, so yes, if grit is what this woman is, then sweep her out and give it to me."

And so, to keep from drinking all of the vodka and to draw his mind far from the ravagement of his body, he told Gregor about the woman of whom he dreamed. Spoke of her on long drawn breaths as the colors flowed and mingled beneath his skin, in ways he had never spoken of her, spoke memory on drifts of pain and the ether of vodka until the words themselves became a bridge from the past into the unrecognizable present.

His tale wove on through the night, a river of history, and he found himself speaking of things he'd forgotten, and places he had been, people he had loved, and those who had loved him in return. He spoke of his sons, on that same river that the vodka bore him down so swiftly and ably, and they were stars in the current of memory.

Gregor had placed a mirror above Jamie's chest when he was done, and Jamie had gasped aloud at the colors, the forms and shapes that scrolled across his chest and down his left arm. The colors were brilliant: blood crimson, vermilion, ocher, lapis lazuli, amethyst, emerald, sapphire and violet.

"Now you are done—now you are *vor* like me, and so we are family forever." Gregor put his large hand over Jamie's heart as he said this, and their eyes held, Jamie knowing he must not look away, no matter if it felt as though the man was pulling out the fine threads of his soul and wrapping them tight in his fist.

The night had seemed without time, something removed, bewitched, as though it were still happening and always would be. Gregor had been right. What he had done had bound them together in some strange way, and Jamie was afraid he was never going to escape the ties of it.

It was a full week later before Violet spoke to him again. He had attempted to apologize for his shortness with her, and though she had accepted said apology she had maintained a cool distance since. He was sitting outside one evening, quiet, watching the light fade from the sky, streaking it with long washes of lavender and heated crimson like the tail of the mythical firebird. Violet came and sat beside him just as the moon rose above the smoking stacks of the huts.

"I'm sorry," she said stiffly, "that morning—it was none of my business what you had done. I forget sometimes that you might want privacy, might cling to whatever shred of it is possible in this hell we live in."

"No, it's I who needs to apologize. You caught me at a very vulnerable moment that morning and I didn't want to be seen. So when you stepped out I was angry because I had hoped that night would not exist beyond my leaving the hut. But that was only a very stupid and momentary hope."

"No, not stupid. It is only natural to want some part of one's life for oneself, even if it is the very dark parts. For a very long time I kept Andrei to myself, the very idea of what we had would be soiled by this world..." her small white hand indicated the world that surrounded them—the world of barbed wire, machine guns, quotas, and a forced communal life that made it next to impossible to have a private thought, much less a private life.

"I admit I was jealous and I know how that sounds. Because I know the circumstances and that if you had any other choice..." she trailed off, sensing his discomfiture. "Still, I felt like he had something of you that I was not allowed."

Jamie felt a hot, not entirely pleasant moment of confusion. "What aren't you allowed?"

"Intimacy with you," she said bluntly. "You and I have been nothing but awkward with one another since your illness and yet you—you allowed that man to—"

"Don't assume you know what Gregor did to me, or I to him," he said sharply.

"Of course," she said, embarrassed at her faux pas.

"Violet, what about Andrei?"

"Do you think," she said bitterly, "that he's not making love to Ilena several times a week? Do you actually believe that a married man can be faithful to a mistress?"

"No, but having sex with me isn't likely to improve that situation," Jamie said, rather too aware that he was cutting off his very pretty nose to spite his lovely face.

"One has nothing to do with the other. A month ago it might have, but now... now I find it's about you, and has nothing to do with Andrei. I know right now you may not want anyone to touch you, but I think about it a great deal—touching you, being touched by you. I'm sorry, Yasha, this is the last thing you need to hear after what happened to you, but I seem to lose the ability to hide my thoughts around you. Even though it wasn't me that you were making love to—that time when you were sick—I—I—can't seem to put it out of my mind."

"I think I better show you just what Gregor did to me," Jamie said firmly.

He almost laughed at the startlement on her face, but knew there was really no laughter in this situation anymore for either of them. He pulled his shirt off over his head and heard her gasp before he even laid the worn garment aside.

"That bastard!"

She was silent for several minutes, grey eyes round with disbelief and then slowly she began to take in each picture, each story that had been carved and ink-bled into his chest and arm. A small and perfectly executed field of skulls curved in a crescent across his left pectoral, trailing from the bottom of these was a vine twined with violets, done in a purple that was almost black. Partway along the vine, nestled amongst the flowers, was a barbed wire, each point prinked with a delicate flower. Jamie knew the story each flower told, and knew that she could read the truth there on his skin.

She paused at a wolf's head inside a perfectly aligned, eight-pointed star. The wolf was close-mouthed, but its eyes bore out from his skin with a look of cold sovereignty.

"It means, Gregor said, 'man is wolf to man', and that I must remember that in all future dealings with him."

"So he didn't—you didn't?"

Jamie laughed. "No, we didn't in any way, shape or form. But I will carry his calling card on me for the rest of my life."

And so she came to the last of his story, a heart stabbed hard by a gilded dagger, a delicate lily carved at its base. The heart formed like the rough of a raw emerald, ragged about its edges but glowing at its center.

"It's beautiful," she said tracing the vine with her finger, eyes following in a manner that made Jamie's breath short. "You're beautiful, Yasha."

"As are you," he replied softly, and brushed a hand along the line of her chin.

She smiled sadly and then clasped her small hands together. His skin felt bereft where her touch had left him. "I must tell you something, Yasha. I am pregnant."

His mouth opened in shock, a tumult of things to say tumbling through his mind. He immediately dismissed all of them as inadequate.

She flushed. "It is Andrei's child. I am too far along for it to be yours."

"What will you do?" he asked.

She smiled up at him, a thing of such sweetness that it pierced him to the core.

"Doesn't it seem to you, Yasha, that life like this, life formed through two people loving one another is a miracle, particularly in these surroundings?"

"It does," he said simply, for Violet needed no lecture on the feasibility of having and raising a child in their current surroundings.

"So I will have this baby and we will see what we will see."

It was, he thought to himself, Russian fatalism at its best. He only hoped, having much experience of loss in this area, that what they would see was a living, healthy child. That would be a miracle, and they all needed a miracle though they tended to be a little thin on the ground here in the camp.

He reached over and took one of her hands in his own, knowing she needed reassurance and knowing he was the only one, in Andrei's absence, who could provide it.

"We will get through this together, Violet."

She smiled at him, copper hair a dim glow in the night.

He was grateful that she did not ask him how they were to get through it, for he had no answers for her.

Chapter Fifty-one

late May 1974

The Piano

WHEN GREGOR DELIVERED, JAMIE HAD TO ADMIT, the man did it with incomparable style. The piano was old but in good shape, a baby grand. And after three days of cursing and sweating and appealing to the gods of music, Vanya, who had long ago been trained in the art of tuning by his grandfather, had assured him the tone was now pitch perfect. Jamie and Violet had spent time after dinner each night polishing and oiling the cabinet until it gleamed with a rich luster befitting such a beautiful instrument.

Jamie requested Nikolai's company after the evening meal. Nikolai was busy tamping down his after dinner smoke and looked up at Jamie with a quizzical expression.

"Just trust me, it will be worth it."

The inside of the common hut smelled richly of piano oil and Nikolai, recognizing the scent at once, turned sharply to Jamie before striding forward, then stopping short halfway across the room. He turned back to Jamie, his entire frame a study in emotion—joy, fear, anger.

"What—what have you done?" The anger was there, but not primary. Jamie had expected it and did not reply. It took Nikolai a few moments to walk to the piano and a few more to put one trembling hand to its surface. It gleamed like a living thing. Nikolai stroked it slowly, as though he felt it a creature of flesh and blood that needed both time and reverence.

"Why, James?" he asked simply.

"Because I wanted to hear you play."

"What if my hands and the keys no longer know each other?" Nikolai asked, his normally stoic countenance completely abandoned at the feel of the ivory under his crooked fingers. "I am afraid, James. Don't you see? My music was my soul, and they took my soul out, scalpel cut by scalpel cut over the years."

Jamie shook his head. "No, they didn't. Tell me they broke your hands, your body, tell me they laid the lash upon your spirit, but you will never convince me that they took your soul. You're too much of an old son-of-a-bitch for that to be true."

Nikolai laughed and Jamie felt relief that his gift had been accepted. The old man sat down on the bench that Vanya and Shura between them had built. Jamie left him there, for this was not a moment to be shared with anyone. He looked back only once, as he crossed the threshold of the building. Nikolai sat, head bowed, crabbed hands resting on the keys, but not playing, not yet. Then Nikolai closed his eyes and threw back his head, tears streaming in an unceasing river through the fissures in the old man's face. The mere touch of the instrument beneath his hands had set in thaw the river that had been frozen so long ago inside the man. Jamie closed the door quietly and left Nikolai to reacquaint himself with his soul.

HERE IN THE CAMP ANYTHING MIGHT BECOME AN EVENT, and so something as momentous as Nikolai playing to the public, even if it was the gulag public, took on the air of a party. Even Gregor had his hair slicked back and a clean shirt. This did not preclude him from winking at Jamie, but Jamie knew such actions were no longer meant to intimidate, but were only part of the strange friendship that had been struck up between them. Violet's face was flushed with anticipation and nerves on Nikolai's behalf, worried that she had not massaged his hands enough over the last couple of weeks. Vanya was seated next to her, fretting about whether he had gotten the tuning just right and Shura wore a tie, a gaudy green thing gained in one of his infamous trades. He also exuded a festive air that was infectious. The Commander sat apart, hands folded in his lap, his expression as unruffled as a lake on a still morning. But he was here, he had allowed this event to take place and Jamie was grateful to him for it. To be grateful to one's own jailor was a new experience in grace for him, and it was a measure of how life had changed that he could even recognize it as such.

It was natural that Nikolai should turn to his fellow Russians for music, for inspiration, and so the evening's programme began with Rachmaninoff's technically demanding *Etudes Tableaux*, and flowed on into Prokofiev, Tchaikovsky, Rimsky-Korsakov and the lesser known Alexander Borodin.

As his hands warmed, he flowed on into other composers and pieces: Bach's *Prelude in B Minor*, Schumann's gorgeously manic Piano Concerto Op. 24, then Beethoven and Liszt, Chopin and Berlioz, the music both transcendent and earthly, both angry and melancholy, and so achingly beautiful that the rugged old prisoner seemed a hybrid—half human, half angel.

He returned to the Russians to close out the evening, finishing with Rachmaninoff's *Vocalise*. Jamie had heard it played many times on both violin and piano, but had never heard it as Nikolai played it, bleeding the keys for all the emotion they could render. Through his playing, he was reconstructing the Russia before the Revolution and all that it had been, that firebird that might yet, through whomever of her artists survived, rise from the ashes of Stalinist destruction. He was playing for his Katya.

There was a hush at the end, and Nikolai looked around, startled out of his reverie. Jamie sensed that he had been so lost in his performance he had forgotten his surroundings entirely and was now surprised to find himself in the dingy common room. His fingers still rested on the ivory keys as though he were afraid if he stopped touching them they would disappear. Now that he had music once again, he would need the sustenance of it daily. It was good to need things. Jamie had long understood that, but only here in Russia had he seen the absolute necessity of it in a human life.

Jamie began to clap, and then the others took it up, but Shura stood, his hand clasped over his heart, tears running from his eyes into his beard. His big sentimental heart had been denied music for so long that having it, hearing it played at this virtuoso level had been more than he could manage. Nikolai looked at him and smiled, for there was no greater accolade than Shura's tears were giving him.

After, they filed out slowly, restless, for such music stirred a person's soul opening wounds best left untouched. To merely go back to their meager beds and lie awake for hours in the dark, still hearing that sublime music, note by painful note, over and over in one's head did not bear thinking about.

Outside in the dark, with the stars appearing beyond the deep feathery tops of the firs, one could pretend for a moment that one did not see the tall fences topped with barbed wire. One could not deny the music though, for it had pierced each of them too deeply.

Violet came and stood beside him, as was their habit now, to drift together whenever they happened into one another's orbits. She was silent, for words would seem trivial after such a fiery display. Except perhaps for the ones he was about to utter. He found himself quite ridiculously nervous.

"I think we should marry," he said quietly. There was a shocked silence from Violet.

"Why?"

"Why not? I think it would be good for the child as it gets older to know he or she has a father and a name that is his to keep. Our world is here for the present and possibly forever, so we must live and quit pretending the only life that is real is the one out there. Here and now is what we are granted."

"You don't speak of love, I note."

"Would you like me to? I could, but then I might insult your relationship with Andrei, not to mention your intelligence."

The silence this time was so long that he thought he might have to break it himself with an apology and a withdrawal of his offer. He could only make out her silhouette in the dark, and so could not read the colors of her skin, nor the expressions of her face.

Finally she spoke, words delicate as ether, but decisive all the same. "I think I should like you to speak of love one day, not tonight, for I do not think you are ready to say such words and mean them. Just be certain, Yasha, that it is not the music speaking, but yourself."

"It is myself. I am no fool. I know that music makes madmen of us all, but this idea was in me before tonight."

"Will you give me a day or two to answer? There are things I must think about before I say yes or no."

"Of course," he said, surprised that he was stung by her hesitancy. It was ridiculous, for he was hardly offering her the moon on a plate, only half a meal that had already been picked over by other hands.

She leaned up and kissed him on his cheek, her hand brushing over his before she turned and fled into the night.

Chapter Fifty-two

May 1974

Papa

HER ANSWER, WHEN IT CAME, TOOK A UNIQUE FORM. Under the softened regime, most of the prisoners spent their evenings—what there was of them—outdoors, soaking up every minute of sunlight to hoard against the days when it was not so plentiful. He and Violet often spent them together talking, walking the perimeter of the fence or working together in the garden. With Violet's advancing pregnancy, this consisted more of her directing Jamie while she sat on the bench by the garden's fence, her hands rubbing the small mound of her belly. Tonight, she had asked that he meet her in the ring of pines where they might have more privacy. He agreed, knowing that she had decided. He felt like a ridiculous schoolboy, thrumming with nerves and wishing the interview was over and done.

She was waiting for him, sitting in the shadow of a large pine, the scent of its sap heady in the late spring evening.

"Yasha, I have something to give you for safekeeping." She sat still in the shadow and he could not see her expression, only heard the serious note in her voice. In her hands she held a bundle of what looked to be letters—letters that had been cherished and read many times. Sacred too. He could tell merely by the way she held them in her hands, as though she were surrendering some part of herself.

"Come sit, for I would tell you what this is—this thing I wish to give you."

It was not a direct answer, but Violet was Russian so it was to be expected that she would answer in her own fashion.

He joined her under the old pines, the evening's sun hazing through the branches, golden and liquid, seeping into their bones.

"These letters that I would give you—they are from my father and they are for my son or daughter. I would wish to give them to him or her myself one day, and likely I will, but on the chance that I cannot for whatever reason, I would have you do this."

He took the bundle from her hands. It was tied together with a ribbon, dark blue and much tattered and soiled, the paper of the envelopes almost like silk from their many handlings. He could feel the reluctance in her even as she let them go, as if a part of her own history was now handed over and out of her keeping.

"Those letters are all from my Papa. I find it hard to explain adequately how much he meant to me, how much I loved him. These letters were all I had of him after I was ten. It has been so long now since he was taken from us—from me, that I do not know if my memories are true or merely dreams."

She took a breath, slightly ragged as though it caught in her throat and put her hand to the cross she never took from around her neck.

"My Papa was magic, much like you, Yasha, as though God put a little extra something in when he made him, a little more stardust, a little more laughter, a little more sadness too. He was so smart—too smart for his own good in the end, I suppose. I don't think he ever really believed in the Party, but he was brilliant and they wanted such men on their side from the beginning. He had his degree in economics and there were people always on the lookout for men such as him. He had vision—such vision of how things could be, how we might change things in Russia. He understood the cycles of capitalism and how the right marriage with socialism could create something new, something that included all the people from the sorriest peasant up to the intellectual cream. He felt certain if we could just hang on, something was coming, that things were going to change. He was right, but it was too late for him, as it turned out. One day he was a party star, the next he was not. They came and took him in the middle of the night, as he stood, without any winter clothing. I remember clinging to him, sobbing, and him saying, 'Hush my little Violushka. You must be strong. Smile for Papa, so that is the picture he takes away with him. I will only be gone a short time. You will see, this is just a mistake.'"

She shrugged. "Well, it was a mistake, of course, but that did not matter. They charged him with belonging to an illegal organization—but I think this organization never existed. They made it up to put him away. It was how things were, one day Stalin loved you, the next day he thought you were a danger to the regime and he would sign orders to have you put away or shot.

"My Papa was sentenced to eight years in a special isolation camp in an old monastery." She looked up at the tall tower that loomed above them, for the irony could not escape either of them. Like father, like daughter.

"He wrote me every week, without fail, and they were—are—the most wonderful letters. He filled them with bits about his day and the birds and insects and all the plants around the monastery—he drew them too, he was quite a talented artist—but you will see that if you look at the letters. He wrote for me a story, just a little bit in each letter, about a fox named Aleksei that went off into the world in search of an ideal land where people and animals and plants lived in harmony and love. He meets many other animals along the way, some good, some bad, but all with something to tell him, a story he can tuck in his packsack and take along with him. Of course the fox never made it to his destination, for there was no such land. I didn't know at the time that he was teaching me all the life lessons he couldn't be present to give me in person—he was doing his best to raise me from a thousand miles away. I think—" she put her head down, the words catching in her throat, "he knew he was never coming back, that he would never see me grow up and so he gave me his world through the story, so that I might always have his advice, his beliefs, and maybe sometimes even the answers to the questions a girl will always have for her papa."

"There is one letter I would like to read to you, if I may?"

"It would be my privilege to hear it," Jamie said quietly.

She slipped the last letter from the pile, leaving the rest still in his hands. She opened it carefully, and in the fading light, the bold hand of her father's writing sprang off the page. The paper was rough, but worn soft from the years. It was likely that her father had written on whatever came to hand. The ink was a coarse black, but the writing itself certain. A crumbled bit of plant lay cupped in the seams, a tinge of lavender left in it.

> *Dear Violushka,*
>
> *Happy Birthday, my love!! How were your summer holidays? Did you swim, did you find turtles in the pond and dig potatoes and beets with Dyedushka? Did you grow stronger and even smarter? Did you read any good books? Did you look up at the stars at night and remember the stories Papa told you about them?*
>
> *I hope you are studying hard and doing well, though you must always remember to have fun and to laugh—it's just as important as the studying. Be good to Mama and Dyedushka, for I know how dearly they love you, my little redheaded girl.*
>
> *Try not to forget your Papa, and when you think of me, know that I am traveling with Aleksei in search of that better land. But I am always holding you in my arms as well, such things can be managed between dreamers, you see. I send you a million million kisses.*
>
> *Your own Papa.*

"It was the last letter I had from him, for he was shot the very next day.

It was only two weeks later that Stalin died. Of such things are our tragedies made."

She stood and walked away then, leaving him holding her history in his hands. It was an answer as only a Russian woman could give it. And he realized that he felt quite happy with what she had not said and even more so, with what she had.

Chapter Fifty-three

August 1974

Another Country

WHEN HE FIRST HEARD THE HORSES, JAMIE STOPPED ON THE ROAD, though he risked being shot for so slight an infraction. He wondered who they belonged to for he could hear two, whickering at each other. There were no farms nearby of which he was aware, but then beyond the camp and the forest, he had not seen any of the surroundings. The sound of the horses caused a rush of homesickness to flood him, for the security and peace of his stables, and the simple pleasures of exercising a horse and brushing it down afterward. Because a horse never required anything of you beyond care and feeding, it never asked questions you had no answers for, it never asked you to give more than you had.

Then he saw the horses standing sturdy, one pewter, one chestnut, both tense with readiness beyond the perimeter of the camp. A visceral rush began deep in his blood. It was an old connection, one he had always had with horses. They represented far more than a mere animal to him, for he had grown up with them, slept between the hooves of an unbroken stallion once when he was four and awakened unharmed. Holding their reins was Andrei, gilt-headed in the sun and gesturing toward him. Jamie wondered for a moment if lack of proper nutrition had finally taken its toll and he was now hallucinating. He turned to the guard behind him and the man nodded that he might go. Jamie moved off toward Andrei, feeling the strange itchy spot on his back that he always got when a man was behind him with a loaded gun.

"What the hell are you doing here?" he said in English, his throat rusty with his own language. He felt a desire to laugh, as he often did when Andrei pulled one of his more outrageous acts.

"I was owed a favor," Andrei said. "This is how I chose to call it in. They won't allow us to go without guards, Yasha, but I told them they better give me bloody Cossacks for the job because they were going to have to keep up. Well, shall we?" Andrei offered the pewter's reins to Jamie. The horses were chuffing and stamping in the warm summer morning and Jamie felt a lurch of anticipation akin to that of a child at Christmas. For once, he knew, he was not going to weigh the cost to others, he was just going to do something that he wanted to do and damn the consequences.

He mounted the pewter, a lovely mare that flashed silver under the sun, who reminded him of Phouka, and hence, of Pamela as well.

They started out at a canter, the horse liquid in joint and pace beneath him. He felt something upwelling in his soul, a feeling he hardly recognized as happiness. Soon the pace increased, Jamie letting the horse have its head, leaning in tighter to its body, stretching out with it, becoming one and allowing sense to overcome and master reason. Faster and faster, the landscape changing from the rougher forest floor to low scrub, the low scrub giving way with a suddenness to wide open, unending land that was like a freefall through air, just as frightening and every bit as exhilarating. Beside him, a furious grin on his face, Andrei matched his pace, the red legs of his pony a blur of earthbound flight. The guards pounded madly behind, but fell further and further back. They did not matter. Nothing mattered but running and the space within which to do it.

An ocean of grain billowed in front of them, rising and falling, moving with the tip and tilt of the planet, just as they did. Everything was movement and light. There was no thought in such extreme physicality, only the sheer joy and terror of taking a horse to its limits, of going beyond the limits oneself, where you knew you were courting death so closely that you could taste the dark intoxication of it on your tongue. The air was so clear that it magnified everything in passing, pure as vodka rippling down his throat and leaving a clean icy wake all the way to his bones. It was both refuge and escape. He heard Andrei laugh as they had once when they were boys together and found himself laughing in response for no reason at all.

The horse had more heart than any he had ever ridden. She responded to his slightest movement like a finely tuned engine, needing no more than a nudge with his knee to check left or right.

The grain bowed down in great golden rippling waves as they galloped through the field, and he could smell the August heat rise from the ripe heads at their passing. Overhead the sky was a blue that was painful in its intensity. He could feel the immensity of the country beneath him, a country that curved around half the globe and still was as small as the limits of a forest camp.

They halted at the edge of the fields, beyond lay—what? Another country, another life that he had once lived and no longer recognized. And yet that did not lessen his longing for it.

Andrei was looking at him strangely, a look made of equal parts expectancy and something darker that Jamie could not, did not want to identify.

"You can go," Andrei said, still gasping, sweaty hair plastered to his head in silver whorls.

"Go where?" Jamie asked, though he understood all too well what Andrei was offering.

"Go home," Andrei said, eyes bright and hard with the physical pleasure of the ride, and dark with anger. Andrei knew about the marriage proposal. Somehow, he was certain of it.

"I can't, you bloody fool. The guards will kill me before I've gone twenty feet."

"Maybe," Andrei said, suddenly very still, his horse glimmering with sweat beneath him, "or maybe not. You have roughly five minutes before they catch up. Do you want to miss this chance, Yasha? What if it's the only one I can provide you?"

Jamie reined the horse in sharply. "What the hell are you up to, Andrei?"

Andrei's face was inscrutable, pure Soviet iron, without give or the ability to change form or shape. "I'm telling you to go while you still can, my friend."

Jamie looked west for a moment, careful to keep the yearning from his face. Of course, it was this ache for home that Andrei understood all too well. That was why he was putting him to this ultimate test.

Andrei cantered away, keeping himself removed, leaving Jamie on the precipice of his own yearning. The horse strained as though she were entirely in tune with his wants, as though they really were one creature who wanted nothing more than to keep running. He knew the odds were better than even that the guards would kill him, and though he knew that should make his decision easier, he found it did not.

The wind picked up, flowing past his senses, and he thought for a moment that he could smell the West in its threads. The scent of far oceans and familiar things. Of home. He allowed himself the vision of it for a moment—to go home, to be free, to make his own decisions. And then the vision was gone, burst like the illusory bubble it was, upon the harsh currents of reality. For that was another country, far gone from him now.

He couldn't go no matter how badly he wanted to, no matter what called to him from that world and that life. He could not let Andrei go back to the camp and tell Violet, Nikolai, Shura and Vanya that he had left them without so much as a goodbye. He hated himself for it and he was certain Andrei did too.

The guards had arrived, their grey presence restoring reality, tamping down its edges and making it clear to him that Andrei had been willing to risk the guards killing both of them today in order to make a point. Just what that point was, was less clear. Though the slight ache inside told him he understood, even if he was not yet willing to articulate it to himself.

He felt as if the weight of Russia itself sat upon his shoulders, heavy, dark and bleeding. He wanted to keep going, to run the horse until she died beneath him, and then walk the rest of the way home if that was what it took to leave this graveyard of a country behind. But he could not, and it seemed without even his own volition the horse turned, pewter coat gleaming like armor under the Soviet sun, and trotted back to where Andrei waited.

It was not the first time Jamie's own nature had been used against him and it wasn't likely to be the last. It was also, as Andrei well knew, the worst form of betrayal he could have inflicted upon him.

Had the ground opened then and pulled him down to hell, it would not have mattered for Russia had swallowed him whole and he knew, as the horse picked up her pace, steadily bearing him back toward the camp, that he might well have turned from his last chance to go home.

Chapter Fifty-four

September 1974

Married

THEY WERE MARRIED AT SUNSET, WHEN THE AIR WAS WASHED and hung with gold and red and lilac silks of cloud and silence. A normal Soviet wedding service was a perfunctory and utilitarian sort of thing, devoid of emotion, and culminated in a visit to the nearest statue of Lenin. As the state was not present to perform the wedding, it was makeshift, and in the end quite lovely. Shura performed the rites, and though it was simple, there was nothing perfunctory nor emotionless about it.

It had taken some time to get the license, though this wasn't uncommon in the Soviet Union, and given their special circumstances Jamie knew they were lucky to get one at all. So it was late September and the autumn already well set in before they were able to marry. Violet was only a couple of months away from her due date and Jamie had worried the license would not come through on time, or that they would be denied the privilege of marrying outright. It was important to Violet to be married before the baby arrived. In this way, she felt he was then officially the baby's father. A sentiment he was certain Andrei would not share.

The common hut, which normally sported a bleak, decaying atmosphere, was charming tonight, the sagging framework hidden by the sunset pouring in at the windows, its crumbling wooden bones made soft with the touch of candlelight.

Gregor had presented him and Violet with a set of traditional Russian wedding rings which he had Dima make, a man who specialized in fashioning every piece of scrap metal to be found into various items of use. Each ring was made from three interlocking bands, traditionally in gold, but here in a scrap of copper Dima had salvaged.

Jamie, waiting for his bride, thought briefly of his first marriage. How very young he and Colleen had been, how nervous he had felt that morning until he caught sight of her coming up the aisle. It wasn't likely then he could have imagined standing here in Camp 642, with a vor for his best man, a dwarf officiating, a Soviet clerk serving as witness, and his morning suit now replaced with a white *kosovorotka*, the traditional Russian men's shirt, and rough black trousers.

Despite the gap of years and customs, he felt a buzzing of nerves all the same. Over the decades the gulag had spawned all sorts of relationships and forms of marriage, some conducted purely by letter, and lasting for years. Some made by couples who had never seen each other's faces, who said their vows on opposite sides of a wall, who would likely never touch nor see one another. He could understand the need for even that much. People craved love, no matter how dire their circumstances, for love was the only thing that could keep them human in such conditions. It had also afforded the women some protection from the sexual advances and often outright rape of other men. Camp relationships were all the *zeks* had, and they were taken very seriously.

Vanya came in, grinning and nodded to Nikolai, who began to play his own rendition of the wedding march. Violet entered, one hand held ruefully to her belly, a clutch of late roses from the garden in the other. She wore a dress of palest buttercup yellow and above it her copper hair gleamed in the flickering candlelight. When she reached Jamie, he took her hand and squeezed it reassuringly.

It was simple after that, just the two of them surrounded by those who had formed a strange family from the tattered ends of life in a Soviet labor camp.

In Russia, wedding rings went on the right hand, and it felt oddly comfortable there to Jamie. For this was an entirely different life in another world altogether from the one he had lived in Ireland.

After, there was truly terrible Georgian champagne in tin mugs, and several hearty toasts accompanied by the cry of *Gor-ko* after which the bride and groom were expected to kiss.

Each person kissed them on either cheek and congratulated them on their new marital state—Gregor in his usual hearty fashion, Volodya, polite and shy, but pleased for them and Vanya simply watching their faces with a wistful smile upon his own. Love, Jamie thought smiling at the boy, even in the small doses allowed here could make a man ache for his own lack of it. Shura delighted Violet with bags of herbs that he had specially prepared for her impending motherhood and for the baby.

Nikolai's blessing was last. He took Jamie's face between his hands and kissed him briefly on each cheek. "Be happy, *moy droog*."

Everyone departed into the night, back to the drafty huts, empty mattresses and bittersweet dreams except for the newly wedded couple, who were to spend this one night together.

There was a small hut that sat empty most of the time, unless there was a visitor from the state who, because of the isolation of the camp, had to stay overnight. Valentin had arranged for Violet and Jamie to have it for their wedding night. It had been prepared for them in advance by some kind soul. The small tin stove kept out the chill of the autumn night, the bed made with heavy quilts and pillows. There was a kettle and tea cups on the table and a small pot of raspberry jam. There were even curtains over the windows, giving the hut a snug intimacy. He handed her over the threshold, stepping in from the dark, starred night behind her and shutting the door.

Violet sat on the bed and sighed, her hand going automatically to her belly to stroke the heavy round of it.

"It was, as gulag weddings go, quite a nice event, don't you think?"

She had meant it as a joke, yet it had been lovely, despite the surroundings.

"It was," he agreed. "Would you like some tea? I'll put the kettle on." It was his Irish soul coming to the fore, he knew. When your nerves got the best of you, making tea bought you the time to steady them.

"Tea would be wonderful," she said.

He put the kettle on and spooned the tea leaves into the samovar.

"You look very well in that shirt, Yasha," she said. "I was feeling very proud of how handsome a husband I have."

He looked at her, serious, giving back the gift she had given him. "I too was proud. You are beautiful always, but especially so tonight."

"Yasha, you are a wondrous liar."

He knelt down at her feet to take her shoes off for her. In another life, he might have given her a string of pearls for a gift, or a beautiful house on a seashore, but in this life there was only the offer of what he could give from the labor of his hands and the wells of his heart. He would have her know that such as he had to give was hers entirely.

"Despite circumstances, I should like to be a good husband to you. If you have expectations, I should like to meet them if at all possible."

"Russians don't have expectations, Yasha. You surely know that by now. Especially here, it is enough to live with one another when we can, day by day. I should like..." she hesitated, and then rushed on with the words, as though she were afraid if she stopped she might never say it. "I should like for it to be a marriage in all senses of the word. After all, we are not complete strangers in that way. I realize you do not remember, but I do." She flushed, a blaze of color along each camellia-skinned cheek. She touched the collar of his shirt in question. He took her hand and kissed the back of it then leaned forward to kiss her mouth. She was warm, so warm and his body kindled bright at the touch of her.

To touch and be touched so was almost more than he could bear for it required that he open up those parts of himself he had put away in Russia. It required that he be entirely present, a luxury that was dangerous in this land. He drew back for a moment, frightened by his own need, for he had not expected it to be so overwhelming.

Violet understood it seemed, without him saying a word, for she stood and went to blow out all but two candles, small stars that glowed golden near the bed.

"I think we are both nervous, so you tell me a story first and then maybe we will relax."

She poured them each a cup of tea, adding a spoon of jam to each saucer. He took the tea gratefully, sitting down on the bed and stretching out his legs. She sat beside him, not touching but close, blew on her tea and closed her eyes, the look of anticipation the one he saw each night before his tales began. This was familiar territory for both of them and he appreciated her wisdom in using it to set the ground beneath this first night of their marriage. Stories were the gateway between worlds and could bridge the distance between friends about to become lovers.

And so he began, each word a span by which they would enter into this new land.

The Tale of Ragged Jack, continued.

IT WAS THE DARK OF THE MOON AND JACK COULD NOT REMEMBER the last time he and Aengus had more than bitter herbs or tough roots or shrivelled berries to eat. He was afraid they were wandering in circles and no longer on the trail of the Crooked Man. He wasn't even sure what world he was in, being that when he went into the frog's hole it had been winter, and then when he and Aengus had escaped a few hours later—by his own reckoning—it had been spring. This whole place, whatever and wherever it was, was entirely topsy-turvy and Jack could no longer decide what was reality and what might be just a dream. It made him feel decidedly off kilter, as though he had suddenly discovered himself walking amongst the clouds with no ground beneath his feet.

It was the afternoon of a day that belonged to some week, or at least he supposed it must, though perhaps days and weeks and months had no meaning in a world where the seasons changed willy-nilly. He and Aengus were both hungry and he hoped they would find something soon: a patch of berries, some apples forgotten on the tree, or a young hare to cook over a fire. The sun was hot in the sky and butterflies floated past him, blue and red, silver and gold. Ahead of them was a scrim of young birch, so new that they seemed hazed with water-green silk, near translucent in their youth. Jack walked toward it, drawn as though he were a skein of yarn being wound in slowly but surely. As he got closer, he saw that the birches were indeed young, but not exactly birches. They were young women, half-frozen, so well rooted in the soil that they would never be able to extricate themselves. Their long arms and fingers had become the branches and twigs, their hair the weeping of leaves.

He approached them sidelong, hoping to get close before he was noticed. Aengus stuck to his side like a cocklebur, a low humming growl setting up in his throat. It was of no use, for with a great sighing creak one birch turned toward him and stared down a long haughty nose at him.

"Who dares to cross this border?" she asked, the voice green and thick with sap, as much a soughing of the wind and a movement of water through wood as *it was words, and yet Jack had no problem understanding.*

"Me and my dog," Jack said, aware his voice was all but lost as more birches turned toward him, their creaks and groans rending the air like a terrible storm.

"Do you and your dog have papers? We need the official forms, dated, signed and stamped by the Ministry of the Oak Warden, or else you cannot cross."

Jack sighed, for he did not have any sort of papers, though it might have been nice to possess such, just as a way of reminding himself who he was. Seeing it on paper would be reassuring: name, date of birth, place of residence. Such things could anchor a boy into the world more firmly. Such things could make a boy real.

"I have no papers. I am just Jack, called Ragged by some," he said stoutly, though his heart quailed within his chest.

Now all the trees were looking toward him, all very officious, all very disapproving. He suddenly felt not to have papers was the very worst thing in the world. Without papers he would have to rely on what skills he had.

"You are," Jack said in a voice as sweet as a harp on the wind, "the most beautiful tree I have ever seen."

The tree blushed a pale green, tossing her leaves over one bent shoulder.

"Flattery will not get you over the border," said another birch who had not spoken up until now, her voice dry as autumn leaves. "Only papers will get you over this border, Comrade."

She was a very fierce looking tree, and when she shifted in the sunlight Jack thought he saw a glint of iron within her pale, peeling bark. What sort of a tree had iron inside? Why a tree like that could be entirely rotten and never fall down.

"What were you thinking, imagining that you exist without papers to prove so?"

It was the tallest birch that had spoken. Her voice was like the rustle of a summer breeze through whip-green saplings. Her eyes were dark as knots and her nose a long slender bough that stretched down toward him as she bent with a great groan to where he stood digging his toes into the soil so that he would not shake before her.

"If I don't exist without papers," Jack said slowly, "then I ought to be allowed to cross the border. Because if I don't exist, I'm not really here, am I?"

This seemed to give the birches pause, for the tallest drew her mossy eyebrows down as though she suspected him of trying to trick her. They put their great shaggy heads together, whispering and rustling, sometimes ascending to strange squeaky sounds that rended the ear. Finally, they moved apart and the tall one, who seemed to be their foremost spokesperson, said—

"You'd best be who you say you are, Comrade Ragged, or there will be great trouble for you. Just this one time, we will allow you to cross the border despite your egregious lack of papers."

He wasted no time starting across the border, the moss squelchy ground that surrounded the roots giving way to his feet. Something moved, curving and sinu-

ous, beneath one foot, causing him to overbalance and fall. His hands sunk into the dripping moss and he felt the movement with his fingers, abrupt and awful. The tree roots were moving and the trees above hissing and laughing, a terrible laughter that sent a strange paralysis through him.

Already one ankle was caught fast in a coiling root, pulling him inexorably down to where he knew he would surely suffocate in the earth and die. Aengus was barking madly and snapping at the roots that coiled and struck out at him, trying to drag him down with his master.

The pressure was terrible, like a horrible squeezing snake sucking the breath out through his skin. He could not believe he had come all this way only to die like this, leaving no trace behind other than a slight disarrangement of earth. Then, blessedly, a hand gripped his hard and a voice said, "hang on tight." Someone was pulling on him, pulling him free of the terrible death-dealing roots.

He scrabbled along the ground, as quick as he could, but one root still clung, fierce as a wolf's fangs, around his ankle. Suddenly there was a ringing sound like that of an axe against iron, followed by a terrible shriek and the root was gone from his ankle.

"Come on, hurry, we have to get you clear of these trees!" There was an arm under him and he pulled himself up, dragging behind the creature that had saved him.

They stopped near a hawthorn hedge, and Jack collapsed on the ground, though he made certain to stay a goodly distance from the hawthorn's roots. The bitter soapy smell of the hedge helped to clear his head. His rescuer was bent over his ankle, inspecting it. It—the creature—was filthy, was his first thought, its hair a great tangle of smokey black and its face and limbs smudged with dirt and the juice of green things. It was not immediately apparent if the creature was male or female, so wild was its countenance and dress. It wore a badger skin tunic and its feet were bare and long-toed as a sloth's. The cloud of hair was so mad that he thought perhaps he saw a wee owl peeking out between swirls of dark curls.

He drew in a sharp breath and jerked his ankle away for the bone was terribly bruised, and while the creature seemed to mean well, it was not gentle in its ministrations. The creature gave him a sharp look and said, "You will have to come with me. I don't have the right herbs to heal you, nor the skill, but I know one who does."

"Thank you for saving me," Jack said. "Might I ask what your name is?"

"Muireann," the creature said and Jack gave a sigh of relief, for though it only meant calm sea, it seemed to him it must surely be the name of a girl. She gave him a very direct look, and he saw that, indeed, beneath the skin and the dirt and plant smears, it was a girl.

He stood, hobbling slightly in her wake. Aengus seemed to have no reservations about this new entity, which reassured Jack that she didn't intend him harm. She set a goodly pace, her legs long and well muscled if slightly scrawny. She wasn't a great talker, for most of the journey was conducted in utter silence, but she stopped to listen a great deal, cocking her head in this direction or that, though he could not hear a blessed thing.

They walked on until the sun was sinking into the west, the dim settling into the valleys and nooks between rocks and grass, and he could sense the small velvety creatures of the twilight come out, peering from behind shrubs, noses twitching at the strangers passing through their realm. He wondered how much further they had to go, for his ankle hurt horribly and he didn't think he could go on much longer. Then without warning she stopped, he looked up from the narrow roadway and gasped.

The mound loomed massively in front of him and his heart stuttered within his chest as he recognized it. The old woman had warned him about the people of the Hollow Hills, and here he had willingly followed one straight home. He remembered the legends from his own place, where it was said if you entered into those hills you would return one day to find your world entirely different, with great spans of time having passed and all that had been familiar, all those you had loved, long disappeared. But hadn't that already happened to him? He no longer knew how long he had been gone, or the way back home. He was already hopelessly lost. All that was left was his pursuit of the Crooked Man. Sometimes, he was so tired and discouraged that he could hardly remember why he chased after such an awful creature.

He followed Muireann toward the mound, for he did not know what else to do, and he was too hungry and too tired, and too homesick to flee on his own into the dark. The land sloped downward as the mound grew ever larger, until it blocked out the sky and the evening's first stars entirely. He followed the girl down a long tunnel into the earth, deeper and deeper until suddenly they emerged into a long hall that seemed lit with a thousand candles, so bright did it shine. It was filled with the most beautiful people Jack had ever seen. A great banquet was taking place and the light, warmth, and smells of cooking meat and ale overwhelmed him, starved as he was. Everything swirled in front of him in a riot of earthen brown, gilt silver and molten gold. The people were dancing, even the smallest of them, whirling like dervishes or skipping lightly in strange patterns. It was dancing of a sort he had never before seen. And the music was like nothing he had ever heard, so sweet and lamenting that it shivered in his spine and made his throat tight with unshed tears. He had never wanted home so badly as he did now, and he felt his heart crack a little knowing how very far he was from his old room and the lilac tree that grew up past his window, his mother's laugh that was like bells on a summer night and the scent of his father's pipe, always letting him know he was safe.

He felt the girl's hand slip into his own as though she sensed how near he was to tears. She pulled him away from the feasting and music and mad revelry, up a set of winding stairs to a quiet room deep in the castle. Muireann pointed out where *he should lie down, and lit a fire in the hearth to remove the chill from the room.*

As he sat down on the bed, an old woman entered the room. Aengus lay down beside him, his one black eye and one blue darting about in suspicion at their new surroundings. The woman was hunchbacked and sprouted three whiskers from her chin: one silver, one gold and one black as night. Her arms were the oddest things about her though, for they started at the shoulder as perfectly good people arms and ended in feathers, as if she were half owl, half woman.

Neither Muireann nor Jack said a word, Jack being too stunned to string a sentence together and Muireann seemingly of the opinion that the woman knew her business and needed no guidance from her. The woman bent directly over Jack's ankle, turning it this way and that with her feathered fingers and making soft sounds, half hoot, half words. Deciding what was needed, she drew a stout length of linen out of her small bag, and laying it on the floor, proceeded to crush a variety of herbs onto it before wrapping it tightly around Jack's ankle. The red-hot pain lancing through it began to subside at once.

"Thank you," he said, very quietly, because her kindness and soft touch had undone him and he did not want to cry in front of her though he sensed she was not the sort of woman to be discomfited by a boy's tears. She brushed a wingtip over his face, soft as a heartbeat, and Jack felt terribly tired, as though her feathers held a sleeping potion. She bundled up her herbs and left.

Muireann had been busy as the woman had tended his ankle for now she held out a goblet to him, a fine silver-chased thing, blackened about its edges with age and use. He wanted the liquid in that cup more than he had ever wanted anything, for his thirst was raging in him, but he remembered all the warnings about the people of the Hollow Hills and shrank back from her offering.

"I know what you've heard, Jack," she said simply. "I know why you're wary, but it's not as you think. Time won't suddenly melt away because of a drink nor a crust of bread—as much as one might wish such things could be, they simply aren't, neither in your world nor in mine."

And so he took the goblet, because he was here and tired and so thirsty and he wanted to believe the girl's words. It held water, water cool across his tongue, water that tasted softly of other things: flowers, honey and the shape of the snow-flakes it had once been.

She gave him bread after that, with some cheese and apples, and they ate together. For Aengus there was an earthen bowl of water and a bone still heavy with meat. After he had eaten his fill, Jack had no memory of the room around him or even of lying down, but he slept for what seemed a long time and no time at all, Aengus tucked up tight to his chest.

He awoke on a mattress stuffed with oat straw, the scent of rosemary surrounding him. He sat up and looked around, confused at first, his hand automatically reaching out to touch the rough reassurance of Aengus' coat. He appeared to be in a tower, built of crumbling stone that had not been repaired in many long years.

Small flowers sprouted out of the cracks and a large tapestry covered one wall. At first he thought the wind was moving it, for the tower was airy to say the least, with breezes playing through the cracks and holes.

He walked to the deep window seat and looked out over the land below. The morning was new. There was still dew upon the grass. The river that wound through the meadows beyond was little more than a hazy silver ribbon. But... hadn't they descended a long track into the mound? How was it that land, trees, and a sinuous river now appeared before him? He rubbed his eyes but the countryside remained, verdant and beautiful, hazed with sun and summer's warmth. He turned away from the window, disturbed. How could it be summer already when it had been spring only yesterday? Had he slept that long?

He turned to the tapestry, needing to ground himself in something unchanging. It was an old tapestry, tattered, that told the tale of a Knight and a Lady—for weren't those always the best and the oldest of tales? He crossed the room to look more closely at it, for the wind was moving it in soft, slow ripples, obscuring some of the pictures. What he saw there froze him to the spot. Everything in the tapestry **was** *moving, and it wasn't the simple movement of the wind—the knight trotted up to a castle gate, small puffs of dust rising then settling in the wake of his horse's hooves, a lady leaned sighing from a tower window, her long hair rippling in the breeze. Small men and women tilled fields, herded cows, or stood in the doorways of tiny huts, smoke coiling from tilted chimney pots. Jack looked closer at the Knight, so close that he could smell the horse and hear the chuff of its breathing and the rattle of the Knight's mail. The Knight turned in his saddle, as though he sensed Jack's gaze. Jack drew in a short, sharp breath of shock. He knew the Knight, knew that face, had seen it before... then he realized, it was his own self, aged many years, as though he had waited a lifetime here at that castle gate and was now old and tired, an eternal knight errant, instead of the young man he truly was.*

The Knight rose up on the miniature spurs, and Jack wondered how it felt in that world? Was it as if threads were being strained each time they moved, or was that simply their world and they moved with ease inside it?

The Knight was trying to speak to him, but it didn't matter how close Jack got to the tapestry, he could not understand what he was saying. It seemed urgent though, as if he were trying to warn him. It was then that Muireann came into the room, considerably tidied from the night before though he still thought there was a tiny owl hiding amidst the curls on her head.

"Good morning, sleepyhead," she said. He looked at her more closely than his exhaustion and pain had allowed the night before. Her eyes were the color of spring gooseberries, her skin as pale as new snow and her hair as dark as... well, as night. She had a tiny face, delicate even, when her expression wasn't as fierce as it had been last evening.

"It's summer," he said, feeling strangely awkward suddenly.

She smiled, and it was like watching a translucent blossom open under the sun. "Of course, it's summer," she said, "what other season could it possibly be?"

Jack thought there was likely no answer to that so he kept his tongue still. She had brought breakfast and he was ravenous. They sat on the floor of the stone tower, amid the flowers growing from the walls and the watery breath of the mosses and feasted on bread, fruit and strong ale that was as dark as Muireann's hair. After, she held out her hand to him.

"Come away with me, Jack. I have much to show you."

And so he took her hand, which fitted into his like a puzzle piece into the center of a picture and followed her down the tower stairs into her world.

Later, he could never account for the time spent there. It would drift about in his memory like a rowboat without oars on a summer-calmed lake and he would only recall snatches. For instance, he remembered the wizened man in the white robes teaching him about the stars one night, yet the constellations were all muzzy in his head later. Still, he knew they weren't the same ones as at home, for in this land they called them by other names—strange ones; names from myth and legend, names of famed hunters and large animals. In his land, they called them by homely names so that the night sky might be a place of comfort when the sun disappeared. There was the Hearth, which was the main constellation of the winter skies, with its blazoning and umistakable five central red stars. Then there was the Arbor of Roses, an arcing constellation with a string of pale pink stars woven through it like a net of roses. Or his own favorite, the Apple Tree, so named for its main trunk of golden stars and the great spray of silver that looked like an apple tree in the torrent time of spring blossom. There was even a small cluster of golden stars near the top which was the Honeybee Nebula.

Time too was different here and there weren't the usual ways by which to reckon it. Surely the sun must have shone, but he could not remember it ever overhead in that strange land, nor the moon either—it was as if the entire place existed in between in some odd twilit realm where enchantment was endless and trickery the order of the day.

At times, it seemed that the castle and its environs were filled with lords and ladies richly dressed, with jeweled crowns upon their heads and the finest furs for cloaks, with scepters made of twined golden snakes topped with a silver apple that shone as bright as the full moon. At others they would be simply garbed, their clothes old and shabby, blending with the earth and the landscape, their scepters merely old gnarled sticks.

Muireann became the locus of this odd world for him, and it was her hand he took to roam in meadows heavy with the loveliest of flowers, or to swim in the cool waters of the lake that lay along the border of the land. Sometimes he caught her watching him with a look of such sadness in her face that he felt bewildered by it, for what was there to be so very sad about in this lovely drifting land?

When he was away from her he had an odd feeling of urgency, though it seemed as soon as one came over him, she would find him and take him by the hand once again, pulling him into the revelry or encouraging him to stay for just one more night, to sleep in the sweet bedding and dream the strange floating dreams that held the drift of the planets in their very core.

It came to him one day that he no longer had any idea where the path out of this world lay, and wasn't sure it mattered either. This last feeling disturbed him most, for if he had strayed so far from home and all that he loved, it should matter. He ought to have a great purpose for breaking his mother's heart. He still needed to find the Crooked Man and take back his dreams, yet here in this strange land it seemed far less urgent than it had when he had begun his journey.

Part Eight

When the Road Bends...
Ireland – May-December 1974
London – November 1974
Paris – November 1974

Chapter Fifty-five

May 15th, 1974

The Strike

THE PALE MAN DID NOT VISUALLY TRANSLATE WELL on a black and white television set, but his roaring rhetoric wasn't the least bit dimmed by the medium. With every statement he made, the crowd roared ever louder. It was a message of unmitigated hatred, a call to arms and the letting of blood. The blood of the enemy—two of whom were watching on their tiny television some remove from the city in which the man spoke, a city where a crowd of more than a thousand people were responding to his call.

"We have been loyal to Queen and Crown. We have laid down our lives on British battlefields, on ships and land. We know the names of all those places. They live in our hearts, and the memory of all those we have lost: the Somme, Burma, Palestine and South Africa. We gave them the best of what we are and that is the finest any nation anywhere has to offer. And now they abandon us for some weak-willed deal with terrorists, with the Republic of Ireland! So that we may be ruled by Rome? I say... No!"

The roar this time was almost deafening, even with the muffling of miles and the sporadic sound of their television set.

"I am prepared to come out and shoot to kill. Let's put all bluffing aside. I am prepared to spill the blood of the enemy and so are those behind me. We will not allow our province to fall into the hands of murderous terrorists and their allies across the border."

At this juncture, the crowd whipped up to a frenzy, he lifted one hand and struck a small knife across it. It wasn't pure theater, for blood dripped thickly from his palm onto the pavement where he stood, and he managed, Pamela noted with no small cynicism, to get some on his vestments.

"He's just told them to go ahead and kill people, and that he's happy to do so himself," Pamela said, feeling as if her own blood were somewhere in the vicinity of her toes.

"Well, it's not like we don't know what he is, Jewel."

She shivered. Knowing the Reverend was back and in nefarious business was one thing, seeing him in the flesh, if indeed he was flesh (which she begged leave to doubt) was another thing entirely. Northern Ireland, in its current state of a pot continually on the verge of boiling over, was a stage waiting for a man like Lucien Broughton.

By the end of 1972, with the unmitigated disasters of Bloody Sunday and internment blackening the Stormont Parliament, Westminster had rather boldly suggested the notion of power sharing between the factions in Northern Ireland as well as a cross-border alliance with the Republic, thus allowing the Catholic/Nationalist community to feel as though they had not only a say, but a link to the Dàil in the Republic, just as the Unionists identified with Westminster and Britain. The Unionist Government flatly refused to countenance such a thing. The Westminster government had the wisdom to see that there was indeed an Irish dimension to the Ulster problem, and that the flames of Nationalism were not going to conveniently sputter and die away. They saw the possibility of power sharing as a triangle of sorts which would, they hoped, alleviate the tension enough on all sides to quell the violence that had seized the province for so long now. The Loyalist factions viewed this as political appeasement, not only to the Nationalist community but also to the hated and feared Provisional Republican Army. The Nationalists viewed it with justifiable suspicion, and the IRA outright refused to take it seriously. Time had taught them that the Unionists would not share power, and would grip it until their hands were raw and bleeding before giving one inch.

The upshot now being that the Ulster Workers' Council had done what it had threatened all along, shut the province down in an act of defiance against the Power Sharing Assembly. Though they had claimed there would be no intimidation to enforce the strike, word was that the eight thousand Protestant workers of Harland and Wolff had been told that if their cars were in the parking lot after the lunch break, they would be torched. Major industry began to shut down as did the small shops, sometimes with the threat of arson looming over them. Pamela got the call that power to the distillery would be cut the following day. Knowing this was a possibility, she had arranged for a power cut days before. Every day of production lost meant thousands upon thousands of dollars, something she could ill afford at present, for it would be another black mark against her, no matter that she had nothing to do with the strike or its consequences. With Kirkpatrick industries as shaky as they were at present, any setback became a major problem for her.

It was the evening of the third day of the strike and it was looking like it would stick, with roads blockaded and power cut, no petrol, milk spoiling in farmer's barns and cattle going hungry. That evening, car bombs were set off in Dublin and Monaghan during the evening rush hour, killing thirty-three people immediately and injuring a further hundred odd. It was the single worst day of atrocity in the Troubles, a dubious honor, but one some of the

Loyalists seemed happy to embrace.

It came as no surprise that the Reverend Lucien Broughton had chosen to use the strike as a platform to stir more violence and hatred.

"What will it mean, do you think?" Pamela asked, looking at the shocked and angry faces on the television screen, the voices, stunned and agonized, that seemed to all run together.

"If they can't resolve it, it'll be all out civil war," Casey replied grimly.

"You really think so?"

"Aye, nothing less than dissolving the power sharing is goin' to appease the bastards. If the government doesn't give on that, there'll be blood in the streets. But have no fear, they'll get their way. The British inevitably crumble to it. We'll be back to direct rule in no time at all."

"I wish it could be different. I don't understand the hatred. Why can't they countenance the Irish Government having some say? After all, the British Government rules every other damn thing here."

"It's fear, darlin'. Fear of the unknown, fear that things will change and the balance of power will shift. In reality, it wouldn't be likely to change much, but the Loyalist community lives on the glory an' traditions of the past and they see no reason to change that."

"Where do you see yourself in all this, Casey?" she asked quietly, for though they never spoke about it, she knew very well how much he had changed his life for her and for the sake of their home and family.

"What do I wish or what is the reality that I see?"

"Both," she said.

"What I wish is that we could finish this stumble into peace, but I think it's clear that isn't going to happen. The reality is that there are too many people on both sides of this war who want it to keep going on. They need it for some reason. I used to feel the reasons for the fight were clear. I believed in it, thought it was just and right and that the end justified the means, but when the end never comes, then the means are only unending bloodshed. As for my own self, Pamela, I am just tryin' to keep my head down, and keep hopin' for a day when everyone will see how mad all this is. And yet—" he paused and she saw something dark and hard in his face that caused her stomach to clench, "when I hear about yet another young man bein' killed in the streets simply because he's Catholic, I feel a fury that I don't know where to put or what to do with. I feel as if I'm on the edge half the time, an' in danger of tippin' into some dark abyss. So perhaps I am no different than any of the mad bastards out there who keep this wee war goin'."

"I wonder sometimes if you miss it? If you regret changing everything, if the frustration makes you wish that you were still involved?"

He gave her a look of disbelief. "Woman, not for a minute. What we have here—you, Conor, myself—it's everything to me. What sort of fool would

I have to be to think some bloody unending conflict was a good substitute for that?"

"It's only that when we met, you seemed so certain that you wouldn't marry, wouldn't have children. It seemed as though the Republican movement was simply in your blood."

He turned the television off and came to stand beside her. He plucked the tea towel off her shoulder and set to drying the dishes while he answered.

"What ye say is true. It was the world I knew, Jewel. It was who I thought I was, so at the time, it felt inevitable. I remember standin' there takin' my oath over the Irish flag, havin' memorized my Green Book, an' feelin' like at last I could be a man, that I could feel some sense of power. That whole growin' up thing never quite works out the way ye think it will. My Da' never wanted that for either Pat or me. He said it only perpetuated the blood cycle that Irish history has always looped through. He was right, but I didn't want to hear him at the time, I figured it was the words of a man whose time had passed. Lord, what a fool I was. It's a wonder my Da' put up with me."

She reached up and kissed him, touching her hand to his jaw, leaving behind a line of bubbles in the dark of his whiskers.

"You're not so bad. I'm sure your Daddy knew you would end up alright. You had to get your stubborn nature from somewhere, after all."

He smiled at her. "Aye, that's true enough, darlin'. The man was a mite stubborn himself."

"You don't see an end to this—" she indicated the silent television with one soapy hand, "any time soon, do you?"

"I don't know, Pamela," he said, his words troubled in both form and tone. "I don't see how this is goin' to be worked out. What it comes down to is this—no one has the right to impose their will upon another person, especially when that will is imposed with violence, an' that is always the tool that is used here. Violence begets violence. I don't know that I understand how we're to get out of that cycle, without everyone agreein' at the same time, an' that is not goin' to happen."

"Not ever? You don't really believe that, do you?"

"I don't know, darlin'," he said softly. "Maybe I'm just tired an' spoutin' foolishness, only I'm feelin' a wee bit sad about it all. The Assembly was our one shot at some sort of decent representation in our own country, but this will bring it down. They won't stop until they get what they want. Which means we're back to direct rule. We just keep cyclin' through the same events, an' every time it seems we've managed a step forward, something pushes the entire country back two."

"I'm sorry," she said and moved into his arms, giving him the anchor of the here and now in her physical presence.

He sighed, and she felt the rise of his chest beneath her cheek, the thrum of his blood and heart sounding deep within her own body.

"It's what they say about the past, isn't it? It's another country, removed from this one an' best not visited too often lest ye should find yerself stranded there. I fear that's what Northern Ireland is though, stranded in the past."

He held her tightly and kissed the top of her head. Then they simply stood entwined, watching the sun sink into the west in shades of vermilion and gold. And she knew as she watched the movement of color and shadow play over the hills and spill soft through the hedgerows, that he saw something far different. He saw what might be, in a far country which existed only in the heart, a country to which she had no passport. It was her greatest fear—that one day he would finally cross that border and return home no more.

HE AWOKE IN THE WEE HOURS, THE DREAM STILL THICK UPON HIM so that he came up from sleep with the boy's name on his lips. He sat up, half expecting him to still be there in front of him, for the boy to speak and to be alive and whole. He had felt the sun's warmth on the boy's head, smelled the sweet half-grown scent of him. He sat up, swung his legs over the side of the bed and put his feet down. Behind him, his wife slept deeply, the steady breath of her grounding him a bit more. He sighed and got up, found his clothes and put them on. He needed the night air to brush the last of the dream from him.

The air outside was warm and thick with the scent of green things exhaling their watery breath. He took in a long steadying draught of it and headed toward the barn.

He had all but torn down the original structure and made it taller, with a loft for the hay. It was like many of the barns they had seen in the New England countryside during their time in Boston. He had even painted it red—with white trim—to Pamela's delight. It wasn't quite finished inside but it was close to it. Now Pamela could bring her horse home from Jamie's stable, should she choose to do so. Right now, Paudeen was the only occupant, curled up cosily on fresh hay. He looked up, uttered a small *meeehhh*, gave Casey the hairy eyeball and went back to sleep. The barn still smelled of freshly sawn wood and paint only just dried. It gave him a feeling of solidity to be here with beams he had hewn and walls he had raised himself, taking away the ephemeral disturbance of the dream.

He fished behind the beam on which his spade hung and brought out a packet of cigarettes. It had been a week since he'd had one and he felt he could reward himself for his good behavior with just one. He was pretty certain Pamela knew exactly where he hid them but she pretended not to and he pretended not to know that she knew. He lit up with the matches he kept tucked inside the packet and took a long, sweet drag, sighing contentedly and letting out a stream of smoke.

The dream had been of Lawrence. The boy had been standing on a gate, a meadow of wild-flowers behind him, the sun high in the sky lighting his hair to a gleaming copper penny. He had an apple in his hand in the dream, and was trying to tell Casey something, though the words had been lost the way they so often were in dreams. But there had been a sense that he was happy and that whatever he was trying to tell Casey wasn't urgent. Casey had been about to ruffle his hair the way he had done in life when he had awakened. He could still feel the silky softness on his palm, the depth of it over the boy's finely rounded skull.

It wasn't the first dream and he wondered sometimes if he dreamed as he did because he did not allow himself to think of Lawrence often. The lad was always there, of course, but Casey did not allow the memory of that tall, gangling frame and smart mouth to come to the surface any more than could be helped. It still had the slice of a scalpel to his heart, and he could not afford it. But sometimes, inevitably, there he was, as though he had appeared writ in the air, all limbs and elbows and sharp angles, food in his hand, for the child had always been hungry, and Finbar devotedly at his side.

Casey knew he had agreed to the deal with Billy because he had hoped somehow to find vengeance for Lawrence. But after the birth of Conor, something changed inside him and he had known it was not the right thing. It would not honor the boy and it would not bring him back.

Billy's information had been hit and miss, and Casey had never really trusted the child entirely. He had known from the start that the boy was playing to his vulnerabilities by dragging Lawrence's ghost into the situation. He had been careful about what he passed on to Dacy, who was his contact in the Republican world, knowing that the wrong information could backfire and cause a greater conflagration in the end. He had warned David too, but David was as wary as a caged hare in his own particular situation and careful with Billy too. He did not like to think about what David might be doing to keep his cover in that house of nightmares that he was attempting to bring down. The man was decent and Casey had come to have a grudging respect for him. Truth was, he trusted him. He laughed softly to himself and took another pull on the cigarette. He trusted a British agent. That and a dime could get you killed in this country.

Their arrangement was working thus far, with Casey using Dacy as his line of communication into the upper echelons of the Republican movement. He knew who the British were willing to talk to and negotiate with and had made that approach first. It had gone well and there had been, he was made aware, a meeting in England with the Secretary of State and a few names he knew from the IRA. Maybe there was hope for some sort of tenuous bridge to be built. At least not all of Jamie's work from the last few years would be destroyed. It made him laugh at himself to know he was holding down the fort for James Kirkpatrick, especially when he considered the hostility of their last meeting. The man had threatened to take his wife from him and Casey knew it had not been an idle threat. Mind, it had the exact effect on Casey that Jamie had intended it should, and he was bloody grateful to the highhanded bastard for the results of that.

Occasionally, through his brother, tidbits of information made their way to Muck as well. It was for him to do with it as he wished but there had only been hints thus far in the articles Muck wrote. Being that Muck's journalism tended more to the incendiary sort, Casey figured he was holding onto the small bait in order to chase a big fish. He had no wish to know what or whom that might be.

He had been chilled by the Reverend on the television. He understood all too clearly that the man was an implacable enemy of James Kirkpatrick, and therefore of Pamela as well.

This latest turn of events, nationally speaking, had made him feel suddenly old. He remembered how it had been, the time he had told Pamela of, what it was to believe so strongly that it was like breathing, not simply words, nor slogans, nor mindless violence. Now he knew that all of it, the posturing, the theater, the voting, the striking, the hate-filled speeches, marches, banners and guns would come down to the same thing—a nation that was lost, a nation that could not rule itself and so must be ruled by the enemy from across the sea, the enemy that occasionally meant well but had no understanding at all of their contrary cousins.

He headed back into the house. He was happy now, satisfied in his family and the world he had built with them. Still and all, sometimes in the quiet of a spring night there were times he missed that fiery boy and his beliefs.

And there was another boy he missed too, the one who spoke words he could not hear in his dreams.

Chapter Fifty-six

November 1974

A Man Uncommon in His Virtues

THE HOUSE WAS AN OLD VICTORIAN MANSION TUCKED AWAY in London's wealthy Mayfair District. The bottom floor was occupied by an elderly woman with blue-rinsed hair, sensible stockings and two cats that often sat on the stone pillars flanking the wrought iron front gate. She had a sharp eye for scoundrels and scamps, and as the neighbors could attest, an even sharper tongue. She had lived in the house a very long time, so long that the shape and form of the neighborhood around her had changed, like a sleeping cat that awakens, stretches itself and resumes its slumber in a different position, but still with recognizable paws and tail. The lady's name was Mrs. Tickle, which seemed rather unsuitable for one so sharp in her dimensions. No one, however, had been brave enough to point this out to her.

On the second floor was a bachelor, an untidy scholar of sorts who lived surrounded by piles of books, unwashed teacups, buttered toast ends, bits of marmalade, and paper with an uncanny ability to go forth and multiply during the night. He was a bit absentminded and tended to waste scads of time looking for his spectacles—inevitably perched upon his head. What his job was, no one knew, only that when he could navigate his way out of his cluttered set of rooms, he spent a great deal of time in the British Museum reading rooms. Neighbors speculated that he must be independently wealthy, though one could not determine that from the state of his clothes or shoes. His name was Mr. Smith.

The top floor of the house was empty and, as far as anyone knew, had never been inhabited. Thick draperies prevented even the smallest bit of light from escaping into the street below and no ghostly faces had ever been seen at the windows.

There was a garden at the back, nowhere near as grand these days as it had been in its Victorian heyday, but well enough kept, though the shrubbery had been allowed to grow high and thick, obscuring even further the neighbors' ability to peer in.

This evening the neighbors would have been rather surprised to see the activity on the third floor. It was a large open space, the walls having been knocked out and the ceiling reinforced with beams to compensate for the lack of load-bearing structure beneath. A large round table dominated the room, which was lit by dozens of candles and a fire in the hearth that made it snug and pleasant. The scents of food wafted up the steep staircase from the kitchen below: the sweet, opulent notes of vanilla, the deeper ones of a perfectly braised roast beef, the breathing flavors of uncorked red wine, cinnamon and pepper, cardamom and roses.

The guests now taking their places around the table came from a wide variety of countries, races, echelons of society and government. They were all present for a common reason—a most uncommon man. Some had known him since his birth, others had witnessed his growing years or groomed him through his adolescence for all that would one day be demanded of him. Still others had met him as a young student and attempted to create for him the spiritual and intellectual environment necessary for his adult life. They had found it no easy task. A few had never met him at all and their knowledge was at a remove. Some loved him and some most assuredly did not. None, however, were disinterested.

They settled quickly and drinks were brought, wine heated with spices in deference to the snow. The fire in the hearth burned high and fragrant, popping with resin from the dry birch that fed it. The chatter was amiable, for many of them knew each other, some through politics and others only through the man they had come here to discuss.

Only one woman sat among them, away from the fire, dressed in clinging crimson wool, her face exquisitely made up but not quite disguising her age. She knew the man in ways the others could not. She had loved him once, she had hated him once, and thought perhaps she still did—hate him and, God help her, love him. It was some small solace to know that he had loved her too, for a time.

Heads turned her way as they always had. A famed beauty in her day, her eyes were the color of the deepest heartsease and her hair fell in waves of winter chestnut to her shoulders. She had been painted more than once, in oils that tried to hold her colors, her delicate tints and the rich fall of her hair. None of them had done her justice. But she was not that bold girl any longer. Life had tempered her bones and skin, her prejudices and desires. Only sometimes, when it could not be avoided, did she remember what it had been to be that young woman, and ached for her.

She seated herself beside the Irish priest, for she had met him once and liked him. He had not judged her at the time and she thought this was a rare quality in a human being, much less a priest. He pulled the chair out for her, his smile crinkling the corners of his eyes. It was easy to see that he was accustomed to smiling and to laughter and his proximity made her spirit feel lighter immediately.

She was here because she was owed a favor and had chosen to call it in by being here tonight. She had been warned only to sit and listen. It had seemed a small enough price to pay.

This proved to be most difficult. It was clear almost immediately that the meeting had been arranged to justify certain actions, or rather the lack of them. She kept her eyes on a man in a grey suit, wondering whether he was friend or foe. She had known him a very long time but had never been able to decide which side of the fence he was on concerning Jamie. He was the one who had owed her a favor from a very long time ago.

Much of what was said was in the form of double talk, the way it always was when any of the shadow forces were involved.

"We need more time," said the grey-suited man. "It's a delicate situation and with the people involved everything must be done carefully."

The Irish priest next to her sighed. There were few people in the world better versed in the uses of double talk than Jesuits, but Jesuits didn't care for it when it was directed at them.

"There is more at stake than we can discuss here tonight."

"We've come about James Kirkpatrick, not about whomever you're intent on protecting or whatever information you're attempting to drown," Father Lawrence said mildly, though there was nothing mild in the man's demeanor. She remembered suddenly that it was he, in part, who had introduced Jamie to the world of boxing.

"It is about the security of nations, not simply the life of one individual."

"Is he inside the Soviet Union?" The priest wasn't going to back down and the grey-suited man was losing patience.

"I can't tell you that. It could compromise other situations that are ongoing."

"Are you saying Jamie is dead?"

She had to admire the priest's pugnacity. He wasn't leaving this place without an answer.

"So quick to throw him to the wolves, my friends?" said a new voice golden as honey. But it was winter honey, frosted along the sharp comb edge.

All heads turned toward the open doorway. Below its ornately carved lintel stood a man who had not been expected to attend this evening, a man who wielded more power in his rough peasant's hands than all the rest of them combined. Suddenly the empty chair on the other side of the Irish priest made sense. For in the doorway, as wide as the doorframe itself, stood the Black Pope, the Father General of the Society of Jesus upon this earth—Giacomo Brandisi, rumored to be the next man to be appointed to the College of Cardinals. Trying to imagine that girth swathed in scarlet was more than a bit overwhelming, the woman thought, as the priest beside her stood to acknowledge the man who had been both friend and confessor for four decades. What might be even harder to digest, for the Pope at least, was how even in a Society famed for its subversiveness, Giacomo had been from time to time considered a rebellious outsider. Yet none who knew him were surprised when he was appointed Superior General of the Order.

"We're hardly throwing him to the wolves. We've met here tonight to see what we can do about extracting him."

"Really? Because it sounded to me like you were justifying leaving him to rot inside the Soviet Union. I suspect you are protecting someone else at Jamie's expense, and I believe that Jamie will have realized that. This man whom you all feel you have some claim upon is not without his own resources. In fact, I would back him in any fight you can name. Do not be so eager to declare him a lost cause. He is a man uncommon in both his virtues and his faults."

A silence greeted Giacomo's words and the woman suppressed a smile. Everyone here knew, whether they liked it or not, what sort of power this man wielded and that he also had the ear of the Pope who in turn had the ear of two thirds of the world. It would not do to upset either. The message could not have been clearer had it been carved in stone.

The conversation changed markedly in tone after that, to practicalities about how to locate one man within an area as vast as Russia. One man, whose various guises made his position that much more precarious, one man—the woman was very aware—who might be far more convenient dead than alive.

SHE DID NOT LINGER AFTERWARDS. She had kept this evening as private as she could since she had something to lose by her attendance, the rest something to gain. There had been no one there that could report her presence back to her husband, for they would not want to admit to having been there themselves.

The meeting had become emotional towards the end, as she had expected it would. It was simply how things were with James Stuart Kirkpatrick. He had always inspired an extreme of emotion in both sexes. Such an extreme in her own case that she had tried to kill herself. In retrospect, she realized that such an act of desperation was an effort to draw him back to her, though had he come it would have been from pity, not love, and that she could not have borne. At the time she had not cared, for she had lost all reason in his absence.

She met him because she had been lost. She had been at one of those country house weekends alone, because Neil, her husband, as always, had business in London that could not keep until Monday. If she suspected that the business concerned a certain bosomy blonde, she did not let on.

Diane Landel, for that was her name, had married well as had been expected of her. She brought to her husband both money and the blue blood
that went back to a remote branch of the Plantagenet family. Neil had been a
rising young star in Parliament at the time, and the sole heir of a grandmother
who doted upon him. Diane had loved him, she was certain, even if she had
been raised not to expect grand passion in a marriage. Marriage was about
connections and fulfilling one's role in the grand scheme of life. Except that
she had been young when she married and not yet asking herself what life
ought to be about.

Then there had been the inability to have children. Doctor after doctor said to be patient and to relax, which after the fourth year of hoping for
a pregnancy had been next to impossible. Neil refused to be tested, saying
there had never been any infertility issues in his family and therefore the
fault—implied though not spoken aloud—must lie with her.

She had been mulling over a variety of thoughts when she entered the
forest, and not paying attention to the pathways her feet followed. She felt
like a princess lost in a fairytale forest, never knowing what adventure lay
just around the next turn in the path, the next crooked tree trunk. The adventure of it wore off an hour later, though, when she realized she was truly
lost. She was flustered at that point, for it was one of those hot, still days
that are slightly breathless, and wondered if she would ever find the end of
this forest. She no longer felt like a lost princess, but rather an overheated
and panicked woman.

She heard them before she saw them, for there was a great deal of laughter,
voices rising and falling in what sounded like very high spirits. She came out
of the wood suddenly, to find a pond sparkling in the bright sunlight and a
group of people, some lying in the grass on picnic blankets, and some running
in and out of the water where three boats bobbed on the wavelets. Her eyes
were drawn immediately to the two young men playing some strange version
of cricket that included the pond and some rather insane maneuvers with
stick in hand. After watching for a few more moments, she realized why no
one else was playing, for the main aim of the game seemed to be how much
bodily harm they could inflict upon one another.

She realized later that it was impossible not to see them, impossible to
look away, and knew everyone present was as riveted as she was. For they
were both beautiful, in that stage of young manhood where they were god-
like: golden, perfect and dazzling in their athletic display, their manic high
spirits and their sheer joy in the mere fact of being. Even then, her eye had
been riveted first and foremost by one in particular. He had been standing on
the branch of an oak that overhung the pond, his shirt plastered to his skin,
his pants streaked with mud and grass and dripping with water, explaining
in rhyming couplets how he proposed to ricochet the ball off his friend's

head before hitting it across the pond and neatly onto the green. The friend, meanwhile, was lining up his own shot and shouting insults back. The man in the tree had looked up, seen her standing on the edge of the wood, and had grinned at her, thus distracting him enough that he was hit by his friend's well-aimed shot—right in the temple. He dropped off the branch like a stone into the water, the friend already splashing in amidst a flurry of expletives that sounded Eastern in tone and none of which was flattering to his drowning compatriot.

She ran with everyone else to the edge of the pond, frightened that he had been killed and that it was, at least in some respects, her fault.

The gilt-headed Russian dragged him to the shore and none too gently slapped his face. A pause, and then a rather rude but very witty couplet finished off the verses the young man had begun on the branch. The Russian swore and laughed.

Diane had found herself equal parts relieved and awkward, hovering near while he lay supine and streaming on the shore. Close to, he took her breath away. He was absurdly young, with the fine skin and gleaming health of one barely past his teens. He peered up at her, shading his eyes with one long, finely-boned hand.

"I might have been killed, and the guilt of it would be on your head."

She began to protest, then saw he was teasing and closed her mouth.

"You will have to stay now, you know. Entertain me, nurse my wound. Besides we have far too much champagne for our own good. You have to stay and drink some."

And so she had, because it was impossible to say 'no' to him that day, and any day after. They had eaten strawberries and drunk champagne chilled in the pond's mossy bottom. He had made her laugh—a lot—something that her husband had never done.

At dinner that night, they were expecting guests, a party of people who were staying at a neighboring estate. Inevitably, for so it seemed at that point, it was the party from the pond. And there he was, lagging in last, dressed impeccably in a summer-weight suit and crisp white shirt. It hurt to look at him, as though it might burn one's eyes and soul to gaze overmuch. In the end, she had looked too long, and paid the price of falling to earth with all the damage that entailed.

But that night had been simply glorious. He had managed to get himself seated next to her at dinner and told her scandalous stories about each person at the table, some she knew to be true, some at which she wondered. She had laughed and drunk too much wine, for he filled her glass each time the bottle passed down the table, or up for that matter.

"Are you trying to get me drunk?" she asked at one point, and he had merely smiled, an expression that went directly to her knees and points somewhat higher.

She had seen the Russian, who was busy enchanting a beautiful redhead further down the table, flick him a look once or twice that seemed to be communicating volumes. Was he warning this beautiful boy off or encouraging him? She rather hoped it was the latter, and yet that was a form of madness that could only bring her trouble.

After dinner, too restless to join the other women in the drawing room, she had gone outside, walking off across the velvet lawn to the shadows that gathered thick and fragrant in the gardens. She drew in the night air, filled sweetly with roses and jasmine. There was music drifting from the open French doors, spilling over the balcony—plaintive, yearning notes, and she wished she were deaf to it. She wished she were deaf to all her senses right now. She wished she were younger and not married. She wished she could run away from her life, her world, herself.

That was where she found him. She had half hoped she would not and prayed that she would, because she understood very well that it did not matter what he asked of her, she would give it happily.

In the end, it wasn't he who asked. He had been, rather infuriatingly despite his slight intoxication and the knot on his head, a gentleman. He was lying on a stone wall lushly bedded with ivy, gold hair filaments of light in the deep shadows of the garden.

"Are we going to sleep together?" she asked, because the dark and the scent of jasmine seemed to allow for such bold questions.

"You're married," he said quietly. "Beautiful and desirable, but married."

"Married and unhappy. Does that help?" she said tartly, angry at him.

He raised one eyebrow. "A little, but I don't sleep with married women, generally speaking."

"Generally speaking? That rather sounds like you have occasionally made exceptions."

He had looked at her quite seriously then, green eyes dark in the night, profile tipped in starlight.

"I think if I take you to bed, it won't be a mere matter of one night for us. That's why I hesitate. Should you ask about me in the circles in which you travel, you're going to hear a great deal to give you pause. Some of it might actually be true, but a great deal won't be. I seem to come with scandal attached to my wings. That's dangerous for a married woman. I will be honest and tell you I don't take responsibility for someone else's vows, but at the same time, I've no wish to be a respondent in divorce proceedings. Still...." He grinned and let the thought linger in the air between them.

And that, as they say, had been that.

The bed had been a revelation, for he was remarkably skilled for a man of his tender years and coupled it with a passion that precluded any artifice.

It did not take long to fall from lust to love and, she was honest enough to admit, she had known the tumble to be inevitable from the moment she had seen him balanced on that branch.

He had given her many things, the absence of which, later, were extremely hard to bear. In the end, they had waited too long to cut the ties even if she had no desire at all to sever what had grown between them. It had been a fool's game and she ought to have known better.

You could write it down like a fairytale, the beautiful golden prince, the well-born young woman with half the kingdom pining after her. Except that in the fairytale everyone always drifted off to live happily ever after and in real life that rarely, if ever, occurred. The princess wasn't already married to someone other than the prince, nor was she older than the prince by several years. And the prince didn't tell her, kindly, gently, that he didn't love her in the right way and that he should never have gotten involved with her in the first place. No, such stories were saved for real life. And real life, this princess had long ago discovered, was hard.

No, a fairytale wouldn't do, unless it was one of the old ones with blood and pain at its root. For princesses do not try to overdose themselves with pills and end up in hospital making up tearful explanations/lies with an extremely sore stomach their only ailment other than a broken heart—which wasn't audible to doctor's stethoscopes, nor visible on their x-ray machines.

Over the course of many years she had kept his memory as distant as she was able, indulging only occasionally, for enchantment remembered at a distance becomes dark. Inevitably, she heard accounts of his life as the years moved along: his marriage, the loss of his sons, the suicide of his father, the scandal concerning that ludicrously young girl who had lived in his home for a time. Sometimes it was idle gossip at a dinner table, sometimes it was told with an edge of malice by someone who suspected her long ago affair. Her heart had ached over the deaths of his children, for she had always felt Jamie should have children, lots of them to fill his beautiful home. Despite often hating him, she had always thought he would make a wonderful father.

The affair had never been spoken of to anyone, not even those who felt themselves her confidantes or might have forgiven her the infidelity, knowing her husband as they did. She had much to protect and even more to hide. For James Kirkpatrick did have a son, living and thriving, a beautiful boy by any account, who had just turned nineteen on his last birthday. A son who was also her own.

Chapter Fifty-seven

November 1974

Waiting

THE RIORDAN LAND WAS ROUGHLY SHAPED like a slice of pie, with the large end a rounded arc that bordered Lewis Guderson's land. The point of the slice was the long windy drive that led up and onto the country road that ran across the tip of their property. The sides of the slice were bordered on one side by a thick copse of pine and a stream that cut off the corner, and on the other a dense wood of oak, hawthorn and, at the very back corner, a small stand of evergreens. Other than the bit immediate to the house, they had left the land as it was. Casey culled the dead wood in fall and Paudeen grazed in the grassy parts, but beyond that it was pristine land untouched for decades. Long ago it had been a working farm but had lain abandoned for so many years that it had grown over in a wild profusion of shrubs and trees and plants.

David had used the Riordan woods more than once to shorten the distance between the wee farm he visited often—only three miles beyond their own—and to where he left his car parked behind an abandoned church, long unused and out of the way but convenient to his own purposes. Few, if any, saw him cutting across country this way, and so he lessened the risk of exposure for himself, and more importantly, for the man he visited.

The warmth of that visit was still there, glowing like his own secret sun between his body and the damp wool of his sweater. There had been no actual sun that day, but that was not a rare thing in Ireland. The woods were dripping with moisture, the air gelid, pregnant with water. The light was heavy—greens and blues, the deep shades that were normally found only in dreams and blood and here on the cusp of winter.

He saw Pamela just as he was about to jump over the stream. She must have noted his approach for she didn't startle, merely looked up at his arrival from where she stood on the far bank, wet to her knees and barefoot in the cold twilit air.

In the aqueous atmosphere, she blended into her surroundings, a creature

of water, a mermaid stranded on land, or one of the selkie women whose hide
had been stolen away from her, preventing her return to her ocean home.
Though his desires did not tend toward women, he could appreciate beauty
regardless of the gender in which it came wrapped. There was something
singular about this woman that made her more than just another lovely face
and form, something that made her stand out from both her surroundings
and the people around her. He thought perhaps it was her inability to be
anything other than what she was. She had never learned how to camouflage
herself from the world.

He crossed over a fallen log and trod through the soaked plant life to
stand beside her, noting that she was damp through but seemingly undisturbed
by it. The scent of waterlogged mint and comfrey rose from under his feet,
a comforting note in the eerie atmosphere. She was, it was apparent, totally
unperturbed by his sudden appearance in her woods.

"It's not what you'd call a soft night," he said by way of greeting.

She turned toward him, a faraway look on her face, as if he were pulling her back unwillingly from a strange land of which he could have no
knowledge. But then she smiled, and the feeling disappeared slowly, like a
ripple on a pond.

"If you mean the evening seems a little bit intemperate to be going about
barefoot, you're right. I was standing in the water earlier."

"Doing what?" The question was out before his good manners could
still his tongue.

"You might think I'm a bit crazy if I tell you."

David didn't laugh, for the atmosphere seemed to forbid such a light act.
He merely waited for her to continue—or not—as she chose. She quirked a
brow at him as if to say she knew exactly what he was doing. Well, he was
learning, he supposed, having spent so much time with the Riordan family
of late, what tactics worked best with whom.

"I have a sense often of being watched, and sometimes I come out here
to challenge it—whatever it is—to come out and show itself, to tell me what
it is that it wants."

"What do you mean? Like the man who was watching you when Casey
was interned?"

She shook her head, her dark hair a billow of ink against the watery
twilight. "No, not that. Not anything human, nothing I can describe without sounding like a superstitious old woman. It's just a sense of something
watching, waiting, a presence that's neither good nor bad."

David, who was normally unflappably upper crust British in his regard
for supernatural phenomena, felt a chill rise up his backbone and crest at the
base of his skull, like a thing with featherless wings had brushed all along
his length. The very land here seemed to hold great reserves of ghouls and

specters and things best not seen, but sensed nevertheless. And so one could not entirely avoid picking up on such things, regardless of the phlegmaticness of one's race of origin.

"Does it scare you?" he asked, knowing that the woman beside him, for all her delicacy of appearance, did not frighten easily.

She shook her head in the waning light, green eyes dark as the night fast closing in around them. "No, it doesn't frighten me. Only I wonder sometimes..."

"Yes?" David prompted, wanting to get in out of the night and thinking that a hot cup of tea was most definitely in order.

She shrugged and gave him a ghost of a smile. "I wonder what it is this presence is waiting for."

The creeping upon his spine became more pronounced at her words and he thought he could feel it himself there in the dim light, this presence of which she spoke, ancient and implacable. He shivered involuntarily. She had said it wasn't a bad presence but neither did it feel warm and fuzzy.

"You haven't asked what I'm doing here," he said, wanting to break the tension and at the same time wondering why he was bringing it up when she had been polite enough to let it lie.

"David, your business is your own. Now, shall we go have some tea, if you've the time for it?"

And that, thought David, told him that she knew exactly what he was doing cutting through her land. He felt a small knot of fear that Patrick knew also but then reminded himself that it would not matter to Patrick Riordan whom he bedded.

"Does anyone else know?" he asked.

"Casey has seen you pass through once or twice. Neither of us has a reason to tell anyone, so you needn't worry. Besides, we've no wish to have it abroad that a British soldier visits our property. It wouldn't go down well with the locals, now would it?"

"No, it wouldn't." He felt a wash of shame, for his thoughts had only been of himself and Darren, not of the risk to this woman and her family.

She turned for the house, and David followed with no small relief toward the warmth and walls that would banish their respective chills.

"This thing, when you challenge it, does it ever come out to tell you what it wants?" David asked, wrapping his coat tightly around his frame and wondering how Pamela managed to look impervious to the wet and cold of the night. He had meant for his question to be light, to break the dark spell of the evening. It did not, however, come out that way, and so she answered him as he had asked.

"No, it doesn't. But I can still feel it. Waiting."

Chapter Fifty-eight

November 1974

When the Road Bends...

A FAINT LIGHT WINKING IN AND OUT OF THE TREES like a particularly impertinent boy was Pamela's only indication that she was nearing her destination. Casey, coming along behind her and swearing vociferously from time to time as thorn bushes caught at his clothing and hair, commented rather mildly, all things considered, that it would be nice if occasionally they could go on a proper outing.

"A meal, maybe the cinema," he said, then halted to peer through the shrubbery at the lights ahead, "ye know, just for the change of pace, as an alternative to crawlin' about in the dark like a couple of thieves or spies. Not that we'd have to give up the espionage permanently or anything, but just now an' again my nerves could do with the rest."

Pamela merely kept walking, for she knew Casey's sarcasm grew with his level of nervousness and wouldn't be helped by protestations on her part. In all honesty, the man had a point. She had been told to meet someone who apparently was without a name, here in the woods that skirted the edges of Jamie's property, in the pitch black of a late autumn evening. It wasn't, to be blunt, a situation designed to soothe anyone's worries. Still, the message had come to her through a friend and she trusted that no harm was intended her.

They came out into the clearing rather precipitately, suddenly seized from behind and pushed out forcibly by strong hands.

Casey swore, and before Pamela could warn him, she found herself looking down at her husband planted on a man's chest with a knife to his throat. Casey Riordan was not the man to attack from behind, though she was a little shocked by the appearance of the knife and wondered when he had started carrying one on his person.

The man pinned to the ground was grinning, white teeth a brilliant gleam in his swarthy face.

"Johnny!" she exclaimed in delight. "Casey, let him up. He's a friend."

Casey removed the knife from the man's throat and helped him up off the ground.

"Sorry, man," he said, "but ye took us rather sudden-like there."

Johnny brushed the leaves from his clothes and grinned. "Ach, that bitty wee knife didn't scare me." He turned to Pamela, one gold earring winking in the firelight, and grabbed her in a bear hug that lifted her right off the ground. He put her back down and held her out at arm's length.

"So, my sweet, have you danced back into my life only to break my heart by dancing back out like you did last time?"

"Last time?" Casey echoed, tone rather grimmer than Johnny's.

"I spent some time traveling with Johnny and his family," she replied. "He taught me how to dance the flamenco."

"In which," the man kissed the tips of his fingers as though recalling an ecstatic vision, "the student far outstripped the teacher."

"You are as much of a flatterer as you ever were." She leaned forward and kissed his cheek, remembering her time traveling the hills and roads of Ireland with this man and his enormous family. It had been a magical interlude, filled with strange adventures.

"It's likely I'll regret askin' this," Casey said, "but how did ye manage to fall in with a band of gypsies? Did they fetch ye direct off the plane?"

"Ah! Ye've not told the man this story?" Johnny asked. "She did the dance of the seven veils for us one night and after that—" he sighed and lifted his eyes heavenward, "we were but putty in her hands. All those veils knotted so ingeniously so that they fell just so... Such a Salome as she was that night there has never been before, nor since. That a *gadjo* could dance with such fire was a revelation."

"Oh, I have no doubt of that," Casey said dryly. "I shall have to ask her for a private performance one of these nights."

"Ye will not regret it my friend. 'Twill put the oil in all yer hinges just to see it."

Pamela felt that it was high time to get things back on a more formal footing before Johnny made any more references to her previous exploits.

"Johnny, you know why we're here?"

"Of course I do, *scumpete*. Just follow me."

They came out into the center of the small clearing, an enormous bonfire in its midst, with hundreds of firefly sparks drifting upward into the frosty night sky. The fire was ringed by caravans, some modern and gleaming with newness, others that had seen many miles of road and field. But there was one that held pride of place, as though the rest were merely courtiers to this queen. It was an old *vardo* in the tradition of Eastern Europe, barrel-topped, painted a vivid red, with gilding and bright blue shutters, an immaculately painted blue door with a brass knocker and a delicate set of stairs leading up to it. There was even an ornate gable peeking out from one end.

Casey had gone quiet as they were directed toward the stairs, as if he sensed who was on the other side of the door. He had never met the woman but he had heard enough about her to harbor some trepidation.

The scent of black cinnamon and rain-drenched gardenias wafted out as the door opened, a scent as exotic as the woman who awaited them. Inside, the caravan was lit with candles that refracted and danced in the glass balls that hung from the ceiling, and the crystals that adorned the candlesticks and trimmed the heavy drapes. A crystal ball sat upon a table covered with a velvet cloth, ancient symbols embroidered into its hem. A silver samovar sat gently steaming on a wee hostess stove.

The woman sat, dark and opulent, in a chair near the stove. The flat eyes of Russian saints lined the gilt-edged shelves above the woman's head, and if Pamela knew her art, she would hazard that they were genuine ikons and not reproductions.

"Yevgena," Pamela said.

"Hello, darlink girl." The woman stood, allowing her robe, lined with some night-dark fur, to fall to the chair in her wake. She had always had a wonderful sense of the dramatic. Dark hair fell in wings to her shoulders, her eyes smoky with kohl and secrets. A Russian by birth, a gypsy by marriage, Yevgena Vasiliovich had been born with drama in her blood, a drama that had played out in some terribly tragic ways throughout her life. History had not been kind to her. She had lost a husband and two sons to the Nazis and been the one real mother James Kirkpatrick had ever known. She had also been instrumental in bringing Pamela back into Jamie's life in a very memorable fashion.

She hugged Pamela to her, enveloping her in scent and warmth, and Pamela felt a sense of relief. If anyone could track Jamie down and return him home whole, it was this woman. She had the sort of contacts the CIA might envy.

Yevgena stood back then and surveyed Casey from the very top of his head to the tips of his toes. To Pamela's surprise, her husband blushed under the scrutiny. She raised her eyebrows, giving him a slight smile. She had rarely seen him flustered by a woman but he most certainly was by this one.

Yevgena smiled, a slow seductive thing, and then gave Casey her hand. He bowed over it and kissed the back of it, for one didn't shake hands with such a woman.

"So you are my girl's husband?"

"Aye, I am that," Casey said, the color still high in his face.

"Well," Yevgena said, a mischievous look in her eyes, "she's lucky I'm not a few decades younger or I might try to steal you from her."

"I'm flattered by the notion," Casey said, rising from her hand and stepping back as one did in the presence of royalty.

"Please sit down, both of you. There are things of which we need to speak."

They sat opposite her on a double seat covered in ruched velvet, the wall above their heads fitted with an ingeniously built china cabinet. Pamela saw Casey take in the construction of the *vardo* with his artisan's eye. The interior was done in highly polished walnut and had clearly been the work of a master craftsman.

"This will be one of the Welsh wagons, no?" Casey asked, peering at a joint in the couch they sat upon.

"Yes," Yevgena said, obviously pleasantly surprised by his knowledge. "How did you know?"

"I saw the wee gilded dragons on the crown boards outside. I know that's a Welsh builder's mark."

"You have the hands of an artist yourself," she said. "The understanding of wood and stone is in your blood, yes?"

"Aye, 'tis," Casey replied and Pamela heard the pleasure in his voice at being so quickly understood.

"Vodka?" Yevgena asked, already uncapping a frosty bottle that sat on the table between them and pouring it into three small glasses. When a Russian asked you to drink, it was only a formality. There really was no question about it, so neither of them bothered to demur.

Casey drank his down in one swallow as a Russian would expect. Pamela sipped at hers and then put it back on the table. The smell of it was strong, which seemed odd as vodka usually was utterly without scent, unless it was infused with fruit or spices.

"So you were right, Pamela. Jemmy is in Russia. Frankly, I had hoped that you were wrong about that."

Jamie had once described Yevgena's voice as akin to honeyed vodka poured through crimson velvet, gorgeous in the moment, but likely to leave a blistering head in its wake. She was a dangerous woman and as much as Jamie loved her, he never made the mistake of underestimating her or her motivations. But in this situation Pamela trusted her entirely for she knew how much this woman loved Jamie—as much as if he were her own son.

"Getting him out won't be easy. To be honest, I do not even know if it is possible. The last place I can track him to is Lubyanka."

Pamela thought she might be sick right there, for Lubyanka was such a chamber of horrors that rumors of its particular terrors had reached far into the outside world. Though she had no idea what the prison looked like, a huge stone edifice streaked with blood and echoing with screams reared up all too vividly in her mind's eye. To survive such a place would require—she tore the thought off before it could root itself in her head.

Yevgena watched the play of emotion as it flashed over her face.

"I did not say it's entirely impossible, child, only that there are road-blocks, and information from within the Soviet Union is at times very hard to come by. It is a little like trying to find one snowflake in a snowball. It is clear to me that someone does not want him found."

"Do you have any idea who?"

Yevgena gave a wry smile. "There are any number of suspects, a wearying variety to be honest. Not to mention the Soviet border is the most closely guarded boundary in the world. Even information has a hard time getting past the Border Guard undetected, so the process is slow to say the least, and any plans we might make must be laid as carefully as though they were being set over a minefield, because in essence they are just that."

"But you can find him?" she asked, her throat so dry it hurt to speak. Casey took her hand and squeezed it.

"There are Romany people everywhere, and we know how to keep our ears to the ground. I will find him, but it will take time and patience. Now," she clapped her hands, "Johnny tells me you have agreed to dance for us tonight."

"I didn't bring clothes for dancing," Pamela protested.

"Ah, that is no problem," Yevgena said and stood. "Come, darlink girl, let us have music and dancing to help our worries."

Casey stood also and bowed over Yevgena's hand once again, kissing it. "It was an honor to meet ye at last."

He left the *vardo*, giving Pamela a quirk of his brow, whether in question or amusement at her having to dance she wasn't sure, but she felt that he was enjoying himself a wee bit too much.

Once the door closed behind him, Yevgena took an outfit out of a tiny built-in closet and laid it out on the bed. Then she turned and opened a drawer, withdrawing an envelope from it and handing it over to Pamela.

"This is for you. Inside you will find a key to a house in Paris, along with other information you will need. It's all I can give you to keep you ahead of the others in this game."

Pamela took the envelope, feeling the shifting weight of the key and the crinkle of several sheets of paper.

"It is Jamie's house now, but once it was the home I shared with his grandfather. I knew Philip through him and I have to tell you, Pamela, this is a man to fear. I want you to understand and take precautions accordingly. He is like a snake idling in the grass—you understand—ready to strike just when you are lulled into complacency. He hates Jamie, he hated his father and he hated his grandfather who was, of course, his own brother. And he hates all those whom Jamie loves."

"I know, but it's not him that I'm most worried about." She told Yevgena then about the return of the Reverend and what she believed the two men were attempting to do to Jamie's companies. Yevgena listened, the violet shadows that clustered near to the candlelight hiding her expression.

Yevgena had taken out a brush and a box of cosmetics while Pamela spoke. She tilted Pamela's head back.

"Close your eyes, darlink," she said. "The Reverend is not as circumspect as he would like to believe, my girl. He is observed at all times."

At the woman's words, Pamela let out a little of the breath she had been holding. It was soothing to have someone brush on color, light as feathers, across her eyelids and cheekbones. Yevgena was humming to herself, soft and low, and Pamela felt the tension begin to leak from her body. It felt as though she weren't herself for a moment, and she realized just how long and how deep the worry over Jamie had become.

"You miss him still—Jamie's grandfather?"

"Yes," Yevgena said frankly, "he is the hole in my universe, the piece of my soul that is always missing. I loved him in such a way that it is hard to say to you what he was in my life, what he still is despite his very long absence. You understand this, I know."

Yevgena poured a golden oil into one hand, rubbing it then between her palms and releasing the scent onto the air. It smelled of the desert and of rain after long sun. She rubbed it through Pamela's hair in long strokes and Pamela succumbed to the pleasure of it, feeling slightly drowsy.

"There, darlink girl, you are ready for the dance."

She met Yevgena's eyes in the mirror. The woman's face was lit in chiascuro, the light of the candles leaving her half in the darkness. The fire-lit side glowed golden, her bones startlingly sharp beneath the surface of her skin. The dark side hid her age, yielding echoes of the beauty she once had been.

"I have been long enough with the Rom that I understand a candle is not wax, it is all flame. I have learned to live in the now and not yearn for what is past and what may or may not be to come. He is still with me. He is always in the now for me and he is always flame."

Yevgena took Pamela's chin in her hand and their reflections flickered back at them in the mirror. Beauty present and past, two ages of woman caught in the shadowy glass.

"We will find him, darlink, we just need time. You have played for time before. You can do it again, no?"

IN A LAND WHERE HALF THE POPULATION FELT DISPOSSESSED, the Pavee were at the bottom. It was part fiction, part mythology and part fact that had put them there. Though they weren't related to the Rom except by lifestyle, they were tarred with the same brush with which the world had always painted gypsies. Casey had heard warnings about them, about the cons and rooks at which they were supposedly expert, but he had always supposed that there were as many con artists who had permanent addresses as there were on wheels.

At times, he thought he could understand such a life: the need to keep moving, to be able to stretch out to new boundaries each day, and to be limited only by the length of the road and the limits of the land. Such a life would free one from certain constraints, though it also imposed new ones: poverty, prejudice, and a lack of any sort of permanence beyond love. Then again, what sort of permanence did life guarantee anyway? And if you had been born to a life of perpetual movement and changing horizons, would you not feel strangled by the lack of such things?

It was then that the music began, distracting him from his thoughts and the particularly potent brew that had been placed in his hand earlier. The drum started slow, like smoke, curling out one beat, a long pause, another beat and the men around him went silent, waiting. The thrum, the anticipation was a tangible vibration upon the air.

A man began to dance, slow formal steps in a call and response with the drum. He realized it was the gypsy to whom he had held the knife, the man his wife called Johnny. He was almost unrecognizable without the grin, and it was impossible to look away from him. He wondered what else the man had tried to teach Pamela beyond dancing. Plenty, he had no doubt.

The dance was a story told through the body and Johnny was master of every muscle within his slender frame. He stopped sharply within the pool of light cast by the fire. A brief flourish of his hand and a violin began on a long note, anticipation and ancient longing in its throat. Then a woman's voice began to flow along that aching violin note, rough and smoky, rising to a ululation that told of such pain and endless wandering without destination that each word struck him to his core even without understanding the meaning.

The air drew taut, suspended, and then he saw her. Barefoot, clad in a red dress sashed with a purple scarf fringed with tiny golden bells. Her eyes were enormous in her face, ringed thickly as they were with kohl, her lips red as blood and full of carnal promise. Her hair fell in a torrent down her back, the sides pulled back and fastened with scarlet flowers. Pamela, but not anyone who looked remotely like Pamela, for he could not find his wife in this woman's face. It both disturbed and excited him. She was something Other, she was every temptress throughout Time: Lilith, Salome, Bathsheba and Delilah. And she was something else beyond that, something powerful that held every eye and kept every breath bated.

Casey watched as the man took his wife in his arms, both of them falling naturally into the formal arc of arms and legs that the dance required. In the firelight her hair shone like a banner of torn silk, her body a perfect fit to the man who was no longer grinning but looking down into her face with the fire that the dance compelled.

They parted immediately, the violin arcing over the drum now, their hands describing individual arabesques upon the air. It was a dance of the dark, of fire that only lit to the edge of shadow, of original sin and man's need of woman. Touching, parting, eyes meeting, the air around them crackling with heat. Advance, retreat, allure, seduce, all the push-pull of the physical courtship.

In his arms again she leaned back, rejecting his advances, arcing over until her hair spilled onto the ground, her back a supple bow of demure regret. And then he pulled her back insistently, one beat at a time, and she raised her arms above her head so that the man could slide his hands along them in a caress that was as old as time. She brought her hands down and touched his face, bending his forehead to her own, then whirled away. The man followed and the dance moved faster and faster until they were a whirl of flesh and fire and flashes of gold and long white leg, hip to hip, cheek to cheek, and Casey saw why they had been such a draw. Half the country would have gathered to see such a passionate display. She was like a mirage rising sinuously from a hot plain, seen from a distance, drawing a man through a desert to find her.

Watching Pamela dance in such a way made him feel odd, as though there was something of her that was foreign to him, a place he had never traveled and did not know the customs nor rituals that would bring him inside her enchanted borders.

Near the end of the dance, the man handed Pamela into Casey's arms in a fluid movement and then danced back to the fire, stamping and tossing his head like a stallion. Though Casey could not imagine trying to match the steps, still he knew how to hold a woman, how to hold this one in particular. When a man knew a woman in this way it was natural to slide into a dance—a soft, slow dance beyond the boundary of the firelight.

He looked down into her eyes, which were dark, the pupils dilated so it felt he could fall into them. She was a stranger entirely, as if she was neither his wife nor the mother of his son but a vessel through which something ancient was being channelled with the aids of fire and drink and the wild, wild music that seemed to go on forever.

She coiled like smoke around his senses until he felt drunk on her, intoxicated by her strangeness, by the night, the music and the madness that seemed to have infected the very molecules of the air. And so he followed when she took his hand and cast a look over her shoulder, hair coiled there, framing the kohled eyes and cherry-bitten lips.

He heard someone call after them, a few sentences in a strange tongue, and the bawdy laughter that followed.

He had not noticed the caravan before, painted a deep blue and standing off by itself beyond the circle of the encampment. Gilded under the full moon and traced with the shadows of the trees that it sheltered under, it sat empty, waiting for them, he understood, following his wife as though in a dream, drifting soft over the landscape and hardly feeling his own movements. The night was held still in the moon's embrace, each blade of grass frosted with a lambent silver glow.

There were lanterns flickering, lighting the stairs into the caravan. He followed her up them and into the snug interior.

A small stove pulsed with heat and the caravan was warm, though he wasn't sure he would have noticed had it been frigid as an ice floe, for his blood was that hot.

"What did she say?" he asked, for the words had been Romany, and though he could not understand the exact meaning, the gist would have been clear in any language.

"She said," she fixed him with the kohl-lined eyes, "that it is a good night for making a baby, for the moon is full and the tides higher than they have been in a hundred years."

Her dress dropped to the floor and he lifted her onto the bed, quirking an eyebrow at her as he climbed up beside her into a nest of quilts and pillows. "Well then, ye gypsy temptress, I suppose we'd best do as we're bid."

Chapter Fifty-nine
Paris Ghosts

PARIS WAS A CITY OF MYTH. CELTIC MYTH AND ROMAN MYTH, ancient gods and goddesses and traces here and there, caught in the periphery of one's vision, of old Roman walls and underfoot, buried in the sediment of human history, entire cities, crypts of bones where lay poets and generals, lovers and liars, saints and thieves. It was a city of sacred geometry and a long tradition of the occult, still evidenced by bookshops devoted to that one subject. It was a city of rebellion, of street fighters, of a population of both kings and *parigots*.

It was a city of ghosts, for one could well imagine Victor Hugo sitting down in that grey shawl, ink pot to hand, and writing the first lines of *Notre-Dame de Paris*, or Balzac fueled by litres of caffeine writing against time and ruin, Baudelaire penning verse that would scandalize a nation, and Colette with her suits and pearls, writing of the flesh in a way no woman had dared before.

If one could crack open the city's layers, one would find history leaved layer upon layer, both golden with promise and fortune and crimson with blood and rebellion. One would find a city forever haunted by its own past.

It seemed inevitable to Pamela, once there in the environs of the greatest *grande dame* of cities, that Jamie, whose past was as much a labyrinth of twisting lanes, dark in the shadows of a tilting architecture, would keep his deepest secrets here. For Paris, like the best of courtesans, knew how to keep a secret safe.

The house was in the 3rd *arrondissemont*, in the old and once venerable Marais quarter of the city. Marais translated literally as 'swamp', and a swamp it had indeed been, but the *quartier* had been occupied in one way or another since the Romans were in residence. It had reached its peak in the Golden Age of the 17th and 18th centuries, when it had been home to members of the *Ancien Regime* as well as a royal stomping ground for Henri IV. After the Revolution the area had gone into serious decline, with many of its old homes razed to the ground. More recently it had become home to a flock of artisans whose skilled hands produced some of the world's most highly prized gold and silver work, enamels, leathers, hats, violins, lutes, jewels, saddles, dyed silks and painted feathers. The artisan workshops that had been plunked down into the courtyards of ancient *hotels*, were called, in a most poetically French manner, 'pustules' while those wedged between the *hotels particuliers* were called 'parasites'.

Jamie's house was tucked into a leafy corner at the end of a curving street. Built in the 17th century, it had only been in Jamie's family since his grandfather had purchased it from an impoverished widow, shortly after WWII. It had been shabbily genteel at that point, but its exquisite bones had been restored with love, good taste and money. It retained the soul of a house built during the Golden Age, however, with organic flowing curves and gilded surfaces. If one was very quiet, one could hear the ghostly echo of gold-encrusted coaches rattling past on the cobbled streets, sense the flutter of ancient love affairs conducted in walled gardens, hear the rustle of pale satins and breezy muslins, smell a waft of *poudre de mille fleurs* borne aloft on a drift of coquettish laughter, and sense the terrible fear that must have gripped the entire city when the Revolution came to tear down the structures of society that had held the aristocracy immutably in place for hundreds of years.

The house itself was pure magic. It was just that sort of house where it was hard to say if the enchantment had been hanging there in the air waiting for the right pair of hands to build it, or if the hands themselves were enchanted that pulled this house out of the airy realm and into that of blueprints, stone and wood, angles and load-bearing walls and trusses, of glass and wrought iron twisted into the shapes of fantastical and grotesque beasts, of steps that went up and then down, that twisted round corners and into nooks, of broad stone sills where a grown person might sit cosily with a book or press a palm to a frosted window pane, hidden behind heavy draperies. Here one could picture a woman waiting for a lover, gazing down at the avenue of lime trees from the octagonal window in the upstairs bedroom. Bare vines rattled against the windows in the November wind, but in the summer their greenery would press against the windows, bringing the outdoors in, making the house seem even more a part of its landscape.

Pamela sat at the desk in the study and watched the sunset lay its water paints over the canvas of bare lime branches and snow, softening the rough trunks and spilling down the twisting drive. It was very peaceful here, so beautifully tucked away that it was hard to believe all Paris was out there, only a brisk walk in the snow and falling light. The twilight stole in softly, pooling on the floor, curling upon the carpets like feline spirals of heavy smoke, slipping over the delicate lip of her teacup and turning its amber contents garnet. It solidified as though smoke took form and sat upon the chairs in ancient costume; waistcoat and brass buttons, silk stockings and embroidered satin. A tendril of twilight slipped off, trailing its finger along her spine, a shiver spreading out in its wake as though a ghost stood behind her and touched her through the veil of two hundred years.

Madame Felicie, the housekeeper in residence, called her for dinner, and she was swiftly returned to the solid world with a dose of hearty Provençal cooking, a beef stew flavored with thyme, garlic, peppercorns and red wine, the latter also in a bottle upon the table, scenting the air with earthy notes. She asked Madame Felicie to eat with her and the woman, after a shrewdly assessing look, acquiesced.

"Have you lived here for long?" Pamela asked, after consuming two full bowls of stew and drinking a glass of the exquisite red wine. No one could ever fault Jamie on the quality of his wine cellars.

"Yes, for a very long time now, Madame. I hardly remember living anywhere else." The woman laid her work-roughened hands on the table, her lined face troubled.

"I think there are things you have come to search out, Madame, and there are things here that Monsieur left in my care, should you come. I would like you to be comfortable, for the story is not a short one nor entirely easy."

Pamela poured them each another glass of wine, feeling the fortification was going to be necessary. Around them, the house seemed to sigh as if it had been waiting for this tale as well. The delft tiles gleamed from behind the stone sink and the wavy thickset glass in the windows reflected back the pleasant surroundings.

"I have to go back a bit. You will understand that stories are complicated beasts with many tentacles and when they are true stories, it is only more complicated."

Pamela nodded to encourage the woman.

"This house originally belonged to Jamie's *grandpere*. He bought it for the woman he loved. It was their time out of the world, *vous comprenez?*"

"Yes, I understand." It was, of course, Yevgena of whom Madame Felicie spoke.

"To begin with, Jamie's *grand-père* was my employer. He hired me for several reasons but the most important one is that I was a nurse. Perhaps just as important was my ability to keep secrets."

Pamela had a sudden foreboding that this story was one of those kind that changed the constructs of the universe, that once heard it could not be unheard, and one could not go back to the former innocence of the world one had lived in before. She bit back the urge to tell the woman to stop, not to tell this tale, to leave her in her innocence concerning things she could not change. But it was too late for that.

"When Jamie was born, it was not, as you believe, a single birth. The other details of his birth are true, that he was born at home to two parents who loved him, but were not perhaps best fitted for such a gifted boy. But there was also a twin sister, born three minutes after him. She too was lovely physically, but she was not gifted in the ways that her brother was and still is. It was as if the universe, feeling that it had endowed the brother with such gifts, was seeking to balance things by giving the sister none. She was like a beautiful vase without flowers, if you understand my meaning."

"I understand," Pamela said through lips that were numb with shock. "Please continue."

"This, of course, is where my part in the story begins. They spirited her away to Paris after the birth. They were an old family, and it was how such things were often managed in such families. Certainly they were not the first to hide a child away. I think Jamie's *grand-père* knew that his son and wife were hardly fit to raise the whole child they had, never mind one that had nothing of wholeness about her. So I was hired and I came here to live in this house with Adele. She was not a difficult child, though now and again we would have some very hard days." She sighed, hands brushing over the worn table, as though she could clear away the long usage and turn it to a glass that would show Pamela the past.

"They did not tell Jamie of his twin, but he was a curious and very determined young man, and one way or another, when he was sixteen he found out, and so he came here to see her on his own. He was so angry—oh, the fight he had with his *grand-père*, I thought the roof would come down around our ears before they ceased—it was, what is the saying, 'anvil and tongs'?"

"'Hammer and tongs'," Pamela supplied. She had rarely seen Jamie angry but on the occasions that he had been, it was a very unpleasant experience.

"Just so, 'hammer and tongs'. For Adele, he was never anything but loving and gentle. You will know his *grand-mère*—his mother's mother?"

"Yes, I know her."

"She would come over for a few months each year, and take care of Adele while I went home to Provençe or on holiday and sorted out the affairs of my own life. When Monsieur Jamie visited here he would look after her with such love. I swear there was a light inside her when he was around that did not turn on when he was absent. I think she knew he was the other half, the whole of their particular equation."

"Once I looked out and they were in the back garden, the two of them. Adele was laughing. It was a strange noise, almost rusty sounding, for I never heard her laugh but for when Monsieur Jamie was with her. On this particular day, the weather was very warm as it sometimes is in Paris in the spring. There were cherry blossoms everywhere, like a snowstorm outside, and Jamie was holding her up so that she might feel the sun on her face. She had that beautiful golden hair just as Monsieur and his *grand-père* had, and it was filled with petals." She took a deep breath and pressed her fingers to her eyes. "I did not have children of my own. Adele was my child. I loved her so very much and I only hope that she knew it somehow."

"I'm sure she did," Pamela meant the words, for the very house around her was the sort of home in which love had been so long fostered that it had grown of its own accord. She knew such houses, for she lived in one herself.

"Though Adele was in so many ways his opposite, like Monsieur Jamie, animals and insects found her most attractive. You will have witnessed this with Monsieur, no doubt."

She nodded. She had seen his way with horses, with children, how if he stood still in the garden for more than a few minutes, the butterflies would land on his head and arms, the foxes would come and sit near him without fear, and deer, shy and beautiful, would take food right out of his hand.

"Once he said to me, Madame Felicie you must not worry about Adele, for this is only her body. The rest of her was stolen away by the fairies when we were born. She was so perfect they had to have her for themselves and so they took her, and left me behind. Some day they will come for her body too and she will dance in marble halls and know neither pain nor fear ever again." Madame Felicie shook her head. "Poor Jamie, to have such gifts and feel that one does not deserve them. The universe, as you know, has seen fit to make him pay dearly for those gifts."

"Where is Adele now, Madame Felicie?" Pamela asked, though she thought she knew the answer. It was lingering in the very air around them. It was, perhaps, the ghost whose touch she had felt earlier.

"She died just over three years ago, Madame. It was pneumonia; her lungs had never been strong. Monsieur Jamie was with her at the end. As much as she was capable of love, she loved him. There was no better hand to hold hers than his, this he knew."

Pamela reached across the table and took the woman's hands in her own. "I'm sorry you lost her but I am certain she knew she was well loved."

"She was an angel, and angels are not meant long for this world of ours. So we must love them as they pass us and thank the Lord for the blessing, however brief."

"Do you have any pictures of her?"

"Of course, Madame. I will fetch some."

Madame Felicie left the kitchen, returning moments later with a photo album bound in pale lavender silk, silver embroidery looping around its worn edges.

The first ones where black and white, a tiny girl in pale-colored pinafores, slight and delicate as a fairy, with a terrible vacant stare. Then slowly she began to grow, and became adolescent, still slight, but tall, as though she would fold up to nothing. The color photos, when they came were startling. She gasped aloud, a thin ache under her heart like a cut from a knife.

"The resemblance is startling, isn't it?"

"Yes, it is." There it was, the beautiful golden hair, the slanted green eyes, the profile that was carved, it seemed, with especial care and love by a Master. And yet... and yet, there was that terrible vacancy in the face whereas Jamie's face was always animated by laughter, by the lift of a sardonic brow, by a supple grace that imbued his every movement and word.

There were a couple of photos of Adele with her grandfather. Jamie and Adele looked a great deal like him. He had been a beautiful man even well past his middle years.

The last four pages of the album were mostly of Adele with her brother, her twin, the golden side of their mutual coin. Jamie always had his arm around her and Adele was often looking up at him, not at the camera. The photos were a little eerie, as though one was truly looking at one person who had been split into two. Jamie's ease with the girl who had been his twin was apparent, and she felt a sharp pang of longing for his presence.

"Madame Felicie, how does this connect to the reason I am in Paris?"

The woman stood and took an envelope from the pocket of her capacious apron.

"I believe I will let Monsieur Jamie tell you himself."

Pamela took the letter to the study, still numb with the revelations of the last hour. She went to the desk where she had sat contemplating the grounds earlier and opened the pale grey envelope. There was no letterhead, for Jamie did not like formality with his personal correspondence. She smiled to see his writing across the page, his hand which managed to be precise and sprawling at the same time. She could see him, golden head bent over the paper, measuring his words and writing quickly in one sitting as was his way.

Dear Pamela,

You will know about Adele now and be wondering how this connects to everything else that is going on. The answer is that I don't entirely know. But if you're here now reading this letter, it means it does connect and is important. I do not want my secrets used as a weapon against you. However, I fear that is what may happen. I wanted to tell you about Adele but it never seemed like the right time and I didn't want the knowledge of it to burden you.

Some time ago, I discovered that Lucien Broughton and I share a birthdate—same day, same year, born only minutes apart. I was born in my home, he was born in a home for unwed mothers. Adele was recorded as having died only moments after birth. This of course is not true, but no one was to ever know that.

I think the Reverend believes that he was the twin that died that day. Of course, that is not true in any way, but it is what he believes. Why is the mystery. Beyond sharing a birthdate and a geographical location, there is no reason for him to think he is my twin. I don't know enough of his life to guess what lies at the bottom of all this but I understand that he believes it to be true. He thinks that I have stolen his birthright and sees himself as Fortune's outcast.

For a long time, because I was young, I saw Adele's life as a tragedy, and because she was my twin I felt that I had stolen from her, taken the life she might have led. I will tell you this, however, she was mostly happy in her own way and her life was a blessing, as most lives are. I loved her, and for me that was a gift beyond price. She taught me that there is more than one meaning to life for there are as many meanings as there are individual lives.

It was as though she was a princess, her body the glass coffin in the fairytale, her spirit roving elsewhere, crossed over into a far land to which mere mortals did not have access. When I first found her I wanted to bring her home, to have her live at Kirkpatrick's Folly as was her birthright and so that she might reside in the heart of a family. This was not to be, as you know, and Felicie showed me long ago that Adele was better off in the Paris house where she had always been and things were familiar to her, where she had her routines and touchstones.

Felicie was right, for there was a strange contentment at Adele's core. Perhaps that was her half of the deal, to have that peace while I took the darkness in exchange for all the other things the universe bestowed. My grandfather told me once that the universe always seeks balance and it seems to be true, as tip-tilty as the world is at times.

If you have to reveal the truth about my sister, then it will have to be. After all, the world cannot hurt her now.

Do what you must with this knowledge, Pamela, and know that you have my blessing as your judgement in this matter is also mine.

Love,

Jamie

She sat for a long time after reading the letter, hearing the soft tick of the clock and the creak of the house around her. She was tired but knew sleep would not come easily tonight. Jamie was right, the world could no longer hurt Adele, but it could still hurt Jamie, a fact of which she was all too painfully aware. Sometimes it felt as though Jamie's world was one of mirrors and the further one advanced into said world the more distorted and shifty the parameters became. How he had managed for so long to keep the many parts of his life separate and balanced was beyond her imagining.

Much later she made her way upstairs to the bedroom that Madame Felicie had prepared for her. It was a beautiful room, well proportioned, with a set of three stairs that led up to a sitting room of windows and comfortable chairs as well as a daintily appointed vanity filled with her perfumes and creams.

She changed into her nightgown, cleaned her face and teeth, and brushed out her hair.

The bed was like a scalloped shell, mother of pearl inlaid into the base, the curtains in hazy shades of blue and grey with hints of pearled lavender and moonlit green. The sheets were fresh and matched the bed hangings and were, of course, the finest grade of Kirkpatrick linen. The pillows were heaped high, and when she leaned back into them they released the sweet scent of lime water. Madame Felicie was a housekeeper that missed no detail.

She had brought books up from the downstairs study, for she rarely fell asleep without the panacea of a story, as soothing to her as a sleep potion. Some in English, some in French, for she had been well enough schooled in the latter to read fluently. But even the delights of reading the letters of Madame Sevigne in the very neighborhood in which she had lived could not hold her attention. Her mind's eye held only the photos of Adele and Jamie, of that strange vacant face which was, like the empty vase that Madame Felicie had compared it to, still a thing of beauty.

The bed was high and she could snuggle deep into the heavy quilts and still see out into the garden. The moon was low, soon to set. It washed the bare lime branches with a soft gilt, tilting over the stone walls, sifting thick in the piles of ivy. It was a beautiful night, clarified in the cold so that the old world hung there visible in the arms of the new.

The last picture in the album that recorded Adele's brief life was of her and Jamie in the garden on a spring afternoon, the abundant green all around them proof of the most extravagant of seasons. Adele was lying in a garden chaise, wrapped in blankets against any stray chill that winter may have left behind. Jamie was seated in the grass beside her, his hands describing airy worlds, his face alight with the creation of something that would give another joy. Adele's gaze rested with contentment upon his face. They were happy, the two of them, captured unaware in that moment.

And around them, caught like silken leaves against the backdrop of virulent green grass and pale winter blankets were butterflies, dozens upon dozens of them. Too early for the season yet undeniably there.

Pamela sighed and closed her eyes to the moonlit garden. Behind her eyelids she still saw the butterflies, delicate upon stalk and leg, feeling every vibration through their wings and seeing no color, only turning to where the sun guided them. They knew the necessity of warmth and sought it always.

"She died only two weeks later," Madame Felicie had said, closing the album as though she could no longer bear to look at Adele's face. "This house felt so empty afterwards. Then, near the end of that summer, I was outside one day and a butterfly lit on my finger and sat there for a long time. I didn't dare breathe nor move for I knew it must be Adele come to say goodbye." The woman smiled in memory. "You will think me a doddery old fool with such fancies. Only sometimes I think I feel her touch in passing or smell her skin, but it goes by too quickly before I can embrace it and hold it to me. That is how ghosts are, passing in a moment, leaving us behind."

Pamela turned in the bed, hearing the echo of Madame Felicie's words. She remembered her earlier fancy of a ghost touching her through the veil of centuries but it no longer felt like an ancient phantom, for the ghosts that dwelt here were real and one did not need to reach far back to find them.

Chapter Sixty
The Black Pope

THE FOLLOWING DAY WAS FILLED WITH ERRANDS, business that needed to be dealt with while she had these few days in Paris. She had arranged meetings with Jamie's French bankers and solicitors, shareholders and vintners. Throughout the entire day the revelations of the previous night occupied part of her mind and she felt as though the golden wraith of Jamie's twin followed her everywhere. She also had the sense that someone far more corporeal was watching her and by lunchtime, over a bottle of Sancerre that tasted like a cold winter peach, shared with one of Jamie's bankers, she realized it was the lumpy little man in the bad suit that she had run into outside the solicitor's offices. She turned around and smiled at him where he sat ostensibly reading *Paris Match* and he disappeared shortly thereafter.

Still, the feeling would not leave her, not through her afternoon appointments, nor over dinner, nor as she walked out in the November evening for a breath of fresh air. It was quiet in the streets, for most people were inside keeping warm, eating supper and looking forward to the warmth of their beds on such a night. She looked behind a couple of times and thought she saw a small figure slide behind a tree, though it might have been a trick of the shadowy walls, overhung as they were with tree branches and bare vines.

She was tired, and she missed Casey and Conor terribly. There were times when she felt that she lived a divided life, a foot in each world, the one she lived with Casey and Conor in their wee home where she was safe and loved, and then the world she stepped into each morning as she drove the winding road up to Kirkpatrick's Folly. She assumed a mantle, particularly since Philip's arrival, that was like to invisible armor and she moved within it with an assurance she rarely felt. Jamie might have believed she was equipped for all this intrigue and financial derring-do but most days she felt that he had severely overestimated her abilities.

The sound of a footstep slightly off the rhythm of her own pulled her out of her thoughts and made her certain that someone was indeed following her, someone far more skilled than the lumpy character in the badly-cut suit. She didn't look around and kept her pace even. At the next corner, she turned quickly, ducking into the first available doorway, that of a grotty hole-in-the-wall bar. The figure came around the corner and she grabbed her erstwhile stalker by the collar, at which it let out an undignified stream of gutter French, impressive both for its invective and array. A delicate and rather grubby face looked up at her and then spat just to the left of her feet. Pamela merely tightened her hold on the frayed collar of its overly-large coat.

"Why are you following me?"

The child looked a touch startled to be addressed in its own tongue.

"Why do you think I am following you? Maybe I am just going the same way as you."

"I saw you loitering by the gates of the house I'm staying in, earlier." She had not seen anyone but suspected that the child had to have been waiting for her there in order to have picked up her trail so quickly.

The child rolled its eyes with great Gallic insouciance. "I am to watch where you go and to deliver you to a certain place when the time is right, Mam'selle." Liquid brown eyes just visible in the glow of the street lantern gazed up into hers in challenge.

"Who hired you to follow me? And where is it you are to deliver me?"

"The priest. He was very tall—and his French was good. *Il est Irlandais.*"

"An Irish priest asked you to follow me?"

"*Oui*, Madame. He was kind and fed me with hot soup before sending me out into the night." The liquid brown eyes beseeched and the narrow frame within the coat sagged just a bit. Pamela knew the child was about to bolt given half a chance.

"You can ease up on the Parisian urchin act. What is your name?"

"Henri." This was said stoutly.

Pamela pulled off the blue toque the child wore and a long dark plait fell over one shoulder and down the back of the worn coat.

"Henri, hmm?"

"Heloïse," the child mumbled, "but I am as good as any boy could ever be at my work."

"I don't doubt that you are. Come with me. We'll find something hot to drink and you can tell me just what the Irish priest looked like and where you're to take me."

They found a small café in one of those crooked streets that still exist in tucked away corners of Paris. Pamela ordered a pot of hot chocolate for the child and herself, as well as a plate of sticky pastries for Heloïse. In the light of the café and without the woolen cap, Heloïse looked ridiculously young, clearly no more than twelve, with a gamine face and the sort of delicate features and clear olive-toned skin that could only belong to a French girl.

Her eyes dominated her face, long thick lashes delineating them as boldly as a stroke of ink from an artist's hand. She was, despite the overly large and bulky coat, quite small and hungry, for the bones of her face lay a little too close to the surface of her skin.

Pamela waited until the child had devoured the pastries and two cups of chocolate before quizzing her.

"So this Irish priest—describe him if you would."

Heloïse swallowed down her last mouthful of chocolate. "He was, like I said, tall. His hair was black and white. He was kind and I do not think he meant you any harm. In fact, it seemed to me, Madame, that he knew you."

"And where did he ask you to deliver me?"

"To the cathedral, but not until tomorrow night. I was to follow you today and tonight and make sure that you weren't being followed by anyone else." She looked longingly at the empty pot. Pamela glanced over at the waiter who was lounging against the bar, talking to the pretty proprietor's daughter. He nodded at her and brought another pot of chocolate to the table a few moments later.

"Which cathedral?" Pamela asked when the waiter had returned to flirting with the owner's daughter.

"Notre Dame, of course," Heloïse said sniffily, as if there were only one cathedral worth mentioning in Paris' church-clogged environment.

From the child's description, it sounded as though the priest was none other than Father Lawrence, a man whom she trusted. He had been one of the most influential men in Jamie's life, having had the teaching of him as a boy. A priest of the Jesuit order, he had been a firm hand and guiding light for Jamie during dark times in his life. Father Lawrence had loved the boy Jamie had been and loved the man he had become as one would a son. She was curious about why he was having her followed but supposed all would be revealed, or rather, being that she was dealing with Jesuits, what he wanted revealed would be so tomorrow night.

"This other man who was following me, what did he look like?" She hoped it was the one in the ill-fitting suit because any more than two people hired to follow her for four days in Paris was an excess of intrigue in her books.

Heloïse assumed a very Gallic loftiness. "*Pah*, he was so obvious I'm sure you knew he was following you. He did not blend in well at all but perhaps he did not cost *la peau des fesse* to those who hired him. Once you started trying on dresses he gave up quickly. By the way, the black dress was lovely but I hope you also bought the green silk organza. The brown was all wrong for you. I do not know what the shop girl was thinking. It drained all the color from your face."

"I did buy both—the black and the green that is." Only in France would the urchin following one also be well versed in fashion and not timid about sharing her opinions on the subject.

They left a little while later, after Heloïse had polished off the second pot of chocolate and Pamela had bought her two croissants for her breakfast.

Outside the fog was gathering in delicate filaments, the grey silk fog of Paris that seemed to spool out of the ancient stonework and up from the twisting arteries of her streets rather than being manufactured in the air.

Heloïse stood for a moment, a subtle hesitation in her manner that Pamela had seen before and recognized for what it was.

"Do you have a home to go to?"

"Of course I do," the girl said, tossing her plait as though insulted by the notion.

"Do you?" Pamela insisted.

The brown eyes met her own with a disarming candor. "Most nights I do. My family are *bateliers* and we live on a *peniche*. You understand?"

She did. The *bateliers* were Paris' boat people who lived on boats from the '20s and '30s and plied their trade on the broad highway of the Seine delivering thousands of tonnes of goods: sand, coal, gravel, flour, potatoes, fuel oil and other staples of life upon land. They were a breed apart, floating gypsies who kept to their own tribe and lived on the knife edge of continual poverty.

"When we are in harbor in Paris I sleep on the boat. When the boat is away I sometimes choose to stay on land until my father returns."

"When you stay on land where is it you sleep?" Pamela asked.

Heloïse shrugged, tucking her long plait underneath her wool cap. "Here and there."

Pamela had her suspicions just what 'here and there' meant, and it did little to quell her sense of worry over the child. She had seen the haunts of children without homes, both here and in Belfast, and knew the frightening desperation that could come when one did not have a place to lay one's head when night fell.

"It is alright, Madame," Heloïse said. "Tonight I have a place to go. I will sleep warm and safe."

"How did you know what I was thinking?"

"You have a most expressive face, Madame." Heloïse smiled and then slipped off into the crooked streets, her slim form disappearing around the corner of a three-storied building, one second visible and the next gone as though she had only been an illusion.

TRUE TO HER WORD, HELOÏSE, HAIR STILL ARTFULLY HIDDEN beneath her wool cap, appeared at the back door of the house the next evening just as twilight was settling into the walls and gardens of the city.

"We go now, Madame," she said, neck pulled down into the collar of her coat, for it was cold, the air thick with fog and the scent of impending snow.

Pamela, well wrapped up in a wool peacoat with a scarf wound around her throat and partly muffling her face, followed the child out into the night. The streets were eerily quiet, their footsteps echoing off the pavement. She had a sudden vision of what Casey would have to say if he knew she was traipsing off after a street urchin on the assumption the Irish priest of whom she spoke was indeed Father Lawrence. It didn't bear thinking about, so she wisely put the thought away.

It was a long brisk walk and even though her legs were twice as long as those of Heloïse, Pamela had to half run to keep up. But within the hour Notre Dame loomed up out of the spectral fog. On such a night as this one could almost hear the ghostly tolling of Quasimodo's beloved bells and feel the medieval walls of the city rise once again out of the past. It was one of those places on the earth, rare, where something seemed to be in the very soil, something sacred that ran in currents inside the earth and hummed beneath a person's feet so that it was unmistakable in its power. Before the great cathedral had been erected this site had been home to a pagan temple and before that there was evidence that Druids had once worshipped within a long-vanished grove of trees. Here Crusaders had bowed their heads and prayed before setting off to sack and pillage in the Holy Land. Here, too, the head of the mystic Knights Templar had been burned at the stake, as he had cursed both King and Pope, inviting them to join him at the gates of heaven—which both had obligingly done within mere months. Here, De Gaulle had knelt in thanksgiving after the liberation of Paris in WWII. Here was the center of France, from which all distances were measured.

Beyond lay the twisting grey-green ribbon of the Seine and the lights of the city. But here on this November night, they might have been swept back to an altogether earlier time, pilgrims on the road to worship, coming to tender their prayers to Saint Genevieve.

The cold and the hour had kept even the faithful to a minimum this night. The long shining marble expanse of the great aisle stretched before them. Above, the soaring ribbed vaults lay thick in shadow. Heloïse seemed Gallicly unimpressed by the grandeur and history. She led Pamela to a bank of candles to the left of the altar, dropped coins into the cup and took flame to light a candle. She looked terribly young in the soft light as she dropped to her knees.

"You do not pray?" she said, small face stern. Pamela knelt beside the child, dropped her own coins in the cup, and lit a candle. It was natural to pray then, for the Cathedral would take one's words upwards so that they might fly toward God. Time dissolved and she felt that strange, still atmosphere that came rarely in life, as though one were suspended in a cocoon of no earthly making. She was startled when a gentle hand touched her shoulder and she looked up into Father Lawrence's rough but reassuring face.

"I'm sorry for the subterfuge, my dear, but it is necessary, as you know."

She stood, glancing at Heloïse. The child's head was still bent in earnest prayer and Pamela was certain she would come to no harm here within the precincts of the Church. She turned and followed Father Lawrence's black-garbed form, their feet tap-tapping against the marble floor.

"You will forgive the drama of the meeting place," Father Lawrence said over his shoulder, "but it seemed best to choose somewhere public that can also provide private corners."

The ambulatory in which they walked was lit with dozens upon dozens of candles, giving it the feel of a long closed honey-comb lined with amber. They walked the entire length of it, encountering only one other person, a priest who nodded and passed them without words.

They stepped out into the dark and she followed him to where a small gate closed off a garden. The church loomed up behind, the flying buttresses and sharp Gothic spire lost in the fog. She shivered. One could feel the stare of the stone gargoyles even through the dark night. She followed Father Lawrence through the gate into a long narrow area, where bare-branched maples were dewed with pearls of fog.

"This is where I leave you," Father Lawrence said, and patted her shoulder before disappearing back through the gate. She was startled, believing Father Lawrence was the man she was meant to meet. Immediately she was aware of another presence and it drew her to the far end of the narrow garden as though she were an iron filing in the face of a magnet. He was seated on a bench and she knew who he was before he uttered a word. Giacomo Brandisi, the beekeeper, the Black Pope—the head of the Jesuit Order. He rose from the bench, a tendril of fog lifting from his shoulders, filling the entire garden with his presence, emanating power and something more, something that felt a great deal like grace.

"Please, come sit with me," he said, his voice warm and steadying to her knees. Raised in the Catholic Church and still familiar with Catholic guilt, she could not help but have a dreadful case of nerves.

Giacomo Brandisi was a large man and that, thought Pamela, seating herself beside him, did not begin to do him justice. His face oddly resembled nothing so much as an olive-toned beehive, rosy-red lips in place of the small arched door. He had no neck to speak of, thus giving the illusion that the concentric folds of fat rose directly from the broad, heavy chest. The eyes, veiled by large, fleshy lids, were the color of smoked gold tourmaline which, his friends and foes knew, could be as melting as warmed honey or as cold as the jewels of Hell.

Long ago, Jamie had briefed her about Father Brandisi, and the tone in which he described him told her that he had great respect for the man. But what lay beyond that she did not know. A mutual esteem, it was clear, but she suspected the rest was very complicated. Jamie had been adamant, however, on one point—that this was a man of whom to be wary, to fear, if only for the reach of his power.

His eccentricities were varied and well cultivated. His nickname, though never uttered in his presence, was The Grand Beekeeper. A poke of derision for the occupations he had kept throughout his lifetime: beekeeper, apiculturist, it mattered not to him what name one gave it, only that they were his solace, pursuits that did not require his mind to move in convoluted circles the way his human charges did.

Behind the honey-toned eyes and the umber nuances of his Sicilian ancestry was a mind as fulgurous and fecund as a meteor in full spate. And rather than resembling his dear, droning friends, his mental machinations were more akin to the manoeuverings of a large, not entirely genial spider. He sat at the center of a society that was renowned for its scholarship, tough-mindedness and dogged determination. He had not gotten there by being anyone's fool. Under his nimble hands lay the skeins of dozens of intrigues, scandals, government secrets, and caught in the multi-layered web were the souls of many he had encountered over the years. Whether Jamie had ever been fettered in that net was not something to which she was privy.

"It is a pleasure to meet at last. I have heard much of you from Father Lawrence."

"It is *my* pleasure, Father General," she said, uncertain of whether she was meant to kiss his hand or if that was only reserved for the other Pope. He solved her dilemma by placing his broad hands on his heavy thighs and leaning forward a little.

"To say that Jamie's past is complicated is, as you will no doubt already know, a vast understatement."

"I see we're not going to waste time on polite preambles," Pamela said dryly.

The Jesuit smiled a broad grin that creased his face and exposed strong, square white teeth.

"You and I are going to get along just fine." He laughed—infectious laughter—and she laughed in response, deciding that he might be a 'meddling bastard' as Jamie had once described him, but she was going to like him. The universe had already decided that for her.

"Let me just say this to begin, there is what is seen, those causes and effects that we understand we are setting in motion, just as whipping a horse's behind sets the cart wheel to going. But there are things beyond that, behind the main picture if you will, that one does not always know one is affecting. Jamie is one who, merely by being, sets things in motion, often things he did not intend to begin. There is, too, a reckless vein in him so that he sometimes sets fire to things just for the pleasure of seeing them burn. I believe the boy has started a conflagration this time that he will not be able to put out. So it is for us to put it out if we can."

"And how is it that we will put this fire out?"

He answered with a statement.

"We have a mutual acquaintance in London. You paid him a visit recently."

Damn it, Jamie had warned her that the man missed nothing. There seemed little purpose in denying it.

"Yes, but it was fairly unproductive."

"Perhaps not so much as it may have appeared, but that is neither here nor there just now." Translated this meant that they should not talk further on the subject now. She had expected the conversation to occur on more than one level and she was long tutored in this art, as he would know and expect.

"There are people who might find it convenient if James did not come home. If he expired and was buried in some unmarked Russian grave. I, however, do not find this convenient. Nor do I believe in walking into conflict without the appropriate arms. There is more at stake here than a man's wealth, or even his life."

Pamela felt a wash of relief begin to run through her veins. The mere sound of his voice made her feel as though the angels were on her side and would help her man the barricades.

"The letter he left you, you should read it."

"How did you know there was a letter?" she asked, for she knew he did not mean the letter about Adele. She wondered if the priest was psychic, for she had brought the letter with her to Paris for safekeeping because she had a feeling whatever lay inside should not be left to the prying of any eyes other than her own. She only half understood her own hesitation about it, only that she felt to open it would be to admit something that she could not. That to break the seal would be to open a Pandora's Box for which she was not prepared.

"Because he would not leave you without some words of comfort and farewell, if that is what he meant this madness to be."

"You cannot really think he meant for this to happen?"

"He tends towards self-destruction. You know this as well as I do. When he was a boy, we protected him from it as best we could. I thought he would outgrow it as a man but it's a dark thing that has a terrible hold on him. In his youth he vacillated between studiousness and brilliance, to being *le bon follastre*—you are familiar with this term?"

"Suicidal clown," Pamela said sharply. "It's a longstanding tradition here in France."

"It also leads to an early grave. This suicidal foolishness was doubled when he was with Andrei. They are of the same ilk temperamentally. This is why Russia is the worst place Jamie could have chosen to disappear."

"This suicidal foolishness, as you call it, is an illness," she said, an edge to her tone. "He didn't choose it. He doesn't walk willingly into that darkness. Nor did he choose to get caught in the Soviet Union."

The Father General eyed her shrewdly, and it felt as though those tourmaline eyes could pick over a soul the way a flood of locusts could strip a cotton field.

"Didn't he, Pamela? Have you ever known Jamie to fall into a trap he hadn't devised in the first place?"

She sighed. The man had a point. She ought to have remembered the first law of all interactions with a Jesuit—don't argue.

"I would just like to find a way to bring him home."

The golden eyes held her own, unblinking. The man would have made a bang-up inquisitor, she decided. People would be admitting to things their ancestors seven generations removed had done, never mind their own sins.

"Home is merely the place where we are loved, and love has the ability to cross time and space, so one is always home if one has ever been loved. It is the place that one builds inside, the fire one tends within the soul. And as such, Jamie is always home. That being said, I should still like to bring him back to his correct geographical location." He smiled, taking the weight from his words.

"I think though, Pamela, you must be honest with yourself. He laid the path for you, after all. Perhaps you must now ask yourself why he did so."

"I know why he did it but I don't accept it."

She shivered, for a sharp wind had come in off the Seine, filled with the scent of northern ice and frosted fields.

"Winter has arrived," he said softly, breath laced with crystals. "But the summer was generous and full, the harvests plenty, so winter's bite will be that much harder. That is as it should be though, for the earth will rest easy beneath the snows."

They sat silent for a long moment and Pamela slowly became aware of a silent exchange taking place between them, something that she could feel in her spine, a shiver that crested in her head, but not one that was uncomfortable or foreboding. So it seemed natural when he held his hands up, the broad, flat palms open to her.

"May I?" he asked.

"Of course," she said, thinking it wasn't likely anyone would find the courage to refuse the man.

His hands covered her head, thick with callouses, heavy with warmth. Her shivers left her. It felt like warm oil suddenly spread out from his palms, anointing her, forgiving her, no matter the length and breadth of her sins. It was the same sense of time dissolved that existed inside the Cathedral, but held within the hands of a human vessel.

"Grace is given to us all, Pamela, but perhaps it is given most freely to those who do not feel they deserve it."

"I just want to be safe, to have those I love be safe. Is that really so much to ask of this life?" It seemed natural to say what was in her heart, simplistic as it might seem, to this man. Inquisitor, confessor, beekeeper, and God's General. Fearsome, but a good man—she would bet her life on it. She was also betting the life of James Kirkpatrick on it.

"Such things are like weighing fire or measuring a bushel of wind, beautiful ideas but impossible in the realm in which we live. We can only live by Faith, which requires much courage of us but is the only passport out of the land of fear. You hold that passport in your hands already. You simply need to open your heart to it."

He was gone then, as though he had never been in the garden at all, though she could still feel the gift of grace he had bestowed upon her, where it had settled like a bright spindle of warmth at her core, in her heart.

Chapter Sixty-one

Christmas 1974

Julian

THE HOUSE WAS ARRAYED IN ITS GLEAMING BEST, the chandeliers lit, the wood polished to within an inch of its life, the wine uncorked and the crates of whiskey sitting in the cold room off the kitchen. Bowls of flowers scented the air, along with the spices wafting from Maggie's kitchen. She was dressed in a gown of moonlit green that had caused her to raise her own eyebrows at her reflection in the mirror when she had first tried it on in Paris. It was cut low and ingeniously darted with a darker shade of velvet. Her hair was up, with a choker of black pavé crystals around her throat and matching crystals dangling from her ears. Casey was going to be apoplectic when he got a view of the neckline on the dress but by then it would be too late to do anything about it.

She checked the dining room one more time. The table blazed with the good crystal and silver, the linens a deep crimson and the decorations simple wreaths of holly with their bright red berries intact. Outside, snow had begun to fall, drifting down slowly in big flakes, softening the fence posts and outbuildings and clinging in all its fugitive beauty on the windows before melting away.

The evening had been choreographed, but in a way so subtle it would go unnoticed. People would only have a sense of enjoyment lingering with them. She had been trained to construct such evenings, first by her father and then, in a more natural fashion, by Jamie. One provided good food, music, wine and spirits, one cultivated an aura of conviviality, and then one got down to business. It was the art of making connections, of promises to meet later, of deals ghosted upon the air, of which the nuts and bolts could be dealt with down the road. It was introducing people who one felt would fit well together, would have things in common, or whose meeting would benefit business even if it wasn't one's own. People remembered such things, saw them later as favors and reciprocated in kind.

Though Casey claimed such evenings made him feel like he couldn't get a decent breath of air, he managed to mingle just fine and told stories that had the entire table laughing. He was very good at making certain no one's glass ever went empty and drawing out those whose tendency was to remain quiet. He also made certain the musicians who had been hired to play didn't indulge too freely in the flow of whiskey and wine.

After dinner, the entire company retired to what had originally been a large parlor, a room fitted out comfortably with leather chairs and couches, an enormous fireplace and floor-to-ceiling windows. A large Christmas tree, a-glow with fairy lights, held pride of place in front of the windows, framed by the falling snow, the flakes so big their starry shapes could be clearly seen through the glass.

Everyone was relaxed and the atmosphere, spiked with generous amounts of whiskey, was as easeful as though the senses had been rubbed down with a double warp of velvet, cut to reveal the pattern only upon later inspection.

Pamela found a quiet moment with Casey and leaned into his side as he wrapped one arm around her. She wanted nothing more than to go home, take down her hair, cuddle her son and sleep for about ten hours straight. Since she had come back from Paris things had become increasingly tense and she was certain someone had gone through all the papers in the study and rifled through Jamie's vast collection of books, looking for something.

"Christ, woman, how often do ye go through such things? I was sweatin' just sittin' there listenin' to them question ye, never mind havin' to come up with intelligent answers an' convince them I was right."

"Oh, once or twice a week," she said a trifle grimly, for the evening, though a success, had drained her completely. "I've got a few things against me in their view. I'm not Jamie, and I'm female and I'm too young as far as they are concerned to know my arse from my elbow, though I think perhaps I changed a few opinions on that score tonight."

"Well, I tell ye yer a better person than me, Jewel. I only just held my-self back from stickin' that bloody Dutchman's head in the punchbowl an' drownin' him. Had he tried any harder to look down yer dress, he would have fallen straight into it."

She laughed, for it was true. She leaned up to kiss Casey's stubbled cheek—and felt him stiffen suddenly, the arm around her tightening.

"Pamela," he said in an odd tone. She followed his gaze to the entryway of the parlor.

The world tilted upside down for a moment and when it turned the right way again, nothing was the same. For Jamie's Uncle Philip had arrived uninvited and brought with him a guest, a boy of about nineteen years of age. A boy with eyes of a dense sapphire blue and hair the color of winter chestnuts. A boy with a pure profile and every bone fitted perfectly to the next. A boy who moved across the room now with a cat-like grace, slender and straight, a natural athlete. A boy who must be Jamie's son. For no relative whose blood spanned farther apart than father and son could so resemble another man, could so embody all those features she had only ever thought to see in one man. He was, quite simply, beautiful, and possibly one of the worst shocks she had ever had in her life.

"Pamela," Philip smiled, yellowing teeth sharp and nasty. "I'd like you to meet Julian. Julian, this is Pamela."

The boy took her hand, though she had no memory of putting hers out to him. Her breath was caught somewhere between her throat and lungs and refused to move. His hand was warm and hers icy in comparison.

One thought with two minds at such times—the mind that wanted to curse and ask why and how and who, and the other mind which was cool and calm, carefully assessing what this might mean, what traps and pitfalls now yawned open at one's feet. One never spoke in public with the first mind, only with the latter.

"How lovely to meet you, Julian. Are you a friend of Philip's?" This was said lightly but with a slightly dubious undertone as to the likelihood of Philip having friends at all.

The boy still held her hand, sapphire eyes bold and face inquisitive. He smiled and it was utterly disarming, just as it was when his father smiled. And his father Jamie must be. She saw that clearly, for the boy had been brought here as a pawn in the Reverend's game, she was certain. Only it was also clear he did not know himself to be a pawn. She wondered if he even knew there was a game, and thought it likely best if he did not. For innocent he would be more amenable to manipulation by his masters, and she had no doubt they had been grooming him for some time in anticipation of this moment.

The second mind spoke to the boy while the first stood back, numb and reeling. He was clearly well educated, cultured, and had been raised with impeccable manners. He had already spent a term at Oxford. Jamie's alma mater. She suspected that was not coincidence. She suspected nothing was.

Philip watched the interplay between them with a look of smugness oiling the froggy sheen of his skin. Julian seemed unaware of the tension that existed between her and Philip but it was likely he was too polite to point it out had he noticed. The game had changed and she was not, despite gypsies and Jesuits, prepared for such a move as this one.

Julian excused himself shortly after, bowing over her hand in parting and on rising up, looked her full in the eyes and spoke in poetry as his father so often did.

"Had the price of looking been blindness, I would have looked."

And so he had some small portion of his father's charm, though not yet his grace. Perhaps never his grace, for it was not a thing acquired so much as innate to Jamie's nature.

"Well, he's not backwards about bein' forwards, I'll say that for the wee beggar." Casey was looking darkly in the boy's direction as he joined a group of people near the window, inserting himself with ease into their midst.

She excused herself and put her half-full wineglass on a table. Smiling all the way to the stairs, she gathered her skirt in one hand and walked up until she was well hidden in the shadows from the upper floor. Then she fled along the hall, certain she was going to be sick. She reached the bathroom and locked herself in, the ball of nausea cold as ice lodged in her chest.

She sat down on the side of the tub, pressing her hand to her chest where her heart was still pounding hard enough that she could hear every beat in her ears. She swallowed, trying to dislodge the icy pain, wishing fervently that she hadn't had the glass of wine earlier. Jamie's son, here in Jamie's home. Oh, that Jamie should be here to see this boy. What would it mean to him? Did he have any idea of this? It was hard for her to imagine that Jamie wouldn't know he had a son, to think that a woman he had once loved could keep such a secret from him seemed beyond cruel. Though perhaps he had not loved her, and that might explain a great deal in itself.

There was a knock on the door and then Casey's voice, quiet, but filled with worry. "Jewel, are ye alright in there?"

She stood and walked across the room to unlock the door. Casey came in and shut it behind him, his face pale beneath the dark of his whiskers.

"It's been the helluva shock, no?"

She smiled wearily. "You could say that."

"Do ye think Jamie knew?" Casey sat beside her on the tub. The lip of it was flat and wide, and as porcelain went, fairly comfortable.

"No, I don't."

He raised an eyebrow in question. "Ye seem very certain of that."

She shrugged, feeling unable to explain. "I think if he knew, he would have prepared me for it and he didn't. The man isn't God. He can't anticipate the consequences of every action he's committed in his lifetime."

"Well," Casey said wryly, "he does a damn good imitation of bein' all knowin' an' all seein' much of the time. Do ye know anything about the mother?"

"No—well nothing other than she must have dark hair and blue eyes."

"Aye, that would seem to be about all the boy took from her."

She looked up at him in question. "So, it's not just my imagination? I started to doubt that he could possibly look that much like Jamie by the time I got to the top of the stairs."

"No, it's bloody apparent to anyone who has ever set eyes on the man. That boy has to be his son. Christ, he even moves like him."

"I noticed that, too."

"Ye'll have to come back downstairs in a bit, darlin'." He squeezed her hand, shoring her up against the evening's disaster.

"I know. I just need a minute to pull myself together." She squeezed his hand back, leaned up to kiss him and then put her forehead against his. "I'm glad you're here tonight. I don't think I would have managed without you."

He put up his free hand and stroked her head. "Well, I'd hate to think ye can manage without me at any time, Jewel, but I know that ye can an' have been in this situation. Give yerself some credit, woman. This hasn't been easy, an' yer man knew it wouldn't be but he felt ye were up to the challenge. An' while I'm not overfond of agreein' with Jamie Kirkpatrick, I do agree with him here."

"I think," she said softly, "I think I have to start considering the possibility that he's not coming back, Casey. I can't hold the companies if it can be proven that Julian is Jamie's blood. It will only be the matter of a blood test and they will have grounds from which to strike hard. Then I have to ask myself as well what Jamie would want, if he had known about Julian? We may have a stronger hold on the house and land, but as to the companies, blood will out, and maybe it's right that it should."

"Take yer time over this and don't assume right away that Jamie would view this boy as a blessing in his life." He gave her a quick kiss and then stood. "I'll see ye downstairs, Jewel."

After Casey left, she straightened her hair and re-applied her lipstick. She knew she still looked pale and shocked but there was little she could do to change that just now.

She hesitated by the window. The snow had stopped falling and a thin skiff of it lay over the lawns. Unbroken by any footsteps, the grounds rolled away from her, a field of silver where the auld ones might dance under the half-moon that waxed in the sky. Below, a soft light came from the stables, creating a small circle of gold in the paddock. She put her forehead to the chill pane and closed her eyes.

Like a small chapel deep in a wood where no wayfarer ever passed, there was a place inside that she kept for Jamie's sons and her own lost babies, each name a folded petal on a delicate rosary: Michael, Alexander, Stuart, Maude, Deirdre and Grace, the last child she and Casey had lost before the miracle of Conor. It was not a place she visited often but she always knew where it was, the shape of it, the doors and windows and the altar, simple, just a place to kneel and remember, to say words that didn't have real form or shape but could only be said in that small, deserted chapel in the forest of the heart.

The prayer she said now was for Jamie and the sons he had lost, both those who had died and the one who had lived. And she prayed that the living son was not a thorn on that petalled rosary that she turned over in her heart.

"Merry Christmas, Jamie," she whispered, soft as the frost latticing and branching on the window. "You have a son."

Part Nine

Russian Fairytale
Russia – November 1974–September 1975

From the Journals of James Kirkpatrick

November 11th, 1974

Born—Nikolai Andreyevich Kirkpatrick, sound of body and certainly sound of lungs, for he has made the entire camp aware of his existence in no uncertain terms, this son with three parents. He is, of course, beautiful and blue-eyed with a quiff of red hair that is Violet's despair, for she had hoped he would be blond like his father. He weighed in at a very respectable 8 lbs. 11oz. and has a hearty appetite.

It is as though we have been given a stay of execution, a stay that allows us to pretend that we are not in a camp from which it seems increasingly unlikely we will emerge. It is at best a game of pretend, yet it is our life at present. There is no knowing if we will be allowed to keep Kolya for more than eighteen months, which has traditionally been when Soviet children are removed from their mothers in situations like ours, and put into the nightmare of state institutions. One does not require a broad imagination to know what a child's fate would be in such a place at such a tender age.

Russians do not live in expectation of happiness. History has taught them far harder lessons. Russians endure, Russians survive, and at the end of the day, that is no small accomplishment. In this country it is often an act of heroism.

But I think in our own way, we have found happiness. Perhaps it is only what is left of my Western naïveté, the part of my philosophy that says man and woman are due some measure of joy in this life, but yet... yes, we are happy in our own way. Stripped down to our essentials and in limbo so that joy is snatched at as bread by a starveling.

This camp exists outside of time, or so it seems to those of us shut up here. It is as though we are beyond the bounds of even Soviet time and space, and live in some strange, dark fairytale buried deep in a Russian bor. Rarely do any officials come here and I know even within a system as secretive as the Soviet one, this camp is beyond the pale, to use a term from my own land.

Chapter Sixty-two

February 1975

Russian Fairytale

JAMIE LEFT THE BATH HUT FEELING REMARKABLY LIGHT in spirit. He had managed a shower in privacy, with hot water and real soap. He was looking forward to cuddling Kolya, having a hot cup of tea, his bed and his wife, in pretty much that order. Valentin, the camp commander, had allowed them permanent occupancy of their small bridal hut and the privacy was a cherished thing, even if it had caused pangs of envy amongst those who did not have such luxuries. He did not feel enough guilt about it to change the situation. Envy in the camp was a given, small shards of it existed everywhere for everything. Envy over bread rations, envy for the extra potato in the bowl of the man next to you, envy for release, even when it was only the release of death.

Shura approached him as he crossed the yard, fine snow falling on his shoulders and frosting the dark waves of his hair. Jamie shivered, still damp from his ablutions, the stubble of his hair immediately stiffened in the cold.

"What's wrong?" Jamie asked sharply, fear already hurrying him forward. Had something happened to Kolya? Had he felt hot when Jamie held him those precious ten minutes before dinner?

Shura held up one thick hand. "It is not the baby or Violet, do not fear."

Jamie's brows rose in query, for the dwarf looked unnaturally flummoxed.

"It's Gregor," Shura said with a heavy breath. "He's drunk and raving and he won't listen to anyone, except, perhaps, you. He has cut his hand badly, and I need to get him calmed enough to clean and stitch it. He's in the banya." Shura gave an apologetic shrug, for few would volunteer to go inside a confined space with an angry Gregor.

"Drunk?" Jamie considered that the idea of drunkenness and Gregor did not seem to belong in the same sentence. He did not think there could be enough vodka in the entire camp to make Gregor drunk. His capacity was legendary.

When Jamie entered the banya, Gregor was quiet, which alarmed him

more than if the man had been raving as Shura had said. But the detritus
of his recent rage lay littered about the place. The structure itself remained
sound, for it had been built to withstand Russian weather and was as solid as
a Shoreland tank. The hut was hot and dry as hell for there was a fire going
strong under the stones and a full bucket of water on the rough floor beside
them. Gregor was partially clothed and seated on the long bench, slumped
against the wall, huge hands lying open on his lap as though beseeching an
invisible guest. Blood dripped steadily from the injured one.

"Gregor." Jamie said his name quietly but with enough authority to
make certain the man heard him clearly.

The man's head rose slowly, like that of an aggrieved titan. His eyes in
the dim of the banya were deep pools with neither fathom nor shore. Jamie
sat down beside him. The animal reek of anger was thick in the air, under-
noted with the sweet copper salt of fresh blood. The stones on the grates were
smoking with heat, making the air thick and hard to breathe.

"What's going on?" Jamie kept his tone as bland as if this were any ordinary night in the gulag. Which it was in many ways.

For a moment it seemed Gregor was not going to answer but then he
sighed, expelling breath that was nine parts vodka into the thick heat of the
banya.

"It is my mother's birthday, or I think it is. I woke up with the echo of
it in my head. This makes me sad and so I drink to drown it and when the
sorrow drowns, the anger surfaces. She was a big woman, the sort that one
sees on Soviet posters—as though if you scratched her skin—you would find
the iron of the nation beneath rather than flesh and blood. I believed for a
long time that she did have iron under her skin. She had beautiful hair though.
It hung to her knees when she took it out at night. I remember lying beside
her, wrapped in it. It was the color of sunrise, all red and gold."

Jamie had a sudden clear picture of his own mother, one of those moments that the mind snatched and stored in the heart so that one could see it
unroll years later as clear and sharp as the moment it happened. She didn't
move like other people. She barely seemed to touch the earth, as though the
strings that bound and held others could not contain her. As though her
elements refused such dull matters as gravity. She had been a being of grace
and he missed her.

"I don't know exactly when my mother abandoned me, but I think it
was June because those first nights in the fields and ditches I remember the
flowers that were blooming. At night they would be all wrapped up tight
like they were holding a secret, but in the morning I would drink the dew
from their cups. It was the only water I could find those first few days. I don't
even know how old I am. Isn't that odd, Yasha? To not even know when
one arrived in this world?"

"It is indeed," Jamie agreed thinking of his own childhood and how there had not always been stability but there had always been love, a roof over his head, food on the table and someone to worry if he didn't come home at night. This man had never had any of those things and the burden of it he would carry for a lifetime. And there was nothing anyone could say or do to lighten that load. There were some things that, because they were lacking, caused a person to carry them for the rest of his life. A parent unable to love her child was one.

"Why do you think she abandoned you? Isn't it more likely that she was killed or taken away?"

"I don't know why. Only that if I ever did know the truth, it left me long ago. Maybe I told myself that she abandoned me so that I would be angry enough to keep going, so the thought of one day finding her and punishing her would goad me to survive."

"What do you remember of her?" Jamie asked.

Gregor did not answer the question at once, but looked long into the cup of his big hands as though he held the past there within them and could read and understand the lines of it only if he looked long enough. "Nothing, just echoes in my head, only half heard, a snatch of a song I think she once sang, a long story that she never finished telling about a boy who was born of a mother but had no father. I think, Yasha, even if I do not know, that boy was me. But how is a boy born without a father?"

Some men wore the protective clothing of quiet citizenship, of belonging to one tribe or another, but in their hearts they were fugitives and always would be. Some men had never known how to find nor wear that protective cloak that hid their inner life from the prying eyes of others, those who would hunt, who only understood the chase. Gregor, despite his bravado, was a fugitive and naked in the world. Jamie knew this because he was one too.

"I remember the forest—it was my first friend. I remember how the mosses whispered to me. Did you know that lichens only grow when a human voice is near? And that some flowers, the most beautiful, grow only in the rot of dead things. Or that some curl their petals up like a young girl ashamed just because of a man looking at her?"

"No," Jamie responded quietly. "I did not know that." He took Gregor's hand, judging that it was safe enough at this point. The cut across the palm was deep and ragged, with the glisten of exposed tendon, pearl white amongst the rubies and garnets of torn flesh. However, it was not life threatening, and there was time for Gregor to say what he needed to say.

"I can still tell you what the light was like on those days, how it rippled and ran before me, and was a living thing, like a playmate that you could never quite catch. How it fell in the hollows and slid over the hills, and how it seemed to point out to me what I could eat—the gleam of it on a berry so that it shone like a jewel and attracted my eye and tongue, how it sparkled like a dance on the water so I would stop to drink. I look back and remember those days as if they are film, a strange story of a changeling like the ones you told us about. I don't know though, Yasha, if I was the real child or the strange one left by the fairies.

"The world is so vast and strange at night, especially to a small person. There is nothing familiar, nothing to which one can hold. I would sing myself to sleep, lisping the words, my own voice seeming too small to be of much use. I remember the strangeness of the night sky, and counting the stars I could not name. But it was not long before the forest became home, before I could smell as the wolf does, and know as the deer when the rain was coming. I could spend hours watching fish swim in ponds and then kill one with my hands and eat it raw. I knew which mushrooms were poisonous, and which were not. I never made a mistake. How I do not know, only that the earth was my mother, the forest my guardian angel. You learn to live in your body rather than your head. You listen to your ears, but also to what your skin tells you. You understand what the birds are saying and can talk to a wolf merely by looking her in the eyes. This happens after a long time with the land, and no human being to talk to, to hear. Language becomes something far more than words. It becomes everything."

Gregor stood and threw the bucket of water onto the stones, now heated to a deadly temperature. The steam billowed out, the stones hissing violently in protest. The heat hit Jamie in a wave and he felt sweat bead instantly across his skin. Gregor sat back down beside him and leaned in, grasping the back of Jamie's neck, putting his forehead, slick with heat, against Jamie's own. Jamie could feel the man's pulse pounding against his temples. The smell of blood and vodka rose between them like a musk, steam floating around them in thick tendrils.

"Tonight, between you and me, no masks, my beautiful harlequin, just truth."

"Just remember that the truth, to quote Heisenberg, becomes less certain the more closely one attempts to know it. Like all stories, truth is subject to the interpretation of the teller."

Gregor laughed, but it was a dark sound. "You are such a bastard, Yasha."

"So are you," Jamie replied.

"The woman will break your heart."

"Perhaps," Jamie said, the taste of blood and sweat in his mouth like an elemental ether. "It is a risk one takes."

"Some stories are written in blood while it is still flowing."

"Stories exist already. How they are written or told is merely a matter of mechanics."

"Mechanics can kill you."

"This I know as well as you do."

Gregor released his hold on Jamie and the two men drew apart.

"You are a storyteller, Yasha, and so you know that even for one man there are many ways to tell one story. Perhaps, no matter how you tell it, it is still the same story at its heart, always."

"Finish your own story," Jamie said, perfectly still, his breathing matching that of the man across from him.

Gregor acquiesced with a sharp-toothed smile.

"I convinced myself that I too was iron beneath the skin, like my mother, that I could not bleed as an ordinary boy, that I was impervious to cold and snow and the dark, black nights. I think it is why I survived. I believed I could not die and so I could not. Then one day I was proven all too human. There they were, standing in the dust of a road, the fields stretched out behind them. They were filthy, clothes too small and torn, a ragged group of children. They were older than me and I saw them as I might have seen an alien from a distant planet. I had not looked in a mirror within my memory and it had been long since I had seen another human."

Through the steam there were the jeweled tones of the man's chest, the domed blue towers, the coiled tail and fiery breath of the dragon—the elements of a fairytale, the cruellest one ever told, because it was true. Indeed, there were many ways to tell a story. Words inside of words like an unending matryoshka doll.

"They were a feral tribe and I was not one of them. Nor could I be. I was frightened but so longed to be one of them at the same time. To no longer be alone. But they feared me as only a mob can fear a single person. They were of one mind and their leader did not want to find a challenge in her midst."

Even at the tender age of five Gregor would have been a challenge, Jamie knew. Much as he himself had been. An entity that existed outside the norm and was thusly, and perhaps naturally, rejected.

"I wanted to show them I was special, thinking that would make them take me in. So I cut myself to prove it, so they would know I was like my mother, that I did not bleed, that I had silver beneath my skin, that I could not be broken no matter what they did to me. I cut too deeply, too bravely. I was foolish. I ran with blood in front of them. And they beat me for it. With sticks and stones and kicks and curses."

"For, of course, there was no iron beneath the skin. There was only a child," Jamie said, only his tone was not soft as it might have been for that long ago child.

"They left me there in that field to die. One could not expect more than that, for they were wild things just as I was, though I learned a valuable lesson that night. I could bleed. I could die. I would never let another person see me bleed. I would give them only the iron of my soul. But you, Yasha, to you

I give blood. And to me, to me you give nothing of yourself."

"You want my blood? I could open my veins to you, allow you to drink me to the dregs. It would not be enough to quench your thirst."

The dark eyes were lustrous with memory and something more, the taut muscle of the big body still as stone. "I know this, my Yasha, but it does not stop me from the wanting of it."

"Life often consists of wanting without having, or at least, I have found it so myself."

Silence reigned for a long moment, their eyes holding through the steam and heat, neither flinching nor blinking. Obsidian to emerald, the language of the ether, no less powerful in its intent and meaning than all the words of the world's infinite lexicon.

"My wolf that I told you of long ago, I found her when she was just a puppy, her mother killed by a hunter, she left for dead. I fed her on my blood those first days, until I could give her the blood of another. It is how she survived."

"I was not aware that a wolf could be suckled on blood." It was given the tone of a question but they both knew it was not.

"Oh yes, Yasha, they can smell it from thrice nine lands, just like in the old tales. And once they smell it, they will come for it, have no doubt."

"Your story," Jamie said, softly, but with a softness that held flint at its core, "is like a pearl dissolving in wine, a beautiful tale perhaps, though not based entirely in truth."

Gregor looked at him long and deep, the dark eyes as unfathomable as the stars to which he could not give names. And then he used the language of the camps to give salve to the wounds of stories that defied all reason, all humanity, to stories that made the teller feel vulnerable.

"If you don't believe it, consider it a fairytale."

Chapter Sixty-three
April 1975
Phoenix in the Ashes

THE WORLD WHEELED ON, STARS FELL FROM THE HEAVENS, tides crashed upon the shores, skirmishes took place upon borders: some lost, some won, some both. In England, there was inflation, scandal, corruption and collusion and a trembling ceasefire with the mad cousins from across the chilly sea. In Vietnam, a war ended and did not end—without resolution, without victory, a thoroughly modern war with all its hideous consequences. In the East, the flow of black gold to the West was lessened considerably. Prices soared and machines were silenced.

And as was wont to happen every year, poets and saviors died, as did musicians and spies, diplomats and artists, soldiers and con men. A President was toppled from grace and a nation lost what was left of its innocence.

The Cold War ground on as it had for many years. It too was a war with casualties, though these were rarely made public and often those who fell in the fight simply disappeared into a chill grave in foreign soil, with their family and loved ones never knowing the truth of their fate. Dissidents were caged in Emperors' prisons under the guise of madness and the Soviet machine, grey as the dullest iron, ground on.

Sometimes men lived to tell their tales, but sometimes they did not.

And in a far corner of Russia, in a small labor camp forgotten by some and remembered by others, none of this was known, for perhaps little of it mattered, for none of those who dwelled there were going anywhere and the world seemed a distant place of little consequence. Time passed slowly here, and dates on a calendar page ceased to have the meaning they had once held. Time was measured by the growth of a child, by the change of seasons, by the falls of snow and the warm winds arriving from the south.

Perhaps these people were lulled by the rule of a benevolent dictator. Perhaps they had forgotten what they needed to, and remembered only that which seemed necessary to survival in a deep, dark forest, forgotten in the empire's hinterland.

Perhaps they had forgotten the one constant of the world, of the universe itself. All things must change and neither happiness nor misery is the natural state of man. The pendulum swings and all things change, and then the pendulum swings again.

It is the way of the world, both this one and that.

IT WAS AN APRIL EVENING, AND THE SNOW WAS IN FULL MELT when Jamie came through the gates after a long, raw day in the forest and saw a familiar figure standing outside the guard's hut. A short, abrasive man stepped away from the figure's side and approached Jamie before he could join his comrades at dinner.

"Comrade Valueve requests your presence," he said in short guttural bursts. Jamie gritted his teeth in dislike. Comrade Yelivosky was short on brains but long on loyalty to the State as well as possessing an encyclopedic knowledge of how to make human beings suffer. He looked like nothing so much as a stunted boar.

Andrei came out on the small porch of the guard hut and walked toward him, hair a-shimmer in the evening air, his walk that of a man who had business to conduct, and not of the pleasant sort.

Jamie heard Gregor say something low behind him, and realized the big man had not gone ahead to the dining hall but had waited to see if Jamie would need him.

Jamie turned and nodded to him. "It's alright."

Gregor gave Andrei a long look and then headed off to eat.

There was shock in Andrei's face at the sight of him. Jamie was all too aware of the sight he must present. He had never regained his weight after the fever and was carved down to his essentials of muscle and bone. His hair, recently shaved, was no more than a bright stubble, hands rough and calloused from his time in the forest. Right now he felt annoyance as he was going to miss his time in the nursery with Kolya before dinner, and from the look on Andrei's face, this wasn't going to be a pleasant chat over a decent meal.

"We need to talk," Andrei said peremptorily. "Follow me."

Having little choice in the matter, Jamie fell into step with Andrei.

"He is a friend?" Andrei jerked his head in the direction in which Gregor had departed, as they walked toward the guard's hut. There was a look upon his face as though he had smelled a three-day corpse.

"He has become a friend," Jamie said, thinking 'friend' seemed a strange word to describe the détente he and Gregor had declared between them.

"This is what you call an alliance? This is what you think is wisdom? You think such a man cares about others, cares whether you live or die?"

"Yes," Jamie said dryly, "it's true love. We're buying a little dacha on Lake Baikal, as soon as Gregor gets parole."

"It's not funny, Yasha," Andrei said prohibitively.

"No, I don't suppose it is."

Andrei paused on the doorstep of the guard hut to glare at Jamie.

"You think someone like that man, that filthy thief, has loyalties? Have you lost your mind, Jamie?"

"Maybe," Jamie shrugged. "What does it matter at this point?"

"You know that it matters, Yasha. You are being ridiculous and naïve and you know it. Do you do this just to anger me?"

"Whether you want to admit it or not, we're in here, not you—so yes, in order to survive I've had to form alliances, make deals, do things I normally wouldn't.

"So what are you now, *vor*?" Andrei sneered.

"In some ways, yes, I guess I always have been. I suspect that's what he recognized in me and it's why I wasn't gang raped and left for dead three days after I arrived," Jamie spat out, suddenly very, very angry. It was true, he realized. His own dark history, his own crimes, the blood on his own hands were the things that had appealed to Gregor enough to stay the invisible knife that was always in the man's hand. He knew the man under the skin and had to admit that the man knew him too.

The ham-hocked Comrade had followed so tightly on their heels that he stumbled into Jamie as they crossed the threshold of the ramshackle building. The guard's hut was empty at present and would afford them the only privacy available in the camp. Inside, Andrei sat, Comrade Yelivosky standing to porcine attention behind him. Jamie began to get a very bad feeling in the pit of his stomach. Still, they might have allowed him the courtesy of a chair, whatever they were up to. It was very warm in the hut. He knew it would shortly make him sleepy and as tired as he was, he might well drop off on the spot.

It was one of the stranger meetings he had experienced with Andrei. The questioning began slowly, questions about the productivity of the timber cutters, about quotas, about meeting required limits, and a great deal more mind-numbing Soviet double-talk. If there was a code wrapped inside this talk, he was too tired and too hungry to decipher it. After he had endured a half hour of it, he couldn't take any more.

"May I go now?" he asked, voice as courteous as a blooded scalpel. "I'd like to have a little of my evening left to me, now that you've made me miss dinner."

"Just what is it you're so eager to get back to?" Andrei asked, eyes narrowed and body leaning forward as though he were barely restraining himself.

"My wife and son," Jamie said, wanting to cut to the real purpose of this visit and force the inevitable confrontation. Andrei would have come on his own had he the choice. He must have been saddled with the good Comrade at the last minute and been unable to wiggle his way free.

Andrei's eyes were the hot blue they always became when he was furious. Nothing could be said in front of the fat wee Comrade. Even Andrei's minders had their limits when it came to loyalty and Jamie had long suspected that Yelivosky had been assigned to keep tabs on Andrei's every word and action. He had the strong feeling something was being telegraphed to him—a warning, a reprimand, a threat? He couldn't tell. His own fury was too full, flooding out from his chest in crimson billows, making him impervious to danger and good sense.

Andrei stood and crossed the room in three strides, then lifted his hand and brought it across Jamie's face with a savagery that rocked Jamie off his feet. He caught up hard on the wall, fighting down the desire to put his hands to his face and check if all his teeth were still in their sockets. The blow had been dealt with unrestrained ferocity and so Jamie knew that it had not been for Comrade Yelivosky's sake but had been delivered out of Andrei's jealousy and rage toward him. Nevertheless, it had served the double purpose of relieving Andrei's feelings and pleasing the Comrade, who had a small smile tucked into his chins.

Jamie used the wall to prop himself up. The pain was already subsiding but the shock to his system wasn't so easily banished. This moment had always been inevitable between him and Andrei, like a song that heads toward its apex from the opening note, to shatter itself in splendor, but shatter itself nonetheless. The prison camp and Violet and now Kolya had only brought it to a more rapid head. But Jamie found a certain reckless thrumming in his blood, for he no longer cared. Instead there was a fury that made him want to wipe that imperious face of Andrei's all over the floor for what he had done to Violet, regardless of the reasons, regardless of the rules and brutality of this country. Andrei might love Violet but it was Jamie who cared for her on a daily basis, who was her husband and who was father to Andrei's son.

Andrei walked in tight to his body, every inch of him a threat. "Stop this defiance now, or I'll be left with no choice but to put you in isolation. Do you understand?"

The chill of Andrei's eyes met his own with the force of a hammer unlocking the trigger on a gun. *Take this no further or I will not answer for the consequences.* Violence often spawned an intimacy that demanded its due, violence that shimmered between them like a deep blue flame, drawing them into a tight vortex that seemed both inevitable and desirable, consequences be damned.

"Fuck you," Jamie said, spitting blood on the floor. "Fuck you—you Soviet whore."

Andrei's eyes were incandescent now with fury, chest heaving with the need to do more than just hit Jamie.

"You want to kill me right now, don't you?" Jamie asked in English so the Comrade could not understand what was taking place, for it had swiftly become personal.

"That's what you do with traitors," Andrei said, voice stripped of its ice and hauteur, down to something so primal that it demanded response.

Jamie laughed, a fine spray of blood flying from his lips as he did so. "I'm a traitor? If I'm a traitor, what the hell do you think you are, Andrei? You've betrayed every ideal you ever claimed to hold dear."

"I might be a Soviet whore, as you call me," Andrei hissed, "but I would never take your woman from you."

"Well, if you didn't leave your woman locked up in a fucking prison I might have higher morals about taking her away."

"So you admit it, then." Andrei looked oddly pleased, as if now he could go ahead and finish Jamie off without troubling his conscience.

"It's a wee bit hard to deny it being that I've married her and that I am father to your son."

It was a few words too far for Andrei.

"Leave," Andrei barked over his shoulder at Yelivosky. The Comrade blanched, but had the sense to exit swiftly, his small ham feet skittering out the door as fast as they would take him.

Andrei shed his coat and gloves, tossing them carelessly onto a chair, a smile of white-hot fury on his face. "I am going to take you apart, you bastard."

"Come on and try," Jamie said, moving out from the wall. He laughed in Andrei's face, knowing it was like the waving of a red rag to a bull and felt a rush of pure adrenaline alongside his rage, something that felt akin to joy.

His training in the ring had never left him and before his journey to Russia he was still sparring twice a week at the gym. His muscle and sinew responded instantly to Andrei's attack, feinting and coming back with a jab that wiped the surety from Andrei's face. But Andrei was no slouch with his fists either and he had the advantage of proper nutrition and rest on his side. He landed a blow to Jamie's ribs that made Jamie catch his breath and hold it for a moment. It exploded out a minute later as he planted a right uppercut to Andrei's face, the jolt of it carrying all the way along his arm.

Andrei called him a very impolite Russian word, dancing back from him and regrouping. Jamie pressed his advantage—following, crowding the man, not giving him a moment to recover from the blow—the urge to inflict damage, to hurt, to maim so strong he could taste the delicate blood flavor of it on his tongue.

Like fire forced through a narrow glass aperture, love subverted will become a self-destructive flame that emerges darker and with greater force, consuming all in its path, cracking and melting the vessel in which it is held, laying waste to things that are too fine and fragile to survive such force.

There was neither the grace nor the choreography of fight that was an art within itself. This was fury and hurt and betrayal and a terrible grappling of flesh and bone. And a great need to wipe free the mind and emotional terrain of one's soul of all history with this person, a repudiation of all the higher feelings one had held for this 'other'.

They fell across the floor, clumsy-footed as bears now, stupid with anger. The stove stood in the center of the room, a rotund belly-barrelled thing, balancing on delicately artful legs so that a good wind might have knocked it over. They hit it with the force of two freight trains in rushing motion, uncaring of damage inflicted or havoc wreaked.

The scent of scorched skin and hair stirred up in the mix of blood and sweat and raw anger. Hell smelled this way and they were locked tight in one of the inner circles. So much so that neither noticed the small, blue flames creep out from the coals that flew across the floor, settling with appetite in corners, under papers, along ancient and moth-chewed boards, expanding with silent rapidity.

Jamie's breath raked in and out of his lungs like salt on a wound. His hair was wet with sweat and his hands were slick with blood. He felt roaringly alive, felt the whisk of blood through vessels and saw every detail of the room around him, though Andrei was the focal point of it all. There was a burn on his back that throbbed, not yet with agony, but soon.

There was a ribbon of blood running from the corner of Andrei's eye and Jamie's mouth was awash with the particular salt of that same fluid. He laughed, the sharp-edged feral laugh of a man caught up in the potent intoxication of violence. It was a high unlike any other, and one didn't feel pain during the execution of it. Unfortunately, when the adrenaline ebbed, the pain came on with the force of a steam train.

The entire wall behind Andrei was sheeted in flame, glowing crimson and flickering tautly on skin and hair. He could feel the strength and hatred of it, how it consumed without guilt or thought. It fed in his veins, heating his blood beyond thought and reason.

Andrei rushed him, yelling something in his face, shoving him hard so that he was flying backwards, barely able to keep his footing. He couldn't understand what Andrei was saying, only saw his lips moving, for the blood pounding through his head deafened him. They stumbled through the door, ashes and soot and bright, stinging sparks falling on their hair and skin and clothing.

They fell into the filthy snow in a tangle of limbs and rage, Andrei's legs scissoring him through the air and squeezing his ribs until they gave. He rolled away from Andrei, through the snow, ash thickening the air until it was as heavy as overcooked oats in a man's mouth. He slid sideways and fought for purchase, Andrei as slick and slippery as an eel, snapping and sliding under him. Andrei was still yelling but Jamie couldn't make sense of the words, couldn't understand anything but the singing fury that coursed through him like the thunder of a forge anvil. His arm was across Andrei's throat, an iron bar, his entire body pulsing with the savage power of it. He would kill Andrei and then the guards would kill him, and it would all be done.

Then with a rush of fire the anvil came down on his own head and the world spun briefly, stars and water and fire, before it all went black.

HE CAME TO IN A POOL OF SLUSH, HEAD FILLED WITH LEAD SHOT... or so it seemed. He was both boiling hot and freezing cold. Someone was saying his name, the soft Russian diminutive and for a moment he thought he smelled dark cinnamon, then realized it was only ashes and blood that were clogging his airways.

"Yasha!" The voice was imperative with panic. He risked cracking one eye though the pain it caused hardly seemed worth it.

Andrei was above him, and behind Andrei, like particularly ugly and brutish angels, hovered the faces of Vlad and Boris, the bumpkin farmer boys who had been fated to serve out their conscription here on the edge of a frozen world, guarding an encampment of lunatics, poets and thieves. It all had a comfortingly Irish feel about it, so he risked opening the other eye and immediately wished he had not been so foolhardy.

Andrei glared at him then turned to the Russian version of Tweedledee and Tweedledum, to yell at them with such ferocity that both were stumbling backward at a run before he got halfway through his castigation of them.

"For the love of all that is holy, will you shut up!" Jamie said acidly, in Russian, which proved, he thought rather smugly, that his brain was still in working order even if it did feel a wee bit too large for its packing crate at present.

"You could have killed me," Andrei said. Jamie squinted up at him, noting the thick smears of bloody soot on his face and what might have been a ring of bruises across the width of his neck.

"I wanted to," Jamie said, then rolled over to spit a mixture of blood and soot onto the ash-speckled snow. "It was a near thing." His face stung and throbbed in places too numerous to count. He would be avoiding mirrors for the next while. Just as well, he supposed, that the camp had none.

"Christ," Andrei said, with a wheeze that might have been laughter, "I needed that."

"So did I," Jamie said, taking slow stock of his injuries before daring to sit up. He had yet to get past his head and all its various cuts, contusions, bumps and bruises. "You've loosened my teeth, you bastard. And I think I've got a broken rib."

"One of my fingers is broken and I think I'm blind in my left eye. Rest assured that you gave as good as you got."

"Once the swelling comes out, you'll be able to see again," Jamie said unsympathetically.

"I can see well enough to know the devil when he's in my view," Andrei retorted with a noise that sounded suspiciously like amusement.

"He is not nearly as handsome as me," Jamie said, coughing as ash drifted into his open mouth.

"Well, if anyone would know, it's you," Andrei said and collapsed on his back in a pile of filthy snow. "Come, Yasha, the snow will numb your bruises."

Jamie was too tired to argue and crawled toward the drifts of snow farther away from the fire. Andrei lay winded in a patch as fluffy as cotton, looking like Picasso's version of a snow angel.

Andrei sat up long enough to bark sharp orders at the guards, who had retreated to the edge of the firelight, uncertain what to do. This hail of verbal bullets seemed to help them decide and they headed for the sanctuary of the bell tower. Comrade Yelivosky was treated to an even more blistering tirade when he poked his snout out of the security of Valentin's office. It was odd but not entirely surprising that no one was willing to interfere.

"They only wanted to put the fire out, and possibly put a bullet through me," Jamie said.

"Let the fucking thing melt into the ground. It's too late to save it now and besides, how often do we get the chance to be warm in this country? If I can't kill you, they sure as hell aren't getting the pleasure of it."

Jamie laughed, causing his ribs to move in the manner of glass ground over glass. He settled his bruised and battered body back into the shell of snow.

They lay thus while the fire died slowly back, having consumed all but the framing of the hut. It stood in a shining pool of water, reflections of crimson, gold and emerald oiling the surface, as beautiful as a Monet painting.

Above, the sky had turned its face to night, the stars so clearly imprinted upon it that it seemed they had been placed by an ancient hand merely for man's pleasure. It was a spring sky, he noted, the wheel of the year was turning even in this frozen land. Orion was low in the sky while Gemini took center stage, with the bright stars of Castor and Pollux, the heads of the celestial twins.

When Andrei spoke, his voice had changed remarkably, as though he were no longer the same man who had entered that hut a scant hour ago. He sounded hollow, as though he had become a straw man.

"Do you love her?"

"Yes, I do."

"My boy—what is he—how..."

"He's beautiful, healthy as a horse and he looks like a bloody Cossack, just like his father."

Beside him, in the pooling slush, Andrei was still, face turned up toward the heavens.

"I remember the first time my father took me out to see the stars. We sat on the roof of our dacha and he pointed Orion out, and told me the story of the great blind hunter. At first, I was enchanted, but then I got scared because for the first time the vastness of the universe struck me and I felt so small. Even my father looked small and I knew suddenly he could not protect me in a space so very large. All my life I have been trying to break that space down into something more manageable, something that could be categorized, put into a book, labeled and made palatable to human fears. A fool's errand, I see now. I still look at the stars and feel small, but now they make me feel hopeless as well. They never used to do that. Because now I know I will never show my son those stars."

Jamie contemplated the blaze of Betelgeuse, clear red beating against the tops of the firs so that it looked a living thing capable of fire and mayhem. The sky was the only thing that represented freedom to him these days, that and the thought that the same stars shone over the heads of those he loved who were far away. There was some small comfort to be taken from that.

"I will show them to him, if I am able. But, perhaps you—"

Andrei cut him off swiftly. "No, Yasha. We will not speak of it. It's impossible."

Jamie, having long been a father who had lost sons, was familiar with that tone of voice. He would speak of other things. It would not lessen the wound but it would distract for a moment.

"I—I had an experience when I was sick last year," he said, feeling the onrush of emotion that had often taken him unawares since Kolya's birth.

"Yes?" Andrei prompted.

"Do you think it's possible to reach out across the miles, across the breadth of the planet and make contact with someone without the aid of telephone or letters, for two souls to touch simply through longing?"

"Will you tell me what happened, Yasha?"

Jamie told the story in brief, realizing how small and beggared the words were in comparison to what he had felt that night, had known in that time out of time. That he had not only touched, felt and smelled Pamela, but had heard Casey, had felt the brute strength of a man with whom his relationship had been less than cordial and could certainly never be described as close.

"Doesn't this point to the likelihood of it being a real event? She is the common thread to which you both hold. It would seem that the three of you are bound together and so are inseparable. And he would be there to keep her safe, from what you've told me. Were it merely a dream, I doubt you would have brought him into it."

"But couldn't it have been the fever affecting my brain?"

"To the point where you held her scent on your hands long after? No, I don't think so."

Andrei was silent for a long space. "Yasha, I have told you much of my work—or as much as I was allowed over the years, but even that barely touched either surface or truth of what we have been doing, studying, testing—all of it, both that which we can prove, and that which remains a puzzle that only tantalizes without resolution. All of this has only made the world in which we live, the universe itself, a greater mystery than it was before. The older I get, the less apparent are the answers. If indeed, the answers exist. But... there have been thousands of studies on one variant or another of this exact thing you speak of. And yes, there is proof that people can communicate across vast distances, even across time."

"And yet..." Jamie said, but found suddenly he did not wish to express any skepticism, nor feel it to be truthful, and knew he must accept the incident for what it was, whatever the small fold of time and space in which it had occurred.

"There is no reason not to believe, Yasha. You know it was more than a fever dream. You know it happened, even if the truth of it only resides in your cells and memory. After all, what is love? Can we touch it, hold it, show it to people in a tangible form? No, but we know it exists, and that something invisible is the greatest power in the universe should tell us all that we need to know or ever will need to know."

"You are waxing romantic tonight, Andrei. Where's your hardheaded Soviet philosophy?"

"I am not Soviet," Andrei said, "I am Russian, and we are the world's biggest romantic fools. And when things are ending, one finds a truth that one did not perhaps seek. It is no less true for all that. Truth and beauty does after all exist outside the confines of political boundaries and history."

"Do you truly believe that, Andrushya?"

"I will tell you what I believe," Andrei said softly. "I believe that somewhere out there you and I are still those two boys, daring the wind, ready to dive into a deep blue void just to know life. Somewhere both within and without we still exist as those boys, just as this night will echo somewhere always, and so we are always here and there, forever. Those boys are not ghosts. It is now, here, that I am a ghost and yet the world would tell me that the only reality is the present moment, that I am imprisoned by each minute. You and I know this is not so. Don't we?"

And suddenly he felt it, the eternal moment they had forged on the tower that night. Andrei was right, that would exist forever somewhere, somehow.

"I am sorry I could not be the raven that bore you out of here, Andrushya. I am more sorry for that than I can ever tell you."

"You are no raven. You are like the phoenix, Yasha. It is why so many are drawn to you. You are the fire that warms chilled souls, that can draw the ghosts in from the night. It is why I loved you from the first. It is why I am here now and it is why I do not know how to forgive you, or myself, for I have loved and hated you in equal measure all these years. I think now though, it is love that will remain with me when you are gone."

"It is all there ever was, Andrei. We just weren't wise enough to see it."

"You are the only friend I have left on the planet, Yasha. If you are still my friend, that makes me far richer than most men. Especially here in this country. Are you still my friend, Jamie? After all this?"

Jamie swallowed. He knew Andrei was asking for a real answer, that the question was merely what it was, stripped of their past and all the wrongdoing that existed between the two of them—simply 'are we friends?' And it was *his* decision and that alone told him how precarious Andrei's footing felt to the man right now.

"*Vsyegda*," Jamie said softly. Always.

Andrei smiled, but it was the smile of a ghost.

"When you go, take them with you. Take them for the sake of that boy one night in Paris, if not for the man he became."

"Am I going somewhere?" Jamie asked, tone light though his heart began to thud.

"Yes, Yasha, just be ready. I don't know the time nor will it be exact when it arrives—just be ready to go. You will have to prepare Violet as well."

"Andrei, what the hell do you have planned?"

Andrei laughed. "It is not so much a plan, Yasha, as an act of desperation."

"Do I take your love to her?" Jamie asked.

"No, I no longer have the right to say it... to feel it cannot be helped, but to say it is a sin now."

"Andrushya..." he began, but halted, without words, the space in his chest empty and quiet with regret.

From his bed of snow, Andrei spoke, words softened by resignation. "It is as it should be, Yasha. Only one can rise from the ashes we have made and it is you who were created with the feathers of the phoenix."

"And you?" Jamie asked, because the words were inevitable between them, always had been. Because here under the stars there was no room for anything but simple honesty.

"Someone must be the fuel, Yasha, for the fire to continue to burn."

And that, thought Jamie, watching the stars raining cold fire above him, was the answer that ended all questions between them, forever.

Chapter Sixty-four

June 1975

The Clerk's Tale

IT WAS QUIET IN THE GREENHOUSE, the lilac twilight that the Russians called *sommerki*, laying a soft haze over the plants and buckets of compost, the watering cans and assorted tools. He had come this evening because Violet wanted a sprig of chamomile for Kolya's gums. Volodya was inside, hands black with dirt, humming a tune to himself. He was tending an orchid, a gift that the commander had given him for his name day. Jamie had always liked the small, bookish man and sometimes brought him tea in the evenings, as he was always to be found here with his flowers.

Two months had passed since Andrei's visit, and there had been no word, no coded message to tell him that escape from this place was imminent. Such things were complicated, he knew, and so he had put his impatience and fears in a tightly locked room that he kept within his mind and found a strange peace existed in the place beyond.

He handed Volodya a cup of tea, the steam wafting off it in elegant curlicues.

"How is the boy?" Volodya asked, and took a small sip of his drink before setting it aside. He picked up a brush so delicate it looked to be composed of no more than a few hairs. Each of the man's movements was precise if slightly fussy, though Jamie knew him for a kind-hearted person who would not undertake the smallest of jobs without ensuring it was done well.

"He is fine, just cutting a tooth, and fussy with it. I rubbed his gums with vodka, as per Gregor's instructions, but Violet wants the chamomile for a tincture for him."

Kolya, thank heaven, despite his genes, was a very contented baby who had more fussing aunties and uncles than any child needed.

"Volodya..." he began, and then thought better of his curiosity for the clerk was a very private man and he had no wish to intrude upon such well-guarded territory.

Volodya turned, brush in hand and smiled. "It is alright, Jamie. You are wondering why I am here? I wondered if you would ever ask for my story. Though it is not terribly exciting, for you know small things can imprison a man in this state."

"I wasn't thinking you were a murderer or anything," Jamie said, smiling, and then abruptly flushed, for what if the small clerk was indeed guilty of murder?

Volodya raised a dark brow at him. "No, I am not a murderer."

He paused to sip his tea and then picked up a pair of tweezers that Dima had fashioned for him in exchange for a dark pink orchid for the woman he was courting. Volodya removed the pollinia from a snowy white orchid and placed it with the care of a watchmaker into the stigma pocket of a deep lavender plant. He then recorded the date and details of the cross pollination in a small cardboard-backed book he kept for the purpose.

"I want to make an orchid the color of the twilight here," he said, and sat on an upturned bucket, gesturing to Jamie that he should do the same.

Jamie sat, breathing in the scent of the soil and water and thick waxen petals.

"I was a postal clerk in a small village near to the Finnish border. I never longed for much, just a fire of my own, some books, flower seeds for the summer and to take care of my mother, who was old and had the rheumatics very bad.

"It wasn't a bad life, though there was never anything in the stores, but we made do. And we always had a garden filled with potatoes and dill, beets and radishes and onions, and we kept cows for milk and meat. In the summer the woods near where we lived were filled with berries and mushrooms. That and vodka and what else does a man need?"

"Shura tells me he's never seen anyone with your feel for flowers, not even Violet."

Volodya smiled, his lean cheeks pinking with pleasure. "I love flowers and they seem to know that and so respond accordingly. It was flowers that were my downfall and that landed me in here."

"Flowers?" Jamie echoed, wondering how even the Soviet Union could prosecute you for growing flowers.

"Yes, flowers. Armloads of violets to be specific. Well, that and a woman." Volodya went even pinker at the admission, as though he had just confessed to congress with a sheep.

"She was my boss at the post office and I think I fell in love with her the minute I set eyes upon her. I kept it to myself for a very long time. It was enough to admire her from afar. I would leave small things for her, from time to time, anonymously in her work locker so that she might know she was thought of most kindly. I made her ornaments for *Novyi God*—small, delicate things from twisted wire and birch bark. It was harmless and I think she enjoyed the mystery of it.

"One day, deep in winter, she was lamenting the snow, the white un-changingness of it, how dirty it looked by that time of year and how she longed for color and greenery. To her it was only a passing thing. To me it was a dream I could give to her."

He sighed and brushed a few bits of dirt from his worn trousers. His small face was dreamy, as though he saw the woman in front of him now.

"She had eyes like velvet—deep and lush—you know the sort of eyes in a woman where you think you could happily drown for the rest of your days?" Volodya looked up, face still flushed, but with memory now rather than embarrassment.

Jamie nodded, for every man knew at least one such set of eyes.

"She lived in a tiny house near the edge of the village. She had a little walkway from the gate to her door. I filled it with violets so that the snow was purple with them—I had to time it just right, so they wouldn't wilt before she could see them. And then I hid myself so that I could watch her reaction. I saw more than I had bargained for. She was surprised and delighted. She stood there in the snow and cried and then picked up the flowers and held them to her face as if she could will spring if she could only breathe the scent of the violets in deeply enough. I should have left then, but I was drinking in her reaction the way an alcoholic drinks in his first vodka of the day. So it was that I was still there, crouched in the dirty snow behind a clump of shrubbery when a car pulled up. It was the car of a party official, for it was much better than what any of us could purchase. I had not known, though I suppose it was common gossip, that she was the mistress of a party official from Kiev. He stepped out and she ran to him, thanking him, thinking of course that he—her lover—had done this for her.

"He was furious, for he thought she was playing him for a fool. That she had another man partaking of her favors. He hit her across the face, first one cheek and then the other. She fell to the ground and then he started kicking the violets at her and calling her a whore. I knew what I risked if I went to her rescue but I couldn't just sit there in the bushes and watch him beat her. So I charged him—I hit him in the face as hard as I could manage. But he was a big man and I am not terribly strong.

"She reviled me, even spit on me as I lay bleeding in the snow. Well," Volodya shrugged, "what else could she do? She had to prove to him that she had no feelings for me, that I was less than dust beneath her feet. The things she said..." he closed his eyes, lean face pale once again, "I still cannot take them from my mind. For when someone is that vehement and the curses come so readily to their tongue, you know they have always, in some part of themselves, thought this of you.

"Two weeks later she accused me of rape which was, of course, completely untrue. But here I am nevertheless. She was badly beaten and I think it likely she had been raped, only not by me but by her lover. In Soviet courts though, if a Party *apparatchik* accuses you, you are always guilty."

He looked at Jamie, setting his teacup to the side, the scents of recently dug soil and petals surrounding them. His small, neatly trimmed mustache trembled slightly with emotion.

"All my life, humiliation is my companion. It rises with me in the morning and I taste its bitter gall in my throat at night. I ask myself many times, what is it in me that makes others want to shame me, to deny the little bit of dignity the world allows a man?"

"I don't know, Volodya," Jamie said quietly, for the world did seem to visit such things upon certain people. And dignity, in such a place as the Soviet world, might be the only bastion a man had between him and outright brutality. It wasn't much in the way of a shield but it was necessary all the same.

He left him then, the small dignified man, taking the chamomile Violet had requested with him.

He could see it clearly, the dark blush of violets in the snow, the sensitive man who had summoned all the romanticism of his nature in one poetic gesture and had it end in blood and cold, humiliation and imprisonment. It was a most Russian story in the shape of its tragedy and pathos.

He looked back, the dim now sifting up from the ground, more lavender than lilac, and saw Volodya in outline, still sitting as he had left him amongst his flowers and his ruined dreams.

Chapter Sixty-five

September 1975

Destroying Angel

SINCE THE ADVENT OF VALENTIN AS THEIR CAMP COMMANDER, they had been allowed to forage for edible things in the forest. Hence, one Sunday in September they were allowed out—with guards—to pick mushrooms, a delicacy that Jamie discovered was dear to the heart of each Russian. Even Nikolai, not given to overt emotion, was apt to go into raptures about the various kinds, shapes, flavors and medicinal values of each grubby fungi.

When Jamie, basket in tow, asked how he was supposed to know a good *gribny* from a bad one, he was confronted with several faces looking at him as if he was an idiot or a strange species of human that they had never stumbled across before.

"I've never picked mushrooms before," he said, feeling that this was a weak explanation for a profound lack in his character, but possessing none better, it was all he could say in his own defense.

This brought forth more strange looks, then laughter and shaking of heads. His sense of being the village idiot heightened considerably.

Violet smiled up at him from under the rim of her drab cap. "It is something we all do as children—go mushrooming, for food, but also for fun. When we live in cities, the Russian soul still longs for the earth, for the muck of soil between our fingers and the scent of the forest in our noses."

It was a theme common amongst the Russian people, that of their country as mother and provider, their connection with the land remaining many generations after they had left for the city. Every one of them was a peasant at heart.

"We have so much war and lack of food," Nikolai told him as they walked together, "that we must forage everywhere for things to eat, always. The forest provides much food and so we accept that bounty. In a famine nation such as this one, you learn to eat all that the earth puts forth and to use what isn't edible for other purposes. It is said that many mushrooms is a sign of war, for they will be needed in the terrible times to come. In the summer of 1940 there were more mushrooms growing than even the old ones could ever remember seeing."

The day was beautiful, cloudless and sunny, not hot as the summer had often been but one of those rare and perfect autumn days with the leaves at their peak glory in golds and russets. A gentle breeze whispered through the pines, and rustled the birches. The scent of decaying leaves and vegetation was ripe and warm on the air.

When he wondered aloud why they didn't stop in any one of several likely-looking clearings, he was told very earnestly by Violet, "You can smell when it is the right place. You can feel that it is a mushroom patch."

The funny thing was he *could* smell them at once—a change of light and air as much as scent. The light was low, filtering through the trees, leaving small fields of shade deep in the verdure of the forest floor. The air was thicker, heavier, and fecund with dark life.

Violet took him in hand and showed him how to find the mushrooms. How the slightest curve often differentiated them from the pile of browning leaves in which they nestled. How certain ones favored particular trees: the *berjozovik* living with the *berjoza*—birch tree, the *podosinovik* growing with the *osina*—aspen. The odd nature of others—the spindly *opjonka* that only lived a few hours before melting into a pool of inky fluid, the slick, slimy ones that Russians called 'fat of the earth.' Soon he could wander off on his own, and tell the good white ones from the beautiful death-dealing ones and was even lucky enough to stumble, in a boggy crag, upon large black ones that Violet clapped her hands over as if he had just presented her with a basketful of pearls. He began to feel slightly less idiotic and somewhat smug.

The sun was strong by late afternoon and induced a certain laziness in all. The desire to stretch out in the velvet grass and mosses and have a nap, to store some of that golden heat, to be pulled up out of the marrow on the long, dark winter days that were soon to come was overwhelming. Even the guards looked relaxed despite their guns slung at waist-height and arcing through the prisoners every few moments.

Once his basket was full he went to sit by Nikolai, who was resting against the broad trunk of a birch, the gleaming silver of his hair contrasting against the parchment pale bark.

Nikolai acknowledged his presence with a grunt and a pat on Jamie's shoulder. Jamie smiled in return and offered him two of the biggest black mushrooms, which Violet assured him were a delicacy beyond price.

Nikolai waved them away. "You keep them for Violet and the baby. They will need the extra when winter comes."

They sat for a stretch, content in the drowsy stupor the autumn sun had created. It was small things that gave pleasure, counted like beads on a string. A basket of mushrooms, heat, no deaths in the camp for the last two months, the way the sun turned Violet's hair to a blazing penny as she explained the finer points of a hairy-leafed plant to Vanya. Jamie smiled at the picture the two made.

"On days such as today," Nikolai said, "I am reminded of what it is to be young. I remember how sweet it was and I feel it in my bones for a second, but then it is gone and it leaves only bitter residue behind."

For Nikolai this was unusually garrulous and Jamie wondered what had brought it on. The old man had mellowed of late, partly because of the return of his music, Jamie suspected, but in larger part because of Kolya. He had been pleased when they named the baby after him and had taken to spending his evenings rocking Kolya, and singing old Russian ditties to him in a rough voice that was quite beautiful. The piano and the child together had brought a softness and a life out in him that had been well hidden before.

Nikolai's eyes were closed as he basked in the sun. His skin was like whisper-thin vellum, with fissures running through it as deep as the bark in an oak tree. He looked terribly frail suddenly, as if every trial and tragedy and all the terrible years in the gulags had risen up from within him and showed themselves now on the map of his body and face. His cough had been worse with the chillier nights and mornings, and sat deep in his chest, an implacable old enemy that Nikolai claimed he would be lost without. Jamie feared it would be the companion that killed him.

"We all die some day, Yasha. It is not always a bad thing," he said as if Jamie had spoken his thoughts aloud. He reached over with one gnarled hand and touched Jamie's hair, softly, like a benediction from a father to a son. "Go and be with your wife. It is a lovely day. Do not waste it. They are rare enough."

It was good advice. Violet was in a dappled patch of woods, tall silver birches surrounding her like a dryad in an old tale. She was utterly absorbed in her mushroom picking and so did not notice his approach until his shadow fell across her own.

She looked up at him, white camellia face haloed in copper hair, and smiled. It was an expression of such sweetness that he felt his heart miss a beat before resuming its normal tread. She flushed, and looked back down at a patch of delicate mushrooms as fragile and ephemeral as fairies at dusk. He pulled her to him and kissed her swiftly, feeling the softness of her body against his own. She laughed up at him, smears of dirt on her fair face, smelling pungently of pine and earth and water, and then pulled his face down in her mucky hands for a kiss of much deeper proportions. Her mouth tasted sweetly of the overripe cloudberries she had been eating and of the dense earth in which she had been digging. She swayed against him and he had to clamp down on a wild desire to take her down in this patch of bracken and make love to her.

She must have read his thoughts for she pushed him away and smiled, her eyes telegraphing that they could resume what they had begun later. They continued their mushroom search, with Violet providing him with botanical information on a variety of plants and their uses. She could set up shop as an herbalist and do well for herself, Jamie mused, for it was clear that she had an understanding of plants that was rare.

"Those are bad," Violet pointed to a small cluster of brown mushrooms that looked rather innocent.

"Poison?" Jamie asked, watching a butterfly hover over a late blooming patch of cornflowers.

"Poison—yes," Violet said, "but good in very small amounts for bad headaches and for great stiffness." She nodded toward Nikolai, and Jamie understood that she meant these were medicinal for arthritis.

"You know how to make medicine from them?" Jamie asked, pausing as the butterfly landed on his forearm and balanced there for a moment, its delicate abdomen pulsating and its celadon wings impossibly fragile. Two more joined it within seconds and he sighed. He hated to brush them off, for to touch them was always to risk damaging them, but he knew how this usually went with him.

"My mother told me that butterflies were guardian angels and that when you saw one go by, you knew you were safe, for it was keeping a close eye on you. Your angels are plenty," Violet said, looking at him in a way that made him slightly uncomfortable. He could not explain this to anyone, but he thought perhaps it was nothing very special, only rare in that animals and insects and people knew they could trust him and so could venture close without fear.

The sunny day and the promise of a feast of fungi seemed to have mellowed even the guards' collective mood, for they allowed Shura and Violet to cook an entire feast of mushrooms—under two sets of watchful eyes and machine guns—but nevertheless, allowed it.

Back in the camp, the dinner was hearty compared to what they were used to, the earthy smell of the mushrooms mixing lushly with the warmth of the garlic and the rich oil of butter. From somewhere Gregor had produced a bottle of *okhotnichaya*—hunter's vodka, a brown brew flavored with ginger, cloves, lemon peel and anise, topped off with wine and sugar. It tasted ambrosial to Jamie's tongue, and along with the food gave him a feeling of sated well-being he had not known in a very long time.

After dinner, Gregor sang a couple of songs, his voice deep and growly but well-suited to the *sturm und drang* of Russian folk music. Then Shura stood up on the table, his hand over his heart, dark eyes glowing soporifically with the drink and food. He sang an old Georgian song, beginning low and whispery which befit the song's melancholy yearning. There was a bit of muttering at first, for *Suliko* had the misfortune to have been a favorite of Stalin's, proving as always that the old monster had an odd sentimental streak.

"I was looking for my sweetheart's grave,
And longing was tearing my heart.
Without love my heart felt heavy -
Where are you, my Suliko?

Among fragrant roses, in the shadow,
Brightly a nightingale sang his song.
There I asked the nightingale
Where he had hidden Suliko.

Suddenly the nightingale fell silent
And softly touched the rose with the beak:
"You have found what you are looking for," he said,
In an eternal sleep Suliko is resting here."

Later, Jamie could not have said just when the tenor of the evening shifted, for all had been mellow goodwill for a time, with laughter and conversation that was as good as any he had known in the many circles he had traveled within in his lifetime. Perhaps it was after the song, for it had cast a strange mood over them all and turned the atmosphere of the evening ever so slightly, bringing the darkness down earlier than intended.

He was turned from Violet, listening to a story Gregor was telling about a hunting trip in Siberia, when he felt her hand convulse in his own.

"Yasha." Only two syllables, but a harbinger of disaster. Jamie looked around to see what had put that tone in Violet's voice. A rush of icy adrenaline washed his cells as he saw what had Violet's small face white with tension. Gregor had stopped speaking and silence spread down the table like dominoes toppling slowly toward disaster.

Volodya, the small shy man who had once filled a snowy walkway with flowers for a woman who could not love him, was standing up. His entire frame shook with suppressed emotion. A lifetime of it, to be exact. In his hand he clutched that day's ration of bread.

"Listen people—let us talk about bread, let us talk about this miserable scrap of life we call bread and how it has ruled all our lives for so long now."

Faces around the table turned to stare, uncomprehending and frightened, the relaxation, the camaraderie melting away like snow touched to a fire. Volodya stepped up onto the table, carrying with him the burdens of humiliation and survival in a country where survival came at a very high cost.

"Every day it is the same thing—bread rules our existence from morning to night—the questions, the hope—will I get more today? If I toady to the foreman will he share his ration, if I do a favor for a guard, will he look the other way when I take that extra bowl of soup because for once the bastard cook miscounted heads? Bread," he crushed the heel in his hand, "goddamn bread—is this the measure of a man's life? Is this the soul that is left of Mother Russia, a lousy few grams of goddamnable bread?" He flung the bread across the room, raising his fists to heaven in a boundless anger. "Is this all there is for Russia—a fucking moldy heel of bread?!"

"He must stop," Violet said tightly and Jamie squeezed her hand under the table, knowing that there was no way to stop Volodya now because he was set upon his course. He gave her hand another squeeze and then stood. Even when the odds were entirely against a man, he must try to avert complete disaster.

Volodya took no notice of Jamie's movement. One of the guards was barking commands now, a mixture of fear and fury in his words. Jamie spared him a sideways glance and then looked back up to Volodya.

"What is a man's worth? Is it measured in grams, in bread that a dog would turn its nose from were it not starving? Is it measured by unfulfilled dreams? Is it measured by all the days lived without freedom? How was it measured for all those ghosts in the bell tower? They ring the bells sometimes at night—ring them until there is no sleep. I hear them so often now. Do you?" He looked down at Jamie, his eyes fever-bright.

Jamie had drawn even with Volodya, taking care to keep the guards within his view. He thanked God that it wasn't Boris and Vlad who had been assigned to supervise the small feast, for he had no doubt either would be happy to put a bullet in his spine.

He held out a hand to Volodya. "Come down man," he said softly, trying to provide him a way out of the fraught situation that wouldn't end in tragedy or humiliation. They had only a few minutes grace before the guards would change their mind about dealing with the situation themselves.

Volodya looked him directly in the eyes, his deep blue ones alight with a despair so pure that Jamie felt his heart plummet. And then he spoke, words low and quiet so that only Jamie might hear him.

"I have doused the light and left open the door
For you, so simple and so wondrous."

He recognized the quote, and understood its import all too well. He kept his hand up to the man, praying that he understood it was his only hope for salvation. Long minutes passed, the tension crawling up the very walls of the dining hall, building thick and black until it seemed impossible that anyone could breathe in such an atmosphere. Jamie could feel beads of sweat begin to run down his backbone but he kept his hand steady and held out to the man. Volodya stared at Jamie's hand as if he could not quite understand why it was there. But finally he stretched his own hand out, and Jamie could feel the guards coil like springs ready to explode behind him.

Volodya slid his hand into Jamie's, grasping it tightly. Jamie grabbed back hard and put his other hand on the man's upper arm, pulling him down to the ground as fast as he could, dropping his own body amid the shouts of the guards and a small cry of dismay from Violet.

He held him down to the ground, his body shielding the man from the guards, hoping to God that they didn't decide to shoot him in lieu of Volodya.

"Stop it, for the love of God," Jamie hissed. "They are losing patience with you." For Volodya was still talking, voice high and hagridden with pain. Volodya ceased at Jamie's admonition, as quiet suddenly as if he were dead though tears ran in an unceasing stream down his face.

"It is too late," he said, and smiled through his tears, but the smile was hollow.

The man's words sent a trickle of ice through Jamie's innards. Volodya seemed resigned but vindictive at the same time, as though something beyond the visible events had taken place and would, like the night-blooming mushroom, only reveal itself in time. Later he would think he should have known, should have understood what the man was saying, but even then, it was too late, just as Volodya had said.

IN THE HUT, VIOLET SAT BY THE LIGHT OF THE FIRE, ROCKING KOLYA. The baby had fallen asleep some time ago, but Jamie understood the need for the reassurance after the scare they had all experienced in the dining hut. He was profoundly grateful for Valentin's latitude in allowing them this space as a married couple. He needed to be with his small family tonight, to banish the darkness that had swum up around Volodya's actions. He still couldn't shake the feeling that he had missed something, overlooked something the man had said or some gesture he had made.

She looked up, a question in her eyes.

"Shura dosed him with a sedative and he's being held in the isolation hut for now."

"Will they punish him further do you think?" she asked, and their eyes met over the baby's head. They both knew the answer, though Volodya had harmed none but himself.

He took Kolya from her arms, holding him fast for a moment, breathing in the sweet milky scent of him, feeling the warm heat of his tiny slumbering form. Jamie's own body relaxed in response and he put his head to the curve of Kolya's, wishing he could always shelter him so but knowing well that he could not. Kolya would soon be a year old, and he was very aware that time was running out swiftly for the child.

He put Kolya in his cot, built with his own hands, with raised sides to keep him safe through the night, and joined his wife in the bed. In the darkness, she stretched out beside him, the scents of the day coming with her. Jamie sighed and turned toward her so that they met along their lengths. Her skin radiated heat and she smelled still of the earth and garlic and butter, and of female desire. She was impatient, seeking reassurance and oblivion from the dark feeling that had fallen like a thick curtain around them all in the dining hut.

Inside, she was even warmer and he groaned softly against her mouth for he knew neither of them was going to last long. He moved slowly, lingering, relishing the feel of her skin under his hands, the small cries she made and how she said his name over and over like a sweet prayer for release. This he gave her, pressing himself against her, feeling the life that beat all around them. It held an edge of desperate relief for the narrow miss they had all experienced in the preceding hours.

"I love you, Yasha," she said afterwards, her forehead leaning damply into his shoulder.

"I love you too," he replied, because it was true.

JAMIE AWOKE IN WHAT SEEMED ONLY MOMENTS LATER to see Shura bending over him, holding a lantern in his hand, a look on his face of utter panic.

"What? What is it? What's happened?" Beside him, Violet sat up, clutching the quilt to her body, eyes wide with sudden fear. Kolya was stirring in his crib, making the small noises that meant he would soon be in full roar.

"Two of the guards, the ones who ate with us—one is throwing up blood," Shura said, and Jamie saw that indeed the man's thick hands were covered in drying blood, black and crimson.

"And the other?" Jamie asked.

"Dead," Shura said bluntly. He didn't need to add anything more, but the words seemed to hang on the air as though he had indeed uttered them. *As are we, once the other guards realize what has happened.*

"He picked plenty of the white ones," Jamie said, remembering with a lurch the strange look Volodya's face had worn when he saw Jamie watching him put the frail white mushrooms into his basket.

"The gauzy looking ones, coming up out of a veil like they are a bride or angel?" Violet asked, her voice sharp with fear.

"Yes," Jamie said, his stomach dropping several inches.

"Those are pure poison," Violet said, grey eyes wide and dark as the depths of a lake.

"Destroying Angel," Shura whispered, his face impossibly white over the broad bones. "They will all die. There is no way to save them from such poison."

Jamie got up and hastily threw on his clothes, shoved his feet into the camp regulation boots and followed Shura out into the night.

Outside the weather had done one of those swift and brutal turnarounds that were native to autumn. It was freezing, the wind howling down like Baba Yaga in a black bitch of a temper. Beyond the wind there lay a terrible silence. He looked about, rain lashing at his face, drawing visibility down to a flickering glimpse of a lit window, and the impression of two pale faces in the dark at the side of Volodya's hut.

"Yasha..." Shura said at his back, a note of warning in his tone, but Jamie was already halfway across the mucky expanse of ground toward the pale faces that hovered in the air.

Suddenly he saw why Volodya was so still, and thought he might be sick there in the freezing cold mud. Volodya was still because Volodya was dead, a bone-handled knife stuck through his throat, pinning him to the rough lumber of the hut, his face horribly blank above the blade.

"What the hell have you done?" Jamie managed to gasp out. Gregor stood in the rain, rivulets gathering in his hair and forming small rivers down his body.

"It had to be done," Gregor said roughly. "It would go much worse with him if they took him. Now it is over. He has had camp justice."

Jamie saw that for Gregor it had not been an act of violence, but rather one of mercy. He was right. He had done what needed doing and he had been the only one with the foresight and courage to see that it was necessary.

"I will help you bury him," Jamie said. Gregor gave him one of those long, unflinching looks that always made Jamie feel like his soul was being scoured, then nodded.

"We will have to do it soon or they will make us leave him to rot, to make a point."

The other guards were nowhere to be seen, though the lights of the infirmary blazed, giving them a good idea of where they were occupied. The fences and fear would keep the inmates in place.

They dug near the edge of the camp, just beyond the ring of pines. The rain felt like needles of ice pouring down Jamie's collar, soaking the earth and making it heavy and cumbersome to move. Winter was on its way, breathing down from the great Arctic plains. Winter in all its killing ferocity, locking them in for another brutal season. He could sense eyes on them but they were left to bury their dead in peace.

Gregor heaved the last spadeful of muck onto the grave and stood for a moment with his head bowed. Jamie bowed his accordingly while streams of freezing rain formed a stream down the hollow of his spine.

"Yasha, you say a prayer. I don't know how to talk to God, but you do."

Jamie looked up and across the mounded dirt at Gregor. The man was perfectly sincere. And so he said a prayer from his own world, a prayer from the West, brought here with a mind and soul that had lived in the light and warmth of those philosophies all its years. As, were God merciful, Volodya should have done as well. American lines for a Russian man. The words came back to him as poetry always did, like a soft breath of air from one of the vortices in his mind and heart, hidden but waiting for the time it was needed.

...This covert have all the children
Early aged, and often cold, --
Sparrows unnoticed by the Father;
Lambs for whom time had not a fold.

THE ATMOSPHERE OF THE CAMP CHANGED SWIFTLY in the wake of the guards' deaths. It came as no surprise to any of them, but it brought with it a cloud of doom that seemed to hang over all their heads. Jamie was banished back to the communal bunkhouse that he had previously shared with Nikolai, Shura, Vanya and Volodya. Even at night, the normal chatter amongst the men was subdued, for they all felt Volodya's ghost lingering in their midst.

His time with Violet and Kolya was severely circumscribed, and often several days would pass without his being able to hold the child in his arms. Valentin had been apologetic but Jamie knew the man was in an untenable position. He had to come down on them all or it was his own head that was going to find its way onto the block, if indeed it wasn't already there. They were all waiting, breath held, for an official visit. The fact that it was so long in coming only contributed to the unease that wrapped around the entire camp.

He managed a few minutes with Violet before nightfall most nights, saying good night to her in a public place, the falling dark the only measure of privacy they were now allowed. In the Empire, you learned quickly to take what you could get and hang onto it with both hands. Around them the camp grounds were uncommonly quiet, the orange glow of the sodium lights falling in patches here and there. The air smelled like the possibility of snow. She shivered and he put his arms around her, wishing he could will his heat into her.

"What is it?" He asked, for he sensed something off in her, some fear that she could not keep from him, though he knew she tried.

She looked up at him, expression pensive. "Last night I dreamt of mushrooms, an unending field of them, Yasha, and I am at the edge of this field but cannot walk into it. To dream of mushrooms is a sign of tears to come. A huge field of them like that," she shivered again and he held her more tightly, "what can that mean?"

"I think it might be odd if you hadn't dreamt of them considering all that's happened in the last weeks."

She shook her head, copper hair a dull gleam in the dark. "That is your rational Western mind speaking, Yasha, but your Russian half knows better."

"My Russian half?" he said, laughing a little.

The face that turned up to his in the dark was entirely serious. "You cannot stay here this long, Yasha, and make a family out of a bunch of prisoners, cannot love us and have us love you without becoming Russian yourself. And once you are Russian, you are Russian forever. This country has changed you. Can you deny it?"

"No, I would never deny that," he said and leaned down to kiss her forehead. She was right. His Russian side had told him there was dark trouble stirring that night when Shura had stood to sing that cursed song. He had known it then but it had already been too late. There was more trouble coming and that was, he supposed, the dark Russian wind rising in his spirit, telling him thus. Though one didn't exactly need to be Baba Yaga reading the portents to know that what Volodya had done was going to come back to curse them all. Even his rational Western mind could see that clearly.

That night it was his Russian mind that dreamt. He was on horseback in a forest, the light an emerald gloom, and catching at the sides of his vision were small creatures, wizened and horrific, whisking in and out of the portentous dim. He had the sense that he was lost, but did not know how he had become so. Just lost in a way that left him without root or ground beneath him. Around him the forest grew thicker and thicker the further he ventured into it. This was Russian *bor*, forests that grew league upon league around the curve of the globe, unending, dense and dangerous.

And then he saw her, a willowy flicker in the trees, the scent of her filling all his senses, green and chill and amber-thick. She was the old forests incarnate, the ones that held witches and winged bears, and lakes so deep that an ever-running chain would never plumb the bottom of them.

He followed, because it was a dream, because he had always been meant to follow, for from the beginning she had been trying to tell him something, to make him understand. It was like following quicksilver; a flash here and a glimmer there, a darting in the dusk. Once or twice he thought he had lost her to the thick gloaming. Then he smelled something, a scent long familiar, one that lived in his blood and marrow, and it was this he followed.

The edge of the forest came up suddenly and his horse stopped under him, whickering gently at the wind that rose from a great sea. The woman stood on the shore, the water lapping at her feet, wind blowing through her pale stripling hair, looking out over the waves with a great yearning in her face.

She turned to him and upon her face was an expression of such exquisite sadness that it cut his heart to witness it. He started toward her but she backed away and disappeared with a flicker of watery green into the forest, which grew thick and dark right to the edges of this strange sea.

He stepped to the edge of the water, felt it foam around his feet, bent and cupped its salt and shimmer to his face. And then he looked up and over the great rolling waves, the swift running verdigris light that ran on into eternity. He understood the yearning in her face. He felt it himself, strong as any swift-running tide, as deep as any cold current.

Beyond the sea, he knew, lay the West. A place he had once called home.

The Tale of Ragged Jack, continued.

EACH NIGHT WHEN JACK LAY DOWN ON HIS BED, *he watched the tapestry as it moved in the soft breezes that stole through every crack in the tower. And he noticed that the Knight's face was sadder and a little older each time he looked, while the Lady retreated further and further into the shadows of the tower. It gave him an uneasy feeling that leaked into his dreams and woke him up in the middle of the night, leaving him staring into the dark. Then day, such as it was, for time was a muddle here, would come and he would go out in the little walnut wood boat with Muireann and she would play her silver pipe, and he would forget what it was that so bothered him in the quiet.*

One night the Knight came to him in a dream, a dream so vivid Jack couldn't be certain he wasn't awake at the time. Even later he would doubt it, for it wasn't fuzzy as dreams often were when he awoke, but a memory with a clarity like mead. In the dream the Knight had been out of the tapestry and they had been sitting together on a fallen tree, thick with moss and lichens, with tiny primroses growing out of the fissures in the bark.

"You cannot stay, Jack—such things are not possible in this land between worlds. She must go on, beyond the Hollow Hills, and you must find the Crooked Man and then return home. You know it in your own heart. You just don't want to listen. Please Jack, if you don't leave, the Lady and I will be trapped inside that tapestry forever, as surely as you will be trapped here with Muireann for all time."

Jack awoke cold and sweaty, the dream lingering all day like a frosted spiderweb around his senses, and he knew no matter how many boat rides they took, or picnics in the great golden harvest field, no matter the enchanted music and the water that tasted like honey and snowflakes, that he could no longer stay here. Only the pathway out seemed to have disappeared, if it had, indeed, ever existed at all. Not too many days later, he caught a glimpse of himself in the still water of a moon-soaked pond and reared back in shock. He had grown older in his time here, his hair grown long and wild, the bones of his face closer to the surface with a scurf of whiskers clouding his chin. He rubbed a hand slowly over his face, wondering when this transformation had occurred. Looking down he saw that his pants were far too short, his shirt threadbare and the sleeves well above his wrists. Aengus too had changed, for he was large now, and there was the odd grey whisker in his muzzle.

At dinner that night, his long hair tidied back in a knotted cord of leaf stems, his clothes replaced by green and brown pants and long shirt from the woman who wove such things, Jack sat beside Muireann, who looked especially pretty with her hair combed for once and a crown of myrtle leaves and strawberries woven amongst her curls. The long hall was unusually subdued. There was none of the music that normally accompanied dinner and though the goblets were filled with mead and peat whiskey, not many were drinking. Even the talk was low, people whispering to their neighbors and friends, many simply looking off into the distance, the food on their plates congealing.

"What's going on?" Jack asked Muireann, noting that she too was unusually pensive.

She shook her head, expression troubled. "There's been talk about moving on, all of us, to the Western Islands, over the Great Sea. Those islands can't be found by any but our own people and once we're there, there is no coming back, not ever."

"Why now?"

"Because Jack, no one believes in the auld ones anymore. People have forgotten us and so you will notice that this world around us is beginning to decay. If they don't leave, they fear that one morning they won't be here either. They will simply have disappeared like smoke in the night."

*"Why do you say **they**?" he asked, a chill wind crossing his bones.*

She stuck her chin out stubbornly. "Because if they go, I'm staying here with you."

"You can't stay, Muireann, nor can I."

The stubborn look remained, the gooseberry green eyes gone dark the way they did when her anger was stoked.

He put out a hand and waited patiently until she took it.

"I need to show you something. Will you come with me?"

She nodded reluctantly and he led her out of the long hall, up the winding stair where the ivy grew thick through the cracks, silver berries ripening with autumn's approach. He was certain it must be autumn this time, for the air smelled faintly of smoke and leaves turning brown and gold, and in the fields the pumpkins grew fat and indolent and the wheat was bowed down with grain that filled the air around with the scent of winter bread.

Inside his tower room it was chilly despite the mellow evening sun setting beyond the thick walls.

"I need you to look at the tapestry, really look and see the story it is telling us."

She quirked the fine lines of her inky brow at him but looked at the tapestry. At first she furrowed her face, and tilted her head, jarring loose one of the strawber-

ries in her crown. He saw her take it in piece by piece, the Knight forever riding up toward the Castle but never arriving. The lady's hair like a silken banner rippling in the wind.

"She—she looks like me—only older," she backed away from the tapestry, eyes wide with consternation. "And the Knight—he..." she trailed off, her eyes flashing angrily at him. "Why did you show me this?"

Jack sighed. It was in her nature to be difficult. He wished just once, though, she wouldn't be. This was the hardest thing he had ever said to another, and the worst of it was he didn't want to say it, not in the least.

"I think what it is trying to tell us, is that if we stay here together," Jack said, "we will be trapped forever—we—we can't stay."

Muireann shook her head. "You can't know that—it's just a tapestry, Jack, and those figures are made of thread. They aren't really us."

"Maybe not us, exactly," he said slowly, "but an echo of what we will become if we stay. It's as though someone, maybe us in another time, left this as a warning so that we wouldn't stay, wouldn't have to suffer this fate."

"Suffer?" she said, small face piqued at his words. "Is that what you consider staying with me? Suffering?"

"No, only it's not the life we're meant to lead. We can't stay here alone in a world that soon won't exist. You know without the magic this place will fade away and then we'll be stuck in a dreadful limbo."

"At least we'd be together," Muireann said, though he heard the first tremor of doubt in her tone.

"We'd be alone, just you and me, forever," Jack said. "I know it seems like what we want, and I think for awhile it would be like a lovely dream, but then when you couldn't ever wake up from it, it wouldn't be so lovely anymore."

She shook her head, the myrtle crown tipping to one side, the berries woven within it bruised and spoiling now. He looked about and realized that the tower was missing half its roof. Surely it hadn't been that way yesterday, or even this morning, had it? The lichen grew thick as sin along the crumbling stone, and the ashes in the hearth were scattered about the floor. And he understood suddenly that this world was undoing itself, even as he stood within it looking at the girl he loved.

"It is all ending now, Jack," she said and the anger had been replaced by a solitary tear the color of a new violet that hung trembling upon her pale skin. "Why did you have to say anything? It was all perfect before."

"No, it wasn't, Muireann, and you know it as well as I do."

"Why, Jack?" she said quietly and it broke his heart to hear the disillusion in her voice, as though she had truly thought they could stay here together, forever.

"Because the world is ever-changing. That is the one certain thing about it, and we either change with it, or crumble to dust."

Once the decision was made by the Fair People, the world around them seemed to decay ever faster, the tower merely a half-shell of stone and pearl, a little less of it each day. One of the great battlements disappeared over-night, and the moat dried up to weed-scummed puddles. The fields lay fallow and cold, with dead leaves huddling in drifts in every corner. The sky at night was dark, with fewer stars each time Jack looked. Soon the signs of leaving were unmistakable as the Fair People pulled up the corners of their enchantment, tucked it into their moss-weave bags and prepared to travel far and away.

Jack lingered, and was painfully aware of his lingering, for he did not know where he was meant to go when the Fair People left him behind. He did not know how he was to wander paths and cross water without Muireann's grubby hand within his own. He wished courage was a thing a boy could take out and polish, and make it shiny and strong once again.

On the last night, when all the horses were shod and the bridles gleamed like the few stars left in the sky, and the last of the berries had long been culled from the woods, Jack went in search of Muireann. There was a saying from his own world that he had never really understood, but thought perhaps he did now—she was extremely conspicuous by her absence.

He found her on the edge of the woods, sitting in a heap of leaves so high that he would have walked straight past her had Aengus not snuffled her out and bounded in, sending the leaves flying in several directions. She was hunched up, slender arms wrapped around long bruised shins, gooseberry green eyes hidden on her scabby knees.

"What's wrong?" Jack asked, for like most boys, he often only saw the obvious and not all the underlying currents that might suck a boy under for asking such tomfool questions.

"What's wrong?" Two green eyes came up and scorched him where he stood. "What's wrong? I'm leaving tomorrow to go that way—" she pointed her hand to the west, where the mists rolled in even now, hiding the land that lay beyond the great Western gates, "and you're leaving to go that way!" She waved vaguely in the direction that encompassed the other half of the world.

"But you knew this yesterday," Jack said, "and you weren't angry then."

Muireann gave him a baleful glare. "Honestly, Jack, sometimes you are stupider than a toe-berry newt. I wasn't angry because I still was hoping. Because until today I thought maybe you would be able to come with us. But I—I asked, and the old mother said it's not possible. Only those with the auld blood can manage the crossing. They said it would kill you. And I cannot live in your world either, the old mother says. I would start to fade as soon as we crossed the border, and then one day you wouldn't be able to see me and I would live like a ghost, neither seen nor heard, just a drifting thing with no place to be at home."

"I already knew that, Muireann," Jack said gently, and realized as he spoke the words that it was so. The knowledge had been there all along, within him. It was why he had so often felt that drag of melancholy upon him, like a heavy shadow, pulling forever at his heels.

She threw a fistful of leaves in his face and turned her narrow back on him. He sidled up beside her, huddling against her for warmth and put his hand where she could take it if she liked—which she did not for some time. But as the great carousel of the sky turned from a lambent blue to gold to lavender to crimson to velvet soft night, he could feel some of the hurt and anger go out of her. At long last, her hand crept across the ground toward his and took it, and she lifted her face up to the dark sky and sighed. They lay that way, silent, tired and connected through their two hands, like a small defiance set against the looming of their parting. They slept a little, Muireann turning into the curve of his shoulder as naturally as if they had slept that way every night of their lives.

The morning, as morning often does, came early and too soon. Even the sun seemed to be sad, taking its time coming over the horizon, like an old man with sore knees and knobbled back, but coming on inexorably nevertheless. Beneath them the earth stirred under its mantle of leaves, the pulsebeat of it still there, but not as strong as it once had run.

Jack yawned and turned to find Muireann already awake and watching him. The green eyes were soft as spring in the first light of the day. She smiled, but it was a sad smile and held not an ounce of her usual mischief.

"I don't feel as if I'll ever really belong to myself again," she said, soft as a feather drifting down the air, and Jack noticed that the myrtle leaves in her crown had changed over the night to a deep and shimmering crimson. "I told the old mother this and she said that when you love someone who belongs to another world, you inhabit a strange place of neither here nor there, where you have a foot in this place and a foot in that. The problem with straddling such a border though is this—worlds break apart. They go off on their own way, and the person trying to inhabit both places is rendered in half, heart shattered into terrible pieces like garnets crushed and blown to the wind. Perhaps one day, one might gather all those pieces together again. But regardless of what binding agent one brings to those shattered bits, and no matter how they might glimmer in the moonlight and smell of palmed roses, still there will be some missing, dust that is gone forever on that wind, into a far country from which they can never be retrieved."

They ate bread for their breakfast and a handful of dried-out berries that were sharp with the taste of late autumn. They were quiet, for all had been spoken between them, and words felt awkward, as though they would overspeak and destroy a fragile balance that was keeping them upright and moving forward.

At the last she placed a flower in his hands, a flower the petals of which glowed pearl-white as a slice of moon.

"Take it to remember me," she said, and curled his fingers around the flower.

"I don't need anything to remember you," Jack said. "You're in my heart for always. I can feel the shape of you there. What you put in your heart stays there forever."

"Yes, you do need it, Jack, even if one day it's only withered petals that cause

you to scratch your head over why you keep them in your pocket, or where you picked such a flower, for when we leave this place, we go to a country from which we can never return. Once we go through the Western gates, we are gone forever from the minds and hearts of man. Only a few will remember us, and even they will think we were merely stories made up to frighten children or to explain that which is not easily explained."

Jack folded the flower in a bit of woven cloth and tucked it in with the thread the old woman had given him.

He kissed her, a first kiss and a last. He wished the taste of her would linger on his mouth and never leave him. He wished he could take her to his own home, but knew that what he had said before was equally true for her as it was for him—his world was not for her.

And then one of the old women, gnarled and soft brown as winter moss, nodded at Muireann, and Jack knew it was time for her to leave. She gave his hand a last squeeze, all her heart there in the gooseberry green eyes, breaking infinitely into the smallest pieces.

He watched the leaving until the mists rose up and swallowed them all. Muireann turned back at the last, her face as sorrowful as the starless heavens. And then she too was gone into the mists, where neither time nor tide could fetch her back.

Jack slept in the room he had been given in the castle for the last time that night. For a long time he watched the tapestry, the wee figures moving, the Knight cresting the hill before the Castle and disappearing, with only dust left behind to tell of his ever being there. The lady was no longer at the window. There was only a blank of threads both black and gold where she had stood, though some of the threads were torn. Outside his tower window the wind grieved, for it had witnessed the Fair People leaving this land and knew they would not come this way again.

In the morning, he awoke to find himself in a narrow hole dug in the side of a mound, cold and filthy. He sat up and rubbed his eyes, Aengus was already up and out, hunting no doubt. There was no sign of the castle and tower, of the sweet timothy and clover mattress or the Knight and his Lady. No great hall, no fireplace filled with hazel and apple wood, no tankards of honeyed mead, nor silver trays bearing steaming goose and hare. There was no music, no harp by the fire, no lute playing enchanted notes to fuddle his head and brim his senses.

He might have believed that it had never been a real place, nor the lords and ladies real beings, except that he had a terrible raw pain around his heart that had the shape of Muireann at the center of it.

He set off along the path, one that led up along a rocky highland and knew, with a bone and marrow knowing, that he was on the final leg of his journey to find the Crooked Man.

Part Ten

Butterfly
Ireland – January-August 1975

Chapter Sixty-six

January 1975

Firelight

CASEY SAT AT THE TABLE, a sheet of paper beneath his hand and a pen poised above it, but for the moment, still. His son slept soundly on the sofa, wee face burnished in the firelight. Both he and Conor had been restless earlier and he had thought to spare Pamela their wakefulness, so had come down to the kitchen for a cup of tea. He sat holding Conor for a long time. The boy was content enough, once he was changed and given some milk, to sit in his father's lap and watch the flames making shadows upon the wall. Casey loved the firelight, for it had always seemed to him it created an enchanted boundary, inside which all that existed was what the firelight touched and held safe from tomorrow.

Conor had eventually drifted off, his wee body a sweet comfort in its boneless weight and warmth, leaving his father to his own thoughts—which were in a vein far less comforting.

Casey was well used to trouble. One could not live in this country and be otherwise, though it touched a man in deeper and darker ways when he had a family to protect.

He knew the source of his discomfort and he knew what his wife thought of it as well. She had made her feelings clear, which he had expected. He had been offered a contract, a good one that in another country he would never have had to question.

Pamela had been huddled over a set of proof sheets with a magnifying glass fitted to her eye when he approached her. He shuddered to think what it was she was looking at, though she didn't bring the gorier aspects of her work home. The film for those went directly to the police labs.

He had sketched the outlines of the project, telling her the positive aspects first. He had wanted an optimistic view of it but his wife, familiar with his ways, had asked a trifle tartly,

"If it's such a good contract, why is it you're hesitating over it?"

"Well, it's only that I don't know if I should take the job on or not," he said, hands flat on the table in front of him but thrumming with a tension that vibrated the very air around him.

"Whyever not?" she asked, green eyes bright with suspicion. Damn the woman, he wouldn't be getting any sort of optimism from her.

"Because it would be a subcontract for the Simon brothers."

"Oh," she said faintly. He could see she was shocked he would even consider such madness. The Simon brothers, of good Catholic stock, had constructed a small empire building structures for the security forces. They were rich men by Belfast standards and marked men as well, marked out by the IRA as traitors helping in the oppression of their own people. Scarce two months past there had been an attempt on Mag Simon's life. A motorcycle had pulled up alongside his car while it was parked outside a construction site, the gunman emptying half a magazine through the driver's side window and killing Mag's twenty-five year old shop manager, who'd had the bad luck to borrow his employer's car on the wrong day.

"You can't do that," she said, her voice harsh with fear.

He rubbed one hand through his hair, knowing he was setting it on end and that he no doubt looked like an annoyed porcupine—which wasn't likely to further his case with Pamela.

"Well, part of me says the same, an' part of me says it's different. It's not a contract to rebuild somethin' that the 'Ra has bombed. I'd not be that much of an eejit. It's a deal of money, Jewel. Money like I've not seen before an' a chance to get the business on a solid footing. It's not for the security forces—they knew better than to offer me such a thing—but for an American firm that's settin' up offices here an' wants to use local builders."

"I don't think it matters much what the building is. You know anyone who's connected even tenuously with the Simon brothers becomes a moving target."

"Aye, I know that, an' I don't."

"What the hell is that supposed to mean, Casey Riordan?"

He gave an inward wince. When she called him by his full name in that tone, it didn't bode well for the direction of the conversation.

"It's a good opportunity an' it would be a couple of years of guaranteed work. I want somethin' more for us than survivin' from one payday to the next. I want to give ye all ye deserve, and I want to know that Conor can have an education an' a chance to be anything he's a mind to be."

"He's not even two years old yet," she said sharply, fear winding its tight wires through her vocal chords.

"Aye, an' how long have we known one another woman? Close on seven years now—an' it seems both a lifetime an' a day. The time goes past quickly, does it not? Opportunities are never lost, Jewel. They're simply picked up by other people. An' maybe this is my gift horse."

"If you'd take a moment to look in its mouth, I think you'll find its teeth are razor sharp."

He had gone to her then, knowing that she was afraid for more than one reason. He put his arms around her, lending her his strength for what he said next.

"Besides," he had said, tone soft, "we've another wee mouth on its way."

"What! It's too early to know for certain..." she had trailed off under the scrutiny of his gaze and he saw that she knew too and was afraid of what might lie ahead, despite how well things had gone with Conor.

"No, it's not." He touched the side of one breast lightly. "Yer gypsy woman was right. It was a good night to make a baby."

He had known for a few days now that she was pregnant again, for he had watched her get out of the bath one morning and seen the changes in her body. He had noted how she held herself differently as though she were being more careful than was her usual manner. She always seemed suddenly and infinitely fragile to him when she was pregnant and he wished there was a way to shelter her and keep her safe, just as her body sheltered their child.

She had cried a little then, because he was right, because she was terrified and overjoyed all at the same time.

Then she said the thing that he had known she would say, and was prepared for.

"I make more than enough with my work for Jamie."

"I think ye can understand, Jewel, if I would rather not use the man's money to keep my own family."

"I cannot lose you, Casey," she said, stiff and unbending in his arms. "I won't lose you. I couldn't survive it."

"And I can't stop livin' in order to survive," he said. He had thought she might hit him then, for her face had gone deathly pale and her eyes turned the deep, heavy green they did when she was incoherent with fury.

In the end though, her need of his reassurance now that the pregnancy was an acknowledged fact was greater than her anger. They had made their peace for the present, in the way that they most often did, and he had felt beneath his hands and lips the changes in her body that he had seen before.

He was not fool enough to think the conversation was at an end, but he thought perhaps he was going to take the contract, for otherwise there was no work to be had for more than a few days here and there.

The fire was simmering low, the cherry red of the coals now faded to an umber-edged gold. There was no more putting off what he had come down here to do. He sighed and confronted the blank white of the paper with a determined stare. There were things that needed saying, much as a man might not wish to say them, much as a man might feel superstitious about such acts. Still, he was a pragmatist and pragmatists knew not to put off to tomorrow what a man ought to do today.

He put the pen to paper and took a deep breath.

Dear Jamie, he began.

Chapter Sixty-seven

March 1975

Invasion

SPRING CAME EARLY THAT YEAR. By March the grass had greened, and in the fields small balls of wool began to appear, wobbling against the legs of larger balls of wool. The fields shimmered pale silver and green under the rains and there was the sense of expectation and energy that the season always brought. Already the crocuses, snowdrops and hellebores had bloomed, wetly defiant through the storms of February.

With the ending of winter, Pamela emerged from the nausea that always plagued her early pregnancy and felt a resurgence of her own energy. The doctor had assured her that the baby was doing just fine and she could resume all her normal activities as soon as she felt able. If only the doctor could convince Casey that all was well she might actually have a hope of getting back to normal. As it was, the man was worried enough for ten people. Certainly there was reason. She had hoped that the successful pregnancy and arrival of a hearty, hale baby in the form of Conor would go some way toward soothing his fears, but it had only had a marginal effect.

It was a day late in March and she and Conor were spending the morning out of doors, for the sun was warm and the soil rich with light and the promise of growth to come. And Conor loved the dirt as much as any wee boy did. She put him on a blanket in the grass with a few toys and Finbar keeping guard beside him, as the dog always did. Casey, never one to wait, had already turned the soil and tilled in the compost and manure in anticipation of setting in his early crops: potatoes, broad beans, onions and leeks. The seedlings were already well started and taking up much of her kitchen counter space and spare room. The potatoes would be sown directly, but the cut seedlings were set out in the cool dark of the shed, ready for their planting. Because he planted the potatoes in raised beds, they went in early, for there was no fear of frost nor of compacting overly wet, cool soil. For the last month, he had been eyeing the sky and feeling the soil, as well as consulting the Farmer's Almanac for the precise phase of the moon under which to plant. When she had made a sarcastic comment about expecting to find him with his head down a well, shouting out questions and waiting for an oracular reply from its depths, he had merely raised an eyebrow at her and said she wouldn't be complaining when she'd fresh fare in the pot and on the table before anyone else.

To one side of the garden, raised up on chunks of wood, Casey had piled hazel and willow wands. The stouter hazel would be used for heavier plants such as beans, while the willow would be woven around a wigwam support of hazel for the peas and sweetpeas to wind their fragile tendrils about. Already the rhubarb was sporting a soft pink blush at its base, the leaves a tender, crumply green, and the sea kale had been set out under buckets to force the shoots and retain their flavor. They would be the first greens on the table for it was only the shoots that were edible.

She took Conor in after they had their lunch, relishing the grubby warmth of his hand in hers. He would be two years old in a few more weeks. Like his father, he was an early riser, and was active from the moment he opened his eyes. Fortunately, this caused him to nap soundly for a good two hours in the afternoons, affording her some quiet time to start dinner, finish chores around the house or, of late, to sit down with a cup of tea and a book, though she rarely got past a page or two before nodding off herself. Today she hoped to make some progress on a sweater she was knitting for Casey. It was wine-colored and knit in a thick wool that would keep him warm on the chilliest days. Since her first few tangled and epithet-ridden projects, she had acquired some skill with the needles and had progressed from scarves to socks and then to a wee blue sweater that would fit Conor come the autumn. This was her first attempt at a full sized article for an adult, and despite ripping out a few rows each day, she was making steady progress on it, and the color looked beautiful against Casey's dark hair and eyes.

The kitchen was peaceful when she sat down, the kettle starting to bubble on the Aga, and the spring sun lighting the floors and counters to a soft glow. She sighed and stretched her legs out in front of her, feeling sleepy but not truly tired. She rubbed an open hand over her belly, the occupant within quiet and tranquil. This baby seemed only to come to life when she herself lay down at night. So far it was only the soft movements, like tiny hops within that rippled outward, reassuring in their regularity.

She picked up her needles, the weight of the garment a satisfying heft. She had measured it against Casey the previous afternoon when he arrived home from work and it smelled still of his day, of his work, of him: the wood, stone and water; the oil he used to keep his tools in working order; the ink from the blueprints he handled daily and the darker, deeper and entirely subtle scent that was uniquely his own. It alternately soothed her and caused her pulse to run ragged, so that Casey, through what he assured her was no fault of his own, often found himself in bed before he was allowed his dinner. Today, the scent had the latter effect and she buried her face in the wool, breathing deeply and wondering if Conor might be an accommodating lad and sleep through his Daddy's arrival home.

She shook her head and smiled. The second trimester of her pregnancies was often a time of erotic wool-gathering on her part. She knit a few stitches on the sweater and laid it back down. She took the wine-colored wool from the top of the basket and picked up what lay underneath, twelve balls of the most perfect, star-dusted pink imaginable. Softer than silk and spun fine as webbing. It had arrived in the post along with a wee lavender sweater set, complete with booties and bonnet and a pair of very fine needles. There was no letter nor card to accompany it, but she knew all the same from where it had come.

The wool lay in her hand, so light that it barely registered. She wanted to use it to knit into something perfect for a baby girl, but superstition held her back. Guilt too, if she were being honest with herself, because she wanted a daughter very badly. It had not mattered to her with Conor, girl or boy, all she had prayed for was a healthy baby who would survive. But this time was different. She had wondered, in part, if she was trying to recover something from her own youth, that somehow having and loving a daughter would heal the loneliness of her childhood and make up in some way for the lack of a mother in her own life. She had lost three daughters: one to abortion, for that pregnancy had been the product of a brutal rape; then wee Deirdre, lost when the pregnancy was five months along, and she had thought herself safe; and last, the baby they had named Grace, who had been lost when Casey was interned during the sweeps of Catholic males two summers past. In the matter of children one was never safe because love itself was fraught with all sorts of dangers. That was the risk one took with love.

As was now common any time she had five minutes to think, worries about Jamie's companies crept in. With the introduction of Julian, everything had changed. Everything she had been certain of in this protracted struggle no longer made the same sort of sense, nor did it seem entirely just. She could not ask Jamie what role he wanted Julian to play, and what if, God forbid, something irrevocable happened to him? What should she do regarding his son—of whom, she was certain, he did not have the slightest knowledge. The last couple of months had consisted of a shell game where the stakes were very high and amounts were changing hands that made her feel more than a little nauseous. It felt like playing chess with a blindfold and pieces that could not be recognized by touch. The pattern of the board itself changed with every shift of the wind. Without Robert, she wasn't sure she could continue. Giacomo Brandisi's support had stiffened her spine, but the advent of a son of Jamie's blood might change even his stance.

As for the son himself, there had been no further meetings and she could only assume he had gone back to Oxford for spring term. Philip had been rather conspicuous by his absence as well, though he was still making his presence felt through his solicitors. The very lack of threat made her feel extremely uneasy because she knew they would not desist until they had what they wanted, though what that was precisely was even less clear than it had been, previous to Julian. She sighed, shutting the thoughts off, as it was like being on a hamster wheel, never resulting in forward movement no matter how fast her thoughts might spin.

She eyed the sweater pattern, orienting herself to where she had left off, and began to loop the wool until her hands found the lovely purling rhythm of knitting that felt so peaceful. She was several rows in and had forgotten the tea when there was a knock at the door. She frowned and laid the sweater aside, not feeling up for company. It was likely only Gert, whom she loved dearly, but this afternoon what she wanted was quiet, not a long Germanic sermon on the care and feeding of the pregnant woman.

Finbar stood and padded behind her to the door, a low growl emanating from his deep chest. She took him by the collar, glad of the security of his presence but not wanting him to eat some unsuspecting salesman on the doorstep, either.

It was not Gert who stood on the other side of the door but two men she did not recognize. Her first instinct was to shut it firmly for their faces were not friendly. The smaller of the two must have sensed this for he pushed his way in immediately, taking her by the shoulder and shoving her deeper into the house. She stumbled slightly, then caught herself, her hand going instinctively to her belly, curving out in barely visible pregnancy. She took her hand off immediately, not wanting them to know that she was in one of the most vulnerable states a human could be in.

"Get the fockin' dog away or I'll kill him," the small man said, his hand emerging from inside his coat with a snub-nosed pistol. She dragged Finbar, growling, teeth bared and feet planted in stubborn outrage, into Lawrence's old bedroom. She felt terrible doing it for the dog had not gone into the boy's room since his death and he began to whimper immediately, dark eyes filled with betrayal. But she had no doubt that the men would, if threatened, kill him.

"I'm sorry, boy," she whispered before shutting the door on him, only to hear his paws scrabbling wildly behind her.

"Get out of my house," she said with a bravado she did not feel. They seemed to fill up the entire space with menace and the promise of violence.

"Now is that any way to treat guests in yer home?" the taller one said, winking at her, a nasty smile splitting his pale face. He looked like a stork. The shorter was silent, but looked about as persuadable as a pillar of granite—and about as intelligent, she thought, noting the dull, small unwavering eyes that stared at her.

"What the hell do you want?" she asked, backing into the kitchen until the solidity of the counter was there to bear her up. There were knives in the drawer behind her but she knew she would never reach them before the men were on her.

"Yer husband is late on a payment, an' we've come to collect," the man said, his eyes making a slow survey of her from head to toe, as if to say he'd be happy to take the payment out of her.

"What payment are you talking about?" she asked, feeling the shadow of suspicion that had been in the back of her mind these last months take a more solid form.

"Has he not told ye? Well, we'll leave that to him to explain when he comes home. Until then I believe we'll keep ye company, myself in here and my partner in the yard so we can see yer man comin'."

"I don't know what your business is with my husband but I'd like you to leave." She curled her hand through the drawer pull, wondering if she would have time to yank it open and grab a knife, or if she would only be handing them a weapon to be used against her in doing so. Finbar was barking now, a hoarse, desperate sound as though he smelled her fear through the wooden barrier between them.

The tall man walked toward her, menace oozing from every pore. He was lean and bony, but she knew that was always deceptive, for he would still be stronger than she was and that was all that mattered.

He swept his arm across the countertop next to the big window and all the wee pots and trays filled with seedlings tumbled to the floor, breaking their delicate stems and necks, dirt scattering across the shiny pine planks. Then he grabbed her arm hard, twisting the fingers that were still curled inside the drawer pull.

"Don't even fockin' think it, lady," he hissed, his breath in her face reeking and sour. She twisted a little in his grip, her fingers feeling like they would break if he applied even slightly more pressure.

She took a breath, her insides unmoored as though they had turned to ice water, the baby a hard ball of fragility in the midst of this. "Please go," she said, voice barely above a whisper, for her throat was thick with fear.

In response to her plea, the man merely let her go and went to sit at the table, making it clear he had no intention of leaving. The squat block of his partner moved off out the door to watch for Casey's arrival.

She rubbed her hand, flexing the fingers to be certain they weren't sprained. The middle one was slightly swollen and throbbed with every overcharged beat of her heart but it was straight and she was quite certain it wasn't broken.

As she stood feeling down each bone in her hand, her brain flitted through what few options she might have for getting this bastard out of her house. Certainly there was no way to physically remove him unless she had a weapon of some sort and could surprise him with it. Even then, she was taking a huge risk that he would simply grab it from her—unless it was a weapon that required too much risk for him to attempt to take it.

She took a deep breath, stiffened her spine and said, "I'm going to put the kettle on. Would you like a cup of tea?"

The man gave her an odd look, as well he might with this sudden about face. "No, I don't want no fockin' tea, an' don't get any notions about throwin' the kettle on me once it's boiled neither."

"This is my house, and I will have a cup if I like," she said tartly. "If you refuse to leave, then the least you can do is accept what hospitality is offered. Or did your Mammy not teach you the least bit of manners?"

"Fine, make a pot of tea," he said, clearly exasperated by her behavior. "But make a fockin' wrong move an' ye'll be sorry."

She nodded barely controlling an urge to spit in his face. Just then the baby moved, a slow soft ripple that sent a surge of fear through her system for what she was about to do. She prayed that Conor would sleep through this because if either of these bastards took so much as a step toward the stairs she was going to have to kill them, no matter what it meant for her.

It wasn't tea leaves she wanted, but rather what she had stowed behind the tea in an old biscuit tin.

She reached back as far as she dared into the cupboard, making a show of not being able to find the tea. She could feel the man's eyes on her back. A fine trickle of sweat ran down her spine and nausea churned her stomach. The baby was making little hiccupy motions inside, jarred no doubt by the massive amount of adrenaline coursing through its mother's body. She stretched just a tiny bit farther and felt the edge of the tin. Her bruised fingers clawed at it, hoping to God that she wouldn't just push it farther off.

"What's takin' ye so long?" the man asked, irritably.

"The Lyons is at the back of the cupboard," she said trying to feign as much nonchalance as a woman with a thug in her house was likely to be able to feel.

The gun had been there in the cupboard, up high, since the last time she had lived here on her own and someone had been watching her from the woods around the house. She wasn't going to be without protection and she knew if she had to put a bullet in this man, if he forced that decision upon her, she wasn't going to hesitate to do so. The tin was in her hands now and she took it down, casting a glance over her shoulder.

He was looking toward the door, giving her the opportunity to ease the gun out of the tin and take the safety off. She took a quick breath and crossed the floor in two strides, jamming the gun into the man's ear. He froze in place and put his hands out to the sides. She stepped back so that he couldn't grab her and take the gun away. Just then, Conor started to cry.

"Alright then lady, take it easy. Ye could hurt yerself with that gun, likely as hurt me." His eyes flicked toward the stairs as though he were weighing how distracted she was by her child's cries.

"I know how to use it, you bastard, so don't even think about trying to take it. You're in my home. Do you think I'll hesitate to kill you? I suggest you move toward the door slowly and then get the fuck out of my house and yard. Now."

Conor was working himself up to a full throttle panic, as if he sensed that below stairs something was very wrong. She was nearing complete panic herself and she knew the man would use it to his advantage if the opportunity presented itself. She could not allow it to happen. She had to get him out of here.

She pushed him toward the door, finger slick on the trigger. At this point it seemed as likely she would kill him by accident as by design.

"Open the door," she said. The man did as bid and opened it, stepping out carefully with his hands up in the air, so his own partner wouldn't take a shot.

"Go down the stairs and move across the yard. Don't even bother to look back. Just get the hell out of here and take your partner with you."

"We'll only be back later, missus, an' yer man can't be here all the time."

"Next time, I'll shoot you on sight."

She gave him a shove toward the three stairs that ran down to the yard, desperate now, for Conor's screams had escalated, with those awful silent gaps that meant he wasn't breathing between cries. Sweat was pouring down her back and sides and her hand was so slick on the gun that she was afraid it would slip right out of her grasp.

The man took the stairs slowly, or so it seemed to Pamela, whose heart was pounding as adrenaline poured in unceasing waves through her body. She felt as though an invisible cord stretched between her and Conor and it yanked at her with each scream.

The ground exploded near the man's feet as he came off the final stair and he jumped sideways, stumbling and nearly losing his balance. For a second she thought she had squeezed the trigger accidentally, then realized the explosion of dirt had resulted from a bullet coming from a completely different direction.

Apparently the man thought the same for he said, "Jesus—I'm moving just as ye told me to."

"Not fast enough for me," said a voice from the edge of the tree line. The other man, hands firmly trussed behind his back, walked out with a knife to his throat. Holding the knife was her husband. Out from behind

Casey stepped Lewis Guderson, racking another cartridge into the shotgun he had pointed directly at the tall man's chest. Owen stood on the tree line, a shotgun held at the ready. Casey's face was dead white but set in lines of rage of a sort she had seen on him only twice before.

"Go inside, Pamela." Casey said, and his voice brooked no opposition. "Lock the door and stay away from the windows." She ran back into the house, wrenching open the door to Lawrence's old room, barely feeling the tread of each stair as she took them as fast as her shaking legs would allow. Finbar streaked up behind her, as intent on the dreadful crying as she was.

She scooped Conor up and held him close to her body. He clung to her, his tiny fists gripped tight in her blouse. His howling slowly came down out of the rafters, reducing to snuffles of anxiety within minutes.

"Oh baby," she said, "Mama is so sorry." She rocked him and felt his body slowly relax into her own. His skin was clammy with fear, hair damp from the exertion of screaming.

She held him tightly and walked to the tub. The only window in the bathroom was up high and therefore not a danger.

Conor clapped his hands excitedly as soon as she shut the bathroom door. "Mama, baf, baf!"

His tiny face was still streaked with tears, but his snuffles were eclipsed by the thought of a bath. Like her, Conor loved water, and was never happier than when he was in a tub filled with it. Right now, it was likely the best thing she could do for him.

She half-filled the tub with warm water, adding in a little of the lavender oil she often used for its calming effect.

She made happy noises at Conor as she washed him and played with him, but her mind felt as though it were on a greased track, sliding out of control. Three men well armed against two who were unarmed, for she had seen Owen pat down the man on the ground as she was running into the house.

It seemed unnervingly silent, and she could not hear so much as a voice, nor the crank of an engine starting. She would have to wait until Casey either walked in through the door, or he did not.

Conor would happily play in the water until he was entirely pruned, but right now she didn't mind. The water was still warm and there was nothing else to do but worry and try to resist the temptation to look frantically out the windows.

She laid her head on the side of the tub, watching Conor. He happily smacked the water, shrieking with delight when it splashed back up into his face, and conducting a long conversation with a rubber duck—which mostly consisted of Conor saying 'bad' to the duck and then slapping it firmly on the bill. She put a hand to her belly as though she could cradle the inhabitant within and keep it safe from harm.

"Keep us safe," she said softly, though she wasn't certain if she spoke to God or her husband. Nor was she certain either of them could.

OUTSIDE THE YARD WAS QUIET, FOR AGAINST TWO SHOTGUNS and a large knife there wasn't a great deal to say. Lewis and Owen stood with shotguns trained on the two men, faces impassive. That they would not hesitate to shoot was clear.

For his part, Casey was struggling against the terrible red surge he had known only a few times before in his life. That fury urged a man to kill, to do it quick and clean, and have it over with.

"Do not mistake me," he said, to the man who knelt at his feet facing away, Casey's blade drawing a thin line of blood from his throat, "for I will kill ye an' have little compunction about it. Should ye make the mistake of goin' near my wife or son again, ye are as good as dead. An' it matters not who ye send after me, I'll survive what I must to have my revenge on ye."

He pulled the knife away, though the desire to kill was still there throbbing in his fingertips, pulsing hard in his chest and throwing its red brand across his eyes. That these men had the gall, the nerve to come upon his own land and threaten his family, to bring weapons into his place of sanctuary, made him angry enough to have killed them with his bare hands.

Clutching his throat, the squat man stumbled toward the lane, his partner following. Lewis kept the shotgun trained on them both until they were gone from view. Casey followed to the head of the lane, keeping the house in sight. He stood for a time, blood coursing heavy beneath his skin, feeling the vulnerability that lay in loving others, in being human, as the rage ebbed away and the reality sank in.

He turned and walked back toward the house. It lay in the last slant of the day's sun, emerald green sills and door gleaming in the light, the whitewash dazzling and the scent of the earth slowly wakening sharp on the air. This house and the people who lived within it were everything to him. The thought that he might have lost them all today was enough to put a man on his knees.

"Go see to Pamela and the wee lad," Lewis said, blue eyes scanning the scrim of the trees as the light of afternoon sank down between needles and feathery boughs and was absorbed into leaf and earth.

Inside the house was quiet, the Aga humming to itself as though nothing had taken place this afternoon. One of the kitchen chairs lay over on its side and a cupboard door stood open. Scattered across the kitchen floor were all the fragile seedlings he and Pamela had so carefully planted—tender stalks crushed, soil scattered and packed by a square boot heel. He righted the chair and closed the door, then cleaned up the worst of the dirt and small broken pots and plants. He only wished he were able to rid his wife and child of what had happened here this afternoon so easily.

He found Pamela upstairs in Conor's room, holding him in her lap. Finbar lay at her feet, growling low in his throat until he realized it was Casey. Just the sight of his wife, with their son's head resting sleepily on her breast, was enough to make him grab for the doorsill in relief. He smelled the warm, herbal scents of a recently bathed child.

"He wouldn't settle," she said quietly. "I just wanted to give him back his sense of security. He was crying so hard, Casey. He couldn't understand why I didn't come."

"I'm sorry, Pamela. Is he alright now, then?"

She nodded, her head still bent over their son. He realized that it wasn't just gazing at Conor that had her avoiding his eyes, for he saw the tight set of her shoulders and the stark white of her skin.

He knelt by them, putting his hand to the soft spring of Conor's curls, feeling the reassuring heat and thrum of the laddie's pulse so close to the delicate network of bone. Conor eyed him warily, as though he distrusted everyone but his mother just now. Casey didn't dare touch his wife yet for he could feel the anger coming off her in waves, and while he knew much of it was still directed at the departed thugs he also was wise enough to know part of it was for him. They sat that way for long minutes, both silent.

Dusk had begun to gather softly in the corners of the room when Pamela stood and patted Conor's back. Conor had screamed himself into exhaustion during the panic for his mother, and his bath, a dry set of clothes and a full belly had put him directly back to sleep. She laid him gently on his bed and pulled his favorite blanket up over his deeply breathing form. Finbar settled beside the bed, his narrow silky face alert and on guard.

"Go put the kettle on, please," Pamela said. "I'll be down in a minute."

Casey went downstairs and did as bid. Outside he could see Lewis still on guard by the front door. He put the kettle on and got out the whiskey bottle, for his nerves could use the analgesic of a small glass.

He heard Pamela's light tread on the stairs moments later and turned to face her.

She stood at the bottom of the stairs, the bones in her face stark against the white skin. She looked exhausted and terribly fragile. He held himself back from going to her, knowing she had to come to him if she so chose.

She walked toward him and though her tension telegraphed itself clearly, still he was shocked when she slapped him across the face, hard enough to rock him back on his heels.

"You goddamn bastard!"

Casey winced slightly and put a hand up to his jaw. He didn't say anything because he knew she was right, and that she was reacting out of the aftermath of terror, of fear that her children, both the one upstairs in his bed and the one she carried in her belly, might have been harmed if not killed outright. He had felt the same rage, but she was pregnant, vulnerable and angry that he hadn't been able to protect her from these men invading their home. He knew, because he was angry at himself for that very thing.

"What the hell is going on at the construction site that you didn't see fit to tell me about? Goddamn it, man, why didn't you say something? No more secrets, we both promised. How long has this been going on?"

And so he told her, about the graft, about the payments, and about the fear and worry that had ridden him like a demon these many months. He knew he was bald in the telling, yet there was no way to cushion it. There never was in this country. By the end of the telling, Pamela looked ready to hit him again but began to shake instead, and he automatically reached out to catch her, afraid her knees were going to drop her to the floor. He could feel the resistance in her body, though he knew what she needed right now was comfort and assurance, which he was bloody well going to give her whether she wanted it or not.

"Pamela, ye can rage at me later. Ye can slap me senseless if ye feel it will help, but right now, woman, can ye just let me hold ye? For my own sake as well as yers."

She looked up at him then, and he thought she saw clearly how terrified he was too, because she moved into the shelter of his arms and let him hold her tightly to his chest.

He breathed deeply of her scent, familiar but changed since she had become a mother, and a comfort to him in all its varying notes. He could feel her pulse slow with the reassurance of his touch. This he could do for her, little that it was. Because he couldn't be here all the time, and well those bastards knew it. Next time he would not be caught unawares because there wasn't going to be a next time. He and Lewis would see to that between them.

He had a sick knot in his stomach, for he knew only too well how much worse this situation might have been. If Owen hadn't called simply because he had a bad feeling about two men who had stopped into his pub for a pint that afternoon, if Lewis hadn't been there in time to grab the second man and hold him at gun point until Casey arrived.

His wife was no stranger to violence. She had been raped by four men years earlier, and it was a tragedy that haunted him—the fear that it would or could happen again. She had come out of the rape a survivor, had moved through it and then beyond in a way that had told him how very strong this woman was. He had never truly forgiven himself for being absent the day it happened, for as irrational as it might seem, he always felt that had he been with her he could have prevented it happening, or at least died in the effort.

In his arms, his wife had stopped shaking, though she still held tightly to him as if he were the anchor that held her to earth just now.

He placed a palm over her belly in gentle protection. The words he wanted to say were stuck tight in his throat, rammed there and choking him. Pamela must have sensed this for she placed her own hand over his.

"We're alright, Casey. Stop thinking about everything that might have happened." She squeezed his hand and he lowered his head in gratitude, knowing his strength often depended entirely on this woman, the touch of her, her limitless capacity for forgiveness, her instinctive understanding of the words he could not say, and her love for him.

"Casey," she said, moments later, in a quiet but grim tone. "I need you to take me upstairs and make love to me."

"What, now?" he asked, shocked at the suggestion. Lewis was still out front and would be for the duration of the night. He meant to join him as soon as Pamela was calmed.

"Yes, now. It's either that or I hit you again."

He laughed, though it was strained. "Well, when ye put it that way woman, I don't see as there's much to the choosin' here."

"I need to feel you against me, inside me. I need to know that we're okay."

"Alright, darlin', alright," he said smoothing the hair from her face, and kissing her forehead gently. He understood the need to touch, to be as close as it was possible for two human beings to be, to regain some ground in the intimacy that had always been their innate language.

He took her upstairs and laid her across the bed, realizing that he needed this too, to know that the heart of what they were was still here and safe, that the bastards had not touched what was sacred.

He made love to her gently, carefully, worried about the baby and that this afternoon's events might have a price that neither of them could afford. She cried near the end, wrapping her arms around his neck and pulling him tight to her body. He kissed her tears away, heart beating strong against hers. Pulse to pulse they lay, he holding her, wishing he could infuse his strength into her. He put his mouth to her ear, breath still warm with exertion.

"What is it, Jewel?"

"I'm so afraid that I'll wake up and find out we didn't make it through this afternoon."

"Hush *macushla*," he said softly. "'Tis alright. I'm here with ye. I'm here."

"I'm sorry I hit you earlier. I was just so afraid for the babies."

"'Tis no matter," he said softly, and meant it.

He waited until she fell asleep, exhausted by both the day's events and pregnancy, before slipping out of the bed. He dressed, checked that Conor was still sleeping and then went outside.

Lewis sat, shotgun still canted and ready, in the shadow of the pine copse.

The sightline from there was broad, covering three angles of the house and with a view to the road lest anyone should chance to come down it. Owen wasn't to be seen but Casey knew he was just out of sight in the crook of a tree, watching over this family that he and Gert had adopted as their own.

Casey sat beside Lewis, a strange calm coming over him. It was fully dark now but the moon was high enough to provide light by which to see. No one could approach the house without them knowing.

"You have to take care of this situation now," Lewis said. The taciturn old Swede was always a man of few words, but one rarely mistook the meaning of those he did speak. "The threat you made this afternoon, you have to carry through on it or they will be back, and it will be much worse next time."

Casey didn't answer, for the man was right. But vague words of agreement had no place here, nor did Lewis expect them.

"Sometimes people are just evil, and it is no sin to kill such people." Lewis had lit two cigarettes and held one out to Casey.

"I'm afraid I'm a wee bit too Catholic to see things quite so black and white," Casey replied, taking the proffered cigarette and drawing deeply on it.

"It is what I did, long ago. It is why I left my own country and came to live here."

"What do you mean—what you did?"

Lewis looked at him, blue eyes without expression. "I disappeared people." He stood, but his eyes never left Casey's. "I have to go home and feed my animals. Owen will take the next watch." He nodded toward the pine copse where a small ember glowed and just as suddenly winked out.

Lewis cracked the shotgun, preparing for the walk home.

"Was it a long time ago, this job of yers?" Casey asked, quietly.

Lewis' eyes were still and cold as a Nordic lake in winter. "It was, but it's not the sort of work a man forgets how to do. And I was very, very good at my job."

Somehow, Casey thought, watching the straight-backed old Swede walk off into the trees, he didn't doubt it for a second.

Chapter Sixty-eight

May 1975

At the Center of the Night

DAVID CURSED THE LUCK THAT HAD BROUGHT HIM HERE, standing on a dark country road somewhere just this side of the border with the Republic. His cover story had, of necessity, included a few dropped hints that he knew his way round making simple explosives—which he did, as it was part of his training. That did not mean he was comfortable with the use of them.

The plan was simple enough but hardly foolproof. They would stake out this road, posing as part of the Security Forces, and while the vehicle they had picked out was stopped and the occupants thereof being frisked and questioned by the roadside, he, David, was to be installing the fifteen pounds of gelignite housed in a briefcase under the driver's seat. It was set on a clock timer and would detonate on the other side of the border. The idea was that this would implicate the band in the van—their chosen target—for carrying explosives. The band was, of course, Roman Catholic to a man. David felt the sophistication of the plan was somewhat lacking, but this dirty war had little in the way of sophistication and plenty in the way of effectiveness.

David had alerted his superiors to the presence of the bomb. They, in turn, had alerted Irish Customs, who were meant to confiscate the vehicle and hand it over to the bomb squad. His personal plan was to make damn sure the bomb was disconnected before it left this dark roadway. He wasn't taking chances with any poor sod's life and fifteen pounds of gelignite. This made it doubly unfortunate that Lenny McAskill had been picked to come along on this mission. Lenny, who was every unfortunate stereotype of the hard man Loyalist fanatic. Lenny, who was, David felt quite certain, a complete psychopath. Lenny who did not trust him, David aka Davey, one little bit.

Lenny was a member in uneasy standing of the Ulster Defense Regiment. The UDR had been linked in the past with the British Security Forces and with the Redhand Defenders. Some said if the Army wanted a filthy job done, the UDR were the men they applied to, not openly, mind, but covertly and with complete denial afterwards. But even these men, green bereted and copiously tattooed with a variety of lurid symbols, were a tad nervous around Lenny McAskill.

Lenny sat beside him in the ditch, adjusting a pair of sunglasses that David felt were a tad redundant considering the pitch-black quality of the night.

Their target was a band—the 'Havana Nights'—a regular sort of dancehall band that added spice to their repertoire with some Latin-based rhythms and drums. Their one big hit had charted in the UK in 1969 and they had been slogging the circuit of sweaty dance halls and grotty pubs ever since. Their only crime was the fact they were Catholic and their schedule was easy to track.

David was aware that Lenny was watching him as closely and carefully as an owl sitting atop a barn roof watches a mouse cross the yard below. It made what he needed to do that much more difficult.

The road was empty this time of night so that when the white van came along it was easily spotted. Lenny and Boyd stepped out, hands up and guns slung waist-height in the particular stance of British soldiers. The van slowed immediately, though David knew the occupants had to find it strange to see security forces on this stretch of deserted road at this hour of the night. Still, not to stop was to risk being shot through the windows.

Boyd ordered the band out of the van and David was chagrined to see that some of them were little more than boys. If this didn't come off as planned, if anything went wrong, he would be directly responsible for their deaths.

He tried not to see their faces nor smell their fear. It made it too personal and he knew that was the road to certain disaster. Boyd nodded to him and he started his walk up the side of the van, the longest in some ways he had ever taken though few steps were involved. He hardly dared to breathe. Packing this much in explosives was a tricky proposition, akin to walking a high wire when your shoes were made from blown glass.

The driver's door was open, the light creating a small hollow vacuum at the center of the night. He set the briefcase down with the gentle delicacy normally reserved for the newly born and let his breath out a little.

He could feel Lenny right behind him, the man's body heat, thick and swampy, encroaching into his space. He was going to have to wire the explosives, so that Lenny wouldn't suspect his true mission here.

"Listen, man, could ye back off a wee bit? I'd not like to blow the both of us to kingdom come an' yer makin' me nervous with yer hoverin'."

Lenny gave him an arch look and backed away, heading toward the rear of the van and the roadway. It was ominously quiet, with only Boyd's oily tones coating the night. The members of the band were silent and David had to will himself not to turn. The very air was taut with menace.

There wasn't a great deal of time to do this, but he would never be able to live with himself if he didn't disconnect the wiring and the van blew up before reaching the border guards. He took a deep breath, steadying himself though the sweat was beading on his forehead. From the rear of the van he could feel Lenny's stare and knew the bastard distrusted him to do the job. He eased the wires back out of their housing just a touch, enough so there was no contact point.

There—it was done. He clipped the briefcase shut and pushed it back under the driver's seat. It was then the gunfire started. He crouched low and ran for the back of the van, peering into the dark where the bullets were sharp red traceries splitting the fabric of the night. All was confusion, Boyd shouting to cease fire, but the man with the gun—Lenny—wasn't listening. It was too late anyhow, for David's sight had adjusted in time to see the last member of the band topple forward into the ditch.

He thought he might be sick, but he had become so accustomed to senseless violence that it no longer affected him as it once would have. It had all gone to smash and now there were five innocent men lying dead in a ditch because of this disturbed bastard.

He didn't even realize he was moving until his fist hit Lenny's face, a satisfying crunch of bone and blood. His arm was grabbed and held back before he could land another blow, for he would not have stopped on his own until he had put the bastard to the ground.

"What are ye doin'?" Boyd demanded, keeping his hold on David's arm.

"What am *I* doin'? It's him that's focked up the entire plan, isn't it? I thought the aim was to blow up the van when it reached the border, not kill a bunch of boys that had barely the whiskers to shave."

The air was charged with violence, that particular scent of sweat and testosterone that made the very particles around a man throb with the need for action, for blood against his knuckles, something to relieve the crimson tide that surged in his body.

"Aye, it was, but plans change." Boyd turned away from him then, leaving David speechless with fury. He had been used as a dupe. And now there was the blood of five innocent men on his hands.

Lenny grinned at him, a fine spray of blood drying on his face and into his clothes. David did not return the smile, cover be damned. For he knew now without a doubt, that there would come a time and place where this man would kill him, or he would have to be the one to kill.

Quite frankly, he looked forward to the day of reckoning.

Chapter Sixty-nine

June 1975

Butterfly

LATER, HE WOULD THINK HE HAD BEEN TIRED, had been focused on other things, had been aware of his surroundings but in a hazy, dreamy way that had been more about what awaited him at home than what was happening in his own vicinity. He knew better, always had. Still he was merely a man and a man sometimes was weary, sometimes had better things to think about, sometimes forgot. He shouldn't have forgotten, but he did.

PAT WAS WRAPPING UP THE DAY'S WORK, including a stack of paperwork that made him feel as if he were one of the lesser lawyers in *Bleak House*. Kate had already left for the day, putting a cup of tea to hand for him before exiting through the back to the mysterious person who drove her to and from work each day. Pat had watched out the door with no small curiosity about who it was that Kate relied upon. All he could determine thus far was that it was not her brother. He was familiar enough with Noah Murray's face to know it wasn't him. He was certain the man must know of his sister's activities though, for Noah wasn't the sort to allow so much as a mouse to move in his vicinity and not take note of it. Pat had been half waiting for months now for him to show up and threaten to part Pat from his ability to breathe.

He was ready to lock up, his cup rinsed and put away, the paperwork still unruly but with some progress made, when David entered the back door as though a banshee were after him. David's face was pale, dark dyed hair rumpled and sweaty. Pat had never seen him so rattled. It didn't do a great deal for his own equilibrium to see the man so.

"What the hell is it, man? Ye look as though ye've seen a troop of ghosts."

"You need to come with me. I can't tell you why right now, so don't ask me."

The look on David's face told Pat he was worried about listening devices.

Therefore he didn't ask questions, merely retrieved his coat, locked up the front door and exited through the back with David.

Once in the car, a Citroën that had seen far better days, David merely gave him a steely look and shook his head. So the car was possibly bugged as well. Pat sighed. Sometimes it felt as though the entire city was monitored by one huge listening device—which considering all the towers, was more or less the truth.

They went north beyond the city, David driving with his usual suicidal intent, so that Pat wasn't certain if his panic was due to what lay ahead or merely a certainty that death was rushing at them full throttle, about to come through the windshield.

They traveled the coast near to Ballycastle, a stretch of beauteous rocky headlands which were lost on the occupants of the car. David bypassed the town, following farther along the coast as the road narrowed.

When they slowed at last, Pat could see the hazy outlines of the great rocky upthrust that was Rathlin Island. David pulled down a narrow pathway where they bumped and jolted all the way down to the sea. There a small motorboat was waiting, bobbing on the waves.

Pat felt his initial worry upgrade itself to a full blown case of panic as they got out of the car. He looked at David for explanation. While he did not share his brother's phobia of the sea, he wasn't so fond of it as to be delighted at the thought of taking a wee craft out onto those treacherous waves.

"It's your brother. He was taken this afternoon. I've had someone keeping a watch because I had intelligence that led me to think he might be in some danger."

Pat didn't need to know more than that. He got into the boat without further question, David tossing him an oilskin coat that lay in the bottom. He had a good idea who had an interest in taking his brother and why. David cranked the motor and they roared off into the fading light, the sea choppy and grey beneath its frail hull.

Rathlin Island sat six miles off the Antrim Coast across a rough stretch of water poetically called the Sea of Moyle. In terms of time, the island lay much farther away. It seemed of another century altogether. Enormous cliffs of limestone and basalt loomed up from the dark sea and small white dots swarmed the cliffs. The island was home to colonies of puffins and guillemots, kittiwakes and falcons, thousands upon thousands of them. The noise of them came across the water, audible even over the thrum of the boat's motor, ghostly aerial specters that belonged to the world of air and water and rock. Pat shivered, his hair and any skin that wasn't covered with the oilskin coat already soaked and salted.

It was on Rathlin that Robert the Bruce had hidden, having fled the wrath of the English after the battles of Methven and Dalry. It was here as well that there had once been a thriving industry during the Neolithic Age, making axes from a fine blue stone called porcellanite. Like most sites in Ireland, it had its share of blood history as well, with the English massacring the women and children of the MacDonnell clan who had once sought refuge upon the island and had been hunted down with no more impunity than if they had been seals or otters.

The tall cliffs were pocked with caves, some huge, some barely large enough for a man to crawl into, some long collapsed beneath the weight of the stone above. Some were stranded high up the cliff walls, relics of a time when the great glacial seas had been far colder and far deeper. A natural stepping stone as the island was between Scotland and Ireland, the caves had become a refuge for men on the run, women forced into hiding and even—it was said—the Children of Lir. Though personally Pat thought, looking at the foreboding shadow cast by the cliffs, the tale about the devil living here seemed more likely than a band of enchanted swans.

David began to yell over the roar of the motor, reasonably certain that even the British Army couldn't manage listening devices on the open sea.

"I have someone keeping an eye out because I was worried something like this might happen. I got a call early in the afternoon, that your brother wasn't where he was meant to be. Being that that's totally out of character for him, I knew something was wrong. Then someone called in to the local police that they'd seen something that looked odd being brought ashore here. I know certain lads of a particular organization occasionally use the caves here to hide contraband of various sorts, the ones high up and hard to access. I suspect they may have brought Casey here. But I think they'll not have used the caves high up. It'll be the ones at sea level we need to search."

Pat didn't need to ask why they would use those caves. For when the high tide came in, which it would do within the hour, a man, if he couldn't move under his own power, would either drown or be bashed to death against the cave walls. Then the body would be swept to sea and conveniently disappear. If the man were already dead, it would solve the same problem.

He took a deep breath, swallowing a spray of sea water and trying very hard not to visualize what it would take to render his brother unfit to crawl from a cave with the high tide surging in.

David had slowed the boat and was running parallel to the cliffs, eyeing the rocky foreshore with no small worry.

"Here," Pat said.

David gave him a questioning look and Pat shrugged, shoulders tight as stone.

"I don't know why. Just a feeling that we should start here. We have to ask if anyone has seen anything, otherwise we've not a clue to go on, and precious little time."

David nodded and eased the boat into the small shoal area. They climbed a set of rock hills and found themselves in the small settlement Pat had noted, within moments of tying off the boat. The village was very little, only a huddle of six cottages, faces turned inward like malcontent sheep, each cottage thickly thatched and whitewashed, with wind-blasted backs and chimneys currently puffing smoke as it was nearing teatime for the occupants.

Pat knocked at the first door and got no answer, though it was clear there was someone inside the small house as there was a visible twitch of a lace curtain. Next door was the same.

"Somethin' has happened here alright, or they're accustomed to treating strangers with a cold shoulder. Meaning they're either paid to keep quiet or scared into it."

On the fourth door, Pat pounded hard enough to wake Robert the Bruce himself, should his spirit still be lingering round. An old man, who had evidently forgotten to put his dentures in, popped his grizzled head out of the top of the half door.

"D'ye think I'm deaf or are ye only tryin' to make me so?"

"I want to know if ye've seen anyone or anything unusual today, someone who normally wouldn't be around the island, or didn't belong."

"Well, there's yerself," the man said, and spit casually to the side of the door.

Pat drew in a short, impatient breath through his nose, eyes black with anger.

"Listen, tell me if ye've seen anything or I'll make certain yer missin' more than yer teeth before I'm gone."

The old man eyed Pat up and down, taking in his size and general air of ferocity.

"Ye've not the most charmin' way of askin' a question, but aye, I'll have seen something today that was out of the ordinary way of things. It's best if I don't go into details"—he flashed a look at the cottage across the way and Pat turning, saw another curtain twitch—"but if I were you, an' lookin' perhaps for a man, I'd head to the point out there." He nodded curtly toward the headland some distance up from the huddle of cottages, visible nevertheless. "I was out walkin' the cliffs earlier an' saw some men that had no business hereabouts except of the wrong sort, if ye take my meanin'. They had a man amongst them that didn't seem to be there voluntary like. 'Twas a distance off, ye'll understand, but he seemed to be like yerself in appearance."

"What's the quickest way to get where I'm going?"

The old man looked ruminative for a moment. "Ye look to be a strong lad, so best if ye see if ye can go straight down the cliff face. There's a big cave at the bottom, but the tide is comin' in and it fills to the top at the peak. There's a narrow set of footholds, not so much stairs as toeholds, but manageable. Watch ye the birds though, they tend to get just the bit agitated when a human comes into their territory. Have yer friend here bring the boat round."

"Why do ye think it'll be that particular cave?" Pat asked.

The blue eyes were cold but frank. "Because it's the one to use if ye want to kill a man an' leave no trace of the body."

Pat nodded. "Thank ye for speakin' to me. It seems it might have been dangerous for you to do so."

The man squinted one watery blue eye at Pat. "I'm too old to be intimidated. No one is goin' to tell me whom I can talk to, an' if they don't like it I've got an old rifle here they can have a chat with. Now best ye hurry. The tide is on the rise already."

They ran across the headland, the wind scouring the cliff top. Pat's heart was in his throat and he hoped to hell Casey was where the man thought or there was no way to reach him before he drowned. There were few deaths his brother would fear more than one by water.

At the edge of the cliffs, they looked down. The sight took the breath from the both of them.

"Christ," David said, "I don't know if I can even get the boat in there. It's a half mile back to go get it, and by the time I..."

Pat finished his sentence for him. "It would be too late. I'll climb down. The old man said it could be done."

"He did," David agreed, adding, "but we're talking about someone without a tooth to his head. Patrick—" David seized his arm with one hand, pointing to the sharp rocks near to where the cave's entrance ought to lie.

Below, so small as to seem little more than a speck borne on the tide, was a dark head, only just above the waves that were coming in ever higher, rough with grey bearded crests.

"Casey," Pat breathed, and all hesitation left him. His brother appeared to be barely clinging to the rock, possibly even unconscious, and Pat knew instinctively that he wasn't going to be able to hold on much longer. Pat stripped off his shoes, socks and jacket, flung them aside and took the measure of the cliff. It was extremely steep and slick as ice with bird shit. The shit of thousands of birds to be precise, most of which seemed to be shrieking, wheeling and diving in the air at present. They were going to be pissed as newts when they discovered him in their midst. He sized up the chutes of stone one last time, determining the best path, or the least suicidal might be more accurate. He then turned to David.

"Go back and bring the boat around. I'll grab Casey and swim out beyond the rocks."

"Pat—" David began, but stopped at the look on Pat's face.

"He's my brother. There's no choice about it. Just don't be too feckin' long about fetchin' the boat, aye?"

"Alright, I'm gone. Just don't break your damn neck, Patrick Riordan, or I'll never forgive you."

"I'll bear that in mind," Pat said and then he was gone down over the cliff face.

IT WAS THE SLAP OF THE FIRST WAVE IN HIS FACE that brought Casey back to a hazy consciousness of his surroundings. The second one slapped harder and brought him up choking on salt and the taste of kelp. The pain came flooding in with the consciousness and he thought drowning might not have been such a terrible fate, despite his lack of love for the sea. And drown he would if he didn't get up and away from the water, for he realized each wave was just a wee bit higher. The tide must be coming in. There was enough light playing upon the walls for him to realize that there were no watermarks upon them, which meant this cave filled to the top when the tide peaked.

Already the water was at least three feet deep and he knew his time was running out quickly. The thought of trying to drag his body through that churning, freezing green mass was more than just formidable, it seemed downright impossible. He didn't know if he had the strength for it. Then again, he would drown if he stayed here. Then again, he might well drown if he went. He wasn't certain he could walk, and swimming against the tide was going to be more than just a wee bit difficult.

He slid into the water, gasping as the cold verdigris filled his mouth. Everything hurt. He could barely lift his arm to pull himself up and get his head above the water so that he could drag in a ragged breath. His chest felt like it was filled with glass and he wondered if they had broken all his ribs. His left hand didn't bear looking at, so he didn't. The water was cold enough that it numbed his extremities, which was a blessing.

The water was higher already, flooding in fast with the racing current. Those off Rathlin were particularly vicious and bloody cold, not to mention as temperamental as a woman, going this way and that and confusing the hell out of a man.

A rock scraped his side hard and caught in his shirt, the tide flooding over his head immediately. He couldn't take in enough air to buy time and his fingers, broken and numb, were hardly functioning at all. He twisted sideways as sharply as he could and felt the shirt rip away. The water was nearly to the cave ceiling now and he would have to dive down to get under the lip of the opening. He was so tired, limbs dragging as if they were weighted with iron. He might well just sink like an anchor straight to the bottom.

He managed the dive in the end, though he was certain he wasn't going to bob back up once he was under the stone overhang. When he did come up, his lungs were filled with an icy fire that felt as though it were going to burst out of his chest. One leg was dragging badly, the knee next to useless.

There were rocks not far beyond the entrance. If he could just make it to one of them, he might cling there for a bit, weigh his options, and pray to God someone saw him before the sea took him. He struck out for them with what strength he could muster, kicking hard with the leg that wasn't hurt, though that was a relative term. He bobbed up and down with the waves. At the top of one it seemed like the rock was right there. On the next he was spitting out water, feeling the stream of salt in his nose and eyes, and it would appear leagues beyond his reach.

He wanted the things a man always wanted in these moments, respite, time to clear his head, a surge of strength, his Daddy, his wife, to hold his son and be bloody anywhere else but here in this predicament. But in the perverse way that the universe often worked, he got a rock with a seal sitting upon it instead.

The seal looked at him as though it were of two minds whether to slap him over the head with a flipper and watch him sink or just let him go down on his own. He pulled himself up as far as he could onto the rock, knowing that it too would be under water soon enough. But he couldn't go any farther right now. He needed to rest a bit, and then... well, best not to think about that overmuch, as there weren't really any options beyond trying to make his way around the island to a place where there was a spit of land not drowning in tide. And that he could not do. He hadn't the strength. He had heard that drowning was a peaceful way to go and he hoped it was so.

It was, he thought fuzzily, rather beautiful out here, wild and majestic, a reminder of how small man was, how insignificant in the grander scheme of things. The pain was manageable now, mostly because he couldn't feel his body except for his heart thudding heavily in his chest. Pamela was going to be furious with him, and the wee lad and the new baby... Christ, he couldn't think of it. He laid his head against the rock, feeling the soft slickness of kelp beneath his cheek. If he was going to die, then out here, free and at the mercy of the elements, was preferable than at the hand of a hate-filled man. If it must be, it was better so.

The dark, when it came, was fast, but quiet and gentle with him.

THE BIRDS WERE SCREAMING, panicked at the strange human only a few feet away from them. Pat could feel the flap of their wings, their piercing shrieks deafening. His hands were slick with fear and bird shit, but he kept moving slowly and carefully. The sun had slipped down the horizon and left the chutes of stones thick with shadow. His world had been reduced to a claustrophobic whirl of feathers and thick webbed feet, of fear and cacophonous noise, enough to make a man lose his hold and fall to the rocks below just to make it stop.

He paused and took a breath, only to find himself face to face with a puffin that seemed none too pleased about Pat's loitering on his bit of rock face. The bird was on a ledge roughly eight inches deep, one that Pat had been standing on a few minutes before. The foothold he had now was just the wee bit more shallow and precarious.

The puffin eyed him with gravity and, Pat thought, a tinge of hostility there deep in its tragic gaze. Eye to eye, despite his superior weight and height, he felt rather at a disadvantage. It was the lack of wings and the sheer drop of the cliff below him into the boiling maw of the sea. The puffin waddled forward and spread its wings. Pat could not back up. Then the puffin jumped up onto his head, flapped its wings twice and settled there as though it had mistaken his curls for an ambulatory nest.

There was simply no dignity in being done to death by a puffin. It was too dangerous to flap his hands about, as the drop to the rocks was far enough to do permanent damage. If the damn bird wanted a ride down the cliff-face Pat had no choice but to be his chariot. He took a tentative step down, foot searching delicately for purchase, and found it on a narrow two-inch wide shelf. The bird sat complacently through his movement, as though this were a Sunday jaunt and he a stoic gentleman taking in the sights upon the head of his footman.

The rest of the journey down was accomplished with a great deal of cursing under his breath, two slips that caused him to pray wordlessly and with great fervency, and the puffin remaining throughout, clutched to his scalp. There was no shore here so it meant a drop straight into the water. Already he was in past his knees, the tide surging hard enough to knock him into the cliff face each time.

He gently shook his head, praying that the puffin would take a hint and fly away home. It tottered to the edge of his skull and, bending over, looked upside down into his face.

"Ye have to go, wee fellow," Pat said, and the puffin, apparently of an agreeable frame of mind, went, with two vigorous flaps launching itself into the air. He eased down into the water, needle cold and over his shoulders. He would have to swim straight out. He could see the top of Casey's head, indigo amongst the sea clogged greens and blacks and rippling colors of the world of stone and water.

The sea here was no gentle maid with sandy shores beckoning. It was roiling and green-black, foaming like mad horses on the gallop and cold as a siren's heart. There were rocks just under the surface, like steel-clawed maenads, waiting for a man to float too near. Pat let go of the rock he was holding and surged out toward his brother. It only took a moment to lose his bearings. He got his head up high enough to spot Casey's head again and continued toward it. The cross current was strong though, and he had to compensate by pulling hard to the right so that the sea would pull him back to the left and he would hopefully end up where his brother was.

The current was pulling hard on his legs and he was choking on the waves that slapped him in the face every time he came up for air. He couldn't see Casey any longer and felt panic begin to course through his muscles. Had the man slipped off into the sea? And if he had, how the hell was Pat to find him beneath the waves? He looked up, eyes stinging and blurred with salt, and found that the rock his brother had rested upon was next to invisible. Panic seized him, sending a surge of adrenaline through him giving him the energy he needed to swim the final length to the rock, only to find it submerged under a few inches of water and his brother nowhere in sight. He dove under the water, the swift-building waves pounding at him, making it impossible to see more than a few inches around him. He reached out, touched the rock, hoped to God it was the same one, and felt down it as far as his lungs would allow. He came up again, drew breath into sheared lungs and felt the force of the bright green breakers, cusped with foam, push and pull to the tilt of the world.

Down again, past the thick satiny mermaid ribbons of kelp, into the deeps where far below, if you believed the legends, lay a lost land where those with the ears for it could hear the bells that still rang in drowned towers. Down, down until his lungs were heavy as stone and aching with tension and then, miraculously, a hand, barely clinging, caught there by some wisp of fate. Pat grabbed onto it and pulled up with all the force in his chilled muscles.

They broke the surface of the waves, coming from the chilled lands below into the twilit air of the world above. Pat grabbed the rock with one hand and pulled his brother to him with the other, turning his face upward to the sky so that he might breathe, if indeed he could.

He couldn't tell if his brother was alive or not. Casey was so bruised and battered that he was almost unrecognizable and what Pat could see of him was fish-belly pale, tinged green about the edges.

He heard the rumble of the boat then and looked over the rock to see it breaching the dark green waves that parted over its hull like horses composed of mercury, shimmering and scattering to the edges and converging again on the plane of the sea.

He swam, towing his brother with him, out beyond where the rocks could savage the boat's hull. His muscles were screaming with exertion and cold and it seemed to take an eternity to reach the small, bobbing craft.

David pulled Casey in, with Pat providing as much leverage as he could from below.

Once in himself, he collapsed beside his brother, streaming seawater, so cold that he could not feel anything other than fear at how still Casey lay in the bottom of the boat. David was bent over him blowing and compressing his chest.

"I'll do it," Pat said grimly. "He's my brother."

Life/Death. The line was so fine and he had been near it more than once himself. He understood the siren call that existed on the far side, how it seemed at times simpler just to let go, let the tide take you where it would. But he was not going to allow his brother that luxury today. He started the compressions, timing them ruthlessly, determination and fury informing every cell of his being.

A thin stream of seawater trickled from Casey's mouth. His face was still that dreadful shade of white with the bronzy green tint around the edges. Pat prayed, a rosary of grim panic turning over and over in his head and heart. Breathe, press, press, press, breathe, the rhythm of it the only thing in the universe. He couldn't feel the boat rocking beneath him, nor the wind that whipped them nearly blind. Waves were coming up over the side so that Casey lay in a foaming pool with fronds of seaweed clinging to his clothes. As though he had left the core of himself behind in the drowned abyss below, with its bells that forever haunted the place between worlds.

"Pat..." David ventured.

"Shut up, do ye hear me? This is not happening. He is not focking dying from drowning. I won't have it," Pat said and went back to breathing for his brother, moving his chest with as much force as he dared to exert, being that the man's ribs felt like shattered glass under his flesh.

"Don't you goddamn dare," he hissed and hit Casey's chest with the flat of his palm. "Ye don't get to go this way, not now, so just get that out of yer head, ye bastard."

The trickle of water turned to a stream, gushing out and causing Casey to choke. David turned him on his side, slow and deliberate. Gasping, he fought for air, the terrible blue-green of his skin slowly turning to white.

When Casey's breathing steadied, David eased him onto his back once again. He still looked utterly drained, horribly pale, dark hair threaded with fronds of kelp. He looked like a merrow brought up from the bottom of the sea after a particularly rough night on the tiles. He looked, thought Pat, like Holy Hell.

One dark eye cracked open and sighted itself hazily upon Pat's face.

"I thought if ye were swearin' it had to be serious." The eye closed then and did not open again for the rest of the agonizing ride over the waves to the mainland. Pat couldn't tell if Casey was unconscious or just ignoring him. Either way he was relieved in small measure, for he knew his brother was in very bad shape. But at least he was breathing now.

On shore it was twilight, coming on for a dark night with neither moon nor stars in the sky. That was for the best, for they did not need witnesses. They transferred Casey, barely conscious, to the car.

"I think it's best if we get him to a safe house," David said. Taking in the look on David's face, Pat knew the man had good reason to suggest this.

"All right. I know where to take him, but he needs the attention of a doctor first."

"I know someone who can take care of him and won't ask questions." There was a curious flush on David's face.

"Do ye?" Pat said. "Ye'd best call him then."

THE RIDE TO KERRY WAS THE LONGEST PAMELA HAD EVER UNDERTAKEN in her life. It felt as though they would never arrive and that Casey might slip away while they were taking back lanes and stopping for cows and sheep to meander with maddening slowness across the roadway. Pat seemed to feel it too, for he used the horn more than once and cursed softly under his breath a time or two.

Pat had called her late in the evening when she had begun to truly worry why Casey had not come home. He had let her know her husband was still alive, but beyond that had not given details. She spent a sleepless night and left first thing in the morning while Conor still slept. Gert had come the night before and so she left her son in the woman's capable hands.

Pat met her at an agreed-upon spot just as the sun rose. She left their car there, tucked into a swathe of hedgerow, and joined Pat in a car she did not recognize. He handed her a note that said they were going to Casey, in Kerry. She had merely nodded at him, understanding implicitly why they could not speak.

When they came up over the final rise on the looping road down to the cottage and the sea spread out before them, she heaved a sigh of relief. Her chest was tight with apprehension and it took everything she had to not get out and run the last few yards as Pat slowed the car.

Father Terry was inside, making tea in the kitchen. He still looked like a scarecrow, all angles and black cloth, but she had known few men in her life who exuded a sense of comfort the way this man did. She felt a little of her worry ease from the minute he hugged her and raised a grizzled brow at Pat.

"He's alright, lass. He's just woken up. He's in the bedroom."

She removed her rain-sprinkled jacket, put it over the back of a chair and took a deep breath before opening the door to the bedroom. The sight that met her eyes made her bite down hard on a gasp. It was as though a masterwork in oils had been desecrated in some way, a beautiful canvas that had been painted with heavy viscous oils in all the darker colors: the ebonies and earths, the cobalts and ochres and deep crush of violets. As though all those colors had been spread in plenty with a brute hand, and then smeared with water and oil. And amidst all this, the thin lines of alizarin crimson where cuts had only just glazed over, the skin so thin that the brush of a moth wing might open them up again, causing them to well with blood. A large bandage was wrapped around his ribs and his left hand was completely swathed in gauze and tape. The right had two fingers splinted. One swollen eye slitted open.

"Christ, Patrick, I told ye she wasn't to come here." The words cost him, she could see, for they came out slowly and slightly slurred.

"Aye," Pat rejoined, standing with one hand on her shoulder to steady her. "Have ye tried to stop her from doin' something she's bent on recently?"

"Point taken," Casey said, and attempted to sit up. She was at his side without even being aware of moving.

"What the hell happened? Jesus, Casey." She burst into tears from the sheer relief of seeing him alive, but also for the beating he must have taken at those bastards' hands.

"Patrick, Father Terry—could ye give us a minute?" Casey asked softly and the men melted out of the wee cottage.

"It looks worse than it is, darlin'. Come here. Let me hold ye."

This was accomplished with no little shifting and a few muffled curses on Casey's part as he moved over so that she could sit on the bed beside him and then pulled her into his arms. He winced as she touched his ribs but wouldn't let her pull away despite his obvious pain.

"A few of my ribs are broken, so I feel like I'm made of shattered glass inside. God woman, it feels good to have you here, much as I didn't want ye to see me this way."

"Who was it, Casey?"

"I don't know an' that's the honest truth. 'Twasn't the bastards that came to our home, but likely someone sent by them or whoever their boss is. They jumped me when I was lockin' up on the site. They had to have been sittin' there waitin' for a bit to know I was alone."

She sat back, careful not to jar him, wanting to assess the damage now that the initial shock had passed.

One eye was swollen completely shut and was the color of a plum. There was a nasty cut through the eyebrow above said eye and a split in his bottom lip that was going to leave a permanent scar. He had an ugly lump on his jaw but it appeared unhurt beyond that. His nose, by some miracle, was untouched.

Further assessment, which caused Casey to utter several very descriptive expletives, brought to light that he had three loose teeth, stitches inside his mouth, and a deep livid bruise inside his right ear.

"Jesus Christ," she breathed out, trying to take in the extent of his injuries and deciding it could only be absorbed in small increments. There wasn't an inch of him that wasn't battered or bruised in shades the human body should never achieve. There was a particularly red-black one peeking out of the bandage over his ribs that made her draw her breath in, shaking with fury. How dare someone hurt him this way, how dare they take this body that she so loved, that she depended upon for so many things, and hurt and maim it. She touched the edge of the deep crimson bruise and he gasped, arching away from her.

"Oh God, I'm sorry," she said. "I didn't mean to hurt you."

"Ye didn't, it's just that it feels like an ox stampeded over my kidneys an' they're a wee bit grumpy about it. At this point, I'm just glad I can still take a piss without bleedin' to death."

"What did the doctor say?"

"Well, he shook his head a great deal, but in the end he said I'd live, even if it seemed a somewhat undesirable state for the first few days. He'll be back day after tomorrow to look me over again. He could save himself the trip. Time is all that's needed. I do wish they hadn't broken my damn fingers though. It's hard to deal with buttons or zippers or anything else."

She bent her head and kissed the back of his hand, though there was a good half inch of gauze between her and his skin.

"Ye seem very calm, Jewel. I was certain ye'd be furious with me."

She shook her head. "No, not right now. Right now I'm just glad you're alive, man. Later, I'll probably be furious, but that can wait."

She gingerly removed herself from his arms and stood, taking care not to jar the bed, no easy feat with how awkward her own movements were becoming.

"Do you think you might manage a wee bit of something to eat? Gert sent some of her beef broth along. I'm going to go heat some up for you and see if your brother is hungry."

"A wee bit, maybe. The inside of my mouth still hurts like hell."

She leaned down carefully, hands pressed to the round of her belly, and kissed him softly over each eye. He looked up at her, a battered warrior, bruised and broken in some places, but unbowed. It relieved some of the tension in her body to know that he would survive this with his spirit intact. That, above all, was what mattered.

"Pamela, now that ye've seen me an' ye know I'm goin' to be fine, ye should go back home to Conor."

"*I* am not going anywhere, Casey Riordan. I am here until you are well enough to be moved home. Pat can bring Conor here. But you are not moving out of my range of vision for the foreseeable future."

Casey opened his mouth to protest, and then taking in the look on her face, promptly shut it. "Alright," he said, in an unusually meek tone. She thought it was a measure of how weak he was feeling that he was so uncharacteristically agreeable.

A half hour later, she shut the bedroom door quietly behind her. Casey was sleeping heavily, though with a slight rattle to his breathing that worried her. He had managed half a bowl of broth before pushing it away and turning his head. She suspected what little nourishment he had been persuaded to take had been for her sake and not because he was hungry. He was also in a great deal more pain than he was allowing her to see. She suspected this was half the reason he wanted her to go back home.

In the kitchen, Pat sat by the table, looking at her questioningly.

"He's asleep for now," she said. "Pat, I need you to do me a favor."

"Anything, Pamela, ye know that."

"I want to keep him here for awhile. I—I can't go back to Belfast. Will you bring Conor here to me? Gert won't mind having him for a wee bit, until you can get back."

"Aye, but d'ye think ye'll be able to keep Casey here for long?"

Her voice was grim when she answered. "Oh, he's going to stay whether he bloody likes it or not. I refuse to go back there until *I'm* ready."

"And what if," there was a deep sympathy in the dark eyes, "yer never ready?"

"Would that be so terrible, Pat? To live out here? Surely there are buildings that need repair and houses to be built? I can still work for Jamie. I don't need to be in his house to sign papers and conduct meetings."

He looked at her face for a long moment and nodded. "Of course I'll bring the wee laddie here to ye." He forbore to say anything else and she thought, not for the first time, that he possessed a quiet wisdom that his brother sometimes did not.

❄ ❄ ❄

AFTER PAT LEFT, WITH ASSURANCES HE WOULD BE BACK the next day with Conor and Finbar, she felt suddenly afraid, as though she did not know what to do, how to deal with the shattered body on the bed, a body that she knew better than her own in many ways, and yet frightening to her now with all its injuries. This sudden feeling of fragility had come upon her more than once during this pregnancy and she felt herself wanting to wrap herself around this person in her body and just hide away from the world that seemed ever more chaotic and frightening to her with each event that whirled out of the maelstrom of Northern Ireland's politics and violence.

She set about tidying the cottage, washing up the few dishes from the meal she had managed to convince Pat he needed before setting off back toward

Belfast. Then she swept the floors and contemplated washing them, though without a mop and with her stomach the size it was, it seemed unlikely that she could manage it. It was all in the cause of avoiding her husband, she knew, of staying busy enough with mindless tasks that she didn't have to absorb what had happened to him, to them. Because it terrified the hell out of her.

She looked around the small room, taking in its corners and shadows, the cream colored dishes with their garland of blackberries and ivy, the deep stone sink and the ancient dripping tap. They had spent their first week as a married couple here, both euphoric and frightened by the bold, sudden step they had taken. Yet in many ways it had not seemed sudden at all, rather inevitable, for she had once told Casey she had been married to him from the minute she saw him. The ceremony had only made it a legal arrangement, for it had always been binding.

Outside, twilight had taken hold, softening the outlines of trees and plants, painting long watercolor blues and purples across the horizon. On a distant hill, she saw a man walking, the space between cottage and man rendering him small and still like a figure in a painting. Beyond was the sea. She could hear the shush and roar of it in her inner ear, feel it along her skin, a pricking awareness that called to her despite her worry.

"Ye've washed that countertop five times now, Jewel. Ye'll wear it out if yer not careful."

She started slightly, for she hadn't realized he was awake. She could feel him watching her and knew that her tension was telegraphing itself to him despite the fog of the painkillers.

"Pamela, stop. Just quit bustlin' about. I know what yer doin', but it won't help."

She turned to find him braced in the doorway of the bedroom, bruises not as prominent in the dim light but the lines of his body speaking eloquently in the language of pain.

"I think I'm afraid to stop moving," she said quietly, "afraid that I'll fly into a thousand pieces if I stop to think, or breathe deep or truly look at you. I feel like I'm made of glass, very thin glass, that's been blown beyond the limits of its strength."

"Then come here an' let me be yer strength," he said.

She shook her head. "Look at the state of you, man. I don't need you to be strong for me right now. I just need you to heal and be well."

"I'm workin' on that love, but in the meantime, d'ye think ye might come and lie with me? The pain eases when ye touch me."

She helped him back to the bed, not an easy task as he shouldn't have been up at all, and it took every bit of his strength to make his way back to a prone position. She knelt on the bed, still feeling as though she were porous material, something through which every wind and storm might easily pass, shattering her internal landscape beyond her control. Casey raised his right hand, thankfully the least damaged of the two, and touched her jawline, fingers tender despite the splints and bandages.

"Will ye do somethin' for me?"

"Of course."

"Take yer clothes off—an' ye needn't give me that look," he said in response to her raised eyebrow. "I only want to look at you an' the babe."

She took her clothes off and put them on the chair beside the bed, then lay down beside him.

He did just look at her for a few moments, silent, his field of vision restricted to his left eye, and that only a slit through which he could peer. But flesh had a sight of its own, and so he touched the round of her breast, soft as a whisper, his hand coming to rest on the swell of belly under which their child stirred and turned, a small fist making contact with the bruised and broken bones of its father.

"Hello, wee love," Casey said and bent his head to kiss the taut skin that lay between him and his child. "Daddy has missed ye."

She cupped the back of his head, careful where she touched, hoping to impart through her hands some form of healing to counteract the hatred that had been inflicted on his body.

Beneath Casey's lips the baby, butterfly-winged, fluttered softly and then stretched until it seemed the flesh that separated child from father must dissolve. She realized with shock that Casey was crying, the tears running hot and salty down the slope of her belly.

She reached down and laid her hand carefully over his, wishing she could grasp him tight to her body and keep him there, safe. But knowing also that she could not do that, and realizing it was this in part that made their love a thing of both painful fragility and overwhelming strength, like a butterfly that a light touch could damage, yet was strong enough to cross continents and oceans in order to find its way home.

"I thought I had died, Pamela."

"What?"

"When I went down in the water, I blacked out an' was certain I was dead. Only there wasn't light the way people say, just all these stars, billions of them, rushing past me an' a great wind, cold an' streamin'. But none of that mattered because I could only think of you an' the babies an' that I was leavin' ye all alone. An' I swear, mad as it sounds, I could feel the pain ye felt because I was gone, or maybe it was my own pain at losin' all of ye. I only know I was as alone as I have ever been in this world, an' I was afraid."

She took a careful, quiet breath, fighting the tears that surged behind her eyes.

"They held a gun to my head for a good bit, even pulled the trigger, but the chamber was empty. I'm not sure why the man didn't pull it again."

"Oh, Casey… I wish I had been here right away. Pat said you made him wait the night."

"I was afraid, Jewel, of what it would do to the baby, that maybe the shock would cause ye to lose her."

"Her?"

"Aye, that's my wee girl in there. I know it sure as I know the sky is blue."

She closed her eyes for a moment, swallowing hard. Seeing him, normally so strong, broken down both physically and emotionally like this was almost more than she could bear. She wished she could cradle him in her body, keep him safe from the world the way she did their child.

"Just forgive me in advance, Jewel, because I'm goin' to say all sorts of silly, sentimental things to both you an' the babe. I'm still half off my head with painkillers an' it's all wantin' to pour out of me, an' I don't think I'm able to stop it."

"Say what you need to, man. You're safe here."

The night had risen up from the deeps of the earth and closed in around the cottage, soft and protective, as if the dark were a sea of safety and refuge and they here secure on an island of linen and pillows and woolen quilts. Pamela felt her anxiety ebb with the loss of the light and relaxed, breathing in Casey's scent, a thing that always calmed her body, even now with its coppery salt notes of blood.

He did say a great many sentimental things to both her and to the shifting mound of her belly, but none of them seemed the least bit silly. She stroked his back softly while he did so, watching the play of firelight on his body, the bruises and the weals of blood, and thought, not for the first time, that love was a strange and mysterious force and that the weight of it could feel like salvation or damnation, changing from minute to minute.

His voice became increasingly drowsy, the gaps between words longer with each half-phrase or sweetly mumbled tenderness. Outside was the world with all its troubles and violence, its heartache and loss, and the gut-wrenching fear she knew every time this man was gone from her for too long. But for now the firelight held them softly in its heat, gilding the bruises and hiding the worst of Casey's pain as well as her own tears.

"Go to sleep," she said softly. "I'll watch over you. The troubles will keep for tomorrow."

Chapter Seventy

July 1975

The Force That Through the Green Fuse...

THE SUMMER PASSED QUIETLY, WITH A STRANGE PEACE settling over their household. Sometimes Pamela felt as though they were in a state of suspension, a warm bath of happiness and ease.

Casey was healing up far quicker than she had expected when she first surveyed the severity of his injuries. His bruises were still visible but fading quickly under the ministrations of the sun. Two of his fingers were still splinted but with far less bandaging now. His ribs still caught him if he moved too swiftly or turned too sharply. Most importantly though, his spirit was intact and when she looked into his eyes he no longer looked away as he often had those first few days, when he had not wanted her to see the fear there. In typical fashion, he had found work restoring an old cottage three miles from their own for an American couple who planned to retire to Ireland.

She wondered if Pat had had a word with Casey, for when he had brought Conor to them he had gone into the bedroom with his brother and not come out for a good half hour. She had heard their two voices raised in anger and Pat reappeared looking things not lawful to be uttered. But after that Casey had agreed to stay the summer. She had not questioned it for fear he would change his mind.

The summer weather, in most un-Irish fashion, had been sublime and they had all turned nut brown in the sun, returning each night to the cottage, sandy, salty, sleepy and perfectly happy. Conor had taken to the sea with a vengeance, squealing in utter delight each time it hove into view. Casey, watching with a wry smile, had quirked a brow at her and said in a dry tone, "If he wasn't the spit of me, I would think ye'd been consortin' with a merrow, the way he loves the water."

One night after her men were asleep she had slipped quietly out of the house and down to the strand, lit by rippling shadows, as small clouds chased across the face of the moon. She waded into the water as far as she dared—her swimming abilities not quite what they normally were—and stood letting the salt water flow and ebb around her. Her body caught the rhythm of the sea and surged with it in tides of amniotic fluid. The entire planet this night seemed neither more nor less than a mother itself, a great womb, its tides akin to the blood that sluiced through her swollen veins, its salt the exact ratio of her own tears. It lapped against her skin, tracing the places her husband had left evidence of himself, the salt and musk of his body still lingering, making her body flush in remembrance and stretch with a satiety that felt utterly in tune with the night and the surge of the tide.

She felt sheltered, enfolded in the mystery of this oldest mother of all, the one that never abandoned her children, though she could treat them with the disdain of ten thousand furies. The concept of Earth as mother was not new, but it was the first time she had felt the bone-deep truth of it with every breath and each hot salt shimmer of blood that rushed in and out with the tide.

There were times she thought she caught a glimpse of this woman, an image caught deep in dreams but living always at the root of the female memory, held there in the cells and the spine, the heart and the womb, of the mother that cradled all and made of life a sacred, if difficult, thing. There was a rhythm to the earth, to the rain and the sun, that seemed purely female, a rhythm of fertility and rest, of the force that drove the green fuse through the flower, to paraphrase Dylan Thomas. It was a rhythm she felt herself when the baby moved or stretched in one of those watery balletic turns that made her body feel every bit of its oceanic makeup.

She had awakened this morning with a great restlessness in her limbs, remembering from the pregnancy with Conor that though it heralded the imminence of birth, it could also last several weeks. Nevertheless, she had craved movement and freedom, so when Peg came by offering to take Conor for the afternoon she jumped at the opportunity to leave the environs of the house and yard.

An oak wood lay not far from the cottage. Kerry was a mix of shore and wood, of ocean and thick greenery that grew rampant in the summer time. In spots, the rhododendrons filled up entire mountainsides, making them as impenetrable as a jungle.

Today, there was a heaviness in the air, as though it too were pregnant and filled to the brim with water and life. As she stepped out into the cottage yard, the scent of thyme and lavender, steeped in sunlight and humidity, flooded her senses. With it came the knowledge of the force that lay coiled at the root of every living thing that moved on two legs and four, things which swayed to the passing wind, to the patter of raindrops, and lay hushed under the winter snows, of all things being connected at their core as though everything had roots that stretched down to some central point in the earth.

Yet the forest was its own world, with its own secrets and hierarchies of life and drama. It was part of what she loved about her walks there, as though she had stepped into a realm separate from the one where she was behind on the laundry, hadn't seen her feet in three months and didn't know what to make for supper. For her it was like crossing from one country to another, where all the customs were different yet somehow deeply familiar.

The property was bounded on one side by a farmer's fields and low stone walls, on another by a small peaty-gold stream. The other two sides led out into small wildernesses where a person could walk without running across a trace of civilization—unless one counted the small holy well that was all but grown over with moss and the detritus of many seasons.

She had discovered the well early in the summer on one of her rambles and knew it was ancient, possibly one that had been consecrated to the Goddess rather than the newer Christian deities, or to Brigid, who was merely a newer face of the Goddess. That it had lain undiscovered for many years was apparent, but the sense of something *other* lingering in the air around it was not diminished by the years that had passed. Today she would go there, perhaps leave some small offering on behalf of her unborn child.

So with Finbar at her side, long nose stretched joyously into the air, she struck out west of the property where the boundaries of cultivated land soon gave way to moss and stone, the wicking of water and the slipping shadows of trees.

Today the forest seemed very still, as though the entire world within it paused at the approach of human feet. Music halted, breath stopped and wine, in the act of being poured, froze in midair. She sometimes had that feeling even in her own home when she had come in after chores or errands—a stillness that spoke of action abruptly halted, pipes and flutes stopped mid-note, and a curtain would flutter as though a light breeze had passed. It was not an ill feeling, rather that some*thing* existed side by side with them in the air and upon their land. And though to say that such presences were benign did not seem right, nor were they in any way malevolent. It was so with this wood as well.

She stepped deeper into the bottle green dim, stooping with care to pick the mallow that grew with such abandon this summer. Finbar bounded ahead of her joyously, picking up sticks and dropping them to bound onto the next one. High in the oaks the blackbirds were voicing shrill complaints at the intrusion.

She hummed to herself as she walked, secure in the knowledge that Conor was well looked after by Peg who, while not as grandmotherly as Gert, was genuinely fond of Conor and was happy to take him any time Pamela was willing to part with him for a few hours. Pamela wondered if she saw some echo of her Brendan in his small great-grandson's face.

A breeze fluttered by, moving the curls against her neck and providing a welcome coolness. It was humid in the wood, with the damp of all things green and the soft decay of fallen trees. A shimmer of silken pewter flashing in and out of the maidenhair ferns and the dappled hollows and mossy edges of long buried stones told her that Finbar was on the trail of some small creature.

She held her face up and took a deep breath, relishing the moisture. The mottled, watery light was soothing, relaxing something in her core that she hadn't been aware was tightly held. The scent and mystery of plants was nourishment to her soul. She felt at home with green things, aware however that they held their own counsel and secrets, whispered about in the night on wind and through water. She rarely felt more relaxed than she did in the company of plants.

It was good to move about without the constraints of yard or child—or husband, come to that. Casey had become particularly strict of late, insisting that she have a lie-down the minute he came through the door at night, while he started supper. Though that might be more in the way of self-preservation on the man's part, she thought, cooking not being her forté by any stretch of the imagination. Still, she enjoyed the wee bit of solitude a nap provided, for Conor was as busy a tot as Casey admitted he himself had been.

As glad as she would be to have this pregnancy successfully come to its end, still she had enjoyed this time with Conor and with Casey too. Two babies meant ten times as busy and distracted, at least that's what other mothers told her. Besides, and here she smiled softly to herself, her husband was the sort of man who truly appreciated a pregnant woman and her hormones. Mind you, it was not as if they were the sort of couple built for abstinence, pregnant or not.

Her musings were brought to a halt by a sharp bark from Finbar up ahead, invisible in the heavy foliage. A small spike of adrenaline shot through her. At this stage in her pregnancy, it was hard not to feel vulnerable to unexpected events. She moved toward the echo of the dog's bark, reverberating like a warning and thrumming at the base of her spine, a delicate ache that she only now realized had been there all morning. The sense of something *other* being present grew heavy again and she glanced about, a shiver threading its way down her spine and settling in with the ache. There was no one to be seen, but it wasn't the sense of human eyes watching that put the fine hairs up on the nape of her neck. She would find the dog and go home. A cup of tea was sounding far more sensible than a walk just at present.

Finbar was scrabbling at the roots of an enormous oak that stood alone in the midst of ash and elm. The floor of the forest here was smooth with moss and fern and the still, heavy light that seemed to come up from the ground rather than down from the sky. Fairy light, Casey would have said, and not that of good fairies either.

"Finbar," she said sternly, "come on, boy. We need to head home."

Like most males, Finbar had finely tuned selective hearing. All around his paws lay a welter of torn moss and black soil. He kept digging and whining, deep brown eyes looking up at her as if to ask why she didn't help if she was in such a tearing hurry to leave. Last time he had dug in this agitated fashion, he had emerged with a cow skull. She strode—as well as her belly would allow—over to him, only to have him back away from the hole he had dug and growl low in this throat, hackles up.

"What is it, boy?" Finbar had crowded close to her legs, a fine trembling apparent beneath his rough hide.

Where Finbar's paws had scrabbled, the turf was overturned, and underneath it lay a flat stone. She bent over to look, for there were strange markings on it, cut deeper into the rock than any scratch Finbar could possibly have inflicted. She lowered herself awkwardly to the ground, hoping she would be able to get back up. She ran her fingers over the damp, cool surface, feeling the pebbled dirt roll into the crevices of her palm, her fingertips easing into deeply scored lines that held no random shape. She looked more closely, bending sideways to avoid the great mound of her stomach. The carved lines looked human in shape, crude, but with the definite outlines of arms and legs and head with a burst of hair. A woman, from what she could make out, a woman pregnant like herself, for where the midriff ought to be was a great round of belly. She wondered briefly if this had been some sort of fertility stone, where women came to offer sacrifices during times of barrenness. She touched the woman's belly, noting that the center held a deep hollow. No sooner had her finger traced the bowl, than she felt a sharp pain in her own belly, deep and low, striking with a hard resonation like iron against a bell.

She took in a breath, a small shot of panic echoing through her, spreading its dark sibilation in her blood. Surely not *now*—she had a couple of weeks yet to go, though Conor's birth had been early and precipitate. She sat on the ground, focusing on taking several deep breaths and praying there would be no more pains, or that the next one would be greatly lessened in strength.

She closed her eyes, turning inward, feeling her way toward the center to see if she would know if it truly was time or if she could get up in a few minutes, damp and green-streaked in places but little worse for the wear.

All she could sense for certain was that she was in a great deal of trouble if this was the real thing. It was a good mile back to the house, Casey wasn't due home for some time yet and Peg fully expected her to be absent for several hours.

"Alright, Pamela," she chided herself aloud, setting off a cloud of rooks, swooshing from the treetops in startlement. Beyond that the forest was unnervingly still, as though it were waiting for something. She tilted up onto one hip, the ground soft and damp beneath her, and made it to her knees before the next pain hit with the force of a wave. This was definitely the real thing, one of those bone-tearing pains that made you remember exactly what was so difficult about giving birth. It was then that her water broke, spilling between her legs onto the ground.

A terrible panic engulfed her, her entire body shaking from head to toe with utter and complete terror. What if something went wrong? There was no way to get help. It wouldn't matter how loudly she screamed in the next few hours, no one was likely to hear, unless someone was out for a walk in the woods.

Women had given birth alone before and survived it. She was young, in good health, and strong, all things in her favor, yet these things seemed of very little comfort at present.

She managed to crawl to the base of the large oak tree under which there was a broad space, soft with moss, sheltered by the tree's great branches.

"Oaks for protection," she muttered to herself, thinking any wee bit of superstition or myth that might help her now was more than welcome.

She took the cardigan she wore off and spread it on the ground, sat upon it and braced her back against the trunk of the tree, easing herself to the edge of her sweater and pulling her knees up toward her body, praying with every fiber of her being that the baby was still the right way round. She took several deep breaths, steadying herself between contractions, striving with every last cell not to give in to the panic that waited to engulf her like a rogue wave and pull her out into the great ocean of terror that awaited her if she gave in.

Her vision seemed oddly delineated, as though the trees had been cut to loom large as in a stage set for some dark and forbidding scene in a Wagnerian opera. The clouds above ran in long shreds and the lovely, mild summer day looked to be brewing itself up for a nasty storm. Sweat was trickling through her hair now, gluing her dress to her body and making the tree slippery behind her.

She knew the fear of death was never far off during labor, but that small bit of knowledge did little to comfort her in her current predicament. Because she was all too aware that under such unsanitary conditions, without help, the odds of something going awry were much higher.

She didn't notice the rain when it began to fall until it had built up enough force that it ran in small streams down her face and trickled into her open mouth. It was a relief, the cool taste of it, for she was as parched as though she were crossing a desert. Desperate sobs sounded in her ears and she could hardly understand that it was she making those noises.

The pain was like lightning now, with little space between strikes. Her backbone felt as if it were breaking. She pushed her heels hard into the soil, feeling the moment nearing, the urge to push irresistible now, accompanied by that terrible burning that told her the baby was crowning.

Where was Casey? Why wasn't he here? Damn the man for not knowing what was happening. If she were to die and leave the baby here alone, how long could it survive? She couldn't judge anymore how long she had been laboring and the storm had darkened the sky so she couldn't tell by the light or the lack of it.

"*CASEY RIORDAN YOU BASTARD!!*" she yelled, finding some small relief in the yelling yet wanting to break down and sob for him as well, wishing he was here with the rain lashing them both so he could hold her hand and tell her all would be well. Even if that was a lie, because the man could make her believe all *would* be well just by his presence and strength.

Suddenly there were hands on her own, cool and dry, and a face swam into her fevered vision. A woman with a face wondrously calm and smooth. She had warm brown eyes that Pamela thought she could fall into, would happily fall into if only this pain would cease.

"Another minute and it will all be over. Just look in my eyes," the woman said, in a voice so soothing that Pamela immediately felt a calm descend over her. There was a strange sensation emanating from the woman's palms and pouring into her own blood. She was certain there was something odd about this personage, but was too distracted to understand what it was. Nor did she particularly care, for it seemed the woman knew what to do, and having another human being there was a great comfort.

Time abandoned her, minutes blurred into an agony that seemed eons in the making. There was only the primal struggle that took one across the boundary between life and death and reduced everything in the universe to bare essentials. She could hear the woman's voice, encouraging her, reassuring her that only a few more pushes would see this child into the world. All the world was this ring of fiery pain and all she wanted was to come out the other side of it.

Her body strained to the point of breaking and suddenly there was the precipitous drop in pressure and pain... and the small sounds of the newly born.

"Tis a girl. I'm goin' to wrap her up in my coat an' then go for help."

The woman used her own mouth to clear the baby's nose and laid her on Pamela's stomach, the cord between mother and daughter still pulsating with life. Pamela reached down a hand, shaky with relief and fear and the heady exhilaration of having just given birth, and touched the small, firm body of her daughter.

She looked up at the woman, a question written plainly on her face.

The woman nodded. "She's fine—healthy an' a good weight. Now stay ye still with yer wee lass an' I'll be back as quick as I can."

Exhausted and bloody, with the fragrance of birth heavy in the air around them, Pamela settled herself, with her daughter snug to her chest, against the bulwark of the tree to wait for help to arrive.

She didn't want to uncover the baby, for the breeze that blew had a cool edge. But her wee face poked out of the coat, perfect as a petal, framed in hair that was dark and slick with amniotic fluid. Pamela suspected when it dried it would wisp into a corona of curls just like Casey's. Then the baby opened her mouth small face bunching up like a tiny wrinkled cabbage and let go a howl that shook the birds from the trees. Her lungs were healthy to be certain, and wee feminine self notwithstanding, she had the look of her father about her.

Above the wind had settled, the sun came out again, dazzling the raindrops into diamonds while the leaves overhead swayed gently. For a moment, just a second, she thought she saw the face there, outlines shimmering in the air, of the mother of all—a face indescribably old and equally as beautiful. And she gave profound thanks to that force, the very root of life itself, which had delivered this particular flower safely through the green fuse of life.

CASEY RIORDAN ARRIVED HOME TO FIND THE PLACE BUSTLING with females. Peg and a woman he did not recognize were busy in the wee kitchen, the scent of a trout baking and potatoes steaming on the air. His heart had been in his throat since Father Terry had come to find him and tell him that he was a father once again, his wife having given birth in the middle of the bloody forest.

At the sight of his raised eyebrow and tentative greeting, Peg said, "She's in the bedroom an' all is well. Go on through, man."

Heart thumping hard, he entered the room to find his wife sitting up against well-plumped pillows, head bent in rapt absorption over a tiny bundle. Conor was snuggled into his mother's side, eyes wide with wonder.

His eyes met Pamela's and he shook his head. "Jaysus woman, yer goin' to give me a heart attack with yer antics one of these days, ye know that?"

She smiled, face drawn with exhaustion but lit from within by that distinctive glow new mothers always wore.

"Come and meet your daughter," she said quietly, moving the blanket away from the baby's face.

"My daughter?" he queried and went to kneel by the bed.

There were no signs on the baby of her dramatic entrance into the world. She was the color of a pink pearl, delicately flushed, hair a tiny corona of black curls. She finished eating with a small smacking sound and a tiny hand came up out of the blanket, waving about as though she sensed a new arrival. Pamela handed Casey the small, red-wrapped bundle.

"Here she is, Daddy."

Casey held his daughter close to his chest, the warm, soft weight of her dispelling the last of his fear.

"D'ye think just once, ye might try givin' birth in a hospital with a doctor to hand?" he asked in the aggrieved tone of a man who never could expect to find his wife in the place where he had left her.

"I hardly planned it this way," Pamela retorted, "but all turned out well. Oh, look, her eyes are open."

Casey looked down and found himself gazing into the darkest, most beautiful eyes he'd ever seen. The baby was squinting at him—in the way that newborns do, her small mouth a round 'O' as she cooed at him.

"Oh, an' who's a love then, angel?" Casey cooed back.

"That's you done for, man," Pamela said, smiling at the picture of her big husband and wee daughter.

"Well, look at her, will ye? No man will ever stand a chance. We make awfully beautiful babies if I do say so myself."

He gathered Conor onto his knee with his free hand, tucking him in snugly next to his sister, wanting him to know he had not been forgotten in the excitement.

"Well, laddie, what d'ye think of yer wee sister?"

"She's aw'fly small," Conor said, looking dubiously at the tiny creature on his father's arm.

Casey smiled down at his son's tousled head. "Aye, she's small now, but before ye know it, she'll be big enough to play with ye."

Conor looked up at his father with doubt written plain on his features that so small a creature could ever be counted upon to play, and then slid off his knee with the pronouncement, "I's hungry," and headed off to the kitchen where he knew the women would feed him.

"D'ye think we ought to call a doctor in, just to be certain yerself an' the baby are alright?" he asked.

"No, we're both fine. The woman who found me in the forest is the local midwife. You will have seen her in the kitchen. What are the odds that she would be out walking in the woods at the same time I was? She's checked both Isabelle and me out and we're fine."

Isabelle had been a long ago ancestor of Casey's, and Pamela had picked it out as the only name she wanted should the baby be a girl.

"Look at us, will ye?" he said softly, for the baby was asleep again in that abrupt way newborns have, eyelids of domed pearl closed tight against the world in which she had so abruptly arrived. "All domesticated."

Pamela's eyes met his and held. There were words that could be said, but did not need to be spoken aloud, for their shared understanding was such as to make it unnecessary. It had not always been an easy journey, this marriage of theirs, but it had been worth every step taken to have brought them here to this place.

He leaned forward and kissed her, breathing in her scent in all its complexity; the fresh green of it, the sweet milkiness of motherhood and the salt notes of extreme physical exertion.

She took his hand in her own and he knew she felt his fear, the worry of what giving birth alone and stranded in the woods might have resulted in.

"It's alright, Casey," she laughed shakily. "I wouldn't choose to do it that way again, but it's alright now."

"Yer the point on which this universe of ours turns, Jewel—don't ye forget it."

"I won't. Same goes for you, man."

He squeezed her hand and leaned his forehead against her own. Between them, the baby snorted in her sleep and pursed her lips as though in disapproval. Around them the evening settled in, warm and safe, beating at its core with the heart of this, the life they had created together.

Chapter Seventy-one

August 1975

Summer's End

PAT SPENT THE SUMMER LIVING AT CASEY AND PAMELA'S HOUSE, telling himself it was easier to tend to the animals and the garden and house if he simply lived there. Notwithstanding the fact that Lewis and Owen had assured him they could divide the chores between them if he wanted to get back to Belfast and his life there. The truth was, part of the attraction of staying on the premises was the proximity to Kate's home. Not that he could visit her, not that he dared visit her, but more often than not she found a way to the house in the hollow several times a week. Though her brother disapproved of her friendship with Pamela, still he didn't outright forbid it. A friendship with himself, Pat knew, was likely to be another matter altogether. Though were he being scrupulously honest with himself, he wasn't sure what he and Kate had was, strictly speaking, a friendship. He had plenty of time to think about it, being that he was lucky to find one functioning channel on his brother's television and the radio was almost as quixotic in its reception. He had managed to distract himself a couple of evenings by reading a volume of fairytales that appeared to have been written by Jamie. Other than that, he found his mind wasn't willing to be diverted from its preferred course, which appeared to have settled itself around Kate.

She was, he thought, the most maddening woman he had ever met. Stubborn to a degree that even he and his brother might have baulked at, headstrong, frustrating, pushy and with an extremely firm opinion on her at all times. Oh, the woman could hold her tongue when she wanted to put a freeze on a man, but she rarely deigned to keep it still otherwise. She had the Fair Housing Office working with an efficiency that would soon render him obsolete and she had sorted him out here too as to regular meals, ironed clothing and adequate sleep. And yet—and here was where the damned honesty with himself came in—he didn't seem to be leaving or telling her to mind her own business and let him be.

He was rather sad that the summer was coming to an end, in fact, as it would put paid to their quiet evenings in Casey and Pamela's house. He did miss his brother and Pamela, especially wee Conor and now, Miss Isabelle, but their return would change things.

He had taken Kate with him to visit the new baby one Saturday and they had a lovely day of it, wandering the shore with the wee family and endlessly admiring the baby. They had stayed to dinner and the talk had flowed easily around the table, well peppered with laughter and the music of the two women's voices and the sweet cooing of the baby. Casey was a good father and Conor went to his Daddy as often as his Mam, but watching Casey with Isabelle was something else altogether, for the man was utterly and totally besotted with his beautiful baby girl. Pat was vastly relieved that his brother had healed up and was entirely back in his own skin, both physically and emotionally. Watching all of them, healthy, happy and whole, he thought it was a pity, much as he would miss them, that they didn't stay there in Kerry forever.

The two brothers found themselves alone in the kitchen after dinner. Pamela was rocking an overly stimulated Conor to sleep and Kate was cuddling Isabelle. Casey and Pat were doing the washing up.

So well did Patrick know his brother that he only waited for the raised eyebrow in his direction before saying, "Don't be after makin' too much of it. I only asked her to come down because she was mad to visit the baby."

"I didn't say a thing," Casey protested, though not with a great deal of vehemence.

"No, but yer thinkin' it."

"Yer as bad as Pamela, thinkin' ye know every thought that flits through my head."

"In this case, I do know," Pat said, "so don't be thinkin' I've got some grand romance goin'. We're just friends."

"Then ye'd best be careful, boyo, because she's not lookin' at yerself as though yer merely a pal."

"She's not," Pat said with some irritation, "lookin' at me at all."

Casey flicked soapsuds in his brother's direction. "Ye know what I mean, ye wee smartarse."

Pat did not reply, for he was beginning to be aware that Kate's feelings were not entirely platonic. But he wasn't sure if he was ready to face just what that meant, for he could not think of a woman in that way without seeing Sylvie in his mind's eye and the price she had paid for loving him. Casey, sensing his discomfort, had dropped the subject and continued to wash the dishes, chatting mildly about the garden, the weather and the children.

Only his brother's words could not be unspoken, and they had stayed in his mind ever since. It was at times such as these that he missed his father. Truth be told he missed the man always, but especially when he wanted Brian there to tell him what to do. Not that his father would have, but he might have led a man in the right direction. After a certain age Brian had told both of his sons, *'If yer askin' for my permission, ye don't need it any longer. If yer askin' for my approval, ye won't necessarily get it.'*

It was a night a few weeks after their visit to Kerry. Kate had not been in to work that day as she stayed at the farm on Fridays through the weekend. He often wondered how she explained her days in the city, but she didn't speak of it so he did not ask. Sometimes this summer, she would be waiting for him on those Friday evenings, seated neatly outside the door on the bench under the overhang of the porch where Casey sat to remove his dirty workboots, or in the barn fussing over that demon horse, Phouka, who seemed to be only slightly less enamored with Kate than he was with Pamela.

A storm was coming in when he got home, the air near to crackling with it. He could feel it all along his nerve endings, like quicksilver chasing in rivulets over his skin. The bench beside the porch overhang was empty and he felt a pang of disappointment. Perhaps she would not come this evening. It wasn't as though they had a standing appointment, after all.

He fed and watered the animals, which went some way toward alleviating the hum in his body that he told himself was entirely due to the impending weather. There was a homely comfort in mixing Paudeen's feed and tending to Phouka's stall. Phouka was grazing in Mr. Guderson's field and would only be in for the night. Rusty followed him about the entire time, meowing and generally making a feline nuisance of himself.

Inside he made himself eggs and sausage for dinner, looking out the window every few minutes to check, he told himself, the advance of the storm. The wind had picked up considerably and the clouds on the horizon were black outlined in silver. It was going to be a terrible one. He was going to have to catch that demon, Phouka, and put him up in the barn.

Phouka, like the bad fairy for whom he had been named, proved very hard to catch and cantered around the field neighing and kicking his heels up. The rain broke just as Pat, sweating and swearing, got him into the barn and settled for the night. The horse gave one long last whinny as Pat shut the barn door and then the rain broke in a deluge so thick that he could hardly see across the yard. The dash to the house was enough to leave him dripping in the entryway beyond the porch.

He stripped off his shirt and pants in the boot room and dried down with the towel Pamela left there for the purpose. There was an old flannel shirt of Casey's hanging on a hook and he shrugged it on over his damp skin. He put on clean blue jeans and filled the kettle, thinking he should probably do some reading as outdoor work was going to be out of the question for the rest of the night. It was dark as the underside of a nun's habit out there already and the rain pounded the earth, the sound echoing back up like a thousand military drums. His skin still felt as though quicksilver ran beneath it, crackling and dividing, making him as restless as the trees and animals. He reached for his books nonetheless, a good hour of reading about torts law ought to bleed the restlessness right out of him. He was only just settled so when several things happened at once.

Thunder boomed so loudly it rattled the thatch of the roof. Rusty bolted hissing off the kitchen sofa, tripping Pat, who had risen from his chair, as he shot across the floor. Pat knocked his head hard on a post. The lights went out and there was a knock on the porch door. He was clutching his head, biting down on calling the cat several unflattering names as he opened the door. Through the haze of pain in his head he saw Kate, clutching a bag to her chest. The light outside was blue and she was outlined as though someone had taken a luminous pen to her and drawn her bold against the wild night. He pulled her in, and slammed the door behind her. Her very arm seemed to hum with the storm's electricity where he touched her.

He was as blind as Kate in the dark that clapped down inside the house but he took her by the hand and guided her carefully into the kitchen. He rummaged about, stubbing his toes and cursing under his breath, until he found the box of candles his brother kept handy for emergencies and lit a few of them, scattering them around the kitchen.

"Are ye mad, out in the storm like this? How the hell did ye get here?" he asked, an irrational wave of anger washing over him at her foolhardiness. "Come sit by the Aga an' I'll get ye some towels."

"I walked," she said simply.

"On yer own?"

"Yes."

Looking at the white set of her face, he decided that calling her a damn fool woman could wait, even though he felt sick at the thought of her out in the storm, unable to see more than the most basic outlines of things. He got the towels for her, keeping back one to blot at his own head, which appeared to be bleeding—damn that cat anyway, and himself having just climbed a treacherous elm two nights past to rescue him.

"I was goin' to have some tea. I'll make ye some to take the chill out of ye."

"I'd prefer something stronger, if ye have it," she said, head coming out of the thick folds of the towel like a woodland flower emerging from the soil. He noted that her customary brusqueness was absent. He poured a couple of inches of Connemara Mist into one of the crystal whiskey tumblers Pamela kept out on the sideboard, handed the tumbler to her and watched as she swallowed it down in one go. Apparently the woman was not in a sipping frame of mind.

"Once more, if ye wouldn't mind," she said and held out her glass. Pat refilled it and, placing the bottle on the table, sat down across from her. She swallowed this one just as quickly and took a deep breath, her eyes hidden in the chancy light of the candles.

"Will ye want to talk about what's upset ye?" he asked, wondering what on earth had finally managed to discombobulate the woman.

"No, I don't. Suffice it to say I've had a wee bit of a falling out with my brother."

Pat quailed inwardly at the thought of what a 'wee bit of a falling out' with Noah Murray might consist of.

"About what?" he asked, though he knew with a fair degree of certainty what it was they had disagreed over.

"'Tis of no matter, an' that's not why I've come here."

"No?"

"No. I—I—" she stuttered slightly and Pat raised an eyebrow. The woman truly was addled tonight. It must have been a regular donnybrook with her brother.

"I should like to stay the night, if that's alright. An' yes, before ye ask, I do mean what ye think I mean by that."

Pat felt as though he had been hit hard in the solar plexus. He had not expected that of all things.

"How would ye explain that to yer brother?" he asked and his voice was gruff enough to make her flinch.

"I told him I'm staying in town tonight with our cousin. He's too angry to check, but if he does, she knows to say that I'm there but not willin' to speak to him."

He put a hand to the table to steady himself, feeling as if there were not adequate oxygen in the house.

"Patrick, I know how you felt about your wife. I'm not trying to replace her, nor make you feel such for me. I just want this night with you before the summer is over, that's all."

"That's all, is it?" he said softly, but inside his heart was hammering and he felt lightheaded. "I—I'll need a minute, Kate," he said, feeling as if the walls were closing in around him.

She nodded, but he could see the hurt in her face, as though her lack of sight had left her without the ability to hide what she felt.

He stood, realizing he was still only half-dressed, shirt unbuttoned, feet bare. He walked outside, stepping off the porch into the torrential rain, drumming hard into his skin. He put his hands to his head, trying to find his breath. He was reeling from her words and the effect they had on him. He wanted her—aye, he had known that from almost the first time he met her, though he had not been able to admit it, but the thought of bedding another woman—a woman who was not Sylvie—stopped him cold. Yet, where the hell had he thought this was leading? The nights by the fire, the meals together, working side by side each day, their walks in the woods with him guiding her every step though he well knew she did not need the help. He had been aware of her as a woman right from the start. She had been much more than a stranger he had met at Pamela and Casey's house one winter's afternoon.

He put his head against the stone wall of the house, letting the rain sluice down the back of his shirt, wishing it would cool the fever in his skin but knowing it would not. He swallowed, his chest tight with desire. Aye, he wanted her all right, as badly as he had ever wanted anything in his life. But did he have the right, even if she was willing? The look on her face cut him to the quick, and he knew he had hurt her far more than he had ever thought he could. It wasn't realistic to think that he could remain celibate for the rest of his life, as much as the idea had appealed in the wake of Sylvie's death. If he said no tonight, he knew there was no way they could go on, as if she had never offered herself to him in this way. Kate's rather brutal honesty simply wouldn't allow for that. It took the wind from him entirely to think of never seeing her again. But that, he was all too well aware, did not justify taking a step such as this if he wasn't ready.

And then he heard it, his father's voice in his head, a memory culled from the depths by need.

'Love is rarer than ye think, laddie. It's a gift, an' if the universe sees fit to present ye with it more than the once, well then, count yerself as truly blessed an' grab it with both hands.'

His own voice then, still in his head, but coming from the depths of his soul.

Sylvie... Sylvie... Sylvie... please understand... please let me go... I have to keep living...

She was still seated by the fire, pale as the driven snow but with two streaks of clear deep pink flaring in her cheeks. She was brave, this Kate, for she met his eyes as he entered the house, his body soaked with the cold rain, and he knew she saw him clearly in the only way that truly mattered between two people. He went to her silently and knelt on the floor at her feet. He took one slim hand in his own and put it to his chest so that she might feel his heart beat and know what her words had done to him. She left her hand where he placed it and with the other turned his face up toward her own. Her hand slid along his jawline, soft as down, and her fingers curled into his wet hair as she bent her head toward his. The quicksilver beneath his skin ignited, flooding through his body, setting fire to his blood.

"Trust me," she said softly against his mouth.

And so he did.

Chapter Seventy-two
Times Gone and Still to Come...

CASEY LOVED THE WALK HOME FROM THE HOUSE he was working on each night, even when the weather wasn't as fine as it was this evening. He liked the time to review bits of the day, to go over the plans once again in his head, to think of the pleasing heft of the stone and the warp of the wood and how it satisfied something deep in his soul to build something, to see something go up instead of being blown down. He thought it fair to say he had not missed his wee, hard city this summer.

It was his favorite time of year, August, when everything was rich and heavy, ripe in the fields, awaiting harvest and the longer, cooler nights. The hedgerows rustled in the breeze and he could smell rose petals that had tumbled to the wind somewhere nearby. Living here in the west for the summer had been an exercise filled with memory for him, as he had always spent his summers in the west as a boy, summers that were now held in an amber haze in his memory, fixed and perfect in their lineaments.

There had been a summer that his father could not come out to the country with them and so they had gone alone, himself and his brother—himself fifteen at the time and Patrick, eleven. They had lived in an old cottage stranded high on a mountainside where the mist wrapped around them before the light left the sky and didn't clear off until late the next day. They lived off the land, snaring rabbits, occasionally stealing milk from the cow in the field at the foot of the mountain and growing a wee garden themselves because he had to—even then—plant something, nourish it and bring it to fullness.

They lived in perfect isolation, with the wind and rain, the sun and the stars, so close to the earth and the sky that they lost sense of being something separate from it. Thoughts there were huge, too big to be real, so you let them go with the clouds and the wind, and savored the lingerings of them sweet in your chest. They had read books by candlelight, told each other blood curdling stories and then regretted it until the dawn broke the dark of the night. They had talked about dreams, both those that were realistic and those that they had understood, even then, weren't likely to come true.

Women had been a theory, a dream that summer, not a reality but something perfect, lovely and transient as angels and the scent of flowers in a meadow. They had talked about what they wanted in a girl, what they hoped for and what they thought the shape of their lives with such a woman might be. Truth be known, he would have been happy with anyone halfway decent looking, under the age of thirty and over the age of fifteen, as long as she came equipped with breasts.

Now he knew that women were like a road, beckoning a man on to somewhere grand, over the next hill to a horizon that may or may not exist, may or may not be a blessing. They were earth under a man's feet and sun thick as honey on his shoulders. His woman though, ah, his woman was like the sea that she so loved. She was depths so deep he could not find the limit of them. She was mystery and shifting light and soul restoring dark. She was movement and change and sometimes he longed to drown in her—and sometimes he was terrified of doing just that.

He paused at the edge of the garden to watch her now, their wee girl in her arms while she displayed enormous interest in the rather large snail Conor was showing her. Never once, even during that enchanted summer so long ago, did he imagine a woman such as this, nor did he have the faintest idea how much one could love a woman. He did now. He could feel her awareness of him and knew she had sensed his presence, turned her thoughts to him as naturally as a flower toward the sun, sensing before sighting. He walked across the field toward her.

Conor tumbled pell-mell at him, and he swept him up into his arms before the child fell. Conor was like himself, trying to run before he could properly walk. He smelled of grass and dirt and water, and Casey breathed him in, grateful for the solid warmth of his son. Isabelle was already squeaking, aware that her Daddy had arrived home, wanting his attention for herself. She was a tyrant—a wee, gorgeous tyrant—for whom he was an utter slave, and he would have it no other way.

His wife smiled in greeting and raised her face to him, emerald eyes soft as the sun that misted down around them, and he leaned in to kiss her, to put his hand upon her and lose himself as he always did with her, as she, in her turn, did with him.

And he knows, given the choice, he will choose to drown every time.

Part Eleven

Belfast, For My Sins
Ireland – September-November 1975

Chapter Seventy-three

September 1975

The Trustees

THE HALL IN WHICH THEY MET WAS OLD AND DRAFTY, with a low ceiling and a stink that was made up of the component parts of wet wool, male sweat, cigarette smoke and one that David could only identify as that of hatred. It underlay everything that was done and said in these meetings and he swore it lingered in his nose for the entire week after.

Tonight, the smell was especially pernicious. The hall was dim, lit only with candles arrayed around the room and stabbed into sconces on the walls. It gave the building the feeling of an unholy Sabbat... which was what it was, more or less, he suspected. There was a heightened tension in the room that told him this was not the ordinary bi-weekly meeting of the murder club, as he had come to think of it. Even the night outside had a spooky feel to it, the way nights in autumn sometimes did. For if the veil between this world and that was at its thinnest this time of year, then it surely allowed as much evil to drift across as good. David gave himself a shake, thinking he had lived too long in this country and was becoming as superstitious as an old woman descended directly from the Celts.

He pinched the bridge of his nose and sighed inaudibly. Coming here always gave him a headache.

Around him were arrayed bankers and teachers, civil servants and men whose only occupation seemed to be that of hired killer. Each wore an air of expectancy, and David wondered just what or whom they were waiting for tonight?

A reading of the previous meeting's minutes, as ridiculous as they were, brought a note of reality into the hall, and David relaxed enough to let his mind wander.

This assignment was going to cost him, regardless of what he had thought going in. A man could not see this much ugliness, could not be touched by it in the way he had, and remain unaffected. If indeed it didn't outright kill him.

He didn't know how much longer he could hold Boyd off either. He could hardly pretend to be some virgin schoolboy untouched by the world, and to fend off the man's advances was becoming more and more difficult. He had awakened four nights previous to find the man sitting on the side of his bed, his hand under the blankets, fingers groping about the strings of David's pyjama bottoms. David had barely restrained himself from hitting him across the face and then choking him to death. He had been well trained in all the arts of both defense and offense, and could have accomplished the task given five minutes. But killing the man would most certainly blow his cover. So he had lain there in the dark, allowing the man to touch him, to fondle and grasp, all the time hearing the man's breath shorten and tighten, and feeling a revulsion so deep within him that he was afraid the taint of it would stay, like poison in a well.

There was a weight to such things, he knew. The way stones dropped into a bucket eventually displaced the water within, so such things displaced a man's humanity, drop by drop, until one day feeling did not come so easily as it once had. David had always thought the lack of feeling was weakness rather than strength, because it bled a man until he no longer knew right from wrong, or perhaps worse yet, no longer cared for the difference. For himself it had always been an occupational hazard, and he had guarded against it. Only lately it had not been so easy. But that was the smaller picture, the personal one he kept within a locket, rarely opened.

The broader picture, the one that had him here tonight was a movement that lacked any sort of vision. The Republicans had their messianic core of a united country, of a right denied for hundreds of years. The Loyalists had no such thing. They had fear and anger, disguised as bravado and domination. There was no coherency and so the movement was propelled by all the wrong things: self-interest, money, power, prestige and revenge—all of which provided the perfect recipe for schisms without number. This particular schism was bound by blood, and by keeping secrets that David was certain were going to turn his own hair white.

The talking had ceased and David pulled his mind back to the present. A man entered, accompanied by a cold breeze, as though premonition followed him as closely as a forked tail followed its chosen demon. David shivered despite the close and fetid atmosphere of the building.

He had never seen a man so pale, so lacking in that indefinable thing that made a person human and recognizable as such. He moved, he breathed, and David had to assume that there was blood flowing through his veins, but it wasn't apparent on his surface. Jamie had warned him about the Reverend, but even Jamie's rather unflattering portrait of the man had not prepared David for the reality. Here was the one man who could bring cohesion to this movement, a cohesion in which all parties were bound by hatred and mired in the past, but cohesion nonetheless. It was, in part, what David feared about him.

The Reverend certainly knew how to speak the language of this particular tribe. From a whisper of brimstone to a high-pitched hiss, this man could gather people into the palm of his lily-white hand and make them move to his commands. David supposed evil had its attractions, though for himself revulsion was all he felt in this man's presence. Revulsion and fear.

David had grown so used to rhetoric that he only half heard the words until a name leapt out at him with the force of a hammer right between the eyes.

"...We're going to attack Noah Murray's farm," the Reverend said, white face aglow with a very special sort of pleasure. David felt sick. Sick and stunned, to be fully accurate. The man must be insane. Noah Murray was the most feared godfather that the Republican world had, and for good reason. David had seen the results of the man's handiwork twice now, and neither was an image he was likely to banish from his mind, ever.

"Noah Murray is the beating heart of the IRA in South Armagh and we need to rip that beating heart out and crush it beneath our heels in order for the Fenian bastards to understand we mean business. Our Protestant brothers in South Armagh have lived under the chill of his evil shadow for too long now."

The man was mad. There was no denying it, and yet it seemed that he, David, was the only person in the room who was disturbed by his rhetoric and fanaticism.

"Only so many of us can fulfill this mission. The men who do this must be chosen carefully, for their loyalty, for their commitment to the cause of freedom for Loyalist Ulster, for their understanding of the blood sacrifice of our ancestors on British battlefields. After careful prayer and contemplation I have chosen the men who will take on this sacred mission." He paused for effect and David felt as though the room paused with him, the very molecules of the air halting to wait for his pronouncement.

The names dropped one by one, blood into a living pool of men. He felt relief in some as their names were not called, jubilation in others as their names were spoken in that soft, sibilant voice, insistent as the snake in Eden. Then he heard the words he had not thought to ever hear.

"Davey MacNee."

The Reverend's eyes, as blank as the center of a dead star, met his own, and David knew that he was going to have to be very lucky indeed to survive this mission.

Twelve of them in the end, like the disciples. Only it was not their leader who would be the ultimate sacrifice, but themselves. He understood why he had been included. He understood that the Reverend was not fooled by his cover. He understood he would have to go anyway. Lenny's name had been spoken too, and David knew this was no coincidence. The moment of reckoning had come. He stood with the other chosen—or damned, as it were—and waited for what came next, knowing it wouldn't be pleasant. It wasn't.

Held in the Reverend's pale, fine-boned hand, the knife glowed, reflecting like a slice of starlight in the basin of water that was placed below it. David swallowed. They were going to sign their pledges in the most lasting ink of all—blood. A blade of fear sliced through his belly. He would have to do it, there was no way out of this sickening ritual. God knew he had done worse in the name of his job.

The candle flames threw out long shadows, thick on the air, so that each man became a looming monster against the smoke-blackened walls. Perhaps they all were monsters, David thought, himself included. Monsters in the guise of ordinary men.

His turn came all too soon. The Reverend took his hand, gripping it tightly, the lightless eyes boring into his own. David felt sick, and as though he wore a mask that was slipping sideways off his face, revealing his truth to this man. The Reverend had dipped the knife in the water and raised it now to score David's hand, but it was not the small cut each man before him had endured. Rather the Reverend cut him to the bone on his palm, the cut long and flowing with blood.

"I'm sorry, the knife slipped," the Reverend said, his smile stating that it had been anything but a mistake. David merely clutched his hand around the blood and pain and said nothing. He signed his name to the covenant and left the requisite blood beside it. Nauseated by the pain and the insanity of what these men had just pledged themselves to, he felt as if time had shifted, and it was hundreds of years ago, with war bristling on the borders, and the land soon to be washed in blood. Only it would be guns and bombs rather than swords and the hangman's noose that made it flow. He felt very small and ineffectual in the face of such hatred.

Lenny was standing beside him, grinning that horrible death's head grin of his.

"Hurt, Davey-boy?"

"Not a bit," David said, though his hand ached as if it had been jointed neatly as a Christmas ham. His arm was slick with blood up to the elbow already.

"You can go now," the Reverend said, his voice so cold it was like ice spreading out geometrically along every nerve ending in David's body.

Their eyes held and David did not blink, but nor did the Reverend. For a moment, the man let him see what lay behind the façade of his preaching, his rhetoric, his pale, cool demeanor.

David turned and left, knowing the man watched him until he was out of sight. His gaze was like a shiv, sharp and cold in David's spine.

He caught his breath on the pain in his hand as he walked out of the building and up the road. He was out in the cold in more ways than one. It had never been in his mandate to get involved in quite this manner. He was under no direct orders, and was largely considered off the grid. There would be no backup, no one who knew where he was or where to look if he disappeared entirely off the face of the planet. He couldn't even tell the people dearest to him in the world, for fear of involving them and bringing a rain of fire down on their heads along with his own. He had long known it, had left a letter in Pamela's keeping, to be delivered to the small grey farmhouse at the end of the crooked lane if he should someday go missing, though he had never felt the possibility of it as viscerally as he did this moment.

He recalled a long ago conversation with James Kirkpatrick. The man had fixed him with that light-spilling gaze over the top of a tumbler of whiskey.

"All spies are whores, David. It's just the method that varies. Only you can decide when you're in danger of losing your soul to it. Only you can decide when the price becomes too high."

David stopped at the verge of a laneway, and looked up into the sky. The night was so very big, the sky dark as Hell's own basement. His day of reckoning was here, and he thought perhaps the price was, indeed, too high.

Chapter Seventy-four

September 1975

A History of Ashes

THE CALL CAME IN THE NIGHT, one of those three o'clock in the morning phone calls where one's heart leaped directly into one's throat at the thought of what a ringing phone could portend at such an hour.

Casey shot out of the bed with the reflexes of a father who dreads his small tyrannical daughter awakening. Inevitably, as he ran down the stairs to the kitchen where the telephone pealed on shrilly, another sort of call, equally piercing entered the fray. Pamela, adrenaline coursing like thoroughbred racehorses through her system, got up and fetched her small, angry daughter from her crib.

Casey didn't return until Isabelle had been changed, and had been nursed enough to alter her furious cries to soft coos. Pamela burped her, rocking her back to sleep, her small downy head on her mother's shoulder. Casey had banked the fire in the bedroom's hearth before they had gone to sleep, but Pamela felt a terrible chill nevertheless.

The look on Casey's face did little for the adrenaline-charged equines in her blood.

"What—what is it?" she asked, through lips that were stiff with fear. Isabelle was squirming slightly, sensing her disquiet.

"It's the distillery—there's a fire. Apparently it started a few hours ago, or so they think as it's well caught. I'm so sorry, Pamela."

The next hour was a blur. Casey called Gert and she arrived within minutes to watch over the children.

They saw the glow of the fire on the horizon long before they reached the distillery site. Pamela felt the ball of ice in her intestines grow larger. The fire had to be huge to cause that sort of light in the sky.

When they arrived, Pamela quickly saw it was even worse than she had feared. Four hundred years of Kirkpatrick history was already well on its way to becoming no more than a very large pile of ashes. She could not even begin to think of all the people whose well-being depended on the distillery every day.

The fire was enormous, and too dangerous for anyone to get close enough to fight it effectively. The worst was still to come though.

"It's going to hit the washbacks and the stills and when it does the whole place will explode," she said, fighting back tears. "There's no way to stop it."

Casey did not reply because there was nothing to say. A force of nature this big had an inevitability about it that made one stand back in equal parts awe and horror. They stood on a hillside above the distillery, a safe enough distance, but they were able to feel the terrific heat that rent the night in two.

The explosion came only minutes later and it sent out a roar that echoed off the surrounding hills, shooting up a ball of flame that looked like a star exploding, ready to pull the universe into the vacuum it would leave behind. A series of smaller explosions followed, like a string of fireworks streaking the air with jets of gold and vermilion.

The outlines of the distillery, the oak beams and river stone, stood out in relief against the flames. It was, Pamela thought, a scene of utter beauty and utter destruction.

"I'm goin' to go down an' see what's what," Casey said. "It'll start to die back now that the stills an' washbacks have exploded."

She clutched at his hand, grateful for the warmth of his skin. Her own was cold and numb.

"Just be careful," she said.

She sat there for a long time on the hillside, as the night faded behind the flames and dawn rose. Dew was thick in the grass while smoke choked the air. Autumn was in the dawn, in the chill shadows that didn't rise until later in the morning, in the feel of winter reaching out with steely fingers. She felt stunned, as though someone had hit her hard with a large object and left her bruised and unable to think coherently. She had half expected Philip to show up and gloat. Then again, he might wish to keep himself as distant as possible from a conflagration that he likely had a hand in setting.

Though Jamie's empire was far flung, the distillery was the root and soul of it, the beginning and the legacy that had been handed down generation after generation. Under the harsh reek of the smoke, she could smell the melting copper of the vats and the heady burn of the grain itself, the vapor of the angel's ether rising in the air.

The fire died back slowly, leaving only a frail skeleton behind in the form of structural beams. The stones had cracked in the enormous heat and were scattered within the ruin and the surrounding yards.

She stood, still numb, but knowing she had to go down and speak to the firemen now that it was safe to approach, and start to make a series of very difficult decisions.

Casey was cresting the hill, the morning sun rising behind him, crimson through the ash that clogged the air. His own face was streaked with cinders, eyes wells of exhaustion.

"Jewel, I've a wee bit of bad news."

"The distillery is gone. It can't get any worse."

"Oh, aye, it can," Casey said grimly. "There's a body inside."

"ARE YE FEELIN' ANY BETTER?" Casey asked from the bedroom doorway. Pamela removed the cold cloth from her eyes and looked at him. It was several hours since he had delivered the news about the dead body. Following upon that they had spent three hours in the police station, trying to answer questions for which they had no answers. Pamela had not voiced her suspicions, because she knew there would be neither proof nor trail leading to the guilty party. He was too careful and calculating for that. She had little doubt that he, the man who had engineered this disaster, would know the identity of the mysterious corpse which had kept them at the police station so long.

She patted the bed beside her, indicating that Casey should come sit.

"Is Isabelle awake?" she asked, for she had nursed the baby—outraged at the long delay between meals—before lying down, and she had no idea how much time had passed as she drifted in and out of sleep.

"No, she's sleepin' fine in her cradle. Conor's playin' in the kitchen an' Gert an' Owen are still here, so don't be after worryin' yerself over the wee ones, darlin'."

His face was hollowed out with worry and exhaustion, and though he was freshly washed, she could still smell smoke on him. She felt as if it was soaked into her very pores, and that she would smell the phantom of this fire for years to come.

"Can ye manage a bit more in the way of bad news then?"

"Aye," she said dryly. "I can manage."

"The police have called an' they think they've maybe identified the body." The tone of his voice warned her.

"Who?"

"Jamie's uncle."

"Oh, Christ," she said and sat up. For a moment black spots danced in front of her eyes and she thought she might faint but Casey's hand on her back shored her up.

"How did they identify him?"

"There was a ring on the corpse. It was melted down a bit, but after they had a good look at it, they made out the initials P.K. There was a sapphire in it, they said."

There was no doubt then, for that was Philip's ring.

"Who can have done this, Casey? With all the legal wrangling Robert and I have been doing, it's going to look very bad for us."

"I would think ye need look no further than the man's partners in crime, if ye wish to know who killed him. But that," Casey said, with a tone of finality, "is for the police to solve, not you. This has gotten, if ye'll pardon the pun, far too hot a situation for ye to be dealin' with. It's time to back off an' reassess, Pamela. Whatever Jamie might want an' however much the distillery meant to him, he would not want ye placin' yerself in harm's way an' nor do I."

She closed her eyes. She was, admittedly, exhausted and at the limits of what she felt she could effectively do. The loss of the distillery was a blow she had not expected and felt unable to absorb just yet. Every time she closed her eyes, she saw the smoking skeleton that was all that remained of the four hundred year old building.

She could almost hear Jamie's voice in her ear telling her not to worry, that they would rebuild. Only it wasn't *they* or we or us. It was herself, making decision after decision that was affecting the long and storied history of Jamie's empire. Every step felt like she was further out on a high wire, without a net beneath her feet.

"Robert is downstairs havin' a tea with Owen. Will ye come down to see him or will I send him up?"

"I'll come down," she said grimly. "Just give me a minute to change and make myself decent."

Casey gave her a worried look, and she summoned up a watery smile. He raised an eyebrow, clearly unconvinced, before taking himself back downstairs.

She had not liked Jamie's uncle in the least, but she had not wished the man dead. It took this game to a new level altogether, one at which she did not wish to play. It told her without doubt that the other side was willing to kill to win. Though she couldn't see what killing Philip accomplished for Lucien, she knew his hand was the one upon the sword hilt.

She was also keenly aware that the game was too far gone to take herself out of play. Now it was simply a matter of the last few moves and hoping they were the ones that would bring the whole thing to an end.

Chapter Seventy-five

September 1975

Day of Reckoning

IT WAS COLD, THE GRASS THICK WITH DEW, fog still hanging in great sheets like diaphanous laundry that one could not escape. The men crept forward in utter silence, dew spangling their beards and hair, coating their faces fine as gossamer. Spiderwebs lay in the grass in small patches too. Dusted with the diamonds of dew and frosted ever so slightly, they were a note of beauty in this chill aching morning. David licked the water from his own lips, grateful for the cold of it. His throat was dry and his head thick with foreboding. Around them, the trees were dripping with the weight of water, soft thuds against the leaf-thick loam.

It was a daft plan. He noted with no small cynicism that the man who had authored it was rather conspicuous by his absence today. He thought perhaps they did not understand the nature of Noah Murray and had made the mistake of thinking him like all other Republicans—capable of bleeding and dying. David, having a somewhat better knowledge of the man, tended to think he was half supernatural with his ability to sniff the wind and know what was coming and to avoid capture both of the legal and illegal sort.

They fanned out from the trees into the open now, where the spine tingled with the lack of cover. David crouched low, the gun a natural part of his body, an extension of flesh into steel. He moved lightly on his feet, back and forth, so that anyone watching could not pinpoint him too easily in their sights. However, one would have to be supernatural to see through this bloody dripping fog. The man next to him was swallowed whole and swiftly into the fog's belly as if it were a living thing with an appetite so voracious it did not take the time to chew.

His hand thrummed with pain, finger stiff on the trigger. He hoped to hell he could move it when the time came. The cut had not been healing well and had been recently cut open again and properly debrided. The memory of that was enough still to make him feel sick. Darren had done it, after insisting on unwrapping the bandages to see how bad the injury was. He had tied the hand to the table and told him to look away. Being that the man was a vet (but no slouch in the treatment of humans either) David had done as he was told—and had thrown up on the well-scrubbed floor a few minutes later. That had been before the stitching, for which Darren had given him a local. David had wishfully mentioned tranquilizers and got the rise of a pale brown brow. He had felt the stitches, as Darren had to do two levels of them in order to properly close the flesh over tendon and bone. He was on enough antibiotics now to kill a bloody horse but took them meekly enough. When it came to the authority over bodily woes, the British super spy bowed before the wisdom of the Irish vet.

A soft bird call reached him on the wind, breaking into his ruminations. But it was no ordinary bird unless the bird was featherless and distinctly humanoid in shape. He knew a signal when he heard one. Three high notes and one low. He stopped for a second, confused. Understanding came swift and deadly, for the final note had only begun to die away when the fog was ripped to shreds by the insect whine of bullets.

David hit the ground, the dew soaking him instantly. He tried to discern where the bullets were coming from—direction, how many guns, how many were automatic fire—but it was useless. The mayhem was too great. He could feel them coming though, many men walking through the fog with purpose and the ability to see their blind enemy. He knew this was not so, but felt it nevertheless. He raised his own gun and shot blind, using senses other than sight. He could do that, put his 'feelers' out into the field ahead, judging by sound and echo where the barrage was coming from. What his senses told him was not a story designed to comfort. There were large numbers of men with automatic guns simply spraying the ground and air ahead of them.

It became clear that Noah Murray had been waiting for them, biding his time, knowing that they were coming and thus giving him the advantage of being entirely prepared. Noah Murray would not show mercy. He would kill every last one of them. They would be fortunate if they weren't tortured for several days before receiving the merciful bullet to the back of the head. What this meant was that there was a traitor within their own group, one beyond himself.

David had been in firefights before and had long known the way a person's insides shrank tight to his bones as if seeking refuge from harm. He knew fear and all its vagaries well but he had never known a day like this one. Death sat upon his tongue, and it tasted like ink spilled in blood—sour galls and copper and something darker, like fate.

It was hard to think, to formulate a plan, to know how to get out when bullets razed the air like hail, leaving molten trails near ears and shoulders and all too fragile organs. But he knew he had to think and act, for that was his job.

In his mind, he saw the land from above, the location of the buildings, the drainage channel, the stone walls that served as fencing for the cattle and the approximate distance to the ditch and the edge of the forest.

He started to crawl backwards toward the former, tendrils of fog still clinging to him, leaving drops of water in his hair, trickling down his collar and chilling him to the core. The ground was soggy, the morning not warm enough to dry last night's hard rain.

It was an eternity to get to the ditch, crawling in a zigzag pattern being rather difficult yet it was too risky to stand. He found the ditch by falling into it, hitting his back on the far side with a distinctive *whomph* that winded him.

There were several men in the ditch already. He didn't even have time to catch his breath before Lenny went on the attack.

"Fuckers knew we were here—how the fuck did they know?" Lenny asked, and though the question seemed general, David felt the man's eyes boring a hole into the side of his face.

"Yer quick to accuse, Lenny. Maybe yer the guilty one."

David looked round in surprise. It was the boy he had privately nicknamed Milquetoast for his pale coloring and mild demeanor. The boy who should not be involved in this, who was too young for this much blood and terror, but he was pleasantly surprised by this display of courage. He flashed him a look of gratitude across the mucky ditch.

"Shut the fuck up or ye'll be eatin' yer teeth fer tea," Lenny retorted. Another barrage of bullets closer than the last silenced them all. Noah's men knew they were in the ditch and had probably counted on the fact that they would end up there eventually.

David looked over, counted heads—six of them. Six of the twelve, the rest most likely dead. He couldn't help but speculate how many more of them would be dead before the hour was out. Lord, let one of them be Lenny.

Another spray of bullets bit into the dirt two feet out from the edge of the ditch. Thick clods of mud and grass sprayed into their tight domain. The world was drawn down to this corner, bullets and blood and the heat and stink of the man next to you, the slippery metallic smell of fear like cold iron coated in frost.

He smelled something else suddenly, beyond the fear and sweat and blood. The ditch itself, the water they were all standing in, was not water at all but something flammable. The smell was faint but it was there. David reached down, dipped two fingers into it and knew for certain. It slid like oil, slicking his skin. It was why they had been driven into the ditch—the whole thing was going to go up like a bomb.

"The ditch is filled with gas!" He yelled it even as he scrambled out onto his chest, for the gunfire had not ceased in its fury. He was crawling as fast as he could for the woods, for the water-soaked forest floor and beyond. It was the only hope for any of them. Even as he thought it, he felt the strange silence that preceded an explosion, as if the world stopped for the narrowest second and drew breath like a dragon, before exploding in a universe of fire.

The screams when they came were primal, drawn from the oldest part of the brain, which had always feared fire, had always known flame's danger and pain, even before the first touch of flesh to leaping, dancing crimson.

David made it to the forest's edge, but he still felt the heat so strongly it was like liquid poured over his body, melting his skin, evaporating his hair, pushing him blind deeper into the trees, trying to sink his body into the sanctuary of loam and moss and root. He crawled belly tight to the ground, scraping his hands and face, eyelids so raw they felt fused together until he feared he would not be able to open them when he found the courage to try.

He pulled himself with his elbows when his hands hurt too much to continue. He could feel blood welling from the injured one. Darren was going to be furious to see his handiwork destroyed. The vision of the man's anger, those soft brown eyes that could scathe with a glance, cheered him slightly. He attempted to open his eyes and was relieved to find he could. He sought the shelter of a massive elm, knowing he needed to stand and think for a moment and decide on the best pathway out of this inferno. He had lost his gun during the explosion and he thought of it with regret. It was likely melting in the ditch right now. He felt for the knife he kept strapped to his ankle. That was gone too, lost in that same explosion that had turned the universe on its ear. He checked himself over. There was blood, more than could be accounted for by his injured hand, but it belonged to other men.

His joints were greasy with adrenaline and he knew he needed to move quickly. He was aware which direction to head now that he was righted. It was as simple as going over two stone walls, through a small stream and edging around a field or three and then he would be home and clear.

But life, especially in South Armagh, was never quite that simple. For there under the spreading branches of an oak tree stood Lenny, a smile on his face so cold that it made the morning seem balmy by comparison. His face was seared, eyebrows gone, the rest a raw and terrible red, but his hatred was unimpaired. Here it was then, the moment they both had known to be inevitable.

Beyond Lenny and the treeline, the fire still roared, painting the man in front of him in shades of gold and red. David felt it, the shift that came when the universe distilled itself down to a fine point. Your life or his, your blood or his. But Lenny had a knife and David's was gone. This would not be a dignified death by any means, but he wasn't going to go easy, knife or no. Particularly not at the hands of this insane bastard. The blade came up, a flash of quicksilver in the fog, and he could taste the cold metal of it as it slashed down. He caught Lenny's wrist hard on the downward stroke.

Bone slid against bone, the blade of the knife coming close as a whisper, close as a lover's impending kiss to his throat. He only had one option and was going to have to take it, pain be damned. He grabbed the knife, feeling the slick of the blade in his palm, cutting through flesh like it was butter, cutting through tendons with little more effort. He took the pain and put it away for later. He couldn't afford it right now.

A fight was never a clear-cut thing, a fight for one's life less so. It was a messy, heaving, grunting mass of muscle and bone and blood and often it was only luck that made one man walk away while the other lay on the ground, never to move again. He was smaller than Lenny, but he was also quicker and long trained in the art of disarming his opponent. That skill might help him—or it might not. It all came down to luck and whether it was smiling upon a man. Apparently it was his lucky day for suddenly with a wrench of blinding pain, the knife was his, hilt slick and hot in his good hand, so that he could barely grip it. There wasn't time to think nor plan, only to execute.

The knife went in to the hilt and David felt the impact of it all the way into his shoulder and chest. His hand was numb and wet with blood, his own and Lenny's mingled, one living, one dying.

There was no time to do more than breathe once, twice, to let go of the knife, to back away, to hear the rat-a-tat-tat of automatic gunfire one last time, and then the world exploded in a great blast of bright stars.

DAVID CAME TO WITH A START. He was suffocating and couldn't understand where he was for a moment nor how the hell he had gotten there. He moved convulsively and a weight slid off his chest with a wet thunk. He felt his own chest gingerly. It seemed to take an eternity to bring his hand up. His chest was soaked, but the fact that it was clammily cold told him it wasn't wet with his own blood, or if it was, he wasn't still actively hemorrhaging. He suspected it was the other man's blood.

He sat up, having concluded that his head was more-or-less in one piece. The world swam for a bit and the feeling was coming back into his extremities now that he had removed the corpse from his chest. His hand was frighteningly numb, his legs hurt so badly that for a moment he was scared to touch them for fear they were riddled with bullets. And then he realized that the pain seemed rather familiar. He was sitting on blackthorn branches, the tree looming over him, dark and ominous against a starlit sky. He had been unconscious for a long time.

He scanned the area quickly. It was dead quiet—no pun intended. Noah Murray and his men must be long gone. Around him lay complete and utter carnage. The very stillness told him every man was likely dead, though he checked to make certain that someone wasn't just unconscious. Lenny had fallen onto him, shielding his body from the last of the bullets. The irony of that was almost comical. Beside David lay a heavy branch, cracked at its base where it had torn away from the tree. It had knocked him out, possibly saved his life, though he thought the reason for that was somewhat more mysterious.

It was a gruesome business, checking corpses. He did not bother with the bodies in the ditch, there was no way they could have survived the flames. He tried not to think of Milquetoast and how horribly young he had been. He tended only to the men who had died by fire of another sort. His hands touched blood, bone, intestine, flesh chilled beyond what breath allowed. There was no light whatsoever to guide him. Had Murray's men counted, he wondered? Would they know later, when the deaths were reported, that one corpse was missing?

What seemed a small eternity later, David ascertained that, indeed, everyone was most certainly dead. He took a deep breath, the rank stink of blood gagging him momentarily. It had the effect of clearing his head to an awareness of how horribly awry things had gone tonight. This had turned into what the Americans so succinctly called a 'clusterfuck'. There was nothing he could do to alleviate the damage because he had about five minutes to disappear into the landscape, judging by the dull thump of helicopter blades he heard in the distance, before the wrath of the British army came down on the surrounding countryside. And here, it must be remembered, he did not exist.

He wiped Lenny's blood from his face, shouldered a gun he found in a dead man's hand and, clutching his re-injured hand to his chest, spared a last look for the men who littered the ground before disappearing behind the blackthorn tree, and into the night. He had only a lingering thought for what he had seen a split second before he had blacked out—a man standing against the inferno, eyes the color of gentian, but as cold as an Arctic spring. The resemblance to his sister was uncanny, but with none of Kate's humanity in the man's face. Not blind in the least, he had looked into David's eyes and raised his gun.

And so the question was—why hadn't the man shot him? Why on earth had Noah Murray allowed him to live?

Chapter Seventy-six
Priest's Confession

THE CHURCH WAS CHILLY AND DIM IN THE EVENING LIGHT. At first Casey thought Father Jim wasn't there, but off on some priestly errand of mercy and had left the church doors open for those who wished a quiet sanctuary. He sat down in a pew and took a deep breath, what felt like the first proper breath in days. He could feel knots in his shoulders and all along his spine. The tension in his body had not gone unnoticed by his wife either, and several times in the last weeks he had noticed her watching him with worry written plainly on her features.

He knew better than to hide things from her, or to think that he could. But there was no way to tell her these things: dark whispers, half-felt threats and formless worries. Well, not formless when it came to those grafting bastards, but beyond that, it was only rumor in the form of averted eyes and tight smiles, and men who did not linger to talk to him in the streets, men who once would have. Telling her would have served little purpose other than to deepen the shadows already in her eyes.

The truth was he didn't want to bring this world, with all its brutal and ugly reality, into his home. He didn't want the weight of it on them in every conversation, over every cup of tea, in every room, in their bed.

He stood, feeling a weariness in all his bones he was quite certain he was too young to possess. Father Jim stood quietly waiting for him, shoulders broad but visibly bowed in the dim of the chapel.

"Casey, have you come to see me or are you here for some quiet contemplation?"

"A wee bit of both, I suppose, though mostly I've come to ask a favor of ye."

"Come to my office then and we'll have a cup of tea. It's perishing in here tonight."

Father Jim's office was off the main body of the church and just large enough to contain a desk, two chairs and a small hearth. It was neat and tidy though, and had a warm, pleasant atmosphere that, Casey thought with no small cynicism, relaxed the sinners enough to make them 'fess up promptly. It looked out over a small garden, dripping with moisture this evening, under a pitch-dark sky.

They made small talk until the tea arrived. Hot and perfectly brewed, it steadied Casey's nerves. It was warm by the fire and he felt some of his knots loosen, and his spine sink gratefully into the chair back.

"How did it all start for you, Casey?"

"What?" Startled from his ruminations, he slopped a bit of tea into his lap, the burn of it spreading along his thigh.

"What it is you're here to talk about."

He sighed. He forgot now and again how prescient this man was, even if that was part of the reason he trusted him as he did. His own natural instinct was to blurt out what he wanted, but for some reason he hesitated, for something else lay in the air about them, something as weighty and clinging as sand. So he sought another route toward what he needed to say.

"It's a strange power that country has over a man," he began, words coming slow and thoughtful. "I mean borders are artificial things in a sense, an' yet more blood has been spilled because of imaginary lines set to paper than over anything else, except perhaps religion. We've a fatal dose of both here in this nation. It's a wee bit of dirt an' rock, stuck in the midst of the Atlantic an' of little matter to anyone that lives beyond its shores other than as a sentimentalism they pull out now an' again on a cold day in March or on election day in America. So I ask myself why we're killin' ourselves over it? Why does it matter so much to have a land to call yer own?"

"If we knew the answer to that question, Casey, we would never see another war."

Father Jim had not so much as blinked at this sideways approach. But then, Casey supposed, priests were well used to people rambling round the edges until they could get to the heart of things. His tongue felt awkward, yet there was nothing false about what he had to say, and it bore relevance to why he was here.

"The Provos are fighting for their vision of the future an' the Loyalists are fighting to keep the past intact. It's a losing prospect either way."

"You ought to have stayed away boy, and that's a fact. If you had to come back home, then go live in the Republic where things aren't a matter of life and death every day."

"What of yerself though, Father Jim? This isn't even yer country. The first time I met ye, ye were here on holiday, so why don't ye leave this place?"

Father Jim shook his head, and Casey noticed suddenly how deeply grooved were the lines that bracketed the man's mouth and how much more grey there was in his hair than there had been just a scant few months ago.

The priest sighed, and it was a sound that came up from the depths of his being.

"Because there's something here, isn't there? That even if we left, we'd long for it all the time, no matter if there was an ocean between us and this bloody little bit of land or merely a false border and an hour's trip by car. This place is like a siren that lures you onto the rocks repeatedly and yet you can't stay away, because there's no one like her in the end." Father Jim slapped his hands against his thighs as though he could dismiss his strange melancholy by sharp movement. "But you've not come to listen to an old priest blather away like some great sentimental poet, not that a man can escape poetry in this land. It might be better for us all if we could. What is it that you really want to say to me, Casey? What is the favor you need?"

Casey looked into the priest's stark grey eyes and saw fear and worry there that matched his own. He had come to the right place, for if anyone understood the darkness that lurked on the other side of everyday life in Belfast, it was this man here.

He reached into his pocket and pulled out an envelope. It was simple, plain white and there was no address adorning it, only a name. He handed it to the priest, who looked at him questioningly as he took it in hand.

Father Jim raised a heavy brow. "This letter is for James Kirkpatrick."

"Aye," Casey said quietly. "The fact of the matter is, Father, we still aren't certain where the man is, but should something happen to me an' he is returned by then... well, there's certain things I would have him know, an' I don't think my wife is a likely messenger for that, do you?"

"No, she isn't." Father Jim tucked the letter into his pocket. "Now tell me, Casey, *is* something likely to happen to you?"

Casey gave the priest a hard look, and decided that truth was the best route, for Father Jim would know half-truths and obfuscations when he heard them.

"Well, a man never knows really when his last dance comes up on the card, but in my case just now, there's a bit more to it."

So he told the priest all of it, about how he had been out delivering contracts and had seen his name and dates of birth and death painted on the wall of the two-up-two-down he had lived in as a boy. About the men who had held his wife and children hostage in their own home, about the graft that had been going on now for months on the construction sites, and about the job he had taken on for the Simon brothers.

Father Jim was silent when Casey finished. Then he let out a long breath and shook his head.

"How much of this does Pamela know?"

"Everything except the writing on the wall, so to speak. I can't tell her. She's only just had Isabelle and she's fighting tooth an' nail to keep Jamie's companies together. The police haven't outright accused her of the murder of Jamie's uncle but the suspicion is there. She's too much to deal with as it is. I need to be her sanctuary right now, not more trouble."

"Casey..."

Casey put up a hand to halt the words. "I know, Father. I know the sensible thing. It's not as bad as I've made it sound, only that should somethin' happen, I'd like ye to pass along that letter to Jamie."

"You're a good man, Casey. A good husband and father, and those are no small things to be. Pamela and your children need you, so be careful and do what you must to be there in their lives."

Father Jim poured him another cup of tea though Casey had not asked for it. He knew a delaying tactic when he saw it.

"What is it, Father?" he asked, for the weight was still there in the room, and not all of it was his.

The priest smiled, but it was a thing of exhaustion.

"It's nothing really, only I have come to understand that a person, even a priest, perhaps most especially a priest, can't really ever separate God and the gun here. No matter how a man might try, they come together, don't they?"

"Aye," Casey agreed, wondering what terrible strain was upon Father Jim, and knowing just as certainly the man could not tell him. Only then he did.

"You know wee Liam O'Neill?"

Casey nodded, a dread chill running up his spine, for suddenly he understood the specters that haunted Father Jim all too well.

"A week back, I was taken from here, blindfolded, to a small hut heaven only knows where to hear his last confession. All I could tell was that we were out in the countryside, because it was dreadfully quiet when we got out of the car but they didn't take the blindfold off me until we got inside the same room as Liam."

Father Jim paused, broad hands spread out on his lap, but Casey could see how they trembled.

"When they took me into the room, he was tied to a chair and he was so still I thought he was dead. I was relieved for a split second, thinking it was over already and I wouldn't have to look in his face and tell him there wasn't a damn thing I could do to help him. But he wasn't dead, though he could barely speak and was in and out of consciousness while I sat with him, so it was a patchy thing altogether. The only words I could even make out were, 'help me, Father, help me.' Poor laddie thought I could get him out of there somehow, but even the one window was impossible, tiny and opened the wrong way, no doubt placed in that manner to prevent any sort of escape."

The priest's hands were clenched now as though he were still there in that cottage that would smell of death and all the fear that preceded it in such executions.

"I took that boy in off the streets, found him work, watched him get on his feet, and for what? So that I could stand by like I wasn't even human when they put a bullet through his head after torturing him for two days straight?"

"If ye'd tried to help him, or even told anyone after, they would have killed ye."

"I know that, but at three o'clock in the morning, when I can't sleep, it's not of much comfort."

"No, I don't imagine it is, but it's the reality of it, Father. Would two dead men rather than one make it better?"

"Oh, I see the sense of what you say, man, but it makes no sort of rational sense in a man's mind, this killing of one's own over and over, and for what end? The lines in this country are so blurred that you'll have to forgive me, because I cannot find a purpose that holds the center together."

"Ye'll drive yerself mad, thinkin' there's a purpose to any of it in Belfast. I've lived here most of my life, Father, an' I can't make anything pure of it. Life isn't that way. Life is chaotic and a wee bit crazy an' this city is magnified in those qualities a thousand times over. I wish I knew the key to stoppin' the madness, but I think peace of any sort will be a very long time coming to this land."

"Why did you get involved in the first place?"

Casey shrugged. "My family was always part of the Republican movement, goin' back to before the Famine. It was who we were, just like havin' dark hair an' eyes. It seemed that simple, but of course it's not. The reality is it's a twilight sort of world where things shift an' ye can never really see the horizon an' ye know on some level yer not goin' to reach it ever. When yer young an' impressionable it seems a place to belong, as though it makes ye special, outlines yer life an' sets it apart. There's this shimmer in the air, a sort of transcendent place that is a promised land for a good Republican boy. But if we ever did achieve peace, what happens to all these amateur warriors? What makes us special at that point? An' that's maybe the real fear, more than any other."

"It has to change at some point. A man like yourself, a man who people listen to, could be at the forefront of that sort of change."

"Anyone who pushes too hard for reform at this point is goin' to find himself with a bullet in the brain—an' that's only if he's lucky. I have a foot in two worlds, Father, an' therefore I am standin' firm in neither. That means those pushing for reform, for peace, are only going to see me as a former member of the IRA, an' my old colleagues see me as a traitor, pure an' simple."

The priest looked at him long in the way that priests often seemed to have, as though they saw through to the soul and read it as clear as light upon water.

"Casey—go. That's the only advice I have for you. Get away from it.

Run if you have to, but don't let me ever be in the position of hearing your last confession in a little hillside hut. Do you understand?"

"Aye, but I've no intention of any such thing. I've a family to raise here. Doin' that is all that really matters to me anymore."

"Would that it were that simple for either of us," Father Jim said bleakly, and Casey felt the chill of it deep in his bones as though the words carried the weight of a seer's prophecy.

It hardly seemed the time to tell the man something he likely already knew anyway—that here in this country, there wasn't anywhere to run. There wasn't a corner in which it was dark enough to hide.

He made to leave then, but hesitated in the doorway. The weight was still there, on his back, in his limbs, thick as lead in his heart. For his confession, if it could be considered such, was not complete.

Father Jim waited, allowing him time to weigh and measure the cost of his next words. Priests, in his experience, had waiting down to a fine art.

He turned back to find Father Jim's grey eyes filled with a deep sympathy, as if he already had a good idea of what Casey had to say. He took a deep breath, for he would need his courage intact for the next few moments.

"There's the one more thing I need to tell ye, but this thing I wish to speak of, it will, ye understand, need to be under the seal of the confessional."

From the Journals of James Kirkpatrick

November 11th, 1972

The moon is wreathed in smoke tonight, that eerie green-grey smoke of autumn. It is my final night here for a time, and the house is quiet around me, with only the soft pop of the peat in the fire behind me interrupting a silence that feels too vast.

Moonlight spills through the oaks, pouring soft gilt in through the windows, the light sifting over the spines of the books, dusting the shelves and drifting across the floor. It is the time of day I love best, just past twilight, where time itself is absorbed into the atmosphere and everything hangs still and perfect for a solitary moment.

My mind is wandering tonight, to other evenings spent here, times when I was only a child and times when I was a father for a delicate heart-stopped moment. I know this house so well, the land that surrounds it, the city below that beats with such a dark and bloodied heart.

I think of a spring long ago, spring when the dark green rolled up from the earth, tendriled and vined, thick shoots and frail white ones, all smelling of dirt and water, all smelling oddly like fire. The leaves were a-shimmer, a verdant mist tumbling up from the valley into this mountain retreat. I can still taste them on my tongue, promising so much, as they do every spring even if the promise always fails. Still, it was and is only the idea that matters, not the reality.

I remember myself standing there now, near the windows, feeling the dark rise up in hollows and ribbons, purling from earth, root and water merging with the glass, gathering around me until the dark was in me and I felt as insubstantial as a moth rising into the air, born, living and dying in a matter of days but flying all the same. I thought a breath might dislodge me, send me spinning up into the pale fire of the early stars and strand me out where there is nothing and everything. Where everything spins and nothing breathes, but all dances with a terrible beginning and finality that strikes both awe and terror with a single chord.

I ran away that night, ten years old and in a fit of pique over something I felt my parents did not understand. In truth, looking back on it now, I think I was beginning to realize that my mother was dying but no one was admitting it to me.

I packed up a few things, bread, cheese and water, and headed off into the woods of my childhood. I wasn't afraid, though it was twilight as I tramped off through the forest, for my anger sustained me and chased away the shadows of that woodland realm.

The moon was full that night, so silver as to be almost a strange powdery white. I was hypnotized by it and by the very planet itself.

I came upon a pond I had not discovered before, an oasis in the midst of the forest, lit dappled silver, kissed by the shadows of willows bending to their own reflections. I sat down there by the shore and thought I might grow roots right into that saturated soil.

It became one of those times that come too rarely in a person's life, something of awe and wonder, something that is distilled by time but not diminished. Some moments, fleeting as they are, are thus, even time and the human mind cannot make less of them. For that night I was just another creature on the shores of the universe, the stars small wayposts on an infinite journey.

I stayed all night by the shore of that pond, listening to the sounds the night makes: the sigh of the mosses, breathing out water, the dark earth rolling soft in its sleep, and the scurry and slip of creatures not seen, only heard. I slept too at some point, for when I awoke it was to a morning hung with gold and crimson, as fresh and whole as the very first dawn. I was cold and hungry, but not afraid.

The day did what it always does, restored me to the world of men and math lessons and Latin translation and the need for clean socks and hot tea. I took that night with me, carried it inside, pulling it out now and again when it was needed. For this I know, if I know little else, that each man has his own geography, the one that lies inside, within the vast country of a human soul. It is an unknown land even at the last, though there are roads and half-cut trails, way signs and crossroads where the grass eventually overgrows and the words upon the sign are long since faded into illegibility. But sometimes, late at night, in those still hours so familiar to the insomniac, when the shadows stop and turn slowly upon the floor in a ghostly pavane, one remembers what the signs once said, the turns made at the crossroads and one feels the bittersweet taste of regret and loss for the boy who was left behind on the road.

Chapter Seventy-seven

October 1975

His Father's Son

PAMELA CLOSED THE VOLUME AND SIGHED. The hour had grown late as she read this last entry in the journals and she needed to be home. She lingered for a moment, caught in the bittersweet spell of Jamie's words.

Reading the journals had become a secret pleasure, one she anticipated all day as she made her way through the piles of paperwork that sat on Jamie's desk every morning. Opening the journals had become akin to saying 'Open Sesame' at the mouth of Ali Baba's cave. She never knew what wonders would confront her that day, what adventure or flight of thought would absorb and enchant her. Through the pages she had come to know Jamie in an utterly different way. She was seeing the man who had often lived on the edge of both his nerves and his own mortality, a man who cared too much though the face he presented to the world rarely betrayed that.

Like Ali Baba's cave, the pages were scattershot with pearls and diamonds as well as the more prosaic events of a normal day, the record of a horse newly bought and how it was coming along with its training, repairs that were needed on the house or grounds, or lists of books, plants, parts for a sailboat or plane. In the margins he would occasionally scribble bits of poetry, random thoughts and phrases thrown upon the air like sifted silver, sparkling and transient. A few lines here and there she recognized from the works of Jack Stuart. Most were entirely new to her and she reflected how like Jamie it was to scatter beauty in such a way. He was often profligate with it.

During these last days, Jamie's final journal had been a sanctuary away from the troubles that roiled thick and deep every time she stepped foot into the world. The police had been asking a lot of questions about the fire, in particular questions about her relationship with and animosity toward Philip Kirkpatrick. Though she knew it was routine in some ways, in others she suspected it was not. She had contacts within the RUC from her days of photographing crime scenes. She had been warned—circumspectly—but warned nevertheless, that the police were considering her very seriously as a suspect in Philip's death. Other than telling them the truth, which was that she had not liked Philip in the least but did not wish him dead, there was little she could say to convince them of her innocence. Nor could she voice her certainty that the Reverend Lucien Broughton had arranged the fire and left the corpse in the ashes in the hopes of implicating her.

She stood and stretched. Outside, the setting sun bronzed the black bark of the oaks, the leaves of the lone maple as crimson as a Chinese vase. Casey had warned her that he would be home late tonight, and Conor and Isabelle were safe in the kitchen with Maggie, but she felt a sudden longing to be home in her own surroundings, with the kettle on the hob and the firelight flickering cheerily on the walls. She was just stepping toward the door when Julian walked into the study.

He wore a pair of worn denims and a deep blue sweater that almost matched his eyes. He smiled at her; a quicksilver dazzle that was so like Jamie's that she had to steel herself against it. He brought with him the scents of the stables and fresh air. He had been riding.

He had arrived here at Jamie's house a few days after the fire, startling her and leaving her little choice but to introduce him to the estate staff. Robert had taken it in his usual implacable manner and been polite but not overtly friendly. Maggie, on the other hand, had looked as though she had seen a ghost for a moment and Pamela had feared that the woman's heart was going to fail from sheer shock. She had maintained a reserve with the boy, but Pamela saw her face when she looked at him, and knew the expression for what it was. She felt it too often on her own face not to recognize it when she saw it in another.

They had spoken for a long while that afternoon, she and Julian, a conversation of feint and counterfeint. It became clear over the course of the discussion that if he had not known at Christmas, he knew now that Jamie was his father. Since then he had hired a solicitor, and she knew it was the Reverend pulling the strings, getting ready for his next move in the game. In the weeks that ensued, Julian had gone on to make himself very much at home in Jamie's house. Which might be his right, but she was not comfortable with it. It was not his fault that Jamie wasn't here to meet him, to decide what the parameters of their relationship might be, and she felt that in his absence it was up to her to keep relations as cordial as possible—cordial, but careful, for he was the Reverend's animal whether he understood that fully or not.

This afternoon she had not been prepared for his presence. Going from the suspended beauty of Jamie's words to the chill presence of his son was a little like being showered with a bucket of cold water. She needed a minute to catch her breath but knew she did not have it.

"I've asked Maggie to bring us tea," he said. He sat in the chair Jamie favored, something she suspected he knew. One long leg canted over the other, ankle resting on knee in a pose that was so like his father it caught her breath in her throat.

She fetched the tea herself, not wanting Maggie to carry the heavy tray with her arthritis as bad as it was these days. It also gave her a chance to check on the children. Conor was happily playing with a set of wooden trucks on the kitchen floor and Isabelle was snug asleep in her cradle. She could spare a few more minutes before taking them home.

In the study, she set the tray down on the low table in front of the fire. She poured them each a cup and added lemon to Julian's. She wondered if this too was genetics or a deliberate parodying of Jamie, who also took his tea so. Apparently Julian was used to having all his needs anticipated and smoothly dealt with by other hands, mostly unseen. His hand touched hers, lightly but deliberately, as she handed him his cup. She looked up to meet his eyes and stiffened in response.

There was no mistaking such looks. She was used to them, though did not care for them. But she could not help seeing herself in his eyes for a moment. Dressed impeccably in a mossy-green sweater paired with a pale grey linen skirt, her hair up and away from her face and delicate gold wires in her ears, she ought to have looked entirely respectable. She knew, however, that was not what men saw when they looked at her. She was aware of her beauty and had not been above using it to her advantage occasionally but sometimes, like now, it brought her attention which she devoutly did not want. There were some men who felt beauty was there to be exploited, with no consideration of the human being who lived inside. It was a lesson she had learned early and not forgotten.

"After," he said without preamble. "I should like you to stay on." The intention in his eyes was unmistakable, even if the words were civil enough. She chose to ignore the intention and address the words.

"I wasn't aware I was leaving," she said, wishing that he had found her behind the desk, for she could use the shoring of its solidity right now and the small bit of authority it gave her.

"Well, that will be your choice. As I said, I should like you to stay, so perhaps we can come to an accommodation."

"Julian," she said carefully, "when Jamie comes home, it will be up to him to decide what your role here is. Until then, I am the guardian of the companies and estates. As such even I don't have the power to hand Jamie's home and companies over to you. And I won't."

Julian smiled, an expression of chilled forbearance.

"Philip told me you were my father's whore, so my question," he said, leaning forward to put his hand on her knee, "is do I inherit you along with the house and the businesses? Granted, I may seem young to you, but I make up for it with experience. A man would do a great deal to have a woman like you and, like my father, I can be generous. I don't even mind that you murdered my great uncle."

Young men sometimes made mistakes, said things beyond their ken and experience, and lived to regret it. She had a feeling Julian was not one for regrets. She removed his hand from her knee and placed it on the table.

"Then perhaps it is fortunate that you are not yet a man, and will certainly never be the man your father is if you continue in this vein. In the meantime, do not make the mistake of putting your hands on me again. I have a husband, and whatever Philip may have told you, Casey is the only man in my life."

"That's not precisely true, now is it? Or at least it hasn't been in the past."

She froze, but kept her expression blank. Was it possible this boy knew about Love Hagerty and the sins she had committed in Boston?

"I think you need to remember, Julian, that I am not alone. I might be the only one visible to you, but I am not alone."

"Yes, but if Lord Kirkpatrick does not return home, and it seems less likely with each day that he will, then it doesn't signify how many people you have on your side. None of them will matter in the balance."

"He will return, Julian. I know what you've been told, but if you knew Jamie at all, you would know that he's not an ordinary man and ordinary obstacles and events don't apply to him in the way they do to others."

He smiled, but there was a dark fire in his eyes that spoke of a cold fury, long cultivated, something that went back farther than Philip's tutelage of him. She realized with a chill that his mother had raised him to this and that she must have hated Jamie, for there was no hate deeper or more profound than that which was seeded first by love.

"Philip warned me that you believed in the myth, not the real man."

"Philip didn't know Jamie in the least, and if you believe he did, Julian, more fool you."

Julian took a swallow of his tea, sapphire eyes aglitter over the rim of the delicate cup. She wanted to look away but knew it would be a terrible mistake to do so. She had vulnerabilities with this boy that did not exist with the other people opposed to her. She knew she would never be able to look at him and not see Jamie on some level despite the fact that he was never going to be the man that Jamie was. There would always be that small hope there was some saving grace that genetics had bestowed upon him. There would always be a wish that the beauty of face and form might in some measure be matched in spirit and intellect. She wanted him to be a son that Jamie would love, would be proud of and would someday be able to build a relationship with. She had considered what she owed Jamie in this area, what he might want of himself shared with this boy. He had given her stewardship of his work and his home, he trusted her judgement and her heart, and so if he did not come home, what were her duties regarding his son?

Julian stood, leaving his cup half full. "Hear this, and hear it well, Pamela. I always get what I want, however much time it takes. It would be better to just give it to me now, rather than hurting yourself in an extended fight."

She did not bother to respond, only rose as he left the room. Taking the tea things back to the kitchen, feeling the happy weight of her son clinging to her leg and hearing the gurgle of Isabelle in her cradle anticipating her mother's arms, she recalled the final words in Jamie's journal. And she felt that bittersweet loss and regret for the boy Julian might have been had he been able to be his father's son.

Chapter Seventy-eight
Drawing Down the Moon

ON A SUNNY AFTERNOON IN OCTOBER, CASEY ARRIVED HOME to find his wife and his son taking tea with his mother, and his daughter tucked neatly into the crook of her grandmother's arm.

To say he was shocked was to understate enormously the surge of emotion that went through him, but Pamela caught his eye with a glance that was half warning, half plea that he at least attempt civility for the sake of the children. He took a heavy breath in through his nose, wished violently for a cigarette and walked into the kitchen.

Conor reached up automatically for his father and Casey swung him up neatly, tucking him against his side. He smelled of sticky apples and milk and the sweet green scent that was both reminiscent of his mother and entirely his own. Isabelle set to squawking as she always did when her Daddy hove into view. Where her father was concerned, Isabelle was a wee ten-pound tyrant with the face of an angel, but a tyrant nevertheless. She had established herself early on as Daddy's Girl, and though perfectly content while Casey was away at work, once she knew her Daddy was home, she made no bones about wanting his full attention. Pamela stood, took Isabelle from Deirdre, handed her over into Casey's free arm and took Conor into her own.

He gave her a black look. "A word if ye will, woman." To his mother he said, "Ye'll excuse us for a moment."

Pamela followed him out to the porch and into the yard, letting Conor, who adored being outdoors, down immediately. The boy tumbled happily into a pile of leaves, sat on his bottom and began to sort through them as though in search of treasure.

Casey turned around and glared at his wife before the door even shut properly behind them. His anger was well stoked. Isabelle gnawed happily on one small fist, drool lending a shiny gleam to her ivory digits. She was quiet, as though she sensed the discord in the air between her parents.

"What the hell do ye mean by havin' herself in there to tea?"

She arched an eyebrow at him and he saw that she did not feel the least bit guilty.

"It's only today. We've not been sneaking about behind your back so you can put the outrage in your pocket and keep it for another day."

"Still," he said, "ye might have told her to go on her way when she showed up on the doorstep."

She drew in a patient breath, and fixed him with a green glare the match of his own.

"I could hardly tell her to leave, Casey. If you wish to do so, you'll have to do it yourself. Besides, she came to see Isabelle, and you can hardly fault her for that."

Isabelle cooed as though in agreement. Casey looked down at her tiny face to find her smiling a gummy sweet smile up at him. He sighed. He swore the child was in cahoots with her mother. A breeze touched the soft, downy curls on her head and she gurgled in delight. He could feel the tension at his core give way a little.

"Casey, I don't expect you to forgive her or to have some wonderful relationship with her, but she is the only grandparent our children will ever have and I think that's worth making a few compromises for, don't you?"

He shook his head at Pamela, knowing she was right but not ready yet to admit it.

She smiled at him and reached up to kiss his cheek. "Bring your son with you when you're ready to come in," she said sweetly, and went back into the house. He looked over at Conor, who was gleefully throwing up handfuls of leaves and watching them fall back down around him in a shower of amber and scarlet. He wished he felt even a small measure of that unfettered joy just now.

He hoisted his daughter up onto his shoulder, where she promptly grabbed a handful of his hair and stuffed it into her mouth. She smelled of baby things: talcum powder, fresh laundry, and a flower newly emerged from soil. He breathed it in and allowed it to soothe him.

"Yer Mammy is a wee bit in the way of a blackmailer, no, Miss Isabelle?"

Isabelle gurgled again and he took it for agreement. A blackmailer Pamela might be, but he supposed she was also right. Damn the woman anyway.

Deirdre stayed to dinner, and he managed to be polite throughout, though admittedly not his normally affable self. Her presence put the hackles up on his back, as though he had to defend himself against the slightest thaw toward her. It felt childish and, he admitted ruefully, it probably was.

After dinner, he slipped away outside again, this time without the children, for he needed a lungful of chill air to clear his head. Phouka was in his stall, pewter coat gleaming in the dimly-lit barn. Casey gave him the apple he had tucked in his pocket, hoping it would keep him from grabbing at the cigarettes, something the bloody-minded beast had done not long ago. He had eaten an entire pack and breathed out tobacco fumes for the two days after.

Casey retrieved his cigarettes from their usual hiding spot and found them a bit damp, but, thank heavens, unchewed and still smokeable. He moved out into the night, walking to the edge of the scrim of pine that bordered their wood. He drew deep on the cigarette and let out the smoke in a long sigh of relief.

"Yer wife thinks ye've quit that particular habit," said his mother from behind him.

"Pamela is nobody's fool. She knows I keep a pack for particularly stressful days."

"I suppose ye'll mean my visit," she said, tone dry as a withered grape.

"I suppose I will," he retorted, tone every bit as dry as hers.

He glanced to the side where her profile showed clearly, delicate yet stubborn. Her arms were crossed over her chest as though she were girding herself for what she had to say next.

"I'd like to know the children, if ye'll allow it. I know, Casey, that I can't make amends for not being there for your growing years. No one can turn back time, as much as one might wish to, but I should like to know ye now, as a man. And I should like to be a part of the children's lives, if ye think ye can manage it."

He took another drag off the cigarette, wishing he could block his ears, wishing he could stop being so angry. He wished more than anything that he didn't feel six bloody years old in her presence.

"No one ever tells ye that ye'll make mistakes that ye can never take back in yer life. That ye'll do things that have no remedy to them, ever. And they're done so quick that it's too late before ye even understand the damage those things may incur. That's no excuse. Only I don't think I understood fully that day I left, just what I was doing. I've never stopped regretting it. I was a fool an' maybe ye cannot forgive that. An' no blame to ye if that's the case."

He took a deep breath in through his nose. "Give me a wee bit to think about it, will ye? I think ye owe me that much, at least."

"I owe you far more than that," she replied, and he heard the first quaver of real emotion in her voice.

He did not reply, for she spoke only the truth. The debt between them could never be repaid and they both knew it. Denial would merely be politeness at this point. He took another drag on the cigarette, crushed it out on the woodpile and looked up at the sky. It was better than trying to make small talk when he felt as though he were half choking.

Above their heads, the moon was on the wane, a delicate crescent like a crystal goblet, center poured soft with hazy golden mead.

"Yer Daddy used to do this thing," she said quietly, "when ye were just wee. He'd circle the moon with his thumb and forefinger and then get ye to look through the circle so that it seemed he was pullin' the moon down to ye. Ye truly believed he was doin' just that, drawin' down the moon for ye."

"Aye, well, the man knew how to make magic," he said gruffly. Talk of his father was always a weak spot for him. Whatever else he might think of this woman, his Daddy had loved her, and she had known parts of him that Casey could not. There were questions that itched under his skin like a nettle rash but he could not find the words to form them. He could not ask the questions for which only she held the answers.

He felt a bit like a mule in her presence, truth be told, balky and stubborn. But he knew Pamela was right. For the sake of their children, he needed to construct some sort of a bridge with her, even if it was built out of shaky materials.

"We'll start with maybe a day a week when ye can see them. Will that do?"

"Aye," she said, and the gratitude could be heard clearly. "That will do."

THE FROST CAME DOWN HARD IN MID-NOVEMBER, and the entire country-side took on the appearance of an enchanted fairyland with frost bejeweling the hedgerows and tree roots, and spangling silver threads across eaves and chimneys and round about the skeletons of decaying plants.

The moon rose full as a wind-billowed sail over the hills, shimmering with that deep-forged silver that came only this time of year. It was so bright and big that it looked near enough to touch. It was the night Casey had been waiting for.

"Will ye come outside for a bit, Jewel? I've something to show yerself and the wee ones."

They bundled the children and themselves up against the cold. Isabelle's face, topped with a pink bonnet, looked like a petal slowly emerging from the heart of a flower, and Conor in his corduroy coat and blue woolen cap so resembled his grandfather that it sent a shaft of sweet pain through Casey's being, to see him so.

Outside, a deep calm held the night in its hand, and the entire universe was distilled in silver spirits down to this small corner. To breathe in was to take some part of that distillation into one's very cells, to recall the beauty of it for years to come. With it came the sharp delineation of scents that cold enhanced and brought bold upon the senses: peat smoke and earth, the amber of pine and the soft decay of late autumn.

Rusty sat atop the peat pile, gazing up at the moon, his ragged ears lit so that they resembled cuts of worn lace. Casey ruffled the cat's head, and Rusty gave him a derisive feline look before returning to his lunar contemplations.

Even Isabelle, known to squawk at any change in temperature, was rendered silent by the strange atmosphere of the night and the great swimming orb that rode the horizon.

"Now, son," Casey said in a quiet tone to Conor, "we need to be quiet an' go canny through the trees, for nighttime is when the fairies are abroad an' we don't want to disturb them." Conor's eyes were wide and dark, and Casey squeezed his hand in reassurance. The child did not frighten easily though, never had. He had an inner core that made him seem far wiser than his years ought to allow. In this way too, he reminded Casey of his father.

It was a small way into the wood, this thing he would show them and they heeded his words to stay hushed and not disturb the creatures of the night, fey or otherwise.

It sat in a small clearing, framed by dark pines that rose against the moon in inked shadows. At first it seemed part of the landscape, the remains of a tree long fallen. But then the outlines came clear: the turreted towers, the winding staircases, the lines that followed the crooked ways of wood and moss and lichen and stone, of feather and leaf and moonlight.

Pamela gasped and Conor said, "Da?"

"'Tis a home for the Auld Ones," he said to Conor, kneeling beside his son and taking him in the curve of his arm, relishing the warmth and solidity of him against his side.

"Here, Jewel, give me the baby so ye can have a good look."

Pamela handed Isabelle over and he propped her carefully against his chest, mindful of the wobbly head.

Conor stepped forward from the shelter of Casey's arm and gazed at the fairy house with pure wonder while his mother dropped to her knees in front of it, clasping her hands together in delight.

"When on earth did you find the time to make this, man? It's amazing." Her face turned toward him, flushed with cold under the brim of her red cap, eyes lit with wonderment.

Casey shrugged. "It just sort of grew on its own in the way things sometimes do, ye know? As if they were there waitin' to be built, hoverin' in the air."

It was built from old branches, mosses, lichens, found things: a chair made from a fossilized stone, a bed canopy cunningly constructed of the seed vessels of translucent lunaria, blankets made from the veins of leaves and tumbled delphinium petals, bits of vine twined around wee staircases leading up to each floor and two turreted towers. The roof was shingled with bark from windfalls and it glimmered, frost outlining the rough edges. There was a kitchen with pots and pans made from acorns, a stove constructed entirely of birch bark and small shelves chock-a-block with jars formed from empty seed pods. The floors were strips of driftwood as were the stairs, which twisted and twined around the castle like a vine growing round a tree. There was a laundry room with a scrubbing board of tiny stones and sticks, an ironing board made from a crow's feather, ash bark dressers in little low-ceilinged bedrooms, a wheelbarrow in a potting room built of seashells, a cradle made from a walnut shell and lined with pussy willow buds. One tower was an observatory and Casey had even fashioned small telescopes with discarded ends of brass. The other tower was a library, the shelves crooked and loaded with books made from leaves, and paper threaded with summer blossom. There were titles stenciled on the spines and Pamela read them one by one, understanding dawning in her face and bringing tears to her eyes. There was not, of course, a nail to be found in it as Casey explained to his son.

"Iron has neither mercy nor warmth, and so it is that the Auld Ones cannot bear the touch of it. So ye must never bring it near them nor build them an abode with other than wood and moss and water and bark. And ye must always bring a wee bit of moonlight down to bless the house."

He held his hand up, making a circle of forefinger and thumb, wrapping the moon there in his fingers to give as a gift to his son. Small and straight-backed, Conor stood with his face tilted up toward that great round, cupped now and floating all dusted pearl within his father's palm. It appeared, Casey knew, as though he were setting it gently on the roof of the fairy house.

They stayed for a time in the wood, watching Conor investigate each room of the house and all its wondrous details. Casey sat back on a stump, joggling Isabelle on his knee in an effort to distract her from the cold.

Later, when Isabelle had been nursed and put to bed, and Conor was tucked up snug in his, Pamela came to him and put her arms around him, looking up into his face. He put one hand to the delicate line of her jaw, her skin still flushed shell-pink from the cold.

"I read the titles on the books in the library," she said. "Thank you."

"Aye, well," he said, "it's for Conor an' Isabelle. They can add to it as they like when they're older. But mostly, Jewel, I had you in mind as I built it."

"Why?"

"Because of the little girl that ye were who maybe was lonelier than the woman admits. I wanted to give her some magic an' wonderment."

"I love you, man." She sighed and turned her cheek against his chest. He could feel her blood beneath her skin, the pulse of it against his own and the enchantment of the iridescent night still there in both of them, casting its peculiar, still magic.

"An' *that*, darlin'," he replied, "is my magic an' wonderment."

"I wish," she said, "that I could hold this moment with both hands and that it could be this way always. Just the two of us with our babies, safe and sheltered. Why can't time just stop for a bit?"

*"Stand still, you ever-moving spheres of Heaven,
That time may cease and midnight never come.'"*

She pulled back and looked up into his face. "Casey Riordan, did you just quote *Faustus* at me?"

"Aye," he said, smiling. "All yer quotin' at *me* has worn off over the years, I suppose."

He stroked her hair, the twined silk of it furling soft under his hands. Through the window the moon peeked, slowly weighing anchor behind the pines and the hills. He knew there was no answer to his wife's question; only that all things changed and one could no more stop it than one could halt the waning of the moon or the growing of a child. The knowledge of that was both the bitter and the sweet marrow of life, no matter how silver the night, no matter how the blood sang beneath the skin, no matter the love and the joy, all things changed.

Still, none could blame a man if, now and again, he wished to hold the moon in his hands and stop time for a space. Because wishes were, and always had been, for the impossible things of the human heart.

Chapter Seventy-nine

November 1975

Belfast, For My Sins

I T WAS THE SORT OF MORNING THAT CAME RARELY IN BELFAST this time of
year. The sky was washed a clear, fragile blue and the sun mellowed the
prevalent red brick to a roseate hue. David was struck by the sudden feeling that this was now home. He had been here in one capacity or another,
with only brief absences, for four years. Normally operatives were cycled out
on a regular basis—unless they were so deeply embedded in the community
they'd been sent to infiltrate that pulling them out would collapse the entire
house of cards they had built over their time. His own house of cards was
so high and so fragile at this point that he was rarely even checked on, and
hadn't reported to his superiors in such a long time that he half wondered if
they had forgotten about him entirely.

His life was here now, whether his minders remembered him or not. It
was something they warned you about, something you were trained to steel
your mind against. But operatives were human and formed relationships
and sometimes even committed the cardinal sin of sympathizing with the
natives—to the point where they thought they were one. A mistake like that
could get you killed. He knew this all too well, as he had made just such a
mistake. He wouldn't be here today, walking this narrow little street, watching the gulls wheel overhead, had Pat Riordan not saved his life. He had been
kidnapped by a crew of IRA men down in South Armagh, and taken to a
field to be shot when Pat Riordan had come to his rescue.

There had been no repercussions to his return from the massacre at
Noah Murray's farm. This worried him, and told him it was time to take
his irons out of the fire.

In the wee hours of the morning he had packed up his scant belongings
and left the boys' home for the last time. He had everything he needed now,
all the evidence required to bring justice—albeit too late for some—to the
boys in that castle of nightmares. He had the target lists for the kill squads
too, though he was aware that they mutated all the time according to the

Trustees' current whim. Beyond those two things, there were a few loose ends that needed tying up, some job related, most personal.

He had long ago learned to compartmentalize his life. A man had to in his line of work or he would go mad. The danger was that you compartmentalized to the point where you couldn't remember any longer where you had left certain aspects of yourself, such as your humanity. He had seen more than one man lose that aspect entirely and forget that he was dealing with human beings and that human beings, despite rhetoric and rough tongues, were terribly fragile things.

The building where his meet was scheduled was an old office front, half deserted as so many buildings were in this city. The stairway was narrow and dank with a warren of offices at the top that seemed little more than ratholes. Which perhaps was a bit too apt, David thought, suppressing an unseemly smile before tapping politely on the opaque glass pane with the neat lettering, *George Felton, Building Inspector*. He wondered how many people had wandered in here looking to have a building inspected. But knowing the man behind the door, it was likely he would take a perverse pleasure in conducting said inspections.

A dry voice bid him to come in and he pictured the man behind the voice. He had never known him as anything other than George Felton but David would lay good money that George wasn't his real name. Their interaction had always been scant, as they worked on a cell system and a need-to-know basis that kept contact to the minimum.

Everything about George's personality was bland, down to the dun coloring of his hair and eyes. There wasn't anything about him that a man would remember later and that was what made him good at his job. There was a reason people called agents at this level spooks, for all of them were like ghosts. There were days he himself felt so unreal he half imagined that he was invisible. The only time he truly felt real these days was when he was in the grey farmhouse just beyond the Riordan land.

He opened the door and went in. His boss was seated behind the desk, head bent over an official-looking document. He wondered briefly about him, if he had a family somewhere, if he went on holidays or had fights with his wife. It was hard to imagine, for he had such a dusty appearance that David imagined him here all the time, suspended between their visits, always signing documents, always dressed in the dreadful brown suit that looked as if it had been worn by some British bureaucrat since the end of the Great War.

David placed the canvas bag he had brought onto the desk.

George looked at it without enthusiasm. "What have you brought me, David?"

"It's all there, what's going on in that house, what's going on in much fancier places than that. Everything we need to put all these bastards in jail is there. Everything is documented, dates, times, and the films are numbered."

A silence asserted itself as the man looked blandly at the bag. David got a very bad feeling as the silence stretched too long. His hand twitched, as it was wont to do since the latest series of injuries, and he put it behind his back.

"We can't use it, not if Boyd is in any of these films." The man pursed his lips in distaste, as though he felt sullied by the evidence on his desk. David went cold at the words, a slow understanding dawning on him.

"Why not?" He swore he could feel it, the fragile house of cards falling in, silent but inflicting terrible damage on the way down.

"Because Boyd is our informant on the inside, David. We can't afford to arrest him or make any of his," he cleared his throat, "proclivities public."

For a second David went entirely numb, the feeling that came just before all-out panic took hold. But within the numbness there was fury.

"Then what the fuck have I been doing all this time?"

The man sighed. "There's no reason to use profanity, David. You aren't naïve, you know the game we play over here and you know we often have to sacrifice a few pawns to get at the key players."

"A few pawns? These are boys, George, boys who had already been thrown onto the refuse heap of this goddamn city, and then when they thought they'd found a safe place to lay their head and get some food and sleep, they were raped—over and over again by grown men. In some cases, George, they were killed, though that isn't news to you. What the hell have you had me out there for, if not for this?"

"What do you think, David?"

David had never liked this man, but he had never outright hated him until now.

"Are you saying this was only a distraction so that you could get your ties as tight as possible with Loyalists and then just throw me to the wolves? Was I that big of an embarrassment to you, George?"

"I don't think I need to answer that question, do you? You were kept in the game because we have a larger asset here to whom you were connected. But as he is no longer quite so valuable to us, we no longer have need of your services."

David swallowed, but his mouth was so dry that it was painful and futile. He knew exactly whom George was referring to and knew with a sickening certainty why they felt he was no longer of value to them. But he could not address that here and now, for there were other matters he wanted cleared up before he left.

"Does Boyd know who I am?" he asked.

"No, he doesn't, but I suspect he will soon." The threat was implicit. It didn't need to be put any more directly.

"You're helping them, aren't you? It's exactly as the Republicans suspect, you're actively helping the kill squads go in and out of the Catholic neighborhoods. Those girls who were shot, by the milk van—was that a mistake, George, or do you allow them to kill indiscriminately? Is it a case of any Taig will do?"

"That," George steepled his hands under his chin, his brown eyes flat, "was an unfortunate mistake. The players have been reprimanded for it."

"Reprimanded!" David laughed, a bitter sound like unripe lemons.

"You're not on the board anymore, David. It's time for you to go home."

David opened his mouth to protest, but was halted by the next words George spoke.

"David, I know what happened in that field in South Armagh. I haven't told anyone... yet. Don't make it necessary for me to do so now."

"You're bluffing, George. That field was a complete and utter clusterfuck. I don't even know who killed whom out there that day."

George gave him a long, level look and David saw that he did know somehow what David had done and would have no compunction about sicking the Loyalist dogs on him if he didn't do as he was told.

"I also know about the man in the farmhouse. Perhaps that's an argument you will find more persuasive."

David was not fool enough to think it wasn't a valid threat. So much could be hidden in this country. The army and the Loyalists, the IRA and all its splinter groups could play their deadly games and the blood of them could often be swept to the side, every death seen as just more collateral damage in an unending war. Death was old and well fed here in this province and a man only needed to happen along at the wrong time or be associated with the wrong person in order to step straight into its jaws.

"As I said before, go home."

He wanted to shout at the man that he was home, that he had built the only life that mattered to him here in this rage-torn city. He wanted to say so many things about the horror of what had unfolded over these last several months, about the futility and blind ignorance of it all, but he knew it was of no use whatsoever. He had to leave before he hit the man, or shot him. Both options were highly tempting.

He left the building, his blood still high with fury and walked half blind to his surroundings. He walked for a long time, out beyond the limits of the city into the dark roads that cut through fields and led toward the coast.

He stopped finally when he reached the water, the sound of gulls like a threnody in his own blood. Strangely, beyond the rage there was a sort of relief, a giddy feeling that he was no longer bound in any way. He had been cut loose. They didn't care whether he lived or died, whether they left him bloodied and circled by wolves, and so he did not have to exercise caution anymore. He no longer needed to pretend. He could do what needed to be done and damn the consequences, for he no longer owed his allegiance to any man. If this was all a game, then he was going to finish it.

Chapter Eighty
Check and Mate

T HE LAST TIME ROBERT HAD FELT THIS NERVOUS was when he had kissed Caitlin Meldrum behind her grandfather's sheep shed. His solid and practical Scots nature, however, assured that he did not show it externally. When you played a long game, you waited for this moment, you envisioned it from the first move and kept it in your sights because it was the only way to keep yourself in play.

Across from him, seated at the table like a prince come to demand obeisance from his subjects, was Julian. The resemblance still startled him, though he had only met James Kirkpatrick the one time. He was not a man forgotten once met, and Robert still felt a second's pause each time Julian entered a room. He wished he liked the boy more, for the sake of the father. But he did not. Part of it stemmed from Julian's suing for the right to take over the companies. It was a move that was, at best, indiscreet, though one look at his face told everyone in the room just whom he was. At worst it was robbery, committed while the owner was away. No, he did not like the boy.

Robert noticed that Pamela was careful not to look at Julian too often. There was a weakness there, an understandable one, for that resemblance he had noted. He even possessed the magnetism, though it wasn't of the brilliant golden sort that his father had but an element far colder and darker. Still, Robert was honest enough to admit, it was mesmerizing. He felt a shiver of worry, for the boy did have a compelling case. Blood could take precedence where nothing else would.

He shifted in his seat and turned his attention to the woman he had worked beside for two years now. Still caught in the bloom of new motherhood, she looked to him like nothing so much as a windblown rose, all pale pinks and whites, with the softest hint of green around her edges. She had chosen her clothing carefully, he was certain, for she had left no detail unstudied this day. The dress was of the palest pink, like rose quartz shaded with cobweb silk. Her hair was up and she wore a string of grey-pink pearls at her neck, with discreet pearl studs in her ears. She was most deliberately feminine, choosing to play to her own native strength rather than attempting to join the men by imitating their own qualities.

Gathered along the length of the table sat the board members, those who owned what stock was public in the various entities of Jamie's empire, and the head supervisors from each of the concerns here in Ulster. Robert tried to read their faces and saw a variety of things there, leaves in the book of worry: stoicism, avariciousness, jealousy, curiosity and fear. He had no way of knowing how they would vote and knew they could count on the loyalty of only a few. Pamela would have to convince the rest.

She stood to speak, using no papers nor charts to prove her points. She went over the position of the companies—why Jamie had chosen to leave them to her, their history of friendship, his trust in her judgement, her knowledge of what he wanted, how he chose to pursue certain avenues, and her admittance that while she was not His Lordship's equal in these areas, he had chosen her, he had placed his trust in her. She knew that the claims of blood were ones that must be given careful consideration and their due weight, only perhaps now, when His Lordship was away, was not the best time.

Robert took a mental reading of the room's temperature and felt certain Pamela's calm delineation of the details was swaying the board to their side. Through the entire recitation, she did not look at Julian once. It worried him a little, that, for the boy could not be unaware of it and it gave him power he did not deserve.

But Robert had no compunction about watching him and saw how he sat back in his chair, biding his time, like a cat that had already drunk the cream and couldn't wait for it to be found out.

Everyone stirred slightly, all eyes trained on the boy's face, as Pamela calmly admitted his paternity. Robert could see that everyone the length of the boardroom—excepting the woman who sat at the foot—was disconcerted by his looks.

She sat down when she was done, and opened the floor for questions. Julian forestalled them by rising from his seat, every move sleek with unstudied grace. Some day he would be a formidable foe, but not, Robert thought, just yet.

"I'd like to thank Mrs. Riordan for her comprehensive outline of the current position of the companies and also for her stewardship of the aforesaid during the very long absence of Lord Kirkpatrick. I have no doubt that his faith and trust in her was very well founded."

He had a great deal of sophistication for one so young. He could sway the board. For what she had in store, Pamela was going to need their good faith. Julian could take that away.

"I only recently found out that Lord Kirkpatrick is my father. It has been a time of great emotion, made only more so by the knowledge that just as I found my real father, I also lost him. I think, as much as we would all like to believe that he is still alive and will someday come home—and believe me, no one wishes that more than I do—still, we need to face reality because a company does not operate on emotion, it operates on bottom lines and the ability of the person in charge to inspire confidence. And while I am impressed by Mrs. Riordan's abilities and how well she has done, I think none of us can deny that things have been rather unstable since the reins were put into her hands. This is through no fault of her own, but she has a life that is very full beyond what the company requires of her. Two young children, a husband and a household to run, not to mention her work for the police department."

Two arrows, well placed, the implications clear. They were trusting a mere housewife with the control of an empire. A housewife who did occasional work for the police, who were, for many of these people, the enemy. Pamela's pale cheeks flushed slightly and Robert said a silent prayer that she would keep her cool.

"While I realize that I am an unknown quantity for all of you here," he inclined his head graciously, "still this company and all it encompasses has always been controlled by a Kirkpatrick. This has always been a family run business, with family values at its core. I will endeavor to do my best by Lord Kirkpatrick, to keep the borders of his kingdom well guarded and if, God forbid, he should not come home, to strive always to honor his memory." Robert had to admire the gall of the boy, he had named Jamie king, and by inference, himself as prince.

The boy went on to outline his understanding of the Kirkpatrick holdings and Robert had to admit, that his grasp was impressive. He also painted in broad strokes his plans for the company to expand, to rebuild the distillery, to keep the Kirkpatrick roots as its brand. He had already begun, he explained, the process to change his name. Pamela looked slightly queasy at that particular pronouncement.

She waited until Julian sat down and then smiled at him with the distinct air of a patient elder. Her voice, when she spoke, was gentle. It was hard to remember that she was only a few years older than the boy.

"Julian, your father didn't even know of your existence. We have no way of knowing what his wishes would be in this regard, if he did know of you. While I understand your desire to be part of the company, I would recommend some patience until we hear from Jamie."

"But, Mrs. Riordan, you don't understand. I don't need to exercise patience. I own twenty percent of the companies, making me the largest single shareholder outside of my father." Julian said. He brought it out like a hidden weapon, a dagger that had been coddled close to his chest, jeweled and lethally sharp. The impulses of youth, Robert thought, and felt a small twinge of sympathy for him. It was, however, quickly quelled.

Pamela did not respond at once. Her eyes steeled at the boy's words and she looked at him directly. And then, with a shaft of iron in her own voice, she brought the axe down swift and clean.

"What you own are shells," she said quietly. "Dummy companies with very convincing façades, while the real assets were moved elsewhere. It took a great deal of careful maneuvering on our part, but we managed it. However, we took the time and care to document every bit of what you bought, and how you went about it, not to mention who funded you."

The green eyes were no longer soft. They were an emerald fire clashing with Julian's iced sapphire.

"Please relay this to your puppet master. Did he really think I would stand back and allow him, of all people, to take Jamie's companies? It was His Lordship who taught me how to play, after all. Your mentor thought it was a game. I knew it was war." Her tone was pleasant but there was no doubt of the strength behind it. Not for the first time, Robert understood just why Lord Kirkpatrick had trusted this woman with all his worldly goods, as well as, perhaps, a great deal more.

Julian's face was pale with unpleasant surprise. He looked frostbitten, truth be told. He, through the auspices of the Reverend, had overplayed his hand, not truly understanding of what his opposition was made. And Pamela had played her own game to that one fatal flaw in the judgement of both the boy and the man. Even playing blind a good deal of the time, she had never forgotten where the chink in the opposition's armor lay. Of course, Robert thought happily, it helped when you had the Black Pope on your side, a network of gypsies and friends in various governments and on the boards of large American corporations who were willing to help you play an extended bout of hide-and-seek. That and some more shadowy figures who had owed Pamela favors, for what services he did not care to be overly informed. A wise man did not need to know every detail.

Robert took the room's temperature again, and found shock, some anger and a complete removal of their attention from the boy who so resembled their commander-in-chief to the woman who sat in his chair.

Then she delineated it all, all the moves and countermoves, the feints and double feints that had twisted back on themselves until there had been nights they had both worried they were in a snarl of complications from which they would not be able to extricate Jamie's holdings. They had many handicaps, not the least of which was the need to make sure there was no trail for the opposition to follow. Each move across the board had, by necessity, been made in the dark, with the foil of having to have the board appear untouched come morning... come each and every bloody morning. It was a wonder neither of their respective heads had turned white over the last few months. The entire game had been fraught with roadblock after roadblock, but if they could not go over them they found a path in the long grass and went around, using whatever they might as a means of camouflage.

"You won't get away with this," Julian said, the line of his finely-carved mouth straight with anger and disbelief. "I have resources of which you have no comprehension."

"I suppose you could start all over but I suspect you don't have the resources to do that at present and we, as much as I would dislike keeping this little war going, do have the resources right now and I will use them to the last cent to keep you out."

"This is not over," Julian said, and Robert felt icy cat feet run down his spine at the boy's tone. How had one so young and seemingly privileged been so well schooled in hate and resentment?

"I think, Julian, you will find that it is over. It would be better to acquiesce now rather than hurting yourself in an extended fight. Any further action will be decided by Lord Kirkpatrick."

The boy's face was as still as a death mask with fury. Robert was glad there was an entire boardroom of people here to witness what was taking place. Otherwise, he knew, Pamela would not be safe. He feared she would not be anyway.

"There's still the house and the land that goes with it. Surely my father would want his own blood to keep that legacy now that he cannot." The emphasis was placed lightly, but the 'my father' was not lost on anyone.

"Actually," said a tart voice from the far end of the table, "the land is mine. My grandson leases it from me, but if ye look at the titles ye will find they are in my name. And I," the green eyes were scalpel sharp, "am very much alive and very much blood. As to blood," she paused, allowing the weight of her words to spread the length of the table, "I will say there seems little doubt ye are my grandson's child, for ye look too much like him for it to be otherwise. But I beg leave to doubt that ye've even half of the heart the man possesses. If so, ye've made an extremely poor showin' of it thus far."

Finola placed a sheaf of papers onto the table, her expression a direct challenge to the young man in front of her. Neat as a pin in a dark green blouse and skirt, her hair a blaze of white in contrast to the jade eyes that genetics had bequeathed also to her grandson, she was a formidable presence despite her diminutive stature.

"The deeds to the house an' land. I'm not a grand chess player myself," she said, smiling as though she were merely a sweet old lady, "but I believe this is what is called 'checkmate', is it not?"

"HE TOLD ME LONG AGO," PAMELA SAID, sighing in ecstasy as Casey rubbed the sole of one of her feet, "that he was her tenant. I didn't understand what he meant at the time but it made sense later. He meant for me to remember. He deeded it to her awhile ago, as if he could see into the future and knew it would be necessary."

"Mmphmm," Casey said, for he had never quite forgiven Finola for the strange night in her cottage.

It was evening and the dark had come down some time ago, though Pamela had only arrived home a half-hour before, still slightly giddy with the release of stress and fear. She had changed out of her dress into worn denims and one of Casey's old rugby jerseys then sat to nurse Isabelle who, having gone rather longer than was her norm between feedings, had been shrieking like an irate tea kettle so that Casey was feeling desperate by the time Pamela came through the door. Conor had fallen asleep right after his father fed him his dinner and had been moved into his bed after his mother arrived home.

Isabelle lay quiet now in her mother's arms, sated, dark eyes wide and deep. She gazed upon Pamela's face with an expression that seemed a tiny bit reproachful, as if to say she thought her mother had absconded for good and she was watching her carefully to make certain she didn't bolt again.

Casey worked his fingers into the arch of her left foot and she leaned into his hands, closing her eyes.

"Oh, that's wonderful." She let out a small breathless gasp as he found an especially tender spot in the ball of her foot.

"Ye make that same noise when I put my tongue—"

She opened one eye. "Casey Riordan, don't you dare say it in front of our daughter."

He grinned. "Well, ye do, an' she's not a clue what I'm talkin' about anyway. Do ye, my sweetheart?" He looked down at his daughter, who cooed agreeably up at him. Pamela rolled her eyes.

"Honestly, I think the two of you are in cahoots sometimes."

"At least have the good grace to distract me by finishin' yer tale."

She yawned widely. "Where was I?"

"Ye were at the bit where ye told them how ye'd played bait an' switch with them, an' how yer trip to France played into that."

"You know all this already, man," she said, half exasperated.

"I know, but I like to hear ye tell it. It turns me on to know I'm beddin' a wee Napoleon in the makin'."

"I'm hardly that." She gave him an indignant look. "And you're perverse, just for the record."

"Aye, just how ye like me. Now go on."

She sighed, but saw by the look on his face that he really did want to hear the details.

"We knew they were watching Father Brandisi and Father Lawrence, but I don't suppose it occurred to them to watch a monk who travels to France on a regular basis to see his mother. Brother Gilles handled much of the business in France for us. Of course, I led them on a merry chase when I went to Paris as well. Meanwhile Brother Gilles was there at the same time, making sure the deal over the distillery looked legitimate on the surface. Which it was, actually, only not in the way they believed it was."

"I tell ye, the nerve of the two of ye, Robert an' yerself—brass monkeys!" He smiled with no small pride, one trickster to another.

"Well somewhat, I suppose," she admitted, returning the smile. "Mind you, if we hadn't been able to convince the board today that we had done the right thing, it would have all gone to hell in a handbasket. And it was a bloody expensive shell game. If I think about the money, I get a prickly rash. But there was no other way to make them overextend their own resources."

"So what will ye do with the distillery in France now, darlin'?"

"Make vodka, of course. That was always my intention, I just needed to clear the board before we could go ahead and do it. Father Gilles comes from Picardy where they grow lovely winter wheat. He made the deals that we need with the understanding that we wouldn't be buying until next year."

"Ye have a market in mind?"

"Of course I do. We're going to make it for Americans. Being one myself, I know that anything French is viewed as a luxury item, so we're going to sell them the best vodka the distillers I've hired know how to make."

"I'm proud of ye, woman. I told ye to fight for it, an' ye have. I'll not like to speak for the man, but I know Jamie would be proud of ye too. Where do ye see the boy fittin' in to all this?"

"That will be for Jamie to decide when he comes home. In the meantime, Julian needs time to cool off. Then I will offer him something at the distillery here once it's rebuilt. If it were Jamie's decision, he would want Julian to learn the business from the ground up, just as he did."

"Ye seem just the wee bit more certain that the man will come home than ye did all these months previous."

"I heard from Yevgena," she said. "She has a line on where Jamie might be. He's alive, and that's enough to know that he will survive and come home. And not a minute too soon because I am ready to hang up my Chief Officer's hat."

Casey gave her a lascivious look, wiggling his eyebrows at her. "Do ye still have that hat? Maybe ye could wear it to bed?"

She laughed and threw a cushion at him. He ducked and grinned, doing something to her toes that sent distinct tingles up the length of her leg.

"I've a wee tale to tell myself." Casey said, his one dimple cutting a deep arc into his cheek.

"Do you then?" she asked, feeling as though a rush of champagne had replaced the blood in her veins. She was fizzy-headed with relief.

"Aye, I composed it whilst ye were out conquering small nations an' evildoers. Here 'tis." He cleared his throat.

"This little piggie longed for whiskey.
This little piggie drank ale.
This little piggie had Guinness.
This little piggie drank wine to its dregs.
But this little piggie craved the taste of honey that..."

He leaned in, careful not to disturb the baby who had fallen asleep during their conversation, and whispered the rest of the extremely bawdy verse in her ear, his hand moving from her toes to her ankle and proceeding up the back of her leg.

"Those are not the words I remember from childhood," she said, laughing helplessly.

"Aye, well, I've edited them to suit the purpose," he quirked a dark brow at her and she felt the tingle grow to a thread of desire, taut and warm in her belly.

"And the purpose would be? Aaah—" she gasped, "that is definitely not a little piggy that you're rubbing now."

"Oh, but it does make ye squeal," he said, a thoroughly wicked look in his dark eyes.

She quirked an eyebrow of her own at him, and gave him a slow, unsubtle smile.

Casey, never a man to look a gift horse in the mouth, lifted his daughter out of his wife's arms with as much delicacy as one did with incendiary devices and placed her ever so gently in her cradle, cannily left by the kitchen hearth.

He turned to find his wife lying back into the sofa cushions, hair a mad tousle, cheeks flushed with victory and arousal.

She smiled, eyelids half shut and stretched out a hand. "Napoleon, is it? Well, come and meet your Waterloo, man."

Chapter Eighty-one
Impermanent Things...

THE FIELDS AROUND THE OLD COTTAGE WERE STILL DAMP from the previous night's rain but it promised to be a fine day, especially when one considered it was November and the weather was normally bleak and miserable this time of year. The early afternoon sun had settled in mellow pools along the thick brambles that half hid the old stone walls, and the earthen scent of decayed leaves and grass was thick on the air.

David walked in across the space he believed had once been a garden, for somewhere in its form and shape the land still spoke of hands that had tilled, sown and harvested. Sometimes when he sat quiet enough, he thought he heard voices from long ago: a man calling across the field; the whicker of a plough horse; the sound of a woman chiding children, her voice tempered by love.

He ducked under the old, rotting lintel of the cottage and looked for the stone in the crumbling hearth. It was a primitive form of communication but effective nonetheless. He had not checked the spot in several days. After the massacre in Noah Murray's field, the infection in his hand had gotten worse and required further treatment, an extremely stern lecture and a dose of antibiotics that might have served a horse. In fact, David suspected they might have been horse pills. When he had come around after the stitching and resulting faint from the pain, it was to find that two days had passed. After that, his movements had been greatly restricted, though he had not minded. Then there had been the meeting with George. Beyond that he had not attended much to business.

He had chosen this spot after the original meeting with Casey that Billy had demanded. Casey was well versed in the treachery of his own country and used the isolated spot for a reason. David saw the wisdom of this, as long as one could be certain one wasn't followed to such remote sites. For such a small country, Ireland had plenty of these cottages, long abandoned and swallowed up by feral nature. Home only to ghosts and the occasional badger, they were ideal for the drop off and retrieval of information that had to be kept secret. David liked to come here sometimes when the small, bloody city became more than he could manage and he needed somewhere quiet to think, or not think, depending on the day and its particular horrors. Besides, he was comfortable with ghosts, having been one himself in great part for a long time now. He felt like one more often than not. There were only pockets in his life now when he was certain he was fully human and not something near to invisible, drifting through the edges of life as others knew it.

He turned the stone over to find a wedge of paper, folded as his informant always folded such things, in a sharp-edged triangle.

He opened it and the world fell in, rendering his vision black for a moment as his heart raced out of control. He was on his knees without understanding that his legs had given way, the sharp edge of a stone cutting into the bony ridge of his kneecap.

A name, moved up, as the man who had been designated for the hit could not be found. A name common enough in this country, but not so common at all. Riordan. David swore. Which one? Which—for the love of Christ—one?

He had to find a phone, his mind already flashing through the nearest village, its tiny lanes and tidy cottages. There was a phone outside one of the pubs, he remembered that much. It would have to do. There wasn't time to get to Casey and Pamela's house. There wasn't time to track down Patrick. There wasn't time for anything anymore.

The drive was an eternity and he cursed the narrow, bumpy roads all the way to the village. He knew he must look a madman entirely as he brought the car to a screeching halt outside the pub and rushed wild-eyed to the phone.

His hands were so slick with sweat that he dropped the receiver twice before managing to make a connection. The line in Casey and Pamela's house rang and rang but was not answered. He tried Pat's line and got the same.

He stepped away from the phone and swore out loud. "Fuck! Fuck! Fuck!" He received a filthy look and a stern finger from a poe-faced matron with a net bag of shopping neatly hung over her arm.

Where the hell were the Riordan men anyway, or even Pamela, who might know their whereabouts? The men who had been set loose would not scruple at killing an entire family. He had a sudden vision of wee Isabelle in his arms only a few days ago, and thought he might be sick right there in the street. He had to make a decision, go to Casey's home and warn them or find Pat and remove him from harm's way—if he could, if it wasn't too late—if one of the brothers wasn't already dead. He knew what Patrick would want, knew exactly what he would say. He wished the bloody man would get out of his head.

He had been a fool thinking he had any control over this situation. It had gotten away from him long ago and the strings he had held were always greased with the duplicity that existed between his own government and this godforsaken country.

He put the car into gear, popped the clutch and began to drive in one direction, only to make a U-turn a few feet later. And then David Kendall, who had not believed in God for a very long time, put the gas pedal to the floor and began to pray.

IT WAS LIKE BEING A CHILD LOST IN A DARK FOREST with night setting in quickly, dropping blackness down in great winding spools. His adrenaline had settled to a steady thrum and he felt light and disconnected. It happened sometimes and it usually wasn't a good sign. Today, it no longer mattered. He had not been able to find either of the Riordan brothers, but it had come to him while searching around Pamela and Casey's house that he knew what was wanted, and by whom. He understood the endgame now. When you no longer knew where to go or what to do, you went back to where it all started. And so, as he had always been fated to do, he went back to the beginning.

He moved through the rooms of the Malone Road house one by one. He had dreams like this often, one empty room leading into another, an endless labyrinth of vacant rooms in a house silent but heavy with sunshine and the scent of dust long undisturbed. The dreams had started long ago, after Edward had died. His beloved older brother, his brother with a soul too fragile for the harshness of the world. He shook his head. He could not think of Edward now. He needed to focus, find Boyd and kill the bastard. It was what ghosts did, slid in and took care of business, and disappeared, maybe for good this time.

For so long now he had felt like an impermanent thing, a spider husk driven before the wind, a bird without a map imprinted in its beak and wings, a Lost Boy who could not find his way back from Neverland. It had always been a risk in this job, and once you stepped over that line you could never step back. It was an alternate world. He had slipped beyond the edge place just like in a tale Pamela had told him once, deep in the night by a fire built of earth, tucked away in a watery wood.

There was only one door he hadn't tried. The heavy wooden one on the other side of which lay a set of twisting stairs that led up, up and away to the top of a dusty tower. There was always a tower in the old tales, for climbing up was another form of edge place, of passing from earth to air. He opened the door and it creaked loudly beneath his hand but it did not matter. Boyd would be expecting him and noise would not alert him to anything he did not already know. Still, David took the stairs carefully, hugging the perimeter of the curving brick wall. Up, up and away to the very top.

The room was a perfect round, filled with the late afternoon light like a gourd brimming with poisoned honey.

Pat was kneeling, head bowed, hands tied behind his back and a gun held to his temple. Boyd stood behind him. David's eyes returned to the man kneeling on the floor. He was badly bruised around the eyes and blood trickled in a steady stream from somewhere behind his left ear. Two more men stood against the wall, silent, guns in hand. It explained how Boyd had subdued Patrick in the first place. He never had been able to handle his wet work himself.

"I wondered when ye'd figure it out, Davey-boy."

"I should have killed you two weeks ago," David said. It was a relief to speak in his own voice. To feel the clipped consonants of his upbringing, the gilded edges of the world into which he had been born and which he had ultimately abandoned. He felt a shaft of longing for it suddenly, for the security of having a name and a place in the world.

"Ye should have killed me the day ye met me," Boyd replied, smiling, a slick thing that spread over his face like oil across water.

"What do you really want, Boyd?"

"Ye know what I want, Davey."

Yes, he knew. It was why he was here, after all.

"David, don't. He'll only kill us both," Pat said with a calm tone that was admirable under the circumstances.

"You—shut the fuck up," Boyd said, shoving the gun muzzle deeper behind Patrick's ear. David saw the look on Pat's face and knew it was one of warning. But it was too late for that.

"I want to know how big a traitor ye are, Davey? Will ye trade places with this Fenian scum? Will ye give over yer life to save his?" Boyd was sweating, but his breathing was slow and calm. He was enjoying his moment.

The other men remained silent, as if they had been turned to pillars of salt and were beyond seeing and hearing. He knew they only awaited Boyd's command and they would come back to life.

The lightness in his head increased, almost as if he were floating now. The decision was no decision at all and he wondered how Boyd had known that.

"I will, but he has to be clear of here. You have to let him go without any sort of harm, Boyd. I need your word on that."

"Ye have it."

Somehow David knew the man meant it. Pat had only been the bait. It wasn't his blood that Boyd wanted to spill.

Pat fixed his dark gaze on David's face and shook his head ever so slightly. David felt as if, for a second, the entire world was held within that gaze. It was pleading with him not to do it, not to make a sacrifice on this scale. David gave him a crooked smile and shrugged, ever so slightly. For him, it was already done. The border of that edge place lay far behind him and this was only the passport that would confirm his citizenship there.

"Slide yer gun over to me—I won't harm yer friend here but I need to know ye won't just shoot me the minute he's clear of my hand."

David crouched and slid it across the floor. Boyd managed to grab it without ever taking the bead off Patrick's ear. The pillars of salt were still.

"You need to cut the ties on his hands," David said, the lightheadedness feeling like the soaring beginnings of a fever, removing his emotions from the situation. Fate, he knew, sometimes felt like a fever.

"He'll find someone in the street to cut his hands free—if he can," Boyd said nastily. "I'm not takin' any chances with a bastard his size. Ye come an' kneel over here an' give me the knife ye wear on yer ankle, Davey. Then yer friend can go."

David knelt and one of the pillars of salt came to life, moved and tied his hands behind his back, and all the time he felt a strange tingling numbness climbing his body, like the touch of moth's wings, light and airy.

He could smell Pat, both the sweat of fear and his blood, but also that scent he carried with him always, like a field after the rain came down. David wanted to close his eyes on it and let it be the last of the things he sensed in this world. But knew he could not.

Pat got to his feet unsteadily, wincing as he did so. He was still bleeding from his scalp but it was only a trickle now. He walked across the room, limping slightly. David swallowed and spoke, feeling the barrel of the gun against his own head now and knowing there would be no reprieve, no white knight on a charger. Not this time. Reality was creeping through the fog of the lightheadedness. He looked up at Pat and met the dark eyes with the trust he had known as a simple given from the day he met him.

"Please ask Pamela to tell Darren what happened, to tell him I'm sorry there wasn't time for goodbye. She knows where to go and what to say."

"I will, man. But David—please don't do this."

"Pat, just go, or he will kill us both."

"David..."

"Patrick," David's voice was gentle, but it carried with the force of its conviction in that room, a room atop a tower that already smelled of the blood that would soon stain it. There would be no happy ending for any of them today. Death hovered in the air and it would have its due. "I have no choice. There isn't any way back. This is my mess. So I'm begging you to get the fuck out of here."

Sweat beaded his forehead, his hair slick with it. His arms, tied behind his back were like corded wire, and the pain cleared his head slightly. He saw the sapping of his strength in Pat's eyes as though they were a reflecting pool. He had told him once, long ago, that he was well versed in the art of killing, but what he had not added was that he knew how to die quickly, if he needed to. Only he did not want an audience for it. He did not want that dark gaze as witness to what a man could become in extremis.

"Patrick," David said, the words slipping up into the ether of the tower, "if my friendship has meant anything to you, you'll do as I ask and go. I don't want any of this blood on you."

Pat put his hand to the doorknob. David hoped the man understood that he was giving him his future by this act, keeping him free to live a life of merit, of honor, with the possibility of happiness, however tenuous. He was giving him the gift of a love that had never been welcomed but had always been unconditional and without strings, despite the futility of it. But, as he had once told Patrick, maybe only the fact that it had existed was the thing that mattered. The only return on that love that Pat could give to him was to walk out of this room and not look back. David looked deep into those dark eyes and saw in the single second that held them all hostage, that Patrick understood all those things and knew there was only one choice left to the both of them. He had to leave.

And so he did.

Chapter Eighty-two
Fault Lines

H E MUST HAVE GASPED WHEN HE SAW THE HEADLINE, for Kate turned from the files she was tucking away and asked sharply, "What is it? Is it bad news?"

"No, not bad," Pat said, "only I didn't know that he..." he trailed off, for he had not talked to Kate about David yet, not the fact of his existence nor his demise. And the latter was not something he could speak of just yet, and maybe never would.

The headlines were a clarion, shrieking off the page, a picture of the house on Malone Road, looking entirely grim and foreboding, with the words *'House of Nightmares Tumbling Down'*. The byline was Muck's. David must have taken all the evidence he had gathered over his time in the house directly to Muck. David would do that, to spare him, Patrick, the danger of the middleman this one last time.

Pat skimmed the article. Muck had outed Boyd as a British tout. This made Boyd a marked man who would be lucky if he had another twenty-four hours left on his clock. Pat hoped they were as miserable a twenty-four hours as any man had ever had to endure. The story went on, disclosing the charnel house of perversion that the old mansion had been. Muck left no stone unturned and the worms were all there now in the glare of the media. David had done what he had always aimed to do, and saved the boys in that damned house. Pat wished with every fiber of his being that the man was here to see it. At least David knew Muck had the suicidal courage of his own convictions and that the story would be written. At least he had that much the day he climbed the stairs into the tower.

Kate was standing near him now, wordless, and he thought he might fall to pieces if she so much as touched him. He closed his eyes and she did touch him then, her hand soft on his back. He turned his face, blind and she took his head to her, stroking his hair. David's death had broken open something inside him, something he had held in check since Sylvie had been killed. He could feel it cracking as though his heart were filled with fault lines, his soul composed of shifting plates that were threatening to buckle.

"It's alright," she said quietly and he felt strangely reassured, as if indeed things might be alright now, even if never the same.

"Was he very dear to you?"

"Who?"

"The friend ye lost. I'm blind in my eyes, Patrick Riordan, but not so blind in my heart. Ye've been grievin' these last days. I could feel that clear, much as ye tried to hide it."

"Aye, he was dear. He was the best friend I ever had."

"Ye can break if ye need to. I can bear the weight of it," she said, and he could feel it, the fault lines widening, the plates shifting to build the pressure up until he would not have control of it.

"Can ye?" His words came out half-choked, pushing past his throat thick and pained. "Because I don't think I can."

"Aye, I can, for it's none so hard," she said so quietly that her words fell light as snowflakes to touch his bruised skin, "to bear what ye can of another's pain, when ye love them."

Chapter Eighty-three
The World Both Under and Over

THE AIR WAS ALIVE TODAY, THE BREEZE SWEET BUT BRISK with winter scent. Casey Riordan surveyed his bit of land with satisfaction. The fruits of the garden had long been picked and put up: the burlap bags filled with root vegetables, the onions hanging in loosely plaited bunches, the gleaming rows of jars filled with jewel-toned berries. All of this gave him a deep sense of satisfaction, a guard against the cold season ahead, an assurance of warmth and full bellies to ride out the winter winds and storms.

Velvety grass, skimmed with a milk frost of new snow, filled the hollows and dips between the trees. Beneath the snow the soil contrasted in thick black rills. Irish land had oft been described as black butter for its richness. The irony of such a thing was not lost on any Irish man or woman that a land so fertile, so lovely, was also tilled to its limits in blood and tears, which ought to have salted and destroyed the very soil beneath all their feet and yet still gave in plenty.

He began to walk, long strides into the woods. He liked to check the boundaries of his property once a month, see what might need mending, trees that may have fallen and just generally take stock of things. In his hand, he held a small bouquet of wild things: leaves blushed crimson from frost, silvered twigs smooth as a woman's skin, and the drifting bits of seedpods that remained behind long after the seeds had flown. Today was also a pilgrimage of sorts, a strange pact he kept with a woman who had long flown herself.

He shivered a little as he walked beyond the pine coppice where the branches were feathered with snow. The day was cold, but his shiver had more to do with the fact that there were times in this wood when he felt that someone watched, someone neither evil nor benign, but most assuredly there.

He knew what his wife would say, witchy woman that she was. She would tell him it was one of those edge places where there was a fracture in time or in the world itself that allowed bits of other worlds to flit through, or creep in, she would say, and he could see her in his mind's eye, her eyes dark with enchantment.

"You know when you sometimes catch a wee bit of someone else's conversation, just snatched words, or someone says your name, but no one is there? Or you see someone just for a flash, and then you look and there's only empty air? Those are the cracks in our world. Those are the holes in the borders between this world and that."

The woman knew how to put a chill up a man's spine, that was certain. But he knew what she meant all too well, for he had enough experience of the inexplicable things of the world to know there was much between the earth and the heavens that defied logic and scientific explanation.

A land this old, this rich in history, was layered deep in overlapping worlds. He often had the sense that if he turned at just the right moment he would see creatures from another time and place crossing through the borders of his own, just as Pamela had described.

Such thoughts brought to mind another place, one that belonged to the past, one he hadn't thought about in a long time. Once, when he was a boy, he had been out roaming the woods and had gotten lost. He wasn't one to panic in such situations as he knew that only led to getting more surely lost. On that ramble, though, he had come across an ancient crannog in the midst of a bog. He thought the bog must have been a pond or wee lake long ago but had dried up over hundreds of years and become ground, albeit of the loose and shifting sort. He had very carefully picked his way across that ground, and spent the afternoon inside of the daub and wattle building. It had been a magic place, as if time did not exist inside it and he might have been himself or a woad-faced warrior from centuries long gone. He had never told anyone about it, not even Pat, to whom he confided most things. Over the years he would go there from time to time; it had been a secret that was all his own, a place where he could step out of the world. He considered that this was how it was with Pamela at times, that in their most intimate moments, in their bed and in their life, there came into being a place where they stepped from the world, a place only the two of them could go, a beautiful secret known solely to them.

After checking the borders of the property and making a mental note about an elm that had come down since his last inspection, and a bit of the stone wall that needed mending, he arrived at his final destination.

The tree still held its leaves, though there had been a terrific storm only the week before that had ravaged most of the wood and left the deciduous trees bare-branched in the stark November wind. The leaves were crimson, glowing deep in the glowering wood like blood hung in warm drops against a night-dark windowpane. He shivered again. This bit of wood always put the hairs up on his neck and brought strange thoughts to mind.

He put the wee bouquet there on a soft break in the peat, in which a plant he did not recognize grew, green even now as it lay surrounded by the first snow. He remembered just where the woman lay, just as he remembered the soaked copper streams of her hair, the ethereal ivory of her ancient skin and the strange necklace she wore, in which the flower and fruit and thorn were together, indicating passage into the world of the Others.

He paused there, touching in his heart those he loved, one by one, like the beads on a rosary, those gone: his Daddy, Lawrence, wee Deirdre and Grace, and then those living: his wife, his brother, his son and his daughter. And a prayer for the man who was missing, gone from a tower room in an evil house, leaving no trace of himself behind. People disappeared all the time in this country. He was another to add to the list of those stranded in the twilit borderlands where they were neither alive nor dead, simply gone.

Above, the leaves fretted to and fro, speaking in their own sibilant tongues of the winter come down from the skies. The leaves shone preternaturally against the limitless blue of the sky and it felt as though someone touched him... laid a hand upon his back... light... a woman's touch... but not his wife's. His breath caught in his throat and he felt that he dared not look behind him, not because he was afraid, but because something was there that was better not seen.

It happened sometimes, though never before this vividly, as though an entity brushed him in passing and opened his eyes briefly to other lives, other possibilities. It turned an ordinary moment into one of those fleeting times when all the multiplicity of universes seemed to exist, as though a thousand bridges lay before him and he could choose a different destiny by crossing the span of each one. All lives that had been granted to him at the beginning of time, all the bridges crossed and not crossed, ways by which he would not return, there pulsing in the supercharged air. And then the moment was gone, the leaves merely leaves again, the bridges having disappeared to wherever such things go. The entity behind him had gone back into the fractured air from which it had entered. But he could still feel traces of the moment on his skin and in his blood, a half-bittersweet, half-relieved lingering as such things always were.

"I would still choose this one," he said softly and only to himself, though he felt that someone else listened and smiled at his words.

He crossed himself and stood, leaving the offering to the red-headed bog woman. It was time to go home.

The Tale of Ragged Jack, continued.

JACK WALKED FOR MANY DAYS AFTER HE LEFT THE LAND OF THE FAIR PEOPLE, and he felt its ruin behind him leaving no trace of the magical people who had once lived and loved there. The autumn lasted for a time, the leaves so red they looked as though blood moved within their delicate veins. They fell in great drifts, muffling his footsteps, and at night he and Aengus made their bed in those stacks of leaves, each morning awaking to find a skeletal sheen of frost over them.

When he wasn't sure which way to go, he simply reached into his bag and let the bones guide him. They always helped him decide which way was the right way, even if, he had noted with no small frustration, the right way always seemed to be far more brambly and pitted and dark, whilst the wrong way often went along a gently-graded slope filled with sunshine and a soft way for the feet.

It was a mellow afternoon late in autumn when he came upon a fork in the path he was following. Right there at the crossroad was a treehouse, with a tiny set of stairs winding up from the ground into the thick, sturdy branches of an oak tree.

He stood looking up the stairs and thinking how nice it would be to know whoever lived inside for it looked very cozy and homely. It would be wonderful to have walls around him for a night so that he might sleep sound and not drift under the surface, not even daring to dream lest a predator steal upon him and Aengus. He was about to turn and continue on the path when a voice halted him, a voice he recognized.

"Come on up, Jack. I've been hoping you would happen this way on your travels."

He looked up to find the Owl Woman who had bound his ankle for him in the Hollow Hills. He wondered if he had slipped back somehow, yet the terrain around him remained the same, the stairs still leading up to the cottage in the boughs. The fork still there in the road.

He climbed the stairs, feeling dusty and worn. Even Aengus' pewter coat was a dull grey and matted with burrs. Ahead of them the Owl Woman climbed the long set of stairs so gracefully he was certain she was using flight in some manner *invisible to the naked eye. The cottage, small and crooked, was very high in the boughs, so high that it swayed softly from side to side and Jack couldn't fathom how it stayed put in a storm.*

"It's a thing of the air, not of the ground," the Owl Woman said, and Jack wondered if he had asked the question out loud, though he was certain he had not.

"I thought you belonged to the Fair People," he said when they had finished climbing and entered the crooked hut, tilting a bit to one side. His voice was as gritty as water drawn from the very bottom of a well. He was used to silence these last days, and his throat hurt with the movement of words.

"Like you, Jack, I was not one of them. They allowed me to come and go from their world but I was never one of them. They are gone now?" she asked, and the soft strange piping of her voice was unmistakably sad.

"Yes, they are gone," Jack said, feeling the shape in his heart where Muireann was absent.

"I thought so, for I went to the borderlands two weeks past and all I saw was a hummock of earth and beyond only the empty sea."

She sat down to knit, a long scarf that split in two, one side running out the window to the left of the hearth all the way into the forest, the other side flowing out the door and heading off over the hills. Both sides furled so far he could not see the ends of them and wondered what sort of dread giant needed a scarf of such length.

"I'm glad you remember them," he said, "because I was afraid I had dreamed them."

She smiled at him, pity in her great gold eyes. "Jack, you carry part of Muireann with you. How could you doubt that she was real?"

At first he thought she meant that he carried Muireann in his heart, but then he realized she meant the flower. He took it out of his pocket and unwrapped it, expecting a small withered ball of desiccated petals, but instead found it as whole and fresh as the day Muireann had placed it in his hand. There was even a drop of dew on one petal.

"Be careful with that flower, Jack. It is more than it appears to be."

Though that was apparent, still he asked her what she meant, but she refused to explain further, instead saying she must make supper for she knew how hungry boys were wont to be at his age.

Hunger was the only thing keeping him awake. Beyond filling his belly, he wanted only to sleep, to lie down on the hearthrug beside Aengus who was already snoring and twitching in the deep dreaming sleep of the canine. Today the bones had not spoken to Jack, had not told him which path he was to follow, and this worried him.

"All roads are the same, all arrive somewhere after journey and toil. Only they don't always arrive where we might want or expect. But expectations and wants are shifty things at best, so often we find where we end up is where we needed to be all along. Even if it's not a comfortable place."

Once again, Jack was certain he had not voiced his question aloud, or had he? How could the woman know the questions in his mind to which even he had not yet given words?

"We don't need words between us, Jack. I can see the shape of your worries in the air before me."

And indeed she could, for even Jack could make out the small spiral of smokey threads which writhed in the air, yet if he tried to look at it from any other angle, it promptly disappeared.

The Owl Woman built a small fire in the crooked hearth inside the crooked hut and she fed him soup from a cauldron, soup that tasted of pine needles and roots, dark berries and a sprinkling of something grainy that she said it was best he didn't know about.

He fell asleep to the soft clacking of the Owl Woman's needles, made of bone, he noted, and polished fine from long use. He slept soundly that night in the small hut, up so high that the boughs swayed with the night wind and the stars sprinkled their dust on the rooftop.

In the morning the fire was out but the sun warmed the roof of the little treehouse and the day outside was fine. Looking down he saw something strange, a long skein of knitted wool the color of blackberry wine, running up and away over the hills and down into the great forest beyond. It was neither the fork to the left, nor the fork to the right, but a road in-between.

"I have knit your road, Jack. The one you must follow, the final length of your journey that will take you to your destination."

"And what if I don't know what that destination is anymore?"

"Follow the road and it will find you. That's how destinations are."

After a breakfast of berries and nuts and warm bread sweet with new butter, he made his way back down the stairs and took his first faltering step onto the blackberry path. It was knit tight to last and would serve him well. He turned back once more before he left the Owl Woman. "How do I know when I've arrived, if I don't know what it is I seek?"

"You move forward and you hope. That is all anyone needs Jack, a path and some hope for their pocket. You have both those things now. Just don't look too long into the abyss when you find it, for if you gaze overlong you will end up walking amongst the dead, a ghost stuck between realms."

The Owl Woman kissed him on his forehead and it felt like a benediction, something warm in his veins to take with him and boost his courage when it faltered. Then she plucked a feather from her own wing, leaving a bead of blood like a ruby on the bare spot left behind.

"The feather is for you. It will summon help when you need it most."

"How will I know when I need it most?"

"You just will."

He looked back only once, and found she was standing still, gold eyes watch-

ing him go. She raised a wing in farewell and Jack raised his hand in kind and then on he went, down the hill into the forest's edge.

He was not alone on the road in the days that followed, for there were other wanderers: vagabonds, urchins, wayfarers, medicine men, tricksters, pig herders and gypsies, beggars and seers. Some he avoided, with others he shared their fires and food, giving of his own small store of what he had picked or captured that day. The road grew thinner as he went until there were days when he had to search high and low for a thread snagged in a tree, or a bit of blackberry wine fluff caught on a thistle. But always, if he looked hard enough, he would find a trace of it.

As the autumn passed, with its fires and fallen leaves, its frosts and deep blue skies, the travelers thinned on the road until those left walked with their heads down, muffled in wool and furs, with only a grunt in greeting to those they passed, if that much. The creatures of the woods had gone into their burrows and holes, their nests up high or to the depths of ponds that would soon solidify into ice. Until one afternoon, as the first flakes of snow were dancing light on the air, Jack realized he and Aengus had not seen another soul all day. The woods surrounding them were grey and old, the trunks of the trees stunted and gnarled, reaching up from boggy ground like grasping claws waiting to pull a boy and his dog down.

This must be the November Wood that the gypsies had told him about after he had sought their advice on finding the Crooked Man. One old woman, who reminded him of someone in his life before, had spoken these words to him.

"Such as is dark souls seeks a dark place. I hear he winters in the November Wood, deep in its heart, where neither man nor boy should like to find himself after the frosts come down."

The woman's words echoed as a warning now, as dark, tangly underbrush tore at his clothes, the bog, only partially frozen, sucking at his boots. Discouragement seemed to rise in the greenish-grey mists that the ground exhaled and sank straight into his bones and heart. But he kept going, Aengus plodding wearily at his side, the ground so soft and nasty in spots that he had to lift the dog up and sling him around his neck so that they might continue on.

Somewhere in the late afternoon as the light was fading into a thick and disturbing twilight, they came to the edge of a sluggishly-flowing stream, gelid with ice at its edges. It was just wide enough that Jack did not see how they could cross it. He was tired, so tired and would have stopped for the night and slept right there, using the thick, wet moss for a mattress, except he knew that would be a mistake that could kill both him and Aengus.

He felt something move in his bag just then, and wondered if a mouse had crawled in last night while he and Aengus slept. He opened the flap, his heart dipping a little as he saw the proof of how little food they had left. But then he saw a small glowing light in the corner of the bag and reached in to grasp it and pull it out. It was the thread spun by the woman he had met so long ago, the ageless beauty who had hidden in the sharp exterior of the crone, though perhaps it had been the other way round for all he knew—women could be tricky like that. The thread glowed with a strange light, blue as frost under the moon, and it moved as though it knew the way forward, even if he did not.

He stepped to the river's edge, understanding now what its purpose was. He threw the thread out over the dark water. It flew high, light sparking all along its length and then began to weave itself in the very air, crossing and re-crossing and then fastening itself tight to a rock upon the other side. It had built a narrow bridge by which he could cross the river.

"Wait here for me, Aengus. I have to do this part alone." How he knew this he could not say, only that it was a knowing without doubt or hesitation, something bone deep. "I will come back for you as soon as I'm done." This last was said rather shakily, for he understood the Crooked Man waited for him on the other side of the bridge's span. He must face him alone, or not at all.

Aengus gave him a look of profound betrayal and turned his back on Jack before finding a more stable patch of moss to lie down upon. Curled up around his grievance, the dog was feigning sleep when Jack looked back from the start of the bridge. He took a deep breath and stepped out onto the thread.

It held tight under his feet, strong as wood but swaying slightly. He crossed the river quickly, arriving on the other side to find that winter had been in possession longer here, for snow hid the bleak brown grass, and gathered deep on the withered arms of the trees. The moon was high, a fingernail slice of cold and the hills, hummocked with snow, breathed out chill air that shimmered like diamonds.

He was so still that at first Jack's eye slid past him, thinking he was just another black-boughed tree, but something pulled his eye back and he realized here he was at last, the man he had sought for so long now that he had gone from a soft-cheeked boy to one with a whiskered jaw and broad shoulders in the interim.

"Hello, Jack," said the Crooked Man, his voice no more than a hissing of leaves moving on the forest floor, but crawling straight into Jack's spine nevertheless.

"Hello," Jack said, with an arrow in his own voice, directed right at the dark shape ahead of him, light snow outlining his broad-brimmed hat, his satchel, his long and terrible form. The only response was a thin-lipped smile, revealing a dark hole, a gaping wound in the white night.

Jack stepped toward the Crooked Man, fear gripping his insides like an ague, but knowing this was what he had come for and he could not hesitate, could not let the man smell the fear that twisted his guts.

"You stole something from me long ago. I have come to retrieve it."

"You want your dreams, boy?" The hissing of his voice was less like leaves now and more like a serpent coiling in dry straw. "Come and take them, if you dare."

Jack stepped forward again, then stopped, for the Crooked Man's shape shifted, slowly, almost imperceptible at first, like an atmospheric disturbance, felt long before it was seen. And for one second he was a border creature, neither man nor animal. And Jack knew he had to do something fast, before it was too late and he was prey. Weaponless, a human boy was a fragile creature, all delicate head and yards of soft permeable skin. He grasped the feather from the Owl Woman's wing tight in his hand, for he had need of help now as he had never needed it before.

A wolf appeared on the edge of the forest to Jack's right—a big male, grey as smoke drifting through the dark wood. His eyes were the color of stone, cold and prickling as frost on Jack's face.

There was a wolf at his back and now a wolf in front of him, for the Crooked Man had fully changed into a wolf as black as night. Jack felt as though every inch of him were exposed, no more than blood and frail bone to be left behind for the scouring winter winds. However, he did not feel menace from the wolf now trotting out from the forest's edge, rather a strange pulling sensation. Jack stepped backward carefully, away from the snarling black coil of razor-sharp teeth and springing muscle in front of him and closer to the smoke-colored male who was now only feet away. If this was what the feather had summoned, then he would take its help gladly.

Still he shook so that his teeth chattered against each other. The universe had boiled itself down to this moment because this was life at its most basic—blood and bone and fang and fur, whose belly was exposed first, who staggered first and gave over his throat for the kill. He understood suddenly why the wolf stood patiently there, even if he did not understand how a feather could summon a wild beast. He could do it, could slip into the skin of a wild thing, become that thing, and take it over, until he no longer needed the shield of its fur and fangs. He could become it, but he would lose something of himself in the process. It was inevitable that it should be so. Still, he did not see how else to live through the next few minutes. He could not fight the wolf as a boy. He could only fight him wolf to wolf. He grasped the feather tightly in his hand and let go of himself in a way that he had never known a boy could.

At first he thought he had been wrong, for he lost his vision and was swept with a wave of pain so vast he really believed he was about to die. Was he lost in the jump, falling even now into an abyss from which he would not be able to deliver himself? Had this been the Crooked Man's plan all along?

He landed with a thump that rattled his bones down to their marrow. His sight returned, not in the form he was familiar with but a different kind of seeing, low to the ground, a seeing that took in the slightest stir of wind in the shrubbery, the twitch of movement that told of prey, a scratch on bark, moss turned over by a fleeing paw. A seeing that demanded swift movement, and a terrible stillness like nothing he had ever known as a boy.

The black wolf sprang on him at once, before he had time to fully fit to the contours of his new being, tackling him to the ground in a fury of claw and tooth and muscle that felt like a strangling vine, thick with hatred and venom. Death, he realized could come swift in this moment.

Movement was instinctive, movement was life, and so he moved: twisting, *writhing, fangs snapping, meeting air that tasted of pine and earth, meeting fur and coiling serpent-slippery muscle. Meeting bone, tasting marrow, feeling the give and roll of your own hide and sliding, ripping away from the enemy, even the pain a strange form of joy, because it spurred your own violence, your own blood hunger. It was a state of being in which the senses crossed over, blended and were not one distinct from any other.*

He felt the burning rake of claws gain purchase in his side and then rip out, freeing blood to flow. The black wolf was terribly strong, and Jack knew he would not have more than a fleeting chance to best him. He would have to hope he didn't die before that chance showed itself.

Then the black wolf had him down, flipped over on his back, and the pain in his side was like fire scything his bones from his hide. This was how death came then, swift and under a low, dark sky, the air cold as an icy razor. Suddenly the black wolf whimpered low in his throat and pulled himself out of the fight with a great shudder of his stinking hide. Jack was thrown, rolling over and up, finding his paws sinking into the boggy ground. He looked through the blood haze that clouded his vision to see what had happened, thinking perhaps he had wounded the black wolf more profoundly than seemed possible.

It was as clear as pawprints in the snow that this was not the case. The black wolf looked relatively unharmed but was afraid, lips curled up, baring his fangs, the line of fur down his back stiff as quills. He was looking at the flower that Muireann had given Jack at their parting. It must have been loosed from his pocket when his clothes fell away from his wolf body. He didn't understand what it was about the flower that could possibly be scaring the black wolf. It gave him a chance though, and chance by its very nature had to be seized. So he took the precious fear of the black wolf and righted himself, feeling the slippery letting of blood into fur as he moved.

He stood straight and looked into the black wolf's eyes. They were silver like coins, like the moon, both fathomless and depthless. They stood thus, the wind blowing over and through them and a strange knowing passed between, a language without words, one of instinct and marrow, one that was so old it had been born along with the wind and the seas. It came into his mind in pictures, shadow paintings like drawings on a cave wall seen only by firelight. The flower was Muireann's life, its essence held there within the undying petals, a final gift to him, a cloak of protection and love. He knew this in an instinctual way, just as he now knew that how a raven flew in the wind told of his fortunes in the hunt and that when the ice groaned in winter it was asking for snow to come down and lay its blanket of comfort over it. He knew that the land itself spoke in varying tempers, soft, fluting words for the green of spring, hard and wrath-filled for great cold. Just as he knew that now was his moment to strike, when the black wolf was, for just a moment, afraid.

He sprang and attacked all in one movement, rage flowing like boiling mercury through his blood. When you only had one shot you went for the throat, because it was the only guarantee of death. He bit hard, teeth clamping down, piercing, tasting the hot rush of blood, cartilage and life on his tongue. It was thick and sweet and salt, it was the taste of victory, it was the taste of life. He must not let go, must not allow the Crooked Man to slip away, to haunt his life once again.

He flipped him, the universe tilting as the big black wolf tried to use the momentum to drag him down. It was a feeble attempt, for life was ebbing swiftly now, the way it did in the wild.

Jack felt the sudden stillness, that stillness that went beyond life, the one that only existed on the other side of the boundary. The black wolf was dead. Whether the Crooked Man was or not remained a mystery, one he did not have the time to solve. The pain in his side was tipped with both ice and fire and he was afraid to look at it for fear it was a mortal wound.

He opened his eyes to see his vanquished foe and felt a ripple run straight down his spine, his ruff rising in response. There was no bloody corpse here in the grey woods, no brush of chill wind over cooling fur and blood, just the skeleton of a wolf, a wolf long dead to judge by the roots and tendrils of dying autumn vines attached to the bone, growing round and through it. He shook his head back and forth, retreating from the skeleton. What madness was this? He could not have imagined it all, could he? If so, it meant he was utterly mad himself, a fear, he admitted, that had lurked beneath the turmoil in his mind all along.

He looked down, catching his breath on pain. There were his dreams, wind-rattled against the bones of the wolf. They had changed, for the dreams that the Crooked Man had held inside him were just little rocks, dull and unremarkable, yet still he knew they were his own that had once seemed as brilliant and faceted as the finest jewels. Jack swallowed, feeling sick. Was this what he had travelled all this way for? Was this worth everything he had lost in his journey? The place where he held the loss of Muireann still felt raw around its edges and now he feared it always would. She had known when she gave him that flower that she was giving him her life. And he had been such a fool that he had taken it, not understanding in the least the sacrifice she was making, that she had been willing to die for love. He would carry the wound of that, as well as the terrible beauty, always.

He understood finally that there were no absolute triumphs in any battle worth the blood, because such a fight always took something away before it bestowed victory's thorny crown.

It took some adjustment, going back to his own body, becoming a boy again, fitting spirit to elbows and knees and upright movement. Nose twitching and itchy because it could not scent things from two hundred yards, could not taste scent on the air like a river of perfume. He felt awkward and clumsy and out of

sorts but gradually, as he moved across hills and through streams, with winter's thin light surrounding him, he realized that he had retained some of his wildness. Some strange instinct that had stayed behind in his soul now transferred to his own body. His body healed, though he would always carry a long and jagged scar that ran the entire arc of his bottom rib.

And then one day, Aengus loping at his side, he came up over the rise of a hill, snow swirling down softly through the air... and he was home. There was his house, held safe in the lee of a hill, there the great wood in which he had originally been lost, there the stables and horses, and servants and hearth. There his mother and his father. They were so happy to see him, he felt guilty that he wasn't ecstatic about being home.

After the initial flurry of emotion at his return, his parents, he could clearly see, weren't entirely comfortable with all the changes in him. But then he supposed parents never were. He had changed, indeed it was as the owl woman had said—he had looked into the Crooked Man and the Crooked Man had looked into him, and he had loved and been loved and lost that love. Such things changed one forever, put dents and fissures in the heart which made it both more open and more closed. Other things had changed too, for his senses were keen as a snake in the grass or an owl on the wind. He could hear the grass grow under the stars at night, taste the earth in every vegetable, feel the wind change direction even when he was indoors. He could see the shadows that lurked at the edge of everything: seashore, forests, fields, fences, roads, staircases, closets, bookshelves, and borders. He could not explain the changes to his parents and was sorry he could not. The changes weren't only in him, for Aengus had aged since their arrival home. Suddenly the dog's bones were creaking, his muzzle snowy, his eyes cloudy, and he preferred to spend his days beside the fire in the kitchen, curled up on a bed thick and warm rather than running constantly at Jack's side. Jack felt like he was missing one of his own limbs, an extension of his body that had been both freedom and companionship.

Life took him back eventually, into school uniforms and math exams, into rugby games, and girls and horses and books and cups of tea on cold nights. But even then he never knew when the wild sensing (for so he thought of it) might come upon him and he would think he heard the clack of the Owl Woman's needles and her strange hooting tongue, or a stray breeze would tickle his nose as he was fielding a ball and he would smell the greenness of Muireann just for a second. Or he would see a strange color such as those that only existed in the spinning woman's world. Once he was riding his horse down near the edge of his father's kingdom and he thought for a moment that he saw the leaves flicker with unnatural fire and begin to form a man. But when he checked it was just the wind moving the leaves against a small hummock of earth, though he thought he smelled a strange burning in the vicinity. It no longer frightened him, for now, seeing as he did with different eyes, he was no longer a boy and would never be one again. Some days that made him sad but most days he did not mind so much.

He had known when he returned home it would be to a place strange in its familiarity, for if there was one constant in the universe it was this—it changes. People, landscapes, friendships, dogs and love, it all changes.

But what he had once told Muireann was equally true, true as anything in life, in this world or that, in dark or light, lost or found; the things we put into our heart stay there forever. The mind, well practiced in its mercies, forgets. The heart, that ruthless and tender organ, does not.

Part Twelve

Bread and Salt
Russia – October–December 1975
London – December 1975

Chapter Eighty-four

October 1975

Departures

IT HAD BEEN A WEEK SINCE HE HAD HELD HIS SON. He had not realized how much he had come to depend on those touches of humanity, how deep he had allowed himself to be drawn into the quicksand of human warmth and assurance, of family. He worried that the child would forget him. It was so simple at this age, for memories to slip free, to love the arms that were most familiar, the ones that could be counted upon.

The day had been long, with blue hints of cold in the air, and Nikolai's hands had been so bent and stiff that he had not been able to hold the saw properly. They were under quota, though barely, for Jamie had done his best to make up the slack. It meant less food at dinner and he was already exhausted. He just wanted to go back to their small hut and to their tiny circle wherein, even if safety was an illusion, still it felt real enough to pretend.

Gregor was sitting on a stump outside the communal hut that Jamie shared with Nikolai, Shura and Vanya, big hands latticed and loose on his knees. His face was grave.

"Yasha," the big man said, "we must speak."

"Kolya?" he said, a choking fear rising in his throat, for the baby had been running a slight fever last time he had seen him. But Gregor shook his head.

"Violet?" he asked, aware that his heart was beating harder than it had been only seconds before. He did not like the look on Gregor's face. He had seen such faces before in his life and they never boded well.

"She is gone," Gregor said flatly.

"Gone?" Jamie echoed. "What do you mean—gone?" It occurred to him with a gut-twisting nastiness just how many meanings that particular word held.

"Some men came today while we were in the forest and took her away. Shura told me."

"Men?" he said, starting to feel like a stunned parrot.

"Yes, Yasha," Gregor said patiently, "the sort of men that I believe you are well acquainted with yourself."

It would not do to say the word aloud, but it hung there between him and Gregor anyway. KGB, the secret police. The men who could make you disappear as though you were no more than smoke threshed by the wind, and who could make you wish you had never been born at all before they did so. The question was, why?

"Kolya?" he asked again, a stunning blow of adrenaline hitting him in the stomach.

"He is here. She did not take him."

The relief almost took him to his knees, as did the pain for Kolya. He could not imagine circumstances under which Violet would leave her son behind if she had any choice in the matter.

"Your friend is here," Gregor slapped his hand to Jamie's shoulder, dispersing a little of his shock. "He is waiting in the hut you shared with the woman. I did not wish for you to go in not knowing."

Gregor never used her name. Jamie wondered why he had not comprehended that before. It had been a mistake of rather epic proportions.

"Why didn't you tell me?"

"Because," Gregor replied, "I did not think you told her anything she did not already know."

"You knew?"

Gregor shrugged, eyes unreadable. "I suspected, that is all. I did warn you, Yasha, that wolf is always wolf to man. But sometimes the wolf is a woman."

"No."

Gregor raised an eyebrow. "No? Then consider it a fairytale."

Jamie walked away toward the hut. He stumbled a little and realized he couldn't feel his legs properly. Shock, yes, shock would do that. So might an avoided truth.

Facing Andrei was like walking into a looking glass, for the expression on his face mirrored the one Jamie felt on his own countenance.

"Where have they taken her, Andrei?"

"I don't know. They just told me that I had visiting privileges today. I came and was told she was gone, but had left Kolya behind."

"Andrei—if..." he trailed off. Andrei understood all the implications and hardly needed it spelled out.

Andrei looked at him long, the blue eyes dense with pain and another emotion that looked a great deal like pity.

"They said she did not struggle, but went with them quietly, Yasha. She was not taken by force."

"But she didn't take Kolya."

"I know," Andrei said flatly.

He knew the face he presented Andrei with was a perfect blank, because he didn't know how to feel or what to say. The scope of such a betrayal—if it were indeed such—was beyond his comprehension. If it were not a betrayal, then he could not even touch those thoughts. He could not live and think of such things happening to her.

He heard someone saying 'no' over and over and realized in a dim, distant way that it was himself, and that he could not stop. Andrei was staring at him but he understood. The pain of it was there in his face, burning incandescent.

"Yasha, you have to go. You have to take my son and go. Don't you see? If she is KGB, we don't have much time left. And even if she isn't then you must go before it's too late. They will take him from us, Yasha. He's almost of an age where they will put him in an orphanage and he'll die there."

"But you—"

Andrei shook his head. "I cannot take him, for what if one day I am not there to care for him? I cannot trust Ilena to do right by him. I will not have him suffer for my sins."

Jamie nodded, numb, aware he was in a room, standing, breathing, but unable to orient himself in time and space. Andrei was right. They would have to get Kolya out one way or another. If he disappeared into Russia's nightmare system of orphanages, he would die, or perhaps even worse, survive. He would also be told that his parents had abandoned him and that only the State cared for his welfare.

"What sort of fools were we?" Jamie asked.

"Her story was designed to make us putty in her hands. The father shot after years in a gulag, the harsh mother, the old servant, her rebellion to the State—all of it. When you look at it from a certain angle, they are things for which we both have a weakness. Maybe some of it was even true. Who knows?"

Yes, Violet would have been wise enough to weave in pearls of truth to the chain of lies. In fact, the most effective lies were those that were so close to the truth as to be almost indiscernible from it. In the West, you might share bits and pieces of your life story, casually and without worry but in Russia the rules changed. Here it was not safe to do so, so that people only got the scattered crumbs of another's story, for the core must be held tight against betrayal. Because the core was all you had if you found yourself in the basement of Lubyanka, on your knees, your only company a man they called 'The Electromonter'. Your core was your only refuge when the pain began, and went on for weeks and months, until you were turned inside out and no longer knew your own name or would happily sell your mother for a reprieve or for the privilege of death.

"It is time, Yasha. I am calling in the last of my chips."

"Why do they owe you so much, Andrei?" he asked, uncaring suddenly who was listening or why. He needed to know the truth for once. He was so weary of all the subterfuge.

"It's what I do for them, what is in here," Andrei tapped his forehead. "I've played a long game, Yasha, always staying a step ahead, or even a half-step—or so I thought until today. Once they get everything out of me that they need, my time will be up and they will dispose of me as quietly and as quickly as they can. With Violet and what she may have told them... the hourglass is down to its last few grains. Will you take Kolya if I can get you out? Will you take my son with you?"

"He is my son too," Jamie said. "I would never leave him behind." Because he had decided in that moment that he was going. They could try to kill him if they liked, but he was going.

"I wonder," Andrei said quietly, "if she ever loved either of us?"

"I don't think it matters anymore," Jamie replied. At last he left the hut, the silence between them so enormous it was suffocating.

Outside, he walked, wanting only the reassurance of Kolya—to know that he too wasn't an illusion. The air was cold, the sky a heartless blue that spoke of the winter so close, the winter that would come down like an iron fist. He heard voices speak to him but they lay in some other world beyond a boundary through which he could not understand individual words. It was enough right now, to stay upright, to keep walking, to find Kolya.

Someone touched his arm and he heard Gregor say, "Let him be."

Kolya was in the small hut that served as a daycare. He was asleep. The old woman who watched him took one look at Jamie's face and left in silence. He touched Kolya's back lightly. The baby breathed deep and even, his eyes shut tight, his face a perfect canvas of pure trust.

I love you, Yasha. He shook his head. There was pain in him like a fire spreading beneath his skin. He ignored it and put it aside for later, maybe for never.

Everything here was a Potemkin village, a façade, and when you looked behind it there was nothing, only a grey emptiness that stretched on forever. And more lies, and more façades. And millions and millions of people wiped out as though they had never existed. Of course, one learned to lie and lie well in such a world until perhaps one no longer knew what truth was, or if it mattered. Perhaps he was a fool for believing truth could matter in such a place. He had forgotten for a moment, a moment as lucent as dawn, that this was the Soviet Union.

After a very long time he lay down beside Kolya, allowing the child's even breathing to calm him. He watched the fire flicker through the slats in the potbellied stove, over the red-gold aureole of Kolya's hair. He watched for a very long time and thought no thoughts at all.

IT WAS JAMIE WHO FOUND NIKOLAI, for they always breakfasted together on the bread and thin oatmeal before setting out for their day. Generally, they sat in silence, but there was a mutual warmth of companionship that Jamie enjoyed whether words were spoken or not. It was not like the old man to be absent, not even when his lungs were at their worst.

He had seen him last evening when Nikolai had come to say goodnight to Kolya, as he always did when it could be managed. The old man had stroked his trembling hand over the fine red-gold of Kolya's head, and before he departed to his own bed, he had done the same to Jamie. Jamie swore out loud, seeing the gesture now for what it had been.

He had been so stupid since Violet's departure that he had not been attuned in the way he normally would have been. He had not, he realized, been paying attention.

He stood and walked down the bench to where Vanya sat hunched over a hot cup of water.

"Vanya, did you see Nikolai this morning?"

Vanya looked up with those eyes the color of amaranthine under frost, those eyes that always saw too much and understood a great deal more.

"He left the hut in the early hours and he asked that I do not follow."

Jamie went straight to the common hut where the piano was. Nikolai would seek music, he knew, both as solace and as a pathway to another time, another space.

The old man sat at the piano, fingers frozen on the keys. His head was bowed down, forehead resting against the music stand, hair a blaze of silver against the burled wood. Jamie hunkered down beside him, touching two fingers to the hollow of the old man's neck. He did not need to do it, for there was a look of peace on Nikolai's face that Jamie had not seen in life. He dropped to his knees and took one of Nikolai's hands. Crabbed and now cold with death, it remained curled over Jamie's own and he thought he could sense the final notes held fast, as gold in a vein, within the fingers.

There was a flask on the floor, fallen sideways. Jamie picked it up and sniffed at the opening—vodka and something more that he recognized. He put it back down.

Another link in the chain which bound him broken now, struck off with purpose. A gift from the man who had not been his father, given to him who was not a son. Now, now he could leave and not look back with regret.

Vanya stood in the doorway, red hair a blaze in the morning light. It reminded Jamie of the copper glow of Violet's hair. He put the thought aside, into a room that he had built swiftly in her absence, the door of which he hoped to seal shut one day soon.

Vanya gazed at Nikolai, his face impassive. "It is what he wished for, Jamie. It is best. You would have found it very hard to leave him. This he knew."

Jamie looked at him sharply, wondering if Vanya was making a guess or if he knew more than he should.

"When you go, Yasha," Vanya said softly, "I am coming with you. You cannot expect to manage alone with Kolya in the wilderness, so I come." His voice was modulated so that he might have been speaking of which sort of tea he preferred. Jamie looked into the exotic cat eyes of the man across from him.

"Why are you so certain I am going?"

"Because you have to," Vanya said simply. "Or you will be a dead man."

"Then come," he said, for it was not in him to deny any man a chance of freedom. And now it was clear he could not risk leaving Vanya behind.

Chapter Eighty-five
Dasvidania is Russian for Goodbye...

I WILL LEAVE IT TO YOU WHAT YOU WISH TO TELL HIM. It may be best to let him believe you are his real father, it will be..." Andrei's voice failed him for a minute, "simpler for him."

They were sitting in the hut Jamie had once shared with Violet and Kolya, the stove glowing with heat and a storm blowing up outside that had skirls of leaves dancing past the windows. Kolya was sitting on Andrei's knee, chewing happily on his own fist, blue eyes wide and curious on the face of his father.

All was in readiness, or as much readiness as could be fashioned in desperation and at speed. It had been Gregor who told him, quietly and quickly one evening, that there was a tunnel under the bell tower. A very old tunnel, long forgotten. How Gregor knew about it Jamie was not told.

"I do not know where it goes. I think it is likely that it comes out in the *bor* somewhere. I was never able to explore it fully, so it is a great risk, but perhaps the only one that gives the four of you a chance of getting out before the guards realize you are gone."

"Four?" Jamie said, quirking a golden brow at the man in front of him.

"Ah, my harlequin," Gregor grinned, "do not look so hopeful. I do not speak of myself but of the dwarf. He will go with you and Vanya. He is useful and trustworthy. Besides, you will need the milk goat for the boy, and you will need the dwarf for the goat."

Jamie felt there was no adequate reply to this bit of logic, so made his arrangements with Shura, who showed no surprise at the plans. Jamie was starting to wonder if there was anyone in the camp who *didn't* know about the escape plot. Not that, as plots went, it was terribly sophisticated, a thing both he and Andrei had admitted as they sat here together for the last time.

"He is beautiful," Andrei said simply, not even looking up from the baby's face.

"He is," Jamie agreed. For it was true. Though Kolya was not quite a year old, it was clear already that he had inherited his mother's copper hair and his father's imperious face.

"Yasha, I—I..." Andrei's words halted. "I don't know what to say. All these years and now I am mute... now when it matters most, there is nothing to say. Except for this—raise my son well. Love him as I would have, had I the choice."

"Andrei?"

"Things are in motion over which I no longer have control." Andrei scratched his neck, two fingers flicking quickly at his ear. Two days then.

He saw suddenly the age in Andrei, not by the normal measures of such things but by the shadows in his eyes, by the ghosts that were bound to him by memory and history, by the terrible yearning in his face for the son he would not see grow to manhood.

Jamie went to stand by the window, unable to bear either the look on Andrei's face or the broken Russian words that he whispered to Kolya. He knew only too well what it was to say goodbye to one's son forever.

"One day..." Jamie began and Andrei summoned up a ghost's smile.

"One day, when the guards are asleep and the sun no longer shines at midnight and we can fly like the raven... I will see you then, my Yasha."

Andrei passed Kolya into Jamie's arms and the boy wrapped his arms around Jamie's neck, laying his head on his shoulder.

And so it was time.

"There aren't any words," Jamie said, feeling a terrible pain in his chest. "other than I love you brother, and goodbye."

Andrei kissed both of his cheeks and then his lips, then bent his head to his son and kissed his forehead. Kolya gurgled with delight and Andrei closed his eyes in pain as he turned away. Jamie took one last look at the man with whom he had finished his youth.

"Hurry, Yasha, and remember us from whom you part. Hurry, you that are going away."

It was fitting that a Russian goodbye should consist of poetry and heartbreak, for of what else was this land made?

Holding Kolya close to his chest, Jamie left the building.

THE FOLLOWING NIGHT ALL WAS IN READINESS FOR THEIR DEPARTURE. They had done all they could, carefully stowing things away in corners and holes where they would not be seen by the guards, who were suspicious of the slightest variation in routine.

He was moving from the dining hall back to the hut, wondering if he would be able to sleep, knowing it was unlikely in the extreme but at least it would provide him with several hours to worry about all the variables over which he had no control.

He sensed rather than saw Gregor near the doorway of the hut, for the big man was well hidden in the deep autumn shadows that gathered thickly at twilight. He halted, for there were things to be said. But Gregor spoke first.

"Smells like snow."

"It does," Jamie agreed, for the air had that strange stillness to it and the fresh smell that presaged snow. It had been a warm day, with sun enough to feel it in the marrow of their bones, but the twilight had brought a raw dampness. Yes, it would snow. But he thought it wasn't likely that Gregor had been waiting out here to discuss the impending weather.

The big man leaned up against the side of the hut, drawing hard on his cigarette. He passed it to Jamie, who took a grateful drag, savoring the harsh edge of Russian tobacco.

"So, tomorrow you go. Before dawn is the best time. We will say prayers that the real snow holds off a bit longer, yes? It is not a good time of year for travel," he laughed. "Are you sure you won't stay until spring?"

"I thought you didn't talk to God," Jamie said.

Gregor looked at him, dark eyes distant. "When I am little boy hiding in the forest, and wandering the roads of this land, I am always praying for someone to come and rescue me. Those are not the kind of prayers that a man forgets. Those I will say for you, Yasha, if you promise to say ones for me, for my black soul."

"Always," Jamie said, and meant it. "You could come with us, Gregor. There is always a place in the world for a strong man." The offer was made in sincerity, even if Jamie knew their odds of getting out of Russia alive weren't terribly high. Still, they were higher odds than staying in the camp was going to allow.

Gregor stubbed out his cigarette against the side of the hut, its coal eclipsed in the dim light, only a tendril of smoke to mark its passing. He took a deep breath and stretched his back, reaching his arms out wide.

"I am thinking Russia is only country large enough for Gregor. I am thinking that a Russian soul withers up and blows away in a foreign place. So I will stay, but you, Yasha, you will go home, because this land is not yours."

"Gregor, if you stay—" Jamie stopped, no one knew better than Gregor what the cost of staying was.

"It is as you said to me—a man who lives by the sword must also die by it. This is justice. This is balance. This is what the Russian soul understands. This is a good death. Now give me your hand."

Jamie put his hand out, feeling the brutal strength of the fingers that touched his own. Gregor sliced his hand before he realized that the man held a knife. Gregor then sliced his own, a thick line of dark blood welling up instantly across the broad, hard palm. He grasped Jamie's hand tightly, the slickness of blood, hot and viscous, binding their two hands together. His eyes were hard as onyx as they held to Jamie's.

"Soon, my brother, we will both be free."

He pulled Jamie to him and gave him a hug that would have crushed him had he not been braced for it. Then he shoved him away toward the hut, voice rough. "Go now."

Jamie walked away feeling slightly bruised, his hand burning like he held Greek fire in his palm.

"Yasha!"

Jamie turned back. Gregor stood tall, strong as an oak, giving off the illusion that he would always be so.

"When you say those prayers, stand beside the sea."

Jamie nodded, for it was all Gregor needed. He knew as he walked to the hut for the final time that his freedom had been paid for in the most precious commodity of all, that of life itself.

THEY ESCAPED IN THE PRE-DAWN HOURS. The fires had begun in the deep of the night, set off like a chain of finely-tuned explosions. They had been ready to go, to slip, fine as sifted fog through the old chapel and down the long stairs into the bowels of the bell tower.

They were all sleepless and strung with nerves like catgut on a violin except for Kolya, who by grace was in the deep and silent sleep of the very young. It would not last. And so they must flee without a backward glance lest they be trapped forever in the underworld of the Soviet Empire.

Not to look back was impossible, for his eyes were drawn as he paused on the threshold of the chapel, back to where the flames shot high and gave the lie of a false dawn. There he saw Gregor, a Slavic Hephaestus, pure element, heat and forge, mercury spilling deadly and smoking into the forced channels of imprisonment.

But in the last moment, lit scarlet and searing, a burning chiascuro of outlawry and rebellion, stood a man who bowed to no authority greater than his own.

Soon, my brother, we will both be free.

Chapter Eighty-six
Beauty

HE AWOKE JUST BEFORE DAWN. Shura and Vanya were still asleep, Kolya too, mummified in the skins that kept him warm through the bitter nights. Jamie took a deep breath of the chilly air and walked toward the rim of the lake, a silver scrim against the horizon.

An angular shape hovered at the edge, taking awkward steps on legs too long for anything but flight, a lone heron picking its way through the reeds. It was in silhouette, only the tips of its feathers delineated in the vague promise of dawn. He wondered if it was sick or wounded for it ought to have been long gone by now, flown south for the winter, not picking its way through icy water that would soon freeze at the edges. Jamie stood still, mesmerized by its alien presence.

The trip through the long dank tunnel underneath the crumbling monastery had been fraught with anxiety at every step. There had been no way to ascertain ahead of time whether parts of the tunnel had collapsed, or been flooded and washed away over the years. At more than one point, they had been in water up to their knees, and then had to crawl through other sections digging rock and soil out with their bare hands. Agrafina, the goat, had not been overly happy about the dark nor the crawling through narrow earth-choked gaps and bleated until they thought they would either go deaf or the guards would be able to hear her through the several feet of earth.

When they found the end of the tunnel, they had bided their time until dark would soon be falling, and emerged into the gloom of a stand of fir. It had been eerily quiet as they stood there under the great fronded boughs, drinking in the amber scent of them and working out which way to travel. They had to avoid patrols that might be out hunting for them while they kept to a northwest heading.

They set out at once, Kolya quiet and wide-eyed, belly full of rich goat's milk. He had proved to be an exceptional traveler considering the brutal pace they had set from the beginning, and slept at his regular times strapped to

Jamie's front or Vanya's back.

Last night they had stopped by the edge of this lake, mirror still and reflecting back a sunken world of crimson, scarlet and gold, the sinking sun mixing with the foliage in a dazzling display. He stood here now on its shore, uncertain what it meant to go home, particularly when you could not find any remnant of that place inside you anymore. But like this heron, he could not remain stranded here in this land for fear of being permanently frozen.

How long he stood there he did not know, silent, waiting for something he did not acknowledge but which he realized was speaking to him nevertheless.

The heron rose, carved against the sky in silver and ink, rose into the curtains of dawn, limned in mists of pearl grey and a strange shimmering verdigris that gave way to a stain of pink that spread and deepened, strengthening like a single chord rising above a symphony. The bird's wings swept in tempo, rising, rising until the stain burst and became scarlet, vermilion, sienna and gold, and the world hung for an instant shivering on that one note, the heron flying into the face of the sun.

The sight of it cracked something inside him, something he had kept still and frozen since coming to Russia, that thing that resided within a man's soul that stood in awe at the profound and churning beauty of the world. He had not wanted to know if he could still feel beauty, could still ache for all that the world was and all that it was not.

He had moments like this in his life, a handful, in which he felt as fragile and transparent as tissue, as though the universe flowed through him in all its beauty and transcendence. Against this he had no defense. It was as painful as it was beautiful, for such moments did not repeat themselves in their entirety, but came differently, giving him the understanding of how much he had changed in the intervening time.

He felt as empty and light as a milkweed pod scoured clean by autumn's rough winds. He turned away from the lake and the heron as it floated up and away, a mere black speck against that violent and shimmering sun, to begin the day's journey.

Chapter Eighty-seven
Bread and Salt

THEIR DAYS HAD ACQUIRED A RHYTHM OF SORTS, which helped to stave off the worst of the exhaustion that seemed to travel no more than a few steps behind them, a weighty shadow they could not shake but could not afford to have catch up either. He did not always know where they were. The need for stealth and passing villages in the night like a sneak-thief made navigating their way that much more difficult. Yet he found if he shut down the thoughts in his head and listened to what his body and skin seemed to understand, he knew instinctively which way to go. He had taken to standing at each invisible crossroads and closing his eyes. The other two knew to be silent and Vanya would take Kolya from him, walking off a way and singing in a low, gravely voice that Kolya seemed to find quite enchanting.

He would stand still and bring his instincts to the fore. He was reading the night sky in this same way, dividing it into thirty-two separate sections, able to impose the vision of those imaginary lines onto the sky itself and thus know exactly where a particular star would rise and where it would set, and use this lineation that arced across the sky as his baseline. It was not that hard once he got the worrying portion of his brain out of the way and relied on memory and the knowledge that was innate inside of a man. If he could steer a course on the trackless wastes of the ocean then he could do it in the trackless wastes of Russia too.

It was not all so easy. There was the day they almost ran into a squad of Red Army soldiers. It had been a near miss, for they were tired and had come to the stumbling point when no one spoke and they each just kept putting one foot in front of the other until they had to stop for the night or Kolya's lusty cries forced them to.

They had been walking in heavy woods where the debris of the forest floor muffled sound and hid intruders. The canopy above their heads kept the weather off them and muffled every sound so it felt like walking on cotton. Unfortunately, if they could not be heard until the last minute, the reverse was also true.

They were on a twisting path, all of them silent with exhaustion, Kolya a dead weight against his chest when he had just known——there was a bend some small way ahead and he could feel a group of men coming. He turned, putting his fingers to his lips and indicating that they should all move quietly off the path into the dense trees. A fallen tree a few feet off the path became their hiding place. There was no time to go deeper into the woods where they might manage to lose themselves in the gloomy green twilight.

They crouched there behind the rotting log, the scent of moss and decaying wood heavy in their nostrils, hoping and praying that the soldiers would move past swiftly. But one stopped to smoke. He was young, as soldiers were, blond hair shorn close to his skull, the tip of his nose red with cold. His eyes were the ice-blue of the Slav and strangely innocent. Behind the tree, they all held their breath, the lazy curls of smoke from the soldier's cigarette hovering around their heads. He leaned on the other side of the fallen log, so close that Jamie could hear the soft snick of his lips on the cigarette. Kolya stirred against Jamie's chest, about to make the fretful noises of the not-quite-awake-but-assuredly-hungry. Jamie felt his heart seize in his chest and promptly lodge itself in the vicinity of his throat. He slipped off his mitten and reached into his pocket, heart pounding, for the crust of bread he replaced every other day. He crumbled it and slid his hand inside his coat, feeding it into Kolya's mouth, and hoping to God it would be enough to stopper him until the damn soldier moved on. He kept crumbling the bread and feeding it to Kolya, one bite at a time, piece by piece, trying to buy their survival.

Kolya managed a squeak that floated out past Jamie's thumb and they all ceased to breathe. Even the goat, Shura's large hand around her muzzle, was round-eyed with horror.

The soldier, in the act of putting out his cigarette, looked around, eyes sharp now and seeming to hone in straight at their ragged group. Jamie wondered wildly if one could smell hunger because if so, he was sure the stink of the three of them would lead the soldier straight over the log and into their midst.

But the angels seemed to be on their side for the soldier shrugged and moved off down the trail to join his squad. It took another minute to resume breathing. Kolya was wriggling like an infuriated bunny trapped in a burlap sack and it was only a matter of minutes before he howled, the bread having done little to appease him. Jamie had his hand lightly over the boy's mouth, feeling the small furious bursts of his breath on the edges of his cold hand. Their time had almost run out.

Shura milked the goat right there into their one bottle and maneuvered the nipple into Kolya's mouth before Jamie took his hand away. Relief swept through them all as Kolya clamped fiercely onto the nipple without letting out another peep.

Three bodies collapsed limply against the log, damp with sweat and shaking at how near they had come to discovery. As soon as Kolya was fed, they moved back onto the path, walking as swiftly as they dared.

Later, when they had chosen a hollow in the forest for their bed and lit a fire, Vanya asked him, "How did you know, Yasha?"

"Know what?" Jamie asked, the heat of the fire making him drowsy. He didn't have first watch so he could lie down with Kolya and sleep for a few hours.

"That the soldiers were coming. We had just enough time to hide and then there they were."

"I—I'm not sure," Jamie said. Now that he thought about it, it had just been a feeling or rather, he had been able to feel them coming—through his feet and on the surface of his skin—and he had known it was a large party of men. It was as Gregor had said; *You learn to live in your body rather than your head. You listen to your ears but also to what your skin tells you. You understand what the birds are saying and can talk to a wolf merely by looking her in the eyes.*

That night it snowed, the first serious snow of the season and a good eight inches of it. Now they would be far easier to track if indeed someone was on their trail. The snow was going to make everything a great deal more difficult. Jamie only hoped that the cold would not follow on its heels because in the state they were in, a few cold nights were likely to kill them.

Shura noticed the wolves first, five of them, wraiths that slid in and out of the blue shadows cast by the birches and firs. Jamie had once heard that wolves could smell death's approach and he worried that this was why the pack trailed them. But he could no longer remember if this was fact or something he had read long ago in a fairytale. One thing he knew for certain, wolves understood fear, and could feel the fine trembling threads of it on the air each time it fluttered inside a man's heart.

"I don't think it's usual for them to follow men like this," Shura said, dark eyes troubled. One did not need, Jamie thought, to be a mind reader to understand what he was thinking. If the wolves were tracking them, it was because the wolves had decided they were worth the risk of attacking. "They are generally timid around men. If they attack it is usually children or women they go after. But I am small and so is Kolya. Vanya is pretty enough to be a woman and Agrafina—close your ears, my little darling—is not even a substantial breakfast in their view. Maybe they are thinking you are the only man here, Yasha." This did little to quell the icy feeling in the pit of Jamie's stomach. "Also I fear it is because we have the perfume of weakness," he ended grimly, and no one needed his speech corrected to understand exactly what he meant.

The forced march was taking its toll on all of them. They were weary, hungry and afraid that they would perish one by one with no one to mark their passing but each other. The wolves on their trail underscored the general feeling of desperation. It had been impossible to catch any game with wolves so near and they hadn't had a decent meal in several days. If Agrafina hadn't been so necessary to Kolya's survival, Jamie knew the goat would have found herself over a fire by now.

Four days after their encounter with the soldier, they stopped mid-afternoon on a large outcropping of rock. Kolya needed to be fed and changed from the small store of cloth diapers that they washed and hung to dry each night over the fire.

Jamie also needed to regain his bearings, to know how many degrees to tack into the wind (to use terminology with which he was comfortable). A thick silence had fallen over all of them some hours back and he knew they needed to rest and regroup before continuing.

"Yasha."

Jamie turned, hearing the warning note in Shura's voice.

Not far away was a ridge thrusting out of the snow, bony as a hunched spine. On it the wolves stood still as gelid water, their fur silhouetted in the blue light of Russian winter. The leader, a big male, had a huge ruff the color of smoke and long, white legs. Jamie could feel the wolf's contemplation upon his skin, that act of instinct that allowed the wolf to decipher weakness, to judge when and how best to strike.

It seemed hours passed before the big male broke his stare and turned away. The rest of the pack followed, slinking through the gathering shadows, layered now in deeper blues and bruised greens as night approached. Not weak enough yet, not yet ripe enough with the reek of hunger, Jamie thought. But soon they would be, and when they were, the wolves would be ready and waiting.

Jamie breathed out the frosted air he had held during the silent standoff with the wolf and turned to Shura and Vanya. They presented a woeful picture, exhausted to the point of standing still and allowing themselves to freeze. The only visible bit of Vanya was his eyes, rendered a darker amethyst by the contrasting blue of his face rag. Shura, who had to struggle with both the goat and the truncated length of his legs, sat in the snow, hat skewed to one side as if even its normally unsinkable pompom was defeated. Kolya lay against Vanya's chest, head on his shoulder, in a silence that was unnatural in one so young. Even the goat looked melancholy, and Jamie knew they had to snap themselves out of the mind set into which they had fallen. Were the wolves to eat one of them now, the animals would likely commit some form of lupine *hara-kiri*, from ingesting the black gloom that seemed to infest all their cells.

"I suppose," Vanya said in the vague, weary tone they had all adopted, "many of them are dead now."

Jamie did not respond and Shura merely looked down at his mittened hands. Vanya did not need anyone to agree with him. They all knew it was true. They had to put aside the sacrifice that had put them on this road. It would drive a man crazy to acknowledge it too soon and they could not afford such things just now. Certainly, he could not think of Andrei, yet... Andrei, who had provided the fire to release the phoenix... Andrei who had not intended that he should leave the camp that day after he had come with men well-bribed to help him create the distraction that would release his son and his friend.

Jamie took Kolya from Vanya. It wasn't his turn but the young man's face was pinched with cold and exhaustion and he gave Jamie a weak smile of gratitude.

"Get up. We need to keep going," Jamie said, though he wasn't certain he could find his feet at this point. Still, if they moved, they would stop brooding and it was imperative that they find somewhere better than this windswept rock to break for the night. Ahead was an unbroken line of pine trees. They would head there where the thick stand would provide both shelter and fuel for the night. He stood, grateful that Kolya had succumbed to the prevalent mood and gone to sleep. Now he would only have to put up with Shura's monk-like chanting, an act, which he claimed, kept his spirits aligned with the universe, and Vanya's grim mood.

The wind was picking up, blowing sheer against their faces and nipping sharply at their ears. Not sharply enough to drown out the bickering twosome behind him, but at least he was spared every other sentence or so.

"...I swear if you quote that damned poet to me one more time, I will show you what sacrifice is—literally."

"Ours is not a caravan of despair, my friend," Shura said, and even Jamie thought he might choke him. Some months ago Shura had discovered a volume of Rumi in the Commander's library, and had been quoting it liberally ever since.

He turned to tell them both to shut up, before he knocked their miserable Slav heads together when the ground abruptly vanished from under his feet. One minute he was on solid ground and the next he was falling through space, clutching Kolya as tightly as he could to cushion the impact. He hit the ground on his rear end and fell backwards, the baby bumping against his chest but not taking any of the brunt of the fall. He looked above them and saw three gaping holes. They had wandered off the edge of a sharp-edged bank that had been hidden by the fresh snow. Jamie looked around. They were in a shallow valley, filled with snow and pine trees.

Vanya caught his breath first and came to check if the others were safe. Kolya had been stunned into silence and Jamie checked him over immediately.

Other than having had a good fright, the baby seemed to be fine. Jamie was marginally less so. It felt as if he had been pulled over a bed of large stones by his feet, which wasn't too far from what had happened. He sat up carefully, one hand still cupped firmly to Kolya's head. He hurt all over, but no bones seemed to be broken.

"Shura?" he said, for he could not see the man anywhere. "Where the hell is he?"

Vanya shrugged, his eyes scanning every bush and shrub. "How far could he have rolled? I know he's built like a barrel but you'd think he would have bumped into a tree along the way." Vanya's tone was dry but Jamie saw the tension in his face as he looked around. There was a long slide in the snow and then a blank space as though the man had slid all the way down and then bounced off into invisibility. Jamie stood, joggling Kolya instinctively though the baby was still quiet, his dense blue eyes enormous in his face and his bottom lip, red as a cherry, starting to wobble the slightest bit. Jamie rubbed his back, hoping to forestall a full-blown wail, though the poor lad deserved one.

"Hush, *moya sladkaya*," he said, softly, for Russian was the language of comfort to Kolya. He continued to murmur silly things in the pidgin mix of Russian, English and Gaelic he had been speaking to the boy from birth. It calmed Kolya and he put his arms around Jamie's neck, clinging tight as an eel round a mussel, but he did not cry.

Without warning, Shura popped out of a dense stand of pine, his hat, woolen bobble in place, now righted on his head. He had a smile on his face.

"Where were you?" Vanya demanded, tone angry and accusing.

"I merely rolled somewhat further than you," Shura said with great dignity, "but that is to be expected given my resemblance to a barrel with legs."

Vanya had the grace to flush.

"Wait until you see what my tumble has uncovered, though! Come! Come!" Shura gestured with impatience, his face alight. Jamie and Vanya followed, ducking under the snow-laden branches and through the dense patch of pines. They came out into a space that was a clear and narrow ribbon through the trees, perfectly straight in its lines. Jamie felt a small thrum of excitement low in his belly.

Shura had uncovered a few railroad ties, half rotted away, but instantly recognizable.

"It's a rail line, one of those ghost ones that Stalin had built," Shura said. "Don't you see? We can follow it. It should take us right to the border, or close enough. We'll have to leave it before we get there, it's too dangerous on the border itself but for now it's a marked trail. This has to be one of the lines meant to reach Leningrad."

They could indeed follow the rail line, but it might lead nowhere. Under Stalin, many such rail lines had been built with *zek* labor and they had simply gone nowhere but into the wilderness, ending abruptly. It was rumored that more than one hundred thousand prisoners lost their lives building rail lines that were never used—made to work in all conditions, temperatures below minus sixty in the winters, swarms of flies in the summer that drove men mad, mud into which a man could sink and drown. Sufficient time had not been granted to construct the lines properly and as a consequence bridges collapsed, embankments washed out and bogs swallowed the lines whole. Cars had often been abandoned mid-track in the middle of a wilderness that swallowed them within a few years.

But for now, it was their best chance. They struck out northwest, where the rail line ran through the thick stands of overgrown pine. Vanya had taken Kolya back and Jamie missed the weight of the baby, for the boy had become both a comfort and a part of him over this last year. He felt so protective that he could not sleep at night unless Kolya was tucked up beside him, his heavy breathing weight the thing that kept Jamie tethered to the planet, traveling along this invisible road leading, he hoped, out of the Soviet Union—hopefully before the wolves shed their reservations about eating them. They walked heads down, for the snow had begun to fall thick and fast, large, wet flakes that clung to their clothes and eyelashes. They walked in silence much of the afternoon and Jamie was considering that it was time to stop and set up whatever sort of camp they could manage when Vanya exclaimed aloud.

"Yasha—look!"

Jamie looked up, wondering what the hell it was now: a tribe of bears, a herd of moose, half the Soviet Army? He cleared the ice from his eyelashes, peering through the thick fall of snow to make out the humped form of something very large ahead... and smiled.

There it was, one of the abandoned rail cars that apparently dotted the countryside, right here with pine trees growing up to the doors and rust coating its sides. Tonight they would sleep soundly and not have to worry about either the wolves or their fire dying down.

The doors were stiff with long disuse and screeched as Jamie and Vanya pried them open, setting off a shower of rust into the pristine snow that coated both the car and the tracks below. Inside it was filthy with time and neglect but it was only a matter of securing a few pine branches and sweeping things down. A tiny stove stood in the corner and a clouded mirror hung askew on one wall. There was a table too, and a chair that had long ago succumbed to the depredations of rot and insects, suggesting that someone had sought sanctuary here for a time and made of this rusty car a home. It begged the question of what had happened to that person, though no one voiced the question aloud, for superstition about their own fate prevented such queries.

Shura took Agrafina with him to find some leaves and shrubbery that she could eat, while Vanya went to forage for more wood. There was a small pile of dry kindling and split birch to start a fire, which Jamie did before changing Kolya and feeding him.

They ate sparingly but well that night. Shura managed to trap a wild hare in the woods and cooked it with some roots, which were bitter, but at least filling. An old tin bucket proved sturdy enough to hold water so they filled it with snow and melted it down enough times for each to have a bit of a wash.

It was Jamie's turn to take the first watch so Shura and Vanya bedded down right after dinner and were asleep in a matter of minutes.

Jamie sat on an upturned birch log and hoped that he could stay awake until it was Vanya's turn, for the warmth and relative safety of the train car had a soporific effect. The night breathed out chill vapors but inside the train car it was warm next to the potbellied heater, glowing red with birch logs. Kolya was fed and Agrafina was curled up in a corner sleeping the sleep of a righteous goat. Shura had found her some grass in a relatively snow-free patch under a birch tree. Kolya slept deeply, face gilded soft in the light of the fire. His hair was coming in thickly, a rich, deep red-gold like coins immersed in whiskied honey. His weight was low but should they survive this trip, that could be remedied swiftly enough.

Jamie was too tired to rein in his thoughts completely, though he did manage to hold them back from Violet. His strength was low and he knew he could not endure that just now. The grief was a double-edged axe above his head, ready to drop and obliterate him should he allow it. But home—that he might manage tonight. Home. It seemed a ridiculous notion—a house, warmth, as surreal as the villages they passed by in the dark of night. As if it were only a place he had dreamed once and vaguely recalled. It was enough right now to imagine that he might get there and be able to sleep and eat and drink an entire pot of tea.

He wondered what had changed in his absence. How old would Pamela's child be? How would Patrick be managing now, with time and distance from Sylvie's death? How had his businesses fared in Pamela and Robert's hands?

During his musings, his eyes were drawn over and over again to the corner where the mirror hung. He realized he had not seen his face in some time.

He approached with a certain amount of trepidation. The mirror was dusty and slightly green around its edges and he had to give it a good rub with his coat sleeve before it gave him any sort of reflection. He took a deep breath and looked.

He stumbled back, entire body tingling with shock at the sight of the stranger in the mirror. The man facing him bore little resemblance to the man who had entered that long, low cabin so long ago. His beard was full and incredibly scruffy, a fact for which he was currently grateful as it had shielded his face from the worst of the wind. His hair had grown out unevenly over his ears. He looked a perfect madman, the bit of skin he could see reddened and cracked from the cold and constantly living in the elements. He might have just crawled from the cave, wild and stinking and without a trace of civilization upon him. He sat down on the birch log again, his entire body shaking, wishing suddenly that Shura was awake to distract him with Gregorian chanting or that Vanya would say something sarcastic and take the sting from the reflection he had just seen.

He then made the mistake of looking at the table. They had not sat at it for dinner. Lacking chairs, there seemed little reason to and they were used to merely sitting in a circle and shoving their food in with their fingers. But now he took in what sat upon the table and felt what was left of his defenses crumble.

For there on the blackened wooden top, long wrapped in cobwebs and dust, sat the traditional offering of Russians to strangers: flowers, bread and salt. It was then Jamie cried, cried the tears that he had not cried in all these long months of stone and cold. For though the flowers were long wilted to mere skeletons, and the bread would, at a touch, turn to dust and the salt was clotted with damp, still these were signs of humanity, of a fruitless hospitality for someone who might never come. Yet, it had existed, and still did somewhere in the cold reaches of this godforsaken land.

Chapter Eighty-eight
... Away Homeward With One Star Awake

AWAKENING AFTER THEIR FIRST NIGHT IN THE TRAIN CAR, it was to find another foot of snow and more still coming down in great drifts, and that the entire car was circled in the large and discomfiting paw prints of wolves. They were still exhausted and knew it would be beyond foolhardy to venture out across the land right now. Wisely, the decision was made to hole up until the weather settled. It gave Jamie a chance to reassess the direction in which they were traveling and re-orient himself within the landscape.

The snow continued to fall for three days. The train car was well hidden and might be entirely shrouded in snow if it didn't stop soon. It wasn't likely anyone could track them here but Jamie was seriously considering that there might be a homicide within the car if they didn't leave soon.

"I swear on my mother's grave, I'm going to choke him if he doesn't shut up. Doesn't he know what country he's in? He must be a spy," Vanya said, narrowing his eyes at Shura, who was whistling a jaunty Georgian tune. "No Russian has ever been *that* happy."

"No, you won't choke him because if anyone is going to kill him, it will be me," Jamie rejoined darkly, adding another chunk of pine to the fire, causing it to spit and hiss.

Vanya grunted as if to say they would see about that, should the moment present itself.

As though he sensed the short string by which his life currently dangled, Shura turned and grinned at them both, the ball of wool on his cap bobbing in a ridiculous manner, his one gold tooth gleaming against the rapidly falling dark.

He had just finished cheerfully regaling them with the umpteenth story of wolves killing humans. The last had been about a wolf that bodily lifted a young farm worker by the throat and scaled a meter high fence with her still clenched in its jaws. Pursued by angry peasants, it had still managed to carry poor Anya several hundred meters into the forest before abandoning her lifeless and bleeding corpse. Being that their wolves were still vividly present, Jamie and Vanya felt the stories were in somewhat dubious taste. On top of that, Kolya had been fussing all afternoon and seemed utterly inconsolable.

"Shura, could you sing something?" Jamie asked. "Maybe that will calm him." While also putting a halt to the lurid lupine tales, Jamie hoped. Vanya breathed a sigh of relief and settled back into his wrappings looking, even after all their time in the wilds, like an exotic and elegant creature, something dreamed of by Diaghilev.

Shura chose a song Jamie himself had taught him months ago. He was shocked that the man still remembered it.

She stepped away from me and she moved through the fair
And fondly I watched her move here and move there
She went away homeward with one star awake
As the swans in the evening move over the lake.

Shura's voice rode the dark over the softly sibilant movement of the fire, the notes seeming to dance upon the air then fly up the chimney with the sparks toward the star-salted sky. His deep voice melted the lyrics into something unbearably poignant. During the music, Jamie could feel Kolya's weight shift to that dream-filled landscape of a baby's sleep.

By unspoken consent, they all bedded down without the usual nightly exchange of words. Jamie took the first shift tending the fire for he didn't slide as easily and deeply into sleep as Shura and Vanya. He wanted time to sort his thoughts and to plan, as much as one could, for the next day. Tonight though, his thoughts were not ordered and tended toward panic—like a bird with wings that suddenly cannot fly but is stuck firmly to the edge of a cliff, with only one way off it.

He had walked the track that day and found that it ended abruptly some small way up the line. If his calculations were correct they should be near the border, soon to slip out from under the dark penetration of the Empire's eyes. But if outward signs were any indication, they seemed still to be stumbling through the vast white wasteland of Russia. How easy it was to make a miscalculation, in a country this large, was only too apparent to him and was a thought that had hagridden him since the beginning of their mad flight.

He gave himself a mental shake, knowing he needed to focus so that his worry and panic would not communicate itself to his companions come morning. He had to look like a man with a plan whether he had one or not.

He added more wood to the fire, every cell in his body protesting against leaving the warmth of the furs. It was colder tonight. It was officially winter, Russia's longest and most merciless face. The train car was warmer than being outside in the elements but it was still very drafty, the rust having eaten almost through the walls and roof in places. Through one such hole he watched as the fire stirred and caught, releasing a rush of sparks in violets and golds, small transitory constellations into the night. He watched them rise until they winked out far above him in the night sky.

He crawled carefully back into the furs. Kolya, small chubby fists clubbed under his chin, did not stir. Already changes were occurring in him—a more stubborn set to the chin, his legs lengthening, his eyes not as dark as at birth, but of a hue that mirrored the skies. Bits of his mother and his father, heart-breakingly present.

Because his mind had been rigorously molded by Jesuits, Jamie had long had the ability to compartmentalize his thoughts, to tuck away grief and yearning and to move forward into the future with his baggage safely stowed. But Russia had stripped him of some of that ability, the camp honing and whittling away at his essence until he was down to his essentials. But without the guards he had previously used to navigate through the shoals and razor sharp reefs of emotion. It was as though he was missing a layer or two of psychic skin, and could not deflect pain and worry, as he had once been able to do. So during his shift of caring for the fire, his thoughts finally found their way to Violet.

He missed the weight and warmth of her beside him at night, missed the security that had been found there, missed the soft half-spoken murmurs as one or both of them slid down into sleep. In their sleep and the mingling of dreams under a billion stars, they had become one, or so he had thought. And now he did not know how to let go of her hand, even though she was gone, far gone and he could not find her no matter how much he might search amongst the snow and the trees and the great cathedral of frosted air that hung there around him.

> *I dreamt it last night, my true love came in*
> *So softly she came that her feet made no din*
> *As she laid her hand on me and this she did say*
> *It will not be long, love, 'til our wedding day*

THE HOWLING OF THE WOLVES WOKE HIM BEFORE DAWN. He sat up and checked automatically for Kolya. The baby was there snug by his side and still fast asleep. He had eaten well the night before and should be good for another hour or two before his belly woke him.

Jamie slid out of the furs and pulled his coat on over the layers of sweater and shirts he wore to stay warm at night. The fire was glowing with coals so he loaded it up from the stack of dry pine they had brought in from snags yesterday. Both Vanya and Shura were still soundly asleep, the security of the train car allowing them to dismiss the wolf howls from their dreams.

He wrapped his scarf securely around his mouth, ramming his woollen cap down over his ears so that a minimum of skin would be exposed to the frigid air.

The snow had stopped and the air was incredibly clear, the dawn just nudging its way up along the horizon, a narrow band of pale grey showing through the trees. The air was cold enough that a breath of it sent crackles of pain through his lungs.

The wolf was sitting only twenty feet away, his shadow blending with the colors of the morning and the dark hollows beneath the trees. He was silent. It had to be one of his companions that Jamie had heard howl. He could feel the unwavering, golden eyes alight in the pre-dawn dim. There was no sense of threat, as though the wolf were merely curious, or drawn by some inexplicable force to stand here eye to eye with him. It was the big male with the smoke-blue ruff and white legs and underbelly. The leader. It was odd for him to be away from the main body of the pack, sitting here solitary. The wolves had to be far outside their territory after following them for five days.

A bare flicker in the corner of his eye and he knew it was too late even as he turned to face the black wolf that had used Jamie's distraction to creep slowly through the trees. Some part of him acknowledged his fate. To die here in the open was not the worst thing that could happen to a man. He had prepared Vanya for this possibility so that he might lead Shura and Kolya out of this land. The border was very close. Jamie knew it with a surety that had eluded him only hours before. The two men could care for Kolya until they reached the sanctuary of his home. This too he had told Vanya. For there was a woman there who had the care of his home and interests, and though he did not tell Vanya this, a part of his soul. She would care for Kolya for the sake of their friendship.

Even as he turned the wolf was at full arc, black body stretched in the moment before the kill. Jamie could see death in the clear amber eyes.

Death did come, with swiftness and brutality as was so often its way in this frozen land. But it was, this time, not calling upon him. The wolf at its apex, teeth bared, dropped to the ground by his feet with an audible thump. An arrow, still trembling, stuck deep into its side.

He saw them then, hidden in the snow and shadow, tribesmen, dressed in reindeer coats and breeches with the soft boots that allowed them to walk in silence across the snow and ice. They emerged like shadow dancers and for a moment he thought they might be a mirage from too many days in the blinding white of this land. Their arrows were nocked and ready for flight, a short trip between their draw hands and his tender flesh. He didn't know what they wanted and did not know how to ask. He put his hands into the air, to show he had no weapons, no defenses against their greater numbers.

He thought of Kolya still asleep in the car behind him, of Vanya and Shura still unconscious too. He supposed if they wanted him dead, they could have allowed the wolf to do the job for them and just picked up the remains after.

He stood quiet, allowing them to approach, their arrows still nocked and at the ready. He could feel his heart thudding slowly, his blood chilled and his mind fixed to a calm point like it often was in situations fraught with danger.

They were arguing about what to do with him, he realized. Though their language was unfamiliar the movement of bodies was universal in its speech. One man seemed to favor simply trussing him up and leaving him for whatever wolves might still be lingering. The other reached up, tore Jamie's woolen cap off and pointed to his hair, saying something sharp. The other man shrugged, then reached up casually and hit Jamie over the head with something hard and heavy.

Chapter Eighty-nine
The Mother

HE AWOKE TO THE SOUND OF WATER POURING INTO TIN. He opened his eyes and quickly shut them again as the room swung around him. He opened them more slowly the next time and realized it wasn't a room at all, at least not one of wood and lathe. He was in a tent—with a pyramid roof, its walls hung with skins that looked like reindeer. Being that his last sight had been of the reindeer-drawn sledge he had been thrown into, this made a cautious sense.

He attempted to sit up and found his head would allow it, though just. A woman in skins was filling a tub with steaming water, the high planes of her amber face glistening with the heat.

But before she cooked him in that tin pot there were things he needed to ascertain. He wasn't certain where he was, nor just who had kidnapped him. Nor, more specifically, why. He sat up fully, finding himself on a bed of skins and naked as the day he was born.

He made a noise and the woman turned to him, her face young and sweet. He cradled his arms and said the Yakut word for 'baby'. It was a guess but it was the right one. She nodded and cradling her arms in return said a few words which Jamie thought meant food and sleep. She motioned in confirmation pointing to her breast. He heaved a sigh of relief. Kolya was safe and fed. He then said the word for 'friend', and stuck up two fingers. She again motioned food and sleep. So Shura and Vanya were somewhere nearby as well and safe.

She left towels and a pungent brown cake of soap and indicated that he should now bathe. Knowing that his charges were safe and that Kolya had been fed, he immersed himself in the hot water with gratitude. The fire was built up high and kept the tent very warm. It was a bit like being drunk on the sheer sensual bliss of heat after so much cold.

He considered his position. It wasn't likely that his captors would bathe him first in order to execute him, hygiene hardly being a requisite for a well-placed arrow in the chest. Then again if they were going to commit atrocities upon him first, they likely wanted him to be less offensive to their senses.

He washed with the brown soap and a rough cloth and felt as though he were washing off the last several weeks and emerging new-skinned into something else. By the time he got to his toes, he thought he might just go back to sleep right here in the warm water. They could cook him if they liked.

He did fall asleep for a few minutes but was jolted back to reality when the girl returned. She mimed getting dressed, placing a pile of clothes on the sleeping skins and using hand gestures accompanied by words which, despite his very limited knowledge of the Yakut language, made it clear that his presence was desired by someone important in the village. Likely their headman, Jamie thought.

He dressed in the clothes she had left, supple hide pants lined with fur, an old and faded cotton shirt, well worn but clean and smelling of pine and smoke, an overshirt of fur-lined leather and boots that were heaven on his feet. A reindeer coat and mittens in the same material completed his ensemble. It was all wonderfully soft and warm; he hoped that Kolya and Shura and Vanya were as well looked after.

The girl waited for him, pulling back the flap of the tent just as he was puttling the boots on. She gestured that he should follow her. Outside, the night was lit by fires and lanterns, the moon full above, turning the snowy fields around to gilt. A strong scent of animal and urine came from the west, and he heard the sounds of reindeer grunting and feeding.

He wondered how far off he was in his reckonings. The Yakut traditionally lived in the east, not here in what he had hoped and prayed was somewhere near the Kola peninsula. The Yakut were nomads and since the Revolution had been badly scattered and depleted due to collectivization and extermination. It simply wasn't possible that he and his small band had wandered into Siberia. Surely even as sleep and food deprived as they were, the Ural Mountains would have caught their attention.

Along snow-crusted paths he was led to a tent in the center of the village. The girl pulled back the tent flap but did not enter, pointing with her hand that he should go in alone.

The tent was firelit like his own had been and beyond the fire, sitting on a pile of skins was a very old woman, her hair so white it appeared blue in the shadows. So not a head man, not a council of elders, but maybe the shaman, for though the Yakut's medicine and folklore came down through both the men and women, women were considered the more powerful. And this woman, despite being very small and fragile-looking, emanated power like few people Jamie had met in his lifetime. Her face was framed by the fur-ruffed collar of her coat, the high bones beneath still speaking of beauty and dignity. Her eyes were pools in the firelight, black as currants and set deep above the winged cheekbones.

She gestured that he should sit across from her on a pile of skins similar to hers. He sat, bowing his head to her so she would know he understood he was with someone of great importance.

She studied his face for several moments and Jamie looked back into her eyes, allowing the regard. Finally, she took a deep breath and said something to herself. Jamie didn't catch much of it other than the word, he thought, for 'sun'. This guess was confirmed when she leaned over and touched his hair, allowing it to lie on the palm of one hand as she smoothed it with the other. He supposed men with golden hair were in short supply in these regions but she seemed more than normally fascinated. Having little choice in the matter, he merely sat and allowed her attentions.

She sat back soon enough and addressed him in Russian; flawless Russian with the north winds in its threads. Most Yakut of her generation would have been educated in Soviet schools, inculcated into a regime and culture that must have been more foreign to them than if they had been transported to Mars. But she was of an age to be rooted firmly in her own culture before the dislocation had occurred.

"You are welcome here."

He replied as he thought right. "Thank you, Mother. I am honored to be your guest."

She nodded, for this was so. Jamie knew that to the Yakut, especially a shamanness such as she, the mental and spiritual abilities of a white Westerner were laughable, that he was little more than an intelligent dog in her view. He wondered, not without some trepidation, what she wanted with him.

Outside, a lone drum began to beat slow, in tempo with blood and heartbeats, primal in the spine and cells. She reached to the side and poured something from a vessel that sat beside her on the floor into a horn cup and handed it to him.

"Drink this," she said. "It is what is necessary for you and me to speak directly."

He took the drink and neither inhaled nor looked too closely at it. He did not know its component parts, though he had a very bad suspicion about them. He could not refuse it, however, for to do so would be to insult this Mother. The taste could not be avoided, sharp and astringent with the flavor of smoke and earth at bottom. He finished it and set the cup down, wondering how long it would be before it took effect. He was not frightened, for he had known such things before, but considered that it was unfortunate that he had not eaten much in many days. The Celts used this too but they had smoked it or used it in steam lodges. The effect, he believed, was much the same.

It occurred to him while his faculties were still in normal working order that he knew who had Yakut relatives—many times removed—but had them nonetheless. So it wasn't likely they were going to cook him. But anything else was entirely possible.

The Mother took his hands and smiled. Afterward, he never knew if she spoke aloud or if she merely thought the words into him, but he felt them, their shapes and rhythms, rather than hearing them through his ears. "Come dream with me, son of the green land."

The drums were louder now and felt as though they beat inside his head, in his blood, each thump pulsing through vein and cell, into muscle and bone. Suddenly, without moving, they were in a field and the moon was bright overhead, pouring silver over them, over every hump of snow and sparking off the coats of the great beasts that moved amongst and around them.

They walked to the edge of a body of water, a lake that lay uncommonly still in the dark night. Jamie felt a sudden rush of vertigo, for the night was reflected perfectly within the bowl of water and it seemed that they stepped out into nothing, stars above and stars below, everything falling away, forever, into infinity, including himself and the woman whose hand held his own. The sense of falling was disturbing at first but then it felt natural, as though there were no bottom to hit, nothing to harm in this universe of stars. He simply had to let go, for he was too tired to do otherwise. He closed his eyes and surrendered to it.

The stars were a river, a great serpentine flow of fire and ice, stretching and roiling out to the edge. The colors that rippled and burst before his eyes were like nothing he had ever seen before. They defied description, and there were no names in his lexicon fit for such wonder.

The woman who stood before him looked like the Mother, old and wise beyond time and the boundaries of human thought. Yet he understood it was not the woman who had taken his hand, but someone—something far older who had existed forever. She held a spindle in her hands, a thing that gleamed and spun and threw out light in great shudders. Suddenly she drove it down through the ground at her feet. The ground opened and then came a flood of light and dark, of the sun and the moon. Mountains formed beneath her feet and the oceans flooded all around them, smelling of life and birth. Coiled around her foot was a serpent, a sign of the infinite and of boundless wisdom.

She touched his face and he knew that it was both women that touched him, one through the other, but the touch held peace within it and the agony of life itself, which was both its terror and its beauty.

"There are endings," she said softly. "Sometimes the thread snaps but in that ending is always the thread that will be spun into a new beginning. The thread is infinite and always in the act of creating. For you, this is a time of both ending and beginning."

And then he began to laugh, for covering him, resting with feet so light they

*were like velvet-shod calyxes, were butterflies, hundreds of butterflies in all the
breathing colors of the universe and the river of stars that he waded within.*

HE AWOKE NEAR MORNING, THE LIGHT STILL DEEP BLUE but with ashes
around the edges that told him dawn was on its way. There was a girl in the
skins with him. He had not wanted this part, not at first, but his mind had
failed to communicate this adequately to his body and his body, missing its
appetites, had done what was necessary.

It was the girl who had filled the bath and taken him to the Mother.
She slept deeply, bare-skinned as he was, warm and smelling sweetly of sex
and some unidentifiable perfume. He fell back into the swaddled arms of
Morpheus feeling strangely peaceful.

When he next awoke, it was morning and there was still a woman in
the tent but it wasn't the soft-skinned partner of the night before. There
was only one woman to whom that perfume belonged, the scent of dark
cinnamon on gardenias.

"Yevgena," he said.

"Open your eyes, Yasha, your breakfast is here."

He opened his eyes. Above him was a pair of dark eyes framed by high
and disdainful cheekbones, unmistakably Russian but clothed comfortingly
in the robes of his childhood.

Clad in furs and a red hat, her dark hair and eyes were a solid point in
the universe. And when she wrapped her arms around him, he too instantly
became real. Because it was Yevgena and because he was tired and weak he
could feel the tightness of engulfing emotion in his throat. She merely held
him harder, hands rubbing his back, murmuring a soft, throaty shush into
his ear that was as comforting as hot tea and vodka.

"We will feed you and then we must leave. I have transportation waiting,"
she said and he could tell by the edge in her voice that she was near tears but
would not do that to him just now. He sensed something else below that, as
if there were words that must be spoken but that she would not utter yet.
An uneasy feeling slid through him, for what news could cause such worry
when he had survived the gulag?

"I'd like to get dressed," he said, for something must be said, must be
done, before she told him news he was not ready to hear.

She smiled at him. That smile from his childhood that had always made
him feel safe and loved.

"I will turn my back. Will that do?"

"That will do," he said and stood as she turned, slipping into the furs,
the boots, the leather, his stomach suddenly loud at the thought of food.

They ate well of the soured mare's milk and fried bread and cold, roasted meat which he knew now was reindeer. There was tea after, hot and sweetened with honey. It tasted like nirvana.

His brain felt like it had been scoured with a wire brush, scrupulously gleaned for every bit of lint and ephemera it held as well as the more concrete things. Which wasn't, it had to be said, the optimal state in which to meet with his godmother.

The girl brought Kolya to him after breakfast. She said something in Yakut and Jamie understood that Kolya had been fed and had slept well, wrapped tight in furs alongside the woman's own child.

Yevgena saw the look on his face. "She was widowed last year, her husband lost to the sea. If she has given you comfort, know that you also have given such to her."

The woman's eyes on him were soft, and he remembered particular moments from the night, and returned the look in kind. He was grateful, for somehow the night had removed some of the thorns from his soul. She was a stranger and she had done this for him. He thought somehow that she understood this.

He held Kolya facing forward on his lap, the boy's hair a halo of copper in the morning light.

"And who," Yevgena said, as a startlingly blue pair of eyes goggled at her, "is this?"

"This," Jamie said softly, "is my son—Nikolai Andreyevich."

Chapter Ninety
The Summons Home

I T WAS, IN THOSE FIRST HOURS, almost more than he could manage. It was life returning: the business of it, the details, the responsibilities. But Yevgena had fed them out as on a fine line, invisible on its own but freighted with news, gossip, and correspondence. He ought to have known, and had he been sharper, less distracted, he would have understood that beneath the glittering waves of all these morsels lay the dark water hiding, as was its way, the monster whose presence was felt long before it was seen. She had given him those two days in which to sleep, to mend a bit and to readjust a little to the idea of returning to the West, to home, to civilization as he understood it. Only he thought, perhaps he no longer did.

Two letters, written on his own personal letterhead and therefore they could only be from one person. But why was Yevgena acting as though she carried an incendiary device? He took the letters, his eyes still on hers, questioning.

She merely looked at him and then quietly left the room. They were in his Paris house, having felt it was not wise to stop on their flight from Russia until they were very far away. He glanced at the clock on his nightstand. It was nearly noon and he had slept twelve hours.

One was written in a hand he recognized vaguely, the other in Pat Riordan's broad and immediate slash. He felt something seize just below his breastbone at the sight of that bold writing—Pamela? No, he could not countenance that. He opened the other letter first and understood why it had seemed somewhat familiar, like an echo so far back in his mind that it was barely registered much less heard. It was from Robert who was, despite his own lengthy absence from the land of the living, his secretary.

Jamie took a deep breath and began.

Dear Lord Kirkpatrick—the title alone made his head swim—he had been Yasha for so long that the thought of any of the many names and titles he carried in this other world had the effect of either making him want to laugh or hide somewhere for a good, long time.

He resumed, eyes taking in the neatly-blocked letters as well as the sense of the man writing them. Economical with his words—well, he would be from what little Jamie knew of him.

> *I hope this letter finds you well.*

That, thought Jamie, was a matter entirely up for debate.

> *We are, of course, rejoicing here to know that you are safe and whole and will be returning to your home soon.*

The 'we' gave Jamie pause—who was 'we'? Robert and Maggie? Montmorency and the horses?

> *Not wishing to waste your time, I will get down to business.*

How very Scots and thrifty of him, Jamie thought, picturing the small owl face of the man he had met so briefly under less than ideal circumstances.

The wee Scot had a very to-the-point style and Jamie felt that he had a good grasp of what had taken place in his companies in his absence.

> *It was wise of you to appoint Mrs. Riordan as your legal heir in your absence. She has been most astute from the beginning, making the hard decisions when they had to be made, but also exercising compassion when it was a personal matter. She has proven herself tough in negotiations too, though I daresay that her face alone addles her opposition so much they barely know that they've agreed with her before they are being hustled from the premises with whiskey in their bellies and yearning in their hearts.*

Yes, Jamie thought wryly, no doubt they did leave in that state. Though he had never known Pamela to indulge in vanity of any sort, still she was shrewd enough to use her looks when she needed to. He could well imagine some of the tough foremen from the linen mills being entirely discombobulated in her presence.

> *She has a mind that adapts readily to the ups and down of the markets, both those of goods and finances. She tells me she was well trained by you to understand these things, and that now she knows why. I am politely paraphrasing here, of course.*

He laughed out loud, for he could well imagine just how Pamela had reacted to the news that she had the running of his home and businesses.

I shall miss working with her. We have formed a well-functioning team these last two years and I have become very fond of her and her family. I look forward, however, to working with yourself whom, I am assured is no slack taskmaster, and I am informed that I will not have time to miss her. I think she underestimates her charms, though. I will, of course, miss the children as well for I have come to regard them as part of this house and its daily rhythms.

Children? Jamie's eyes slid further down the page. So Pamela and Casey had another child. The thought of it made him suddenly feel unmoored from the earth, as if he had been gone so long that nothing would be familiar upon his return. Nothing *was* familiar, that was already too apparent. He wasn't sure he even wanted to go home, and he knew how irrational that was considering how much he had missed it these last three years. But Russia had turned him into someone else, someone unrecognizable in the mirror even now that the small niceties of shaving and showering had been re-introduced to his world.

I must tell you now so that you are prepared when you come home, that the distillery was destroyed by fire, and in the ashes was found the body of your Uncle Philip.

How the hell had that happened? He didn't feel any sadness on behalf of his uncle for the man had spread a taint by his mere presence, one from which Jamie's spirit and self had always recoiled. The distillery though, he did regret. It had been part of his home and he had spent many soothing hours there, both on his own and in years past with his grandfather.

He returned his attention to the letter. Robert continued with a brief summary of market reports and investments. There was a summation as well of the threats against the companies and the two years of sleight of hand in which Pamela and Robert had been engaged to save it. He felt sick at the thought of the threats she had been under.

Jamie paused here, feeling suddenly that the Scot was trying to lighten the blow of something that was stated further down in the letter. An ominous feeling had lodged itself at the base of his spine and was building with each line his eyes took in.

There were a few more lines that provided a pathway toward his final words, which Jamie skimmed, not really taking them in. And here it was, what wasn't being said.

I feel it is best that you read Patrick's letter. This is not informa-

tion that is mine to impart and so I will not. If you have read
his letter first then you will know why I urge you to come home
as quickly as you can.

Jamie looked at the dark lettering on the white field of the envelope and
knew he had never wished to read anything less in his entire life. The weight
of it hung in the air, unavoidable, inescapable. He had felt it when Yevgena
placed it in his hands, that it contained news that would shift the axis of the
universe and that it had already done so to those he loved in Ireland. He realized suddenly that he was gripping Robert's letter so tightly he had torn the
paper in two. If, after all....no, he would not think it, would not allow the
thought to even rest in his mind for a moment, lest it take seed.

Read the letter he must though, there was no avoiding the world anymore.
He opened it and one thin sheet fell out. Only a few lines, most definitely
the economy of that was a harbinger of dread news.

Dear Jamie,

We are so relieved that you are well. I write this in haste to go
in the package with Robert's letter. How to say this, without
baldly shocking you—which I know you do not need—but there
is no way to sugar-coat things. Casey has gone missing and I fear
he's dead. The circumstances surrounding his disappearance are
strange, and yet I cannot see how my brother could still be alive
and not come home nor give his wife and children a sign that
he is alive somewhere.

I know you will be wondering how Pamela is managing. The
answer is that she's not. She's frantic and in complete denial. The
look in her eyes is something I can hardly bear to witness. I don't
know what will happen if—but, no, I won't write those lines
here. The children are too young to understand, thank heavens.
Will this be a blessing for them, I wonder, and then my heart
plummets to know that if Casey does not come home they will
have no memory of their father.

I know you haven't had time to adjust to the idea of coming
home, but for Pamela's sake, and I admit, for my own, please
hurry. We need you.

Patrick

He scanned the letter twice more, rapidly, but the words remained in
place, stubbornly insistent, unchanging and irrevocable.

He stood from the bed, took clothes from the closet, put them on, all without a sense of breathing or moving, as though the world hung in a horrific state of suspension.

"Yevgena," he called out.

She opened the door as though she had waited outside it, knowing he would need her.

"You know?"

"Yes," she replied, black eyes liquid with sympathy.

"Why didn't you give these to me, as soon as we arrived?"

"You know why, Jemmy. You're still too weak but I felt I had no choice. You must go home. You are needed."

Jamie functioned through the brutal discipline of his mind in the next hours, arranging a plane, arranging transportation to the plane, calling on every resource of his vast holdings to get back to Ireland as quickly as possible.

But once on the plane from Paris to London, with Kolya fast asleep on the seat beside him, he found he could not escape his thoughts nor the fears of what he would find when he arrived home.

It was as he slipped toward sleep himself that they came to him—his ghosts, both the living and the dead: Violet, Andrei, Nikolai, behind him now; Pamela and Patrick and their fears and loss in front of him. And he remembered the last words the Mother had spoken to him.

"It is you who holds yourself there. It is you who must let them go, or they will become yor and be trapped here. It is not the dead who cling to the living, but the living who cannot let the dead go. It is not time yet but one day you must do what is right for them and allow them to move on. It is the living who have need of you. It is to them you must go."

And so he would go back to his life, to whatever form and shape that might now take. The ache of loss was an open wound still but at the heart of this pain was that fragile seed of peace, a sense that eventually he would come to a place where he might embrace his ghosts and then release them.

For now, however, he would carry them with him, for he was not ready to let them go.

Epilogue

JAMES KIRKPATRICK WAS FATED TO MAKE ONE MORE STOP before reaching home. An official summons had greeted him when he arrived in London and he had been all but manhandled into an anonymous black car. Politely, for his abductors were British after all, but with a firmness that told him they would knock him out and truss him up if that was what was required to buy his acquiescence.

They drove in the back entrance, but back or front, Jamie recognized the tall ugly shadow of the building to which he was taken. He sighed. He had been afraid of this, but had hoped to slip through England before they were aware of his presence.

It was all familiar, including the room they took him to and the man who entered a few moments later. Aubrey Fielding, for his sins. The man was an officious bastard and Jamie had never been fond of him. They could hardly be serious about allowing this man to debrief him. Whatever he had been to them before Russia, he was now a free agent and he would not answer to any man he did not wish to, including British prats who couldn't see beyond their pointy bureaucratic noses.

The questions began simply. No doubt the man thought he could lull him into actually answering something if caught unawares by the sheer mind-numbing stupidity of what he was saying.

"Why were you so long in the Soviet Union?"

It was one question too far. The camel's back snapped. "Are you serious? Taking an extended tea with Brezhnev—what the fuck do you think I was doing?"

The man in front of him spluttered and Jamie thought of how much easier it had been to deal with someone like Gregor, direct and to the point. He turned to look up at the corner where the camera sat.

"Richard, could you please relieve me of this nitwit? If you want to know anything, come in and I'll tell you face-to-face but I am not talking to this ass for another minute."

Within seconds, a tall man entered at the door with the stoic face of a professional spy handler. "Aubrey, you may leave. I will take over from here."

Aubrey, knowing an unequivocal dismissal when he heard it, left, but not without considerable gritting of his teeth.

"Really, James, you were a bit hard on the boy," Richard said, seating himself on the corner of the desk. It was a tactic he used occasionally to place himself at a casual advantage over the men and women who sat in the brown leather chair. But he did not fool himself for a minute into thinking he could intimidate the man who sat there now.

"Living in a gulag will shorten your patience for idiocy considerably." Jamie said.

"Yes, I'm sorry about that. We wanted to extract you but the stars never seemed to align in a manner that allowed us to do that, without compromising other operations."

"By which you mean that you have a Russian mole working for you and you couldn't risk him in order to help me. Don't think I will forget this, Richard. You might want to ask yourself about your other man in Russia too. Somebody told the Soviets where and when I would be over the border."

Richard had already considered this possibility and had a very good idea who had done it. However, it was not something he could discuss with this man. At least not at the present moment with cameras running.

"I've been instructed to tell you that we will do everything within our power to make your return as comfortable and as easy as possible."

"Richard, the only man who instructs you is the PM."

"Well, he wants you to know that we are at your disposal as far as we are able."

The green eyes narrowed. "I didn't come back alone." His voice was quiet. It carried like a scythe through sun-blistered wheat.

"Ah," Richard tapped the blotter on his desk with a heavy gold pen. "So I heard. What exactly do you want?"

"Asylum and citizenship papers for my Russian friends, for whichever country they may choose to call home."

"I think something can be arranged. For now though, you will find them waiting on the plane for you. Your secretary, who is a bit of a highhanded bastard if I do say so myself, sent your plane over to bring you home. What about the baby?" he asked, wondering if the man before him would answer truthfully.

"The child is my son and will therefore be a citizen of Northern Ireland. You know where to send the required papers."

"Of course," Richard said. They would do what this man asked for some time, he supposed. They owed him enough to fear him. "Your friend—I'm sorry. But we were right about what they had him doing?"

"Yes, you were. Satellite weaponry, fairly advanced. Keeping his knowledge in his head was the only thing staying his execution. But of course they will have their ways of prying it out of him now that he has nothing left to lose."

The conversation that followed was brief. Richard asked what questions he could and Jamie either answered them or did not as he saw fit. All his answers consisted of a few words and hid far more than they revealed. Richard, however, was patient, and knew now was not the best time to get what they needed from this man. At the end of the interview—which might have been, Richard thought, quite the most barbed of his long career—His Lordship James Stuart Kirkpatrick stood, impeccable in a dark grey suit, well barbered and the epitome of a civilized gentleman. But when Richard looked into the green eyes, he saw something that bore no taint of civilization.

Jamie took something from his pocket and placed it on the desk in front of Richard. Two chess pieces—a white knight and a black knight.

"What you want is inside the pieces," Jamie said. "Now, I really must go. It has been a pleasure but one I fear that we will be foregoing in the future, Richard. Because I quit."

Richard sat watching the door long after it had closed behind Jamie. He understood the man's anger. They would have to give him time and space in which to allow that anger to die down, but if he really thought he could just quit this particular job, he had, as the saying went, another think coming.

The direct line on his desk rang, interrupting his thoughts of the man who had just exited. The Prime Minister. He sighed. He would want answers but Richard had very few to give him just now.

Jamie stopped outside the great ugly tower known as Century House and took a deep breath. It had started to snow while he was inside, just a flake or two drifting down through the air, silent and transitory but beautiful in their passing. It calmed the anger burning in his chest a little. He waved away the car they had provided and walked into the grey chill of a London afternoon. He started across Westminster Bridge and stopped midpoint to watch the river flow past. Snowflakes touched its grey surface like miniature dancers, and then disappeared.

He stood for a very long time while the light faded, the snow fell thicker and faster and the lights of London came on around him, their reflections glowing in the river like drowned stars.

He had a sense, as he had twice before in his life, of being cut free of the earth, adrift and unacquainted with his own self. Russia had changed him. He felt it in every cell and thought. It remained to be seen what the outlines of this new man, carved by the silver stylus of struggle and hardship, his charcoal swept away by the barbed feathers of Russia itself, would look like or how he would deal with the world he had left behind seemingly so long ago. The shading of his soul had been sifted fine, like smoke, darker in its folds and drifting corners, painted over and over in the shades of blood and loss: vermilion and cinnabar, ivory and black and the crumbling ends of charred bone.

But he thought, perhaps remaining somewhere, spindrift and often invisible, was the *azzuro oltre marino*, the blue of such depth that it was considered the most valuable color of all. The core of the soul as rendered by the artist.

It was time to go. There was a flight to catch and a home to return to and there were friends who had long required his presence. He began to walk, alone in the midst of millions of people, snow shrouding his shoulders and hair.

His feet were toward the West but his head turned one last time back to the East... because once he had a friend there in those snowy wastes. Once he had a friend...

Good night sweet prince;
And flights of angels sing thee to thy rest...

THERE WILL ALWAYS BE AND THERE WILL ALWAYS NOT BE a world under, beyond the border of the maiden birches or at the bottom of the sea. There will always be and always not be a crone in the heart of the dark forest and sometimes she will be good and true and sometimes she will not. This is, after all, the way of the world. This is balance and the world ever seeks it.

There will always be and not be crumbling towers and damsels in distress who long to be unshackled. There will always be and not be birds with feathers of flame and plain-faced girls of cunning and wit and old men who roam the pathways of the forest and sea. There will always be and not be figures who are dark and lurk below the horizon. There will always be a castle and a woman who waits for a knight to crest the far hills. Sometimes he will arrive and sometimes he will not.

For this I know and tell you as the one truth of the world, both the over and the under—all things change. It is the one sure thing and happiness is not a natural state any more than misery, no matter how man might long for it to be so.

There will always be worlds within worlds and the suspension between the two. The priests call such places purgatory, but I know there will always be twilight borderlands, the edge places of this world and that. It is there you will find me, waiting for one who wanders too close to where the veil between worlds thins so fine you might pass a needle through it without so much as a whisper of protest. A needle or a man.

Write my name with ink upon paper and you will scent the smoke of my arrival. For I am the Crooked Man and I come by crooked ways.

About the Author

Cindy Brandner lives in the Interior of British Columbia with her husband and children and several animals. Flights of Angels is the third novel in the Exit Unicorns series.

www.exitunicorns.com

CPSIA information can be obtained
at www.ICGtesting.com
Printed in the USA
LVOW01s1515051016

507534LV00004B/126/P